MICHAEL KORDA

SUMMIT BOOKS

THE
FORTUNE

NEW YORK · LONDON · TORONTO · SYDNEY · TOKYO

A SUMMIT BOOK/LINDEN PRESS
SIMON & SCHUSTER BUILDING
ROCKEFELLER CENTER
1230 AVENUE OF THE AMERICAS
NEW YORK, NEW YORK 10020

PUBLISHED BY SUMMIT BOOKS

SUMMIT BOOKS AND COLOPHON AND LINDEN PRESS ARE TRADEMARKS
OF SIMON & SCHUSTER INC.

DESIGNED BY EVE METZ
MANUFACTURED IN THE UNITED STATES OF AMERICA

ACKNOWLEDGMENTS

TO JONI EVANS, FOR HER UNFAILING ENTHUSIASM AND ENCOURAGEMENT; AND TO LYNN NESBIT, FOR ALWAYS BEING THERE.

FOR MARGARET, WITH LOVE.

FOR DICK SNYDER, IN FRIENDSHIP.

*"He that is without sin among you,
let him first cast a stone at her."*
John 8:7

THE FORTUNE

"**I**f the girl's father is so bloody rich, what's she doing in a hellhole like this?"

Martin Booker was too tired to answer the pilot's question in a hurry —besides, he was a lawyer. He never spoke without thinking first.

The landscape below reminded Booker of paintings of the surface of Mars—a dusty, barren wasteland in which the desert stretched for miles to meet jagged, rocky mountains, on the other side of which were yet more miles of monotonous desert, then more mountains. From ten thousand feet, it was impossible to see any sign of life; the only movement visible was an occasional cloud of dust.

Even though he wore sunglasses—which the pilot had insisted he buy in Nairobi before taking off—the glare was blinding. Thanks to modern technology, he had been in New York less than twenty-four hours ago—yesterday's *Wall Street Journal* was still neatly folded in the briefcase beside him. He was exhausted, deyhdrated, miserably conscious of a rumbling discomfort in his guts, a dull pain in his sinuses, a headache. He hoped, without conviction, that he was only suffering from jet lag.

"You'd have to know her father to understand," he said at last, raising his voice to make himself heard over the noise of the engines.

Strictly speaking, he reflected, it wasn't the whole truth. You would have to know the whole goddamned family and its history, all the way back to the time when a young bookkeeper named Cyrus Arthur Bannerman saw his chance to begin one of the great American fortunes, and took it.

And of course you'd need to know the girl.

Booker knew the girl. Or thought he did, anyway—had even been in love with her once, perhaps still was. She had loved him, too, he was sure of that.

Could he swear to it in court? he wondered. But like most of the things that really mattered in life, it wouldn't hold up in court—there were no depositions, affidavits, or other documents to present as evidence. They did not give a course in feelings at Harvard Law School. The law wasn't comfortable with emotions, and neither was he, which was perhaps why he had lost her in the first place. . . .

He tried without success to imagine Cecilia Aldon Bannerman, Radcliffe, Class of '77, living somewhere down there. He had been at her coming-out party. *Vogue* had named her "Deb of the Year." She had been the only girl he knew at Radcliffe with her own Mercedes. The income of her trust fund, which Booker now handled, would have enabled her to live comfortably, even extravagantly, anywhere, if she chose.

"I don't care *who* her father is, she's bloody mad, if you want my opinion."

Booker didn't want the pilot's opinion. He shaded his eyes and stared out the window at a line of green wavering in the heat haze on the far horizon. "What's that?" he shouted, more out of a desire to change the subject than from any curiosity.

"Lake Turkana. They used to call it Lake Rudolf—the Jade Sea. We're almost there now."

The pilot banked into a tight turn and dropped toward the lake, the size of which astonished Booker now that he could see it more clearly. At its far end, a range of mountains was visible. "The Omo River's up there," the pilot shouted. "That's where Kenya, the Sudan, and Ethiopia meet. End of the bloody world!"

It looked to Booker even less inviting than the desert they had just flown over.

He remembered her at the Devon Horse Show, a tall, angular girl, biting her lips with tension as she took her Thoroughbred hunter over the last fence to the polite applause of the well-dressed crowd. "The gal's mother had a damned good seat, too," her Aunt Katherine had growled down at him, he remembered, from the tailgate of her specially built pre-war Rolls-Royce station wagon, which she insisted on calling a "shooting brake," in the English way. "All the Bannerman gals have good seats," she added. Then, after a pause: "The men ride like sacks of coal."

Booker did not ride, had never been near a horse until he met Cecilia. He wondered if it would have made a difference had he learned to ride. Probably not, he decided.

"Hold on tight!" the pilot shouted.

Booker's stomach lurched as the pilot cut the power abruptly. The lake stretched before them, to Booker's eye more the color of canned split-pea soup than jade.

"Look out for a boat your side," the pilot said. "That's the only way to find the strip."

Booker peered through the Perspex, saw a dot on the water ahead and pointed. Below them, anchored in the water, was a large fishing trawler—or rather a shape that reminded Booker of a trawler, for it was deeply encrusted in some grayish substance, as if it had been dipped in molten rock and allowed to dry. The pilot slid below the level of the mast, then banked sharply toward the shore. Hundreds of birds rose from the trawler, flapped listlessly for a moment in the hot air, then dropped back onto their perches.

"Bloody UN wanted to teach the Turkana to fish commercially," the pilot said. He laughed. "They sent a team of Norwegian fishermen here. Flew the trawler in, in pieces. Assembled it on the spot. There's so much bird shit on it now, it's a wonder it hasn't bloody sunk. . . ."

Bird droppings, Booker thought. He had been traveling for twenty-four hours to see guano! "There must be fish in the lake?"

"Oh, the bloody lake is full of fish, mate. Big buggers—two, three hundred pounds. No problem there. What they forgot is that there's no bloody road to Nairobi. There's no place to ship the fish *to!*"

"So the Norwegians went home and left their boat here?"

"No, they're still here, poor sods. They're trying to build a plant to freeze the fish, but everybody's lost interest. That's Africa for you. . . . Here we are. Home, sweet home."

Immediately in front of them Booker saw a dusty airstrip, marked at its edges with rusty, empty diesel oil drums. At the far end, a corrugated iron shack shimmered in the heat. Beside it stood a mast from which the pale-blue flag of the United Nations drooped listlessly. Dozens of naked black children ran across the strip, waving. They appeared from nowhere, as if they had been hiding in the sand.

At ground level the heat was instantly intolerable. Booker was drenched in sweat in his three-piece suit—even the pilot, in his short-sleeved bush shirt, was dripping wet. "It must be like an oven out there," Booker said.

"One hundred twenty degrees, mate—at least that, at noon."

"And at night?"

"One hundred twenty. It's always one hundred twenty, day or bloody night. Here we go!"

The tires thumped against the hard-packed dirt, sending a cloud of dust over the wings, the brakes squealed, the pilot cut the engines back to idle, and raised a finger at the children who were running alongside the airplane. "One day, one of the little bastards will get himself cut to pieces by a prop," he complained. "It's the only way these people learn anything."

He switched off the engines and reached across Booker to open the door. It was like opening the door to a blast furnace, Booker thought, remembering a tour he had once taken of a steel mill the Bannerman family owned in Pittsburgh. The heat here was like an explosion, instantly drying the sweat off his body, leaving him so weak that he almost fell off the wing as he climbed out.

"Steady on, mate!" The pilot jumped down and guided Booker into the shade of the shack, where he stood for a moment, panting for breath. Inside was a dusty Land Rover, the hood open. A tall, blond, bearded man with bright blue eyes stood beside it, wiping the grease off his hands with a shop rag. He wore abbreviated shorts and sandals, and it took Booker, even in his befuddled state, no great effort to guess that this was one of the unfortunate Norwegians.

"What ho, Karl," the pilot said cheerfully, apparently unaffected by the heat. "Can you run us up to the refugee camp?"

The Norwegian's expression was melancholy to begin with, and became a shade more so. He shook his head. "The car is *kaput*," he said. "I thought maybe you bring parts."

"Never mind. They'll have heard the airplane. Somebody will turn up."

"Maybe. They are very busy."

"How far is the camp?" Booker asked. He had nurtured the hope of a car, perhaps even one with air-conditioning, a cold bottle of beer. A few hundred feet away the lakeshore festered under layers of decomposing fish, their huge skulls glittering in the fierce light. The stench was overpowering.

The notion of waiting seemed unbearable. Even in the shade, the ground burned through the soles of his hand-lasted black shoes. He felt an itch and looked down to discover that his hands were covered with thousands of tiny green flies, then realized they were on his face as well. He tried to brush them off, but they simply settled in a thick layer, swarming busily around his eyelids and his nostrils.

"Lake flies," the Norwegian explained. "They don't bite too bad. . . . The camp is maybe ten kilometers." He pointed toward the rocky wilderness. "Over there."

Booker could hardly imagine how anybody could live "over there," let alone large numbers of refugees. "How big is the camp?" he asked, wondering if there was a shower, perhaps even an air-conditioned building.

"Big," the Norwegian said. "Several hectares. There are thousands of people there, living in tents—the lucky ones, anyway."

"Tents? Thousands of people? Out *there?*"

"They walk across the border from Uganda. In Uganda there's a drought, tribal warfare, civil war—even cannibalism, they say. The Kenyans don't want them here, so they pen them up. If they escape from the camps, the Turkana kill them. There's hardly enough food or water here for the Turkana to begin with, so you can't blame them." He shaded his eyes. "I think you're in luck."

Far away, between two rocky ledges, Booker saw—or *thought* he saw—a puff of dust. He looked harder until his eyes began to ache, then saw a black dot. It grew larger. To his acute disappointment, he could see it was an open Jeep. The thought of driving ten kilometers in it made his head throb.

"Got a couple of beers for us, Karl?" the pilot asked.

The Norwegian shook his head mournfully. "Not until the next plane. Anyway, the generator is *kaput*, too. No ice."

The Jeep bounced across the runway, accompanied by the hordes of naked children who had materialized again, as thin as scarecrows. Booker wondered how they could run in this heat. He could hardly even stand. The Jeep pulled to a stop, the driver stood up, and as soon as Booker saw her he felt instantly revived, as if he were back in Kiawa again on a cool autumn morning, watching from the steps as Cecilia and her father mounted their horses for the opening meet, with the hunt and the hounds before them on the vast lawn, and the Bannerman lands stretching as far as the eye could see, the gentle, rolling hills glowing red and orange in the clear light. . . .

Then she had worn a black hunting habit, a top hat and a veil—the Bannerman women were expected to ride sidesaddle for the opening meet of the Kiawa Hounds. It was just one of those "things," of which there were legion, that made the Bannermans different from other people—even from other *rich* people.

She had always been thin—none of the Bannermans was fat, as if being overweight was a problem that did not affect people of their class and wealth. Now she was thinner than ever, her skin covered with dust and flies. She wore baggy khaki trousers and a pale-blue work shirt streaked with sweat. Her head was covered with a kind of burnoose, faintly religious in effect, like the headdresses worn by some of the more liberated orders of nuns. There was a frayed Red Cross armband on her sleeve.

He stepped out to the edge of the shade where she could see him more clearly, trying to think of some way to break the news. For nearly two days he had been thinking of very little else, but now that he was here, none of the phrases he had composed seemed possible to say, or even necessary. She would guess, the moment she saw it was he.

She stopped only a few feet away, still in the sun. She bit her lip, just the way he remembered she had at Devon, when she won Reserve

Champion, and on the day they broke up. "Martin!" she said, in that quiet voice he remembered so well, which seemed so unemotional to strangers, but was always trembling ever so delicately on the brink of revealing her feelings—something no Bannerman was supposed to do. "Is it Father?"

Booker nodded. He hoped his expression was appropriately mournful, despite the flies. He himself felt no grief for Bannerman—not many people did—but he knew Cecilia would.

"How bad is it, Martin? Does he want me?"

Booker cleared his throat. He wished there was a way to tell her without the pilot and the Norwegian listening, but he could not bring himself to step into the sunlight. He felt ridiculous, too, surely the only man in hundreds of miles wearing a dark-blue three-piece suit and holding a black leather briefcase under one arm. "Cici, he's dead," he said gently at last.

He had decided not to say more than he had to about Bannerman's death. There would be time enough for Cici to learn what had happened. This was not the moment.

They stood there facing each other for a moment in silence, then Booker stepped out into the sunlight and put his arms around her as she began to cry.

She was the last of Arthur Aldon Bannerman's children to hear of his death. And the only one to cry.

AMBASSADOR ROBERT ARTHUR BANNERMAN had heard the news of his father's death two days earlier in Caracas, though he was not immediately informed of the circumstances. They would later strike him as richly ironic.

He was not in the residence when the news came. It was his custom to leave the embassy at six if there was no official entertaining to be done, with strict instructions that he was not to be disturbed unless there was an emergency. Few emergencies were likely to trouble the relationship between the United States of America and the Republic of Venezuela, which was one reason why Robert Bannerman had been appointed to the post.

There were other reasons, none of which included any special talent for diplomacy on Robert Bannerman's part. Every Republican President felt a natural obligation to "do something" for the Bannerman family, which had never failed to support even the least promising of Republican presidential candidates. To many people, indeed, the Bannermans were almost synonymous with the Republican Party—the wealthy East Coast internationalist wing of it, anyway. Arthur Bannerman, the ambassador's father, had coveted his party's Presidential nomination for years, though less patrician Republicans joked that he expected to be crowned King Arthur by acclamation at the convention —and indeed it was difficult for most people to imagine his pressing the flesh at primaries, or horse-trading with cigar-chewing pols. The Bannermans, like the Lodges, the Cabots, and the Saltonstalls, loved the Republican Party, but from a distance, and with a well-justified suspicion that their feelings were not reciprocated.

Arthur Bannerman's loyalty—and perennial disappointment—called for some reward, however, and since he owned several thousand acres of Venezuela, it seemed only fitting to make his elder son ambassador to that country.

It was not a post that Robert Bannerman wanted, or one his father thought him particularly well suited for, but Robert had accepted it nevertheless, partly out of a sense of noblesse oblige and partly because he felt something at least was owed to him after two unsuccessful—and expensive—attempts to win a seat in the United States Senate. Besides, it was an offer he could hardly refuse if he had any further political ambitions, and it was well known that his eye was on the governorship of New York State—a subject about which the President had been sympathetic, if slightly evasive, when he offered Robert the ambassadorship. "After all, Bob," the President had said, with a flash of his famous smile, "you've got the looks, the money, a famous name . . . besides, you can probably commute to Albany from Kiawa every day in half an hour—nice work, if you can get it."

Robert Bannerman winced when the President called him "Bob," but did his best to hide it. Like his father, he never allowed his first name to be contracted and hated familiarity, but he could hardly correct the President.

Robert shared the President's opinion of his advantages. He *was* good-looking—he knew that. His name *was* famous—though he had long since learned that was not necessarily an asset in politics. One day, when his father died, he would have control over one of America's great fortunes. In the meantime he was stuck with the crippling debts of two primary campaigns and a Senate race, paid for out of his own pocket, and an ambassadorship to a country whose capital resembled Miami.

He made the best of it. Americans might have ambiguous feelings about the morality of great wealth, but in Venezuela the rich did not suffer from self-doubt. They spent lavishly, lived for pleasure, and paid no taxes, without apologies or guilt. It was a society tailor-made for a handsome wealthy forty-year-old divorced ambassador whose qualifications included polo, golf, and a legendary way with women.

.   .   .

WHEN THE NEWS CLATTERED over the AP ticker in the Chancery at midnight, the ambassador's personal assistant broke into a sweat. He knew where to *find* Ambassador Bannerman—it was common knowledge among the embassy staff. He also knew there was nothing more likely to provoke the ambassador's wrath than being disturbed. Still, it was his duty, the young man told himself. He tore off the news bulletin, folded it in his pocket, and went down to call for an embassy car.

The big apartment building on the Avenida Generalísimo Jiménez, a towering modern structure of daringly curved concrete, marble and black glass, was set in one of the most luxurious private gardens in the city. It would not have seemed out of place in Los Angeles or Miami except for the fact that the driveway was blocked by a steel gate, beside which was an armored plate booth with bulletproof windows, manned by armed guards. The Venezuelan upper class took no chances when it came to security. They kept their money in Switzerland and New York, and turned their houses into fortresses. *"Après nous le déluge"* might have been the national motto.

At the sight of the diplomatic plates, the guard pushed a button to open the gate. The car swept up the driveway, between the rows of floodlit palm trees and fountains, and stopped in front of the marble entrance.

The ambassador's own car and driver were not in sight. Most of the Caracas beau monde knew he kept a lavish apartment here, but he tried not to advertise the fact. He was always driven here in a plain, unmarked sedan rather than his official limousine, and invariably without a police escort. It gave the embassy security staff nightmares, but Ambassador Bannerman considered it was their job to protect him as best they could without interfering with his life.

The ambassador's personal assistant hurried through the lobby, ignoring the uniformed doormen, stepped into the elevator, and pushed the button for the fourteenth floor penthouse. The doors slid open silently; he stepped out onto the thick plush carpet of the hallway and pressed the unmarked doorbell. There was no reaction. He pressed again. He heard a click as the peephole opened.

"What the devil are you doing here?" the ambassador asked, his voice muffled by the closed door, but not so much that his irritation couldn't be heard.

The young man broke into a sweat. He didn't feel it was appropriate to break the news through a closed door—that seemed wrong, somehow. "I have an urgent message, Mr. Ambassador," he whispered, putting his face as close to the door as he could.

"Urgent? Is it from the Secretary of State? I talked to the damned fool yesterday, and he didn't even seem to know where Venezuela *was!*"

"It's personal, sir."

"Personal? What the hell is it about?"

"I think you should read it yourself, sir."

"Oh, very well."

There was a clatter of chains being unfastened and locks turning; then the door swung open, revealing a glimpse of Ambassador Robert Bannerman's luxurious bachelor pied-à-terre and the ambassador himself, wearing only a towel wrapped around his waist. He glared unpleasantly at the young man before him. "It had better be important," he said grimly. "Hand it over."

"Robert, darling," a clear, high-pitched feminine voice called out, presumably from the bedroom. "Is something the matter?"

"Nothing, dear. A message. I'll only be a moment."

There was a rustle of silk and a sudden scent of expensive perfume. A beautiful young woman appeared behind the ambassador, her long blond hair in disarray, wrapping herself in a man's dressing gown. "My husband hasn't returned from Paris early, has he?" she asked anxiously. "Tell me the truth!"

"No, no, I'm sure it's nothing like that," the ambassador said impatiently, unfolding the piece of paper.

"It's not bad news, is it, darling?"

In the dim light it was hard to tell, but the young man was *almost* sure it was the wife of Manolo Guzmán y Pereira, the oil tycoon, and reputedly the real power behind the new government. If so—and a closer look told him it *was* so—the ambassador was taking a very undiplomatic risk. He shuddered to think of the political consequences if Guzmán ever found out the American ambassador was sleeping with his wife.

The ambassador's expression was ambiguous, but not by any stretch of the imagination grief-stricken. "A family matter," he said to the woman. "Nothing for you to concern yourself about, dear."

He handed the news bulletin back to his assistant. "Go back and send a cable to my grandmother," he ordered. "Tell her I'll be home tomorrow night."

He began to close the door, then opened it again a fraction. "Don't just stand there with your mouth open, man. What is it?"

"I just wanted to say how sorry I am, sir."

Ambassador Bannerman nodded. "Quite," he whispered gravely. "Thank you. It's a great tragedy, of course. Still, life must go on."

The door slammed in the young man's face. He heard the locks being turned and the chain refastened. Then he heard—or thought he heard —laughter, and after a few minutes, a groan of pleasure, followed by the voice of Señora Guzmán shrieking, "Ay, you brute, Robert, at least wait until we're back in bed!"

Just to reassure himself that he had not given the Ambassador the wrong message, the young man opened the piece of paper and read it again. But there was no mistake.

Arthur Aldon Bannerman was dead of a heart attack at the age of sixty-four.

The AP message did not say where he had died.

PUTNAM BANNERMAN II, the ambassador's younger brother, learned of his father's death at dawn, on the way to Central Park for his morning run.

He was not an enthusiastic runner. As a young man he had been something of a natural athlete, good at all the sports young men of his class were supposed to be good at—though without the fierce competitive edge that had made his older brother legendary at Groton and Harvard. Putnam was the bigger of the two brothers, with the build of a quarterback, but it was Robert who scored a famous last-second-of-the-game touchdown for Harvard against Yale, and went on to become one of the country's highest-ranked polo players.

Even now, at the age of thirty-six, Putnam still had an athlete's muscles, without any need to maintain them by exercise, but unlike his older brother, he was beginning to put on weight—not much, but just enough to push him into the park every morning, in an old college sweatsuit and sneakers, with a towel wrapped around his neck. He refused to buy fancy running shoes—he preferred to think of himself as being "in training," as opposed to running, though what he was in training for was unclear, even to him.

He stood on the pavement under the awning of his building on Central Park West, breathing in the crisp morning air and trying to convince himself that he was enjoying himself. He was not an early riser when it could be avoided, but he had told so many people about his morning run—and how much better he felt for it—that he now felt obligated to do it.

He wished the idea had never occurred to him in the first place; then he thought about the fact that his trousers felt too tight around the waist these days, took a deep breath, and did a few knee bends to limber up, aware that the doorman was staring at him with amusement from the warmth of the lobby. Putnam waved at him—he prided himself on getting along well with everyone—ran in place for a few seconds to show he meant business, then started up Central Park West toward Tavern on the Green, where he usually began his run.

He jogged up to the corner, smiled as he passed the dog-walker, punctual as always, with half a dozen Labradors, golden retrievers, and a chow at her heels, reminded himself as he did every day that she would make a great picture, then paused at Sixty-sixth Street, waiting for the light to change. He glanced at the headlines in *The New York Times* behind the glass window of the newspaper-vending machine on the corner, preparing himself to sprint across the avenue as soon as the light turned green, and stopped dead.

He leaned over to peer at the front page. The glass was dirty, and somebody had scrawled "Get the rich off our backs" across it with a thick felt-tipped marker pen—still it was possible to distinguish the familiar face of his father staring back at him, flashing the smile that many people, years ago, had believed would take him to the White House if he wanted to get there badly enough.

These days the photograph usually accompanied stories in the Arts & Leisure section about the Bannerman Foundation. "Putt" (as Putnam was called in the family) knew there could be only one reason now for it to appear on the front page.

It occurred to him that he had not listened to his messages on the answering machine last night—the light had been blinking rapidly in the dark when he fell into bed. He had ignored it deliberately.

He put his hand automatically to where his pocket should have been, but of course it wasn't there. He carried no money when he was running—only his key, looped around his neck on a string. He wondered if he could borrow thirty cents from the dog-walker, but she had already vanished around the corner.

He thought a moment about the absurdity of the situation—a Bannerman obliged to beg a total stranger for change! He looked up and down the street, but there was nobody in sight, not even the doorman, who had gone off somewhere. He tried to pull open the door of the machine, but it was firmly locked. He gave it a kick. Nothing happened —it had been built to withstand casual urban violence.

"Shit!" he said. He put both arms around the machine and lifted it up. He was surprised at its weight. He clasped it in a bear hug, bending his knees, raised it chest-high, grunting with the strain, then dropped it back on the pavement. The glass door popped open, scattering copies of the *Times* onto the street. A taxi driver slowed down to see what was happening, took one look at the spectacle of a sweating, red-faced, unshaven man trashing a street vending machine, and sped away from trouble with a screech of tires.

Putt picked up a copy of the *Times* and ran back to his building. "I didn't have any fucking change on me," he explained to the doorman, who had reappeared in the lobby, attracted by the noise outside.

"I didn't see nothing, man."

Putt nodded. One of the few things he liked about New York was the fact that nobody ever saw or heard anything. He did not know his neighbors' names, and if they knew his, they never mentioned it. It was one of the reasons he lived on the West Side, to the horror of his family, to most of whom Central Park West might as well have been Calcutta or Beirut.

He read the story quickly in the elevator. The facts of his father's life he knew, and skipped over. The facts of his death were obscure. A "family representative"—Putt guessed it was Uncle Cordy—merely reported that Arthur Bannerman had died of a heart attack. The details of the funeral would be announced later.

Putt glanced at the message light on his answering machine, blinking away furiously now, no doubt signaling a new flood of calls ordering him back into the family fold. He broke into a cold sweat at the thought.

He went into the kitchen, poured himself a glass of orange juice and sat down to read the rest of the story. He knew what he was doing—it was the old familiar pattern of temporizing, delaying, avoiding to the last minute the necessity of confronting the family, and the inescapable fact that he was part of it. He had done it a thousand times before— when he was expelled from Groton, when he ran away from military school, when he became the first Bannerman ever to flunk out of Harvard. . . .

Of course it had never worked—not for long, anyway. No matter how far he ran, the family eventually caught up with him. He glanced at the photographs he had taken, thumbtacked to the wall, reminders of the days when he thought he was doing something that mattered: a Marine, his face blank with grief and horror, holding a poncho over his dying comrade; a Vietnamese family watching as a soldier set fire to their hut, their eyes reflecting the flames; a boulevard in Saigon, empty except for a single body sprawled in the center, next to a shattered bicycle . . . they were the mementos of a kind of love affair, reminders of an excitement that he had once felt and could no longer reach.

His father had supported the war—backed it to the hilt, *believed* in it, long after everyone else knew the only thing that mattered was to bury the dead and go home—but he—which was perhaps worse—had seen it close up for what it was, and loved it all the same. It was as if it had been waiting for him, the noisy climax to a decade of rebellion, the logical destination of all those years of motorcycle accidents and expulsions from school, of rock concerts and drug trips. He and his generation had made a profession of tempting fate, and fate had caught up with them at Khe San and Danang, at the Citadel in Hue and in the Bloody Triangle. He had once gone home wearing a grunt's T-shirt with the slogan "Born to Lose." His father—no big grin on the old man's face that day—had snapped, "Take that damned thing off—no Bannerman can ever say *that* about himself!"

He opened the second section, found the end of the story and folded the paper back. At the end of the column was a brief paragraph that caught his attention. "A spokesman for the Emergency Medical Service reported that a family representative had summoned an ambulance at 9:00 P.M. last night after the billionaire philanthropist was struck by a heart attack at the apartment of a friend, but Mr. Bannerman was already dead when the ambulance arrived. 'We made it to West 68th Street in twelve minutes from the time the call was logged,' the driver said, 'well below average. There was no delay—the guy was just dead.'"

Putt closed his eyes and thought about running away. The income from his trust fund was more than enough to keep him out of the country for a year. If he hurried, he could be on his way to Mexico or Europe in a couple of hours and stay away until things had settled down. Then he thought about Cici, and knew he couldn't go.

He sat for a moment in the kitchen, surrounded by expensive appliances that he had never used, trying to sort out his feelings about the death of his father. Did he feel grief? He could not be sure. He had grieved at his mother's death—run from that grief into a wildness that increased his pain, rather than drowning it as he had hoped. Somewhere along the way he had grown indifferent to any death but that, as if death no longer had the power to shock him. It sometimes seemed to him that almost everyone who had mattered to his generation was dead —Janis, Elvis, Otis Redding, Lenny Bruce, John Lennon, Jack and Bobby and Martin Luther King. . . . Not since Custer's last stand at the Little Bighorn had so many Americans died with so little to show for it.

He had watched Bobby Kennedy die through the viewfinder of his Nikon, pushing and shoving for a tighter frame, numb to everything but the photograph—a true pro—and he had loved Bobby as much as he could bring himself to love any politician, to the rage of his brother and his father, who hated the Kennedys.

He walked into the bedroom to search for the clothes he would need —anything, he reflected, rather than push the button on the answering machine and hear those familiar voices announcing, with various degrees of self-importance and urgency, a new family drama, and pointing his duty out to him.

Did he still have a decent white shirt? he wondered. It had been years since he had worn one. He seemed to remember giving the last one to a girl who liked to wear men's shirts in bed. He would have to buy a couple of white shirts on his way to Kiawa—he refused to think of it as "home"—and a black tie.

Then, as he blew the dust off a pair of plain black shoes—the kind his father would have approved of, with plain toes and five eyelets—it suddenly occurred to Putt what was so puzzling about the story in the *Times*. The idea of Arthur Bannerman's having "a friend" on the West Side was absurd. To the best of Putt's knowledge, his father never went west of Fifth Avenue, except for the occasional obligatory formal evening at Lincoln Center, of which he was, naturally, a trustee, as he was of countless other institutions.

Nothing that Putt could imagine would have brought his father to the West Side, to die within three blocks of Putt's own apartment. A woman? That was possible, of course, but the kind of woman Arthur Bannerman knew lived on Sutton Place or Fifth Avenue, not the West Side in what must be, he guessed—for it was Putt's neighborhood—a walk-up brownstone. And how, he wondered, had "the family representative" known it was necessary to call for an ambulance?

He stripped off his running clothes and rewound the tape on the answering machine. The first three messages were from Giselle, his about-to-be ex-girlfriend—exactly the ones he had been determined to ignore, the first two begging him to call her back, the last, predictably, telling him to fuck off. The next messages were from Cordy DeWitt, asking him to telephone "at once," with increasing exasperation, but it was the last message on the tape that got Putt dressed in a hurry. The voice was unmistakably that of his brother, Robert, and it said, "Read the goddamn papers, why don't you—then get your ass up to Kiawa on the double before I send the Marines out looking for you."

Putt was out of the shower, dressed and weaving his silver Porsche 930 Turbo in and out of the traffic on the West Side Highway in less than half an hour.

He was on the Taconic, across the Dutchess County line, before he remembered that he still didn't have a white shirt.

"DO STOP FIDGETING, Courtland."

Courtland Cross DeWitt suppressed a sigh and removed his fingers from his gold watch chain. He placed his hands behind his back, where they couldn't be seen, and glanced out the window, wishing he were elsewhere.

Before him, the low, rolling, wooded hills stretched to the Hudson River, five thousand acres of land, all of it owned by Arthur Aldon Bannerman—the *late* Arthur Aldon Bannerman, he reminded himself.

Arthur's grandfather, Cyrus, had acquired the land, and named his estate Kiawa, after the Indian tribe that had once lived here before they were dispossessed by the Dutch. He sent to France for an architect to design his house, to Italy for the stonemasons to build it, to England for the landscape architects and gardeners to give it a proper setting. The result resembled a vastly enlarged French château of the seventeenth century and was, for many years, the largest private residence in the United States.

It was one of the most famous houses in America. When King George VI and Queen Elizabeth came to Hyde Park to visit the Roosevelts, the royal couple had expressed the desire to see Kiawa, and had been driven over to have tea in this very room—though without Mrs. Roosevelt, since Putnam Bannerman, Cyrus's son, hated FDR and the New Deal, and often referred to his neighbor, the President, in public, as "the greatest fraud and hypocrite since Pontius Pilate."

Somewhere beyond the golden hills, glistening in the autumn sunlight after a light morning rain, was the Kiawa home farm's prize herd of Black Angus, and beyond that the stables and paddocks of Kiawa Stud, where two Kentucky Derby winners had been bred (the Triple Crown had always eluded the Bannermans, as if to prove that money couldn't buy everything). Farther still was the Gothic church the first Putnam Bannerman had built—some said in an attempt to expiate the sins of his robber baron father.

At this very moment, it occurred to DeWitt, a grave was no doubt being dug for Arthur Bannerman. The staff of Kiawa was so large that it included all sorts of people whose crafts had long since ceased to be in demand, most of them passed on from father to son. Somewhere on the estate there was a man who repaired carriages, as well as a harness maker, a blacksmith, a stonemason. Were there gravediggers as well, he wondered, or did some of them simply double as gravediggers when the occasion arose? The thought depressed DeWitt, who was almost the same age as his deceased brother-in-law.

He turned his attention back to the old woman sitting in front of him, resigned to the fact that Eleanor Bannerman would probably be around to order his burial, just as she was her son's.

At the look in her eyes he suppressed an urge to straighten his tie and put his hands in his trouser pockets. Eleanor Bannerman's eyes could best be described as "piercing," though that word hardly did justice to them. Courtland had long ago learned to read them, and at the moment they signaled impatience and anger. He did not expect tears, of course. If Eleanor ever cried, she would do it in private. She had so far buried a husband, a son and a grandson without anyone in the family's having seen her cry.

Old as she was—eighty-six, as of this year—there was nothing confused in that demanding stare. She not only had all her marbles, he reflected, she had everybody else's as well. Though he was six feet three inches tall, senior partner of a distinguished law firm, and by now a wealthy man in his own right, he stood before her like a naughty child, trying not to fidget.

His mother-in-law was hardly more than five feet two, perhaps less, but she had such presence that few people ever thought of her as small. She sat there on a petit-point Louis XV sofa, her hands neatly folded in her lap and her knees pressed together, dressed in a Chanel suit of a brocade so stiff and heavy that it was a wonder she could carry the weight of it. Her white hair was formed into a coiffure as elaborate as Marie Antoinette's. Her diamonds glittered in the morning sun from the tall windows: a heavy necklace, an immense old-fashioned bracelet, like a jeweled handcuff, three rings on each hand, diamond earrings the size of walnuts—her "daytime" jewels, as she called them, a small part of the fabulous collection she had amassed over the years.

A man came up from Cartier once a year in a limousine to clean her diamonds, and stayed for a week to do it, like the man who came up regularly from New York City to look after the hundreds of antique clocks—for Eleanor Bannerman insisted that all of them should chime simultaneously. The only standard she knew was perfection, and she accepted nothing less, which explained why the manner of her son's death seemed to her like a personal affront.

Courtland DeWitt had married Elizabeth Bannerman, the elder of Eleanor's two daughters, almost forty years ago, but he was conscious of never having been able to meet his mother-in-law's standards of perfection. The only consolation was that her children and grandchildren had done no better. He thought of his wife's sister, Katherine; he thought of Arthur's youngest son, Putt; he thought of poor Cici, far away in Africa, trying to exorcise the Bannerman family's wealth among the starving Ugandans. He cleared his throat.

"As I was saying . . ." His voice boomed out, the courtroom voice which in his younger days had kept juries awake through the most somnolent of trials. He coughed and lowered it to a more conversational tone before she could remind him that she wasn't deaf. She suffered, in fact, from none of the infirmities of age, much to DeWitt's annoyance, since he had acquired no small number of them himself, though twenty years her junior.

". . . As I was saying, I think we'll have to face the music."

"*Music?* Whatever can you mean? We're threatened with a disgraceful scandal. I asked you what we can do to prevent it."

"That's my point, Eleanor. I don't think there's anything we *can* do to prevent it. By the time I received the call, poor Arthur was already dead."

"Then why did you telephone for an ambulance?"

"I didn't know he was dead. I only knew he'd had a heart attack. He might have been alive, after all."

"You should have gone there yourself."

"I'm not a doctor. My first thought was to get help to him. By the time I got to the apartment, the police and the ambulance people were already there. Of course, the moment the police heard the name, they came in droves—a full inspector showed up. It didn't take them long to realize that Arthur had been dead for an hour or two."

"Surely you ought to have been able to deal with them? When Uncle

John died in the Harvard Club, my husband called Mayor LaGuardia and said, 'John Aldon passed away in his sleep.' And the Mayor told the police to put it down that way. One has to be firm with these people."

DeWitt fiddled with the change in his pocket, then thought the better of it and stopped. He longed for a cigar, but it was out of the question in Eleanor's presence. At Kiawa, cigars were permitted only after dinner, when Eleanor and whatever other ladies were present withdrew to leave the men to their brandy. DeWitt remembered Uncle John's death all too well—John had left his wife after a bitter quarrel, and taken a room at the Harvard Club, where he drank himself into a stupor at the bar, then went upstairs and fell asleep in the bath, leaving the hot-water tap running. Unfortunately, the boiler had been turned up too high by a careless janitor, and John was boiled to death.

"Wealth doesn't command the same respect it used to," he said gently. "Besides, there were some rather—embarrassing—problems. Arthur had been dressed, you see, *after* he died. And the police couldn't help noticing that, once they started to examine the body."

He paused. There seemed no point in telling Eleanor that Arthur's shorts were on back to front and that his waistcoat buttons were done up unevenly. The inspector, a burly man with the face of a prizefighter and a detective's knowing eyes, had taken him to one side in the bath room, puffing on the cigar DeWitt had offered him. "You'll never get away with it," he whispered. "Those are young cops out there. They'll want to get their names in the fucking papers. And those two spics from EMS—they're not dumb. They'll be over at the New York *Post* to sell the story as soon as they've left the goddamn body in the morgue." He flicked the ash off the end of his cigar into the toilet. "Poor guy—he thought he was coming, but he was going!"

Luckily Eleanor Bannerman did not ask for details. Like a lawyer, she knew better than to ask a question when she wasn't certain she would like the answer. "Can't it be kept out of the press?"

"Frankly, I don't think so. By tomorrow the tabloids will be having a field day. 'Billionaire's love nest.' That sort of thing. And that will be only the beginning, I'm afraid. Somebody is bound to ask whether Arthur might not have been saved if the girl had called an ambulance right away."

"And why *didn't* she?"

"She panicked. She's very young. There was Arthur—forgive me, Eleanor—dead in her bed. Or dying, perhaps. She tried to cover up what had happened by moving him to the living room and putting his clothes back on. She may have been thinking of his reputation, you know."

"Or her own. Will she talk to the press?"

"No, I feel sure she won't." Courtland DeWitt stood on tiptoe for a moment, stretching his muscles. Despite the heat from the fireplace—Eleanor Bannerman hated cold rooms—he felt chilled. He nerved himself to go on. "There's a more serious problem," he said, gathering up his courage.

"More serious than my son dying in the bed of some little tramp? What on *earth* can you have in mind?"

DeWitt stared at the carpet in front of him as if he were trying to memorize the pattern. He could feel his courage, such as it was, ebbing fast. "Well, she's not exactly a tramp, Eleanor," he said cautiously, taking his hands from his pockets and rubbing them together.

Eleanor Bannerman's eyebrows were small works of art, plucked and shaped into elegant, thin curves. They might have been painted on by one of the old masters, so little did they resemble ordinary human eyebrows. She raised one gracefully. She was not about to help him out.

There was a long silence during which DeWitt could hear the clocks ticking all over the house like some kind of Chinese torture. Then, as if on cue, they burst into song—chiming, ringing, whirring, and playing music in a deafening chorus.

DeWitt tried to look her in the eye and failed. He glanced at the Bannerman tapestry, for which Cyrus Bannerman had outbid Frick, a fifteenth-century Flemish rendering of the expulsion from the Garden of Eden, then back at Eleanor. His mother-in-law's expression seemed mirrored in the face of the angel with the flaming sword.

"The fact is," he said at last, "the girl claims they were married."

PART ONE

THE
FIRST
STONE

1

She was alone at last. An apartment of her own in New York had once been among the most glittering and improbable of her dreams. Tonight it seemed as cold and unfamiliar as a stranger's.

She had never been burglarized, though burglary was a major topic of conversation among her neighbors; this was the West Side of Manhattan, after all, so she knew plenty of people who had been, and most of them said that it felt like a kind of violation to find your apartment ransacked by strangers. The place you thought was safe, they agreed, no longer was; you could never feel the same about it again.

Elizabeth Alexandra Walden understood that feeling very well now, though all her possessions were intact. There was a smell of stale cigar smoke in the air, the furniture had been moved out of place, the carpet was covered with footmarks; a half-empty Styrofoam container of deli coffee stood on the antique chinoiserie lacquer table, where it would certainly leave a ring, and several crumpled Polaroid film wrappers lay on the floor. Everywhere she looked, the ashtrays were not only full, but overflowing.

She wondered if tidying up would make her feel better, decided it wouldn't, then started to do it anyway, just as her mother would have expected. City folk might allow themselves the luxury of wallowing in their grief, but farm folk kept their emotions to themselves and got on with the chores.

She remembered once when she was four years old she fell and skinned her knees; her father picked her up, dried her tears and said to her solemnly, "Farmers' daughters don't cry, Lizzy." She knew he meant it—her father meant everything he said, though he never said much. She had felt guilty about crying ever since. She had not even cried at his funeral.

Tonight, she told herself bitterly, her father would have been pleased with her. She had held herself back from crying, even though she knew the absence of her tears shocked everyone—the police, Courtland DeWitt, even the paramedics. Tears were expected of her. Stubbornly she had refused to oblige.

For hours she had longed for them to be out of the apartment with their equipment, their cameras, their questions, and their knowing, scarcely veiled tones of accusation, as if *she* were somehow responsible for Arthur Bannerman's death. Now they were gone, and she could almost have wished them back. Anything—almost anything, anyway— was better than being here alone, unable to cry.

With a sense of purpose that she recognized as misplaced, she cleared the debris, washed the ashtrays, polished the lacquer tabletop until every mark was gone except the damned ring, vacuumed the rug.

Once she had shared an apartment in the Village with a girl who responded to emotional crises by covering whatever flat surfaces were available with contact paper. Sometimes, she would work right through the night, as silent and unreachable as an autistic child, totally absorbed in the task of lining the inside of the kitchen drawers or the closet shelves. Alexandra moved on when her roommate began to cover the bathroom walls and ceiling, but now for the first time she understood what was behind that mindless activity.

She had no idea of the time, though she guessed it must be near dawn. She should have been exhausted, but instead she was driven by a kind of manic, pointless energy, plumping pillows, moving furniture back and forth, even polishing the silver picture frame that contained the only photograph she had of Arthur Bannerman and herself to- gether.

It had been taken at a ball at the Metropolitan Museum of Art, and, to her regret, there were several other people in the picture. Arthur Bannerman was standing next to her, but a little apart, as if he were anxious to keep some distance between them in public. His hands were firmly jammed into the pockets of his dinner jacket, possibly to restrain himself from putting his arm around her, and he was looking straight at the camera. There was a faint expression of irritation on his face at being photographed.

Anyone looking at the picture would have thought they were total strangers, which was no doubt exactly what he had hoped to convey. It was a disappointing memento, but it was all she had, except for his gifts —and all she was *going* to have now, she reflected, wiping the glass clean with a cloth.

She allowed herself to look at the telephone on the antique desk that she had bought after so much hesitation. She was too much her father's daughter to feel easy about spending money, even when it was an unexpected windfall.

More than anything, just at the moment she wanted to talk to somebody, anybody, who could offer her comfort and understanding without asking too many questions. The list of people who could be counted on for that, she decided, was not long to begin with, and even shorter in the middle of the night. She thought of her mother, but if there was one thing her mother would have plenty of, it was questions, and most of them would be difficult to answer.

Whatever the time was, her mother would probably be awake, even allowing for the fact that it was an hour earlier in Illinois. On a dairy farm life revolved around the animals; a man who wasn't milking his cows by three in the morning in the summer, or four in the winter, wasn't much of a dairy farmer. Even now, though she didn't need to, her mother rose every morning at three, went down to the kitchen to heat herself a cup of coffee and drink it alone at the big, scrubbed pine table, opposite the place where Alexa's father had sat every morning in his clean overalls—he believed in starting out clean every day, however messy the work—freshly shaved and impatient to get on with the milking.

Alexandra tried to think of an easy way to break the news to her mother that she was a widow, but since she hadn't yet told her she was married, it was a difficult proposition, not made easier by the fact that Arthur had been more than twice her age—a lot more—older, as it happened, than her mother.

She could almost hear her mother's voice, asking questions which would at first seem naive and innocent, but which always led her inexorably to the truth. Alexandra's mother seemed to many people in Stephenson County more than a little out of touch with reality—had seemed so even when she was young—but behind the puzzled expression, the big, innocent blue eyes, and the general impression she gave of being a sheltered Southern belle, incapable of dealing with the facts of life, she was, Alexa knew, as hard as nails and twice as sharp. What she did not want to know she affected not to hear, but it was impossible to hide anything from her for long.

Alexa could guess just what her mother would say: "I don't know what your father would think, Liz"—a ritual phrase, even now, when he had been dead for six years, which allowed her not to say what *she* thought. Alexa had stopped thinking of herself as "Liz" or "Lizzy" or even "Elizabeth," years ago. Now Elizabeth (or worse, Liz) seemed to her a different person altogether from the one she had become, making communication with her mother even more difficult.

Alexa had been taught "never to put off to tomorrow what you can do today"—virtually the household motto, as it was for every farm family—but she had learned a lot since coming to New York, and putting off things when you could get away with it was one of them. She would have to tell her mother, and the sooner the better, but just at the moment she was in no mood.

She picked up the telephone, touched the buttons, and listened to the ring. There was a click, a pause, then the sound of Madonna singing "Material Girl" for about thirty seconds—Simon Wolff changed the music on his tape at least twice a week to show he kept up with things. "For we are living in the material world, and I am a material girl," Madonna sang, a sentiment with which Simon would certainly have agreed, followed by Simon's own voice—cautious, neutral, giving away nothing, asking the caller to leave a name and number. Typically, Simon did not say that he was out, or would be back soon, or even give his own name.

Simon did not believe in telling anyone more than was absolutely necessary. He was the kind of man who not only had an unlisted telephone number but peeled the labels off his junk mail before throwing it away, just in case somebody might go through the garbage and find his address.

"Simon, it's me," she said, after the beep. For what seemed a very long time, there was no reaction, except for the hissing of the tape. She rubbed the dust cloth over the leather top of the desk impatiently. Could he be asleep? But even under normal circumstances, he was an unapologetic night person, for whom four in the morning might as well have been the middle of the day. Or did he simply not want to talk to her? That was certainly possible, but unlikely. If there was one thing Simon enjoyed, it was involving himself in someone else's drama. Give him a breakup, a divorce, or a suicide attempt, and he was at your door in nothing flat at any hour of the day or night.

She heard him pick up the receiver at last. In the background she could hear what sounded like a movie sound track. In her mind's eye she could see him lying on the enormous bed in a terry-cloth robe, switching restlessly from one cable channel or taped movie to another, waiting for dawn and the two or three hours of sleep that were apparently all he needed. Simon's bedroom was a kind of high-tech playground, which one of his friends had once described as looking like a Japanese trade fair. On the wall opposite the bed was a giant television screen; the headboard and night tables resembled the control panels of a space shuttle. The ceiling was mirrored, the walls upholstered in black leather, the furniture chrome, glass, stainless steel. There was too much of everything: erotic sculpture, cunningly lit by concealed spotlights, revolved on Lucite pedestals; holograms glowed against the darkness of the walls; neon objets d'art blinked on and off.

"For God's sake, Simon, it's Alexa!" she said impatiently.

There was a pause. "Are you alone?" His voice was even more remote and cautious in person than the one on the tape of the answering machine.

"They left hours ago, Simon. I was waiting for you to call."

"Are you crazy? For all I knew, the police might have picked up the phone. Are you all right?"

Was she? In a sense, she was, yes. She had managed to clean the apartment, had she not? She had not fainted, or taken an overdose of pills, or burst into uncontrollable tears. On the other hand, she hadn't been able to make herself touch the bed, let alone lie down on it, and could not even begin to think about the future, which was going to present itself, in one form or another, the moment the sun was up.

"Hello? Are you there?"

"I'm sorry. No, I'm not all right."

"What happened?"

"It was awful. You'd have thought I killed him! Nobody even *listened* to me—not even Arthur's brother-in-law."

"DeWitt? Yes, he's a cold fish, that one. Did they believe your story?"

She trembled for a moment, remembering the panic she had felt when the doorbell rang, knowing it was the police, whom she had summoned, that it was too late to undo what she had done, that she was stuck with her story.

"No," she said. "The uniformed cops, the first ones who came, they might have believed it, but I don't think it fooled the paramedics for a second. Then an inspector arrived with a couple of detectives. He knew exactly what had happened. I could see it in his eyes."

"Forget his eyes. Did he *say* anything?"

"He didn't accuse me outright, no, if that's what you mean. But I could tell from the kind of questions he asked what he was thinking."

"Don't worry about what he *thinks*. Cops are paid to think the worst. Did he ask you if anyone else had been in the apartment?"

"Yes. Over and over again."

"What did you say?"

"I said no, I'd been alone."

"Good girl." He paused. She could hear a clicking noise and guessed he was changing channels with the remote control of his television. "Of course," he continued, "I never thought they'd buy it. I did warn you."

She said nothing. It was undeniably true.

"It still baffles me, frankly—your caring that much about Bannerman's goddamn reputation. Not many people would have taken a risk like that for the old man. It's a side to your character I hadn't fully appreciated. I keep forgetting you come from the Midwest."

"I told you. I loved him."

"Yes, I know," he said impatiently. Talk about love never failed to irritate Simon, who denied the emotion existed, or that it made any sense if it did. He liked to claim, with some pride, that he had never experienced it himself, yet was perfectly happy. "We've been through all that, it's simple. Bannerman was a father image—an attractive older man, stupendously rich . . . textbook psychology, absolutely familiar stuff to any Freudian . . . "

She hardly bothered to listen. Simon was a tireless explainer of other people's emotions.

Much of what she had learned about life since coming to New York she owed to him, but on the subject of love she did not think he had anything useful to teach her. Once they had been lovers (a word Simon used only in the physical sense), and from that experience, too, she had learned a lot, much of it unhappy. She did not hold that against him, however. "I don't need a lecture, Simon," she said. "Not tonight."

"That bad, was it?"

His tone was sympathetic, as near as he was ever likely to come to offering an apology. You could say what you liked about Simon, she thought—and most of the people she knew had plenty of bad things to say about him—but you couldn't beat him on intuition. Perhaps because he had so few emotions himself, he was quick to read other people's. Naturally manipulative, even where his self-interest was not directly at stake, he was acutely sensitive to people's feelings, a good listener in a city where most successful men were too busy talking about themselves to hear a word that was said to them.

"That bad. Worse." She was silent for a moment. When she spoke again, her voice was lower, more urgent. "Simon, I can't stay here," she said, almost whispering.

"Come again?"

"I can't stay here alone!" she repeated, aware that her voice was trembling on the brink of hysteria, but unable to control it. "I thought I could. I was okay so long as I was busy cleaning up, but as soon as I stopped, I knew I had to get out of here."

"Calm down. You'll feel better about it in the morning. Trust me."

"I'm not waiting for the morning, Simon."

He sighed.

"Simon, I want to come over there! You can put me in the spare bedroom. Or I'll sleep on the sofa. *Please!*" She paused. "I don't want to be alone, Simon."

"Hey, calm down, I understand. I just don't think it's a good idea."

"I don't care. Anyway, *why* is it a bad idea? Have you got someone there? I don't mind that, for God's sake!"

"No, no, that's not the point. Have you looked outside?"

"Of course not. Why?"

"Well, look! I think you'll find a mob of reporters camped at your door."

Her throat tightened. She put down the receiver, went to the window, and pulled back the curtain. It was impossible to look down at the entrance to the building, but there were at least a dozen men and women on the pavement opposite, including a television news team with a minicam and lights. She felt like a trapped animal. She went back and picked up the telephone. "You're right," she said softly, as if the press outside could hear her.

"Of course I am. You're *news!* My advice is stay put."

She considered his advice for a moment and rejected it. If she had learned anything about Simon in two years of working for him, it was that he would go to any length to keep his name out of the papers. And hers, since she worked for him. Most of the people he knew worked hard to get themselves mentioned in *W*, or on Page Six of the *Post*, or in Liz Smith's column; Simon worked full time to avoid any mention of himself, or his affairs, even in the business section of *The New York Times*. A crowd of reporters would have the same effect on him as a lynch mob.

She had no desire to step out of her front door into a barrage of questions and the glare of lights, but it was better than sitting here, trapped in the apartment where only a few hours ago Arthur Bannerman had died in her arms. "The worst they can do is ask questions," she said more firmly than she felt. "There's no law that says I have to answer them. I'm not going to stay penned up here forever, so I might as well get it over with."

"Be realistic. It's four in the fucking morning. You'll never find a taxi. And if you do, they'll follow you."

Alexa recognized without difficulty the note of caution, like an alarm bell ringing in the distance. Earlier on, Simon had stuck his neck out for her, against his better judgment; now he was ducking. She fought down the impulse to shout at him, knowing it would do no good and only make her feel worse. "I'll get there somehow," she said. "I'll lose them in the park if I have to."

He laughed. "The park? It's a DMZ this time of night!"

Simon was one of those New Yorkers who took a romantic pride in the city's dangers, real and imagined, and he approached a two-block walk down First Avenue as if it were a heroic adventure fraught with peril. His apartment was equipped with enough burglar alarms to protect a missile base; he practiced the martial arts; he had a carry-pistol permit. To the best of Alexa's knowledge, he had never been in Central Park, but it was only natural that he would regard it as a combat zone. "I'll be all right there, Simon," she said. "The muggers go home to bed when there's nobody there to mug. They have business hours like everybody else."

"For Christ's sake, Alexa, your boyfriend was one of the richest men in America. By tomorrow, the whole goddamned world is going to know he dropped dead in your apartment. And it won't take them long to guess he died in your bed. People would think that even if it *weren't* true. In twenty-four hours you're going to be a media celebrity, darling. Like it or not."

"He wasn't my boyfriend, Simon."

"Well, whatever."

She drew a deep breath. "He was my *husband*."

Simon was silent. For a moment, she thought the connection had been broken. Then she heard Otis Redding singing "Try a Little Tenderness" faintly in the background. Presumably Simon had switched from whatever movie he was watching while talking to her to a tape—a sure sign that he was concentrating, his eyes closed to think better. It gave her some pleasure to realize that she had at last managed to shock him.

"What do you mean, 'husband'?" he asked.

"I mean we were married."

"You're kidding me."

"No."

"When, for Christ's sake?"

"Yesterday."

She could hear the noise of his breathing, drowning out Otis Redding. "Why the fuck didn't you tell me?"

It was a good question. She was not proud of her behavior in the past few hours. It had been irrational to insist on dressing Arthur and moving him into the living room—though she still felt that he would not want anyone to have found him lying naked in her bed. Dignity was important to him; the idea of dying while making love to a woman young enough to be his granddaughter would have seemed to him like a joke in bad taste, whether he was married to her or not. Even Simon, whom she had called as soon as she could speak, understood *that*.

It was even more irrational to conceal the secret of their marriage once he was dead. A promise was a promise, and she would never have broken her word to Arthur, but death surely released her from that obligation—made it, in fact, impossible to keep. "Arthur wanted it kept secret until he had a chance to tell the family," she said. "They were all going to be together for his sixty-fifth birthday, you see, and Arthur was going to do it then. . . . "

"I see." He did not sound convinced. "Does DeWitt know?"

"*Nobody* knows. Well, the judge. And his secretary. And Arthur's chauffeur. He was the witness."

"You'd better get over here," Simon said. She noticed his reluctance had vanished completely. "The sooner the better."

"What about the reporters?"

"Push right through them. Don't answer any questions. Keep moving. Give me—oh, say twenty minutes. I'll be waiting for you in the parking lot outside Tavern on the Green."

His tone was brisk but friendly. Alexa had no difficulty in guessing that as the widow of the late Arthur Aldon Bannerman, however recent and embarrassing the circumstances of her widowhood, she was very much more welcome than as an unmarried front-page scandal. She was resentful, but not so much that she was tempted to ignore Simon's quick change of heart. His self-interest was instinctive, so natural that it was impossible to resent for long. In any case, she was in no position to quarrel with him. She needed a friend and an ally, even if his motives were not entirely pure.

She allowed herself a touch of malice. "Aren't you worried about their following us?"

He ignored it. "I'll take them up to Harlem, or even the Bronx, lose them in the streets up there, then come back to the East Side."

Given a practical problem, Simon was unfailingly resourceful, particularly if it involved any kind of adventure; the only thing he truly feared was boredom. "Wear running shoes," he advised. "First thing in the morning, you'd better call DeWitt. It's important he hears the news from you."

"I don't see why . . . " Alexa started to say, not at all sure that she wanted to start the first full day of her widowhood by confronting Courtland DeWitt, whose behavior toward her she was not prepared to forgive, but Simon was already in charge—off and running, as he liked to say about himself. "Twenty minutes from *now*," he said, interrupting her, and hung up the phone.

She looked at her watch, a thin, flexible band of gold scales, with a face so small that it was almost impossible to tell the time—her first present from Arthur. It was typical of him that he had not gone to Buccellati or Tiffany to buy her a present, but instead had given her an infinitely more valuable heirloom. The watch was one of a kind, designed by Cartier in Paris, so unique that when she took it to the Cartier service department on Fifth Avenue, the manager himself came over to examine it and offered to buy it back for the Cartier collection if ever she wanted to sell it. She did not ask what it was worth; the bill for cleaning and regulating it came to nearly five hundred dollars, which she herself paid without telling Arthur.

Ten minutes to go. She gave a moment's thought to her appearance. What, she wondered, was the appropriate look for pushing your way through a crowd of reporters in front of a television camera? The only people she had seen doing it were top-level mafiosi on their way to the grand jury, who usually tried to cover their faces with a coat or windbreaker. She was not about to do that.

Nor, despite Simon's advice, had she any intention of wearing running shoes on national television. She slipped out of the jeans and sweater she had worn through the night—she had not wanted to face the police in a dressing gown—and put on a pleated gray flannel skirt, a silk blouse, high suede boots, and a tweed jacket. There was no point, after all, in dressing like a teenager or a tramp for the media. She picked up her sunglasses and balanced them on her forehead to hold her hair back. She knew better than to cover her eyes—sunglasses worn at night would look like a sure sign of guilt on camera, and she told herself she had nothing to feel guilty about.

Taking her gloves and her handbag from the hall table, she opened the door and went downstairs, conscious, even as she reached the hallway, that the television lights were going on, that the reporters outside were crowding against the frosted-glass doors.

It occurred to her, as she braced herself for the ordeal, that she had come to New York in the hope of being famous. Now fame was about to touch her at last.

For all the wrong reasons.

BEYOND THE FAMILY CIRCLE, Putnam Bannerman was treated like a reasonably intelligent—and talented—adult. He was a successful photographer, wealthy in his own right, more than capable of looking after his own affairs and dealing with the large and small problems of everyday life. He was treated with deference by his bank manager, his maid, his agent, and with varying degrees of affection and admiration by a large number of women. He had only to come home, he reflected, to be treated like a child, or the village idiot.

As the youngest of Arthur Aldon Bannerman's children, he was used to being left out of family councils and was hardly even resentful when it happened. All too often, in the past, they had been about him.

He had solved the problem by staying away, and already he regretted having come back—though in the circumstances he could hardly have refused. He had paid his respects to his grandmother—who told him to find a white shirt and put it on—and exchanged a few words with his brother Robert, who was hard at work "handling things," as if their father's death was a diplomatic crisis.

Robert had taken over his father's study—a dark, paneled room full of leather-bound account books and political mementos—from which he emerged from time to time to announce that he had just talked to the President or that Courtland DeWitt was on his way up from New

York with important news which he didn't want to discuss on the telephone. DeWitt's arrival—and sudden departure—seemed to have created a *real* crisis, and Robert was now upstairs behind locked doors with their grandmother, while the servants walked around on tiptoe, communicating in sepulchral whispers, as if even the slightest noise would bring the wrath of God down on their heads, which, given Mrs. Bannerman's mood, was probably the case.

The news that his father had died in the apartment—possibly even in the bed—of a young woman did not shock Putt. He was surprised, no doubt about that, but in some ways it seemed to him the best thing he had heard about the old man in years. He had assumed that his father was well past that sort of thing—that his life consisted of board meetings, black-tie dinner parties with people his own age, and the kind of stuffy social functions that revolved around the opening of a new wing at the Metropolitan Museum, or the acquisition of a major work by MOMA.

On the few occasions when he had seen his father in the last few years, he had seemed old, tired, and bored, a man firmly planted in a routine that gave him little pleasure and almost no excitement. Putnam did not find that surprising—his father was in his sixties, after all, still smarting from his final, failed attempt at the Presidency, though concealing his disappointment with his usual well-bred self-control. He was healthy, even vigorous, but Putnam had given no thought to his father's sex life, as if the libido had been drained out of Arthur Bannerman along with his presidential ambitions.

Of course children always found it difficult to imagine their parents' sex lives—Putnam, though not a parent, was old enough to know that —but in Arthur Bannerman's case his dignity, his overpowering presence, and his contempt for any behavior that did not live up to his standards made it even harder to think about his having the same needs and weaknesses as lesser mortals. It was like trying to think about George Washington with his teeth out or his pants off.

Putt was amused at the thought of all those lectures about his own morals over the years, but not, he thought, bitter—especially since they had had no effect. On the whole, he was glad that his father had managed to get some enjoyment out of the last years of his life.

He sat in a state of suspended animation, waiting to hear what was going on upstairs, feeling out of place in the big library, a room that had been firmly out of bounds to children, and which he associated with stern lectures on the need to change his ways and act like a Bannerman. His great-grandfather had bought the room, with its Grinling Gibbons paneling and elaborately carved ceiling, from an English duke, and had it shipped to Kiawa, along with its priceless collection of books and manuscripts, as well as half a dozen craftsmen who labored for two years to reassemble it. It belonged in a museum, and Putt wished it were there.

He got up, opened one of the cabinets to reveal a television set, and turned it on for the news—at Kiawa, modern appliances were scrupulously hidden away, in deference to Eleanor's belief that anything made of plastic should be used but not seen. Guests had been known to prowl around the house looking in vain for a telephone, not realizing there was one in the drawer of their bedside table.

He settled back to watch. The lead story was a shooting in the Bronx —how his father would have hated coming second to a shoot-out between the cops and a crazed Hispanic! Not as much, however, as he would have hated what followed: There was some footage of Arthur Bannerman at the Republican national convention, the year Richard Nixon swamped him; an aerial photograph of Kiawa that established the Bannermans as one of the richest families in America, for those who didn't already know; then a shot of a brownstone on West Sixty-eighth Street, where he had died—as Connie Chung announced, with a knowing smile—"in the luxury apartment of a close friend, model Alexandra Walden."

There followed several glamorous photographs of Miss Walden, who was certainly a knockout, Putt thought. The black hair and pale-gray eyes gave her face a startling, almost feline quality, and there was nothing to complain about in the full lips and the high cheekbones— but she didn't have the remote, cold grace of the best models. There was real bone and muscle under the sleek skin. She would have needed to drop five or ten pounds to be a top high-fashion model, and anyway, the top models were now fourteen or fifteen years old, skinny children with pouting, adult faces. An extra five or ten pounds would probably have given her a crack at being a Playmate, though the face was a touch too classy for *Playboy*, he thought. The last photograph showed her in a Kamali bathing suit in which she did not seem entirely at ease.

He heard footsteps behind him, but his attention was fixed on the screen, where the television minicam had caught her pushing her way through a mob of reporters in the middle of the night, a harshly lit mob scene. The camera zoomed in on her face; her expression was grimly determined, though the big, pale-gray eyes showed a trace of panic— or perhaps grief, it was hard to tell.

"How well did you know Mr. Bannerman?" a reporter shouted, his face pressed close to hers.

She shook her head and pushed toward the minicam.

"What was the nature of your relationship?" She was surrounded now, hardly even visible behind all the microphones and tape recorders held close to her face.

"Leave . . . me . . . alone." Her voice was firm, distinct, by no means hysterical. She ducked suddenly, bumped into the minicam, said "I'm sorry" to the invisible operator, or perhaps to the world at large, and vanished out of focus into the darkness at a run.

"Father had better taste than I would have given him credit for." The familiar voice was whipcrack sharp, each syllable as clear as a bell, a trace of Harvard and Groton in every vowel, a voice that sounded as if it was giving orders even when it wasn't.

Putnam looked behind him. Robert was standing there, faultlessly dressed as always. "A damned good-looking girl. Not at all common, wouldn't you agree?"

Putt turned down the sound. "I guess."

"You *guess?* Why the lukewarm reaction, Putt? You *don't* think she has class?"

"Okay, she does, for God's sake! What the fuck does it matter?"

Robert smiled—the knowing, superior smile that always made Putnam feel he was back in the nursery, at the mercy of his elder brother. "Well, it's going to matter, you see. More than you might think. It turns out that young Miss Walden *claims"*—Robert's expression was ironic as he emphasized the word—"that Father married her."

"*Married* her?"

Robert sat down, cocked one leg elegantly over the other—he was one of those men whose clothes never seemed to lose their creases or get wrinkled like ordinary people's. Put him in a rainstorm and he would still manage, without any noticeable effort, to look as if he had just stepped out of his London tailor's in a brand-new suit. He lit a cigarette. He seemed to be having a good time, which Putt recognized as a danger signal. "That's just the kind of intelligent comment I was hoping for," Robert said. "I can always count on you in a goddamn crisis."

Putnam struggled with the thought that his father might have quietly married a woman thirty—no, forty!—years younger than he was. Marriage in the Bannerman family was a serious and solemn business, rather like marriage in the British royal family—only certain other families were considered acceptable; birth, breeding and old money were, of course, required, while the marriage itself involved careful orchestration, a major family gathering, the work of dozens of heavyweight lawyers and—first and foremost—the advice and consent of Eleanor Bannerman. It was not by any means unknown for Bannerman men to have mistresses and girlfriends—though no scandal had ever touched the lives of Putnam's grandfather and great-grandfather except for the kind of financial scandal that infuriated muckrakers and an occasional Senate committee—but Bannerman marriages were the equivalent of alliances or mergers, not to be undertaken lightly, which was one reason that Putt had never married. "Jesus," he said. "Do you think it's true?"

"DeWitt seemed to think it's not. Of course he's an asshole."

"What does Grandmother think?"

"Well, to put it bluntly—she's pissed off. She'd disinherit Father, if he were still alive and she could. *She* thinks the girl is pulling a fast one. Out for money or publicity."

"What do *you* think?"

"It's certainly a possibility. I can't imagine Father going down to City Hall to marry a girl young enough to be his goddamn granddaughter, can you?"

Putt thought about it. Robert, as the eldest son and heir apparent, had a greater stake than he did in believing the story was a fabrication. "I don't know about that," he said, trying to remember what his father had told him the last time they met. "He was kind of, you know—different, the last time I saw him. He talked a lot about happiness."

"Happiness? *Father?*"

"I saw more of him than you did." That was putting it tactfully, Putnam thought. The estrangement between Arthur Bannerman and his eldest son was total and complete; each of them was firmly entrenched in his position, and there had been no peace feelers from either side in years. Putnam did not see his father often, and only when summoned, but Robert did not see him at all. "Father always seemed very lonely to me, you know. And *bitter.* But when I went up to the apartment to have a drink with him—oh, maybe six months ago—he was very, ah, laid back. He was looking forward to his sixty-fifth birthday, you know. He talked about putting things right with you."

"With *me?*"

" 'Enough's enough, I'm going to bury the hatchet with Robert,' he said. I thought, Christ, that isn't like him at all. Then I thought, well, maybe he'd had a couple of fucking Scotches before I got there, good luck to him, but he didn't seem drunk, you know? I mean, it's not a word I'd normally use about Father, but he seemed almost—mellow. I kept thinking, he's trying to tell me something—but whatever it was, he never did."

"*Mellow?* I'm not sure *I* know what you mean. We led different lives in the Sixties."

"Yes. My side won, too."

"Could he have been in love?" Robert asked, ignoring Putnam's reminder of their old political differences.

"Well, it didn't occur to me at the time, but, yes, I guess he could have been. Come to think of it, he was wearing a striped shirt."

Robert raised an eyebrow.

"I don't mean *narrow* stripes. I mean the kind that Turnbull and Asser makes—big, wide stripes, bright red on cream, the kind of shirt a Hollywood movie producer would buy in London. It didn't look like something Father would pick for himself in a million years."

Robert sat silent for a moment. He glanced at his own spotless white cuffs. His clothes were as conservative as his father's, his taste molded by family tradition and the demands of politics. Old Cyrus Bannerman had worn the fashions of his youth throughout his long life—he was perhaps the last man in America to be seen in high-buttoned boots and a stiff white collar; his son Putnam wore a dark-blue suit with a vest, even at Kiawa; Arthur Bannerman wore double-breasted suits long after most people had abandoned them, and usually dressed as if he was on his way to a board meeting or his own inauguration.

Robert put out his cigarette, got up, walked across the room and stood for a few moments in front of one of the big windows, his back to Putnam, looking out at the hills. He ran one hand over the paneling, touched the intricate carving lovingly with his fingertips, then clasped both hands behind his back.

Putnam felt a familiar jolt of fear and guilt, then realized why: their father had always stood that way, a tall, somber figure, his hands behind his back, looking out at Kiawa to collect his thoughts before he turned around to deal with one of his children.

From the back, Robert might almost have *been* his father: the same broad shoulders and erect posture, the same strong, nervous fingers, which were the only visible sign of an otherwise well-concealed tendency toward nervous tension. As a child Robert had been judged "high-strung"; great efforts were made by nannies, tutors, headmasters, and athletic coaches to correct this, despite the fact that Arthur Bannerman himself and Arthur's father, Putnam—were also well known to be moody and "difficult" in private. Men who lived on their nerves, they were given to unpredictable bouts of black depression, as if the strain of living up to Cyrus Bannerman's name and fortune was more than they could bear. "There's a lot of dead wood here that needs pruning," Robert said, apparently to himself.

Putnam wondered whether his brother was thinking about the trees or the staff. The major difference between the two of them was that Robert was the heir apparent and had always wanted to be.

If John had lived . . . but he had not. Putnam wondered if there would ever be a time when that thought stopped occurring to him, many times a day—and not only to him, but to everyone else in the family, including Robert. *Especially* Robert.

John, with his easygoing, happy-go-lucky charm, his sense of humor, his passionate causes, the Golden Boy who was never in awe of the fortune, secure in the knowledge that it would one day be his, and that he would know exactly what to do with it. . . .

Everybody loved John, even Robert—though Robert could hardly conceal his envy, or his bitter resentment that a mere accident of timing had placed him second in the family. He drove himself hard to beat John at everything, but even when he did, it was a hopeless task, because John did things effortlessly, whereas Robert had to sweat, fight, and train, with a grim determination that often made even his victories seem worthless. He challenged John at everything from swimming, climbing trees, and arm wrestling to who could drive the fastest, but John hardly seemed to care whether he won or not, as if he were simply indulging Robert's passion for competition, so that it always seemed, even when he lost, that he *could* have won if he had cared to try. He did not exactly take Kiawa or the fortune for granted—he was far too intelligent for that—but he managed to give the impression that there were more important things in life than either, unlike Robert, whose obsession with what was not going to be his was obvious to everyone.

Of course, Kiawa, like the fortune it represented, was too big to "belong" to any one person, but control over the intricate spiderweb of trusts, corporations, and foundations of which it was a part traditionally went to the eldest direct Bannerman descendant, along with limited but very considerable power to make financial decisions on behalf of the family.

Putnam knew his family history: Cyrus Bannerman had thought long and hard about the fate of his vast fortune, and although there was nothing aristocratic about the emaciated old man who spent his last years in the dark little study upstairs, hunched over his ledgers like an accountant, wearing a green eyeshade, sleeve garters, steel-rimmed reading spectacles, and a celluloid collar, he understood the many advantages of the English aristocracy, whose works of art he had bought up at such a furious pace. Even a fortune as big as the one he had amassed would be dispersed in two or three generations if it were shared equally between his descendants, and his object was to keep it together.

A deeply religious man, in the spirit of his times he came to think of his wealth as a kind of religion. Money was not only power, it was, in his eyes and those of the Lord, *good*—therefore diminishing it, or wasting it, was a kind of blasphemy. Still, though he was richer than all the English dukes put together, he was not a duke, nor did the laws of the United States lend themselves to the creation of dukedoms. He arranged matters so that the income from a part of the fortune would provide, by means of interlocking trusts, for the needs of his descendants, while control over the bulk of it would pass from father to eldest son—or daughter, if there were no sons.

There were loopholes, of course, problems which even Cyrus Bannerman couldn't solve for the generations to come. Each heir would have to protect the integrity of the fortune—which they always referred to, modestly, as The Trust—by insisting on a long, complicated prenuptial agreement, and it was the need for negotiating this instrument that made Bannerman marriages resemble business mergers. It was, in part, as Putnam knew well, Robert Bannerman's disastrous marriage—

and subsequent divorce—that finally turned his father against him, for the choice of the right woman was the first and most important responsibility of a Bannerman heir.

Robert turned around to face his brother, the expression on his face hard, unyielding, judgmental. "You should have warned me about Father, goddamn it," he said.

It was odd, Putnam thought, that just when you were beginning to feel sympathy for Robert, he invariably did or said something to erase it. Vanessa, Robert's ex-wife, once confided that Robert was simply unable to accept love; he wanted it, she said, even demanded it, but when it was offered, he rejected it.

"I don't mean he isn't good in bed," she had whispered to him once in her husky, breathless voice, "but a girl needs some affection too, right? I mean, there's more to marriage than fucking. . . . "

After a couple of drinks, Vanessa specialized in the kind of intimate revelation that made her luckless partners at the dinner table squirm and blush—she had once been heard to say, in one of those brief hushes in the conversation that sometimes occur between courses, how unfair it was that while most men liked receiving oral sex, they hated giving it—but Putt felt she had summed up Robert's character perfectly. He skillfully trapped you into showing that you cared for him, then kicked the chair out from under you and made you feel like a fool.

Now, Putnam controlled his natural reaction to hit back, knowing it was exactly what Robert wanted him to do. "I wouldn't have phoned you just to say that Father was wearing a striped shirt and looked happy," he said. "I mean, it didn't seem to me such a big deal at the time."

Robert nodded—as much of an apology as he was going to offer. "God," he said, "if I'd had my way, this would never have happened. It ought to be a family rule: Past a certain age, the head of the family is put out to pasture, or shares the responsibility with the next generation."

"You'd never agree to that when it came to your turn."

Robert gave a grim smile. "Goddamn right." He walked over to the big antique desk and pushed a button. "I'm going to have a drink, whatever the goddamn time is. All I can say is: I hope Grandmother is right."

"Meaning?"

"Meaning that the girl just invented this story about the marriage. Worse comes to worst, we can pay her off. That's probably all she's looking for."

"Frankly, she doesn't look like that kind of girl to me."

"Grow up! There isn't any other kind. Some of them have a higher price than others, that's all."

Putnam did not agree but was not about to argue. After all, he had not been married to Vanessa or obliged to negotiate a separation agreement with her; that experience would certainly color anyone's opinion about women. "I'll be curious to meet her," he said cautiously.

"*Meet* her? For God's sake, don't even think about it. Everything has to be at arm's length, between the lawyers. The last thing we want is to *meet* the bitch! That's probably just what she wants. Eleanor made it absolutely clear to DeWitt that under no circumstances was she to appear at the funeral. But I can't imagine she'd dare to show up here, can you?"

"No way," Putnam said loyally. But looking back at the television footage of Alexandra Walden facing the press, he wasn't so sure. There was something in those eyes that made him uneasy. It occurred to him suddenly that it was exactly the same kind of determination you could see in Eleanor Bannerman's eyes.

He wondered if Robert was underestimating the enemy again.

2

"All I'm saying is, I don't think this is a smart move."

"I've never been good at the smart move, Simon. You know that."

"Is that a fact? For somebody who's no good at smart moves, you have a way of landing on your pretty little feet. You married one of the richest men in the country, for example. The Bannermans wouldn't be the only people to think *that* was a pretty smart move."

"I don't owe anyone an explanation. Arthur asked me to marry him, and I said yes. Is that a crime?"

"Not in my book, no. His family may not feel the same way."

"Whatever they feel, they can't treat me as if I didn't exist!"

"If you say so."

"Simon, I have a right to be at Arthur's funeral. More than that, it's an obligation. Arthur would have expected it. Surely the Bannermans, of all people, will understand that!"

"Maybe. I'm not sure *I* understand it, you want to know the truth. They made it pretty clear they don't want you there. When you turn up, they'll assume you're making trouble—or looking for publicity."

"That's ridiculous. They've never even met me."

"Met you?" He laughed. "If you think you're going to have a heart-to-hearter with Eleanor Bannerman at the funeral, forget it. Tell me again what DeWitt said."

She didn't reply at once. The two days since Arthur Bannerman's death had been an ordeal, and DeWitt seemed to her to have gone out of his way to make things worse. She was willing to concede that this was possibly not intentional—DeWitt's manner was cold, unsympathetic, and supercilious, but she had no reason to believe that was anything more than a combination of his natural style and their difference in age. He made no secret of the fact that he found the relationship between her and Arthur Bannerman almost as distasteful as the circumstances of Arthur's death—not that he blamed her for what had happened. His tone toward her was partly avuncular, partly that of a bully trying to see how far he could go, and always infuriatingly condescending. Perhaps unwisely, she retaliated by tuning him out, so that it was not easy now to remember exactly what he *had* said. "About what?" she asked.

"For God's sake! Wake up! About the funeral!"

"He said the family would prefer me not to come. That there was no point in upsetting Arthur's mother."

"That's *it?* Just an appeal to your finer feelings? It doesn't sound like DeWitt to me."

"Well—he more or less told me to stay away if I knew what was good for me. And he asked if I needed any money to 'tide me over.' "

"Over what, I wonder? I don't suppose you asked how much it was worth to the Bannermans to have you stay away?"

"Oh, of *course* not! I mean, it was all so horribly creepy, I didn't really pick up on what he'd meant until later. I nearly threw up."

"DeWitt was just doing his job. First he threatened you, then he tried to buy you off. The old one-two. Par for the course."

It occurred to Alexa—not for the first time in the last couple of days—that Simon could be even more insulting than DeWitt, but then she was used to his know-it-all cynicism, most of which she took with a grain of salt, and without too many bruised feelings. She had never had a gift for making friends with other women, so there were none toward whom she could easily turn in a crisis. In any case, during the year or so in which she had known Arthur Bannerman, such friends as she had had dropped away. When she was not working, she was with Arthur, and since he was anxious to keep their relationship a secret for as long as possible—more out of the fear of appearing ridiculous than for any other reason—she had lost touch with most of the people she knew. In New York, it was all too easy to lose friends: people led busy social lives; for a month, perhaps two, they might wonder what had become of you, but soon they lost interest and moved on to new friendships. In the end, there was simply no one to whom she could turn *except* Simon, who, since he looked on his friends as assets, never let one of them go if he could help it.

She pushed her sunglasses back and stared through the windshield at the autumn leaves, the colors as bright as a child's painting. During all the years she had lived in New York, she had always wanted to see the leaves turn—it was one of those things that made the Northeast different from home. In New York it was a seasonal ritual: Come October, everybody said, "Let's drive up and see the autumn colors," but somehow nobody she knew ever actually *did* it. Things got in the way, and suddenly it was too late—the trees were bare, and everybody was making plans for skiing trips that wouldn't happen either.

When Arthur had learned that she had never been "Upstate" to see the autumn colors, he promised she would see them at Kiawa—where, naturally, they would be at their finest—and here she was, looking at them just as he had said, though in circumstances he could hardly have imagined. . . .

"It's beautiful, isn't it?" she said.

Simon had many interests, but an enthusiasm for the country was not among them. He shrugged. "If you like that sort of thing." The downward curve of his mouth made it clear that he did not—in fact his whole appearance seemed out of place here, as if he did not belong to the same world as the trees in their autumn foliage, or the tourists in station wagons who were slowing down traffic on the Taconic and getting in his way.

Simon drove the way he did everything—fast, skillfully, and with more daring than was necessary. Somebody who did not know him well might have been impressed, even frightened, by the apparently casual way he took risks, but Alexa knew better than anyone that he was always in complete control, even when he was showing off. He loved to make things look easy—in one of the many expensive boarding schools where he had spent his childhood, he had been taught that a gentleman must never seem to be *trying*. His ethics were debatable, but he clung to the belief that he was above all a gentleman.

He was a flashy driver, and liked flashy cars. In fact, Alexa thought, almost everything Simon liked was flashy, from the wine-red Maserati Quattroporte in which they were now sitting to his Cartier sunglasses and diamond-studded gold wrist-chronometer. He changed down expertly and hurtled past a Chevrolet, one hand on the wheel as he lit a cigarette. The speedometer needle spun toward three figures; he smiled with satisfaction, then blew out a puff of smoke.

He spoke to her without taking his eyes off the road. "I've heard of crashing a party," he said, "but never of crashing a bloody *funeral!*"

He spoke with a clipped British accent—a sure sign, she knew, that he was prepared to be difficult. Normally, his accent was vaguely mid-Atlantic. In various moods he affected upper-class British, or tough, street-smart New Yorker, laid-back Sixties, even Hollywood minimogul. He could be almost anything but himself.

"Whose side are you on anyway?" she asked, more impatiently than she had intended.

"Don't be an ass! Who did you call when Bannerman dropped dead —in such indecorous circumstances? Who helped you put his clothes on and move him to the living room? I thought that was a bad idea at the time, if you remember, and I was dead right. I think this is a bad idea, too."

She could not deny it: Simon had performed above and beyond the call of friendship—and of his own cautious better judgment. She owed him, and even though she knew he would certainly find a way of collecting, sooner or later, and in spades, she was still in his debt. "I'm sorry," she said quietly. "The last couple of days have been rotten."

"You won't get an argument from me. I'm just not convinced you're going to improve on them by going up to Kiawa to do the widow number for the benefit of the Bannermans."

He unbuttoned one of his kidskin Hermès driving gloves to give her a pat on the thigh, a small familiarity to show he was willing to forgive and forget, and a reminder that they had been lovers.

"All the same," he said, returning to his theme, "it's not too late to turn back. A nice drive in the country. Nothing wrong with that."

"I'm going there, Simon. Like it or not. If you don't want to go on, leave me here. I shouldn't have too much trouble hitching a ride."

She flicked down the sun visor to look at herself in the vanity mirror as if she wanted to confirm that she wouldn't be left for long by the side of the road. The two days since Arthur's death had taken a certain toll, she thought. Her face was paler than usual, the high cheekbones more pronounced, there were dark circles under her eyes.

She was not a particularly vain young woman, but she was realistic about her looks. She knew that men found her beautiful, and she enjoyed the fact, but in truth her face had never completely satisfied her. The nose was too straight, she thought, the lips too full, the mouth too wide. There had been half a dozen girls in school whose snub-nosed faces and blond hair she had envied, and still did. She had come to New York four years ago with the ambition of becoming a model, only to discover that the ladies at *Glamour* and *Mademoiselle* and the agencies thought she was too "exotic." They wanted girls with nice tans and blond hair, Cheryl Tiegs look-alikes. Her pale skin and the curious contrast between her light gray eyes and dark hair were too unconventional to please them. "It's a *Vogue* face, honey," a sympathetic photographer told her, "but you're too big in the bazoom and the tush for a *Vogue* body."

It was just those things that turned off the fashion world which attracted Arthur Bannerman's attention to her. His wife had been tall, thin to the point of anorexia, with the kind of aristocratic WASP good looks that so often turn into hardness past the age of thirty-five. Almost all the pictures Alexa had seen of the late Mrs. Bannerman showed her on a horse, looking as thin as a rail, and irritable about having to sit still for the photographer. During Arthur Bannerman's presidential phase, she had apparently treated the press and the voters with such obvious disdain that Arthur eventually campaigned without her. Even before her illness, she had starved herself, and Arthur, who enjoyed his food enormously, whether it was dinner at Lutèce or a club sandwich in front of the fire, had been delighted to find that Alexa not only *liked* eating, but could eat as much as she pleased without putting on weight. "The one word I never want to hear from your lips is 'diet,' " he told her shortly after the first night they spent together.

It hurt her that nobody—not Simon, not DeWitt, not the press— gave any thought to the possibility that she *loved* Arthur, or that she might feel any grief at his death. Even her mother, once Alexa had nerved herself to call her, seemed to think that the whole thing was a mistake, further proof that her daughter had no gift at all for picking the right man. She assumed that Arthur Bannerman, being rich and old, had in some way taken advantage of Alexa. What little she knew about him she had learned from seeing him on television during his political campaigns, when even his supporters came to the conclusion that he had no natural gift for the media and tended to come across as an arrogant WASP aristocrat.

The newspapers took much the same view. Reading between the lines, most of the obituaries described a man who was cold, haughty, ambitious, born with a golden spoon in his mouth, and who felt the White House should be his for the asking. The fact that he had been a liberal and an internationalist at just the point in time when the Republican Party turned to the right was ignored; his philanthropy as well as his enormous involvement in the arts were written off as the guilt offerings of a man who was too rich for his own good.

This was not the man she had known, and it puzzled her that the newspapers' view of him was so different from hers. He had talked enough about his own family to make it clear that they too had a very different opinion of him. She knew—or thought she knew—as much about them as she did about her own brothers, perhaps even more, for she had been, in the last six months or so, as much his confidante as his lover, as if what he needed most was somebody to talk to, somebody who *wasn't* in the family, or one of the family retainers—the small army of lawyers, financial advisers, and elder statesmen that guarded the Bannermans and their fortune from the outside world.

"Are you listening, or am I talking to myself?"

Whatever Simon had said, she had missed it, lost in her own thoughts, which were, she recognized, hardly profitable. "I'm sorry," she said. "I was thinking."

"Good. Thinking is just what you *should* be doing. If you think hard enough, you'll see I'm right. The reason it's stupid—sorry, a *mistake*," Simon went on cheerfully, "is that the Bannermans have the big guns.

Why cross them? Let them come to you. They'll have to, sooner or later."

"That's pretty much what DeWitt said."

"Well, he's not a total idiot, Alexa. Admittedly he's screwed up all around so far, but then this kind of thing isn't his specialty. Just because he's made a mess of handling the press doesn't mean he's wrong about the best way to handle the Bannerman family. Of course, considering the kind of press he's got them, DeWitt's probably not any more popular with the family than you are, just now."

It was on the tip of Alexa's tongue to say that she had more reason to complain about the press than the Bannermans did, but it was not a subject she wanted to pursue, even with Simon. There was hardly a newspaper in the country that hadn't carried her photograph on the front page in the past forty-eight hours, as the story of Arthur Aldon Bannerman's death unraveled.

Simon had warned her from the very first that there was almost no possibility of avoiding a scandal, and Simon had been right. The idea of dressing Arthur and moving him to the living room had been, as he had predicted, a wasted effort. Keeping her out of sight only whetted the media's appetite.

DeWitt had urged her "to keep a low profile," and she had done her best, hiding out in Simon's apartment while the press dredged up whatever few facts they could about her. She was described as a "glamorous model"; people she hardly knew gave inaccurate and misleading accounts of her relationship with Arthur Bannerman; her mother, tracked down by an enterprising New York *Post* reporter to the farm in Illinois, refused to comment.

The element of mystery only made the story hotter, of course—as DeWitt had failed to foresee. "If they can't find you, they'll eventually lose interest," he had told her. "When things have cooled off, perhaps you can talk to The Family." DeWitt always referred to the Bannerman family in unspoken capitals, as if there could be no other. "It's not in anyone's interest to let this become a circus, after all."

His argument seemed plausible to Alexa—a "circus" was the last thing she wanted, and she knew it was exactly what she was going to get if the press found her, with herself as the main attraction. She was prepared, if only out of respect for Arthur, to keep silent about the marriage until it could be revealed in some dignified way, and was not about to call a press conference to announce the news herself—which, she guessed, was exactly what DeWitt feared she would do.

The result was that her side of the story remained untold—everyone assumed she was Arthur Bannerman's mistress, or a "kept woman," even some kind of call girl. It was beginning to make her angry, not only at DeWitt but at herself, for having been so naive.

Simon cleared his throat. "DeWitt will have kittens when he sees you."

"I don't give a damn about DeWitt."

"You know what your problem is?"

Alexa didn't know—didn't want to know—but she resigned herself to listening.

She looked out the window, wondering how much farther there was to go. A sign reading "Schultzville" flashed past. She could see a farm on the hills, overlooking the parkway, though it looked nothing like the farms of her childhood spread out across the plain. This one consisted of a neat white green-shuttered house set among trees, with a red barn, a picket fence, a small apple orchard, horses and cows, a farm from a children's picture book. She had no romantic notions about farms.

"Your problem," Simon continued, without waiting for a reply, "is that you're a romantic. Deep down, you believe the Bannermans are going to greet you with open arms. Well, you're wrong. The rich—the *real* rich, I'm talking about, you understand—are selfish and cruel. I went to school with them, so I know. Don't you ever forget it."

"Arthur wasn't."

Simon took both hands off the wheel in a gesture of exasperation that sent the car leaping into the next lane. "Maybe he wasn't to *you*, but the poor man was hopelessly besotted with you. What I'm trying to say is that you can't judge the rest of the Bannerman family by your relationship with Arthur."

"I'm not afraid of them, Simon, if that's what you mean."

"Well, you ought to be. The old lady's supposed to be a fire-breathing dragon. As for Robert, I know him slightly. He has a well-deserved reputation for being a real bastard."

"I know about Robert," she said, conscious that she sounded a little smug—but Arthur talked about his children often—too often, she had sometimes thought.

"But you don't *know* him."

"I guess I feel like I do. You couldn't spend much time with Arthur without the subject coming up."

"He must have really hated his children. Robert particularly."

The idea surprised her. During the past two days, Simon had been so busy protecting her—and himself—from the press that they had hardly had an opportunity to talk. Now that they *were* talking, she found herself resenting his questions. "Hate?" she asked. "What makes you think that?"

"Oh, come off it, Alexa. Everybody knows that! Bannerman and his three kids! There was a long piece about them in *New York* a couple of years back. 'Trouble in Paradise,' I think it was called. Robert threatened to sue, but I don't think anything came of it. Arthur Bannerman's relationship with his children is one of the staples of high-level gossip writing, right up there with the von Bulow marriage and what happened when old Seward Johnson married his Polish maid and left her the billion dollars his children thought they were getting. . . . I've heard Arthur never spoke to Robert again after Robert's divorce."

"I know *that's* not true," she said, suddenly tired of the whole subject. It would take forever to persuade Simon he was wrong, and it didn't seem worth the effort.

"He didn't do a damned thing to help Robert's campaign. He wouldn't even appear at rallies with his own son!"

"Oh, Simon, it's not that simple. Arthur thought he'd be a liability. He didn't want Robert to run, but once Robert decided to, Arthur worked behind the scenes for him. Arthur told me he'd phoned every damn Republican in the state—and then phoned them again to make them promise they wouldn't tell Robert his father had called!"

"Is that so?" Simon asked resentfully. He hated to be told he was wrong. "I certainly never heard that. How about Robert's divorce? The story was that Arthur agreed to give evidence against his own son, for Vanessa's side."

"For God's sake, Vanessa's lawyers *subpoenaed* Arthur! He didn't have a choice. He told me that being served with a subpoena as he was going into the Metropolitan Club for lunch was the most shameful moment in his life. At the deposition he said, sure, he didn't see eye to eye with his son, everybody knew that, but he wanted to go on record that his daughter-in-law had the morals of a streetwalker. I guess that's why they decided not to call him as a witness in the end."

"It still doesn't sound like a happy family to me."

"Well, I don't suppose it was. Neither is mine. Neither is yours, from what you've told me. Anyway, the real problem with Robert wasn't his divorce, or the Senate campaign. It went way back. Arthur's wife was dying of cancer, you know, while he was out campaigning. I think she probably hid how serious it was from him at the end, or maybe he just didn't get the message in time—anyway she died before he could get home. The children never forgave him for that. And they blamed him for John's death, too."

"*John?* Who was he? I thought there were just the three children?"

"Four. John, Robert, Cecilia, Putnam. John was killed in a car accident."

She stared out of the window, conscious of the fact that she hadn't really told Simon the whole story, didn't *want* to tell him. There was no way to give him a crash course in the Bannerman family psychodrama, and she didn't much feel like trying. She had started off thinking that Arthur had been victimized by his children, then decided they had been victimized by *him*, and finally reached the conclusion that they had probably been victims of one another, or maybe just of the family name and fortune. Certainly the Arthur Bannerman she knew was a very different person from the one his children had fought against nearly twenty years ago.

Besides, as in every family, the relationships were more complicated than they looked to an outsider, or than anybody in the family would admit. Arthur saw in Robert, his eldest now, and once his favorite, a rival who might succeed in politics, where he had failed. Cecilia, who blamed her father for a whole shopping list of failures, loved him more than any of the men in her life, but quarreled with him every time they met. Putnam loved his father, but, like Cecilia, seemed unable to live on the same continent with him. . . .

Alexa wished she could take off her shoes and scrunch up with her feet on the seat and arms around her knees, the sunroof open, a Bruce Springsteen tape playing at high volume, but she could hardly do it in a suit, hat, and high heels. There were things she had missed, being a part of Arthur Bannerman's life—the kind of small, casual freedoms that other people her age took for granted. It was a trade-off she had made knowingly, and had come to terms with eventually, not without difficulty, but she thought it gave her a special insight into the problems of Arthur's children, grown-ups now as they were, who had been enclosed from birth in the Bannerman family's special world, without a choice, unlike her.

"Did he tell you a lot about the family?" Simon asked.

"Well, sure. I didn't pump him or anything. He *liked* to talk to me about it. I know nobody will believe me, but a lot of the time we just sat in front of the fireplace with a drink and talked. It was a new experience for him, I think."

"Did he ever talk about money?"

"He didn't need my help to look after his investments, Simon."

"That's not what I meant."

She could read Simon's mind like a book—she knew exactly what he meant and wanted to avoid the subject. "You have to understand," she explained. "Arthur wasn't interested in money. He didn't talk about it because it was always *there*. You turn on the faucet and water comes out. Why think about it? I don't mean he didn't pay attention—he wasn't like an oil sheik. I mean, you knew him, Simon. He didn't drive around in a Rolls-Royce, or overtip. He added up his check in a restaurant like anybody else, and always made sure he got his money's worth when he bought something. The Bannermans came from Scotland originally, after all."

"I know that. Everybody knows that. I wasn't talking about his restaurant checks, for God's sake! I sold him a couple of pictures, and he drove a pretty hard bargain. . . . But are you telling me that with all those goddamn fireside chats, he never mentioned what he was going to do about you? He must have made *some* provision for you?"

"He said that if anything ever happened to him, I'd be taken care of —that it was all very complicated, but for now I'd just have to trust him."

"And did you?"

"Yes. I did. Why wouldn't I? Anyway, I wasn't expecting him to die at any moment, and I'm sure he wasn't either."

"For all you know, you're a rich woman."

"And for all I know I'm not. I want to go to the funeral. And I want people to stop treating me as if I were some kind of freak or—*femme fatale.*" She waited for Simon to correct her accent. French was not her strong point. For once, he passed up the opportunity, as if his attention were elsewhere. "After that, I'll worry about the rest."

"Jesus Christ!" he exclaimed. He pulled over to the side of the road and stopped the car. "Will you look at *that!*"

For the first time in all the years she had known him, there was a touch of awe in Simon's voice, as if finally something had impressed him.

She looked out in the direction he was pointing. To their left the neat fields stretched out for miles toward gently rolling, wooded hills; at the top of the farthest hill, overlooking the Hudson, a silver ribbon on the horizon, was an enormous house—the largest house she had ever seen —the weathered stone glowing golden in the autumn light. The sun reflected off hundreds of windows. She shaded her eyes. She could make out a huge, ornate greenhouse, marble terraces the size of several city blocks, formal gardens, stone steps that seemed a mile long, decorative pools with ornamental fountains sending up jets of water, lawns so green that they might have been freshly painted, long alleys of ancient trees.

In the distance was another building—a kind of medieval castle, with turrets, a moat, and a drawbridge—and beyond that, half hidden in the woods, a steepled church, with a long line of black limousines gleaming in the sun.

It was like nothing she had ever seen. She sat there for a moment, opened the window, sorted out the familiar country smells. For the first time she felt a touch of fear, shocked by the sheer size of Kiawa, and the wealth it represented, as if the Bannerman fortune was real to her at last. For a moment she was almost tempted to take Simon's advice and turn back. Then she pulled herself together and reminded herself that she was Arthur Aldon Bannerman's widow, whether they liked it or not.

She looked in the mirror and made sure her hat was straight. She pulled the short veil down—something she had only seen done before by Joan Collins on television, who seemed to have the knack of hats with veils. Veils, however short, were not something her generation wore, and it had not been easy to find one at short notice, but Alexa guessed they would be expected at a Bannerman funeral.

She put one hand on Simon's, pressing it hard.

"Let's get on with it," she said, with more courage than she felt.

ROBERT BANNERMAN stood on the flagstone steps of the church his grandfather had built, his handsome features composed in an expression of stately grief.

He was flanked by his cousin, the Reverend Emmett Aldon DeWitt, and by the rector; below the three men, in the gravel courtyard, the more distant Bannerman relations milled around, greeting each other with a heartiness that would have seemed to a stranger inappropriate for the occasion.

A funeral was a rare opportunity for the descendants of Cyrus Bannerman to confirm to themselves and each other that they belonged to one of America's most famous families—that Kiawa, and all it stood for, was part of their heritage. Some of them were important, many merely rich nobodies, the kind of people who spent the winters in Palm Beach and the summers in Maine. None of them was poor by the standards of the world—almost everybody in the family was a beneficiary of at least one trust fund—but only the children and grandchildren of Cyrus Bannerman had a direct connection to Kiawa and the fortune itself.

"It is easier for a camel to pass through the eye of a needle than for a rich man to enter the Kingdom of Heaven," Emmett DeWitt intoned in his reedy voice. "I thought that might set an appropriate tone to the service."

"Fighting words, here, Em. They'd lynch you. And I'd tie the noose. Think again."

"Don't worry, Robert. I decided against it. I thought about what Eleanor would say."

"That will do it every time, old man."

The Reverend Emmett DeWitt did not normally flinch from his Christian duty, even where the sensibilities of the family were concerned. When Seymour Hersh revealed in the *Times* that the Bannerman Foundation owned shares in South African gold mines, DeWitt did not hesitate to organize a picket line and march at the head of it conspicuously—all the more so since he was over six feet four. He led the welfare mothers of nearby Hudson on a protest march to the gates of Kiawa when their abortion-counseling service was closed down, and staged a sit-in of the elderly poor in the lobby of Arthur Bannerman's apartment building on Fifth Avenue when the *Post* discovered that Arthur Bannerman planned to tear down a lot of old, decaying West Side tenements and build a museum on the site.

DeWitt was one of the best-known clerics in the country, constantly in demand for campus lectures, television talk shows, and marches on nuclear-power plants. A celebrity priest, he preached to his flock from "The Phil Donahue Show," the pages of *Playboy*, and peace rallies, rather than from the pulpit of his fashionable East Side church, where the parishioners regarded him as a traitor to his class and theirs.

DeWitt towered above Robert Bannerman and the rector, neither of whom was short. His curly red hair rose above his head in two peaks, leaving a bald spot in the middle, which gave him, from a distance, a certain clownish appearance. In contrast to the rector's high church magnificence, he wore a simple black robe, with a large peace symbol around his neck in place of a cross. The eyes behind his thick glasses had a lunatic intensity that terrified strangers.

"I would have thought we could expect the President, or the Vice President—certainly the Governor," the rector said, a hint of disappointment in his voice. Having no choice, he had accepted with good grace the fact that Emmett DeWitt would read the service. It was a family tradition that as long as there was a Bannerman relative available in holy orders, he would conduct the funeral services for a death in the family. Emmett DeWitt's opinions were offensive to most of his relatives, and seemed to Eleanor eccentric to the point of madness, but he was an ordained Episcopal minister and the son of her eldest daughter, so the matter was therefore beyond argument.

The rector was least likely of anybody to argue. For more than a decade, the Episcopalian Bishop of Albany, his nominal superior, had been trying to close down the Kiawa church on the grounds that it was hardly more than a private chapel for the Bannermans. Eleanor fought the bishop tooth and nail. She withdrew her contributions to various Protestant charities, lobbied successfully to have the church declared a historic landmark, and finally sued the bishop, who gave in at last to superior secular force. "Leave it alone as long as the old lady is alive," he was reported to have told the diocese's lawyers.

Robert Bannerman reflected that this might well have served as the family motto. As long as Eleanor lived, nothing at Kiawa could be changed. Servants were kept on long past the point of usefulness, the stables were full of horses, even though there was seldom a call for them, a dozen gardeners were employed to sweep every pathway clean of leaves and twigs, maids cleaned bedrooms that would never be used and lit fires that would never warm anyone. . . .

Robert found it hard to imagine Kiawa without Eleanor—and suspected that he was the only member of the family courageous enough to try. His father, almost to the very end, submitted to Eleanor's wishes; indeed, Robert could not help wondering if his father's shameful affair was not his first, and, as things turned out, final and fatal, act of rebellion. Certainly Cici and Putt would never question their grandmother's hold over the family, any more than the rector, who was waiting patiently for Robert to reply.

Robert cleared his throat. "Given the circumstances of Father's death, it seemed more sensible to have a private ceremony, Rector. The President *offered* to come, of course, but Grandmother suggested a memorial service later on in New York might be more appropriate, when all the fuss has died down. . . ."

"Oh, quite," the rector said, beaming. Eleanor Bannerman was his bread and butter. If she had suggested a funeral service in Swahili, to be held on top of the Empire State Building, the rector would have found a way to approve it.

"Has anybody talked to the young woman?" Emmett DeWitt asked. He had been raised among his cousins, the Bannerman children. Physically awkward, Emmett had been Robert's victim in countless nursery games and practical jokes. Emmett therefore took a particular pleasure in bringing up the subject that would surely cause Robert the most pain.

Robert gave him a cold stare, sufficiently reminiscent of the nursery to make Emmett wish for a moment that he had not asked the question. "Your father spoke to her, Em. I gather from him that she's a tough little cookie."

"My father said *that?*"

"Not word for word, no. But that was the impression he gave me— that she was cool as a goddamn cucumber. She didn't shed a tear! Unusual for a young woman of twenty-four who's standing over the body of the feller she's been in bed with, wouldn't you say?"

"Perhaps . . ."

"No goddamn 'perhaps' about it, Em. We're dealing with a tough customer. Let's drop the subject, shall we? Here come Cici and Putt."

Robert descended to open the door of the limousine, followed by Emmett, his robes flapping behind him, his cheeks flaming red. From earliest childhood he had been unable to conceal his feelings for Cecilia Bannerman, but while she had always stood up for him against Robert, she never allowed the relationship between them to go beyond cousinly affection, to his regret.

She stepped out of the car, looking more frail than ever after thirty-six hours of nonstop travel. Her face was darkly tanned, but not the kind of tan that comes from lying on a beach covered with Bain de Soleil. Cecilia's skin was etched, darkened, and dried by the wind and the tropical sun; far from making her look healthy, it merely made her seem ill, feverish, burned out. Always thin, she now seemed to Robert emaciated. Her eyes were huge, as if the flesh around them had been burned away; they were deep pools of hurt, like those in the faces of the starving children she had gone to Africa to save—unwisely in Robert's opinion. There were dark circles under them, as if she had been crying most of the way home. The black dress she wore was too large for her. Eleanor's maid had done her best with Cecilia's hair, but the sun had bleached it to the color of wheat straw, and it had been roughly cut for comfort in the heat, rather than by a fashionable hairdresser. She had hidden most of it with a veiled hat, but the general effect made her look like a waif.

She stood as stiffly as a soldier on parade, determined not to show weakness, trying, as always, to live up to the standards of her grandmother. If you took a fall, you remounted your horse and went on, and worried about your injuries later. It was the family creed: a stiff upper lip, a straight back, no tears or complaints in public, as few as possible in private, for that matter. He put his arms around her and held her. For a moment, she resisted, then he felt her give in and relax. He kissed her. "Welcome home," he said. "I missed you."

"I should have been here," she whispered. "I should have been with him."

"Don't blame yourself. It wouldn't have changed a thing. And stop trying to be so goddamned brave, will you? If you want to cry, cry. That's what funerals are for."

He moved her gently toward the steps, the others following at a discreet distance. It was generally accepted in the Bannerman family that to the extent that Robert had any finer feelings at all, they were for Cecilia. She could do no wrong in his eyes. Physically they resembled each other closely. Tall, fine-boned, athletic, each seemed to find in the other qualities they lacked in themselves. Cecilia leaned on Robert's toughness, his refusal to settle for anything less than getting his own way; he seemed to need her sensitivity and fragile emotions, as if he knew that protecting her brought out the best in him as nothing else could do.

Robert planted himself firmly in the middle of the steps, still holding Cecilia's hand, while others grouped around him, as if they were about to re-enact Custer's Last Stand. He glanced at his watch. "Is Grandmother on the way?"

"Don't worry. She'll be here on the stroke of twelve," Putt said.

Robert nodded. In the Bannerman family everybody except Putt took punctuality seriously—and even *he* felt guilty about it when he was late. Eleanor, naturally, carried punctuality to its extreme limits: not only was she never late, she was never *early*. You could set your watch by her, indeed, it paid to do so, since hers was regularly checked against the time signal.

"I still can't believe it's happened," Cecilia said.

Emmett bowed his head. "In the midst of life we are in death."

Robert gave him a sharp look. "Try not to be a horse's ass, Em. Stick to peace rallies, why don't you?"

Cecilia ignored their bickering—she was so used to it, in fact, that she hardly noticed. "I was thinking of *how* he died. It seems so unlike him. The girl, I mean . . ."

The men, except for the rector, exchanged glances. Cecilia had idolized her father, even when they fought. She could have forgiven him anything except the ordinary human weaknesses. It was no doubt impossible for her to imagine him going to bed with a young woman in her twenties, let alone dying there.

"Well, Father wasn't exactly a monk, you know," Putt said. "Nothing wrong with that."

"He must have been out of his mind," Cecilia said. "It would never have happened if I'd been here."

"He looked okay to me, Cici, honestly. I don't think he needed you to chaperon him."

"You don't know what you're talking about, Putt," Robert said sternly. Even to himself, he sounded just like his father, right down to the hard, clipped tone of authority. For a moment he felt an uncomfortable sense of oppression, as if he were playing a role, but then he told himself he was the head of the family now. "Father was a sick man," he said briskly. "Out of his head. Senile. That's our story. That's the *truth!* Stick to it."

"All I'm saying . . ."

"Don't rock the goddamned boat, Putt!"

Robert's warning came straight from their childhood—and their father—and had the heavy weight of family tradition behind it. Bannermans did not rock the boat. A certain degree of eccentricity was permitted: Uncle John had raised buffalo on his estate in the mistaken belief that they would replace beef cattle; Emmett was the family gadfly; Arthur's younger brother, Aldon, who was reputed to have kept two Chinese mistresses, died in a fall while climbing Mount Ararat in search of the remains of the Ark—but where the family was concerned, the Bannermans closed ranks.

It was ironic, Robert thought, that his father had in the end rocked the boat so hard that he'd almost sunk it—but then he had never been convinced that his father was altogether reliable when it came to the interests of the family. It was for that reason that Robert had tried to gain control over the fortune while the old man was still alive—an unthinkable breach of family tradition.

And if I'd succeeded, he told himself bitterly, we wouldn't be up shit creek now. . . . But of course success was never in the cards, as he should have known—better than anyone. Family tradition gave each heir absolute control for life, subject only to Eleanor's formidable capacity for interference. In the end she always won. She was willing to work at it twenty-four hours a day, unlike her husband and her son, who eventually became bored with the responsibility of increasing a fortune which was already more than they could handle or give away. The truth was, he knew, that they were afraid of the responsibility, while Eleanor, even though she hated change, was not.

Robert was not afraid of making changes, nor did he fear taking the responsibility. In the days when his father had been a child, Kiawa was still patrolled by mounted armed guards, Pinkertons accompanied the Bannerman children everywhere, and Cyrus slept with a revolver under his pillow. Great wealth had made the family fearful. People threw rocks at Cyrus's limousine in the early 1900s, and while his physical courage was never in doubt, he was determined to protect his family from the hatred of his fellow Americans, which explained why he chose to build Kiawa—nearly a hundred miles from New York City, with its own private railway station, thanks to an accommodation he made with the New York Central—and fought to prevent the building of any highway linking Albany and New York. Cyrus scrupulously read the endless stream of hate mail that was sent to him and did his best to ensure the family's safety from mob violence, assassination threats, anarchist attempts, Senate investigations and—after the Lindbergh case—kidnapping. He had never sought popularity, so he didn't mind being hated, but the feeling that Kiawa was an armed camp in a sea of hostility inevitably had its effect on his son, Putnam, and grandson, Arthur, both of whom sought, in different ways, to soften and humanize the family's public image.

Times had changed. Robert knew that. Great wealth was no longer unpopular; a Bannerman, if he played his cards right, had as much chance to succeed in politics as anyone else. Besides, there were plenty of oilmen and conglomerateurs who had as much money as the Bannermans, or more, and nobody hated *them*. He glanced at his relations in the courtyard below and felt a profound contempt. Most of them represented the past: he recognized Chauncey Bannerman, his cheeks flushed with a lifetime of pursuing—and consuming—the perfect martini, a nonentity who made a profession of sitting on the board of directors of any company that was willing to pay for the magic of the Bannerman name in its annual report—exactly the kind of person who gave the family the reputation that Robert knew he had to overcome. There was Makepeace Bannerman, yachtsman and banker, whose loans to any tinpot dictator willing to hang a decoration around his neck had brought his bank—and much of the Third World—to the brink of financial catastrophe. Makepeace didn't look worried. Why should he? Robert asked himself. The American taxpayer, the World

Bank, and the IMF would undoubtedly bail him out. He could see his cousin Martha, standing beside her fourth—or was it fifth?—husband, and Uncle Ralph, his mother's younger brother, a bore of international reputation whose only interest in life was big-game hunting, who had built what amounted to a small museum to house his trophies. . . .

He stared ahead, watching the driveway for the approach of Eleanor's car, ignoring his relatives completely. There would be time enough to shake hands with them after the funeral, when they all trooped into the house to eat and drink. He sighed at the thought, then consoled himself with the fact that at least they didn't know as yet about the girl's claim to have married his father. The thought of having to receive their hypocritical sympathy and condolences graciously was bad enough without that additional humiliation.

Fossils, fogys, clowns! he told himself savagely, living on money they didn't even control, secure in the knowledge that failure, self-indulgence, and lack of initiative would never make them poor. . . .

He longed for a cigarette. All his life he had fought against falling into the same trap as they had. He sought risk—the big gamble, with real stakes. He understood better than anybody why his father had sought the Presidency, and how much it had cost him to lose; he even understood the reason for his father's failure—he had not committed everything to it, make or break. He played by the rules, and in the end he lost by them.

Once, Robert remembered, long ago at Harvard, when he still played poker, he lost three nights in a row. "You shouldn't play poker," the winner, a boy from Wisconsin, had told him, counting his own winnings. "I'm not saying you're not a good poker player. You know the moves, you understand the game—*but to win, the money has to matter!* You have to know that if you don't win this hand, you don't *eat*. You play for the goddamn farm, or you always lose."

No Bannerman since Cyrus had been willing to play for the goddamn farm.

All or nothing now, he told himself.

THE CLOCK in the church steeple whirred and began to strike twelve; the rector smoothed his robes like a plump bird grooming its bright plumage; the Bannerman relatives in the courtyard fell silent. Emmett and the rector descended the steps shoulder to shoulder, followed by Cecilia on Martin Booker's arm, then by Putt and Robert.

On the stroke of noon, an old Cadillac limousine—Eleanor Bannerman was of the opinion that Rolls-Royces were for the *nouveaux riches*, except in England, and did not believe in getting rid of a good car merely because Detroit had brought out a new model—pulled to a silent stop in front of the church, the back door of the car exactly even with the steps. Daley, Eleanor's elderly chauffeur, still in active service despite cataracts and rheumatism, got out slowly and opened the door for her. Courtland DeWitt emerged from the front seat to stand beside Daley.

As the echoes of the last chime faded, Eleanor Bannerman emerged at last, dressed head to toe in black, her long veils floating in the mild breeze. Courtland, towering over her, offered her his arm. She ignored it, raised her veil to peer at the servants and make sure they were all present, then paused briefly to acknowledge the presence of cousins, nieces, nephews, and distant relatives. Old as she was, there was not a face to which she could not put a name, not a soul whose life, financial situation, and marital status she did not know by heart. Far more than Kiawa, she was the symbol of that intangible web of power, money, and tradition that made them all, in their own eyes and hers, special.

Behind her, two identically black-clad figures appeared, one short, the other as tall and athletic as a man—Elizabeth Aldon Bannerman DeWitt, Eleanor's younger daughter and Emmett's mother; and, a head taller, striding beside her as if she were wearing boots and spurs under her long dress, Katherine Aldon Bannerman Scott, Eleanor's elder daughter. Katherine gave a hearty wave in Cecilia's direction, dropped her handbag, and scooped it up with a gesture that suggested she was more used to a pitchfork or a shovel than to feminine accessories.

The limousine pulled away silently. Eleanor shook hands with the rector and gave Emmett a warning glance. "None of your nonsense, mind, Emmett," she said loudly enough to make him blush. "I won't have it."

"Yes, Grandmother," he said meekly.

She did not pause to listen. Mounting the steps with remarkable speed for a woman of her age, she was followed by DeWitt, her daughters, her grandchildren, and Booker. At the top, she paused for a moment, as if to inspect them, and gave Booker a look that made it clear she did not think he belonged here with the family—that he would have been down in the courtyard, where he belonged, if Cecilia hadn't insisted on his accompanying her.

Satisfied with the rest of them, she stood for a moment, the elbow of her right arm turned outward slightly in anticipation.

Robert allowed himself a thin smile, then moved forward to take her arm in his, as head of the family. Over the years he had developed a kind of admiration for his grandmother, even a certain affection— something he could not have imagined feeling when he was a child. He was her favorite since John's death, he knew that—but of course she did her best not to show it. Eleanor Bannerman did not indulge those whom she loved—she simply set higher standards for them. He remembered Cecilia, as a horse-crazy child, running into the house one morning to announce that she had taken her hunter over a course of three-foot-six jumps. Eleanor had merely nodded as if she expected nothing less, and ordered Cecilia's instructor to raise the jumps another three inches the next day. In her own eccentric way she made exceptions—Putt, for example, or Uncle Ralph—but what she could forgive in them, she would not tolerate in the heir apparent, or in Cecilia, for that matter.

"The hearse is late," she said.

Robert, who had been working for nearly forty-eight hours to arrange the funeral, felt a sudden, irrational spasm of guilt, a sensation so well remembered from his childhood that it was as if he had been dropped thirty years or more back in time. He was about to say it wasn't his fault, but of course that excuse had never satisfied her then, and surely wouldn't now, nor was it suitable for a man of his age, or in his position. "I can hear the car now," he said. "I told them to make it a few seconds after twelve, to give us time to get in place."

He felt uneasy with the lie—he knew it wasn't worthy of him and, worse still, guessed he hadn't fooled her for a second. Still, he had given her an answer, and she always respected that.

"This afternoon, after everyone has gone, I want to see you," she said. "And the rest, too," she added. "Courtland has news for us."

"Good or bad?"

"That remains to be seen. He's still waiting for a call from New York. . . ."

Robert did his best to control his emotions, reminding himself that he was in full view of the entire family. He braced himself stiffly, unwilling to show the slightest tremor or trace of fear. He was perfectly sure the marriage was a hoax, a sordid little plot, and only wished he hadn't been stuck up here at Kiawa, making the funeral arrangements, while DeWitt, that senile incompetent, was left to deal with what really mattered. He heard the sound of tires on the gravel, this time for real. "They're here," he said, with relief.

His grandmother nodded. Her arm in his, she turned slowly, adjusted her veil with her free hand and stood ready to receive her son's body.

Robert felt her hand, elegantly gloved as always, squeeze his hard, as if she were signaling that she needed his strength, his presence, his support, for the ceremonies that lay ahead, or perhaps just to let him know that she felt grief.

He peered at her face, but beneath the veil he could see no sign of tears. Then the car's chrome grill flashed in the sun through the gap in the trees, and the moment was gone. Whatever had passed between the two of them was over with, and she was in full control of herself again.

For a single second—a fraction of a second—she had shown him weakness.

Robert had never been so shocked in his life.

"YOU CAN TELL these are the *real* rich," Simon said. "I mean, in Bel Air they have electric gates, alarms, guards with dogs. All the Bannermans have is a cattle grid. Christ, there aren't even any 'No Trespassing' signs! They're so rich they're not afraid of anybody."

She paid no attention. Now that she was here, she felt a sensation of panic, something like stage fright. She had assumed vaguely that there would be a large crowd and that she could slip in unnoticed, but something about the look of Kiawa itself gave her a warning that this might not be easy. Everything here was orderly, planned; nothing had been left to chance. The winding gravel road took them through thick woods, but there was no sense of nature's disorder—even the trees seemed to have been placed where they stood by design, and though it was autumn, there were no fallen leaves or broken twigs on the road.

In whatever direction she looked, there was evidence of the small army of Italian stonemasons that Cyrus Bannerman had brought here at the turn of the century, in much the same spirit that Pharoah had brought the Jews to Egypt to labor on the pyramids. It was one of Arthur's favorite stories, perhaps because it showed his grandfather in a more benign light than the usual picture of him as a desiccated robber baron.

Cyrus, Arthur liked to say, would have made a good general. He marshaled his army of laborers, built housing for them, even created what amounted to a navy—a whole fleet of barges to bring huge blocks of granite down the Hudson from quarries he had bought to ensure an unlimited supply of stone for Kiawa. He focused on Kiawa the same energy and attention to detail that had made him a billionaire, and built on such a scale, and with such massive solidity, that it was as if he wanted to ensure that his descendants could never alter what he had done.

Vast as the place was, there was, curiously, no feeling of space, none of the emptiness of nature. It was as if Cyrus had been determined not to leave anything out, to have within his view every kind of landscape and architecture. The car swept through miles of thick pines, as dark and threatening as a fairy-tale forest, then around a large lake, in the center of which was an island with what looked very much like a miniature castle on it, and on in a straight line between green, sweeping fields in which herds of cattle grazed.

"Even the bloody cows look clean," Simon said.

"Steers. It's a beef herd. Black Angus."

"One up for the farmer's daughter."

As a farmer's daughter, she could recognize breeding on the hoof when she saw it. Where she came from, Black Angus were looked down on as a rich man's hobby, the kind of animal a dairy farmer might admire at the County Fair, the way he would give an admiring glance at a fancy Corvette in the Chevrolet dealership before buying a new pickup truck. Black Angus were for gentleman farmers.

She glanced at her watch. "We're going to be late," she said. "Are you sure this is the way?"

"I'm going by what I saw from the hill." Simon glanced in his mirror. "There's a limo behind us, so unless he's lost, and just following me, we can't be far out."

He turned a corner sharply, crossed a stone bridge that seemed several times too large for the stream beneath it, speeded down a long, tree-lined alley, at the end of which a state trooper in full dress waved him on.

"Getting there," Simon said. "I'll park, then you mingle with the crowd and slip in. Don't make a big production number out of it. Play it by ear, right?"

She was more than willing to play it by ear. The Bannermans would surely notice she was here, but hopefully not right away. They might talk to her, they might not, but the ball would be in their court. She intended to arrive quietly, keep a dignified distance, try not to seem either obvious or timid, and wait to see what happened.

There was a sharp bend ahead. "I hope that's the bloody parking lot coming up," Simon said. He took the bend fast, then suddenly braked hard, scattering a shower of gravel. "Oh, shit!" he said.

She stared through the windshield in horror, aware that it was too late now to make a tactful entrance—or to withdraw. Not more than fifty feet away, the immediate family of Arthur Bannerman stood before the church door, at the top of a flight of broad stone steps, staring directly at her.

Lined up on either side of the steps were at least forty or fifty mourners, all of them facing the car with expressions that ranged from outrage to surprise. Except for the quiet hum of the car's engine, there was not another sound. She imagined she could hear a collective gasp—some people indeed had opened their mouths, as if in shock—but in fact the silence was complete and deadly. The arrival of a spaceship in the courtyard could not have been greeted with greater incredulity, or hostility.

In the middle of the steps stood a small, erect figure swathed in black, her eyes fixed on the far horizon as if the car which had arrived so inopportunely did not exist.

Alexa had no difficulty in recognizing Arthur Bannerman's mother. The old lady was exactly as Arthur had described her—and it was also in keeping with his description that she did not allow herself to show even the slightest trace of surprise or annoyance. At first glance she seemed frail, but even from a distance it was possible to guess that the frailty was deceptive—there was something about the way she stood that suggested a strength hardly less than that of the great trees around the church.

Alexa had seen enough photographs of the Bannerman family to recognize Cecilia and Putnam instantly, yet they were not at all what she expected them to be. Like all parents—like her own—Arthur had talked about them as if they were still children. He knew better, of course, but sometimes, hearing him, it was easy enough to imagine that Putnam had just been expelled from Harvard, or that Cecilia was still a young girl having trouble in school because of her famous name.

It was hard to reconcile these wavering images with the real figures on the steps. Putnam, for example, looked older than she had expected, and larger, with the build of a football player who has let himself run slightly to seed. Arthur had often complained that he had "too much boyish charm for his own good," but if that was the case, there was no evidence of it today. His face looked flushed and puffy, as if he had a hangover.

Cecilia was even more of a surprise. Instead of the awkward adolescent girl whom Arthur had usually seemed to have in mind, she was a tall woman of at least thirty, far too thin for her height, which was considerable, but immensely graceful. To Arthur, his daughter may have remained an ugly duckling, but in fact, Alexa thought, she had obviously long since grown into a swan—and indeed there *was* something of that graceful bird in Cecilia's long neck, her fine bones, the narrow, tapered fingers. She was what *Vogue* would call "a classic beauty," perhaps a shade too cool and regal for modern tastes. She would have seemed intimidating, except for her eyes, which had the nervous, hunted look of an animal caught in a trap.

A heavyset man in his late thirties with dark hair and wearing glasses, looking somehow out of place among the Bannermans, stood close beside Cecilia with his arm around her waist as if he were trying to protect her. She did not look pleased—she seemed, in fact, to be trying to move away from him without making an obvious fuss about it. Alexa guessed that this was Martin Booker, Cecilia's one-time fiancé, the lawyer who did most of the real work for the Bannerman family in DeWitt's law firm, and with whom Arthur had had frequent conversations.

In the moment of slow-motion paralysis that followed her traumatic arrival, Alexa saw these people with sharp, intense clarity, as if a flash-bulb had just gone off in their faces. They were different in many ways from what she had imagined, but it was the man standing next to Eleanor Bannerman, his arm in hers, who caused a sinking feeling in the pit of her stomach.

Nothing had prepared her for the startling resemblance between Robert Bannerman and his father. They had the same face: the finely chiseled straight nose, the square, thrusting jaw, the wide mouth, above all, the piercing, cornflower-blue eyes. Like the rest of the family, Robert had fine, straight blond hair. Arthur's had turned silver—the kind of silver that has nothing in common with "gray"—but otherwise they were almost identical, except that Robert was, of course, leaner and younger. His face was less lined, the planes of it sharper, but she imagined it was like seeing Arthur Bannerman as he must have been twenty-five years ago, right down to the same curious habit of raising his chin so that he looked down on most of the world through half-hooded eyes. It was the eyes, she knew, that made Arthur seem more arrogant than he was, arrogant even when he didn't mean to be—though in Robert's case, she thought, something in their depths suggested that *his* arrogance was the real thing.

She heard a horn sound behind her. Simon, who usually liked to be in charge, gave a small shrug to indicate that he didn't know what to do next; then an elderly man in a dark suit, clearly some sort of servant, rushed to the car, a look of panic on his face, and opened the door. "Leave the keys in, I'll take it," he said breathlessly. "Hurry! The hearse is right behind you!"

She had expected to have a moment or two to prepare herself. She had imagined parking the car discreetly, sitting in it for a few minutes to summon up her courage. She hesitated.

"Come on, for chrissake!" the man shouted. She jumped out quickly, joined by Simon, who for once looked bewildered, as his car shot out of sight with a roar.

She had not given any thought to the question of whether or not Simon would accompany her into the church. She suspected, now that it was too late, that he would have preferred to remain out of sight in the car. She also knew it would have looked better for her if he had. Her status as widow could only be prejudiced by the presence of Simon as her companion. For a second she wondered if passing him off as her brother would work, but there was no time now to prepare him for the role, and in any case, Courtland DeWitt and Robert knew better. She already could see DeWitt leaning over to whisper in old Mrs. Bannerman's ear, his long, sad face like that of one of the more lugubrious breeds of hound.

She heard the sound of tires on the gravel. She and Simon could hardly stand in front of the steps, blocking the way—that much was obvious. Summoning up her courage, she mounted the steps, Simon in tow, silent for once, just in time to see six men in dark suits slide the heavy, ornate casket out of the hearse. They hoisted it to their shoulders, then bore it slowly up the steps, passing so close to her that she could have touched the casket. She could see the finely grained wood, the bronze handles, the elegant carving, could even read the small brass plaque engraved in Gothic letters with the legend "Aurora Casket Company, Aurora, Indiana—Nationwide."

She felt tears coming, and fought to keep them back. Aurora was not all that far from home. She remembered her father's funeral on a day of sweltering Illinois heat, the mourners her father's neighbors, big, serious men, with large work-hardened hands, awkward in their best suits and anxious to get back to their farms as soon as they had paid their respects, and their wives, in flowered dresses and hats, fanning themselves with round paper fans, courtesy of the funeral home, glad for a chance to get out of their kitchens, even for a funeral. There had been just as many pickup trucks as cars outside the church, and the grave was bordered with Astroturf.

It was impossible to believe that the casket her brothers had carried with such ease contained her father—it was not until they lowered it with slings into the ground that she finally accepted his death. The thought that Arthur Bannerman was lying inside *this* casket, stretched out on plush satin, doubtless dressed in one of his dark-blue suits—but surely not, she guessed, in any of the shirts or ties she had bought him —was just as impossible to accept. Big as the casket was, it did not seem big enough to contain him.

She *knew* he was dead, had seen him die, after all, but the knowledge that he was there, not more than a few feet from her touch but beyond reach forever, made her feel more alone and frightened than even her father's death. She did not need Simon's Freudian explanations to know that she had sought in Arthur Bannerman a second father, and found, against the odds, love.

She dabbed away her tears with a handkerchief and followed the casket up the steps in full view of the family. A part of her hoped they would accept her, but she knew that was wishful thinking. They knew nothing about her—and what they did know, from the newspapers and from DeWitt, was mostly wrong—while she knew much more about them than they could possibly imagine. Arthur had given her what amounted to a crash course in the history of his family, and it had not occurred to her that he must have had a reason for doing so, a purpose in mind for her. Did he have a premonition of death? He had never talked about his health, and for his age he was remarkably robust—but it now seemed to her that he had been determined to tell her as much as he could, as if he felt the pressure of some uncertain deadline. She had promised to carry out his plans; now that she was here, she wished she hadn't given him her word.

The Bannermans didn't seem any better prepared for it than she was. They moved into the shade of the church door, under an elaborately wrought wooden canopy, as if they were determined to protect the casket from attack. Behind her, the Bannerman relatives from the courtyard were crowding up the steps now. Retreat was out of the question. She could not have turned back without pushing through them—it would be like pushing through a subway turnstile against the flow, an undignified shoving match.

She saw Courtland DeWitt appear before her, his normally sallow face red with anger, accompanied by the young man who had been hovering over Cecilia Bannerman. "I thought we had a deal," DeWitt said. "You'd better go now."

Here, at least, was an enemy she recognized, and about whom she had no ambiguous feelings. "I never agreed not to come," she said. "You heard what you wanted to hear. I said I'd think it over, and I did."

"You haven't done yourself any good, young lady. Mrs. Bannerman is furious. You can't go in, and that's that."

"I'm *going* in. Arthur would have wanted me to, and you know it."

"I know nothing of the kind! Wolff, I expected more common sense from you. Talk some reason into her, man."

"Well, I've been trying to do that all the way up the Taconic . . . "

Alexa moved forward blindly, ignoring Simon. One of the Bannermans, she knew, certainly the old lady, might have been able to talk her out of going into the church, but not DeWitt, who had treated her like a tramp in her own apartment. Besides, now that she was close to him, she could see a trace of fear in his eyes. It had been his job to keep her quiet and keep her away, and he had failed. No doubt a large part of old Mrs. Bannerman's rage would be directed at him. "Get out of my way," she said firmly, "before I make a scene in front of all these people. *That* ought to make the papers, don't you think?"

DeWitt apparently knew better than to argue with an angry woman. He looked at her, recognized that he was not going to get anywhere, and gave an imploring glance at Simon, who shrugged his shoulders to indicate that he was powerless, or perhaps simply not to blame.

She advanced along the porch as DeWitt retreated in front of her. The organ began to play—she recognized "A Mighty Fortress Is Our God," a hymn that had been played at her father's funeral, though she doubted that it had quite the same weighty significance for Episcopalians as it did for Lutherans. Here it was background music, chosen, no doubt, for its ponderous tones; in her father's church it was always the culmination of the service. Her grandfather had always sung the words in German—or Swiss-German, more exactly, for long ago the Waldens had fled to Switzerland to escape persecution in France, and the house in which she was born was still full of nostalgic reminders of their homeland: a cuckoo clock, dark oil paintings of cows in the Alps, beer mugs depicting Wilhelm Tell shooting an apple off his son's head and other patriotic scenes from Swiss history, a family Bible printed in Gothic German script that was only taken out for special occasions.

Even from the outside, looking into the dark interior, it was easy to see that the Bannerman church was very different from the one of her childhood. It took no skill as an antiquarian to guess that the magnificent stained-glass windows were medieval, and surely priceless. In their light, the ancient carved wood, the brass, and the polished stone gleamed sumptuously. At the far end, in front of an altar that would not have seemed out of place in a European cathedral, was a lectern in the shape of an eagle, the outstretched wings of brass glowing like the sun.

Although it was cool on the porch, DeWitt took the handkerchief out of his breast pocket and wiped the sweat off his forehead. "Let's be reasonable," he said.

"I'm *being* reasonable. I'm going to sit down."

"What seems to be the problem?"

She turned in panic at the sound of the voice. It was Arthur's—the same clipped, precise articulation, the unmistakable Harvard vowels, the same self-confident tone that carried easily above other people's conversations, even, in this case, the organ. For a moment she could almost have believed it *was* Arthur, appearing beside her, then she realized that the man's hair was blond, not silver-white. Robert Bannerman was staring at her. He seemed more amused than angry, to judge from his expression.

"I was explaining to the—ah—young lady, that she can't come in," DeWitt stammered.

Robert Bannerman raised an eyebrow. He gave a small smile—*shared* it, in fact, with Alexa, as if they were accomplices in some way. He laughed. "She doesn't seem to have taken it to heart, old man."

DeWitt's face turned pale, then darkened again. Clearly there was no love lost between the two men. "Your grandmother's wishes were explicit, Robert," he said. The dislike in his voice was obvious to Alexa. Was there a split in the family ranks? she wondered. Whoever DeWitt spoke for, it was apparently not Robert, who showed his frank contempt for his uncle by continuing to smile, ignoring DeWitt's anger as if it were beneath his notice.

"I'll speak to Grandmother later," Robert said. "In the meantime—" he turned his attention to Alexa—"you and your friend had better come in and be seated. We don't want a quarrel in public."

He nodded courteously—almost a small bow. "If you don't mind, however, pick a pew at the rear of the church. There's no point in pushing Grandmother too far. Take my word for it."

She took his word for it. There was something about him that made her willing to listen. Like his father, he had a way of suggesting that what he wanted you to do was exactly what *you* wanted.

He took her arm gently and guided her to a pew at the back. Two elderly couples squeezed more closely together, more from the fear of sitting next to her, she suspected, than from any need to make room. "It's always sensible not to overplay your hand," Robert said pleasantly, letting go of her arm. "I'm sure we'll meet again."

"I suppose so, yes."

The cold blue eyes flickered. Robert Bannerman was still smiling, but for a fraction of a second she saw the anger in them, then it vanished as if it had never been there. "Count on it," he said, and turned to make his way down the aisle toward the altar, where his grandmother sat motionless, waiting for him.

Alexa sat unmoved through the beginning of the service, uncomfortably aware that those who could do so inconspicuously were staring at her from behind their hymnbooks. She rose for the Lord's Prayer, sat when everyone else sat, rose again while the congregation sang a hymn —this time, one she didn't know—then sat again. She had hoped to be moved, hoped in some way that the service would reconcile her to Arthur's death, or at least help her understand her own feelings about what had happened, but it seemed to her as meaningless as her father's funeral. She found no comfort in the prayers and hymns—they were just a ritual to be endured before the body was lowered into the ground.

There was a rustle of anticipation in the congregation as Emmett DeWitt mounted the lectern, his head towering above the eagle's wings. She knew him by sight, of course—he was a celebrity in his own right. Arthur, she knew, had a certain affection for Emmett, whose command of the media he envied. Arthur had rather liked the idea of having an eccentric in the family, provided it wasn't one of his *own* children, and she knew he had often defended Emmett against his father. She had once overheard him saying on the phone, "Courtland, you leave Emmett be, or by God I'll take the family's legal business elsewhere, brother-in-law or no brother-in-law."

She watched with curiosity now, as Emmett stood in silence, patiently waiting until he had the full attention of his audience. Despite his peculiar appearance—the strange hair, the fanatical gleam in his eyes behind the thick glasses, the hollow, sunken cheeks, and his ungainly height—he had great presence. She could sense the anticipation in the church, an unnatural quiet—perhaps it was because Emmett was a kind of religious practical joker, who loved to shock his listeners, but also because he had the actor's gift of making you wait for his line. He coughed. He studied the ornate ceiling. He held out his arms in a blessing that made him look for an instant like some large, ungraceful bird, a stork perhaps, preparing to take flight.

His prominent Adam's apple bobbed a couple of times; then, drawing a deep breath, he turned, staring straight at her, his arms still raised, and in a voice of operatic power, directed toward her, he intoned, "He that is without sin among you, let him be the first to cast a stone."

There was a moment of silence—then, from all over the church, a low hum of whispering. She saw every head in the church turn toward her except Eleanor Bannerman's.

For a moment she was tempted to rise and leave. She could feel her legs trembling. Worse yet, she could feel herself blushing.

She tried to fight it back, hoping it was something she could control. It was not. She focused her eyes on the back of Eleanor Bannerman's head, then sat rigidly, not even hearing the rest of Emmett's sermon, conscious only of her own determination to sit through the ceremony to the end without tears.

"AH, EXCUSE ME."

She turned to find Martin Booker standing behind her on the porch. He looked nervous, as if he didn't like whatever he had been delegated to do.

"Robert—ah, the ambassador—wanted me to make sure you and Mr. Wolff found your way to the Pie."

"The Pie?"

"The *Bannerman* Pie. Cyrus Bannerman built a graveyard for his descendants, you know. It's circular—well, you'll see. It looks a lot like a pie, as a matter of fact. . . . "

Booker's attitude was solicitous, if slightly superior. Alexa hated being treated as if she were stupid merely because she was pretty. She searched Booker's face for a sign that he was doing so, but found nothing there except a certain amount of embarrassment at his own role. Or, she wondered, was he simply feeling out of place here like herself?

Arthur had countless ways of determining whether or not someone came up to Bannerman standards. He did not think of these as prejudices, nor did he necessarily think the less of people who flouted them, provided they did so out of ignorance. Still, he believed in them firmly. Bannerman men did not wear cuff links in the daytime, tie clips ever, or button-down shirts; they wore plain black shoes with five eyelets and were never seen wearing a hat. He had hundreds of such opinions, big and small, and clung to them stubbornly. He did not appear to have shared them with Booker, whose gold tie clip and cuff links glinted in the sun (they were a set, which was, she remembered, even worse in Arthur's eyes) and who carried a black homburg hat by the brim carefully, as if it were someone else's. Unaccountably she felt sorry for him.

"I didn't mean to sound like a tour guide," he said.

"A tour guide? Or a guard?"

He revolved the hat. His fingers were long and thin—musician's fingers, she thought, rather than the stubby, practical ones she associated, for no particular reason, with lawyers. He was taller than she had supposed, now that he was not standing with the Bannermans, and good-looking, in a dark, rough-hewn way, with black hair, thick eyebrows and the kind of five o'clock shadow that resists even the most careful of shaves. He had a habit of rubbing his hand over his chin from time to time, as if he were wondering how much his beard had grown in the last few minutes. He did so now. "Both," he admitted uncomfortably. "I'm to find a place for you and Mr. Wolff to stand . . ."

" . . . And to make sure we stay there?"

"Something like that, yes. You surely weren't expecting old Mrs. Bannerman to greet you with open arms, were you?"

"I don't know what I was expecting. I *wasn't* expecting to be humiliated from the pulpit, anyway."

"By Emmett? He's a crackpot. Besides, he probably meant well. He's always on the side of the underdog."

"Am I the underdog?"

He scrutinized her carefully. "I'm not sure," he said cautiously. "Follow me, please."

He led her through a set of elaborately gilded wrought-iron gates and onto a gravel path at the edge of the graveyard—which was, indeed, shaped like a pie. Simon followed, a little sheepishly, as if he did not want to be here but also didn't want to be left behind.

Shaded by huge hemlocks, the graves of three generations of Bannermans were arranged within a large circle and divided by bordered pathways into four sections. At the center, on a block of rough-hewn granite, she saw what was unmistakably a life-size bronze statue of Cyrus Bannerman, dressed in a business suit of old-fashioned cut and seated in a bronze desk chair. One hand rested on his knee; in the other he held what appeared to be an accountant's ledger. He faced Kiawa, but his eyes were directed downward toward the book, as if to demonstrate to his descendants that business came before pleasure.

The sculptor had tried for an expression of nobility, but either his abilities or the subject had failed him. The face, though dignified, had a crafty look to it, that of a man who has mastered his own weaknesses and in doing so has learned exactly how to turn everybody else's to his advantage.

Arthur had often talked to her about the old man, with a false affection that failed to conceal his fear of him, even sixty years after Cyrus Bannerman's death. He told her that Cyrus liked to test his grandchildren with trick questions; if they were unable to answer them correctly, they got no dessert. By then, of course, Cyrus was so old that he had outlived all his enemies: it was longevity as much as wealth that eventually made him respectable. Chiseled into the base of his statue was the cheerless inscription: "Work, thrift, family."

To one side of Cyrus, but a little lower, stood his eldest son, Putnam, Arthur's father, looking away from Kiawa as if the sculptor had managed to capture his lifelong dream of escaping from the responsibilities of the fortune Cyrus had handed down to him—a dream which was never realized, for Putnam spent his life sitting behind a desk, working like a clerk to manage the wealth he was unable to enjoy. He gave away millions of dollars to foundations, museums, universities, and hospitals, but the fortune piled up income faster than he could get rid of it, until the task finally broke his health, forced him to withdraw into seclusion, leaving his wife, Eleanor, to take over the task until the next generation was ready for it.

Arthur's life, she knew, had been formed by the example of his father, whom he idolized and pitied. He himself was determined not to be crushed by the responsibilities of the Bannerman fortune when it came to him. He refused to spend his life looking after it, or giving it away, or apologizing for it. The memory of his father, that sad, lonely figure, hunched over his desk day after day, trying to master every detail of an empire that no one man could possibly run single-handedly— except perhaps for old Cyrus himself—haunted Arthur's youth, indeed, still haunted him when he and Alexa had met, had played, in fact, no small role in their relationship.

"Quite something, isn't it?" Booker asked with a certain pride, as if he were already a member of the family. He would give his eyeteeth to be, she decided.

"It's a little depressing." Everywhere there were markers, ranging from the elaborate ones at the center of the Pie to small marble plaques at the outer edges. A large urn, supported by weeping maidens in the Grecian style and shaded by a willow tree, marked the grave of Elizabeth Putnam Bannerman, Cyrus's wife.

Alexa looked down and saw at her feet a rectangular marker, rather bigger than most. The inscription read simply: "John Aldon Bannerman, 1944–1967." There were no engraved words of wisdom, no statue, she noticed, for Arthur's boy, whose death had apparently caused such a rift in the family. At the head of the marker was a rosebush, though it bore no flowers at this time of year.

There was no evidence of flower beds in the Pie—possibly Cyrus had never intended it to be a cheerful place. The lawn was as scrupulously tended as that of a golf course, the borders of the pathways were lined with dark privet hedges trimmed as straight as a ruler. Around the outer edge was a black wrought-iron fence topped with gilded spikes. She wondered what would happen when the Pie was filled up. Would the Bannermans have to be buried one on top of another?

"This seems as good a place as any," Booker said firmly.

He had chosen the spot, Alexa thought, with some care—far enough from Arthur Bannerman's grave to make her presence inconspicuous, and directly behind Eleanor Bannerman so that she was out of the old lady's immediate sight. At the same time, it was not at the extreme edge of the Pie where, she judged from their expressions and clothes, the family servants and the local people who depended on Kiawa stood.

She was tempted to push forward toward the gravesite, if only to test Booker's strength of character, which seemed formidable, but then she reminded herself that she had not come here to make a scene or stake out a claim as a star mourner. She was here for Arthur's sake, and for Arthur's sake she would stay in the background, out of his mother's sight.

"Close enough?"

"I came here to say goodbye to Arthur. I can do that just fine from here, thank you."

"Well, sure . . . I didn't mean . . ."

"Maybe you could stand back a little so I can see? Is that too much to ask?"

He cleared his throat and stepped behind her. Ahead of her, about fifty feet away, she could see the grave. It had been dug very close to old Putnam Bannerman's monument, right at the center of the Pie, its edges covered with rich turf. She could hear the rector reciting a prayer. Emmett DeWitt stood behind him, his eyes staring up at the sky as if he were in direct connection with God, while the rest of the immediate family grouped itself around old Mrs. Bannerman, facing the two clergymen.

There was a moment of silence; then the pallbearers appeared and began to lower the coffin into the ground on slings. Alexa closed her eyes. That had been the worst moment at her father's funeral—the slow, inexorable descent into the ground, the final realization that he was gone forever, *buried*, that it was too late to put things right.

She remembered the dull thud of the clods of earth, hard from a long drought, as the gravediggers covered her father's casket. The sound had haunted her for years, still did sometimes in her dreams. She felt herself break into a sweat at the thought of it, and opened her eyes.

"Are you all right?" she heard Simon whisper. "You turned white as a sheet, a moment there."

She nodded. She found it difficult to catch her breath, harder still to speak. She clenched her teeth and made herself look at the lid of the casket as it disappeared into the ground. She waited for the awful sound of earth being thrown on it, but instead, Robert Bannerman simply stepped forward, accepted a small silver scoop from one of the pallbearers—from where she stood, it looked more appropriate for a tea service than a funeral—stooped down to fill it with earth, and emptied it silently into the grave. He handed it back, dusted off his fingers, and stepped back.

The Bannerman family moved away from the grave. To her relief, the business of filling in the grave was apparently not part of the ceremony.

She took a deep breath. She felt sad, drained, suddenly exhausted, glad the casket was gone from her view. Whatever it was she had come here for had happened. She wanted to go home.

"Sad, isn't it?" Booker asked, though he didn't sound sad at all. "He'd always hoped for the full works, I guess—caisson, black horses, boots reversed, flags at half-mast all over the country, the Marine band playing 'Hail to the Chief' in slow time. . . . He might have had it, too, if Hugh Scott hadn't gone back on his word and delivered the Pennsylvania delegation to Nixon at the last minute."

"Was it really that close?" she asked, interested despite her growing irritation with Booker's lack of sympathy and love of his own voice.

"You're too young to remember. He looked like a winner to a lot of people. Not to the pols, though. They didn't want a President who was so rich they couldn't control him. And Arthur didn't really have the killer instinct, you know. He left the dirty work to Robert, but he didn't want to know what Robert was doing in his name. Of course, Robert was too young to be handed that kind of responsibility. Did Arthur talk much about it?"

"Some. Not much. He once told me that losing the nomination was the best thing that had ever happened to him. 'If I'd won,' he said, 'I'd have gone into Vietnam lock, stock, and barrel. People would have ended up hating me just the way they hated poor Lyndon.' "

"That doesn't sound like him to me. I mean, the Vietnam thing, sure. He stuck his neck out for LBJ right to the end. Even for Nixon, during the Cambodia invasion—and he hated Nixon worse than the Kennedys or LBJ. I didn't see that much of him the last year or so, but he never struck me as the kind of guy who was philosophical about losing, frankly."

"He was with me."

"You must have had a good effect on the old boy."

"Nobody else here seems to think so," she snapped, angered by Booker's flatfooted cheerfulness. Not only was he unmoved by Arthur Bannerman's death but he seemed to think she was, too. He behaved as if she were a spectator, without feelings. She also doubted whether he would have allowed himself to call Arthur "the old boy" to any member of the family.

He looked at her more closely and rubbed his chin. "I'm sorry," he said. "I realize this is difficult for you."

"Difficult?"

"Well, given the circumstances . . ."

"Circumstances?"

Booker rolled his dark eyes soulfully. "Of his death, I mean."

"Does it really matter *how* he died? Arthur loved me, and now he's dead. I'm sorry it embarrasses the family, but that's the way it is." She stared at Booker as if his opinion mattered to her. "He loved me and he married me," she said quietly. "Whether you believe it or not. That's why I'm here."

He coughed. "Yes, of course . . . I understand . . . you must feel . . ." He studied the hat in his hands for inspiration. "It's a great loss," he said. "For everyone. For you too, of course."

"Thank you. I'm glad somebody finally said it."

Booker sighed. He had the resigned expression of a man who was used to guessing wrong about women, however smart he was about the rest of life. "You're not exactly what we—what I—expected. . . ."

"What *did* you expect, Mr. Booker? Just out of curiosity. A chorus-girl type? A brainless model? I would have thought you'd all have given Arthur credit for better taste than that?"

"Look," he said, on the defensive now, "you can't expect anybody here to put out the welcome mat for you. The general feeling is that Arthur was off his rocker."

"Is that *your* feeling, Mr. Booker?"

"Maybe not, but I only work here. Look, we got off on the wrong foot. I'm sorry."

He did look sorry, she decided. His eyes had the look of a guilty cocker spaniel's. Now that she was looking at him more closely, she saw that he was quite good-looking in his own way. Under different circumstances, she decided, she might like Booker.

"I think we'd better go now," Simon said from behind her, speaking up for the first time since they'd left the church. His tone was urgent.

Booker looked around, then nodded. "Good idea," he said. "I'll show you where your car is."

She glanced over his shoulder, wondering what had attracted Simon's attention, and saw Eleanor Bannerman, methodically making her way around the Pie to accept the condolences of the mourners. She was walking briskly, pausing with each person only long enough to nod or say a word of thanks. There was nothing haphazard about her path. She had obviously set out to cover each section of the Pie, and was moving toward them on a collision course.

"I'm sorry, Mr. Booker," Alexa said firmly, "but I haven't the slightest intention of moving."

"Booker is right, Alexa," Simon said. "Time to go, for God's sake! You don't want a scene with the old lady."

"Simon, if you want to hide, there's a tree over there. I'm not going to. I'm not going to run away from anyone."

Simon shrugged and apparently resigned himself to his fate. Not twenty yards away, Eleanor Bannerman was bearing down on them, followed by her daughters and her grandchildren. Simon's fear was contagious. For a moment, Alexa almost wished she had retreated out of sight, but then she reminded herself that she had nothing to fear. What could old Mrs. Bannerman do to *her?* She would probably walk right past her without a word.

Alexa could see her clearly now. Mrs. Bannerman had raised her veils so that they flowed behind her in the breeze. In one small gloved hand she carried a pocketbook made of jet beads, with a diamond clasp. Around her neck she wore three strands of black pearls. The veils were pinned to her black velvet hat with two matching diamond brooches.

Close up, Alexa realized for the first time how diminutive the old lady was—it was impossible to imagine her giving birth to Arthur, giving birth at all, come to that. And yet, by some trick of bearing, she did not seem *small*—she had the kind of presence that makes height inconsequential.

It was easy enough to see that she must once have been a great beauty, with her fine bones, her fierce blue eyes, and her swanlike neck, and in her own way, she was still beautiful. Age had not made her ugly, as it did so many old people—it had simply given her a beauty of a different kind. The fine skin was almost translucent, stretched tight over cheekbones like those of a cat, her eyelashes as dark and thick as a model's, and clearly her own. Her face, too, was as carefully made up as any model's. Age and mourning had not prevented Mrs. Bannerman from putting on her lipstick, eyeliner, mascara, and powder, nor had it affected her skill in applying them, which, with her ex-model's eye, Alexa could see was considerable.

Mrs. Bannerman looked straight in front of her into the middle distance. For a moment Alexa wondered whether the old lady had seen her—certainly the blue eyes didn't even flicker in her direction as Mrs. Bannerman approached without slowing her pace.

Then, as she was about to pass by Alexa on the gravel path, she stopped as if she had forgotten something, and turned to face her, hardly more than two feet away. Alexa felt herself blush under the scrutiny of Mrs. Bannerman's eyes.

The faces of the other Bannermans registered a variety of emotions, from nervous embarrassment to outright hatred, in the case of Cecilia, but Mrs. Bannerman's was an elegant mask, registering nothing at all except, perhaps, the slightest trace of annoyance, like that of someone who has just noticed something out of place in a room, a picture not hung quite straight, or a speck of dust on a polished table.

There was a long pause, a silence so complete that Alexa could hear Booker breathing hard beside her. Mrs. Bannerman's eyes were as unwavering as those of a bird of prey. Her neatly black-gloved hands were clasped in front of her, holding her small purse. Only her veils moved in the breeze.

"The photographs in the newspapers don't do you justice," she said at last in a voice that was astonishingly clear and firm for someone her age. She spoke with old-fashioned precision, rather slowly, and while her voice was not particularly loud, it seemed to Alexa that it carried like an opera singer's so that it could be heard right across the Pie.

"Thank you," Alexa said, though she was not sure it was meant as a compliment. There was a great deal more that she wanted to say, but she felt as if Mrs. Bannerman's formidable presence had turned her to stone.

"You had no business coming here."

Alexa summoned up her courage. "I *had* to be here," she said, aware that her voice was hardly more than a whisper. "For Arthur's sake."

She watched the old lady's eyes, and for a fraction of a second she thought she saw something change in them, like a puff of breeze on a hot summer's day ruffling the surface of a pond and changing its color briefly. Was it respect? Or anger? Or perhaps a grudging admiration for the fact that she had spoken up for herself?

The moment passed. "I see," Mrs. Bannerman said. "Good day." She suddenly seemed tired to Alexa, as if the strain of the day had finally caught up with her. Even her voice was a shade less crisp and self-assured. Had the old woman recognized something in Alexa that she had not expected to find? She looked faintly puzzled, or thoughtful, like somebody who was trying hard to remember a name or a face and was unable to make the connection. For a moment Alexa thought she was going to say something more, but instead she turned away and proceeded down the path, less briskly now.

The immediate Bannerman family followed her in a dark flying wedge. None of them turned to look at her. It was as if she simply did not exist. All over the Pie, the mourners were talking now, moving slowly down the paths in groups of three or four, greeting each other, but nobody came near her, nobody even dared to look in her direction, clearly all too eager to get away. The spot she stood on, with Booker beside her and Simon behind her, might have been contaminated ground, dangerous to approach.

She stayed put with her unwilling companions until the Pie was empty except for the three of them, and only then did she turn to Simon and say, "Let's go home."

3

Robert Bannerman stood in front of the fireplace, a drink in his hand. Despite the fire, he felt chilled. He wondered if he had caught a cold—after all, there was a considerable difference in temperature between Caracas and Dutchess County—but since he prided himself on never being sick, he dismissed the possibility. Eleanor looked chilled, too, he thought. Remarkable as her health was, it had been a long day for a woman of eighty-six, particularly with over a hundred people to feed, some of the more privileged or important of whom were spending the night here before starting home. The door opened. An elderly, red-faced man looked in, muttered, "I'm sorry," and closed it again quickly at the sight of Robert's face.

Robert tried to remember who he was. Cousin Amory, former MFH of the Rombout, who had once ridden his hunter into the Saltonstall house during a dinner party and jumped the horse over the dining table without knocking over the silver candlesticks or breaking a piece of china? Or was Amory dead? Robert couldn't remember, didn't *care*, but as the new head of the family, these were exactly the things he was supposed to know. Without any visible effort, his father had been aware of every birth, death, and marriage in the family, probably because Eleanor kept him up-to-date.

The hell with it, Robert thought. He sipped his Scotch and gave some thought to ordering another. On the mantelpiece beside him was a small silver serving tray with a miniature decanter. Kiawa was perhaps the last private house in America where spirits were served in individual little crystal decanters just big enough for two strong drinks. At Kiawa, no guest ever saw a bottle—they were kept in the butler's pantry where,

Robert was quite sure, the servants helped themselves, despite a complex bookkeeping system designed to prevent just that, in which every drink had to be accounted for.

Robert knew it was time for a real housecleaning, from the investment decisions of the Bannerman Foundation to the kitchen of Kiawa, where the cook, he had no doubt, was stealing the Bannermans blind. He could hardly wait to get on with it.

He faced his grandmother in her red-and-gold "Chinese room." The walls were covered with priceless chinoiserie panels, looted from the siege of Peking, for which Cyrus Bannerman had outbid three museums and William Randolph Hearst, whom he despised. Putnam Bannerman's collection of Chinese porcelain was displayed in glass cabinets. It was said to be worth a fortune, but to Robert's eye it was merely a lot of useless and highly breakable vases, the kind of thing that belonged in a museum and would go there just as soon as he got the chance to donate it. Half a dozen antique clocks whirred, ticked and chimed at regular intervals, getting on his nerves.

In front of Eleanor Bannerman, on a lacquer table, sat a tea service, with china so delicate that it was almost transparent. Behind her was a long table covered with silver picture frames of different sizes, according to some rating system of her own, a kind of gallery of the dead: her own brother John, Robert's mother, *his* brother John, his grandfather Putnam, seated as usual at his desk, and, of course, Cyrus Bannerman himself, in old age, looking like an Egyptian mummy, everything about him wrinkled and aged except the eyes, which stared at the photographer shrewdly, as if he were thinking, "Old as I am, I can buy you, or sell you, or ruin you, if I please."

There were no photographs of the living. Robert wondered how long it would be before his father's photograph was placed there, and whether Eleanor kept a stock of Cartier frames in various sizes just to be ready for a death in the family.

The two largest photographs, he noticed for the first time, were those of his brother John and old Cyrus. Was there a significance in that, he wondered? Cyrus he could understand. It was well known that Eleanor worshipped her father-in-law, whose single-minded ferocity and cold cunning were so lacking in her husband. The old robber baron was said to have adored her, too, shown toward her, in fact, an affection he denied everyone else, certainly his son, even his wife, who in photographs always looked as if she were terrified of him.

The size of John's photograph was harder to explain. Had John been one of her favorites among her grandchildren, or was it just that he had been the eldest, and therefore the heir? Robert tried to remember, but he could think of nothing in the past to indicate that she preferred John, or had ever taken his side. It would be interesting to see what size frame she would use for his father, he thought, then decided that he didn't care. There was too much of the past in this room, and most of it was better forgotten.

"I'm glad it's all over," he said. "I was afraid Cici couldn't sit through it."

"At least there were no surprises in the will," Eleanor said. "I thought Courtland did the reading with great dignity."

"I suppose so, Grandmother."

"I wish you wouldn't be so disagreeable to him. He *is* your uncle."

"I'm not sure he's the man for the job, that's all. Booker does all the work." DeWitt, he told himself, would be the first to go—DeWitt who had fought him tooth and nail when he tried to take on some of the family's responsibilities, DeWitt who had screwed up—no other phrase could describe it—the whole business of the Walden girl's claim to have married his father. If DeWitt had been on the ball, he would have been over at her apartment before the police arrived and paid her off on the spot. He should have sent Booker, Robert told himself.

His grandmother poured herself a fresh cup of tea. She looked as if she could use a drink, Robert thought, but she seldom drank, except for a glass of sherry before dinner or a sip of champagne on special occasions. "Courtland surrounds himself with good people," she said. "His firm has an excellent reputation. All lawyers are fools, of course, but one can't get anything done without them. At least we *know* Courtland's limitations."

"Unfortunately, he doesn't."

She looked at him shrewdly. "Few men do." She put her cup down, her diamond bracelet clicking against the porcelain. "Did you know your father seriously considered disinheriting you? I'm a little surprised that he changed his mind and did nothing."

Robert stared at her. The thought had never crossed his mind, and it came as a sudden shock, a sense of betrayal that left him breathless. "I don't believe it," he said angrily. "He never even hinted at it."

"He felt—what were his words? That you'd tried 'to pull the rug out from under him while he was still alive and kicking.' He wanted to punish you, you see. I don't think you ever appreciated just how angry he was."

"He couldn't have done it, surely? It's never happened."

"Whoever has control of The Trust can do what he likes, Robert. You know that. You've been thinking about nothing else these last few days. In the end, though, I suppose your father wasn't strong enough to break with family tradition. You're very lucky."

"You could have warned me."

"*Warned* you? I warned you at the time. You wouldn't listen. You never do. I told your father that just because you were a young fool was no reason for him to be an old one."

Robert felt as if he were suddenly standing on quicksand. He had fought with his father, yes, but he had also fought *for* him. Even when things were at their worst, he had always assumed there were certain rules to the fight—that he was the heir, and eventually everything would come to him. To a degree, after all, that was what the quarrel between them had been about. Robert had always thought of it in Shakespearean terms, with himself in the role of Prince Hal, and he felt sick at the possibility that he had misjudged things so badly over the years. He thought about the scene over his mother's death, about the campaign—he had wanted the nomination more for his father than the old man had wanted it himself, had he not? He thought about John's death and shivered. Never once had it ever occurred to him that his father might disinherit him, no matter how bitter things were between them. "God *damn* him!" he said fiercely.

"I won't have you speaking that way of your father in my presence."

Robert swallowed. He had gone too far. There were things that were unimaginable, and raising one's voice to Eleanor Bannerman was one of them. "I apologize, Grandmother," he said.

"You'd do better to learn how to control your temper."

"I'll do my best. Tell me, if Father *had* decided against me, whom would he have picked? I can hardly see him relying on Putt, whatever he thought of me."

"Of course, Putnam would have been out of the question. Despite the way he died, your father was not altogether foolish; he knew per fectly well that Putnam could never have handled the responsibility, wouldn't want to, for that matter."

"Well, then . . . "

"He gave serious thought to Cecilia."

"*Cecilia?* But that's ridiculous!"

Eleanor looked at him coldly. "Really? Why?"

Robert emptied what was left in the decanter—a finger or two of Scotch—into his glass and drained it in one gulp. He could feel it burn its way down, and gasped for air. He felt weak in the knees at the thought of the Bannerman fortune, with all its responsibilities, passing to Cecilia, of all people. The notion that his father could even have contemplated anything so absurd, so humiliating, so *treacherous*, was like an unbearable pressure on his chest. He could feel his heartbeat racing, the veins in his temple throbbing, his throat dry. He took a deep breath, which made him dizzy.

He fought back an impulse to do something, *anything* to relieve the pressure—hurl his glass at one of the cabinets with his grandfather's stupid Chinese knickknacks, scream, burst into laughter. The last seemed the most appropriate, but he gained control of himself at last and did nothing. Perfect composure, grace under pressure, was what Eleanor demanded, and goddamn her, that was what she would get.

"Well, for one thing," he said, as calmly as he could, "Cecilia has never shown the slightest interest in financial matters. And she's—well, fragile."

"Fragile? Cecilia has simply been emotionally overprotected all her life, that's all. In large part by you, though your father was just as much to blame. She has common sense and good instincts. The rest can be learned. None of you men thinks a woman is capable of taking on great responsibilities. Your great-grandfather knew better than that. I remember walking with him once, here at Kiawa, before he was confined to a wheelchair—he took my hand and said, 'Eleanor, I'd leave the whole damned thing to you, but I can't do that, so you'll just have to look after Putnam and keep his backbone straight.' "

She smiled at the memory. "I did, too, but God help me, much as I loved your grandfather, I often thought I could have done a better job of it, left to myself. And people thought *I* was 'fragile,' too, overprotected. Well, of course, in those days women of our class *were*. They were *expected* to be silly, delicate, romantic creatures, to faint and have vapors. . . . Poppycock! Sara Roosevelt had twice the backbone of her husband *and* her son Franklin—and more common sense, too."

She paused for breath, which was just as well, Robert thought, since he was unprepared for feminist arguments from his grandmother, of all people. The truth was that he didn't think Cici—or any woman—was equipped to deal with the problems of the Bannerman family's fortune. He had nothing against women and was perfectly prepared to admit that many of them were more intelligent than most men, but other things being equal, there was a level at which men operated better. He could not prove it—he was too smart, too much the politician, ever to be tempted into an argument on the subject, least of all with his grandmother—but deep in his heart he believed it to be so.

"You may be right," he said diplomatically. "In any case, Father apparently changed his mind. Or thought better of it. He left things in my hands, in the end."

"Subject to certain restrictions, yes."

"I'm aware of them."

Subject to certain restrictions. Robert knew them by heart, resented every one of them, had long ago worked out ways of getting around the more onerous ones. The responsibilities that accompanied control of the Bannerman fortune were immense, and were complicated by the fact that each Bannerman had sought to make sure his heirs would preserve the fortune intact. The heir to The Trust was an autocrat in theory, but in practice he was bound by such a tangled legal web that it would have been difficult for him to make a significant inroad on the fortune itself. Nor had it ever been necessary. As the heir, Robert would receive, as his father had, not only a substantial income, but Kiawa itself, as well as Seal Cove, the Bannerman summer "cottage" in Maine —not to speak of Beau Rivage, the family mansion in Palm Beach, which Cyrus had commissioned the Mizners to build when he could no longer bear the Dutchess County winters, or the old Bannerman house on Fifth Avenue, which had been leased on advantageous terms to the Venezuelan Mission to the United Nations, and of course Arthur's twenty-five-room duplex at 967 Fifth Avenue overlooking the park. None of these things could be sold without the agreement of so many people that it would be almost impossible to do.

Wherever you looked, there were obligations, from the Bannerman Foundation, which had long since acquired an autonomous status, independent of the family wishes or opinions, to the pension funds for retired Bannerman employees. Bannerman money had built hospitals, schools, universities, funded theaters, museums, and scholarships, so that the family's reputation for wealth grew in direct proportion to the amount that was given away. His father had lived like a king—and with all the obligations of a king, too—but would have been hard-pressed to raise $10 million in cash without a major family struggle. And $10 million was what Robert needed, at the very least, if he was going to pay off the campaign debts of his Senate race and make a serious stab at the governorship. He thought about his debts, about the commitments he had made, about the people he had made them to, and gritted his teeth. There were things you had to do in politics that you couldn't tell anyone about—that it didn't pay even to think about

"It's a heavy responsibility," Eleanor said, looking straight at him as if she could read his mind. "Your grandfather used to say it was a *moral* responsibility far more than a financial one. I remember when your father inherited, he was overwhelmed at first."

And remained overwhelmed, Robert thought bitterly, right to the end. "I think I'm quite prepared, Grandmother," he said.

He expected her to hit back, prepared himself for the blow, but for once she said nothing. He reminded himself that in his grandmother's opinion, it was *she* who was in charge, and of course there was some truth to that, particularly in recent years, as his father began to lose interest. DeWitt, the financial people, the bankers, they all suspected she had the last word and knew she, at least, was *interested* in what they were doing—more interested, in fact, than they would have liked. Robert guessed there was a lot going on that his father hadn't known, didn't *want* to know—particularly with a young girlfriend to take his mind off things.

"There's a great deal to be done," he said. "Father lost interest. You know it as well as I do."

She shrugged, a delicate, almost birdlike movement of the shoulders beneath the dark silk suit. "He grew bored with it, poor man. That's why he went into politics. I always thought it was a mistake. Your great-grandfather and your grandfather had no political ambitions. People tried to persuade your grandfather to run against Franklin Roosevelt for the governorship, you know, but he wouldn't hear of it. He felt that being head of the Bannerman family was much more important than being governor. He had too much contempt for people who can be bought to *become* one."

"I don't know about FDR, but I don't think Father could have been bought," Robert said stiffly.

"My poor boy, of course he could. The moment he ran for office he was for sale, just as you are. Just as Franklin was. Oh, don't look so shocked. Not for money, I know that, but there are other ways of buying someone: praise, flattery, the applause of the mob. Political ambition is a terrible thing. Look what it did to the Kennedys. Your great-grandfather and your grandfather didn't care a hoot what people thought about them, or wrote about them—they were above all that."

"Times have changed, Grandmother," Robert said gently. He understood her feelings, but he also knew they were irrelevant. When Cyrus was alive, his personal fortune had exceeded the net worth of any corporation in the country. He bought and sold United States Senators, newspaper editors, even Presidents, shamelessly, always through agents, for he was too proud to deal directly with any man he could buy. He was like a spider, the center of whose web was a simple, windowless closet of an office on lower Broadway, furnished with a battered rolltop desk, a single cheap wooden chair, and a brass bell to summon the office boy for fresh ink.

There he sat, absorbing distant tremors that meant little or nothing to other men—a fall in the price of guano in Valparaiso, storms in Kansas, a bankruptcy in the City of London, the rumor that a dry well in Ponder, Texas, was not as dry as it was said to be—fitting all the pieces together like some invisible jigsaw puzzle that he carried in his head, then, by some rare gift of imagination, or perhaps simply fierce, single-minded concentration, writing out his orders to buy, sell, foreclose, in a neat copperplate hand on carefully torn scraps of waste paper, notes that often brought ruin to his competitors, or to millions of small investors, sometimes even to governments and countries. Today America was controlled by faceless corporations, any one of whose minor subdivisions far exceeded in wealth the Bannerman fortune, while the politicians Cyrus had despised wielded the power of a government that was bigger than anything he could have imagined.

The Kennedys, goddamn them—the old man, anyway—had been right: power no longer lay in money but in politics, provided you had the guts to use it. The fortune was no longer an end in itself—it was just the means to something else, and there was no point, no glory, in spending a lifetime wet-nursing it for the next goddamn generation. Robert knew his father had understood that—understood it better than anyone—but he would never admit it, or commit himself heart and soul to the consequences. He was like a priest who no longer believed in the teachings of the church, but didn't have the guts to leave it.

Once, when he was a child, before he went to Groton, Robert remembered that he had been punished for not writing his daily expenses in the little black leather notebook that was part of family tradition (at the end of every week's entries there was supposed to be a certain amount, at least 10 percent of one's allowance, put toward "savings"), and he summoned up the nerve to ask his father if *he* still kept a notebook for his daily expenses, knowing perfectly well he didn't. "I did when I was your age," his father said, his anger at being challenged blunted by what Robert took to be shame, perhaps even guilt. For they both knew it was not an acceptable or a truthful answer. Cyrus and Putnam had written their daily expenses into little black notebooks until the day of their deaths, as if it were a religious duty, which in their terms perhaps it was.

His father, it was clear to Robert, had wanted his sons to do what *he* had been unwilling to do, but could never bring himself to say so. Robert wished there had been time to have it out to the end, and for an instant saw his father's face, as clearly as if he were in the room, heard the familiar, impatient voice. . . .

"I *said*, I don't think times have changed for the better." His grandmother had raised her voice. "Are you *deaf?*"

"No, no, I was just thinking. . . ."

"There's no point in my talking to you if your mind is elsewhere. It's extremely rude. Tell me, if I have your attention at last—what did you think of the girl?"

"The girl? She seemed quite pretty."

"That was not what I had in mind."

"No, quite. Well, I thought she showed guts, frankly."

"Guts? Certainly it was bold as brass to come here uninvited, but she was not at all what I expected her to be. I would like to know more about her."

"So would I."

"I asked Courtland to find out what he could."

"DeWitt's useless for that sort of thing, Grandmother. Booker might do—though I notice he couldn't keep her out of the Pie."

"Mr. Booker is a lawyer. He could hardly be expected to manhandle the young woman to her car. Plainly, she has a mind of her own. Besides, you're hardly in a position to criticize. *You* put yourself out to be charming to her, I noticed."

"Oh, hardly."

"I'm not blind."

"I thought it was wise to prevent a scene."

"She didn't seem to me about to cause one. On the whole, she handled herself surprisingly well. I wonder that she decided to come. It can't have been easy for her."

"I expect this fellow Wolff put her up to it. I know him slightly. They're probably in this together—were from the beginning."

"Do you think so? I wouldn't be so sure."

"Well, this claim of marriage . . . that's exactly the kind of thing Wolff would dream up."

"Is it? Then you think there's nothing to it?"

He stared at her in astonishment. "Good God!" he cried. "You don't think she's telling the *truth*, do you? It's surely obvious that she's lying."

"I hope you're right—but then good judgment on the subject of young women has never been one of your strong points, Robert."

He felt his cheeks flush. His grandmother had never forgotten—or forgiven—his marriage, or the subsequent scandal of his divorce, which played no small part in his defeat as the Republican (Conservative) candidate for the seat of junior United States Senator from New York.

It dawned on him that his grandmother had actually considered the possibility that the Walden girl was telling the truth. Of course, he himself had considered it briefly, then pushed the idea firmly back, willing himself to dismiss it as absurd—but if Eleanor was able to sit there calmly on her heirloom sofa and mention it, then the possibility had to be taken seriously.

Like a piece of chalk scratching on a blackboard, her remark set his nerves on edge. He felt his instincts awaken, as they always did when there was a danger to his plans. If she *had* married his father—the thought was ridiculous, of course, out of the question—then what? Could one prove the marriage had been invalid? For what reason? He knew already that DeWitt would be no help. He would have to turn to other people with fewer scruples, more guts. He thought about Roy Cohn and made a mental note to call him in the morning. Roy was tough, God knows, whatever else people thought about him. Or that fellow Gruttman, a courtroom spellbinder. . . .

A *fighter*—that was what was needed, the sooner the better. And if you wanted a fighter—a real, street-smart fighter—you needed a Jew who was still trying to prove that he was as good as anyone else, or better.

An image of Roy Cohn's face—the broken nose, the perpetual tan, the scars, the eyes as hard and cold as stones on the beach—came to his mind, then faded suddenly to the brilliant sunshine of Miami, a darker face, a neat black moustache, gold chains, brilliant white teeth, eyes like pools of darkness. Ramirez and his friends . . . why the hell hadn't he thought of them before? Was he slowing down, getting old? The Cubans owed him one—owed him *several*, goddamn it!

The girl had been his father's mistress, for Christ's sake! Who *else* had she fucked, who else was she fucking, what was her real story? Those were the questions you asked when you had trouble on your hands. The first rule of politics was to get the dirt on your opponent, even if you didn't need to use it: the secret bank accounts in the Bahamas, the little apartment in a discreet residential hotel that even the wife—*especially* the wife—didn't know about, the girlfriends or the boyfriends, the little mistake with drugs at college, or with some young man in a bus-station men's room, that always lay never quite hidden in some forgotten police file somewhere . . . doctors' records, telephone conversations, bankbooks, love letters unwisely written or kept. If you wanted to go for the jugular, you started at the soft underbelly of human weakness, greed and passion. Everyone had something to hide, if you looked hard enough, Robert told himself, as if it were a mantra. Ramirez was the man to talk to. He would call him tonight . . .

His grandmother sighed. She seemed suddenly exhausted, as if her formidable energy had been depleted. "The girl reminds me of somebody," she said. "I can't put my finger on it. Well, never mind. I'm getting old. I *am* old. So is Courtland, for that matter. Tell Booker to find out what he can. Discreetly. He's up to that, is he not?"

"I think so," he said without enthusiasm.

"You've never liked him because he's in love with Cecilia. He would not be my first choice for her either, as you know, but she could do worse."

"I don't agree."

"She can't go on being a spinster for the rest of her life just to please you, Robert. You've always been the most selfish of my grandchildren. And the most headstrong. Tell him to find out what he can."

"I'll take care of it."

She looked at him keenly. "Keep out of it yourself, Robert. Let Booker handle it his own way."

"I have friends who can dig up the facts about her quicker than Booker. It's quite simple to do—well, never mind how. It's best not to *know* how these things are done."

"That was your father's view, certainly. He believed it cost him the Presidency, as you may recall."

Robert bit his tongue. His grandmother, with her usual skill, had touched a nerve that was still raw more than ten years after he had made the headlines during his father's campaign with the news that he had bugged the Nixon delegates' rooms at the Miami convention. Few people thought that the exposure of Robert's activities in the national press was the *only* reason his father had lost on the first ballot, but it had certainly done him no good.

"As you wish," he said.

"I mean what I say, Robert. Don't think you can fool me the way you did your father." She rose stiffly. For a moment he was almost tempted to rush to her help. Was it out of respect for her pride that he didn't move to help her—the knowledge that she hated weakness, and hated it most of all in herself? Or did he simply feel, the hell with her? He couldn't decide. He had never been able to sort out his feelings about his grandmother, not as a child, not now, possibly not ever, he decided.

She walked slowly to the door and opened it, then stood for a moment, looking at him across the room. "Have you heard from Vanessa?" she snapped.

"A cable."

"She would have done better to return the jewels."

Robert shrugged. No conversation with his grandmother was complete without some mention of the jewelry that Eleanor had presented her granddaughter-in-law with at the time of the marriage, with considerable reluctance.

Cyrus Bannerman, on one of his trips to Europe, had somehow acquired the matching diamond necklace, tiara, bracelet, and earrings presented to the Empress Marie-Louise by Napoleon on the birth of their son, and brought it back to America despite an outcry from the French government and the Paris press that briefly soured Franco-American relationships.

Eleanor had not worn the diamonds for years, and Robert had persuaded her with great difficulty to let Vanessa have them. It had been "understood"—by everyone except Vanessa—that the jewelry belonged "in the family," not to any one person, let alone Vanessa, but she had walked off with them at the time of the divorce and now claimed they had been a gift. Not only had she taken them to France, but she rubbed salt in the wound by wearing them at every possible occasion, despite a lawsuit to recover them which had dragged on for years.

Part of Robert's irritation with Booker came from the fact that Booker was in charge of this expensive piece of litigation, which had limped its way through the American courts and was now proceeding even more slowly through the baroque and incomprehensible legal system of France, with the maximum amount of publicity and no discernible results. Vanessa's photograph had appeared in *Vogue* only last month, the full set glittering around her head and graceful neck, at the *Bal des petits lits blancs*, looking, Robert had to admit to his rage, more ravishing than ever.

"We'll get the damned things back," he said grimly—though, in fact, he was by no means optimistic about it. Getting anything away from

Vanessa once it was in her hands was no easy task, and it was not made easier in this case by the French government, which took the view the diamonds should never have left France in the first place and were now back where they belonged, in a way.

She nodded. "We'll see," she said. "I've heard that before." She paused on the threshold. "I can't help thinking you've allowed yourself to be beaten once by a pretty young woman." She looked at him like a general inspecting a soldier on parade and not at all pleased with what she saw. "I hope you won't let it happen twice." She walked out and closed the door behind her quietly.

She never needed to slam a door, he thought, pushing the button to summon the butler for a fresh drink at last, thank God.

Why should she? She always had the last word.

"THANK YOU for seeing me on such short notice," Alexa said.

"Any friend of Penelope's a friend of mine, Miss Walden."

"Penelope and I aren't exactly *friends*, Mr. Stern. She's a friend of Simon Wolff's."

"Whatever."

Penelope Moritz was an attractive woman in her forties who appeared from time to time at Simon's parties, and had once managed his art gallery. For almost twenty years, ever since graduating from Barnard, she had been Abraham Lincoln Stern's mistress, and still lived in the hope that he would eventually leave his wife and marry her.

It was rumored—Simon swore it to be true—that Penelope had furnished her Sutton Place apartment as an exact duplicate of Stern's so that he would feel at home there, and certainly it was around the corner from Stern's town house so he could stop in every evening while he was walking the dog.

It was one of those New York "arrangements" which seemed to Alexa designed to provide the maximum amount of stress and tension to everybody involved, rather than any measurable increase in happiness, but at least it might give Stern, she thought, some understanding of her own ambiguous position.

Stern was tall, stooped, thin and, in fact, rather resembled his namesake, right down to the big ears. It was difficult to see at first glance just what it was about him that had kept a good-looking and intelligent woman in what amounted to bondage for the better part of her adult life, but Alexa had learned not to question such things. They happened, that was all. Something not dissimilar, after all, had happened to *her* when she met Arthur Bannerman.

Stern had, at any rate, a kind of lugubrious, weary charm, and the kind of intense energy many women, including herself, found attractive. He was a lawyer's lawyer, a defender of great causes, who pleaded regularly before the Supreme Court. Most of his cases made the headlines—he left the routine legal work to his juniors and took on only those clients who interested him.

His office in the Seagram Building, overlooking Park Avenue, was decorated to look as "traditional" as possible. The walls were paneled in dark wood, the furniture was massive—huge tufted leather chairs and sofas, a partner's desk the size of a compact car, the walls hung with dark oil paintings of eighteenth-century gentlemen, presumably lawyers, in powdered wigs. Stern, like so many successful people in New York, had long ago recreated himself in the image of his choice, a bright young man from Washington Heights who had managed to turn himself into his own idea of an English gentleman, his suits, shirts, and shoes made in London, his office decorated as if it had been in his family since the eighteenth century.

Alexa wondered how Penelope Moritz, with her twentieth-century greyhound figure and passion for David Webb jewelry and expensive shoes, of which she owned hundreds, fit into all this—but then Penelope had her own fantasy, which was that her role in life was that of the central figure in a great romance.

Stern placed his long fingers tip to tip and smiled encouragingly, more like a family doctor than a high-powered lawyer. "I knew Bannerman," he said. "I know a lot about his family, in fact. Not that we were close, you understand. I used to meet him from time to time at B'nai Brith dinners, the Alfred E. Smith Memorial Dinner—that sort of thing. When he was running for President, he felt obliged to reach out for the Jewish vote, you know. I never felt his heart was in it, frankly." He paused. "Don't misunderstand me, please. I quite liked the man, even if he did always call me Abe. I suppose he thought I'd be flattered. I can't think why. I would never have called him Artie."

She laughed. "No, he wouldn't have liked that at all, Mr. Stern."

"Otherwise, he had great dignity. And more honesty than most rich men. He would have made a very poor President. Well, never mind. How can I be of service to you?"

"I'm not sure, actually."

Stern took off his horn-rimmed glasses and rubbed the welts on the bridge of his nose. With his glasses removed he seemed so fatigued and worn down with care that any woman would be flattered by his attention, which perhaps explained how he had been able to hold Penelope Moritz in thrall for so long. "Let me just say, my dear," he murmured, "that if it's a case of 'palimony'—a loathsome word—I'm the wrong man to consult. I don't say you may not have a case, but that's not my kind of case."

"It's not my kind of case, either. I have a whole different problem."

He nodded, waiting patiently to hear what it was. With the deep pouches under his eyes, the mournful lines around the mouth, the high, creased forehead, he could have been an elderly priest waiting to hear a confession, already so familiar with the problems of the secular life that nothing could shock or surprise him any more.

"The thing is—we were married."

"Good God! Married? To Arthur Bannerman?" Stern looked as if he had just received an electric shock. He put his glasses back on and examined her with new interest. "Surely you jest?"

"No."

He was silent for a moment, then shook his head. "Life never ceases to amaze me," he said. "I suppose that's why it's worth living. Let me be the first to offer you congratulations, which I'm sure nobody else has bothered to do. And condolences. Which I don't imagine you've received either. Why was this not in the papers?"

"Arthur wanted it kept secret."

"I see. From the world at large? Or also from his family?"

"From both."

"You'll tell me his reasons—though I think I can guess at some of them. Does the family know yet?"

"Yes. I told Mr. DeWitt. I phoned him when Arthur died. I didn't know who else to call, you see."

"That was a perfectly sensible thing to do. I would like to have seen his face when he heard the news. DeWitt and I are not friends, I must tell you." He switched to a pair of half-moon reading glasses, balanced a yellow legal pad on his bony knee, and uncapped an old-fashioned fountain pen. "What did DeWitt say?" he asked.

"He didn't believe me."

"He's a man of limited imagination. If he didn't have Martin Booker working for him, he'd be lost. Did DeWitt tell the family?"

"Yes."

"Then why has nobody heard about this? One would think it would be front page news. Perhaps not in the *Times*, but everywhere else."

"He asked me to keep quiet about the marriage, Mr. Stern. He said it would make things more difficult for me with the Bannerman family if it became a media event. And I wasn't exactly looking for a media event myself."

"Fair enough, but I don't know if it was so smart to go along with him, frankly. Bannerman's death was a media event anyway. You might just as well have gotten it all over with at once. How long were you married?"

"We were married the day before he died."

He raised an eyebrow. "Well, a marriage is a marriage. Twenty-four years or twenty-four hours, it's all the same so far as the law is concerned. Do you have your marriage certificate?"

"No. I suppose Arthur kept it. He never had a chance to talk to me about his plans, or maybe he just didn't want to, so I'm not sure what to do."

"Well, you don't have to do much except prove that you're a widow. Or challenge them to prove otherwise, in the worst case. Did you sign a prenuptial agreement?"

She shook her head.

Stern stared at her. "You and Arthur Bannerman got married without a prenuptial agreement? Like a couple of teenagers?"

"All I know is I didn't sign anything."

"That's very strange. I handled Vanessa Bannerman's divorce, you know, and I was very impressed by the way the Bannermans protected the fortune from outsiders." He closed his eyes in contemplation. "You might consider whether I'm the man you want, in view of that, by the way. Robert won't like it a bit, nor DeWitt. The old man—forgive me, your late husband—didn't hold it against me. I think he was too angry with Robert to care who represented Vanessa. But Robert's bound to consider me an enemy."

She did not want to make an enemy of Robert—that was the very thing that Arthur had warned her about. But instinctively she trusted Stern, all the more since he had been honest with her. "Do you think it will make a difference?"

He shrugged. "Probably not. It will save time and money that I know the territory. And if Robert goes off the deep end, it won't matter who your lawyer is. My guess, however, is that he will tread very carefully at first. The last thing he needs is another scandal if he wants the governorship. It's strange. He's the one member of that family who has some fire in him, but all he ever does with it is burn his own fingers. But then I speak as a lifelong Democrat. Well, let's get on with it. Did he leave you any papers? Documents, letters, that sort of thing?"

"Not exactly."

"Go on."

"Well, the day before we were married, Arthur went out for lunch, and stayed out most of the afternoon. When he came back, he seemed tired—very tired. He said there were a lot of things he wanted to talk to me about, practical matters, but he just didn't feel up to it. He told me he'd taken out a safety-deposit box in my name, and that he was going to put some things in it, just in case."

"Just in case of what?"

"I didn't want to talk about it. I knew what he meant. I didn't want to spend the evening before my marriage talking about what would happen if he died. I don't think he did, either, because he was quite happy to drop the subject. 'We'll go over it all tomorrow, or the day after,' he said. 'Time enough.' "

Stern sighed. "How often people say that. It's one of the things that makes lawyers rich. In the event, as it turned out, there wasn't time enough?"

"Yes. He gave me the key to the box. I didn't want to take it, but he insisted."

"And have you opened the box?"

"I went there before coming to see you. There was an envelope with my name on it. I thought it might be a good idea to open it in the presence of a lawyer. I don't know why."

"You're a very intelligent young woman," Stern said admiringly, taking the envelope out of her hand. "Arthur Bannerman was a lucky man." He smiled at her for the first time, like a teacher awarding an A plus. Why is it, she wondered, that she was such a sucker for the approval of older men? No, to be absolutely truthful, of *old* men? But she knew the reason all too well. She smiled back demurely, the star pupil, and hated herself for doing so.

The sight of the familiar sprawling handwriting on the envelope depressed her almost as much as its contents were likely to. In her father's effects there had been a letter to her, written on her seventeenth birthday, to be given to her in case of his death. She had torn it up unread, and burned the pieces. She had never regretted it. She had a premonition that whatever Arthur had to say to her after his death was probably something he couldn't bring himself to say to her while he was alive.

Stern pressed the button on the speakerphone and called out, "Miss Barbera, please hold all my calls while I'm with Miss Walden." Then he took a small tape recorder out of his desk drawer and turned it on. "You can't be too careful," he explained, and began to talk into it just like Quincy performing an autopsy on television, she thought.

It occurred to her that it was a series Arthur had been fond of—for it was one of the strange paradoxes about the man that despite his aristocratic manner, which made it appear to outsiders that he lived in some special world inhabited only by the third generation superrich, his tastes, when he was alone, were those of an average middle-class American. He liked watching television, particularly things like "Quincy," "Kojak" (a big favorite of his), "Hill Street Blues," Johnny Carson, and was perfectly content to sit in front of the set with a tray of sandwiches and a Scotch.

"A white envelope from the Harvard Club, addressed to 'Alexandra,' with the signature 'Arthur A. Bannerman' written across the sealed back. I'm opening it." He slit the envelope carefully with an elaborate sterling silver paper knife, probably a gift from Penelope Moritz, who spent most of her spare time shopping for things to give Stern that his wife hadn't already given him. He spread the contents on the desk. "The contents," he said, "a handwritten letter on Harvard Club stationery, addressed to 'Dearest Alexandra." He put it to one side. "A marriage certificate, County of New York, between Arthur Aldon Bannerman and Elizabeth Alexandra Walden . . ." He unfolded a printed form. "A deposit slip, indicating a deposit of two hundred and fifty thousand dollars into an interest-bearing account at the Morgan Guaranty Trust, Rockefeller Center Branch, in the name of Elizabeth Alexandra Walden. . . ."

"Two hundred and fifty thousand dollars?" It was far more money than she had ever had in her life.

Stern continued. A quarter of a million dollars was apparently not a sum that impressed him. "There's a note attached to the deposit slip," he said, still speaking into the machine. " 'This is to tide you over, in case there are difficulties.' Very thoughtful—and smart. Whatever else he planned to do for you, he guessed the family would fight it, so he left you some pin money in your own name. Maybe he *should* have been President!"

He unfolded another, larger sheet of paper and read it with care. "A handwritten document, which appears to be the last will and testament of Arthur Aldon Bannerman. It's witnessed by somebody called Baxter Troubridge, address, Eight Sixty-seven Fifth Avenue. . . ."

"Mr. Troubridge was at Groton and Harvard with Arthur. He was his oldest friend. They sometimes had lunch together at the Harvard Club. I think they were both—Overseers of Harvard, or whatever they call themselves. Arthur thought he was a bore, but they'd known each other for about fifty years."

"I think I get the picture. He goes to the Harvard Club, writes a note to you, finds Troubridge at the bar and gets him to witness the will, puts everything in an envelope, then walks down Fifth to Morgan Guaranty to put it in the safe-deposit box he'd rented for you. I wonder if he had a premonition about dying, or if it was just something he wanted to make sure of before he'd married you. I suppose we'll never know. God, how I hate these last-minute handwritten wills. It's not even notarized."

"Does that matter?"

"My dear young lady, wills have been written on matchbook covers, cocktail napkins, and pieces of tree bark, and still found valid. What matters is the clear intention of the person who wrote it. Still, it's a pity Bannerman didn't find a notary at the Harvard Club instead of Troubridge. What kind of fellow *is* Troubridge, do you know, just in case we have to call him as a witness?"

"I've only met him once. Arthur always said he was a drunk. He was certainly drunk the time I saw him."

"Wonderful! Just what we need! We'd better retain the best handwriting expert in the country right away, before the other side does." He took his glasses off and peered at her. His expression was puzzled, like a schoolteacher facing a bright child who can't understand a simple problem. "You haven't asked the important question," he said. "It's usually the first thing people want to know."

She sighed. She was curious, of course—but the truth was that she wanted to put off knowing what Arthur had done. She did not doubt that he had probably left her a large amount of money, otherwise he would hardly have gone to the trouble of writing out a new will, but the last thing she wanted was a knock-down-drag-out fight to the death with the Bannerman family; nor was she at all sure that she wanted to go through year after year of depositions, litigation, and trials, and the front-page stories that went with it all, a perfect recipe for wasting one's life. And the more he had left her, the harder they would fight.

"It's not that I don't care," she explained. "It's that I don't look forward to fighting with his family over whatever Arthur's left me, and that's what I can see coming. How much money are you talking about, then?"

Stern nodded understandingly. His expression was almost sad, as if he was reluctant to give her bad news. Had Arthur left her *nothing*? That would be surprising—even a little disappointing—but not the end of the world. She had not married him for his money, after all, whatever other people thought.

He cleared his throat. "He left you the whole damned thing," he said. "His entire net estate."

She was silent for a moment, stunned and petrified. If Stern had said a million dollars, even two million, or five million, she would have been surprised, although those were sums of money she could imagine; but "entire net estate" was beyond her imagination—a fortune so great that it had been a burden to Arthur himself. And what did "net" mean, she wondered? "Explain it to me," she said quietly, forcing herself to sound as calm as possible.

"Well, to begin with, you're one of the richest women in the world. 'Net' in this context is simple. A great part of the Bannerman fortune is in trusts and foundations, of course. Each of the children has a substantial trust, for example, and the old lady has a trust left to her by Arthur's father. The Bannerman Foundation is a separate entity, I believe, and there must be dozens of similar things. What's left over, after bequests to friends, relatives, institutions, servants and so on, is the net estate."

"And that's worth how much, roughly?" she heard herself ask.

She felt totally calm, but she knew it was deceptive—that she was really in shock, like the victim of an accident.

"It's very hard to say. The last numbers I read came up during the Senate confirmation hearings for Robert's ambassadorship. He claimed his father's net estate was worth about two hundred and fifty million, but some of the Senators said it was closer to a billion. I suspect it's somewhere between those two figures, but a lot would depend on how you value all sorts of properties. Robert lowballed the Senators, and they tried to highball him. Either way, it's a huge fortune. You're not exactly jumping up and down with joy?"

A fortune. *The* fortune. He had left it all to her, without any warning or discussion. Why? She was not elated. How could she be? It was not like leaving someone you loved a lot of money to enjoy, or to use for security. It was a heavy responsibility instead, one that Arthur himself had in large part walked away from in the last decade of his life, one that no untrained outsider to the family could possibly take on. She had promised to carry out his wishes, but he had never mentioned the possibility of giving her control of the fortune—or "The Trust," as he always called it.

"You'd better read the letter," Stern said, handing it over. "And stop looking so grim. Worse things have happened."

She wiped her eyes—she was almost in tears. She held the letter with the familiar handwriting—she did not need an expert to tell *her* it was genuine—in front of her, blinking until the blur in her vision cleared. A single tear fell on the page, spotting the ink at the end of one word. She blinked and began to read.

MY DEAREST ALEXA,

I am writing this brief note in the hope that you will never have to read it. I trust we will share a long and happy life together and, God willing, that I will have plenty of time to make all the necessary arrangements to deal with my estate and your place in my family. Why should we not? My grandfather lived to 95, my father to 84. My mother is 86, and still, as you will soon discover, vigorous in health and mind—*too* vigorous, possibly! However, one never knows, and I would feel irresponsible if I didn't make some temporary provisions on your behalf. You will find here a new will, hastily drawn. My reasons for it I will write down in detail, together with my instructions to you. It goes without saying that I hope there will be plenty of time, not only to explain what I have in mind for the disposition of The Trust, and your role in that, but also to persuade my family—which will soon be *yours* as well —to accept my wishes. Should I die, follow my instructions, coupled with your own common sense, which is greater than you know. But if the burden becomes too great for you—and it may well—*give it up!* Of all people, I would be the first to understand, and forgive.

With all my love,
ARTHUR

PS: Should you have any difficulty with Robert, go instantly to Baxter Troubridge—but *only* if you're in real trouble. He'll explain.

AAB

She held the letter for a moment, then passed it to Stern, who read it slowly, frowning as if he were deciphering an ancient language. "Was his handwriting always like this?" he asked. "It's very hard to follow."

"Usually it was a *little* clearer than this, but not much. He was born left-handed, you see, and his mother made up her mind that he was going to learn to write with his right hand. So he was forced to do it. I guess that's why it looks so strange."

"A typical Bannerman story. Never give in to nature. I'd like to have some other samples of his writing, please."

"I'm sure I can find a few, but why?"

"They may try to prove that any deterioration of his handwriting was a reflex of his mental state—that he was confused, or ill, or drunk, or maybe even had a small stroke when he wrote the new will, who knows?"

She was momentarily shocked. "But it isn't true. He was fine."

"Truth isn't the issue here. It's what can be *proved*. Let me be frank with you. A judge is likely to take a very skeptical view of the state of mind of a man of sixty-five who marries a young girl and draws up a last-minute handwritten unnotarized will that drastically changes the disposition of a great fortune. We're going to have to prove he was of sound mind and firm intent—in short, that he'd thought this out. He refers to another letter, one he was going to write, and presumably place in the box for you. It isn't here. Did he write another letter, to your knowledge?"

She thought for a moment. "Not that I know of," she said. "He may not have had time. . . ." She felt a sudden, overwhelming sadness.

"Quite." Stern bowed his head briefly in sympathy.

She held onto Arthur's note as if she were reluctant to part with it.

"I'll need to have that back," Stern said.

She looked him in the eye. "What if I tore it up?" she asked. "And the will?"

"I don't think you should. And I don't think you will. You could walk away from all this, certainly, and I do believe you'd like to. Oh, yes, you've convinced *me*, my dear, and I'm not an easy man to convince. I understand how you're feeling. It's a heavy burden, isn't it, with no end in sight and not much reward, when you come right down to it, except a lot of money you don't really want—far more than anybody needs or can enjoy. But he wanted you to do this. It was, not to be maudlin about it, his last wish, so far as we can determine. Unless he was mentally incompetent, which you tell me he was not, I don't think you can ignore it. You can't just pretend he never wrote the note you're holding, or the will. If you do, sooner or later you'll regret it bitterly. Anyway, even if we burned it all, you'd still have the fight of your life on your hands."

He leaned back in his chair and closed his eyes. " 'Estates, Powers and Trust Law, 5–1.1. Absent an agreement with the spouse to the contrary, i.e., antenuptial agreement, a spouse is entitled to a share in the estate of a deceased spouse, if not provided for by the will, to the minimum extent provided by law. . . .' " He paused for breath. "It's the modern equivalent of what used to be called 'dower rights' at common law. Not to get into a lot of legal garbage, but in New York State, if the deceased is survived by children—which is the case here—the surviving spouse is entitled to one half of the net estate. So even if you decided to tear this will up, which as an officer of the court I wouldn't let you do because it's a felony, you'd still get half of the net estate, and you can be pretty damned sure the Bannermans would fight hard over that."

She handed the letter back to him. "I don't have a choice. I gave Arthur my word."

"Just so. The point is, the will isn't what matters. Oh, they'll contest it. I would if *I* were representing the other side. They'll try to prove it's a forgery, or that he was of unsound mind—all that is par for the course. But what matters, what *really* matters, is this marriage certificate. That's the only piece of paper that counts here. It's a ticket to half the estate, even if you don't get the whole thing. If they go after anything, it will be the marriage—because if that's not valid, you get nothing!"

"Well, it's valid all right. We were married in front of a judge."

"Yes, a marriage is hard to attack, I agree. There's undue influence, of course. An old man, a young woman, he's perhaps a little senile, she takes advantage of the situation and gets him to marry her when he doesn't want to—he may not even know what's going on. . . ."

"It wasn't anything *like* that!"

"I'm just looking at it from the other side's point of view. It's a pretty good tactic, there are plenty of precedents, but I think they'll have a hard time making it stick. They'll try, though, you can bet your bottom dollar. Booker's not dumb, even if DeWitt is. We'd better stack up some witnesses on Bannerman's soundness of mind, his affection for you and so forth."

"It was *his* idea to get married. I wasn't sure I wanted to."

"Good! That's just the right thing to say. Let me think a moment. He was a widower, right? No problem there. Have you ever been married before?"

"No, of course not!"

He looked at her shrewdly—his courtroom, questioning-the-witness-look again, a combination of guilelessness and disbelief that made her realize she'd said "No" too quickly, too loudly; that she'd awakened the lawyer's natural reluctance to believe anybody's story, even a client's—perhaps *especially* a client's.

"If you have anything to hide, I shall need to know. I don't want to go into this if I'm walking into a minefield and going to get my foot blown off in court. There's nothing in the past I should know?"

"Nothing that matters."

"I hate qualified answers, my dear. I want you to think about it. Hard. There can't be any secrets between us. That's why lawyers and doctors have an oath of secrecy."

He got up and walked her to the door. "And stay out of, ah, trouble," he said. "They're going to attack your reputation if they can. There's half a billion dollars at stake, and it all hangs on the validity of your marriage. And that may end up hanging on the kind of personal life you've led, so *watch out!*" He paused. "Are you up to it? Do you want to fight? Bare knuckles? No holds barred?"

"I don't have a choice."

"Nonsense! Of *course* you have a choice. There's always a choice. You can give up. We can settle. I can call DeWitt and say, 'Give us a few million and we'll go away.' It's done every day. Just a few moments ago you didn't seem so sure you wanted to go through with this."

"I still don't. I dread it. But you're right. I owe it to Arthur. He trusted me. In more ways than one."

"That's a good answer. The best. And, let me add, in the best Bannerman spirit. He may have seen that in you, you know. In which case, he had a sharper eye than just one for pretty girls. Keep in touch, please."

He opened the door for her ceremoniously. Miss Barbera, who was uncommonly attractive, stopped typing and gave Alexa a look of smoldering jealousy as she shook hands with Stern. She wondered if Miss Barbera, like Penelope Moritz, had also devoted her life to the comforts of Abraham Lincoln Stern.

"Don't forget," he said. "I need to know everything, including the past. Never hold out on your lawyer."

She let go of his hand, half expecting Miss Barbera to stab a paper knife in her back. "It's not that interesting a past," she said.

Stern gave her a reassuring smile. "I'm sure you're being modest," he said gallantly, but his eyes were steady, as if he were searching for the truth. She turned toward the elevators.

"Mrs. Bannerman!" she heard someone shout.

She did not associate the words with herself for an instant. Instinctively she looked around to see if there was anyone else in the elevator, but it was empty. Then she saw that Miss Barbera was holding the door open, her face still resentful, but now touched with a kind of awe. "Mr. Stern asked me to give you his private number," she said, holding out a card. "He says you should feel free to call him any time, day or night, if there's a problem."

Alexa took the card. "Thank you," she said.

"You're welcome, Mrs. Bannerman." Miss Barbera's voice was full of respect for a name that symbolized money beyond her wildest dreams. It was not, Alexa understood, respect for *her*, or even for her recent widowhood—it was respect for the fortune, for the idea of wealth itself. Miss Barbera actually smiled—a smile tinged with a certain amount of envy. The doors shut, and Alexa was alone.

It was only then that she realized it was the first time anyone had ever called her Mrs. Bannerman. She burst into tears and cried on the way down to the lobby.

She walked all the way back to Simon's apartment, still crying, conscious of the fact that people were staring at her, not caring any more.

Arthur Bannerman had never asked her about her past, had not even shown any curiosity about it, perhaps because he was old enough and intelligent enough to guess it was the last thing he wanted to know. And—if she was going to be honest with herself—at least one of the reasons she had agreed, against her better judgment, to marry him, was that it would be like starting life all over again with a clean slate, the past erased forever by the glamorous present.

There was no wiping the slate clean now, she told herself. She was about to become a public figure, like a politician running for office— perhaps was one already.

She told herself not to be silly. After all, she had never done anyone any harm, had she?

But even that wasn't true, she thought sadly, as she sneaked in the back way to avoid any reporters.

Not true at all.

PART TWO

A

PILLAR OF
SALT

But his wife looked back from behind him,
and she became a pillar of salt.

Genesis 19:26

4

The crush of people at the de Laszlo Gallery was so great that it was almost impossible to see the pictures—no great loss, so far as Alexa was concerned. She had learned a lot in the two years she had been in New York, but this did not include an appreciation for contemporary art—certainly not *this* artist's work, anyway. Geza Baldur's canvases were enormous, monochromatic, heavily textured, as if the paint had been smeared on with a trowel. Whatever his technique was, the surface of his paintings seemed to her repellently brown and slimy; she couldn't look at one without feeling the urge to hose it off down to the bare, clean canvas.

It baffled her that Baldur's work received serious attention from the critics, even from the more adventurous collectors, but Simon had an instinct for this kind of thing, and she had none. She liked things to be pretty, and prettiness was just what Simon—and the heavyweight art critics—most despised.

The model agencies and fashion editors had felt the same way about *her*—she hadn't been in New York a week before she learned that being "pretty" was the kiss of death in the modeling business. Pretty girls were a dime a dozen; the lucky ones ended doing catalog work or posing for lingerie ads, if they had the legs for it.

She had the legs, but she had been smart enough to see there wasn't any point to being a model if you couldn't get to the top, and stay there for a while. Looking after Simon Wolff's affairs was a more reliable way of making a living.

She moved in and out of the crowd, making sure the "right" people met Baldur, a hirsute, gloomy giant of a man, as ugly as his own paintings. She was tired but elated. Simon had bought the gallery from old de Laszlo's estate, more for the name and good will than anything else. De Laszlo had been the first to show De Kooning, Pollock, Lichtenstein, Warhol; his gallery had once been the cutting edge of modern art in New York. A brilliant promoter but a miserable businessman, Laszlo operated in a state of permanent bankruptcy, and died venerated but penniless. Simon, who had been dabbling in the art business for years, saw the opportunity and took it. He leased new space on Madison Avenue and Fifty-seventh Street, left Alexa to deal with it, and went off to Europe in search of a painter of sufficient obscurity to make the reopening an event in the eyes of the New York art world.

Little as she cared about art, the gallery was her creation—just as were Simon's disco and his restaurant, for in those ventures, too, he had left most of the details to her. Her job was to solve the problems Simon didn't want to be bothered with, while he got on with the work of finding new and ever more glamorous ways to invest other people's money, even though he thought of himself, always, as an art dealer. What's more, she was good at it, as Simon himself admitted. She had been surprised to discover that she was a quick learner, with a grasp for details, and grateful to Simon for giving her the opportunity to find it out. She learned the art business as quickly as she mastered his other affairs, and it remained her chief concern, if only because it was his. Without the slightest interest in art, he enjoyed being an art dealer, which brought with it a certain social cachet, as well as a healthy profit.

That side of the business he kept strictly to himself. He had been to one of those schools in Switzerland that cater to the international rich, and from it he drew an apparently endless supply of young oil sheiks who wanted to invest in movies, heirs to Greek shipping fortunes who yearned for a piece of a smart New York discotheque, second-generation Lebanese arms merchants who didn't care what they put their money into as long as it was in New York.

Simon's schoolmates had all the money they needed; what they were looking for was a piece of the action in something more exciting than oil, tankers, Swiss banking, or heavy industry, an investment that would get them to the right parties and give them a chance to meet pretty girls under favorable circumstances. The money Simon raised from them was not, by their standards, "serious"—they invested in his ventures for the fun of it, or to prove to their wives and mistresses they were not such dull fellows after all. They were the least demanding of investors.

Simon had drawn up the guest list with considerable care—in this area, at least, he had strong opinions. His investors wanted a chance to meet celebrities; he wanted to attract people who might actually buy Baldur's paintings. It was a delicate task to arrive at exactly the right mix of money and glamour, and Simon had spent a whole long evening on it with her, restlessly moving from his Rolodex to a well-thumbed pile of glossy magazines, throwing out names while she wrote them down. "The Baroness Thyssen, if she's in town. Leo Lerman, of course. Liz Smith. Some pretty girls . . ."

"Which pretty girls?"

"For God's sake, Alexa, *any* pretty girls, provided they're well-dressed. Not Kiki Lobanos, however."

"Why on earth not? You can't get prettier than that."

"I want new faces, not retreads from George Weidenfeld's guest list. Benoit de Montechristo, naturally, Henry Geldzahler, Thomas Hoving, all the art establishment—if you can get one to come, the others all will, for fear of missing something. Jackie Onassis?"

"I already tried. Her secretary said no go."

"Call back. Say that Baldur is looking for a publisher and doesn't want to talk to anybody else until he's seen her. Greta Garbo?"

"I don't think she goes anywhere, does she?"

"Try, *try!* Aha, Arthur Bannerman! Put him down."

"Garbo is more realistic, Simon. What on earth makes you think Arthur Bannerman would be interested in Baldur's opening?"

"How many times do I have to tell you? *Vernissage*, not 'opening.' Bannerman's a major collector."

"Yes, but I don't think he goes out, does he? You're sure you don't mean *Robert* Bannerman? The one who got divorced a while ago?"

"Robert Bannerman has no interest in art at all. I know him." He paused. "The Bannermans," he said, closing his eyes in what looked like ecstasy at the sound of the name. "My God, when you stop to think of it, what a family! All that money. Somebody told me that Hoving once came up with the idea of putting on a special show at the Met of the Bannerman treasures—you can imagine the kind of things they own—but when he suggested it to Arthur Bannerman at a meeting of the trustees, Bannerman just shook his head and said, 'No, I don't think Mother would like it.' " He laughed. "Do you know how much money they have?"

"Simon, I'm not an idiot. I *know* who the Bannermans are. I'm not totally ignorant."

"All right, all right, just put him down and let's get on with it."

She wrote the name down. She would send Arthur Aldon Bannerman an invitation, but she knew it was a waste of time and postage. Simon might get Jackie, in the end—possibly even Benoit de Montechristo—but never Arthur Bannerman. The Bannermans were as close as you could get to royalty in America—so much so that when she looked in the telephone book, there was no listing of any kind under that name. Eventually she sent the invitation to the Metropolitan Museum of Art, marked "Please Forward."

She moved through the gallery now, noting with pleasure that Mrs. Onassis had not only come, but was deep in conversation with Baldur —though how they were able to communicate was something of a mystery, since Baldur spoke no English at all, and those who, like Simon, knew other languages didn't seem to make any better headway with him than Alexa had.

Mrs. Onassis wore black silk trousers and a black silk blouse, with rather modest jewelry for a woman of her means. Alexa caught sight of herself in a mirror, and on the whole thought she was a lot better dressed. She wore a short white silk bolero jacket over a black silk turtleneck, and a Donna Karan black wool-jersey scarf skirt, cut to show rather more leg than she was altogether comfortable about. She spent too much money on clothes, but no matter how much she spent, it was never enough. Simon paid her well, and she was frugal in everything else, but clothes were her one extravagance. Of course, she reflected, you didn't need another.

Once Alexa had dreamed of modeling *haute couture*, but no matter how hard she dieted, there had been too much of her for that. There were two fashion models standing together in a corner of the room, whippet thin, hardly out of their teens, with the bored look that was part of the profession—faces that came to life only when they were being photographed. One of them wore a skimpy Geoffrey Beene dress of tightly knit bronze metallic beads. Her eyelashes were painted bronze to match the dress. The other wore a Mary McFadden dress of creamy lace, trimmed with brightly colored marabou feathers, as transparent as the nightgowns in a mail-order catalog for erotic lingerie.

Alexa tried to look at the two of them without envy and failed. She told herself that she had the kind of figure men, not fashion editors, admired. It didn't help. There was one part of her mind that would always see herself as the glittering center of attraction, strutting down the gangway in some outrageous show-stopper by Valentino or Ungaro or Saint Laurent—the drop-dead dress that is every woman's fantasy, but which only a *haute couture* model can wear.

She edged her way around to where Simon was standing, doing his best to look interested as Sir Leo Goldlust, the British art publisher, declaimed on the finer points of Baldur's paintings, his jowls shaking, the dark, predatory eyes flickering back and forth, always on the alert for the approach of somebody more important in the crowd. "Plasticity," he exclaimed in his guttural voice, as if he had just invented the word. "He has cut himself off from the seductive ease of the palette, shown us that color isn't *necessary* for painting. . . . Everything can be brown, you see. By throwing away color, he forces us to look at the *act* of painting, the bare bones of art, as it were. . . ."

"Quite," Simon said as if he were enraptured. He glanced at Alexa, his expression imploring her to interrupt the conversation.

Sir Leo leaned over, eyes bulging, and winked. "Of course you and I know, dear boy, that all this is terrible *dreck!* Have you sold any yet?"

"Two or three, I think."

"*Mazel tov!* It might be a good time to think of a book of his work, you know. Full color, perhaps with a foreword by one of our eminent friends here—a seventy-five-dollar package for the serious collector, numbered and signed. Possibly it would be in your interest to share the costs. And the profits, naturally," he added smoothly.

"Excuse me, Simon, but you're needed," she said, giving Sir Leo an apologetic smile. Goldlust's suety face showed no sign of irritation at being interrupted. His eyes were already seeking a new opportunity.

"Thank God," Simon said. "He had me trapped." He took two glasses of champagne from a passing waiter, drained one, and offered the other to her.

She shook her head. She had never been able to develop much of a taste for whiskey or wine. She did like the taste of champagne, but not the headaches it gave her. At one time Simon had made it his mission in life to "loosen her up"—in his words—but when it came to drugs and drinking he had failed. Marijuana made her sleepy—besides, she hated the smell. Alcohol made her sick. The more serious drugs simply frightened her. On this, as on many other subjects, they had agreed to disagree.

Simon shrugged and drank the second glass himself. "Great party!" he said casually, as if they were merely fellow guests.

He lit a cigarette and grinned at her, his eyes half-closed in the smoke. Like so many of his gestures, she was sure he had learned it from a movie. Sometimes, watching television late at night, she saw an actor performing a scene that made her think, So *that's* where Simon picked that up from! Though she wasn't certain, she thought this one was early Jean Gabin.

She knew just what he was doing—giving her a put-down, testing, as usual, just how far he could push her. The hell with him! she thought to herself; but the problem was that *thinking* it didn't do her any good, and saying it came hard to a girl who had been brought up in a house where the name of the Lord was never taken in vain and no obscenity was ever spoken.

She had spent weeks putting the party together for him—and he had spent the whole evening avoiding her. Why hadn't he started out the evening by giving her a kiss and telling her what a wonderful job she'd done? She knew the answer to that one—he liked to needle her. Why did she still give a damn? She didn't have an answer, and occasionally it still drove her crazy.

Once—not so long ago—she had been in love with him, had even been able to persuade herself that *he* was in love with her. Now they lived apart and occasionally spent the night together, like people who are unable to give up an old habit. She should have quit, made a clean break, found a new job, a new man, but her unhappiness with Simon was familiar and comfortable, like a pair of old shoes you cannot bring yourself to throw away. They were like an old married couple, used to each other's faults. Was it just that the right man hadn't come along? *Yet*, she added, without much confidence.

"I'm so glad," she said sharply—with Simon, subtlety was wasted. "Now that I've found out you think it's a great party, I can relax."

"I meant it as a compliment."

"A simple 'Thank you,' maybe two hours ago, would have been nice." He sighed.

I am spoiling what should have been a good time, she told herself firmly, staring straight ahead like a cigar-store Indian as he kissed her cheek. "Did I tell you that you're looking terrific tonight?" he whispered.

"No, you didn't," she said, wishing it didn't matter to her.

"Well, you are." He gave her his best Tyrone Power-in-*Witness-for-the-Prosecution* smile. "Look, I'm sorry. I had a lot on my mind. I'll tell you about it later. Come over after dinner, and we'll have a long talk, just the two of us. We'll make an early night of it."

Say no, she told herself, but instead, fatally, as usual, she said "Maybe," and instantly hated herself for it. She knew what the problem was—she had invested so much of her emotional energy in Simon over the past two years that she was reluctant to let go, and apparently not capable of starting all over again with someone else. It was not that she did not meet other men—her reserves were simply depleted, her funds temporarily exhausted. She told herself frequently that she was happier spending the nights at home in her own apartment, with a book or perhaps watching television, and it was partly true, in the sense that she wasn't *un*happy, as she might have been with Simon. In fact, when she was alone she wished she were with Simon, and when she was with Simon she wished she were alone. She hoped she was simply in that limbo when what she needed was a new relationship, and also hoped that she'd recognize it when it came along. She rather doubted it.

"Great!" Simon said, as if she'd agreed, giving her a squeeze.

"Simon, I'm not sure. . . ."

"Well, dinner anyway, Alexa, okay? You've got to eat, right?"

"I'm not sure I'm up to a lot of people tonight, Simon. Maybe we could go somewhere quiet."

"Absolutely!" Simon said enthusiastically. "You're on!" He paused for a moment, frowning, as if he had forgotten something. "Damn," he said, slapping his hand against his temple theatrically, "I'd forgotten. There are a couple of people I *promised* to take out."

"How many?" she asked, feeling foolish for having allowed herself to think Simon would settle for a quiet dinner alone with her. Even at the height of their romance he liked to be surrounded by other people, as she well knew, and still resented.

"Just a couple of old friends, people you know. We'll grab a quick bite and leave them early, I promise. Come on, be a sport."

After all, she told herself, why not? She might have met somebody else during the evening if she'd made the effort, or tacked onto another dinner party if she'd thought about it earlier, but, as usual, she hadn't tried, and now it was too late. The alternative was to go home, put away her clothes, and try to finish the book she'd been reading for a month in one of her fitful attempts at self-improvement. Besides, she was always a sucker for an appeal to her good nature, as Simon knew well.

"All right," she said, conscious that she'd already surrendered, "if it's not going to be a late evening. . . ." She knew it was a waste of time negotiating with him. One of the differences between them was that they might as well have lived in separate time zones. Simon rarely rose before ten and seldom went to bed before three in the morning; she was ready for bed at eleven and usually up at six. She wondered exactly when she had started to keep a mental list of the differences between herself and Simon, and was sad to realize how long the list had become.

Now that he had won, Simon pressed his advantage. "See if Ferdi de Cuinzbourg wants to join us . . . and Dominick Stavropoulos, of course, and Adnan Husseini, if he's free. If Adnan *is* coming, better see if you can get those two models in the see-through, fuck-me dresses as well. Do you think Benoit de Montechristo would come?"

She looked across the room at the director of the Met, an austere, aristocratic figure, moving from painting to painting with an expression that suggested a fastidious nobleman of the eighteenth century examining a group of lepers. "I don't know him," she said. "Maybe you'd better ask him yourself."

"Do I detect a certain lack of enthusiasm?" He raised an eyebrow. "I believe I do," he said, answering his own question. "Or is it just that you feel he'd be out of place?"

"He might." She hadn't the slightest intention of trying.

"Try him anyway," Simon said, reading her mind, as usual, "there's a good girl. Montechristo's in his *forties*, for God's sake. He can't spend *all* his time with old farts like Arthur Bannerman, can he?" He stared at the crowd. "I see *he* didn't show up, by the way."

"Who?"

"Bannerman."

"I never thought he would."

"The hell with him. From what I hear, he's a basket case—halfway senile, and drunk out of his mind most of the time. I've heard Robert is trying to have him committed before he leaves the Bannerman fortune to the ASPCA. Listen, I'll talk to Montechristo—you go phone Trump's and get us a table, okay?"

She watched while Simon made his approach to Benoit de Montechristo, registered Montechristo's Gallic shrug of apology as he declined the invitation to dinner—just as she expected—and went downstairs to the telephone, wondering why she had allowed Simon to walk all over her again.

Behind the big curved desk in the lobby, the receptionist was checking invitations, ticking off the names on her list. Alexa turned to open the door to the office when she heard a deep voice say, "*Bannerman!* I'm sure my secretary replied."

It was a voice that carried without apparent effort. It was not so much that Bannerman raised it—it simply had the full resonance of someone who was used to making himself heard over other people's conversations, together with an accent that stood out so sharply, here in New York, that he might have been speaking some exotic foreign language. Bannerman spoke slowly, pronouncing the consonants with explosive precision, while his vowels seemed to go on forever, a whole, rolling, old-fashioned, unfamiliar register of sounds that was instantly identifiable as patrician. "Aah–th'r Bah–nuh–m'n," he drawled, as if he were giving an elocution lesson. There was a trace in those long-drawn-out, richly modulated vowels that said Harvard, but what the voice mostly projected was the self-confidence of wealth and power.

She turned, expecting to see an old man, and was surprised to find herself face to face instead with a tall, powerfully built man in his sixties with the erect posture and physical presence of someone much younger. Bannerman was built on a heroic scale—he was an inch or two over six feet, and without being in any way fat, gave an impression of immense solidity: a barrel chest, broad shoulders, enormous hands, almost unspotted by age.

It was the head that captured her attention, however—it seemed larger than life, like a monumental sculpture, the features so sharp they might have been carved out of rock. His face was a study in contrasts: a square, aggressive chin and a powerful nose, clear bright blue eyes. His complexion was ruddy—she wondered if it was the result of outdoor sports or merely high blood pressure—and his thick hair was snow-white and cut short.

His clothes were as old-fashioned as his way of speaking. Bannerman wore a plain gray three-piece suit, a white shirt with a stiffly starched collar, a dark tie, and black shoes so highly polished that at first she thought they were patent leather. He somehow managed to be conspicuous by his inconspicuousness.

"Can I help you?" she asked, conscious that she had been staring at him—but then, he must be used to that, she reflected.

He gave her an imperious look—he clearly wasn't used to being kept waiting or asked to produce an invitation. "I hope so. Apparently my name isn't on the young lady's list."

"I'm sure it's our fault," she said quickly, though she was fairly sure it *wasn't*. "Why don't you come upstairs and I'll show you around?"

Bannerman did not answer at once. His jaw was thrust forward pugnaciously and he seemed about to make a scene. Simon's rich friends were the kind of people who were quick to demand that a waiter or a receptionist be fired when they weren't recognized, or didn't get what they wanted immediately, and Bannerman looked as if he was about to do just that. The receptionist was young, pretty, and probably ignorant of any celebrity who didn't appear on MTV or in *Rolling Stone*, but explaining that was hardly likely to placate an angry Arthur Bannerman, Alexa thought. He was rich enough to expect the whole world to know who he was and bow to him.

To her surprise, he did nothing of the kind. He smiled instead—not a polite, formal smile, but the real thing, as if she'd just told him he was the winner at some television game show. He seemed, strangely, almost relieved, as if he didn't want to go upstairs into the crowd alone. Suddenly he didn't look to her like a chilling, forbidding figure any more, but merely like an attractive older man, perhaps a little bit lonely and grateful for company.

"Why, that's damned kind of you," he said. "I'd appreciate that, if it's no trouble."

"None at all. I'd be happy to, Mr. Bannerman."

He beamed at her. "Capital!" he barked. "And your name is?"

"Alexandra Walden."

He shook her hand, a firm, hard handshake, just the kind you'd expect from a former politician, she thought. She was conscious of a certain excitement on her part—she was not exactly in awe of him; still, it was the first time she had ever actually met anybody who bore such a magic name.

She had a sudden flash of memory. Her grandfather on her mother's side, a lively old gentleman from Kentucky with something of a reputation in the family as a hell-raiser in his youth, used to hold her in his lap when he visited, telling her stories and sometimes singing the songs he remembered from the Twenties. One of his favorites began: "If I was as rich as a Bannerman, I'd give it all up for you."

Once she had asked him what a Bannerman was—she was the kind of child who asked questions relentlessly, even when, as was the case with her grandfather, grown-ups wanted to be left alone to enjoy the sound of their own voices. "Why, the Bannermans are the richest people in the world, honey," he answered sharply, as if it were something even a child should have known.

She wanted to ask, *"How* rich?" but from the tone of her grandfather's voice, she knew better than to interrupt him a second time. She could smell the unfamiliar odors of whiskey and cigars on his breath—her father neither drank nor smoked—as the old man rocked back and forth on the porch in the hot summer twilight; then he cleared his throat and, as if he had guessed what she wanted to know, said, "I read in the *Reader's Digest* that if the Bannerman fortune was in dollar bills lined up end to end, it would stretch from here to the moon and back."

Cyrus Bannerman and his fortune were as much a part of American folklore as Paul Bunyan and his ox. She could not get over the feeling of improbability that she was here, twenty years later, actually *talking* to a Bannerman—not just any Bannerman, for that matter, but the head of the family, former presidential candidate, the grandson of Cyrus Bannerman himself.

She accompanied him up the stairs, against the flow of people coming down—for it was close to dinnertime, and most of the crowd was going now. His way of walking was purposeful, the shoulders hunched, the big head thrust forward, the powerful jaw leading the way like the prow of a ship. Bannerman's size and vitality made her feel as if she were being followed by some large animal. It occurred to her that he must be about the same age as her grandfather had been when she snuggled on his lap, listening to his stories, but her grandfather already had the stooped shoulders, the hesitant shuffle, the careful way of approaching stairs that came to most people with age. Bannerman took the stairs like an athlete.

His appearance brought all conversation to a halt. In the hush, people stared at Bannerman as if he were an escaped lunatic. He did not seem to notice; he plunged ahead toward the first painting that caught his eye, while the crowd parted to make way for him like the Red Sea before Moses. She had never met anybody who exuded such enormous vitality or seemed to put so much fierce, concentrated energy into every movement. It was impossible to think of him as old; without apparent effort, he made everyone else in the room seem drab and lifeless. "Star quality," "presence," whatever it was called, Bannerman had it. He reminded her vaguely of one of those older movie stars, big, rugged men who seemed to get better with age, Charlton Heston perhaps, or Kirk Douglas, except for the fact that the fortune somehow gave Bannerman an added luster, an aura that everybody recognized.

He gazed intently at Baldur's wretched daubs as if they were his first view of the Sistine Chapel. *"Mah*-velous!" he said, the big voice drowning out the subdued buzz of conversation beginning again and the clatter of glasses. "Wonderful work, isn't it?"

"Why, yes, I suppose it is," she said cautiously. It was her job to sell Baldur's paintings, but there was something about Bannerman that made it difficult for her to fake an enthusiasm she didn't feel. Size and voice apart, he was like a child in a toy shop. He turned to look at her. There was a glint in the blue eyes—was it shrewdness, a malicious sense of humor, or the cold snobbery of the very, *very* rich? she wondered— that made her glad she hadn't tried to give him a sales pitch. "He's supposed to be very important. To tell you the truth, I don't know that much about this kind of art. . . ."

"Yes, yes," he snapped impatiently, "but do you *like* the damned thing? That's all that counts."

She had a momentary feeling of guilt at the thought of betraying Simon, but she was not about to lie to Bannerman. "Not much," she admitted.

He laughed—a great booming laugh that made several people turn to stare in their direction. "You're honest," he said. "That's damned rare in the art world, let me tell you. Or anywhere else, come to that." He moved on to the next painting and subjected it to fierce scrutiny, leaning over until his nose almost touched the painting. "Why *don't* you like it?"

"Well, brown isn't my favorite color."

Another laugh, even louder this time. Bannerman threw his head back in what would have been a theatrical gesture from anyone less sure of himself. He laughed as if the whole world had been made for his amusement. "Not your favorite color, is it?" he boomed. "Well, as a matter of fact it isn't mine, either, so we have something in common." He stared down at her, the blue eyes reflecting a certain interest—or perhaps it was just a politician's trick, the way of looking at someone as if he or she were the most important person in the whole world. Bannerman's eyes suggested a personality that did not take kindly to fools, strangers, or people who didn't measure up to his standards. "What *is* your favorite color, then, Miss Walden?"

She wasn't sure she had one, but it was easy to guess that Arthur Bannerman's patience with wishy-washy opinions was about zero. "Green," she said firmly, instantly wishing she'd said blue.

He nodded as if it were a matter of grave importance. "Interesting," he said. "What shade of green, exactly?"

She was surprised, even a little alarmed, by the suddenness, or more precisely, by the *intensity* of the question. Was he a little cracked, or senile? Or perhaps drunk?

"Bright green," she said quickly. "Kelly green."

"No Irish blood in your family, is there?"

"None that I know of, no," she said.

"Well, thank God for that." She had the impression she had passed some kind of test, which Bannerman instantly confirmed. "You'd be surprised how many people don't have a favorite color—just hem and haw, you know, if you ask them. People ought to know their own minds and speak up, don't you think? You think this feller Baldur's paintings are ugly, eh?"

"Well, yes, but I don't think Simon—Mr. Wolff—would be too happy if he knew I'd told *you* that."

Another bark of laughter. She was reminded, oddly, of sea lions at the zoo. "Damn right!" he said cheerfully. "Never mind, I won't tell him if you won't. Of course, you've got a point. They *are* ugly, but there's a certain charm to ugliness. Oh, not in women, don't you know, but in art. Disraeli, I think it was, once said, 'I quite like *bad* wine now and then—one gets so bored with *good* wine.' " He rewarded himself for his memory with a good-humored chuckle instead of his earlier full-blown laugh. "It's refreshing to find someone in the art world who doesn't talk up their own goods. I hate being sold as if I were buying a used car."

She was glad that she had passed Bannerman's test, if that was what it was, though it seemed to her unlikely he had ever visited a used-car lot in his life.

They moved on to the next painting. A waiter approached with a tray of champagne. "Mr. Wolff went downstairs a couple of minutes ago, Miss Walden," he said. "He's waiting for you."

She had forgotten all about dinner. "Tell him I'll meet him at the restaurant," she said. "Oh, also tell him I never got a chance to phone for a table." It occurred to her that she should let Simon know Bannerman was here—he would surely come running back upstairs, leaving his guests to fend for themselves. Then she decided to keep Bannerman to herself. It would serve Simon right for being so ungracious to her.

"I'm keeping you," Bannerman said, with an expression of genuine distress. "You go on to your dinner, please. I'll find my way around."

She shook her head. She was enjoying his company far more than she expected to enjoy dinner. "Not at all. Would you care for a glass of champagne?"

"I can't stand the damned stuff. I wouldn't mind a Scotch, if it's not a lot of trouble."

It *was* a lot of trouble, in fact. Alexa had catered the party on the assumption that almost everyone drinks champagne, which was a lot simpler than trying to set up two bars in a long and fairly narrow room. In her experience, if you provided champagne and Perrier, most people were content.

She excused herself, found a waiter, and explained where to find a bottle of Scotch in the office downstairs. When she turned around, she noticed a puzzling social phenomenon—everybody in the room was aware of Arthur Bannerman's presence, but nobody was daring enough to approach him. As he walked from painting to painting, people moved out of his way, so he was always standing by himself in a circle of empty space.

He showed no sign that he was aware of the effect he had on his fellow guests. She wondered how it felt to be an object of curiosity far more interesting to most of the people here than the paintings. Did people avoid him out of respect for his wealth, or were they afraid of being snubbed? He stood squarely in front of each painting, consulting the catalog in his hands, as if he were alone in the gallery.

For a moment she was almost sorry for him, standing there in a room full of people as if he were separated from them by an invisible barrier, but perhaps that was the way he wanted it to be, she told herself—and anyway, it was hard to work up much sympathy for a man with a billion or so dollars. And yet she *felt* sympathy for him, or something like it.

She crossed the empty no-man's-land between Bannerman and the rest of the world and stood beside him. "It's not *just* brown, you know," he said. For a moment she thought he was talking to himself. "The feller uses different *shades* of brown, layers them on top of each other. Damn clever. I wanted to be a painter once myself."

His pronunciation of "fellow" was so odd that it took her a couple of seconds to understand what he was saying. "Fal–er" he said explosively, so loudly that it appeared to have some special significance for him.

The idea of Arthur Bannerman as an art student seemed to her incongruous. She tried to imagine him with a beard, wearing blue jeans, and failed. Then it occurred to her that he was several generations removed from the art world as it was today. She had a fleeting, ludicrous image of him as one of Rodolfo's rowdy friends in *La Bohème*, but that too was surely the wrong generation. She found it difficult to form any picture of what he had been like as a young man, or even what period that might have been. "Did you try it?" she asked.

"Oh, my, yes. When I was a boy, I had a tutor who did some painting, a Frenchman. He taught me to do watercolors—Hudson Valley landscapes, that sort of thing. Gave one to my father for Christmas once. He was damned impressed. When I went to Harvard, I decided to take it up more seriously—oils and canvas, live models, the real thing. Well, when my father heard about *that*, he put a stop to it right away, don't you know? Read me the riot act. No son of *his* was going to waste his time and risk his morals painting naked women. So I gave it up."

"Were you unhappy about it?"

"Oh, when I was a boy, people didn't worry as much about being happy as they do today. I saw Father's point. A Bannerman couldn't be a painter—not then. Besides, I wasn't that good at it. I took it up again when I was in Washington. A feller told me it was good for the nerves. Used to do some Sunday painting with Ike, at Camp David. *He* said it was the only thing except golf that relaxed him, but he always lost his temper when his paintings didn't come out the way he wanted them to. 'God*damn* it, Arthur,' he used to say to me, 'if I could plan goddamn D-Day, why the hell can't I get these goddamn trees to look right?' "

He laughed boisterously. "Now I collect. It's easier, but not nearly as much fun."

The waiter appeared. Bannerman took a deep drink of Scotch, as if he needed it. Alexa wondered if that was the explanation for his ruddy complexion. She watched to see if his hands trembled, but they were as steady as a rock. He clicked an ice cube against his teeth and stared at the painting. "I like this one best," he said at last. "What do you think?"

"Well, it's a lot larger than the others."

"Exactly! *Scale!* There's no point in doing something like this on a small scale, is there? The bigger, the better, don't you know?"

"Surely that depends where you're going to put it?"

"No, no. You can't buy art because it fits somewhere, young lady. Art and decoration are completely different things. My father bought a Baroccio in London—huge damned allegorical thing. When he discovered he couldn't fit it in the dining room, he had the ceiling raised. The painting was more important than the room. Of course, this feller here is no goddamn Baroccio. Still, I like the large one. I might lend it to the governor. I persuaded him to put some modern art in the governor's mansion, up in Albany, you know—liven the damned place up. I can hardly wait to see the poor feller's face when he sees this!"

It occurred to her to wonder if Bannerman's passion for modern art might be a kind of practical joke on a large scale. She knew it was a recent phenomenon—only in the past two years had he emerged as a force to be reckoned with in the world of contemporary art. Before that, his checkbook had always been open to finance the more ambitious acquisitions of the Metropolitan Museum of Art, of which he was well known to be one of the more difficult and opinionated trustees. There had even been speculation—which found its way into the press —that Bannerman's interest in contemporary art was viewed by his friends and family as a sign of madness or senility, though Alexa saw nothing in him to suggest either.

"How much is it?" he asked.

She fished the typed price list out of her handbag. Normally Simon or the gallery manager handled this kind of thing, but for some reason she felt a certain sense of proprietorship over Bannerman. "Fifty thousand dollars," she said. It seemed like a lot of money to her.

Apparently, it seemed like a lot of money to Bannerman, too. He sipped his drink reflectively, went back to the painting, ran his fingertips over the surface and sighed. "Thirty-five would suit me a damn sight better," he said.

She shook her head. It was not her business to bargain on the price. She guessed that Simon would probably be overjoyed to get thirty-five thousand, if he were making the deal himself, but if *she* made it, he would accuse her of having cost him fifteen thousand. Of course, if she lost him a sale—to Arthur Bannerman, of all people—he would be even more furious. She wished she had called Simon back instead of deciding to keep Bannerman to herself. "I'm afraid the price is fifty, Mr. Bannerman," she said, as firmly as she could. "Mr. Wolff has several other parties interested in the painting."

She hoped she hadn't blushed. She wasn't good about lying, even when it was a harmless part of the bargaining process, and something about Bannerman made it even more difficult than usual.

Bannerman frowned. For a moment she felt her heart sink, afraid he was going to accuse her outright of not telling the truth. He leaned close to her. "Is it that damned fool Rosenzweig again?" he whispered fiercely. "He's buying everything in sight for his new museum. Who's going to appreciate a painting like this in Fort Worth, I ask you?"

She gave him her best shot at a knowing smile. Bannerman stared up at the ceiling, stuck his hands in his pockets like her father trying to strike a bargain on a few heifers at the LaGrange livestock auction, except that Bannerman apparently didn't have any change in his pockets to jingle. "Forty," he said, between clenched teeth.

"I can't do it," she said, which was no more than the truth.

He glared at her, and for a moment she was about to say, "All right, forty." Then he smiled. "You strike a hard bargain," he said, with a note of admiration in his voice. "I'll take it at fifty—but mind, I get a ten percent discount."

"You do?"

"Ask around. It's worth ten percent off to say you sold a painting to me."

"I'll take your word for it, Mr. Bannerman. Forty-five thousand dollars it is. Sold."

Bannerman drained his Scotch. "Capital! You've got a deal." He reached out and gave her another firm handshake, as if she were a voter. "You're not a New Yorker, are you, Miss—ah—Walden?"

"I'm from Illinois."

"Illinois. Where?"

"Stephenson County."

"I carried Stephenson County by four-point-something percent in the 'sixty-eight primary. County seat is LaGrange, right?"

"How on earth do you know that?"

"A politician never forgets a victory, however small. Besides, if there were two things my father insisted children know, they were geography and arithmetic. He had a mental picture, don't you know, of every piece of land he owned—and most of what everybody else owned, too. It was all there in his mind. If somebody suggested a plot of land for an industrial park in Cincinnati, say, Father would close his eyes for a moment, then say, 'No, I don't think so, that's bottom land—it will be under water every time the Ohio rises.' Father had never been to Cincinnati in his life, you understand, but he knew the whole damned country so well he never needed a map. He was a much underrated man, my father."

She detected a bitterness in the way he said it. Was it simple resentment at the fact that his father had been underestimated? Or did Arthur Bannerman feel that he, too, had been underestimated, never received his due, because he was born so rich?

It was not a subject she knew how to pursue with him, though she would have loved to. "How did you know I don't come from New York?" she asked, instead, seeking safer ground.

"Well, you don't speak like a New Yorker, to begin with. Anyway, a New Yorker would have let me have the damned painting for forty just because I'm a Bannerman. It takes a Yankee to drive a hard bargain with another Yankee."

It was on the tip of her tongue to say that she was not a Yankee at all, but a Midwesterner—Swiss-Protestant on her father's side, Anglo-Scots small-town Southern on her mother's—but she didn't feel like trading genealogies with Arthur Bannerman and guessed it was just his tactful way of acknowledging her as a fellow white Protestant.

"What does your father do?" he asked. "Is he a dairy farmer?"

"He's dead," she said. "Several years ago," she added quickly, to forestall condolences or further discussion of the subject. "He *was* a dairy farmer, though. How did you guess that?"

"It's an easy guess, my dear. Practically everybody in Stephenson County's a dairy farmer. I remember a delegation of Republican dairy farmers coming to New York to sell me on higher milk price supports in 'sixty-eight—one of *them* was from Stephenson County, Illinois— I'm sorry I gave in. I didn't believe in price supports then, and I don't now, even if they did win me the dairy-farm vote."

"My father voted against you, I'm sorry to say."

"He was a man of uncommon good sense. I'd have found some way to cut back on price supports if I'd been elected, whatever I promised."

"That's what he said."

"Well, I can see where you got your brains from. . . . Great heavens! I'm keeping you from your dinner." Bannerman's face flushed a darker red with embarrassment.

"Honestly, it's all right," she told him. "Simon—Mr. Wolff, I mean —has gone on with his friends. They won't mind if I'm late." She realized she had said "his" friends, as if she wanted to emphasize that they were no friends of *hers*—which was true enough.

"You must let me drop you off. I won't take no for an answer." He took her arm, as if she was, in fact, going to say no, which she wasn't, and turned toward the stairs. People moved out of the way, clearing a path for him again. A few of the more courageous ones said hello. Bannerman grinned back at them ferociously—he had big, square, teeth, dazzling white, and when he smiled broadly, they dominated his whole face, like those of Teddy Kennedy in cartoons. "Hi, feller, great to see you," he shouted indiscriminately, without slowing down. She wondered if he did it because he had trouble remembering names, but that seemed unlikely, given his sharpness of mind. She decided it was either arrogance or shyness—perhaps complicated by a lifetime of knowing that almost everyone he met wanted something from him. He defended himself by keeping in constant motion and by affecting a loud, hearty affability that probably acted as a barrier against any real conversation.

At the foot of the stairs, Bannerman's rapid progress was blocked by Benoit de Montechristo, struggling into a fur-lined overcoat. Alexa wondered if Bannerman was going to say, "Hi, feller," to Montechristo —and for a moment Bannerman seemed tempted. He shuffled back and forth, head pushed forward, shoulders hunched, like a bull looking for a way around an obstacle before making up his mind to charge. Was there bad blood between them? There were rumors that they had locked horns over several acquisitions—and of course Bannerman's newfound interest in contemporary art probably reduced the amount of money he was willing to donate to the Metropolitan, or so she assumed, knowing no more about it than any other reader of *New York* magazine.

Montechristo's handsome face was impassive. "Good evening, Arthur," he said, in the tone of voice of a man who wishes he had left the party a couple of minutes sooner.

Bannerman grinned broadly, the big teeth flashing, grabbed Montechristo's hand in his and pumped it so hard that Montechristo winced in pain. "*Great* to see you!" Bannerman shouted. He squeezed Montechristo's hand again, even harder. "*Really* great, feller."

Montechristo held his ground, standing directly in front of Bannerman so he could not escape. "I've been trying to reach you," he said.

"I've been busy." Bannerman's grin faded.

"There are some important acquisitions to discuss."

"I've been doing some acquiring of my own."

Montechristo raised an eyebrow. "*This* kind of thing? I've heard. You know my opinion."

"I know it well. I hear it from Eleanor, too. In spades."

Alexa found her coat—a plain cloth coat that made her envy Montechristo's fur. She wondered who Eleanor was. She knew very little about Arthur Bannerman beyond the fact that he had a son who made headlines as a playboy and a politician. Was there a Mrs. Bannerman? And why did the question suddenly occur to her?

Bannerman seized her coat and helped her into it. "This is Miss—ah —Walden," he said. "She has just sold me a painting."

Montechristo gave a small bow. "Delighted," he said. "But frankly, Arthur, it saddens me to see you collecting this kind of thing, lending your name to it. . . . There's a man in Zurich who has a Caravaggio for sale—a masterpiece! It's exactly the kind of painting we should be acquiring. Imagine it as the center of a whole new hall . . . 'The Art of the Renaissance,' perhaps. . . ."

"No. My grandfather bailed the museum out after the crash, you have a whole wing named for my father, and one of the museum's largest acquisition funds is named after my mother. I have given the museum I don't know how many millions of dollars over the years, but I want to do something of my own now." Bannerman's tone was just on the truculent edge of rudeness, which Montechristo pointedly ignored.

"Your *own* museum? Like Getty? Or Rosenzweig? But my dear Arthur, this is New York! New York doesn't *need* another museum."

"Who says it has to be in New York?" Bannerman asked mulishly.

"One assumes . . ." Montechristo shrugged, as if he were dealing with a madman. "Well, I hope you're getting good advice, anyway."

"Miss Walden is advising me," Bannerman said. Seeing an opening to Montechristo's right, he swept her past him, and on out into the hallway, where as if in deference to Bannerman's presence, the elevator was waiting, its doors open.

Bannerman seemed pleased with himself, rather to her annoyance, since she disliked being used as a way of shocking Montechristo. "Why did you say that?" she asked him, a little surprised by her own boldness.

He looked sheepish. "I'm sorry," he said. "You're quite right. I had no right to drag you into my quarrel with Benoit."

"None at all. What on earth will he think of me?"

"It's me he's angry at. He's not a bad feller, really. It's just that over the years the Metropolitan Museum has grown used to thinking of my family as the Great Provider. Hoving, and the feller before him, were just the same. Nobody likes to be told 'No'—the directors of a nonprofit institution least of all. Listen, let me invite you to lunch and apologize properly, what do you say?"

She hesitated, but it was exactly what she had been hoping would happen. All the same, she wondered what she was letting herself in for. "Well, all right," she said. Was it just curiosity that she felt? Bannerman inhabited a world so far removed from hers that the invitation was irresistible. How many people she knew, after all, could say they had been asked to lunch by Arthur Bannerman? Even Simon would be jealous. *Especially* Simon, she told herself with satisfaction.

"Capital!" Outside in the street, a car waited, not the kind of stretch limo she half expected, but a simple black sedan. Beside it stood an elderly black man in a dark suit. She had vaguely supposed that Bannerman's car would be something special—possibly a Rolls-Royce—and that his chauffeur would be in uniform, with a peaked cap, but that appeared not to be Bannerman's style. "Where to?" he asked, sitting down in the front seat, while she got into the back.

"Trump's," she said.

"What the devil is that? And where?"

"I know where it is, sir." The black man's voice was low and lugubrious, but not in the least servile.

"Jack knows everything. Helluva feller."

Some of Simon's schoolmates, particularly those from the Middle East, traveled in limousines with bulletproof glass, accompanied by a bodyguard, and Simon himself, though he was not rich, behaved as if New York was as dangerous as Beirut. Bannerman, on the contrary, seemed to take no precautions. His sedan, far from having bulletproof windows, did not even have a telephone.

He turned his head. "Will tomorrow do for lunch, Miss Walden? It'll give me a chance to hand you the check personally. Can't trust the damned mail these days, can you? Can't trust any goddamn thing."

She had no plans for lunch. She briefly considered the idea of playing hard to get and rejected it. "Tomorrow will be fine," she said.

"Capital!" It seemed to be one of Bannerman's favorite words—appropriately enough, she thought. "Tell Jack where and he'll pick you up."

The car pulled over and stopped outside Trump's, and Jack got out to open the door for her. Bannerman turned around in his seat, reached out and took her hand in his. She braced herself for a hearty grip, but instead he held it gently, but firmly, in his. For a moment she thought he was going to suggest she join him for dinner and, to her surprise, rather hoped he would, but after what seemed a long pause, he merely squeezed her hand and said, "It's been a more rewarding evening than I expected."

His hand was strong, though the touch of his fingertips was surprisingly delicate. She felt, somehow, a certain current between them that made her reluctant to leave the intimacy of the car for the glare and noise of Trump's. She squeezed back, ever so slightly, and was rewarded with what looked very much like a wink.

"It's been an expensive evening for you," she said. "But you got what you wanted."

He looked startled. "*Did* I? Ah, the painting, yes, of course. That wasn't what I was thinking of. Well, I'm keeping you from your dinner," he said, letting go of her hand unwillingly. "I hope we'll—ah—get to know each other better. Tomorrow, then?"

She nodded.

"Speaking of the painting," he said, "did you really have an offer from that feller Rosenzweig?"

She smiled and shook her head. "No," she admitted. "He *is* interested, though."

Bannerman laughed and took her hand again, squeezing harder this time, but not by any means painfully. "By God," he said, "you're a girl after my own heart—a real horse trader! I'll have to watch myself."

"You're not angry?"

"No, no. It was worth every penny, my dear. Besides—" he winked —"not everyone gives me a discount, so we're even. Goodnight."

"DISCOUNT? *What* discount? You let the old bastard cheat you. Why the hell didn't you tell me he was there?"

Simon had to shout to make himself heard over the noise at Trump's. She understood that, but still she hated being shouted at. "He was in a hurry," she said.

"You should have told him to come back tomorrow so I could deal with him."

"He isn't the kind of man who comes back tomorrow, Simon. Anyway, you'd have been happy to let Bannerman have the painting for thirty-five, just to be able to tell people you sold it to him. You know that, so don't shout at me!"

"I am *not* shouting!" Simon's voice was loud enough now to attract the attention of several of his friends, not to speak of strangers standing at the bar and the bartender himself. He glared at the bartender, who moved away. "I don't know what the hell's come over you tonight," he said, lowering his voice. "You didn't call for a table, so we've had to wait at the bar for an hour. . . . "

"Half an hour. At most."

"Okay, half an hour. That's not the point. Then you take it upon yourself to sell a painting—to Arthur Bannerman of all people. Did he give you a check, by the way?"

"No." *Should* she have asked Bannerman for a check? Instinct told her that he had probably never carried a checkbook in his life. Would he have been offended if she'd asked for one? Probably not, she decided, but he would almost certainly have concluded that she was hopelessly small-time. She was surprised to realize that Arthur Bannerman's opinion suddenly mattered to her. She hardly knew him, after all!

"I'll tell you something, Alexa," Simon said, shaking his finger at her. "Six months from now we'll still be waiting for that goddamned check. The rich pay late—when they pay at all. I can give you the whole scenario—we'll wait ninety days, then write to him, then a month or two later we'll get a letter from some lawyer saying there was a misunderstanding and offering thirty thousand dollars to settle the matter. Always get the fucking check while the customer still wants the painting!"

She hated being lectured. She felt a sudden disgust with herself. Trump's, with its densely packed, noisy customers and its overbright lighting, was exactly where she didn't want to be. Simon, whom she tried so hard to please—and who remained impossible to please, as usual, except at the cost of total surrender—was also, as usual, treating her as if she were a moron, confident that she wouldn't fight back. She found she had no patience for it. "I'll get the check tomorrow, since you're so worried about it," she said.

"Tomorrow? And how the hell are you going to do that?"

She gave him a look that would have frozen anyone less self-centered in his tracks—but of course it was wasted on him, she knew that. Simon had long since decided that he held her in the palm of his hand, and it was nobody's fault but her own. "I'm having lunch with him," she said. "Now if you don't mind, I'm going home. I have a headache."

If she had hit Simon over the head with a two-by-four, he couldn't have looked more startled. She derived a small degree of pleasure at least from that. "*Lunch?* With Arthur Bannerman? You're kidding me."

"No, I'm not."

"For God's sake, you should have told me, Alexa! What an opportunity! Why didn't you tell him you wanted *me* to come too, for Christ's sake? You don't know anything about art—you know that as well as I do."

"What makes you think he wants to talk about art, Simon? Goodnight."

She turned away. "You're not *going,* are you?" Simon shouted.

"I told you, I have a headache. I'm going home."

"Look, I'm sorry. . . ."

She knew he *was* sorry, too. He was always sorry when he had gone too far.

For once she didn't care a damn.

SHE HAD BEEN in a lot of apartment buildings and assumed that by now nothing in New York could surprise her, but this one took her breath away. The entrance of the Dakota was perhaps more exotic, but here every detail, from the starched collars of the staff to the stained-glass windows and dark paneling, proclaimed "old money" as opposed to new, and lots of it. The lobby bore a distinct resemblance to an Episcopalian church in a wealthy neighborhood: marble floors, carved beams, gilded chandeliers of faintly ecclesiastical design, antique furniture. The doorman, his assistant, and the elevator operators all had a faintly clerical look too: gray-haired, elderly men, wearing white gloves, they looked like ushers at an elegant Protestant funeral, their heads bowed as if the coffin were about to arrive. When the doorman asked her name, she found herself whispering it, as if the decor required a hushed voice and a reverential attitude.

The elevator operator bowed a little deeper, in deference to the very mention of the name, and carefully closed the doors. The operator used an old-fashioned hand lever, and the elevator rose at a pace stately enough not to frighten even the oldest of dowagers, accompanied by the gentle wheezing of ancient, well-oiled machinery.

He opened the grille, and she stepped out into a foyer that was three or four times the size of her own apartment. There was no hallway— the elevator door opened directly into Bannerman's apartment, which presumably took up a whole floor of the building, covering almost half a city block and overlooking Central Park. She could not even begin to guess at its value—millions of dollars, of course, but how many?

At the far end of the foyer a butler waited, bowing deferentially at her approach. A maid appeared to take her coat, then the butler led her through a pair of heavy carved wooden doors, like those of a cathedral, and on through a series of sunlit rooms, each one larger and more elaborately furnished than the one before. She had a confused impression of rich Oriental carpets, marble fireplaces, gold-framed paintings, tapestries, fresh flowers and antique furniture—enough, it seemed, for several museums.

"Mr. Arthur is waiting in the library," the butler said, as if he were referring to God. He led her through yet another enormous room, this one hung with modern paintings, which looked grotesque beside the elaborate, old-fashioned furniture, knocked gently, and opened a pair of double doors.

She supposed that Bannerman's library would be wood-paneled and lined with books, probably bound in leather, but it was nothing of the kind. It was a large, brightly lit room with red walls, dominated by enormous modern paintings, looking more like the Museum of Modern Art than anything she would have associated with Bannerman. He himself, as he rose to greet her, looked startlingly out of place against the bright splashes of color and the amorphous shapes of the sculpture dotted around the room. At the far end of the library a pair of doors opened out onto a small, glassed-in dining room, full of bright abstract paintings and flowers, where two maids were busy around the table. Beyond the dining room was a terrace with a formal garden.

"Good of you to come," he boomed, shaking her hand. He led her over to a pair of chrome-and-leather chairs, more elegant than comfortable, and sat down, pulling up his trousers with a careful, fussy gesture. He seemed pleased to see her. "You'll join me in a drink?"

She shook her head. "I'm not much of a drinker."

"I remember. Wish I could say the same. Well, no, I don't wish it at all, as a matter of fact. My father and grandfather were teetotalers. Dead set against what used to be called 'the demon rum.' Didn't make them any happier, so far as I could see." He nodded at the butler, who raised an eyebrow with what seemed to Alexa a faint sign of disapproval, and returned a minute later with a large tumbler of Scotch on a silver tray.

"I suppose your Mr. Wolff must be pretty pleased with you," Bannerman said.

"Not really. He thought I sold you the painting too cheap." She decided to be frank with him—his bright blue eyes demanded frankness. "He thought I should have asked you for a check on the spot, too."

"Did he?" Bannerman laughed. "He's got a point, you know. On the whole, the rich are quick to collect and slow to pay. That's how they got rich in the first place. The Bannermans are an exception, I'm happy to say. Cash on the barrelhead is the family tradition, don't you know." He took an envelope out of his pocket and handed it to her. "PIF," he said. "I added on the sales tax for Dutchess County—no point paying good money to the damned city if you don't have to. . . . You don't like any of this much, do you?" He waved toward the pictures on the wall.

She recognized a De Kooning, a Pollock, a Motherwell. The others were unknown to her. "I've tried," she said. "Simon—Mr. Wolff—has been working on me for years."

"Has he? But without success, apparently. You prefer what's out there in the other rooms?" He smiled. "The old masters? All those gilt frames and grim Dutch faces?"

She did not want to offend him, but she was determined to be truthful. "Yes, I do. Or the Impressionists." She hoped he had not invited her here to talk about art.

"Because they're pretty, eh? My mother would agree with you. I expect my children would, too, if they bothered to think about it. I like a bit of excitement around me, you see. If you live long enough with museum pieces, you end up *becoming* a museum piece, like old Getty."

"You don't look like a museum piece to me, Mr. Bannerman."

"Capital! But call me Arthur, please. 'Mr. Bannerman' is altogether too museumlike."

The butler appeared at the other end of the room and coughed discreetly. "Ah, lunch!" Bannerman shouted, with his usual enthusiasm. "You must be starved."

She was not, in fact, even hungry. She was, however, more than a little curious to see what lunch consisted of for Bannerman. She expected something elaborate and elegant, the work of a master French chef—and indeed the luncheon table gave promise of an extraordinary meal. Two maids waited to serve them at a table that was laid with dazzling elegance, from the fresh flowers in a vermeil centerpiece to the gleaming silver.

There were three wineglasses in front of her, but Bannerman asked the butler for another Scotch. For a moment she thought the butler was going to object, but he merely gave a small, resigned shrug. Did Bannerman have a drinking problem? If so, he seemed to handle it well enough. To the butler's disappointment, she asked for a Perrier, was informed after some difficulty that there was none, and settled for a glass of soda water.

The tomato soup, served by one of the maids in a splendid tureen, tasted to Alexa suspiciously like Campbell's. She took a second spoonful, and the taste confirmed the first. There was no doubt about it—the soup had come straight from the familiar red-and-white can. Bannerman ate his slowly, blowing on his spoon, while he talked about his collection.

The soup plates were cleared; a maid returned, this time with an elaborate silver serving tray, which when uncovered, revealed two neatly browned hamburgers, accompanied by mashed potatoes, gravy, and frozen green beans. She noticed that Bannerman helped himself from an antique silver sauceboat filled with ketchup. If there had ever been a French chef in Bannerman's kitchen, she decided, he must long since have resigned.

Bannerman ate rapidly and methodically, without any sign of enjoyment, like a child who had been told not to leave anything on his plate. Had he been taught to "waste not, want not" by some governess or nanny sixty years ago?

"Do you usually have lunch here?" she asked, hoping he wouldn't take it as a criticism of the meal.

Bannerman finished his Scotch and tapped his finger against the glass for a refill. "Often," he said. "Too often. There's a staff, you see. They prepare meals. They expect me to eat at home. For a long time it seemed the natural thing to do. Like so many other things."

He sipped the fresh drink. For a moment, he looked sad to her, and suddenly much older. It seemed unlikely that a man with a billion dollars could suffer from anything as ordinary as loneliness, but something about the immense, empty apartment with its echoing rooms and silent servants told her it was surely true. Did Bannerman have friends, hobbies, women in his life? Did he go out in the evening to his club to play bridge, or to see a movie? She wished she could recapture the small moment of intimacy they had shared in the car, but here, in his home, Bannerman seemed more remote.

"Tell me about yourself," he said, as the plates were cleared. "What brought you to New York?"

"When my father died"—she felt the familiar stab of pain and guilt —"I decided I didn't want to spend the rest of my life in LaGrange." It wasn't the whole truth, but it was part of the truth—enough to make conversation.

"In a way, I envy you. To strike out for New York from a small town when you're young—it's quite an adventure. It takes guts. *My* father lived on well into his eighties, you know. I was a middle-aged man, with a family of my own, when he died. Of course I inherited great responsibilities, but then, I knew I would, eventually. There were no surprises, no adventure." He shrugged. "For a time I made politics my adventure, but I leave that to Robert, my eldest, now, damn him. Though he still has a lot to learn . . ."

There was a long pause. "How many children do you have?" she asked, trying to keep the conversation going. Lunch was a mistake, she thought with disappointment. She wished she had gone out to dinner with him last night, when the mood had been altogether different.

"Three. Two boys—grown men now, of course. And a girl—though she's a grown woman, too. Takes after her mother."

There was a hint of bitterness or anger—or at least it sounded that way to Alexa—as he snapped the last words out sharply. If there was one subject Alexa knew about, it was fathers and daughters. She wondered what Bannerman's daughter had done to displease him.

There was a hushed noise of china and cutlery as the maids returned to serve dessert—ice cream and cookies, just right to end a meal that was probably being served at this very moment to millions of American children in school cafeterias across the country. Was it what Bannerman wanted? Did he have simple tastes, or perhaps a nostalgia for his childhood? Or were his meals fixed by some kind of family routine and tradition? The cookies were out of a box. She herself did not mind—if anything, the meal produced a certain nostalgia in her for her own childhood—but she thought it was sad that for all his money, Bannerman's staff could not at least bake him homemade cookies.

Having brought up the subject of his children, he closed it firmly. "How long have you worked for Mr. Wolff?" he asked.

"Almost two years."

"And before that?"

"I was a model." That was not the whole truth. She had done some modeling, but it was stretching things to say that she had been a model. "It was something I always wanted to do, even in school. It seemed as far away from what people did in LaGrange as you could get."

"I'm sure you were very good at it."

"No. It wasn't as easy as it looked from LaGrange."

"I find it hard to believe that you didn't succeed. You're a very— attractive—young woman."

She listened carefully as he hesitated for the right word, presumably rejecting "beautiful" as too extreme a compliment, and "pretty" as trivial. He did not linger on the subject. "Well, we all have our ambitions," he went on, as if running for the Presidency was the same as trying to get on the cover of Vogue. "Working for a feller like Wolff must be an interesting job."

"Yes, it is," she said, with what sounded to her own ears like feeble-minded enthusiasm. It was like having lunch with a distant relative, she thought, one you hadn't seen for a long time—or like a job interview. Bannerman seemed unwilling, or perhaps unable, in the cold light of day, to go beyond the most formal conversation. Was it a job interview, perhaps? It crossed her mind that Bannerman might be looking for a personal assistant of some kind, that this lunch might be a test. "It's very varied."

He nodded. "Wolff is quite the entrepreneur, from what I hear." He gave a small sniff, enough to suggest that he didn't think Wolff's kind of entrepreneurship was altogether respectable, or perhaps that it was too small-time to interest him.

"He's easily bored," she explained. "So he's always looking for something new. That's fun for me."

"Oh, I can imagine . . . boredom is a terrible thing." He paused. "I never used to be bored, you know. Didn't know the meaning of the word. When the children were growing up, the days weren't long enough—there was always something going on. Oh, I was busy: the Foundation, politics, business. Still we had some grand times—Maine in the summer, fox-hunting in the autumn. . . . " He seemed to be talking to himself.

He stared into his empty coffee cup for a moment. "Then, you know, my wife died, the children went their ways, I retired from politics. . . ." He glared at her defensively. "Well, two runs at the Presidency are enough for any man, except Richard Nixon. I woke up one morning and realized I had nothing to do. Oh, there were business decisions to be made, meetings to go to—but in that respect the Bannerman family is like one of those damned space machines, the kind they send to Mars, or the stars. . . . "

He closed his eyes, as if he were trying to imagine the kind of machine he had in mind. He opened them again and smiled at her. The smile, she guessed, was a kind of apology for making her listen to his problems. "What I mean," he went on, "is that the machine flies on forever, on its own course, long after the people who built it are dead and buried, do you follow me? What my grandfather created is like that. It goes on and on, just the way he meant it to. . . . "

Was he drunk? What he was saying was coherent enough, despite his flight of fancy into space, but she could think of no good reason why Bannerman should suddenly have decided to confide in her. In a way, she understood what he was saying. She had seen *2001*—it was one of Simon's favorite movies—and had been chilled by the way the space-ship dwarfed and destroyed its crew, though she found the movie de-pressing and overblown. It was only later that she discovered Simon and his friends had seen the movie through a haze of marijuana smoke —that it had been a cult object for those who came of age in the drug culture.

Was Bannerman thinking of *2001?* Had he seen, without the benefit of drugs, in that vast and lifeless spaceship floating through space to an unknown destination, some sudden vision of what his own life had become? She herself hated things that were huge and beyond her con-trol. As a child, she had burst into tears on the platform of a railway station when the train pulled in, terrified by the sheer size and noise of the locomotive as it screeched and clanged to a halt only a few feet from her like some terrible monster. To this day, she was nervous about threading her way across the New York streets in front of rumbling buses and trucks. Without ever having been on one (or tempted to go on one), she knew she would hate being on a cruise ship, however luxurious.

The fact that Arthur Bannerman seemed to have the same kind of fear made her feel less like a job applicant. Suddenly she was no longer in awe of him. He was a man in trouble, who drank too much in a quiet, steady way, had nightmares about spaceships, and apparently wanted her to feel sorry for him.

"I follow you all right," she said. And with some asperity, "Still, it can't be all that bad, being rich. I mean, it's what everyone wants to be, isn't it?"

"Is it? *Is* it?" He seemed genuinely surprised at the idea. "I suppose it is. Would you believe me if I told you it's not all it's cracked up to be?"

"It sounds good to me."

He laughed. "That's honest. I like that. But if you had money, what would you do with it? I mean money far beyond anything you could spend, far beyond your needs. It's a heavy responsibility, you know— to have what everyone wants, and more. I tried to protect my children from that knowledge—didn't want them to have the kind of cloistered life I had. I don't think I succeeded, frankly. Perhaps it isn't possible, in the end."

Bannerman rose, a little stiffly. Was it age, or the whiskey? He stood behind her as she got up, courteous as ever, and led her back to the library, where he poured himself another drink. She walked over to the window and looked out at the park.

"Magnificent, isn't it?" he asked. "The leaves are beginning to turn. Upstate, they've already turned by now. You should see what the au-tumn colors look like at Kiawa. Have you seen them?"

She shook her head. "Never."

"You must, you must! It's not a sight to be missed, don't you know? Am I keeping you? You must want to get back to your office."

"The office can wait for once."

She turned away from the view. Somewhere across the park, invisible from here, was her own apartment, which might as well have been in a different world. Facing the window was Bannerman's desk, an antique *bureau plat*, of obvious value even to her inexpert eyes. It was clear of papers, a perfectly blank space of polished leather. Did he work here? And if so, what did he *do?*

There were several pictures on it in silver frames. One showed a girl of about fourteen leaning forward from the saddle to pin a ribbon on her horse's bridle. She did not look happy—the face beneath the velvet riding cap was serious, even, in some hard-to-define way, resentful. A folding double frame contained photographs of two boys. One looked exactly like a younger version of Bannerman, with an expression that suggested he was determined not to smile for the photographer; the other was younger, a boy of twelve or so, grinning from ear to ear, the only happy face in Bannerman's gallery of family portraits. In a small, separate frame, of exquisite design, was a photograph of a third boy, the face clearly resembling Bannerman's, but with a suggestion of something secretive and withdrawn in the eyes and mouth, a sadness which came across even in the snapshot.

Bannerman had mentioned three children, but there were four here. She wondered what the explanation for the omission was, and wished again that she knew more about him.

In a much larger frame, set apart from the rest, was a color photograph of a woman in her late thirties or early forties, a formal portrait like the kind one might see in *Vogue* or *Town and Country* accompanying an article on the great houses of the rich. The woman, seated in an elaborate room, was wearing a pale-gray Chanel suit and a single strand of pearls. She was posed as if the photograph had been intended to demonstrate exactly how a lady should sit—knees and ankles firmly pressed together, hands neatly folded in her lap, her back as stiff and straight as a soldier's.

Mrs. Bannerman's eyes were pale gray and her hair was black—the same coloring as her own, Alexa realized, with a slight sense of discomfort. Was that the explanation for Bannerman's invitation to lunch?

She knew how little was required to imagine that kind of resemblance. Often she had seen in older men something that reminded her of her father—she had even seen it in Bannerman when she first met him at the gallery. It was not by any means an exact physical resemblance—for one thing, her father had been a young man compared to Bannerman—though he had not seemed so, of course, to her as a child

—so much as a combination of small details: the neat, slightly fussy way Bannerman cut up his food, which was natural enough in a wealthy aristocrat, but had always seemed unusual for a heavily muscled farmer with the big, gnarled, blunt-fingered hands of a workingman, or the way Bannerman moved toward anything that interested him, a loping, fast-moving gait, head forward, as if he were going to collide head-on with it.

"You're looking at my family?" he asked.

She blushed. Did he think she had been snooping? "I'm sorry," she said. "Yes. Your wife is—was—a very beautiful woman."

"Indeed. A great beauty. She was a Merrivale. From Philadelphia, you know. Her family wasn't at all pleased that she married a Bannerman." He smiled. "It used to be said of old Jock Merrivale, her grandfather, that if he went to heaven, he'd expect God to bow to him. I'm happy to say that there's a lot less snobbery in the world nowadays. In Philadelphia, poor Priscilla was considered to have married very much beneath her."

It was hard for her to imagine anyone more aristocratic, in American terms, than Arthur Bannerman, but it was clear from the way he spoke that he had been slightly in awe of his wife, like many ordinary American men who marry a notch above themselves and live to regret it.

"I've never heard of the Merrivales," she said.

Bannerman gave one of his great, whooping laughs, his face lighting up with genuine pleasure. "Why, bless you," he said. "That's quite the nicest thing I've heard you say. Jock Merrivale would turn over in his grave if he heard that!"

He came over and stared at the photographs on his desk as if he were seeing them for the first time. "Funny thing," he said, "when the children were small, I always imagined we'd be a close-knit family. Thought I'd fill Kiawa up with grandchildren. But I don't see my children much at all, and there *are* no grandchildren, so far. Just a damned big, empty house . . . "

"My mother makes the same complaint about me. Luckily, I have older brothers, so there are enough grandchildren around to satisfy her. Are your children married?"

"Only Robert, the eldest. Married and divorced. Putnam is getting to the age where he will soon be have to be described as a congenital bachelor, I'm afraid. As for Cecilia, she's in Africa, shouldering the white woman's burden, though why she should feel guilty about the plight of the Africans beats me. Her great-grandfather was accused of being a robber baron often enough in his time, but never of being a slaveowner. He was *against* slavery, don't you know? Thought it was an inefficient form of labor."

He stared at the photographs, silent for a moment, then coughed.

"How was your dinner party last night, by the way?" he asked. "I hope I didn't make you too late?"

"I went home instead."

"Ah? I'm sorry."

"It's okay. I wasn't looking forward to it that much."

He nodded. He seemed as conscious as she was that he wasn't making much headway with her. Perhaps it was the apartment, with all the reminders of his family. Or had he simply decided he had gone too far with her last night, and was too polite to have canceled the invitation to lunch at the last minute?

"Indeed?" He leaned a fraction closer. He put his hand on hers, so suddenly and gently that for a moment she was unaware of the gesture. "I've been thinking of you all day," he said. "Last night, too, frankly. I'm not in the habit of flirting, don't you know? I think I've lost my touch."

She laughed. "You were doing pretty well last night."

"Was I?" He was delighted with the compliment. "Well, nobody's told me that for a long time." His hand pressed hers against the warm leather of the desk.

She felt something like an electric shock, the kind you got when you walked across a thick carpet on a cold day and touched a light switch. She turned to look at Bannerman. His expression was grave, like that of a man who has just reached a serious decision after considerable thought, and isn't completely happy with it.

She understood. It had been a long time since she had felt this kind of attraction. Simon had monopolized her feelings long past the point when there was anything left between them to feel. She didn't know what to say to Bannerman. It was not just the difference in their ages. It was impossible to forget that he was one of the richest and most famous men in America, or not to wonder what the implications of those two facts might be in any relationship between them.

She wondered what he would do if she kissed him, but before she could make up her mind there was a muffled knock on the door and the butler said, "Half-past two, sir."

"Damn!" Bannerman exclaimed, jumping as if he had been caught doing something shameful. "What was I saying?"

"That you were no good at flirting."

He shook his head impatiently. "No, no, before that. . . . "

"That you don't go out much?"

"Exactly. And I should, you know. I'm in danger of becoming a goddamn hermit. Trouble is, most of the people I know have one foot in the grave." He waved toward the fireplace, the mantel of which was stacked with invitations. "Dinners to raise money for every damn thing from the goddamn Republican Party to widows and orphans . . . "

Somewhere in the depths of the apartment there was a sudden muffled sound of voices.

Bannerman walked to the fireplace, and for a moment she thought
he was about to toss the cards into the flames. "My secretary puts them
there," he said. "It's a damned middle-class habit, displaying invitations
like Christmas cards, but it's her way of encouraging me to go out."

He picked one up, holding it at a great distance from his eyes. He
shook his head in disgust and fumbled in his breast pocket for reading
glasses.

"The trustees of the Rockefeller Institute. Five hundred dollars a
seat! You'd think the Rockefellers could do without other people's
money, wouldn't you? Here's one for multiple sclerosis. Half of social
life these days seems to revolve around diseases. The Metropolitan
Museum of Art . . . " He examined the invitation more carefully than
the others. "I suppose I might go to this one. . . . "

There was a discreet cough from the doorway. "Mr. Walter Wriston
is here, sir," the butler said. "With some other gentlemen."

"Damn bankers. Tell them to wait." He put the spectacles back in his
pocket and sighed. "I'd hoped to show you round the apartment," he
said. "There are a lot of things you'd enjoy, I think—not like my mod-
erns, you know. *Pretty* things," he snapped, with just an edge of contempt. "Some damned fine Impressionists, a nice collection of Degas
bronzes. Never mind, another time. Sorry to have talked you to death
about my damned family. You're a good listener, and I took advantage
of it. . . . "

She seemed to have lost the moment. Bannerman was playing tour
guide again, his way, she guessed, of putting distance between them.
"No," she said. "I mean, I *am* a good listener, I guess, but I was really
interested."

"You're not just being polite?"

"I'm not being polite at all. Honestly."

"Indeed?" He led her through the door, then paused. "The Bannerman family interests you, eh?"

"Well, it interests everybody, doesn't it?"

"Does it? Of course it does." He took her arm. "If you have a moment, I'll show you something a lot more interesting than Impressionist
paintings." He took a bunch of keys out of his pocket and opened a
door. "After you," he said.

"I don't want you to keep Mr. Wriston waiting on my account. . . . "

"Damn Wriston! All bankers used to know was how to say 'No' to
people who wanted a loan. Now all they do is say 'Yes' to every goddamn tinpot Third World dictator. Mark my words, they'll bring the
whole economy crashing down around our ears. This feller Wriston
and David Rockefeller have done more harm between them than Marx

and Engels. . . . " He switched on the light. "There! What do you say
to that?"

She stepped into a small room, hardly more than a cubicle, without
a window. The floor was of worn, stained brown linoleum, badly
cracked and buckled. Where it had worn through, small patches had
been thriftily tacked over the holes. They did not quite match.

The walls were painted a bilious yellow-green. There were no deco-
rations, no pictures or photographs except for a faded calendar, an old-
fashioned, loudly ticking office clock, and an ancient steam radiator,
from which the silver paint was peeling in strips. There were only three
pieces of furniture in the room: a big, stained, oak rolltop desk, a battered swivel chair and a tall coatrack. On the desk were a lamp with a
green shade, a fresh sheet of blotting paper, and an antique upright
telephone like the ones she had seen in old movies. Next to the desk
was a battered metal wastepaper basket and a glass-domed stock ticker.
It was as cheerless a room as she had ever seen—as austere as a monk's
cell, in its own way.

Bannerman smiled. He stood next to the rolltop desk, his head
slightly bowed as if in contemplation of a religious relic. "Father recon-
structed Cyrus Bannerman's office," he explained. "Had the whole
thing moved up here from Wall Street, with the original walls and floor.
You can still see the scuff marks from Cyrus's boots."

"Did your father use it?"

"Good God, no! He would have felt it was sacrilege to sit behind
Grandfather's desk."

"It's a little bare, isn't it? There's no furniture. Where did people sit?"

"I knew it! You've gone straight to the point. Those who came to see
Cyrus didn't sit. They *stood* beside his desk and spoke their piece, hat
in hand. Then *he* said 'Yes' or 'No,' and they left. He wasn't a man to
waste words—or time. You see the fresh blotter? Every night, before
leaving, Cyrus used to remove the sheet of blotting paper, fold it up,
put it in his pocket, and take it home. When he got home, he burned
it. As a young man, he bought his first mine because he read a letter
his boss had written by holding the blotter up in front of a mirror, and
he never forgot the lesson."

For some reason she shivered. It was warm in the room, but there
was something frightening about this Spartan shrine to the man who
had once sat here patiently calculating, secure in the knowledge that
his mind worked faster than other men's, unmoved by the passions and
hopes of lesser mortals—like a god without mercy or love, she thought.

"You feel it, too," Bannerman said. "It always seems colder in here
than it is. When I was young, I used to think it was Cyrus's ghost
bringing down the temperature like a block of ice. If he *has* a ghost,
this is where it would be, you know—not at Kiawa. He began as

a bookkeeper. Even as a boy, he had a head for numbers. Got a job at a mining company here in New York, in the head office, at five dollars a week. He was so good with the books that they sent him out west to keep tabs on the mine managers, who were stealing the company blind.

"Cyrus was seventeen—a tall, serious boy, with a stiff celluloid collar and high-laced shoes, and they sent him off to California—which was like sending somebody to the moon today—to deal with grown men who wore guns and kept peace in the mines with their bare fists. . . . Oh, they must have laughed when they saw Cyrus, but they stopped once they'd got a close look at his eyes. Even when I was a child, sitting on his knees, those eyes frightened me. They frightened the mine managers, too, by God! Within a year he'd put things in order; by the time he was twenty-one he owned more mines himself than the company he worked for; by thirty, he was one of half a dozen men who owned the country. Rockefeller had the petroleum; Carnegie, the steel mills; Morgan and Mellon had the banks; Vanderbilt and Harriman, the railroads; Cyrus had the gold, silver, coal, iron, and lead. He set the prices to suit himself, and if you didn't like it, be damned to you! When some of the holdouts, independent silver mine operators, refused to do business with United, Cyrus just increased production, flooded the market with silver until the price dropped so low the independents were bankrupted —then bought them out for a song and raised the price again."

He chuckled. "Oh, the goddamned OPEC sheiks had nothing on Cyrus; he would have run rings around them. Abner Chase, who practically owned Montana, once stood in this very office and warned Grandfather to stay out of 'his' state, unless Cyrus wanted the fight of his life. 'I won't fight you,' Cyrus said. 'I'll ruin you!' And he did."

"What happened to Chase?"

"Chase? He shot himself. Took a room at the old Waldorf Hotel, wrote a letter to the *Times* blaming Cyrus for ruining him, then put a bullet through his brain. I think that was the low point of Cyrus's life— as close as he ever came to despair. He was hated, you know—people booed and hissed at him in the streets. He never showed he felt a thing, but it was about then he began to build Kiawa, and started to give away money."

"That's terrible!" she cried out, so loudly that she startled Bannerman. She had no idea what Chase looked like, had never heard of him before, but she knew all too well what a room looked like, smelled like, when somebody had just been shot. She had spent years trying to forget, but it took only one phrase to bring it all back.

"Why, yes, of course," Bannerman said. He sounded a little puzzled. "All that was a long time ago, however. . . . Are you all right?"

She nodded. There was no point in having come this far with Bannerman only to make a fool of herself about something she couldn't even begin to discuss with him. "Did you know him well, your grand-father?" she asked, trying to make her voice sound normal. "Were you fond of him?"

"He wasn't an easy man to be fond of. I'm not sure he *wanted* affec-tion. Or perhaps he just didn't know how to show it—he was a very old man by the time I got to know him, and he'd long since become a kind of institution, worshipped like an idol, by the same damned people who once hated him. Or by their grandchildren, anyway. When he appeared in public, you know, people fought their way past the guards just to *touch* him, as though some of his wealth might rub off on them. Oh, how he must have hated that. Or perhaps he didn't, who knows? Maybe it amused him. Cyrus once told Father that if he lived to two hundred —and I think poor Father was afraid he *would*—the spectacle of human greed and folly would always be enough to keep him amused."

He stared at the desk as if it too were part of the spectacle of human folly and greed—as indeed, she supposed, in a way it *was*—then sighed. "To tell you the truth," he said, "I myself found this room frightening when I was brought here as a child. Now I merely find it depressing."

They stood together on the threshold for a moment in awkward si-lence. "Not many people have seen this room," he said finally, in a soft voice. "Outside the family, I mean."

She took his hand. "I'm flattered."

He seemed to take a long time to think that over, or perhaps he was simply reluctant to let her go. He cleared his throat. "I felt some-how . . . " he began, but whatever it was he felt he kept to himself. The butler had reappeared as silently as a ghost, his expression a warning that even Arthur Bannerman couldn't keep the head of Citibank wait-ing forever.

"I'm *coming*, Martin!" Bannerman snapped. "Show Miss Walden out."

He winked at her. "Mind you," he said, "that's the best way to deal with bankers. Keep 'em waiting. . . . So nice of you to have come. I really enjoyed it."

He stood there for a moment, towering over her, his hand on the doorknob, as if he wanted to say something more. "Jack will be waiting downstairs to take you back," he said, and opened the door. It closed behind him, and she heard his voice, booming and hearty even through a couple of inches of solid oak, greeting the long-suffering bankers without an apology.

So far, on two occasions, she had hardly gotten beyond polite for-mality with Bannerman, who had a remarkable ability to flee from the slightest sign of intimacy.

She hoped he liked her, but the more she thought about it, the less she was sure.

THE VOICE on the telephone was as crisp as a schoolteacher's. "I'm calling on behalf of Mr. Arthur Bannerman," the woman said. "Mr. Bannerman wished me to ask if you would care to be his guest at the trustees' dinner dance at the Metropolitan Museum of Art next Thursday."

Alexa thought she detected a faint note of disapproval in the woman's voice. Bannerman's secretary probably had her own ideas about her employer's choice of companions. "Well, I don't know . . . " she said hesitantly. *Did* she want to go out with him?

The voice at the other end of the line took on an impatient quality. "Mr. Bannerman expressed his very *strong* hope that you would accept, if you were free. Of course, if you already have an engagement, I'm sure he'll understand."

The woman's tone suggested that while Mr. Bannerman might understand, he would certainly not forgive, nor would she. Why am I hesitating? Alexa asked herself. "Well, all right," she said, trying not to sound too eager.

"He'll pick you up at seven forty-five at your apartment."

"Let me give you the address."

"We already have that, thank you," the woman said triumphantly. "Good day."

It was not until she had hung up that it occurred to Alexa to wonder how Bannerman's office had come by her address so easily—she had an unlisted telephone number, so they couldn't simply have looked it up—then she realized how silly that was. If you were Arthur Bannerman, she supposed you could get anything you wanted.

ALEXA HAD FEW WOMEN FRIENDS—certainly none who would know what to wear on a date with Arthur Aldon Bannerman. Clothes she had —her life before meeting Simon had required rather more in the way of formal evening wear than most young women owned, though much of it was no longer in the latest fashion, or the right kind of thing for an evening at the Metropolitan Museum among dowagers and debutantes.

She stopped in at Rizzoli and bought *Vogue* and *Harper's Bazaar*, neither of which was much help, since she didn't intend to spend three or four thousand dollars on a pleated evening dress by Mary McFadden, or a glittering gown of bugle beads by Bill Blass. On a hunch, she picked up a copy of *Manhattan*, which was full of photos of people taken at just the kind of fund-raising parties Bannerman had complained about. Here, as in the pages of *Town & Country*, was a whole world of unfamiliar people, smiling vacuously at the camera in their fancy clothes: Mesa Dadiani and Mr. "Coco" Brown at the Memorial Sloan-Kettering Cancer Research dance; Miss Amanda ("Babe") Saltonstall and Mr. Deems Vandenplas at the Heart Fund gala in the grand ballroom of the Helmsley Palace Hotel; Mr. and Mrs. Burns ("Bunny") Carroll (Palm Beach tans and pale unfocused eyes, like hard-boiled eggs, that suggested heavy drinking), with their daughter Dana (straight blond hair and the kind of nose lesser mortals spent a fortune on plastic surgery to imitate) and Mr. Russell Redbank Reade II of Cravath, Swain & Moore (every inch the young WASP lawyer, boyish good looks turning slightly to fat) at a fund-raising dinner dance for the United States Olympic Equestrian Team; Tampa *(Tampa?)* Pluckett and her fiancé, Mr. Burke Gould (she of New York and Hobe Sound, he of New York and Dark Harbor, Maine), holding up the keys to the Porsche 911 Targa she had just won as the first door prize at a ball to raise money for babies born with a heroin addiction.

Miss Dormaison's emerald necklace looked as if it could be sold for enough to buy the entire South Bronx, right down to the last heroin-addicted mother; Mr. Gould's profession was listed simply as "an assistant to John Diebold and a noted yachtsman." This was not her world, nor did it seem Bannerman's, either. She found it difficult to know what to choose. A full-length gown? A three-quarter-length dress? Black, or something brighter? There *were* people she knew who could have helped her, but they were, as it happened, women she particularly didn't want to reach—she had tried to forget them a long time ago, and hoped they had forgotten her.

She finally got up the courage to put her problem to the only person she knew who lived in the world represented by *Town & Country* and *Manhattan*, even though there was no closeness between them.

Mrs. Eldridge Chantry was a formidable woman in her well-preserved sixties (or possibly her less well-preserved fifties, it was hard to tell), who made a good living decorating the homes of the unfamous rich—she made a point, in fact, of *not* dealing with celebrities, as if to make sure that none of *her* rooms would appear in the pages of *People* magazine. Her clients' tastes sometimes brought her to Simon for a painting, or more often in search of some more exotic object, a neon sculpture or a Lucite chair. She hated such things—her taste ran to eighteenth-century French antiques and Impressionist sketches, on which the commission was also much bigger—but from time to time she was obliged to give way to the fantasies of a client.

"Sis" Chantry, as she was known throughout the trade, belonged to the New York social world by birth as well as by marriage, but she was also a shrewd businesswoman. It was only by chance that she appeared at the gallery one morning when Alexa was there—she normally made an appointment with Simon—but it was clearly an opportunity not to be wasted.

"I won't take off my coat," Mrs. Chantry said firmly after one look at Baldur's paintings. "I wouldn't let a client have one of these if my life depended on it." She clutched her mink to her chest and shuddered. "Gawd! Simon ought to be ashamed of himself."

Alexa seldom found herself in agreement with Sis Chantry on anything, but on the subject of Baldur's paintings they shared common ground. "I hate them, too," she said. She found the perfect opening: "Mr. Bannerman bought one, though."

Sis Chantry raised a plucked and penciled eyebrow. "Which Bannerman?"

"Arthur Bannerman."

"*Arthur?* He must have been drunk. What on earth was he doing here? This isn't his neck of the woods at all."

"He came to the opening. I was surprised myself. He was very nice."

Mrs. Chantry sniffed. "Nice? My dear girl, the man's a monster! Those poor children . . . well, they're grown up now, of course. . . . He treated his wife abominably. Never even came to see her when she was dying! The children never forgave him—haven't spoken to him for years. Cecilia was so upset she broke off her engagement and ran off to Africa, to work with lepers or something. . . . " Mrs. Chantry shuddered. "He's practically a recluse now," she continued. "Drinks like a fish, I've been told. If he bought one of *these* horrors, they ought to lock him up in one of those funny farms in Connecticut and throw away the key."

"He seemed okay to me. Do you know him well?"

"I know all the Bannermans. Most of them, anyway. They're an odd lot. Of course, with all that money, what else *would* they be? Ice-cold Puritans on the outside, but positively seething inside. Look at Elliott Bannerman, Arthur's cousin—pillar of the church, member of the Council on Foreign Relations, on the board of every philanthropy you can think of, and killed himself on his fiftieth birthday! He kept the same mistress for fifteen years—nice gal, a client of mine. He visited her three times a week, always carried a little leather fitted case, like a flute player's, you know, for his *whips!* Had them all made up specially in London, with little gold ferrules so they unscrewed, like a folding billiard cue. Liked to dress up in women's clothes, then have this gal whip him. He gave her two thousand dollars a month, wrote it into his will, too, so she gets it for the rest of her life. Can't say he wasn't generous or loyal, poor man. She was a Woodward, but one of the poor ones. . . . "

Once she was launched on society gossip Sis Chantry was unstoppable, but since she was also a snob, she apparently decided that she had gone too far in talking about Alexa's betters. "Of course, all the best families have something to hide." She made for the door. "They can't be judged by the standards of ordinary people," she snapped, with a glance that made it clear that as far as she was concerned Alexa was about as ordinary as you could get.

Alexa swallowed her resentment—there was no point in being angry with Mrs. Chantry, who was notorious from Palm Beach to Newport for speaking her mind. "By the way," she said, "I'm going to the trustees' dinner dance at the Metropolitan Museum next week. I wasn't sure exactly what to wear. . . ."

Mrs. Chantry stopped dead in her tracks and stared at her. "You *are?*" She gave Alexa a searching glance of reappraisal, like one of Cinderella's elder sisters watching her put on the glass slipper—clearly Mrs. Chantry did not relish having to change her opinion of what category Alexa fitted into. "Well, well," she said, "Simon *has* taken a step up!"

Alexa decided there was no advantage to correcting the mistake, certainly none in saying that she was going with Arthur Bannerman. It did not seem likely that he would appreciate having Mrs. Chantry spread the news.

"Of course," Sis went on, "it doesn't matter what you wear if you're young and pretty. Which you *are*, my dear." She gave Alexa a wink that was uncomfortably explicit—that Mrs. Chantry was a lesbian was common knowledge, except to Mr. Chantry, who had been married to her for over thirty years without suspecting a thing. "Full-length evening dress, bare shoulders, and strong colors, that's my opinion, if you want it. Don't wear white. It's only for virgins and debutantes."

She examined Alexa from head to foot, as if she were seeing her for the first time. "I think you'll do very well, dear." She gave a throaty laugh. "Fresh blood. Nothing like it to liven up all those stodgy old patricians."

She pushed open the door. "Watch out for Baxter Troubridge if he's there. He's a bottom-pincher."

She sailed out on a gale of frankly bawdy laughter.

ALEXA HAD NEVER had an occasion to feel true stage fright, but as she entered the room on the arm of Arthur Bannerman, she understood at last the full meaning of the phrase. There were perhaps two hundred people in the vast, glassed-in annex in which the Egyptian temple of Dendur had been reassembled, all of them staring at her.

It was not a figment of her imagination—the fact that Arthur Aldon Bannerman was escorting her turned every head in her direction. Alexa could tell, just by looking at the faces of Bannerman's fellow trustees and guests, how strongly they disliked and feared him—but why? These people, she felt sure, had not voted for him, probably had never forgiven him for running for office in the first place.

There was nothing remotely stuffy about Bannerman—he had the politician's knack of working the room, even a room this size—shaking hands, beaming, shouting out, "Hi, feller!" as if he were still campaigning for the Presidency. It was odd being next to him as he made his way around the room—she could watch the expressions of disapproval, sometimes of outright hostility, on well-bred faces. At the approach of Arthur Bannerman, people smiled; as he passed by, the smiles very often turned to a look of anger, envy, sometimes even cold, hard rage. What had he done, she wondered, to make his fellow rich so obvious in their dislike of him? He seemed totally unaware of their feelings— unless the sheer determination of his formidable joviality was a calculated response to it.

Bannerman gave the impression that somebody had bet him he couldn't shake hands with everyone in the room in under ten minutes. When he chose to stop, he introduced her briefly as "Miss Walden," with no further explanation.

She caught the occasional name, but soon they began to run together in her mind, with a few exceptions: John Phipps (elderly, tall, balding, looking more like a stork than a penguin in his tuxedo); Mrs. Nelson Makepeace (an enormous bosom, covered with what seemed to be layers of diamonds, the first living human being whom Alexa had actually seen *wearing* a tiara); Mr. and Mrs. Douglas Dillon (she noticed that Dillon took a step backward at the approach of Arthur Bannerman, as if he were afraid of being physically assaulted); Mr. and Mrs. William F. Buckley (looking as if they had been freeze-dried on the spot); Mr. James Bull (who resembled alarmingly the animal of the same name); countless others whose names and faces she had no time to sort out or remember.

Baxter Troubridge, at least, she was not likely to forget, since he was clearly an out-and-out drunk, a big man with the look of a football player running to fat, his patrician features softened by time and liquor to the point where they seemed about to melt. Bannerman paused to chat with him longer—or more willingly—than with anyone else, making it obvious they were old friends. Troubridge, she could not help noticing, was the picture of old-fashioned elegance in a perfectly tailored double-breasted dinner jacket that went a long way—though perhaps not far enough—to disguise his bulk, except that he had forgotten to put in his studs, so that his starched shirtfront gaped open when he moved, exposing a narrow glimpse of his undershirt. He swayed back and forth on patent-leather pumps like a tree about to be felled. "Long time no see, Arthur," he said jovially. He, at least, did not seem to feel that Bannerman was crazy or dangerous.

"Been under the weather, Bax," Bannerman boomed heartily.

"So I've heard." Troubridge's pale, watery eyes focused imperfectly on Alexa.

"Miss Walden," Bannerman said, his way of introduction. He and

Troubridge, she noticed, did not seem to need much in the way of words to communicate.

"Walden?" Troubridge asked, shaking her hand. "*Walden,*" he repeated slowly, closing his eyes for a moment with the effort of concentrating. "You don't hear much about the Waldens lately. One of the oldest Dutch families—as *you* know better than I do, Miss Walden, no doubt. Henry Walden married a Blair, I think, but that was before my time. *His* son married a Peabody—damned silly girl, too, I forget her name. There was a Walden in the class behind us at Harvard, Arthur, who came to a bad end. . . ."

"Mr. Troubridge is a distinguished genealogist," Bannerman explained to her. "Miss Walden comes from Illinois," he told Troubridge.

"*Illinois?*" Troubridge exclaimed, as if Bannerman had said Ghana or Sri Lanka.

"The heartland, Baxter." Bannerman grinned ferociously. "The land of Lincoln. Out there where the real America is! They don't pay much attention to genealogy where Miss Walden comes from, and it hasn't done them a damned bit of harm, by God!"

That was not strictly true, Alexa thought. Genealogy was just as important where she came from as it was to Baxter Troubridge. Stephenson County had its own chapter of the Illinois Historical Society, and there was a definite local pecking order involving the Daughters of the American Revolution, the descendants of the early settlers, and comparative newcomers who had been in the county for only three or four generations, like her own family. No doubt none of this would seem very meaningful to Troubridge, whose touchstone was probably direct descent from the Mayflower settlers, but it meant a lot in La-Grange, even today.

Bannerman took her arm and moved her away from Troubridge, who was rocking back and forth on his feet, presumably trying to remember which of the New York Waldens had picked up stakes for Illinois in the nineteenth century. "Damned old fool," Bannerman said, taking a glass of Scotch from a waiter. "He was a fool at Groton, and a fool at Harvard, and he's *still* a fool."

"But you're friends? You seem fond of him."

"Fond of him? What makes you think so?"

"You seemed glad to see him. *Really* glad, I mean. You have two different kinds of smiles, you know. Most people get the political one, but Mr. Troubridge got the real thing."

He gave her a searching look over the rim of his glass. "You're a very perceptive young woman," he said. "Well, yes, he's an old friend, fool though he may be. The fortune sets one apart from people, you know —always did, even when I was at Harvard. *Especially* there. I'm not complaining, mind. I'm just stating a fact."

"It didn't set you apart from Troubridge."

He laughed. "Well, Baxter doesn't rate money as high as he does blood, you see. In Baxter's book, what matters is Mayflower descent, that kind of thing. From a genealogist's point of view, the only interesting thing about the Bannermans is that my father married an Aldon. The Aldons came across with the Cabots and Lodges, cold-blooded Puritans to a man—and woman. Do you know the first thing the Mayflower pilgrims did when they landed?"

"Got down on their knees and prayed, I suppose."

"Well, no doubt. But right after that, they hanged some fellow who'd been making trouble on the voyage with another man's wife!" He gave a roar of laughter that brought a moment of silence to the room. "There you have it, my dear girl, the future of America, laid out right there on the damned beach, on day one! Prayer, capital punishment, no fooling around with your neighbor's wife, and grab as much land as you can from the natives. And that, in poor Baxter Troubridge's eyes, is what passes for aristocracy and tradition." He took a sip—a gulp, actually—of his Scotch. "I wouldn't have been elected to the Porcellian if Baxter hadn't spoken up for me."

"What's the Porcellian?"

"A club at Harvard. Damn silly thing, but it meant a lot then. They turned down FDR, you know, and he never forgot it. Probably what made him become a Democrat. People like the Saltonstalls, the Chapins, the Minots, the Aldons, the Troubridges, they were as good as *born* into membership, but I was the first Bannerman to go to Harvard, and in those days a lot of people still thought of my grandfather as the Great Robber Baron. Oh, you have no idea how much hate there was then at the very mention of his name."

"That was a long time ago," she said. "Do you still care?"

"Oh, yes, alas. It's only the hurts of one's childhood that matter—and that last."

A small orchestra, hidden away somewhere in the dark arches of the temple, played string music, hardly even audible above the sedate buzz of conversation. Everywhere there were flowers which, combined with the sweeping glass walls and ceiling, gave the whole hall—it could hardly be called a room—the appearance of a huge, exotic greenhouse. Many of the older women wore full-length ball gowns and long gloves; the younger ones wore the kind of dresses that you saw in *Vogue* at the time of the Paris collections, but seldom on a living human being. She recognized, with considerable envy, Dior, Chanel, Yves Saint Laurent, Ungaro, Valentino, Patou, Givenchy—the kinds of dresses that defied common sense, the normal restraints of economics, even the shape of the female body, works of art as useless and extravagant as the temple that overlooked them, the kind of *haute couture* that every woman dismissed as silly and extreme, and of course secretly lusted after, right down to the last twenty-four-karat gold-thread hussar jacket and pleated, bias-cut, panne velvet skirt. They were the kinds of dresses you could hardly even sit down in, let alone get in and out of a taxi in, that could be pressed only by a French maid, and probably be cleaned only by sending them back to Paris on the Concorde—thoroughly impractical, and nevertheless almost worth killing for. . . .

"Not too many people I want to talk to here," he said, looking around him, an expression of cold distaste on his face. "*Society!*" he spat the word out. "Damned if I don't prefer politicians and bankers."

"You didn't seem too crazy about the bankers last week."

"My dear, I've never known a banker who wasn't a criminal at heart. *Damn!*"

With an expression on his face suggesting that he had just smelled something he didn't like, he was looking at a tall, elderly man making his way toward them. Bannerman's dismay—and dislike—were evident. If he had been a horse, he would have put his ears flat back against his head and bared his teeth. Instead, he gave one of his big smiles—the kind that was patently insincere—exposing his square white teeth as if he were in a dentist's chair. He reached out and seized the other man's hand, pumping it as if he were drawing water from an old well. "Hi there, Courtland!" he bellowed—evidently he did not feel "feller" was appropriate in this case.

"I'm surprised to see *you* here, Arthur," the taller man said, raising an eyebrow. As gestures went, it was, Alexa thought, pretty spectacular —Courtland's eyebrows were so bushy that they seemed to have a life of their own, like small furry animals clinging to his brow. Eyebrows apart, Courtland had a noble if lugubrious face—a high forehead, furrowed as if from constant worry, deep lines on his cheeks, a strong nose and chin. He must have been handsome as a young man, but at some point he had settled his features into an expression of somber dignity that was now hardened like concrete, so that even his faint smile had a chilling effect, on her at least, and apparently on Bannerman. The otherwise carefully cultivated dignity of Courtland's face was marred by a well-trimmed moustache, which made him look vain rather than dashing, and eyes that reminded her of a basset hound's. "I'd heard you weren't feeling up to snuff," Courtland said, in a tone that suggested he was disappointed to see that Bannerman was on his feet and breathing.

"Never felt better in my life, Cordy," Bannerman boomed. "Can't imagine who you've been talking to." Courtland winced at the nickname as if Bannerman had stepped on his toe.

"Eleanor, for one. She says it's months since she's seen you."

At the mention of the name Eleanor, Bannerman's face took on a martyred expression. "Well, it's not that long," he said defensively. "A month, at most, I should think."

"More like two or three. She has the impression that you're under doctor's orders—bundled up by the fireplace drinking herb tea, that sort of thing. . . ." Courtland DeWitt stared at Alexa for a moment, then turned to look at Bannerman and raised his eyebrows again, this time even more impressively.

Bannerman blushed—she would not have believed it if she hadn't seen it—a rosy blush, like that of a child caught out in a lie, starting first in his cheeks, then spreading to the back of his neck. He seemed surprised by it himself, as if it was an unfamiliar sensation, something out of his childhood that he couldn't at first identify; then realizing what was happening, he moved quickly to cover it, taking out his white pocket handkerchief and dabbing at his face. "Too damn warm in here," he muttered. He balled the handkerchief up in his hand and stuffed it back into the breast pocket of his dinner jacket, where it made an unsightly bulge.

He had moved just far enough away from her side so that he could have pretended they had just met, and for an instant she thought he was going to do just that. Then he clenched his jaws and introduced her. "By the way, Courtland, let me introduce you to Miss Alexa Walden." He stared at Courtland with unconcealed distaste. "My brother-in-law, Courtland DeWitt," he said flatly. "A lawyer," he added with disgust.

DeWitt gave her a mournful grimace that no doubt served him for a smile and shook her hand with all the enthusiasm of a man who has just picked up a dead fish. "Pleased to meet you," he said, though he didn't look in the least pleased. "Sorry to interrupt your chat."

He looked over her head, apparently trying to see who she was with, but there were no single men of the appropriate age standing nearby. He obviously hoped she would have the tact to leave him alone with his reluctant brother-in-law, who was wavering back and forth like a bull trying to decide between charging and strategic retreat.

"I'd like a word with you, Arthur. You're not an easy man to reach on the telephone these days." DeWitt glared in Alexa's direction, all but ordering her to move on, like a cop at the scene of a crime.

She stuck to her ground. Bannerman, blushing again, this time more sharply, said, "By the way, Courtland, Miss Walden is my—ah—guest." She wondered if he had been about to say "date."

DeWitt managed to raise not just one eyebrow, but both. He could hardly have looked more startled if Bannerman had bitten him—which he seemed to feel Bannerman might do at any moment. "I see," he said. He looked at her with considerably more curiosity. "You're a friend of Cecilia's, of course?"

"No," she said. "I've never met her."

"Miss Walden is in the art business. Sold me a Baldur."

"A what?"

"Damned fine painter. You ought to look at his work, don't you know? Pick one up while prices are still at ground level."

"If it's anything like the paintings up at Albany—the ones Eleanor refused to have in the house—no, thank you."

"You've got a closed mind, Courtland. A lawyer's mind. Is my sister here?"

"I'm on my own. Just came for the dinner. I'll be leaving early. Elizabeth hasn't been feeling well. Don't like to leave her alone too long."

"She hasn't been feeling well for thirty years. Truth is, she's as strong as a horse."

"*She* doesn't think so. She'd appreciate a call from you."

"I doubt that very much. I didn't think anything remains to be said after Elizabeth's last talk with me. I don't need another lecture on my sins as a parent."

"She meant well, Arthur."

"I doubt that even more. I've known Elizabeth longer than you have. Give her my best, however."

A waiter appeared, unbidden, to take Bannerman's glass and exchange it for a fresh drink. Bannerman seemed as embarrassed in front of DeWitt by this as he had been to be caught escorting Alexa.

DeWitt stared at the glass in Bannerman's hand, his expression more mournful than ever, like a doctor preparing to break bad news to a patient. "I believe we're about to go in to dinner," he said pointedly.

"Are we?" Bannerman took a deep gulp of his drink, defiantly. "Then I'd better finish this first, hadn't I?"

"You know best, Arthur." DeWitt's face made it clear he thought nothing of the kind.

"Damned right I do." Bannerman drained the glass, held it out, and, as usual, a waiter appeared as if called by some inaudible signal, to remove it from his hand. "Come, Alexandra," he said loudly, offering his arm. "You must be starving." He did not say goodbye to DeWitt.

"Arthur," she said, as he swept her into dinner, realizing suddenly that it was the first time he had used her first name, "who *is* Eleanor?"

He paused, sighed, stared at the table, then said, almost reluctantly, "My mother. . ."

He seemed unable to finish the sentence, then cleared his throat. "My mother," he said, "is a remarkable woman."

"MOTHER." When Arthur Bannerman spoke the word, his face registered a whole gamut of emotions, many of them contradictory. She thought about it as they danced sedately—and after some hesitation on her part—once dinner was over.

Bannerman talked about his mother with a degree of fear that struck her as amazing in a man who was certainly more than sixty years old. Eleanor Bannerman seemed to represent for her elderly son a tangled web of duties, obligations, and rules, against which he still measured himself—or was measured by her, and mostly found wanting.

Picking at his food, he told her about Eleanor. He did not speak about her with affection, but with awe. It was because of her that the New York State Thruway went up to Albany on the west side of the Hudson, he explained, for its original path would have taken it past or, God forbid, *through*, Kiawa, so former Governor Dewey had been summoned to Kiawa to carry her displeasure to President Eisenhower, who, as a Republican and a general, knew when it was wise to retreat, and ordered a new survey. It was at Eleanor's insistence that the railway station at Kiawa was still in service, complete with a porter and a ticket clerk—even though only one train a day stopped there. Cyrus Bannerman's private Pullman car still stood on a siding there, perfectly maintained, the Bannerman family's legal right to have it attached to any express on the Hudson line having provided a comic, but exasperating, difficulty for the lawyers during the merger of the New York Central into Amtrak. Eleanor's determination to prevent the removal of a small rocky island in the middle of the Hudson River had pitted her against three successive governors of New York State, the U.S. Army Corps of Engineers, and the U.S. Coast Guard, but the island remained in her hands, or at any rate, in her view, while the main ship channel had been dredged at great inconvenience and cost to the taxpayers, on the other side of it. . . .

Alexa tried to stop thinking about this formidable presence in Arthur Bannerman's life and to concentrate on her feet instead, which seemed to be getting in Arthur Bannerman's way. Dancing—the old-fashioned, slow kind—was not something she often had occasion to do, or had ever really learned well. True, back home in LaGrange, girls learned the rudiments of dancing—the kind of dancing their parents and grandparents did—and she remembered shuffling back and forth in the school gym, usually in the arms of another girl while the boys giggled and blushed on the sidelines, to music of another era, but when she was old enough to go to *real* dances, none of that meager knowledge had proved useful. To her dismay, Arthur Bannerman danced with a precision and enthusiasm that put her to shame.

She was grateful for his tact. "I'm a little rusty," she said apologetically.

"So am I. Been ages since I danced," he said, beaming with pleasure —he, at least, was obviously enjoying himself. "Used to love it. When I was a boy, we were taught to dance, you see. A dancing instructor came twice a week to give us private lessons. Mother used to sit and watch us go through our paces when we danced, and with *her* eye on you, believe me you didn't make the same mistake twice. Father loved dancing. For his thirtieth wedding anniversary he brought a full orchestra up to Kiawa and danced a waltz with Mother—just the two of them, alone in the middle of the ballroom, while everybody else stood and watched. I remember it as clearly as if it were yesterday—'The Emperor Waltz,' it was, Father in tails, Eleanor wearing the Bannerman diamonds, with the tiara. She *looked* every inch an empress, you know. Ah, well, I don't suppose the ballroom has been used but once in the past ten years. . . ."

"For what?"

"My son Robert's wedding," Bannerman said with an expression that discouraged further questions on the subject. He moved a little closer, his arm around her waist now, a change of pressure so slight that it would have been invisible to anybody watching them dance, but which she felt—and understood—instantly.

There was nothing overt about it, nothing obvious—it was simply a change of degree in their relationship, a gesture of familiarity. She had only to back away an inch or so, and Bannerman would no doubt move his arm so that only the flat of his hand touched her back again. The choice was hers, and she knew it—knew it instinctively, for in the dances of her generation, there was no place for such a small, subtle touch of intimacy. The direct approach was the fashion.

She allowed her cheek to rest lightly against his shoulder, leaving, as she realized a moment too late, a trace of Lancôme Blush Satin on his dinner jacket.

Bannerman didn't notice. "I'm having a whale of a time," he said. "I suppose it's not all that exciting for you. Pretty girl like you, you must go out dancing all the time, eh?"

"No, hardly ever. Nobody seems to dance any more in New York. Nobody I know, anyway."

"Pity. Ah, they're playing a fast one."

Bannerman held her close—so close that she could feel the studs of his dress shirt against her chest as she struggled to put her feet in the right place. He looked happier than she had ever seen him before, although a little red in the face—then he suddenly drew back, his face a mask. "Damn!" he said. "Let's sit this one out."

She was a little disappointed—she had just been getting in the mood —but she reminded herself that he was over sixty and might be pushing himself too hard.

"Would you like to sit down?" she asked.

"No, no, I'm fine." His tone was impatient, even irritable, and she wondered if she had done anything wrong, or whether Bannerman had simply let himself go too far and now regretted it. "I thought DeWitt had gone home," he said. "There he is, large as life, dancing with some old gal and staring right at us."

She was annoyed. If Bannerman was ashamed of being seen with her, he shouldn't have invited her in the first place. Besides, he was a grown-up man and a widower. Then it occurred to her that it might simply be a question of his dignity, that the head of the Bannerman family shouldn't be seen in public dancing like a teenager with a girl half his age—no, almost a *third* his age—pressed close to him. "Does it matter what he thinks?" she asked.

"DeWitt? No, no, not a damn. He's a horse's ass. Always has been." Some of Bannerman's good humor returned. He smiled at her. "Truth is, I was a little out of breath. Enjoyed every second of it, though. Haven't had such a good time in years."

She guessed it was a polite lie. Still, he put his arm around her waist and pushed a way through the crowd to the bar, where, she was not surprised to see, Baxter Troubridge seemed to have installed himself as a permanent fixture, leaning against the cloth-covered table as if it would collapse were he to step away from it. His face was the color of a ripe plum, but he seemed in full control of his faculties, as if a lifetime of heavy drinking had inoculated him against its effects. He raised his glass. "Saw you dancing," he said. "Damned impressive. All I can do to put one foot in front of the other."

"You don't take care of yourself," Bannerman said. He seemed to relax in Troubridge's presence. "I exercise every morning. Swim four times a week. Got to keep the old circulation going, Bax."

"I try not to disturb mine, Arthur, personally. A nice steady flow is good enough for me. Used to swim, at the Racquet Club, but the sight of my contemporaries in their trunks put me off the whole damned thing. Where on earth do you go?"

"I've got my own pool, Bax," Bannerman said shortly.

Troubridge nodded. "I should have known. I probably did know. One forgets the Bannerman touch. There can't be many apartments in New York that have a full-sized, glassed-in pool above them, but it stands to reason that yours would have one."

"William Randolph Hearst had one, too," Bannerman said with a sharp edge to his voice, though he was apparently used to Troubridge's making fun of him. Troubridge was older money than Bannerman, she remembered, but probably much less of it.

"It's been a long time since I danced," Troubridge said. "Robert's wedding was the last time, I think. How is the boy, Arthur?"

"Doing splendidly."

Troubridge gave a skeptical smile. "He must be what—forty now, at least? How time flies."

Bannerman did not look pleased at being reminded in front of Alexa that his elder son was in his forties. "Robert is forty-two," he said in his coldest and most clipped tone.

"Old enough to run for the Presidency." Troubridge smiled. "Fancy that. Hard to believe, isn't it?"

Drinking had the effect of slowing down Troubridge's facial expressions so that they were slightly out of sync, like a badly dubbed foreign movie. Once he started a smile it stayed on his face too long, as if he couldn't stop it or had forgotten it was there. "What *are* Robert's future plans, by the way? One hears rumors about the Senate, the governorship. When is he coming home?"

"When the President recalls him," Bannerman said stiffly. "He is a United States ambassador."

"He must miss New York, poor fellow. And you must miss having him by your side, Arthur."

"Quite." Bannerman's expression would have been sufficient to make anyone else change the subject, but Troubridge was impervious to it.

"Helluva feller, Miss Walden. You wait till you meet him. A real hellraiser, right, Arthur?"

"I'm hoping Caracas will cool him down a bit."

"Wrong climate, Arthur, wrong climate altogether. You should have held out for the Court of St. James's. Robert would look splendid in knee breeches. Of course, I suppose the divorce ditched that. Eleanor must have taken it hard. How is the old girl?"

"Bearing up quite well. Under the circumstances."

"Tough as nails. She's the eighth wonder of the world. You haven't met her, have you, Miss Walden? No? You've got a treat in store."

The orchestra struck up, and Bannerman grabbed her quite roughly by the arm. "We mustn't keep you, Bax," he said to Troubridge. "There must be other people who want to chat with you."

Troubridge raised his glass as they turned from him. "Sorry about that," Bannerman said. "Poor Baxter gossips like an old woman."

"He seems fond of your son."

"He's Robert's godfather. Always sees the boy's side of things. Robert can do no wrong in Baxter's eyes."

"But not in yours?"

Bannerman gave her a hard stare—a warning that she was treading on forbidden ground, perhaps? "Robert will get his chance," he said, his teeth clenched.

"He looks just like you."

Whatever was left of Bannerman's geniality instantly vanished. His face was as hard as a rock—quite different from the man she was beginning to get used to. "You *know* Robert?" To her amazement, he seemed frightened as well as angry, his voice sharp as a knife. She had the impression that he was recoiling from her like an animal facing an unexpected threat.

"I meant from photographs."

"Ah." He was obviously relieved. "Well, we do look alike, yes. Unfortunately we don't *think* alike."

The music ended. Bannerman held onto her for a moment. There was a bright flash, and he instantly jumped away, turning toward the photographer with an expression of outrage on his face, only to find that it was a young woman. Had it been a man, Alexa thought, Bannerman would have given the photographer a burst of patrician anger, but he clearly wasn't sure how to deal with a young woman. "I prefer not to be photographed without my permission," he said stiffly, "if you don't mind."

"I'm sorry, Mr. Bannerman," the girl said. "I'm from *Town and Country*. We *did* want one of you. If it's all right, I mean."

He stood his ground, hands jammed into the pockets of his jacket, unsmiling, chin thrust forward. "Very well," he said at last. "You may take one only, a group. The first one will *not* be used. Is that clearly understood?"

The girl blushed with anger, but young as she was, she obviously knew that Arthur Bannerman was not somebody who could be annoyed with impunity. His wishes counted for something, and clearly he meant exactly what he said. She whispered something to her companion, who had been writing down in his notebook the names of everyone she photographed, and he quickly moved a few other people over to stand beside them, turning it into a group picture, with Bannerman in the center, glaring furiously at the camera. Alexa stood next to him, but he didn't look at her as the flash went off. Anyone looking at it might have supposed they were total strangers. Certainly there was nothing to indicate that she was with him. "That's it," Bannerman said firmly. "Thank you."

He turned away, determined not to give the photographer a chance at a second shot. "Damned impertinence," he muttered.

"She was only doing her job."

"I made it a rule when I ran for President—I won't be photographed dancing or wearing funny hats."

She did not believe him. Maybe he was telling the truth about his wishes as a presidential candidate, but it was perfectly obvious that he had been reluctant to be photographed dancing with *her*, or even alone with her.

What's wrong with me? she thought. Then it struck her that the real question was, What was wrong with Arthur Bannerman? Did he really think he could take her out and pretend she didn't exist—then lie to her about it as well? How much, in fact, did she know about him? Almost nothing. His loneliness had appealed to her, but for all she knew, there might be somebody in his life who wouldn't appreciate seeing a photograph of him dancing with another woman. Her pleasure in the evening evaporated. She felt used, shabbily treated, and resentful that he hadn't turned out to be the kind of man she thought he was. "I think I'd like to go home now," she said.

He blinked nervously—a little alarmed, she guessed, at the possibility that she might add to his troubles by making a scene in public. Apparently even Arthur Bannerman was afraid of a woman's displeasure. "Are you sure?" he asked. "I mean, it's not that late."

"It's well past eleven. Besides, there may be more photographers coming. I wouldn't want to embarrass you by standing too close when they take your picture."

She could see that Bannerman was not used to being confronted. She wondered if his children had experienced that look—the eyes hooded as he stared down his nose at her, the corners of his mouth turned down sharply, his jaw standing out like a rock in a storm. If so, it was not hard to understand why he and his son Robert didn't get along—and maybe why he didn't see much of his other children as well.

"You're being foolish," he said.

"I don't think so. I don't usually go out with men who are ashamed of being seen with me. It's a new experience. Most men are *happy* to be seen in public with me."

He sighed. "Of course I'm not ashamed."

"Then why the scene with that poor photographer? And why did you stop dancing the moment you saw what's-his-name? DeWitt?"

"It's no reflection on you. You must believe me."

"I don't see why I should believe you. That's the way it looked to me. That's the way it would look to anyone."

"Yes, possibly . . . I suppose you're right. . . ." He had dropped his pose of arrogance. He seemed humble, embarrassed, not about to argue the point. "Listen to me," he said urgently. "You don't understand my situation."

"I understand mine, and I don't like it."

He grabbed her wrist. "I don't want Robert to hear about this," he whispered hoarsely. "Or see a photograph of us together."

She had expected him to mention a woman whom he didn't want to offend, or even his mother, whose opinions he respected so much. "Robert?" she asked. "Your *son* Robert?"

"Exactly."

"Why would he care? You're his father. What business is it of his if you go out dancing with someone? With me?"

He looked at her for a moment in silence, as if he were trying to decide whether or not he could trust her with a secret. He made up his mind, then took a deep breath. "A couple of years ago, Robert tried to have me put out to pasture. A photograph of me dancing with a young

girl, and, believe me, Alexandra, Robert would be on the next flight up
from Caracas and loaded for bear."

It was an expression she hadn't heard for years—one of her father's
favorites. Somehow it erased her anger with Bannerman—that and the
fact that he was the first person who had ever used her full name instead
of shortening it to "Alexa." It was easily apparent that he was telling the
truth this time. She wasn't sure she understood how he could be afraid
of his own son, but clearly he was. "Why?"

"Robert is one of those fellers who's always looking for leverage, don't
you know? He's been pretty quiet down there in Venezuela, playing the
diplomat, but I've no wish to prod him to life again, not just now when
I'm planning a few big changes. . . . Well, no need to bore you with all
that."

Whatever the changes were that Bannerman had in mind, his voice
dropped so low that she could hardly make out the words. "It's not a
good time for me to get my name in some goddamn tabloid, Alexandra.
If it weren't for that, I'd be happy to be photographed dancing with
you. Proud to, in fact. It would do my stock a world of good among my
contemporaries—set their goddamn pacemakers humming with envy!"
He laughed, though a little less boisterously than usual.

She was mollified, though not completely. He had his reasons, she
could accept that, though she wasn't sure she completely understood
them, or that he'd told her more than a small fraction of the truth. She
allowed him to take her hand, but the mood between them was broken,
and they both knew it.

"I suppose it *is* getting late," he said.

She nodded. "I'll get my things," she said. Bannerman waved her on
her way, glumly taking up a position behind a vast piece of ancient
stonework, presumably to avoid having to say goodbye to people he
knew. He sulked among the hieroglyphics like a molting eagle, the
expression on his face quite sufficient to protect his privacy.

She went into the ladies room. Inside, two well-dressed women were
talking to each other in the loud, self-assured voices of the upper-class
rich, as they touched up their makeup. They did not look at her.
"Ghastly evening," she heard one of them say—a lady in a gray silk
Valentino that must have cost five thousand dollars and exposed shoulders and breasts that were suntanned to the color and consistency of
well-done bacon.

"Oh, I don't know, darling," the other woman said. She was a few
years younger than her companion, not more than forty, with the sinewy muscles of an athlete. Seen from the back, she might have been a
professional tennis player, except for a diamond necklace that must
have been worth a fortune. She had the slightly vacant eyes and stiff
posture of somebody who drinks hard and is coasting, late in the eve-

ning, just a hair's-breadth below her limit. "It beats last night—'The Moth Ball,' as Thomas calls it, at the Pierre. All those sweating FFVs in their hunting-pink coats dancing the Virginia reel and singing 'Dixie.' Thomas *loved* it, of course. Anything for a chance to get pissed to the gills with the rest of the Virginia horsey set."

"I used to like that sort of thing myself, darling."

"Well, who didn't? At seventeen. But of course for all practical purposes, Thomas *is* seventeen. He still thinks women and horses respond to the same treatment, and frankly he isn't even all that good with horses, poor brutes. If I had to do it all over again, I'd marry Yankee money instead of Southern charm."

"Well, you've done it all over again, at least twice, darling, so you should know. Speaking of Yankee money, wasn't that Arthur Bannerman dancing with a girl young enough to be his granddaughter?"

"Arthur Bannerman? I thought he was dead!"

"Of course he's not *dead*, darling. He's just in disgrace. There was some dreadful scandal—I can't remember what. . . ."

"Robert's divorce?"

"No, no, *before* that. Anyway, he's been out of sight since whatever it was happened. A girlfriend of mine—Babs Burgess, you must know her, the one whose second husband killed himself skydiving—told me the family virtually had him locked up in a wing of Kiawa like the Prisoner of Zenda, with his meals sent up on trays. . . . Sandy Burgess —whoever heard of a man taking up parachute jumping at the age of sixty, I ask you?—told me *he* had a friend who'd been to Kiawa and said Arthur was mad as a hatter, drunk out of his mind at noon, baying at the moon all night from a locked room in the attic, all that sort of thing. . . . Robert apparently decided his father wasn't fit to handle the family fortune, and there was a terrible row about it."

"It sounds like Thomas's goddamned Southern Gothic family. They all sit down and bay at the moon in Middleburg whenever it's full—but *they* think it's normal."

"Darling, I went to Foxcroft, too. It's perfectly normal down there. It *isn't* normal for a Bannerman."

"Robert's the only one I've met. *He* seemed normal enough."

"If that's what you call normal . . . If Robert ever gets to the White House, he'll have women in and out of there just like Jack Kennedy. There are *terrible* stories about Arthur, you know—Thornton told me he didn't even bother to visit his wife when she was dying of cancer. And he drove one of his children to suicide. Anyway, there he was, large as life, dancing away with quite a pretty girl, in an ordinary sort of way. . . . Strange."

"Who is she?"

"Damned if I know, darling. No serious jewelry yet, so it can't amount to much between them. . . ."

Alexa slipped into one of the toilets and closed the door, hoping the conversation about her was over, when she heard a familiar voice growl, "I can't believe my goddamned eyes!"

She had not seen Sis Chantry at all, had no idea she was here this evening, but there was no mistaking the gravelly chain-smoker's voice. "Did you *see* Arthur Bannerman tonight?"

"We were just talking about him, Sis," the lady in the Valentino said. "Who was the girl?"

"A complete nobody. She works in an art gallery, for God's sake! Frightful modern stuff. And to think she was buttering me up about what to wear . . ."

Alexa felt herself blush with embarrassment. It came as no surprise to her that Mrs. Chantry would think of her as a "nobody," but it was still not pleasant to hear. The hell with the old bitch, she thought. She would find a way somehow to let Mrs. Chantry know she had overheard her remark.

"Yes, but who *is* she, Sis, dear? What's the *story?*"

"I don't know. He met her at some repulsive show. She's the girl-friend of Simon Wolff, the art dealer. Or she *was*—I think he dropped her a while ago."

"Never heard of him, Sis. But how on earth did she get her hooks into Arthur Bannerman, I wonder?"

Sis Chantry laughed throatily. "The usual way, I suppose. But what a cunning little bitch! She never gave me a hint of it."

"Well, she's cleverer than you thought, Sis. One up to her."

"Clever? Bannerman's got one foot in the grave and the other in a bottle. It doesn't take much for a good-looking young gal to pull the wool over an old man's eyes."

"Oh, I don't know," the woman in the Valentino said. "He looked rather sexy to me, even if he *is* a drunken monster."

"Oh my, yes," the younger woman with the stunning diamond neck-lace said in a throaty whisper. "Very much like my father-in-law. Madly attractive. What a shame to waste it on a little tart like that."

Alexa gasped. She was no longer blushing with embarrassment or the shame of eavesdropping—she was flushed with anger, her skin bright pink and burning hot. She hated scenes, and would normally go to any lengths to avoid one, but being called a "tart" was too much for her. She stood up and pushed open the door, steeling herself for an angry confrontation, only to find that she was a moment too late—the three women had left, their bare backs just visible as the door closed behind them. She stood in front of the mirror, glaring at her image until she felt in control of herself again.

It was strange, she thought, but the conversation she had overheard made her feel more warmly toward Arthur Bannerman. She under-stood now his fear of being seen in public, his quick changes of mood.

She did not know him well, but she was fairly sure his reputation was undeserved. Certainly he was not a drunk, nor was he senile, but he must surely be aware of what people were saying about him, and she guessed it must cause him great pain—which of course, being a Bannerman, he could not allow himself to show. She had liked him in the beginning. Now she began to feel a certain respect for him as well.

To hell with what people think or say, she told herself. She walked out of the ladies room boldly, her back as straight as her mother would have wished, and rejoined Arthur. Her eyes fixed firmly on him, she put her arm in his, stood on her toes and gave him a kiss.

"Thank you for a lovely evening," she said.

She knew people were staring at them. She paid no attention. Together, arm-in-arm, they walked down the wide steps to where Jack waited with the car.

"THERE'S SOMET'ING for you downstairs," the superintendent growled. "You wan' I bring it up?"

He had obviously been waiting for her, standing in the entrance hall and wiping the dusty mirror with a filthy shop rag. It was one of Alexa's ambitions to live in a building with a doorman—perhaps not in the same splendor as Arthur Bannerman, but at least somebody in a uniform, possibly with white gloves. The super, though he spent most of his time in the basement, wore several layers of clothes on top of a stained, greasy boiler suit, and a knitted wool watch cap pulled down over his ears, even in the summer. If he had been black or Hispanic she might have persuaded herself it was necessary to like him, but since he was a Central European of some sort and an outspoken bigot, she felt free to dislike him heartily.

From the beginning—and despite tips and Christmas envelopes that seemed lavish to her—he had been uncooperative and surly, apparently convinced that no young woman who lived alone on the West Side could be altogether what she seemed. When packages arrived for her, which was seldom, he usually managed to be absent, so there was nobody to sign for them; if he did accept them, he left them in the hall for her to pick up. It was out of the ordinary for him to offer to bring anything up.

"If you please," she said. It was part of her Midwestern heritage to show extreme politeness to people she disliked—not that it seemed to have any effect one way or another in New York.

She went upstairs and unlocked her door. Before she was inside she heard the super wheezing and thumping his way up the stairs. Usually an interval of hours, or days, followed his promise to do anything, and she was still wondering what had energized him when he appeared at the door, cradling in his arms a bulky package wrapped in brown paper as if it were a baby. "You got to keep 'em cold," the super said, placing it on the table. "The man told me to keep 'em in my icebox till you come home."

"What man?"

"Mr. Johnson. If every nigger was like him, New York would be a better place to live." He paused. "I be up tomorrow first thing, fix the faucet."

For weeks she had been leaving notes to complain that the kitchen faucet was dripping, to no effect. Snoop though he was, the super had a rare talent for vanishing when there was a job to be done, however small. Apparently he had undergone a change of heart—he was positively beaming at her now. She thanked him and closed the door.

The plain brown paper had been neatly stapled with no attempt to simulate glossy packaging. She tore it apart carefully and lifted it off to reveal a moss-filled garden basket filled with orchids—not the kind you saw in florists' shops, which were usually white and lifeless, with their stems stiffly encased in little glass tubes. These were orchids like none she had ever seen, in strange, iridescent colors and shapes, some as tiny as violets, others enormous. They had been arranged with natural simplicity, so that they appeared to be growing out of the moss.

Attached to the basket was a plain white card that read, "I had these sent down from Kiawa." Below that Bannerman had written, in a sprawling hand, "So many thanks, AAB."

She made herself a cup of tea and sat down to look at the flowers, which seemed to light up the room. Flowers as such were no surprise, really. She did not receive flowers every day, or even every month, but it was the kind of gesture you expected from older men—though Bannerman was so much older than most of the men she knew that the phrase hardly seemed to make sense when applied to him.

These flowers, however, represented something quite different. How many people could send for rare orchids from their own greenhouse?

She decided the orchids were a perfect opportunity to call him. Then she realized she didn't have his number.

She turned the card over in her fingers. On the back was a telephone number in the same careless handwriting.

Arthur Bannerman apparently thought of everything.

"JESUS!" Simon said when she told him about the orchids. "I hope you unwrapped them carefully. You never know—he might have put a diamond bracelet in the moss."

"Don't be silly."

"Silly, hell! The Duke of Westminster sent Coco Chanel a box of chocolates with a diamond at the bottom of the box, so she'd find it when she'd eaten all of them. Well, of course, Chanel didn't *eat* chocolate, so she gave the box to the maid, who ate the top layer and threw the rest away. . . ."

"I don't see Arthur Bannerman doing that kind of thing, Simon."

"Maybe not."

Simon's mood had improved and they were back on speaking terms again. She wondered why. Sometimes Simon cheered up spontaneously after they had quarreled about something, but as a rule it required either an apology on her part—and some sacrifice to his wishes —or a piece of good fortune extraordinary enough to make him forget his bruised feelings.

Simon's smile made it clear that he knew something she didn't. She did not ask him what it was—he was never capable of keeping a secret for long enough to make it worthwhile trying to pry it out of him. "I had a call from the Museum of Modern Art," he said. "Apparently someone there was very impressed with Bannerman's Baldur. They want to buy one for the museum."

He cracked his knuckles—a sound she hated. "Do you know what that's going to do to Baldur's prices? Your friend Bannerman will end up with a bargain, once Baldur's in MOMA's permanent collection. Getting friendly with Bannerman was the smartest move you've made in a long time, baby. I'm proud of you." He cleared his throat. "And I'm sorry I lost my temper at dinner. No hard feelings?"

She promised that she harbored no hard feelings, congratulated him on his good fortune, and went back into her cubbyhole of an office.

She did not have a devious nature—she knew that from experience —but it didn't take a Machiavelli to recognize the fine hand of Arthur Aldon Bannerman at work, pulling strings by remote control. He had guessed from what she had told him that Simon was angry with her and had found an easy way to appease him—a way to make Simon *happy* that she was spending time with Bannerman. Some of the credit for Baldur's rise to museum status would fall on her—a nice side effect, designed, no doubt, to make *her* happy. There was a wonderful economy in Bannerman's way of doing things. At the same time, Bannerman had managed to double, or even treble, the value of his painting overnight, with just one call to one of his friends on the board of the MOMA.

She picked up the phone and dialed his number. He answered on the first ring.

"I called to thank you for the flowers," she said. "They're beautiful."

"Aren't they? My father took a great interest in orchids. In his day the greenhouses at Kiawa were famous, you know. He had species and hybrids that didn't exist anywhere else—botanists came from all over the world to study them. Most of that's gone now, I'm afraid."

"I hear the Museum of Modern Art decided to acquire a Baldur."

Bannerman chuckled. "Saw the light, did they?"

"I thought you might have had something to do with it."

"A word to the wise. Nothing more. Your Mr. Wolff should be pleased."

He sounded remarkably pleased with himself. She was about to say that Simon was not *her* Mr. Wolff, but, remembering how easily Bannerman's moods changed, she thought better of it. "I've never seen so many orchids before," she said.

"You shall have as many as you like. Eleanor can't stand them, so they bloom and die. A terrible waste. Like so much at Kiawa." He was silent for a moment. Whenever he brought up the subject of Kiawa, it seemed to depress him.

"I had a wonderful time," she said, to break the spell.

"Splendid. I enjoyed myself, too. Haven't had so much fun in ages. You wouldn't be free for lunch, by the way, would you? There are a few things I wanted to talk to you about. I don't want to monopolize your time. . . ."

She toyed with the idea of saying that she was busy, but decided it wasn't worth the trouble. Lunch with Arthur Bannerman would certainly be more interesting than a tuna salad sandwich at her desk. "I could make it for lunch, sure," she said, in an offhanded tone that suggested she didn't much care one way or the other—there was no point in making it too easy for him, after all.

"You're sure Mr. Wolff won't mind?"

"Simon probably won't even notice." Even if he did, she thought, he would be delighted—her friendship with Bannerman was obviously the best thing she had done for Simon in a long time, from his point of view—a lucky break that might lead anywhere. "He certainly won't mind."

"Ah, good. I'll have Jack pick you up at twelve-thirty. We'll meet at the Foundation."

Why the Foundation? she wondered. The Bannerman Foundation was almost as famous as the Ford Foundation or the Guggenheim. It had begun life as a kind of private think tank for the Bannermans, but by now it was an integral part of American cultural and academic life, spawning research grants, commissions, scholarships, and controversy on every imaginable subject, its headquarters picketed daily by everybody from creationists to disgruntled artists.

She was a little sorry not to be invited to Lutèce, or The Four Seasons, or "21," or wherever it was that Bannerman went when he went out. She liked being admired, and didn't feel it was anything for an attractive young woman to be ashamed of. Frankly, she liked picking her own food from the menu, too, when she was invited out, rather than being served whatever Arthur Bannerman's staff had prepared for him.

She would have to make an effort to pry him loose from his habits, she decided, if they were going to get along.

She didn't think it would be difficult to do.

THE BUILDING was anything but nondescript, but seemed almost defiantly anonymous. Immediately opposite the sculpture garden of the Museum of Modern Art and just down the corner from the University Club, it was one of the most valuable small pieces of real estate in the city, a five-story townhouse, impeccably preserved, the kind of building that any developer would give his eyeteeth to demolish. Polished marble steps led to the kind of ornate doorway with which the nineteenth-century rich announced their wealth—nymphs, muscular gods on horseback, and dolphins, carved in stone, climbed upward to support a glazed bronze ornamental canopy. The art nouveau doors were wrought iron and opaque glass, and they looked as if no normal-sized human being could have moved them.

To one side of the building, at street level, was a more modest door. Jack led her to it, opened the door for her, and left her in an elegantly furnished hallway. There was an elevator door in front of her. She pushed the button and stepped in. It rose automatically. There was a Mondrian on one wall of the elevator. The Bannerman touch, she thought—he put paintings in his elevators that other people would have placed over the fireplaces of their living rooms.

The door opened silently and she walked into what looked like a modern living room, rather than an office. Skylights and hidden lighting made it seem as airy as a greenhouse, though there was something antiseptic about the place, as if the room were unlived in. Arthur Bannerman was standing in front of the fireplace, smiling. "Good of you to come," he said, as if she were here on business. He seemed nervous.

There was a gleaming chrome-and-glass trolley in one corner of the room. He went over to it and poured himself a Scotch, thought it over, and made it a generous double. He opened a bottle of Perrier for her. Had he gone to the trouble of laying in a stock for her? she wondered. She could not help noticing that he had a good deal of trouble opening the bottle. It seemed to be the kind of small, domestic duty he hadn't done for himself in years. He hacked off a ragged piece of lime with the expression of a man who has just completed an act requiring extreme dexterity.

"No servants here," he explained. "Not like the damned apartment, where they're underfoot all the time." He came over to the sofa and patted the cushion, indicating that she should sit down beside him.

There was a crock of cheese and some crackers on a silver plate on the glass coffee table in front of them. Bannerman carefully moved the crackers into a neat row, as if he wanted to keep his hands busy. He did not take one, nor did he offer her any. "Sometimes a fellow needs a place to—ah, get away from things," he said.

"I guess so," she said.

He placed his hand gently on her knee. "Well, it has its advantages," he said complacently. "A nice, private place, right in midtown Manhattan—and nobody even knows it exists."

"I thought the building was an office?"

"Well, so does everybody, damn it. That's the point. Even most of the people who work here don't know about this apartment. Those who do suppose it's for visiting dignitaries—which it is, more or less. All sorts of people have stayed here without the press finding out. Damned useful thing to have, when you're in politics. And in business, these days . . ."

"I suppose so."

"No question about it," he boomed, as if he were trying to sell her the apartment. He drained his Scotch and gave the cheese and crackers a moody glare. There was a key next to the silver plate, fastened to a gold key chain. "I won't beat around the bush," he said at last. "I've been thinking a lot about you." He paused. "You're a damned attractive young woman, you know," he said, in a tone that suggested the fact might have escaped her attention.

What was it about men? she asked herself. They never had a sense of timing. Last night at the party she might have been receptive, before Bannerman had shunted her to one side for the photograph, but today he was as stiff and self-important as if this were a board meeting or a financial transaction. Last night she had found him attractive despite his age, perhaps even—she admitted to herself—*because* of it, but now he was just a familiar figure, an older man coming on to a young woman. She had been through that before, more times than she cared to remember, and it held no attraction for her.

"Thank you," she said modestly. "You must know a lot of attractive women, though."

He seemed put out—which she meant him to be. "I've met my share, yes," he admitted, with just a trace of self-satisfaction. "But there's something about you . . . well, let me put it bluntly. I find *you* damned attractive. I may not be making myself clear—it's been some time since I've had a conversation like this."

"I think it's pretty clear, Arthur." She decided to let him do the work.

"You're not shocked, I hope? You didn't seem to me the kind of young woman who would be, frankly."

"I'm not shocked, no. On the other hand, it's not exactly the most romantic thing I've heard."

"I'm a little old for romance, don't you think? I thought the direct approach might save time. I didn't think your generation went in for candlelight and romantic music. But I wouldn't want you to think I don't have *feelings* about you, my dear. I do. Strong feelings, as a matter of fact."

"Well, that's nice, Arthur. I'm really glad. But what kind?"

He thought about that. "The most, ah, personal kind. Feelings, I must tell you, that I haven't had for years." He coughed.

"I'm not trying to be difficult," she said. "It's just that I wasn't prepared for this conversation. I guess I should have been."

"If my timing is poor, I apologize."

"Oh, don't be so damned *stiff*—I'm not even sure what you're talking about. Besides, you haven't even *looked* at me. If I make you nervous and embarrassed, why bother?"

He sighed. "Perhaps I've gone about this the wrong way. I realize there's a great difference of age between us. . . ."

"Honestly, that doesn't matter to me. You're a very attractive man when you're not being pompous."

He flushed. "I am *not* being pompous."

"Yes, you are. And overbearing." She tried to sort out her own feelings and failed. "I'd like to feel a man can at least look at me, maybe even put his arms around me, before making a proposition."

"You're making fun of me."

"No, honestly, I'm not. But I don't know what you have in mind, or why it's so difficult for you to say it."

He turned to look at her, his expression severe. "I want to go to bed with you," he said slowly and firmly, like a man under oath.

She had known that all along, of course, and if she was going to be honest with herself, she had even been curious about when and how the subject would come up. The odd thing was that she hadn't decided what she would do about it—she'd been too busy allowing herself to be dazzled by Bannerman's wealth, as if being with him were a kind of field trip in sociology. In the right mood, she might have gone to bed with him out of sheer curiosity, but from the beginning she had sensed that Arthur Bannerman was looking for something more complicated than one night in bed. Well, so was she, if she was going to be *completely* honest with herself—but not with a man who was going to treat her as if she were a Merger and Acquisition problem. He had led her to hope for something better than that, and she felt disappointed.

"Arthur," she said, "if you'd asked me last night when we were dancing, I'd have said yes like a shot. But what are we talking about here? What are the terms? Are we going to be friends, lovers, go out together in public, or what? Is it going to be for a day, a week, a month? I'm not setting conditions, Arthur. I just want to know what I'm getting into. I'll be honest with you. There's no shortage of men who want to go to bed with me—or any other reasonably pretty girl—but I still spend most nights home alone. And do you know why? Because sex isn't as important to me as not getting hurt. I've *been* hurt. I don't like the way it feels."

"I haven't the slightest intention of hurting you."

"I believe you. That doesn't mean it won't happen."

"You have my word."

"I have a tendency to expect too much of men, Arthur. That's what I've been told, anyway. In the long run, I don't think I'd be comfortable with a man who wants to go to bed with me but pretends not to know me when there's a photographer around. I've been through something like that before. It didn't make me feel good."

"There are reasons for my being cautious, Alexandra, and they have nothing to do with you. I told you that."

She could tell he was losing his patience, which annoyed her even more. He put his drink down hard. It clinked against the key on the coffee table. She stared at it as if she had seen it for the first time—a shiny, brand-new key, fresh from the locksmith's, on a solid gold key chain from Tiffany.

It infuriated her that he had actually ordered a key for her in advance, like a man hiring a new maid. "Is the key for me?" she asked coldly. "Is that how you usually set things up? I get my own key, so I can let myself in? Do we have a regular schedule? If things don't work out, what do you do? Have the lock changed? Do I get to keep the key chain?"

Bannerman turned red. "My previous, ah, arrangements, if any, are no concern of yours. As it happens, the key *was* made for you, yes. It's purely a practical matter. If it offends you, let's forget about it."

It was his anger that made up her mind. Anger was the one thing she feared in a man, and she didn't need a psychiatrist to tell her why. She had run away from home to escape from her father's anger, then had been dragged back and engulfed by it. For her, a scowl, a tone of command, the telltale signs of rage were what she feared most. She hated the idea of the key, but if he'd put his arms around her and kissed her, she would probably have walked out of there with it in her handbag —she knew that. What she couldn't bear was his anger with himself at needing her, as much as his anger with her for making things difficult. The combination was too familiar for comfort.

She stood up. "Maybe it's too practical," she said. "I *liked* you, Arthur. I don't want to sound foolish, but really I did. If what you wanted was a mistress who'd come and go on schedule, with her own key, then you shouldn't have made me like you. A strict business proposition I think I'd have said no to, but who knows?"

"I am *not* trying to buy you," he said furiously.

"I don't go to bed with men who shout at me, Arthur. That's one of my rules—the most important one. And I think it would have been nice to ask me first before having the key made up." She went to the door. "Look," she said, "I know this hasn't worked out the way you meant it to. Maybe it's my fault."

He rose as stiffly as a soldier on parade. "I'll have Jack drive you back to your office," he said, in his most clipped and businesslike voice.

"Arthur, it's not necessary. I can walk."

"I insist," he said harshly.

There was no point in pushing him too far. After all, she told herself, he had done nothing wrong. A lot of women would have been delighted to slip his key into their handbag and accept the arrangement. There had been times in her life when it would have seemed like a good deal. A few afternoons a week with an elderly, but still attractive, billionaire, in his secret hideaway—what was wrong with that? He was probably generous enough, in the manner of his class—no diamonds or Rolls-Royces, such as one might expect from an Arab oil sheik or a Greek shipowner, but probably a nice little broker's account somewhere, slowly hatching a modest nest egg. She had known women—quite respectable married women—who had maintained just such "arrangements" for years, and seemed perfectly happy. Sometimes the arrangement came to mean more to them than the marriage. Life was full of surprises.

In a way, she was sorry she couldn't just say yes and get on with it. She *liked* Bannerman when he was not being angry and pompous. That was the problem. She liked him too much. "I'm sorry," she said. "I really am."

Bannerman nodded. He had himself under control again, his expression giving away nothing, his dignity restored. "Thank you for coming," he said, as if she were a complete stranger.

That night she broke a small rule of her life and took a sleeping pill, then another, just to be on the safe side, and went to bed early.

She hoped in the morning she would still feel she had done the right thing.

SHE WOKE to the sound of the doorbell. She gathered her robe around her and went to the door. It had taken her a long time to learn the urban survival mechanism, and she had never succumbed to it completely like native New Yorkers. Her door bore the usual clutter of Medeco locks, a chain, a peephole, and a dead bolt; but she often forgot to use all three keys, and almost never bothered with the peephole, which revealed only a dark and distorted picture that would have made her own mother look like a burglar or a rapist. She opened the door a crack and found Arthur Aldon Bannerman standing in the shabby hallway, his face blue in the fluorescent light. "I owe you an apology," he said thickly.

Had he been drinking? But then, he was always drinking, without giving the slightest sign of ever being drunk. "You could have phoned," she said.

"I hate the damned thing. Open the door, please."

She unfastened the chain and let him in. "How did you get in without buzzing from downstairs?"

"Some foreign feller was lurking there. I told him to open the door."

The super, of course, would have been no match for Bannerman. "Can I get you something?" she asked.

"A Scotch." Bannerman examined the living room. "Nice place you have here."

"It's a little small compared to what you're used to."

He shrugged. She went to the kitchen and made him a drink. When she returned, he was examining her books. She wished there was a more interesting selection. She wished the apartment was more glamorous. She wished she wasn't standing there without makeup, in a worn terry-cloth robe that was far too short for modesty.

"This *is* a surprise," she said. "What time is it?"

"I don't wear a watch. It's eleven or thereabouts. . . . Listen to me. I don't usually come barging in like this, but we must talk."

"Must we? We talked at lunchtime. Look, it was probably all my fault, okay? I said so. But you can't just cut me a key and expect me to come around so many times a week like the girl who looks after the plants."

"I never implied anything of the kind," he said stiffly, more angry than ever, it seemed to her. Then he threw his head back and laughed. He caught his breath, finally restored to good humor. "Well, yes, I did, by God. I have only myself to blame. Let me come right out and say it: *I want you.* On any terms."

"I wasn't negotiating."

"Damn it, don't be so touchy. I meant only that we can be friends, lovers, anything you like. You don't have to take the goddamn *key*, Alexandra. The question is: *Will you take me?*"

Without giving her a chance to reply, he put his arms round her and kissed her, squeezing her in a bear hug of surprising strength that took her breath away—and apparently his, too, for he let go of her, picked up his Scotch and took a deep gulp. "I'm out of practice," he said.

"You could have fooled me."

"I meant, I'm out of practice at talking to young women. To be perfectly honest, I've spent the last few years feeling sorry for myself. A waste of time."

"I've been there."

"Where? Ah, I see. One wouldn't know it. You're very young to feel sorry for yourself."

"It isn't a question of age."

"No, I suppose not." He put his arms around her again, more gently this time. "I wouldn't want to be thought of as a foolish old man. . . . "

"You're not."

"Thank you. But what I am trying to say, Alexa, is that I don't care. Think what you like, I want you."

All of a sudden the notion of being alone seemed unbearable to her, even though she had been content enough a few minutes ago. She wanted him, too, and she let herself admit it, *feel* it, and was at peace with the fact, wherever it was going to lead her.

"Arthur," she said, looking up at him, "I'm not promising anything."

"I haven't asked you for any promises."

"Would you—like to stay the night?"

"I should very much like to," he said gravely. "If you'll have me."

He towered over her, dwarfing the small living room, a figure built to the scale of the palaces in which he lived. She stood on tiptoe and kissed him. "Oh, yes," she said. "I'll have you, all right."

SHE DREAMED of a cornfield. She was running through it under a clear blue autumn sky, the air so sharp and crisp that she could almost smell the coming of winter. The stalks were much taller than she was, ready for harvesting, and even the slightest breeze made the leaves move like waves at sea—not that she had ever seen the sea for real.

She carried a Thermos, holding it carefully with both hands—not a small Thermos, like the one inside the lunchbox she took to school, but the kind that men put on the front seat of the pickup in the morning, with enough coffee to last them through a whole morning's work at ten below.

She ran on and on, it seemed forever, down the narrow tracks, with the corn on either side. Occasionally there was a sudden sharp noise as some animal or bird, startled by the sound of her sneakers, made a dash for safety—otherwise there was only the sound of the corn itself.

She felt a sense of urgency, as if the Thermos contained something precious or desperately needed, but the faster she went, the farther the cornfield seemed to stretch, as if it were growing as she ran, while the Thermos itself grew larger and heavier, until she was running with labored breath, running for her life, or someone else's.

She felt something like panic begin to grip her. Her feet slipped on the rutted surface of the track. She heard a voice warn, "You won't make it in time," then she was out of the cornfield in a cleared, open space, the corn surrounding it like high, green walls, and standing in the middle of it was her father, in his shirt-sleeves, a green-and-gold John Deere hat on his head, grinning at her, reaching out to hug her, pick her up, whirl her once around as if she weighed nothing. She felt his arms around her, squeezing her against his hard chest. "That's my girl!" he said, putting her down while she still held on tightly to the Thermos.

A part of her was puzzled by the dream even as it unfolded in her mind. *Had* she ever run out into the fields with a Thermos of coffee for her father? For that matter, had he ever picked her up and whirled her around in his arms? He had been, on the whole, a man who avoided displays of physical affection. You had to work hard to win his approval, and it was given in small doses when it was given at all.

The scene was absolutely clear in her mind, with a sharpness that was almost surreal, like that of an Andrew Wyeth painting: her father, reaching out to take the Thermos from her, the beads of sweat gleaming on his chest, behind him the long snout of the corn harvester towering high above their heads.

The rational part of her mind wondered what her father was doing out there. He was good with his hands—what farmer wasn't?—but time was money for a dairyman: repairing farm machinery was a job for her older brothers, who were hardly interested in anything else; harvesting corn, too, was a job for the boys, or a couple of hired hands, since it merely involved sitting on a machine from dawn until well past dusk, cutting a dead-straight slice off each side of a field, while the ears of feedcorn came bursting out of the tall, curved spout into the waiting trucks, like a golden geyser. . . .

Her father counted time away from his stock as wasted time, so there was no explanation for his being there alone with the machine, and with her, but she felt a kind of guilty exhilaration and excitement at the rare pleasure of being with him. He took the big Thermos, held it in his hands, unscrewed it, filled the cup, and offered her a drink—which was odder still, since she didn't drink coffee—but she took a sip anyway, afraid of spoiling the moment. She tasted it—it didn't taste like coffee at all, or even look like coffee. Quite suddenly there was a terrible noise like a storm, the walls of corn began to contract, turning the clearing into a small room without a roof, squeezing her and her father in. The sky was filled with crows, cawing to each other so loudly that she put her hands over her ears.

Her father was no longer smiling. He seemed angry. A voice which sounded like her own, but magnified as if by a faulty loudspeaker, called out, "It's not my fault!" There was a sudden explosion that made her ears ring. Her father was lying on the floor, covered with blood. She could hear herself shouting "I didn't mean to do it!" over and over again; then she was alone, back in the field again, struggling to break free from the corn, which was suffocating her, while overhead the crows blotted out the sun, laughing harshly. She gave a cry and opened her eyes to find Arthur Bannerman, an expression of concern visible on his face in the dim light, holding her. "Are you all right?" he asked.

For a moment, she wasn't sure where she was. She recognized Bannerman, but she had no idea what he was doing in her bed. Then her mind cleared. She remembered where she was and wondered how long she had been sleeping. "It was a dream," she said.

"A nightmare? You sounded—frightened."

"A kind of nightmare, yes."

Bannerman sat up in bed. His hair was disheveled. It did not make him look younger—or older, for that matter—but it detracted some from his dignity.

There was a suggestion of stubble on his chin and cheeks in the glow of the night-light, a faint, silvery-white trace which reminded her that Bannerman was no different from any other man when you got down to the basics—where, after all, they had recently been. She wanted to go to the bathroom but felt unwilling to get out of bed and stand naked in front of him. It was strange that she had felt no shame in making love to a man old enough to be her father—and then some—but was embarrassed to have him watch her walk naked to her own bathroom. She decided she could hardly ask him to shut his eyes.

"I know a thing or two about nightmares," he said. "Lie back quietly, and we'll talk. It's the next best thing to a glass of milk."

"I need to go to the bathroom first."

"I'll shut my eyes."

"How did you guess that's what I wanted you to do?"

"I'm a lot older than you are."

"And you've done this kind of thing a lot?"

"Not recently."

She stretched out closer to him. "I didn't mean to pry."

"Nonsense. Of course you did. That's all right. I'm sorry to say there hasn't been much to pry into for a while."

"I would have thought women would be knocking your door down."

"I don't mean to suggest that I've been living a life of celibacy since my wife's death. I leave that to my nephew Emmett—though as an Episcopalian priest he's under no obligation that I know of to do so. There's nothing like celibacy for driving a man mad, I've always thought. My eyes are closed, by the way."

When she came back, dressed in a robe now, carrying a glass of milk, his eyes were still shut, his powerful torso propped up on the pillows until he was almost in a sitting position, with the covers modestly pulled up to his neck. Did he normally wear pajamas? she wondered. Probably, but she had none to offer him, and even her robe would be ridiculously small for a man of his size. He seemed to fill her bed with his bulk; the bedroom, which was small to begin with, looked tiny, as if it could barely contain him. He gave the faint impression of a large animal of some kind in a zoo cage. "You can open your eyes now," she said as she slipped into bed.

"Thank God. I'll take a sip of your milk, if you don't mind."

She handed him the glass and giggled. "I wonder what the rest of the world would say if they could see you lying in a bed that's too small for you, drinking a glass of milk."

"I neither know nor care. All my life, people have expected me to act a certain way, and by and large I've failed. I remember when Lyndon Johnson was President. I went to a barbecue at the LBJ Ranch with a lot of other Eastern Establishment figures Lyndon was courting, and there was David Rockefeller, in a banker's suit, trying to eat spareribs off a paper plate with a knife and fork. I asked David why he didn't just pick the damned things up and chew 'em, like everybody else. Well, he looked at me as if I were mad and said, 'Arthur, I'm the head of the Chase Manhattan Bank, for God's sake—I can't be seen in public eating with my fingers!' "

He laughed loud enough to wake the neighbors. "The dignity of wealth—I've spent a lifetime in its service. It isn't worth cat's piss."

He had a rim of milk on his lips, like a child. She found it endearing.

"Sex seems to make me garrulous. I'm sorry. Or perhaps it's age. . . . Tell me about your dream."

"Oh, I don't know. It was just one of those dreams that don't make any sense."

"All dreams make sense. I'm not a Freudian—in my opinion, Freud has caused as much trouble in this century as Hitler and Stalin—but I put great faith in dreams. Tell me about yours. What was it that frightened you?"

"I was dreaming about my father. . . ."

"The dairy farmer who voted against me? Go on."

She tried to explain. "My father was a very religious man," she began.

Bannerman nodded. "So was mine," he said. "We have something in common."

"I don't mean that he had crazy ideas or anything. He wasn't like all these preachers you see on television, but he had strong notions about right and wrong. Most people do, where I come from, but even in Stephenson County he was considered a hard-liner on sin. Not that we *had* a lot of sin, you understand, but the general feeling was that if you didn't watch out, sin would creep in from Indianapolis or Chicago, and pretty soon all the kids would be reading *Playboy* and lose interest in getting up at three A.M. to milk the cows."

"No doubt there's some truth to that."

"Well, sure. Look at my brothers. They all read *Playboy* secretly, and, apart from girls and cars, the only thing that interested them was getting off the farm, and a job where you start work at nine in the morning. What I'm trying to say is that my father didn't believe in churchgoing all that much, but he did believe in toeing the line. He held the boys on a light rein, if you know what I mean—he thought it was okay for them to raise a little hell, within decent limits. But he didn't feel that way at all about girls. And I was his only daughter."

Bannerman smiled. "I like the metaphor—I'm a horseman myself," he said. "I take it, then, you weren't brought up on a loose rein and a mild bit?"

"Curb and chain, all the way."

He laughed. "I felt much the same about Cecilia, which probably explains why she's imitating Florence Nightingale on the shores of Lake Rudolph—without, to my knowledge, any aptitude for nursing. Were you fond of him?"

"I loved him more than anyone when I was little. It's funny, the stricter he was, the more I loved him. And he loved *me*. He tried not to show it—he wasn't the kind of man who hugged and kissed his kids much, you know. He was always kind of remote, as if his mind was on the farm, not on us—but he liked me to be with him, just sitting there beside him in the pickup, when he had to go someplace. He used to let me ride on his lap when he was driving the tractor. He always came to my room to kiss me goodnight—and I never saw him kiss my mother, *ever*. Then, when I was about fourteen, he stopped, and I was heartbroken. I thought I'd done something wrong."

"Well, he was quite right. That's the dangerous age for fathers and daughters. Seen it a thousand times. Don't need Freud to explain that."

"I didn't understand. He'd been so—affectionate, you know. Then suddenly he was withdrawn, almost hostile. I blamed myself at first. Then I decided he hated me. I caught him looking at me with such *anger* in his eyes. . . . So I fought back the only way I could."

"What way was that?"

"I fell in love with a boy in school and we ran away together to get married."

Bannerman nodded. No doubt his own children, being rich, had found far more dramatic forms of rebellion than hers. "How far did you get?"

"We were planning on going to L.A., but we got picked up in Cedar Rapids, Iowa, at a Value-Right motel. Up to then we'd been sticking to the back roads. We got married in Zwingle, on the way. By a justice of the peace. Our folks got it annulled, once they got us home.

"Billy's heart wasn't in it, frankly. I think he was relieved when the police spotted his car in the parking lot. I *told* him not to leave it where it could be seen, but he did anyway. On purpose, I guess. He seemed pretty gung ho, until we got to Zwingle and tied the knot."

"And you?"

"I was scared out of my mind. But I would have gone on to California if the police hadn't found us. It's funny. Nobody at home blamed Billy for what had happened—everybody said it was my fault. Of course, he was the high school football star, and that means a lot in a town like LaGrange, so people figured I'd talked him into it."

"I take it your father wasn't pleased?"

She took a sip of milk. This was the part that she still couldn't face— the part that gave her nightmares. "He came to the State Police barracks to pick me up. He never said a word to me all the way home. His knuckles were white on the steering wheel. When we got home, he said, 'I don't want to hear what you did, or why you did it, or anything else from you.'

"He didn't even look at me—just stared through the windshield, you know? Into the distance, as if he was still driving. Then he got out and went off to the barn."

She shivered. She hadn't described the expression on her father's face. Anger had drained it of blood, and he was pale as a ghost. The only sign of emotion he gave had been a small involuntary twitch to one side of his mouth, which made it look as if he were chewing gum —something he never did, or allowed in his sight.

She didn't say that for the next few weeks her father behaved as if she were invisible—that he spoke, at meals, when he spoke at all, as if she weren't in the room. Neither did she say that her mother thought he was making too much of a fuss, hurting himself by bottling up his feelings.

But that had always been her father's way. His anger took the form of silence, and when Alexa, frightened by what that silence was doing to him, by how much it cost him to keep it up, finally asked him to forgive her, he turned on her savagely, his face that of a stranger, the veins pulsing at his temples. "I'd have let you keep going all the way to California if your mama hadn't been after me to bring you back," he said, in a voice as taut as a stretched cable. There was no mistaking the bitterness in his voice, which, years later, when she had grown up, she recognized as that of a jilted lover rather than an angry father. She should have realized it was jealousy, but she didn't find that out until it was too late.

"And then?" Bannerman asked, putting his hand on hers.

She closed her eyes, didn't like what she saw there, and opened them again. "A month later, he was dead."

"I see."

But of course he didn't, he couldn't. There was no way he could imagine what it was like—the sight of her father lying on the polished wooden floor of his farm office, on which there was never a speck of mud even though there were a hundred cows in the barn, his eyes wide open and suddenly peaceful, his chest a mass of blood, as if it had been crushed by a giant fist. There was no way to describe the eerie quiet, either, after the ear-splitting roar of the shotgun. A stray pellet had hit the old Regulator clock on the wall, stopping its loud tick; even the cows next door were silent, still shocked by the sudden loud noise.

"How did he die?" Bannerman asked gently.

"A shotgun," she said. It was true enough, but it left a lot unsaid.

"Ah." He sighed deeply. "But it wasn't your fault," he said, in the tone of a judge passing sentence. "People are responsible for their own actions. When you're my age, you begin to realize what a waste guilt is. After my eldest son's death, I suffered terribly, but that didn't bring him back, of course. And it made me less of a father to the others, just when they needed me most." He put his arm around her. "One thing I know," he said softly. "Once people have decided to kill themselves, nobody can stop them."

She felt his warmth. "I don't want to talk about it any more," she said. "I don't know why I started to."

"Perhaps it's because you trust me. And because I'm the right age to be a good listener. It's one of the few advantages of age. God knows, I can't think of many others."

She smiled, comforted by his presence. A lesser man would have asked questions, and she was already sorry she had brought the subject up at all. Bannerman didn't push her for more details. "You seem to do all right," she said. "Age doesn't seem to have slowed you down."

"I will take that as a compliment—though in fact it *has* slowed me down. Still, I've never thought that sex was something that needed to be hurried, so that's not all bad."

She stretched out against his body. He had none of the impatience of a young man, it was true, which was fine with her. He seemed perfectly content to lie here, close to her, which, as it happened, was just what she liked. Most of the men she knew would either be up and looking for the telephone by now or getting ready to make love again, whether she wanted to or not.

"You must never be afraid to talk to me," he said, his voice suddenly serious. "I have lived long enough not to judge anyone. One day you'll tell me more. Or you won't. It doesn't matter."

"You might not forgive me if I told you everything."

"Oh, I think I would. But my forgiving you isn't what matters. I'm not God, after all. What matters is to forgive *yourself*. And that I may be able to help you do."

"You already have."

"I am flattered. Perhaps I should hang out my shingle as a psychiatrist."

"I don't need one." She put her head against his shoulder and relaxed. There was nothing about the feel of his body in the dark to give away his age. Solid, she decided, was what he was, in every way. She thought of him as a massive tree, the kind that lasts for centuries, like the great redwoods in California. He had the roots and the strength of those big trees. You could hold onto him and never fall.

She had never felt closer to anyone in her life—not since the days when her father still came to her room to kiss her goodnight.

She slept for once without dreams.

5

Simon almost never came to the office, and from the moment he appeared, dapper as always, it was clear that he wanted to talk.

"I never seem to be able to get you on the phone any more," he said. "I called twice last night—no reply. Shit, that sounds like the Beatles. You *could* turn your answering machine on, you know."

"I wasn't feeling well so I unplugged the phone and made an early night of it." Arthur had not sworn her to secrecy, but she felt uncomfortable with the idea of telling anyone about their relationship, even Simon.

"No kidding? You don't look as if you got a lot of sleep for a girl who went to bed early." He stared at her closely and sighed. "Listen, if somebody else *has* come along, it's not such a big deal. We never made each other that kind of promise, right?"

That was not true. She had made exactly that kind of promise, and so had Simon, though his was admittedly hedged with so many options, escape clauses and qualifications that it had seemed transparently untrue even at the time. She had guessed even then that Simon was only telling her what she wanted to hear, but she had been determined to believe him. She said nothing.

"Is it somebody I know?"

"I don't want to talk about it, Simon. Honestly."

"Look, we haven't been together that much lately. Maybe this is all for the best, right?"

"Right," she said automatically. Simon had a tendency to talk like a self-help book, especially when he was trying to put a good face on things.

"You're not thinking of quitting, are you?"

"Of course I'm not. I didn't even say there *was* somebody else, Simon. You're jumping to conclusions."

"I've got eyes, for Christ's sake. I just don't want you walking out of here because you're in love with somebody else. I need you."

She raised an eyebrow. It was unusual for Simon to admit that he needed her to manage his affairs. Was he in some kind of trouble?

"It seems you made quite an impression on old Bannerman," Simon explained. "I had a call from some high WASP gofer of his. It seems the old boy wants *us*"—Simon emphasized the word "us"—"to go after, and I quote, 'the works of first-rate contemporary artists.' Bannerman is looking for artists 'on the leading edge,' to quote again. High-risk collecting, in other words."

"*Us?*"

"The man was explicit. You and me. Did you by any chance give the old man the impression that you were an art expert of some kind?"

"No. Well, I might have . . . not deliberately."

"Not deliberately? It just slipped out, by accident? You ought to be ashamed of yourself, lying to a man that age. Still, there it is—from now on you're an art expert. Why not? God knows the real ones don't know anything either. I asked if it was true that Bannerman was planning to build a museum, but he didn't know—or wouldn't say. Bannerman didn't mention any of this to you?"

"Not a word."

Simon looked skeptical. "You must have talked about *something* when you had lunch with him."

Simon, she reminded herself, was not yet aware of her fast-developing relationship with Arthur Bannerman. He had been busy demonstrating that *he* didn't need her by simply vanishing from sight, as he often did. Simon's favorite way of punishing her was by a combination of absence and silence—he would go to California or London on business for a few days without telling her, so she would only find out that he was away when he called in, or when somebody else mentioned it. Once it had hurt; now it no longer mattered. "We talked a lot about dairy farming," she said.

Simon took off his dark glasses and stared at her. He hated being made fun of. He looked at her for a few seconds, then decided she was serious. "Whatever works," he snapped. "If you see him again, keep talking cows. *He's* talking about spending five hundred thousand dollars, as a *start!* Listen, I'm going to need your help. He seems to trust you. Does he know what he wants, do you think?"

She looked out at the rainy, windswept street. The pavements were crowded with office workers on their way home.

The Bannerman fortune at work again, she thought. Arthur was using his position to smooth things out for her, exerting a little behind-the-scenes leverage in her favor. It wouldn't even cost him anything in the long run. Simon, with his contacts, would surely find just the kind of art Arthur was looking for, and Arthur's five hundred thousand would be doubled or trebled. The Midas touch was nothing compared to the Bannerman.

"I think he knows what he wants, Simon," she said. "He knows exactly what he wants."

"Will you be meeting him again soon?"

"I don't know," she answered cautiously. "Why?"

"If you do, tell him I'd like to meet him, too. I'd rather not work through some middleman in the Bannerman family's office."

Arthur would almost certainly want to work through a middleman any time he could, but she didn't say so. "I don't suppose I'll hear from him," she said. "I think I just caught his eye when I sold him the Baldur. I wouldn't overestimate his attention span."

"I don't. That's why I'd like to make hay while the sun shines. Still, you never know, do you, with these rich old guys. Look at Timmy de Hartnung! He caught John Paul Getty's eye after Claus von Bulow let the old boy slip out of his fingers—and Timmy ended up buying most of the art for the Getty Museum. Millions and millions of dollars. Timmy's ten percent was enough to make him a rich man. Not counting whatever he managed to steal. . . ."

"I'll keep it in mind."

Simon put his hand on her. "Whoever it is, we're still going to be friends? Aren't we?"

"Yes," she said—and it was true. For all his faults, Simon *was* her friend. Friendship with Simon was something she could handle; it was loving him that had made her unhappy.

"I was never the jealous type," Simon said, congratulating himself as usual on a virtue he didn't possess. "I'm *glad* to see you happy, really. What I mean is, we don't have to be strangers just because you've got someone new. Bring him along for dinner one day, why don't you?"

"Well, not just yet. . . ."

"What's the big secret? It isn't one of my friends, is it? Not that I'd mind," he added hastily.

"No, it's nothing like that."

"Don't tell me he's married? Look, you know me, I'm discreet."

"He's not married, Simon," she said.

"I'm having dinner with a few people tomorrow—Ferdi and Morgana, they're together again, you know, Jean-Claude with his new girl, all people you know. We'll probably go on to Karim Palevi's new disco afterward. Why not bring him along?"

She tried to imagine Arthur Bannerman sitting down to dinner with

Ferdi de Brasse, a schoolmate of Simon's who was in the process of running through one of the largest fortunes in Belgium, and who had been busted so many times at airports for possession of cocaine ("for personal use only, darling") that his family had finally been obliged to buy him a Vatican diplomatic passport; or Karim Palevi, who wore Armani suits over a black T-shirt and favored a black leather tuxedo for formal wear. "I don't think that would work, Simon," she said cautiously.

He gave her the look of a man who thinks he may have been insulted, but isn't sure, as if she had suggested that he and his friends didn't come up to her lover's standards, whatever they might be—an impression she had tried very hard not to convey, precisely because it was true. "Is he rich?"

"Well, he's got a lot of money, yes."

"That's something, anyway."

If only he knew, she thought, watching him make a small production of draping his overcoat over his shoulders in the European style and pulling on his gloves smoothly so they wouldn't crease.

"I hope he's fun, at least?"

"Well, he leads a kind of quiet life."

"If that's what you want . . ."

It had never been what Simon wanted, she thought, as he turned and left. But the truth was, she still didn't have the slightest idea what kind of life she might have with Arthur Bannerman. He seemed to live in some faraway, remote world of his own, and she couldn't imagine how she would fit into his scheme of things.

I've known him for a week, she told herself, and slept with him twice, and already I'm resentful.

She would have to learn patience.

WITHIN A WEEK of the night he spent in her apartment, she was using her key to the apartment above the Bannerman Foundation as if she had never objected to it in the first place.

Sometimes they spent the night together, sometimes not. In that respect, too, Arthur Bannerman was anything but demanding—companionship, talk, her simple presence, were as important to him as sex. There were none of the pressures that usually accompanied a love affair —in many respects, it was just what she imagined a marriage might be after a few years. A *good* marriage, she corrected herself.

True, for a man of his wealth, Arthur Bannerman seemed to have very few pastimes. He did not own a yacht, he didn't play golf, he had no interest in travel. The playgrounds of the rich had no interest for him at all—he had never skied in St. Moritz or spent the summer on the Côte d'Azur; he owned neither a villa in Cuernavaca nor a beach house in Jamaica. While it was hard to put one's finger on exactly what he *did* every day, he was always busy, and by no stretch of the imagination a member of the leisure class.

He had a certain disdain for what he called "rich men's toys," a disdain in which Alexa thought she occasionally caught a note of envy. At one time in his life, he *had* enjoyed himself in the tradition of his class, ridden to hounds, raced horses, sailed in Maine, but even then he kept up the fiction that these were vacation pursuits, as if he led an ordinary working life like everyone else, and had only his weekends and three weeks in the summer to enjoy himself. Now he behaved as if he had retired, though from what it was hard to say.

Still, any fears she had that her relationship with him would involve sitting in the apartment with him in seclusion were, as she soon discovered, unfounded. Bannerman knew exactly where he would be recognized and where he wouldn't, and did not repeat the error of their appearance together at the trustees' dinner at the Metropolitan Museum of Art. They went to the theater, the opera, the ballet, always taking their seats just as the lights dimmed and leaving while the audience was still applauding; they avoided restaurants like "21," Lutèce, The Four Seasons, or Mortimer's, where he would be instantly recognized, avoidance of which didn't matter to him, since he preferred steak houses like Christ Cella or fish restaurants like Gloucester House, full of solid, substantial elderly men among whom he passed unnoticed. Many of them, too, she couldn't help remarking, were accompanied by women young enough to be their daughters, but clearly were not. He always booked a table in another name, and if the management knew better, nothing was ever said. At art galleries and openings they arrived separately and behaved as if they had met by accident; the problem of what to do at cocktail parties never came up, since he absolutely refused to go to any. Slowly but surely, as the weeks went by, the circle of their activities broadened without the slightest sign that they had attracted the attention of the press or anyone else.

He did not make any attempt to interfere in her life, though sometimes, in small ways, he made his influence felt: a Swiss art collector, well known for his unapproachability, wrote to ask if she would purchase a few works by some of the up-and-coming young SoHo artists on his behalf, and provided her with such a detailed list of requests that she could hardly go wrong; a French museum director inquired if she and Monsieur Wolff would be willing to hunt down a list of contemporary artworks, on commission. Almost every mail brought a piece of new business, however small and bizarre, all of it directed to her. "You're on a roll," Simon told her. "You're finally paying attention to what I've been telling you for years."

It was true. He had been after her for as long as they'd known each other to develop contacts and hunt out business, but she had always considered that *his* side of things, while she looked after the details. Now that she was doing as he said, Simon naturally assumed she was simply putting his good advice into practice at last, with unexpected success.

Bannerman himself was silent on the subject. He made it very clear that he expected his good will toward her to remain anonymous and unthanked; nor was he the kind of millionaire to whisk her off to Cartier or Harry Winston and shower her with diamonds—not that that was something she wanted. He provided her, instead, with opportunities, and left it to her to decide whether to take advantage of them or not. In any case, she found it fascinating to watch him adding up his bill at a restaurant, completely absorbed in the task, and all too often discovering a discrepancy, which he never failed to point out. He calculated a 15 percent tip exactly, rounding it off to the lowest number, and complained that anywhere but in New York 10 percent would be plenty.

For a man who spent millions on art and lived on a scale that most kings would have envied, Bannerman's reluctance to spend money on small things was remarkable, as was his strict attention to detail. Even his clothes were regulated by some mysterious schedule; she quickly learned that if he wore a dark-blue suit on Monday, the same suit would appear on the next Monday, and from then on, until it was replaced by an identical new suit. His clothes were all somber, sturdy, and just slightly old-fashioned, and he allowed himself nothing in the way of eccentricity; he adhered strictly to convention, from the white handkerchief in his breast pocket to his well-polished shoes.

By degrees, without giving the matter much thought, she set out to bring him up-to-date. She guessed he could be moved only in small steps; she was not anxious, in any case, to transform him. She bought him a conservatively striped shirt, which he could hardly refuse to wear, then a pair of bright red suspenders, a couple of ties that had just a hint of color—dark enough for any banker, but at least not quite as funereal as his own. "I haven't opened a gift-wrapped package for years!" he exclaimed one evening, taking the ribbon off a shirt box from Herzfeld, where she had selected a checked shirt that was on the narrow borderline between conservative and flamboyant. He held it up. "I'm going to look like Malcolm Forbes," he said. "Never mind. Thank you."

He himself never shopped, it seemed. He loved to send her gifts, but they tended to be solid, substantial objects of great value. Although he had not visited her apartment since the one night they had spent there together, he had an eye and a visual memory that would have put Mrs. Chantry or Sister Parrish to shame. Before long, it was crowded with his presents—an eighteenth-century chinoiserie lacquer table that fitted in perfectly with the colors of her living room, a Fabergé clock, a Degas bronze, a tiny Seurat beach scene. . . . When she lost her watch, he sent her, in a plain envelope, hand-delivered by Jack, a gold Cartier ladies' watch of such exquisite workmanship that she hardly dared to wear it at first, terrified of losing it. "Mother gave it to Priscilla," he said, when she thanked him for it. "Old Cartier himself designed it, in Paris, before the First World War. No point in leaving it to Cecilia—she'd never appreciate it."

There were, she thought, strange gaps in her knowledge of Arthur's life, when it came to his immediate family. Whatever had happened was like an explosion; the force of it had scattered the Bannermans like debris. There had been a time, even after his wife's death, when Kiawa was still the real family home, when the children still gathered there for Christmas or Thanksgiving like ordinary people, when gifts were still placed under the Christmas tree—then all that had apparently stopped dead. Children grew up, moved away from home; all that Alexa understood, having done it herself—but Arthur Bannerman and his children seemed to have moved into separate orbits, leaving nothing at the center but old Mrs. Bannerman living on in splendid isolation in a huge, empty house.

What had he done? she wondered—or what had *they* done, since she had no idea who was at fault—to destroy a family that must not have been very different from anybody else's, judging from the photographs on Arthur's desk? Whatever it was, Bannerman seemed to live in its shadow.

Sometimes it occurred to her that she was better off not knowing.

HIS BIRTHDAY, she discovered, was less than a week away. She wondered if his family would celebrate it, but he made no mention of the date, as if his own birthday was part of that vanished past, something that no longer mattered to him or anyone else. Would he go to Kiawa, to celebrate it with his mother? Would one of his children—the younger boy, Putnam, she knew, lived in New York—ask him out, or visit him?

He mentioned none of these things, so on the day, she sent him a bouquet of flowers and a card on which she wrote, "Happy birthday, I'm inviting *you* to dinner." After a moment of hesitation, she added the word "Love," and scrawled an "A." It was easier to write it than to say it, but the fact that she hadn't ever said it to him made writing it seem false. It was a word experience had taught her to use with caution, even fear, but the card didn't seem right without it.

He was waiting for her, smiling cheerfully, when that evening after work she arrived downstairs at La Domaine. He himself had introduced her to it—the restaurant of choice for a clientele that was almost exclusively rich and patrician, the kind of people who wintered in Palm Beach and summered in Maine and thought of themselves as "Old New York." La Domaine was expensive, dark, and stuffy, elegant without being chic, the kind of place where movie stars, conglomerateurs and publishing executives would be told it was all booked up even if it was empty. There was no trendy *nouvelle cuisine* here—it was *la vieille cuisine* all the way, rich, solid, substantial, for people who no longer worried much about their figures.

"Happy birthday," she said, giving him a quick kiss as she sat down.

"I'd almost forgotten it *was* my birthday, frankly. Sixty-four—no great age, in my family."

She ordered a Perrier and put a small, neatly wrapped box in his hand. He opened it with all the delight of a child, though he was careful to untie the ribbon, fold it up carefully—the Bannermans did not waste small things—and put it away in his pocket. Did he intend to use it again? she wondered. He extracted a small silver penknife from the box, leaned over and kissed her. "I shall use it for cutting through red tape," he said. "The more time I spend with lawyers, the less respect I have for the law. Damned fools, the lot of 'em."

"You're not thinking of your brother-in-law, are you? What's his name? DeWitt?"

"Courtland DeWitt. I could tell you stories about him that would turn your hair. No, Courtland is the *family* lawyer. Takes his role seriously, too—been married to my poor sister for so long that he thinks he was *born* a Bannerman by now. What is it the French say? '*Plus royaliste que le roi?*' He thinks he's more a Bannerman than I am."

"I could see he didn't like *me* one bit."

"Welcome to the club. He feels the same way about me. I warned my sister not to marry him thirty-five years ago, and I was perfectly right. He's been a bad husband, and though I'm in no position to criticize, a worse father. I brought up his boy, Emmett, as if he were one of my own children, and Courtland has never forgiven me for it. Blames me for the way the boy's turned out. . . . "

"That's the priest, isn't it? How *did* he turn out?"

"Emmett's a *radical* priest. A real firebrand," he said, with some pride. Was he glad to have a "firebrand" in the family, or was it simply pleasure at what must surely be for Courtland DeWitt a major source of disappointment and anger?

"You mean like—what was their name?—those priests in the sixties, the Berrigans?"

"Not that kind of priest, for God's sake, Alexandra! Emmett's not a Catholic—even he wouldn't go that far. He's quite harmless. In my experience, most clergymen are crackpots. Emmett merely happens to be a left-wing crackpot."

"Do you see him often?"

"See Emmett? Good God, no! I'm not in need of spiritual advice—not that I'd set much store on Emmett's. Why do you ask?"

"Well, it's none of my business, but you don't seem to see much of *anyone* in the family. I mean, you'd think they'd get together for your birthday. . . ."

He shrugged. "We're not close-knit, you might say. Not any more."

"I don't live at home any more, but I wouldn't forget my mother's birthday. I always call her."

"I'm sure you do. But take Cecilia. I don't suppose there's much she could do about my birthday from her refugee camp in Uganda, you know. No telephone there. Putnam? Heaven only knows where he is, or what he's doing. I don't suppose the boy remembers his own birthday, let alone mine. Robert, of course, knows the date of my birthday perfectly well—he'd probably say a prayer that it was my last, if he were religious enough to pray."

She had not meant to turn the conversation to his family, but now that she had, she was, as always, fascinated. "You don't really believe Robert wishes you were dead, do you?" she asked, aghast.

"Absolutely!" Bannerman replied cheerfully. "Let's order."

She let him order for both of them, knowing that his taste in food, like hers—if anything, more so—ran to the simple and ordinary. He would have been quite at home at her mother's table: soup, steak, two vegetables, gravy and potatoes was what he expected for dinner, and a rich dessert. The Pritikin phenomenon seemed to have passed him by without his even noticing it.

"That doesn't bother you?" she asked.

"I try not to brood on it. Mostly I succeed."

Bannerman examined his smoked trout, then proceeded to dissect it with a surgeon's care, which she found difficult to watch. "Have you and Robert always hated each other?" she asked.

"We don't hate each other at all."

"You said he'd be happy to see you dead."

"Happy? I'm not sure that's the right word. You have to understand that so long as Robert's my heir, my death gives him control of the fortune. That's all he wants."

"Did you?"

He put his knife and fork down. "I'm sorry I raised the subject," he said. "However, the answer is no. I admired my father and had no wish to take on his responsibilities. Robert doesn't admire me a bit and thinks he could do a better job than I'm doing."

"Can I ask another question?"

The trout was removed. Now he contemplated a steak, which she knew from habit he would cut into hamburger before he started to eat it. The knife did not please him. He sent it back and tested the sharpness of the next one on his thumb, an outdoorsman's gesture, like her father testing the edge of an ax. "Shoot," he said.

"How long do we have to be careful about being seen together?"

He sighed. "We are not exactly leading a hole-in-the-wall existence, Alexandra. Do I sense that you're chafing at the bit?"

"Maybe. Not really. But I might some day."

"I see. Well, that is to be expected, sooner or later. The truth is, I don't know. I have certain things to do regarding the fortune. When they're done, I think we can lead a more open life, if that's what you want."

"Is it something *you* want?"

He put down his knife and fork and smiled. "With all my heart," he said. "But it's not the moment, not yet. You'll have to take my word for that."

"Because of Robert?"

"In part."

She picked at her food. She knew it was a mistake to be inquisitive, but she couldn't help it. On the rare occasions when Arthur talked about his family, he avoided the subject of his children and his mother as much as possible. For example, she had heard all about his sister Katherine's notorious marriage to a handsome, white-trash Virginia hunt servant, James "Beau" Randolph, who had absconded with her jewels after a year and gone on to Hollywood to become a cowboy star, and later a successful conservative politician, leaving Katherine to raise racehorses and fighting cocks for the rest of her life—but almost nothing about Cecilia, except that she was in Africa. The Bannerman family was full of eccentrics, and Arthur enjoyed talking about them, but when it came to his immediate family, she knew very little more than when she had first seen their photographs on his desk over a month ago.

"Arthur," she said, "the night we went to the Met, for the dance, a funny thing happened. . . ."

"I behaved badly, as I remember. You didn't find it amusing at the time."

"I wasn't thinking about the photographer. When I was in the ladies room, there were a couple of women talking. And Sis Chantry . . . "

"That bloody bitch! Her husband was a classmate of mine. A pompous ass."

"Well, they were gossiping. About you and me, in fact."

"I see. And you overheard them?"

She nodded. "They had some unpleasant things to say about me."

"Envy, no doubt. There's no unkindness like that of women toward another woman who's younger and more beautiful."

"Maybe so. One of the things they were saying, though, is that your children tried to have you put away, and that Robert was still trying. Are things *really* that bad between you?"

He clenched his teeth. For a moment she thought he was angry with her, as well he might have been, but he seemed determined to be patient. "How I hate gossip! Listen to me, Alexandra—and I don't mean this in any unkind way—my children are not your concern."

"But you don't want them to know about me, do you?"

"No. Not yet. And particularly Robert." He waved at the waiter. "They make a damn good *crème brulée* here," he said, finishing his steak. "I might have it. At my age, there's no point in counting calories or worrying about cholesterol."

"Yes, there is. You're not *that* old." When it suited him, she thought, he played the old man, but it was mostly a role, the way he sometimes feigned mild deafness with strangers to avoid talking to them. We all have our little games, she told herself. Who was she to criticize his?

"Old enough not to care what my children think of me, though. That's what you're thinking, isn't it?"

"No, not really. *Is* it the children? I thought it might be the world, the press, society, public opinion—maybe all of them."

"I don't give a damn about public opinion. Never did. It's why I lost the Presidency, I suppose. One of the reasons, anyway. And I never gave a damn about society, even when I was part of it." He glared at the dessert tray balefully. "I don't care *what* people think of me, to tell you the truth. That's not the point at all."

"No, it's not. The truth is, I was wondering if what worried you was what people would think of *me*."

He stabbed a finger toward the *crème brulée*. His face had gone slightly red—a sure sign that he was upset. He wasn't used to arguments, she could tell, except, presumably, from his own family. Everybody else probably fell in with his wishes and moods automatically. His method for dealing with the few people who talked back was to stop seeing them. For a moment, she thought the anger was going to surface —I've gone too far, she thought—but then his face began to resume its normal color. "I see," he said slowly. "I should have thought of that. You're afraid that I'm ashamed of you? Embarrassed by our relationship? Because of the difference in our ages, perhaps?"

"Maybe."

He shook his head. "Foolishness. I don't give a damn. Neither should you. Here, taste this."

He put a large spoonful of his dessert on her plate, which she tasted without enthusiasm. A sweet tooth was not one of her problems— hadn't been even as a child. She made herself finish it, however, as a gesture of reconciliation, even though she hated being told what to do.

Bannerman ate his with the swiftness and ferocity of a steam shovel, anxious to get it out of the way before he spoke. It was, she thought, pretty much like vanilla pudding, except for the crust, but then, nursery food was what he seemed to like best. He wiped his mouth. "All right," he said. "I'll tell you what I can, so we can talk about something better. A few years ago," he said, his face set for a serious explanation, "I had a bad spell."

"A what?"

"I went through a difficult period in my life. My wife had died. My eldest son, John, was, ah, killed in a, ah, car crash. In circumstances . . . " he hesitated. "Well, never mind the damned circumstances, but they weren't pleasant. I'd lost the Presidency. Looking back on it now, I'm not even sure I wanted to *be* President all that much. But the ambition gave me a sense of purpose, do you see? That's half the attraction of the Presidency, I suspect. It takes your mind off all the normal problems of life and family that you can't solve. It doesn't leave room for any of that—rather like war."

She nodded. She knew nothing about war and still less about the Presidency, but running away from family problems you couldn't solve was something she knew all about.

"Not to beat around the bush, I may have been drinking a little more than was good for me. I let things slide. Made a few decisions I regret. Neglected to make some I should have. A midlife crisis, I believe the psychiatrists call it, in their damn silly jargon."

"That can happen to anybody."

"Damn right. But not everybody has a son waiting in the wings who wants to take over. I'll tell you the truth: Robert came damned close to putting me out to pasture."

"What did he *do*, exactly?"

"Spread the rumor that I was drunk, senile, incompetent; went around the family whispering that I couldn't be trusted to look after The Trust; made certain promises in the financial community about what he'd do once he was firmly in charge. And more. And worse."

"And the others? Your mother? The rest of the family?"

"Eleanor's always had a soft spot for Robert. Can't imagine why, but there it is. By the time I realized what was going on, Robert was damned near ready to have me carted off to one of those high-priced drunk farms in Connecticut and declared legally incompetent by some quack doctor."

"Surely it isn't that easy, is it?"

"It's not easy at all, but it's been done. And Robert's smart enough to know how. It's a lot easier when your own lawyer is working against you, too—which DeWitt was, I'm convinced. I was busy buying up art, you know, had the idea of starting a new museum. It was the one thing that kept me going. Then one day I realized that my staff wasn't following through. I'd bought a very nice collection of modern sculpture from some German feller's estate—expensive but worth every penny—and left the details of the purchase to the people in the office to handle, couldn't be bothered myself, and it was their job anyway. Forgot all about it. Eventually I asked where my goddamned sculptures were and discovered my orders hadn't been followed—that Robert had told the staff not to do it! Lucky thing, really. I lost the collection, but I woke up and realized what was happening just in time."

"What did you do?"

Bannerman's expression hardened. There were times when his face looked like one of the sculptures on Mount Rushmore, mostly when he was thwarted or when he was talking about Robert. "I had it out with Robert," he said grimly. "And I won. By the skin of my goddamn teeth. I have a couple of cards up my sleeve, when it comes to Robert, luckily. Still, things have changed. There are plenty of people in the financial world, even in the family, who'd like to see Robert in charge. He'd use the fortune selfishly, and there's always a profit to be made in selfishness. And he's devious. You'd be surprised how easy it would be for him to make our, ah, friendship, look as if I'm losing my judgment."

She was genuinely shocked. Arthur Bannerman seemed to her, so far, a figure of immense authority and strength. It did not seem to her likely that his elder son could simply push him aside, however he chose to live his private life. "How would he do that?" she asked. "He can't blackmail you for something that's perfectly innocent."

"I never mentioned blackmail. But Robert would twist things. He's artful that way. An old man, a young woman, a lot of money spent on art most people don't understand . . . it would play very nicely in the tabloids."

"What's the art got to do with it?"

"My whole family is against me on that—with Robert in the lead, of course—though it's only a small part of the differences between us. Robert wants to exploit the fortune, and I want it used to do good. Well, never mind. These are my problems, not yours. The main thing is I don't want *you* caught up in a family fight, Alexa. You'd be an indirect target, of course—I'm the only one Robert cares about—still, why risk it? You're far too young to have anything to hide, but Robert's not above inventing something for his friends in the press. So you see, I *do* have my reasons. More than I've told you, to be perfectly honest."

He sat back and sipped his coffee. She found it hard to believe that the young man whose photograph she had seen in Arthur's study was in fact the scheming villain his father made him out to be, but there was no question that Arthur took him seriously. His feelings about Robert were the first sign of weakness she had seen in Arthur Bannerman, and strangely it made him even more appealing to her. She was grateful to him, too, for dealing so tactfully with the possibility that she might have something to hide in her own life—or was he shrewdly aware of more than she knew? It was very possible, she thought. Arthur was anything but the senile old fool his family pretended he was. It might suit him not to know any more than he wanted to know about her, but he was rich enough to find out, if he really wanted to. She felt a slight chill despite the warmth of the restaurant.

"I understand," she said. "I'm sorry I brought the subject up."

"No, you were quite right. I don't want there to be any misunderstandings between us."

He reached across and took her hand in his. "One thing I promise you. Whatever happens, I'm not going to let Robert interfere with my life again."

She had never seen an expression quite as implacable as the one on Arthur Bannerman's face, not even on her own father. There was no give to it at all, as if the edges had been roughly carved from hardwood.

She smiled and lifted her glass to break the mood. "Happy birthday, again," she said.

His expression became less severe, his normal good spirits returned. He leaned over and kissed her. "The first of many more together," he said. He gave a roar of laughter that startled the room. "The hell with Robert anyway! I'm planning to live to ninety. Maybe a hundred, just to spite him."

He gave her the smile that had caught her attention the first time she saw him. His bright blue eyes sparkled; he looked, for an instant, twenty years younger than his age, a wholly different man from the one he had been when he was talking about Robert, and she believed him, willingly, absolutely. He would live to ninety, healthy, hearty, strong as an oak, and somehow they would be happy together, always.

She felt it deep in her bones. . . .

WHEN SIMON ASKED HER OUT for a drink after work, she knew he had something important on his mind, particularly since he chose the Hobe Sound, around the corner from his office. He was not much of a drinker, but he always went to bars for a serious conversation. This one was so dark and empty that the few people who knew of it assumed it was a cover for something, though what, nobody seemed to know. The waitresses were middle-aged, cheerful, and wholesome, no drug dealers hung out at the bar, and far from being gay, the atmosphere was, if anything, lugubrious, and hardly improved by the artificial storm that occurred every quarter of an hour, or the fishing nets and lifebuoys hanging from the ceiling.

She should have guessed that there was no hiding her relationship with Arthur Bannerman from Simon. He could hardly help noticing the flow of mail that came in from the Bannerman Foundation, most of it directed to her, or the occasional gifts she couldn't hide. In the long run it was impossible to hide anything from Simon, and at some level she didn't *want* to hide it from him, not to the extent of lying to him—face to face, anyway.

"It's Bannerman, isn't it?" he asked.

She said nothing.

"I know you," Simon said. "You're the worst liar in the world."

"I haven't lied to you."

"No, but you haven't denied it, either, because you can't. Look, we're supposed to be friends. Friends don't hide things from each other."

She nodded. That was true enough, except for the fact that Simon's life had been full of secrets even when they were living together. Still, there was no point in denying what he already knew, nor was she capable of doing so.

"I should have known," he said, more annoyed with himself for not picking up on the truth than with her for withholding it. "All that business suddenly coming in to you. And the goddamned flowers! I've got to hand it to you: you're a lot smarter than I thought you were. And faster. I don't know why I didn't think of it. I should have remembered, you have this thing about older men. . . . "

"I don't have a 'thing' about older men, Simon," she said indignantly. "What about us? You're not *that* much older than I am."

"Of course when it comes to older men, you may be carrying things too far this time. He must be all of seventy, for Christ's sake!"

"Sixty-four."

"Jesus, Alexa! Sixty-four! I suppose it's none of my business, but can he still . . . ?"

"You're right, Simon. It's none of your business."

"Okay, okay, I won't pry. May I ask why you're keeping it so secret?"

"Because it's important. Seriously, Simon, nobody must know."

"Important for whom? He can't be thinking of running for the Presidency again, can he? I know being head of the Bannerman family is a big deal, but it doesn't require a life of celibacy, surely?"

"He *wants* it kept secret, Simon. It's important to him, so it's important to me."

"Well, I won't tell a soul."

"You have to promise. Please!"

"For God's sake, I promise. When it breaks on page six of the *Post*, it won't be because of me."

"What makes you think it will?"

"Instinct. He has servants, to begin with, and servants love to gossip.

I'm surprised he doesn't want the world to know, frankly. It's not as if he's married."

"He has his reasons."

"The family. I can imagine. And of course he doesn't exactly have a playboy image. It must be a little like having an affair with a bishop. Does he know about us, by the way?"

"I haven't talked to him about us, Simon, and he hasn't asked. But I think he's probably guessed about us, yes. He's not a fool."

"I wouldn't think so. He strikes me as more than usually shrewd, in fact. Hell, why not? It runs in the family. Actually, it's lucky for you, now that I think of it—I mean that he wants it all kept secret."

"For *me*?"

"Don't be naive, Alexa. You know perfectly well what I mean. You get your picture in the papers as Arthur Bannerman's girlfriend, and you're going to be getting a lot of calls from old friends, and some of them won't be phoning just to say hello and offer their congratulations."

There was an explosion of thunder, followed by a lightning flash, and then the noise of a torrential rainstorm, making further conversation, mercifully, impossible. After a minute or so, it ebbed into the pounding surf and the screaming of sea gulls, then died away altogether.

"Simon, that was a long time ago," she said, as the noise ended.

"Two years? Three? That doesn't seem very long to me. And one of the people I'm thinking of has a mind like a Rolodex, right? Never forgets a name, a number, or an insult, however slight."

"I didn't insult her."

"You walked out on her. In case you've forgotten, I was the one who got you out of that particular sticky situation."

"And I've always been grateful."

"And always *will* be, I hope. Somehow, I don't think it's something the old boy would understand quite so easily as I do. My guess is he'd be shocked. Or at least disappointed."

"I didn't do anything that terrible."

"Did I say you did? Only, let's face it, it might look very different to somebody else. Somebody a little more old-fashioned, perhaps? It's just a thought."

The room darkened. The storm swept in again. The miniature fishing port behind the glassed-in wall at the back of the bar lit up with lightning; thunder saved her the trouble of replying.

Simon cleared his throat. "Are you going to keep on working?" he asked.

She was startled. Surely Simon wasn't going to fire her just because she was sleeping with somebody else? "Of course I am," she said. "Why?"

"Well, in the first place, I think I probably ought to give you a raise. You're bringing in a lot of business, and I assume there'll be more."

Privately she thought she deserved a raise even without the new business, but money had never been a problem between her and Simon. He hated arguments about money and was happy enough, in her case, to overpay her so as not to have to talk about it. "What are you making now?" he asked, though he knew the answer as well as she did.

"Sixty."

"Seventy-five okay?"

She nodded. "Seventy-five is fine," she said. "Why did you think I'd stop working?"

"Well, I thought Bannerman might not want you to."

"He hasn't even mentioned the subject. Why on earth would he want me to stop working?"

Simon put on his worldly-wise look, the weary expression of the Great Explainer, his favorite role. "Alexa," he said, "men like Arthur Bannerman expect to pay for their pleasure. No, no, don't look at me like that. What I mean is, there are certain things a rich man *does* in this kind of situation. He gets you a nice apartment, for example, somewhere with a view of the park and no junkie burglars on the street, he gives you an allowance, he opens up charge accounts for you. I mean, the man has all the money in the world, after all. There's a right way to do this kind of thing, and he must know it, at his age."

"Simon, I haven't asked him for anything."

"Well, that may be smart, actually. But what has he offered?"

"Nothing. The subject hasn't come up. It isn't *going* to come up."

"Of course it is. Bannerman's not an innocent. You aren't an innocent, either, let me remind you. Well, on the other hand, now that I think of it, maybe you are, when it comes to money. The least you should have is a nice co-op, a good address, the kind of place where he can come and visit and feel at home. In *your* name, of course."

She should have been angry, but she knew Simon too well for that. He wasn't trying to provoke her. It was simply the way his mind worked naturally. Maybe it was the way most people's minds would work on the subject of herself and Arthur Bannerman, but for some reason hers didn't. "Simon," she said, as the storm began to recycle itself, "I'm not his mistress."

He leaned forward to make himself heard, a puzzled expression on his face. "Really?" he asked. "Then what are you, exactly?"

SHE HARDLY EVEN NOTICED when she started learning from Arthur Bannerman.

Through the endless winter they began, by imperceptible degrees, to build a life around each other. Bannerman did not exactly change his routine, which, like that of a head of state, was fixed by tradition and the needs of his staff, but he loosened it slightly to spend more time with her. When they first met, it had seemed to Alexa that he had nothing to do—indeed, she thought this might be part of his trouble—but as they grew closer, she realized that his workload was considerable. He never went to the family office—apparently he had never forgiven the people who worked there for siding with Robert and Eleanor against him during Robert's abortive attempt to take over control of the fortune —but he received a constant stream of paperwork and visitors from what he referred to as "Indian Territory."

The administration of the Bannerman fortune, as she began to discover, was curiously unbusinesslike. Like a constitutional monarch with a hostile government that wants to overthrow him, Arthur placed no trust in his staff, yet was unable to change it. At first she thought there might be some family tradition that made it impossible for him to fire them, but when she asked him about it, he laughed. "Nothing of the kind!" he boomed. "If I were going to make big changes, I'd have to go down there to do it—and I'd have to talk it over with Eleanor and that damned fool DeWitt first. Not to speak of the fact that Robert would hotfoot it back from Caracas to find out what's going on. It's not worth the trouble, that's all."

The result was that Bannerman had to make his way through an endless pile of paperwork without help from anyone he trusted—a task made more time-consuming by the fact that he was a slow reader. It was as if the chief executive of what amounted to a billion-dollar business was trying to run things out of his apartment with the help of a secretary who came in for two hours in the morning and two hours in the afternoon, and who dealt mostly with Bannerman's personal life, declining invitations, sending cards to the far-flung and lesser members of the family on their birthdays, and acting as a kind of personnel manager for Arthur's servants.

Arthur's routine was to wake at six, read the newspapers in bed until seven, dress, eat breakfast at eight, then devote himself to reading through the piles of letters, memos, and documents that arrived in batches from the family office. At eleven, his secretary arrived, and he worked with her until lunchtime. After lunch he received visitors. At four o'clock he went upstairs to swim for half an hour in his own pool, then took a nap. By six, he was ready for a drink, and if there was no social function on his calendar, dinner at eight, followed by an evening of reading art catalogs until the eleven o'clock news. That, at any rate, had been his schedule until he met Alexa, and it took a good deal of ingenuity to pry him loose from it, much as he complained about the boredom and loneliness of his life. "Habits die hard," he told her, "and the older you are, the harder."

One part of Bannerman's routine which he found no difficulty in giving up was his lunch at home, though it left his servants with time on their hands. Every weekday at twelve-thirty he picked Alexa up at Simon's office, the car waiting downstairs in a "No Standing" zone, apparently immune from tickets. From twelve-thirty to two they went from gallery to gallery, many of them so obscure that Alexa had never heard of them. How Bannerman discovered them was something of a mystery, for that matter, until she realized that he had sources everywhere. When he wanted to know who the hot new painters were on the avant-garde scene he called Hugo Pascal, the enfant terrible of modern art—who was as unapproachable to most people as the Dalai Lama, or Andy Warhol, or Henry Geldzahler—in much the same spirit that he called the Secretary of the Treasury to discuss interest rates, or Henry Kissinger for advice before making an investment in a foreign country.

Proximity to Bannerman gave her a first glimmering of the power of real wealth. His name conjured up an endless list of foundations, scholarships, endowments, trusts, cultural institutions, hospitals, medical research centers, and parks. No Republican President could refuse a call from the head of a family that had been the single largest contributor to the Republican Party year after year, since the turn of the century; no artist would close his door to the chairman of the Bannerman Foundation, whose fellowships kept hundreds of artists alive and whose contributions enabled museums to acquire their work; no head of government would ignore a request from the honorary president of the Elizabeth Putnam Bannerman Foundation for Medical Research, which had built hospitals and educated doctors all over the world, and financed research into every major disease; nor would even the Pope himself be unapproachable to the head of a family whose generosity toward every kind of religious institution was well known, provided it did not require the conversion of Episcopalians into anything else.

Sometimes when they toured the city from one loft studio to another, or from gallery to gallery, he would talk to her about the many monuments to the Bannerman family's largesse that they passed, most of them things she had never noticed before. He was more at ease telling her about the fortune than talking about himself or his children, and it sometimes seemed to her that in some ways she was *replacing* his children, as if he was determined to make her understand just what the fortune involved, since Putnam and Cecilia weren't interested, and Robert was interested only for the wrong reasons.

She expected him to be secretive about his business affairs, if only because that was his public reputation to a notorious degree, but he talked to her about everything, showed her letters and documents, explained them, gave her the reasons for his decisions.

At first it occurred to her that he might simply be trying to impress her—to prove that he was not merely a rich old man with time on his hands, as many people thought, or a mindless figurehead, as some of his family seemed to think—but whatever his motive was, it wasn't that. He didn't have that kind of vanity. She decided it was simply a symptom of his loneliness, the need to share with somebody the concerns of his day, like any other businessman whose children didn't care.

One day, as the car turned down Fifth Avenue, he pointed toward Bergdorf Goodman. "That's where Cyrus built his first mansion," he said. "Fifth Avenue and Fifty-ninth Street, facing the Plaza Hotel. It was thought too far 'uptown' then—very daring. Huge place it was, covered almost half a block, what with the gardens and the stables. Torn down before my time."

"He can't have lived in it long."

"He didn't. Commerce followed Cyrus. Shops. Offices. Traffic in the daytime. Prostitutes in the evening. He felt the area had become 'insalubrious,' to use his own word, so he sold the mansion and built a new one higher up Fifth Avenue, just below Frick's. He had a huge organ, big enough for a cathedral, in the living room, and an organist who played for him in the evenings before dinner, and a greenhouse with his own orange trees. All that's gone, too. *That* house I remember, at least. I was born in it, grew up in it, drank my breakfast orange juice from Cyrus's trees. It had a fence around it fifteen feet high, ornate ironwork, with points like spears. It made a great impression on me as a child—I thought it was to keep us *in*, like a prison wall, and I looked through it at the park and the street the way a prisoner would. I didn't understand that Cyrus wanted to keep other people *out*—he had a real fear of mob violence, perhaps because he had stirred so much of it up himself in the mines out west. And put it down with an army of Pinkertons. . . ."

"I didn't know about that."

"No. A great deal of money was spent to erase the memory, believe me. By the time Cyrus built his mansions on Fifth Avenue, shooting down striking miners was a long way behind him. But not forgotten. There were always armed guards in the house, and Cyrus slept with his old Colt .44–40, fully loaded on the night table beside him."

It was cold and a light rain was falling. Still people were window-gazing on Fifth Avenue—was there ever a time, she wondered, when the windows went unshopped? "Saks," Bannerman said. "Cyrus owned *that* block, too."

"Cyrus must have owned half of Fifth Avenue."

He laughed. "Nothing like half! A quarter, at most. My father sold it off, most of it, and used the money to build charitable institutions all over the city. He changed the face of the city, you know, and in my opinion never got the credit he was owed for it. New York Episcopal

Hospital, for example—Bannerman money built it. There was talk of calling it the Cyrus A. Bannerman Hospital, but Father wouldn't hear of it. On the other hand, there's the Bannerman Home for Foundlings, uptown a little, at Ninety-sixth Street, and the Bannerman Institute for Advanced Medical Research, next to Memorial Sloan-Kettering, and the Elizabeth Putnam Bannerman Pavilion, up at Columbia Presbyterian. Oh, and the Aldon Makepeace Bannerman Hospital for Childhood Diseases, on Fourteenth Street, which commemorates Father's younger brother, who died in infancy. There's the Bannerman Library at Columbia, and the Bannerman Institute for International Relations —which has become a left-wing thorn in our side, by the way. And the Bannerman Center for Industrial Health, next to Bellevue. It was Father's way of making up for the thousands of people who died from working in Grandfather's mines. Oh, there's more, much more. I'm the only one who remembers most of it, and except for Eleanor, nobody else in the family seems to give a damn."

"Surely all that's something to be proud of, isn't it?"

"We were brought up *not* to feel that, as a matter of fact. Father was paying Cyrus's debt to society, no more, no less. Pride was the one thing he wouldn't allow us. Besides, there was a problem Father hadn't foreseen—by then the fortune was so large that it made money faster than he could give it away. He had Cyrus's shrewdness, despite himself —for every million dollars Father gave away, he reaped ten million in increased property values, and since what he gave away was tax-deductible, he paid no taxes. It was like a perpetual-motion machine: the more he gave, the more he increased his assets, and the less tax he had to pay. I think Father was genuinely grieved by it. If he'd been a ruthless robber baron, like Cyrus, he couldn't have increased the fortune any more than he did by philanthropy on a large scale and Christian principles. As it was, he gave away almost a billion dollars in his lifetime, still managed to double the fortune, and considered himself a failure. A cautionary tale."

"What's the caution?"

"That even good intentions have unexpected consequences." He paused. "My children don't understand any of this, you know, not really. Take Cecilia. She thinks the only way to do good is to get out into the world and suffer cheek by jowl with the poor. Well, that's absolute nonsense! Perfectly all right for religious martyrs, of course, but my father did more for people from Kiawa than Cecilia will ever do in Africa. Or take Putnam. He turned against me over Vietnam—mind you, I respect him for it; I might even agree with him now, in retrospect —but Bannerman international scholarships have done more for peace than anything the protest marchers ever did. My children take The Trust for granted. No, that's not true. They *hate* it, in fact, because it makes them different from other people. They don't see it as a great responsibility, something they could *use* for the good of other people, if only they took an interest in it. . . ."

"Not Robert? Surely *he* takes an interest in it."

"Yes, damn him! He's the exception. But *he's* not going to be worrying about the goddamn foundlings, is he?"

He talked about Robert, and the rest of his family, as if she knew them as well as he did. When he admired a dress she was wearing, he was likely to say, "Of course that's not a color Cecilia could wear, is it?" as if she and Cecilia were best friends.

It was like the way he had begun to include her in his decisions. He would hand her a piece of paper, a suggestion from the family office about investing in a new hotel in Kenya (an irresistible combination of help for Black Africa and a good Return on Investment), or increasing the Bannerman Foundation's investment in high technology (the possibility of high profits, offset by high risk), then ask, "What do you think we should do about this, my dear?" as if her view counted as much as his.

From time to time she wondered just what her role *was*, in his mind —and what the rest of the family would say about it, if they knew. She had never thought of herself as a businesswoman, but she was surprised at how interesting it all was. The questions that reached Arthur Bannerman were not those of an ordinary businessman, however wealthy. He was surely the only man in America, for instance, who paid taxes *voluntarily*, though not to the Government—his charitable deductions were so large that they balanced out his tax liability, but he *chose* to give away an additional 10 percent every year as a kind of self-imposed tax.

The flow of memoranda from the family office went far beyond financial matters, however. Should AAB (as he was always referred to in writing) receive the Soviet Deputy Minister for Financial Affairs for dinner, in view of the effect this might have on human rights groups and Jewish organizations, and bearing in mind the possibility of causing offense to the Chinese, who were on the verge of permitting the Bannerman Foundation to reopen its American-Chinese Institute in Peking? Should AAB make a conspicuous investment in businesses owned by Black Americans? What was AAB's view of the fact that a television station of which the Bannerman family owned a significant part was showing X-rated movies? ("I think we're all for that, damn it, aren't we?" he said, with a roar of laughter—though she noticed, some weeks later, that he had discreetly sold off the shares.)

Effortlessly, for she had a good mind, she began to understand the curious rules by which he governed The Trust, almost as if it were a public trust. There were to be no investments in anything that might embarrass the family, no ventures with people whose reputation was in any way doubtful, no full acquisition of major companies (the Bannermans must never be suspected of trying to dominate a business), no high-risk investments (it was more important for the fortune to be preserved intact than to achieve a high rate of growth)—above all, no publicity (the Bannerman name must appear in the press only when money was being *given* away, not when it was being made).

Sometimes she reflected that if the relationship between them had been based entirely on sexual passion, it might have ended quickly. Not that they didn't have sex, of course, and not that it didn't matter, some to her and a lot to Arthur; but there was much more to it than that. She did not feel a strong sexual passion for him, and was secretly ashamed of that—but then, sexual passion, as Simon was so fond of pointing out, had not exactly been the most important thing in her life so far. As a child, she'd seen what it could lead to, and the effect had never quite worn off. What she wanted was a place in someone's life— a *secure* place—and if it included a place in his bed, that was fine with her, she might even enjoy it—but it was never as important as trust, affection, companionship, and the sense that she *belonged* there.

Improbably, she had found all this with Arthur Bannerman, though the rest of the world, if their affair were ever discovered, would probably never understand it. They would see her, she guessed, merely as the mistress of a wealthy man forty years her senior and draw the natural conclusion that there was nothing between them *but* sex, and the most exploitive kind of sex at that, whereas in truth they were more like an old married couple. Or father and daughter, some might think—but she was so repelled by the idea that her mind instantly rejected it.

By degrees, she brought at least some degree of normality to his life. They went for walks, window-shopping, sometimes even stopping to buy, like normal people. She even managed to get him to go to the movies occasionally. Without making a point of it, she took an interest in his diet and kept an eye on the number of drinks he had. He looked younger, thinner, happier, and she was pleased with the change.

She solved the problem of the future by not thinking about it.

ONE EVENING IN MARCH, she let herself into the apartment. He was waiting for her, as always—his sense of punctuality was so strict that he was always the first to arrive.

He was standing in front of the fireplace in his shirt-sleeves, such a rare occurrence—even if they were spending an evening together, he wore a suit and tie—that she wondered if something was wrong. He looked a little red in the face, as if he had been doing some kind of manual labor, but that, she thought, was unlikely.

He came over and kissed her warmly. One of the nice things about him was that he never took her for granted—it was as if every time he saw her was the first time.

"What *have* you been doing?" she asked.

He gave a guilty smile. "Ah. I've got something to show you. I hadn't looked at it in ages, myself. Had it taken out of storage and brought round here."

She looked around the living room, but nothing seemed to have changed—certainly nothing that would require Arthur to move a heavy object. She could sense his excitement, but at the same time she felt a certain unease, which she had been feeling more and more often lately.

She would have liked to ask him if it was wise to overexert himself, or tell him that his color worried her, or ask when he'd last seen his doctor and what the doctor had said, or suggest that maybe a man of sixty-four ought not to turn bright red in the face and start breathing hard because he'd moved a painting or a sculpture by himself. But she knew Arthur would regard that kind of question as an intrusion on his privacy, and in a way he would be right.

"It's next door," he said. "Come." He took her hand and led her into the study, one of those meaningless rooms that had been designed by its decorator with no recognizable human purpose, unless it was for a head of state to sit behind the desk for formal treaty signings. The furniture seemed too big, the pieces too far apart, far too valuable, and too uncomfortable for normal habitation. In the center of the room was a large object covered by a dust sheet. It seemed the wrong shape for a piece of art, but of course, with Arthur, you never knew—his modernism was enthusiastic and uncritical; the more bizarre something was, the more likely he was to be interested in it.

He pulled the dust cover off with a flourish to reveal an architect's model of a strange, squat, windowless building. It was "modern" all right, but not in the usual style of a plain glass box. From certain angles the building looked like an Egyptian temple or a Babylonian ziggurat, with terraces, hanging gardens, carved stone walls and odd overhanging balconies. She did not pretend to have any great knowledge of architecture, but it took no expertise to see that this would surely be one of the most remarkable and controversial buildings in the world, if it were ever built.

"Well, what do you think?" Arthur asked, like a proud father showing off his child.

"It's fascinating." She hoped it was the right word.

Apparently it was. He beamed. "Isn't it just? Makes the damned Guggenheim look silly, doesn't it? Frank Lloyd Wright was all very well in his way, but the Guggenheim was an exercise in senility."

"It's a museum?"

"Well, of course it is, Alexa. Not *a* museum. *The* museum. *My* museum! I'd almost forgotten what the damned thing looked like. I had the model put in storage when Robert tried to take things over. It had become—" he searched for the right phrase—"a bone of contention. *The* bone of contention. I was going to squander millions on it while the Bannerman fortune went down the drain, that sort of nonsense. . . . I was fighting for my life, so I dropped the whole thing. Sorry I did, now that I look at it again."

"How much was it going to cost?"

"Then? About seventy-five million, give or take a few million. Worth every penny, too. Of course, if you include the value of the land and the value of the collection, it's much, much more, but I don't take them into account. I *own* the land, and I already have the art. Damn shame not to put it somewhere, when you think about it."

"Wouldn't it cost a lot more to build now?"

"That's my point. You put this kind of thing off and it gets harder and harder to do. The fact is, it isn't as expensive as you might think. Most of the money is tax-deductible. And the museum itself could be self-supporting. I had a plan to license reproductions of the art, but on a big scale, by mail order, like a book club . . . bring contemporary art into people's homes, by mail order, at a bargain price. Had it all worked out, down to the last penny."

"What would the artists say?"

"They'd get a royalty. I can't imagine they'd complain."

"And your family?"

"Ah. They will *certainly* complain. But I'm sixty-four, my dear. If I want to do it, it's now or never." He sat down on the sofa and patted the seat. She sat beside him and slipped her arm around him. "The truth is," he said, "I'm beginning to feel like myself again. Like Rip Van Winkle coming out of his sleep, do you see? I owe that to you. I've been *vegetating*, like a bump on a log—and there's no quicker way to reach the grave. I don't know how much time I have left to do this, but I mean to do it. With your help."

"*Mine?*"

"I don't see who else I can count on, do you? Everybody in the family was against it last time, and I don't suppose they've changed their minds. Certainly not Robert."

"And you don't care?"

He shrugged. "I do care, very much indeed, but I'm not going to let that stop me. Not this time." He took her hand. "I'm going to make some changes. Changes that should have been made years ago. I want the fortune used to *help* people, not squandered or given away to institutions. If Robert doesn't accept my wishes—" he took a deep breath and paused—"I shall disinherit him, once and for all."

She felt his hand grasping hers hard. She would have liked to say that this was none of her business—that the last thing she wanted was to be caught up in a fight between Arthur and his family over a fortune which had nothing to do with her, and a new museum in a city that already had as many as it needed, or more—but she saw no point in arguing. She felt, despite herself, a slight sense of unease. Once word got out to the family of what Arthur had in mind, there would be hell to pay, and anybody who was caught in the cross fire would get badly hurt.

"Would you really go that far?" she asked.

"If I must," he said. "It means going against family tradition, but trying to grab control of the fortune away from your own father while he's still alive and breathing wasn't exactly traditional either, and that didn't stop Robert." His eyes were hard; whenever he talked about Robert, he became a different person, somehow more remote, harsher. He shook his head. "You know he even went so far as to prepare a plan for carving up Kiawa! 'The Kiawa Development Plan,' if you please. He had architects, contractors, political support in Albany. Barney Roth was behind the whole thing, you know, the big builder who put up that goddamn eyesore on Fifth that's made out of black glass, and he never forgave me. He and Robert would have turned the place into a goddamn corporation and built thousands of houses!" He laughed. "I put a stop to that. I'm damned if I want to see him turn The Trust into some kind of conglomerate, with a board of directors and common shares traded on the goddamn Stock Exchange, but that's what he'd do, or something very much like it."

"How would you leave the fortune instead?"

"I don't know. Or rather, I haven't decided yet. If there were somebody in the family I could really trust to handle things, I would put control in his hands. Putnam is out of the question, unfortunately. I did actually give some thought to Cecilia at one time, but she'd end by doing just what Robert wanted her to. I may have to leave control to more than one person, much as I hate the idea. . . ."

"But isn't that exactly what you just said Robert would do? Set up a kind of board of directors?"

"Nonsense!" Arthur barked. "It's altogether different." But he looked at her with new respect. Was it because she had answered back? she wondered. Or because she'd scored a point? He looked thoughtful. "Of course there's something in what you say," he muttered grudgingly.

"It was just a thought."

He got up and stretched, then began to pace restlessly back and forth. "I should ask your opinion more often," he said. "You've got your head screwed on tight, unlike my goddamn lawyers. That's the trouble with being alone all the time. There's nobody to talk things over with. You start turning things over in your mind without doing anything about them. I've been putting things off, then putting them off again. Well, no more! I feel like a new man."

"I liked the old one well enough."

"You'll like the new one better, I promise you." He stopped and stared at the model. "I suppose we could turn this room into a working office," he said.

"An office?"

"We're going to work, you and I. If you're willing."

"Well, sure, I'm willing, but what are we going to do?"

He laughed, happier than she had ever seen him before. "For one thing, we're going to lay the groundwork for a museum," he said. "Then we're going to decide how the fortune can be used—philanthropy for the Eighties, things that touch people's lives, instead of just pouring millions of dollars into places that already have too much. . . ." He came over to her and pulled her to her feet. "There's a lot to be done, but we'll do it together. Do you mind that?"

"Of course I don't," she said, and it was true—his enthusiasm was not only infectious but it also made him seem quite suddenly years younger.

"We'll shake on it." Then he changed his mind and put his arms around her. "No, we'll celebrate it another way altogether." Gently, but firmly, he pulled her down onto the sofa on top of him, and began to undress her. They had always, until now, made love in bed, undressing separately; and if the truth were known, she had never been enthusiastic about sex in other places, which usually turned out to be uncomfortable.

She kicked off her shoes and pulled down her pantyhose, while he struggled with the buttons of her blouse. There was something so spontaneous and natural in Arthur's sudden need for her that she was carried away by it as she had never been before. She didn't think about his age, or the discomfort of the sofa, or the fact that they were only partially undressed. She grasped him as hard as she could, felt him enter her abruptly, without any of the slow, gentle preparation which was his usual pattern, and heard his breath, harsh in her ear. "By God, I love you!" he said. She wanted to tell him how much *she* loved him, but the words wouldn't come, as if saying them would make it untrue.

She felt safe, wanted, *needed*, just the way she had felt once upon a time, so long ago, with her father. . . . She reached behind him with one hand and touched wood. She, of all people, knew how dangerous it was to think you had what you wanted. And how quickly it could change.

She blotted out the thought by sheer willpower and held tight to Arthur Bannerman as if her life depended on it.

6

"**Y**ou should be wearing a hat," she told him as he loped along the Avenue of the Americas at his usual rapid pace.

"Hate the goddamn things. Make you bald."

"You don't seem to have a problem."

"Perhaps that's why." A cold, light rain came down like mist. He strode through it as if he were taking a walk on his own estate, oblivious to the panhandlers, the crowds, the street merchants, and, apparently, the noise. A couple of elderly Hasidic Jews passed him, bearded, black-hatted, deep in conversation, and he inclined his head to them, possibly under the impression that they were rabbis. They bowed back gravely.

Not a single tenant on this block between Fifth Avenue and Sixth, to the east and west, and Forty-sixth Street, from north to south, had any idea that Arthur Bannerman was their landlord—let alone that his dearest wish was to raze the block to the ground.

The disrepair and general seediness around him seemed to cheer Bannerman up, as if he were the unofficial mayor of a small city of luggage shops that kept their "Going out of business" signs up from one end of the year to the other, porno magazine sellers, and obscure ethnic restaurants struggling to keep one step ahead of the Department of Health. "You couldn't ask for a better location," he said, pausing in front of an empty doorway in which a wino or a drug addict stretched out on a makeshift bed of old cardboard cartons.

"For a museum? I don't see what's so good about it." Her feet were wet, she was hungry, and she didn't share Arthur Bannerman's enthusiasm for walking.

"My dear girl. Use your imagination! What do you think the area north of here was like before John D., Jr., built Rockefeller Center?"

"I haven't the foggiest idea."

"A slum!" he boomed. "Filthy tenements, notorious brothels, speak-easies, the spawning ground of Hell's Kitchen. People said he was mad, and now look."

Two blocks to the north the towers of Rockefeller Center rose into the mist as if they were unconnected in any way to the ramshackle, low-rise world beneath them. "How on earth are you going to get rid of what's here?" she asked.

Bannerman looked surprised. "You demolish, bit by bit," he said. "Buy people out of their leases, relocate them, and so forth. It's a long process, but of course that's the whole point, don't you see? You have to start at some point, or nothing ever gets built."

"And you never started?"

"I did, actually. Years ago. Emmett got wind of it and organized a rent strike—even held a sit-in, or whatever the hell they were called, right there in the lobby of my apartment building. Mother had to fight her way past the demonstrators!" He laughed so loudly that people stopped and stared.

"Of course it wasn't funny at the time," he added. "It was one of the things Robert used against me. Part of the ground swell, so to speak." He paused to look in the window of a shop selling "adult" magazines and videotapes. "When did adult come to mean obscene?" he asked. "Just about here, if I remember the plans, will be the entrance to the sculpture garden. I don't see how anybody can argue it won't be an improvement, but I suppose some people *will*."

"Including Emmett?"

"Perhaps. Though Emmett's attention is turned toward South Africa at present, I believe. What time is it?"

She looked at her watch. "One-fifteen. Why?"

"We're meeting somebody." He gave her a quick smile—even Arthur Bannerman wasn't immune to such small pleasures as having a secret.

"Here?" She looked up and down the street. There seemed nobody in sight whom Arthur would be likely to know, and no place which he would be comfortable entering: a cheap Brazilian restaurant, a narrow shop that sold toy trains, a boarded-up storefront that served as head-quarters for a Fagin's brood of teenage black bicycle messengers. . . .

Farther down the street, Arthur's car was parked. Jack always fol-lowed Bannerman on his walks at a discreet distance, never letting him get out of sight. She had no idea whether this was something that Bannerman wanted or whether Jack simply felt it was his duty to keep his eye on his employer. Arthur never seemed to notice that the car trailed him—he hated the slightest suggestion that he had anything to fear from people and frequently expressed his contempt for the kind of new-money millionaires who surrounded themselves with alarm systems, bodyguards, and attack dogs.

A stretch limousine pulled up in front of Bannerman's car and flashed its lights. Arthur took Alexa by the arm and led her to it. A uniformed chauffeur leaped out and opened the door, and they stepped in. It was dark inside because of the heavily tinted glass, but even so, it was clear that this was the car of somebody whose idea of wealth differed from Arthur Bannerman's: there was a television set with a VCR recorder, several telephones, a fully stocked bar, an odor of expensive leather and fashionable men's cologne.

In the back seat a tall young man sat, dressed in an impeccable dark suit. She recognized him instantly, which was no great feat, since he had been on the cover of *New York* magazine last week and was on the cover of *Manhattan Inc.* this week, besides appearing regularly in every gossip column. David Roth was The Builder, the man who could work miracles in stone and steel, for whom no project was too big, too expensive, too ambitious, too glossy. His grandfather had acquired slums, his father had built thousands of the kind of cheap apartment in which you could hear your neighbors making love unless you kept the television set turned on all night; but Roth specialized in the kind of project that everybody believed couldn't be done, when he wasn't leading a social life that made him sound like a Renaissance prince with a Brooklyn accent. In photographs he looked dashing, but in the aquarium light of his limo his face seemed pallid, pudgy, and more than a little irritable. He had fat hands with rather too many rings, heavy cuff links, a wristwatch that must have cost a fortune. His expression suggested he was afraid he might be the victim of an elaborate practical joke.

Bannerman cocked one leg over the other jauntily and sat back in good humor, as if it were his limousine, while she sat facing the two men. "Damned nice car," Bannerman said. "A television set in it, too. Whatever will they think of next?"

"I spend a lot of time in it," Roth said.

"Of *course* you do, my dear fellow. I would too if I had a car as nice as this. How's your father?"

"He said to give you his best."

Bannerman whooped with laughter. "I'll bet he did! I hear his health is poor. I'm sorry if it's true."

Roth shrugged. "He's had a couple of heart attacks. A quadruple bypass. He's in a wheelchair now. Mother's got him down in Florida, with a round-the-clock nurse and all that. He's bored out of his fucking mind, to tell you the truth."

"How *is* his mind?"

"It comes and goes. Some days he's sharp as a tack. Other days . . . "

Roth shrugged. There was no tone of regret or sympathy in his voice. His father had been a big player once, and now he wasn't, he seemed to be saying. It was a waste of time talking about it.

"I don't suppose he's ever forgiven me for doing him out of this block?"

"You aren't his favorite person, no. He liked it even less that you never did anything with it. He hates waste."

"So do I. Oh, this is my, ah, associate, Miss Alexandra Walden. Alexandra, David Roth."

She said hello. Roth stared at her blankly. The pale-gray eyes took her in and dismissed her. Arthur Bannerman's personal life was of no interest to Roth. He was here to listen to a deal, not to look at a pretty girl.

"What would you say this parcel is worth now?" Bannerman asked.

Roth showed no interest. His suety face was devoid of expression, though his eyes flickered briefly toward the darkened window, as if to make sure that he and Arthur Bannerman were thinking about the same block. "Who knows?" he said softly. "As it stands, it's garbage. The rents probably don't even cover the fucking taxes, and you have to break your ass to collect them."

It occurred to her that she had rarely heard Arthur utter an obscenity, or heard anyone utter one in his presence, but he laughed. "I couldn't have put it better myself," he said. "But the value has skyrocketed in the past five years. Most of a whole block in midtown Manhattan, a stone's throw from Rockefeller Center. I can't tell you the offers I've turned down. Japs, Arabs, conglomerates. Amazing."

"Sure. It would be worth a lot more if you owned the whole thing, of course. But you don't."

"Your father saw to that. I offered to buy him out."

"He offered to buy *you* out, too, if I remember it right. Robert was all for selling."

"Robert wasn't in charge."

"It looked like he was then."

"He wasn't then and he isn't now."

Roth sighed wearily. "No offense, Mr. Bannerman, but I can wait. I've got plenty of other parcels to develop."

"Of course you do. But nothing like this."

"So? You can't build on it, I can't build on it."

"We could *both* build on it, Roth."

Roth's eyes widened. "You're not ˄ developer," he said. "Have you given up on the museum?"

"No. But there's room for both of us. You put up whatever you like —a hotel, or an office building, I don't give a damn so long as it's done with style—not one of your goddamn shoebox buildings—and I'll build my museum."

Alexa watched Roth's face. She wondered if he played poker. He would certainly do well at it, she thought, but she guessed that no card game could interest him as much as the kind of deal he was famous for that involved hundreds of millions of dollars. "I don't like partnerships," he said.

"Neither do I. But this isn't a partnership, Roth. You get what you want, I get what I want."

"I like to do business with people who are hungry, Mr. Bannerman. You're not hungry."

"That's true enough, Roth, but on the other hand, I'm an old man in a hurry. It comes to the same thing."

Roth nodded, acknowledging the truth of that. "There could be problems," he said. "At the city level, maybe. At the state level, for sure."

"I'd take care of all that. It's just a question of speaking to the right people."

"Yes, I guess that's still true for you," Roth said resentfully. "I should have been born a Bannerman."

"It isn't everything it's cracked up to be. And you've done well as you are. How are you getting along with the banks these days, by the way?"

"I hate the fucking bankers."

"My dear boy, who doesn't? But I hear they've become cautious lately where you're concerned."

"Maybe. They tell me I'm overbuilding." He laughed without any trace of humor. "They'd rather give the money to Brazil or Poland and watch it go down the toilet."

Bannerman shrugged. It was exactly his opinion. "Typical of them. Still, I *could* have a word with my cousin Makepeace Bannerman. Or with David Rockefeller. See if I can get them to loosen the purse strings a bit for you, eh?"

"It wouldn't hurt. What do I have to do in return?"

"Keep this a secret, for one thing. For another, you take on clearing the site—the whole thing. My name doesn't come into it."

Roth grimaced. "I get the pickets and the protest marches?"

"Exactly."

Roth sat silently for a minute or so. "You've got a deal," he finally said.

Bannerman nodded, opened the door, and helped Alexa out. He did not shake hands with Roth. The door closed behind him, and by the time they had reached Bannerman's own car, Roth's limousine had vanished into the flow of traffic as if it had never existed.

"He never even spoke to me," she said.

"No, but then, why should he? Roth's mind is on money. He probably doesn't think it pays to let himself be distracted by a pretty girl. I expect he's still wondering why I brought you along."

"So am I."

"It's the best way of learning. You won't learn anything by looking at pieces of paper, believe me. Business is flesh and blood, not paper. What did you think of Mr. Roth?"

"I'm not sure. You seemed to like him."

"He's not half the man his father was. He's also greedy and unscrupulous. But I trust him."

"Why?"

"Because he *is* greedy and unscrupulous—I've offered him half a loaf, and it's more than he ever expected to get. He'd get the whole loaf from Robert in time, or so he thinks, but now that he's seen me with you, he may have doubts about how soon that's going to happen. His father is about my age. He probably expected me to be in much the same condition—instead of which he found me hale, hearty, and with an attractive young woman in tow as my companion. Roth knows that time is money. He doesn't want to wait another five years, or ten. Now that he knows I don't have one foot in the grave, we'll get along just fine, you'll see. Besides, he thinks big. I like that in a feller."

She should have felt some resentment at being used as window dressing, but instead, she had a certain reluctant admiration for Arthur's cunning. She wondered if Robert was as smart as his father.

"Arthur," she said, "what *is* there between you and Robert? It's more than just not wanting him to have the fortune, isn't it?"

"Jack," he said. "Stop the car. We'll walk for a bit."

They got out at the corner of Sixth Avenue and Fifty-third Street. He took her arm as if they were an ordinary couple out for a stroll. He always seemed happiest when he was in motion, and left to himself he would walk for hours, even in the most appalling weather. "I trust Jack," he said, "but there's no point in overburdening him with secrets."

He slowed his pace a little to match hers. "I can't tell you what Robert did. It's a secret I promised myself I'd take to my grave. I've struggled for twenty years to forgive him—and to forgive myself, too, because I share in the guilt—but I can't. But make no mistake about it: Robert will undo whatever I've done unless I make that impossible for him."

"That's the reason for making a deal with Roth?"

"Of course."

"Does the museum really matter that much to you?"

"It matters a lot, yes, but it's not *all* that matters, by a long shot. I don't make any moral claims for building a new museum. I suppose if you really pushed me to the wall, I don't give a damn if the public goes to it or not, let alone whether they like the pictures. It's something I've always wanted to do, and I mean to do it, that's all. It's not as serious an issue as control of the fortune, or maintaining the independence of the Bannerman Foundation. The main thing is to ensure that Robert isn't allowed to pull to pieces what my father and grandfather built."

She squeezed his hand. His fingers were chilled—apparently he felt the same way about gloves as he did about hats. It was turning colder, the mist hardening into real rain, but he didn't seem to notice. "I don't like it when you talk about it, Arthur," she said. "It's as if you're getting ready to die."

"I have things to do, and I've put off doing them, that's all. I don't intend to die any sooner than I have to, thank you."

"I'm glad," she said, a little shortly. "Look, I know the family, the fortune, none of that is really any of my business. But it worries me to see you spend so much of your time thinking about what's going to happen after you're *dead*. I can understand the reasons, I'm not dumb, but I still think it's a little—morbid."

"Morbid?" His voice was glacial.

"Well, unhealthy. I don't think it's good for you."

"What gives you the right to lecture me on what's good for me, may I ask?"

"Maybe the fact that I care about you. I don't see anybody else worrying about you, do you? Frankly, nobody else seems to give a damn —certainly not your family. Sometimes I'm not sure *you* give a damn. You walk around in the pouring rain without a hat; you worry yourself sick about the money you're going to leave your children, when they can't even be bothered to send you a card for your birthday; you push heavy furniture around by yourself until you're red in the face. . . . When did you last see a doctor for a checkup?"

"Doctors are idiots," he snapped, jaw thrust forward.

"Are they? Or is it that you just don't want to hear what they might have to say?"

"I don't propose to be bullied on the subject of my health. By them, or by you."

She kept her temper with some difficulty. If he had been her own age, more or less, she would have let her anger go, or simply walked out. "Arthur," she said more patiently than she felt, "I *care*, that's all. Relax and enjoy it, why don't you? Not everyone is lucky enough to be cared about."

He glared into the middle distance, then sighed. "Point taken," he said. "Forgive me, I'm not used to it. Let me reassure you, however. Much as I despise doctors, my health is good. As for the rest, I plead guilty—with extenuating circumstances. Perhaps it *is* a little morbid to be so preoccupied with what will happen after my death, but I haven't a choice. If I trusted Robert, I daresay I could persuade myself to say the hell with it—let *him* sort it out after I'm dead and buried, why not? But I can't trust him, so that's that."

He paused to stare in a shop window, the rain running off his face. "My damned family," he sighed. "Of course, I shouldn't say that, now that you're practically a member of it."

"No I'm not."

"Not quite, true. The problem is that you're half in and half out."

"*Am* I half in?"

"Oh, I think so," he said firmly. "Unless you propose to pack your bags and move out."

"I haven't moved in yet."

"As good as, or almost."

"If you're thinking of introducing me to your family, Arthur, I'm not ready for it."

"They're perhaps not ready for *you*. But eventually—well, we'll see. I should like to show you Kiawa. Been a long time since I was there, myself."

"I'd like to see it, Arthur—but I don't imagine your mother will roll out the red carpet for me."

He laughed. "No, you're damned right. Damn, I wish I had a family like yours, you know. I'll bet your father wouldn't have put up with a situation like that for one minute, would he?"

"Well, it's hard to imagine."

"Of course it is," he said vehemently. "Impossible to imagine. I'm sure *his* children toed the line. I know those farming families, got a few of them still left around Kiawa, thank God. Salt of the earth. Spare the rod and spoil the child. I'll bet you never disobeyed your father, did you, when you were a child?"

"No," she said flatly, and it was true, up to a point. She reached across and touched his hand, causing him to jump as if from a mild electric shock—he was still nervous about small intimacies in public, though becoming less so. "No," she went on, "I always did what I was told until I grew up."

His hand was cold and wet. She wished he would get inside the car. For a moment, it crossed her mind that this would be as good a time as any to tell him the truth about her family, and what the consequences had been of being a good girl and doing as she was told. But she hadn't the courage, not here, not anywhere, it seemed.

Sometimes at night, when they were lying in bed together, she drifted to the very edge of talking about it, but he was usually sleepy by then, and she was not anxious to spoil the intimacy of the moment.

There was no right time, no right place, and perhaps there never would be. She decided it was just as well. Let him envy her family. He was no more likely to meet what remained of it than she was to be introduced to his—and they were both better off that way.

"Oh, even Robert was obedient enough as a *child*," he said, shaking his head. "That doesn't count." Then he smiled. "I'm doing it again. I promise not to talk about my family for the rest of the day."

The rain was pouring down now—a dim, dismal afternoon. Even Arthur had had enough of it. They got into the car, though it was only a few blocks to Simon's office. She forced herself to think of the work on her desk and was surprised to find that she was looking forward to getting back to it. In some ways Arthur was the least demanding of men, but when she was with him she found herself behaving exactly like a dutiful daughter, and while she didn't exactly resent it—after all, it was her fault, not his—she didn't like it much, either.

"We'll meet for dinner," he said. It was not a question. It half crossed her mind to say no, just to see what would happen, but she had, in fact, no plans, and could see no point in sitting at home with a container of cottage cheese and a stack of magazines just to teach him a lesson. In the past few months, her plans had become his—she had fallen into the habit of living her life to suit his schedule. She supposed that was the definition of being a mistress, which was just what Simon had called her, to her annoyance.

She gave him a kiss and sprinted across the wet pavement before Jack could even get out to open the door for her. Just once, she told herself, she ought to say no, but as she turned under the canopy to wave goodbye, she saw him watching her as he slumped alone in the front seat of the car, looking quite suddenly tired, and much older, and she knew she wasn't going to. He needed her, and he trusted her. Not many people had, she thought, since her father.

She tried not to think where that had led her.

"HERE HE COMES," Simon whispered. "The Baryshnikov of table-hopping." There was a hint of envy in his voice as he watched Sir Leo Goldlust move through the Grill Room of The Four Seasons like a ship of the line under full sail. Sir Leo tacked across the room to pay his respects to Philip Johnson, paused at Cranston Hornblower's table, head bowed in an attitude of worship appropriate before a major collector and patron of the arts, went down the line of banquettes kissing women's hands and shaking men's as if he were running for the Presidency of some Central European country, then proceeded down the middle of the room, handing out snippets of the latest gossip from London like a man handing out Halloween candy to children. He circled around and waddled toward Simon's table at last, though for a moment it looked as if he might keep going right past it, or perhaps pause merely to drop a few names before continuing on his way. Instead, he heaved a deep sigh and dropped onto the banquette beside Alexa, depressing the level of the seat by several inches. "So nice to see so many friends," he said, dabbing at his face with a silk handkerchief.

"I didn't know Philip Johnson was a friend of yours," Simon said.

"He's not a *close* friend, no," Sir Leo said cautiously, "but one naturally wants to pay one's respects."

Alexa guessed that Goldlust probably didn't even know Philip Johnson. He had simply recognized the great architect and had boldly interrupted his lunch.

Observing Leo Goldlust at work never failed to interest her. He was like a cruise director, determined to make even the most mundane of occasions a special event, with himself as the center of attention. For years, Goldlust had been Simon's guide through the baffling labyrinth of the European art world, for a healthy annual fee, plus a percentage of any deals that developed—an arrangement which she strongly suspected Goldlust probably also had with most of Simon's competitors. His knowledge was invaluable, which was why Simon, who avoided lunch dates as a rule, since he seldom got out of bed before noon at the earliest, had insisted on taking Goldlust to lunch. He had brought Alexa along largely because Goldlust liked attractive women, or at any rate liked to be seen in their company. Probably he would have preferred a celebrity, or somebody's rich and beautiful wife, but he was of a generation that had learned to take what they could get and make the most of it.

He kissed her hand, congratulated her on her clothes, gave a one-minute spiel on the Paris fall collections, with obligatory references to the health and state of mind of the top designers, all of whom were naturally his "dear, *close* friends," galloped through a couple of fast stories about how much Mrs. Agnelli had spent at Balenciaga and what the Vicomtesse de Ribes ("Dear Françoise") said to Yves Saint Laurent, and having done his duty by Alexa, settled down to business. You had to hand it to him, she thought. Given the opportunity, he could have probably done the same on the subject of the College of Cardinals if he had been seated next to Cardinal O'Connor at lunch. When it came to conversation, he was like a door-to-door peddler with a different trinket for every child.

"You're buying big, these days," he said. He pronounced it "pig."

Simon shrugged. "It's a rising market."

"Somebody's *making* it rise."

"The Arabs. The New York arbitrage crowd. Boesky, all those people. New money always means new collectors."

"The Arabs buy Impressionist paintings, dear boy, and hide them away because their religion doesn't permit representational art. If you go to Riyadh, they take you to one side after dinner and show you their secret Gauguin just the way a Victorian host would unlock the hidden cabinet of pornography in his library. I don't see them collecting contemporary art at all. Big nudes are what they like."

He smiled and waved at a tall man who stared back without a flicker of recognition. "My old friend John Fairchild," Goldlust said. "I must call him while I'm here or he'll never forgive me."

He turned his attention to the menu and proceeded to order. Goldlust had been knighted by the Queen, for who knew what hanky-panky with the royal pictures, but his title did not prevent him from taking full advantage of a meal when somebody else was paying. "Since you're doing so well, dear boy," he murmured, as he studied the wine list, peering at it through a gold-rimmed monocle, and ordered an expensive claret in guttural French. "I still think there's a shark out there, gobbling up the little fishes," he went on. "Somebody paid a quarter of a million *pounds*—not dollars, mind you!—for Venable Ford's triptych. Three immense panels, my dears, positively *sodden* with paint, great gobs of it."

"A museum piece," Simon said judiciously, with a thoughtful expression intended, Alexa had no doubt, to conceal the fact that he had never heard of the painting, or indeed, the painter. Normally she looked these things up for him so he could always appear knowledgeable, but in this case he was taken by surprise.

Goldlust tore into his roll like a man coming off a starvation diet and snapped his pudgy fingers for another. "Interesting you should say that. I wouldn't have thought so myself. Still, my point was its *size*, not its quality, if that word can be applied to a vast daub. Where could you hang a thing like that, *except* in a museum?"

"Plenty of people have big houses," Alexa said, knowing perfectly well who had bought the painting—for a color print of it was on Arthur Bannerman's desk, and she had commented on how grotesque she thought it was, to his irritation.

"An anonymous buyer," Goldlust said. "A lot of things are being bought these days by 'an anonymous buyer,' and they all seem to end up in storage in New York somewhere. I thought the two of you might have a clue who it was." The dark eyes fixed on Alexa. "There's all sorts of gossip," Goldlust said unblinkingly.

She willed herself not to blush, with some difficulty. She was good at keeping secrets, but no good at lying about them. Silence seemed like the best bet, so she shook her head.

"Gossip's a dime a dozen," Simon said.

"Not so in the art world—it's worth millions. Now you take a man who wants to build a new museum, for example, what does he need most?"

"A lot of money?" Alexa asked.

Goldlust bared his teeth to indicate that he too had a sense of humor. "He needs an adviser. Someone completely familiar with the art world. Someone, let us say, who could not only lay the groundwork for a unique collection, but also serve eventually as the director. Of course, people like that don't grow on trees." His eye caught the waiter. "More bread and butter. I can't eat oysters without bread and butter. Such a person should also be *cosmopolitan*." He gave Alexa his best effort at a self-deprecating smile. "Familiar with many cultures. A man of the world."

"It doesn't sound as if he'd be easy to find."

Goldlust wiped his lips carefully, then used the napkin to dab at his forehead. "Not easy at all," he agreed. "It's the kind of thing I could do myself, but at my age, with all my commitments . . . " He sighed modestly. "Well, the position would have to be very well paid indeed to tempt me. Of course, the opportunity to make a contribution to culture is the chief thing, in the end. Art is not merely commerce, is it? Certainly, under the right circumstances, I can imagine making such a sacrifice, if I were pressed hard enough."

"What makes you think we can help?" Simon asked. *"We're* not building a museum, after all."

Goldlust examined the plate put before him with the intensity of a truly greedy man: duck, *roesti* potato pancake, creamed Jerusalem artichokes. He took a sip of wine and closed his eyes as if he were about to say grace. When he was knighted, there were those in the art world who suggested the motto on Sir Leo's crest should be, "Better nouveau than never," but his true gift was not so much for making money as living off other people's. He ate swiftly, like a man who feared his plate might be taken away from him at any moment.

"A new museum," he said, his mouth full. "When you come right down to it, it's an extraordinarily ambitious undertaking. How many have there been? Serious ones, I mean, with some chance to endure as major cultural institutions? Le Centre Pompidou, of course, but that was done by the French government, an attempt to make the unofficial culture official. The Guggenheim? But that was almost thirty years ago. Norton Simon's museum?" He shrugged. "Very nice, but not altogether serious, and anyway, it's out on the West Coast, a tourist attraction, the Disneyland of the arts. A serious museum must have a purpose, it cannot merely be a picture supermarket, with a sculpture garden instead of a parking lot, or why bother? And it should be in a great metropolis, so that it stimulates creativity. It requires a man of uncommon vision to create something that will endure for decades, possibly centuries, and endow it with the capacity to grow and change. . . ."

He cleaned his plate with a piece of bread, and glanced nervously toward the dessert tray at the far end of the room to make sure it was still there. "Not many rich men have that quality. Take a man like Arthur Bannerman. Does he have such vision? One wonders. What do you think?"

"I don't have the foggiest idea," Simon said.

Sir Leo gave an ironic smile, dismissing the notion that Simon's idea, if he had had one, would have interested him. "I was asking *you,* dear girl," he said, patting her hand.

"Me? How would I know? I've only met him a couple of times."

"Is that so? Ah, the chocolate cake, yes, *mit Schlag, natürlich*, and espresso coffee, thank you. Perhaps a brandy. A Hennessey Five Star will be quite good enough, I think. . . . Talking about Bannerman, one hears rumors he has been seen around town with a rather striking young woman lately. He took *you* to a dance, I hear, at the Metropolitan Museum, of all places."

"That's nobody's business but my own, Sir Leo," she said firmly. "I hardly even know him."

"Of course, dear. And I would be the last to pry, I assure you. Probably the rumors are incorrect. Perhaps it's a different girl he's been seen with, or even *several* different girls. After all, why should a man as rich as Bannerman have only one girl? Still, my thought was that, if you *did* know him well enough to do so, you might put in a good word in my favor, that's all. Let me be perfectly frank—I see no point in false modesty—I *am* the right man for the job."

"I'm the last person he'd ask," she said.

"Well, nothing ventured, nothing gained, eh?" Goldlust sat back and surveyed the room happily. "I shall miss all this next week," he said.

"You're going back to London?" Simon asked, with a note of relief in his voice.

"Alas, not London. Caracas, I'm afraid. Of all placcs."

"What's in Caracas?" Alexa asked, trying to remember of what country it was the capital.

"Well, money for one thing. Venezuela is a member of OPEC, don't forget. Where there's oil, there's new money, and where there's new money, there are people who want to collect paintings." Goldlust called for a cigar and made a small, elaborate ceremony of selecting and lighting it. He puffed at it contentedly, the thick fingers with their varnished nails holding it with surprising delicacy, but his dark eyes were wary, as if there was still something on his mind. "It's an interesting country, Venezuela," he said, blowing a smoke ring skillfully.

"Is it?" she asked. "I don't know much about it."

"By an odd coincidence, the Bannerman family has major interests there. Mostly agricultural. Arthur Bannerman's son is the ambassador there, as a matter of fact."

She nodded with a polite show of interest. She wondered where this was leading.

"I shall be seeing quite a lot of him, I expect," Goldlust continued with a knowing smile. "The Pan-American Institute is putting on a show of contemporary American art. The State Department is very keen on it, since the Russians sent the ballet there last year. Better ballets than bullets, of course, but it's sparked off a cultural cold war. The United States Ambassador is naturally the honorary chairman of the exhibit, so I shall be dining with him. Of course we're old friends. I know his ex-wife, the lovely Vanessa, very well, wouldn't dream of going to Paris without seeing her. . . ."

"What's he like?" Alexa asked, showing rather more curiosity than she had intended.

"Robert? Charming. Attractive. Strong-willed. Very much like Vanessa, in fact—which I suppose was why the marriage was doomed. Of course, Robert's a victim of his family . . . it's very sad. His father always hated him, you know, still does. When he hit rock bottom, after losing the Presidency and after his wife's death—and Robert can tell stories about his father's behavior over *that* which would curdle your blood—Robert tried to help the old man out and damned near got disinherited for his pains. Vanessa always says it was like marrying into a Greek tragedy, and given her relationship with Basil Goulandris, she should know. *She* thinks the old boy is mad as a hatter, when it comes to Robert."

"And is Robert interested in art, like his father?"

"Not in the least. In the case of this exhibit, it's simply noblesse oblige, the obligatory small change of an ambassador's life. Ironically, it's exactly the kind of art that Robert hates, because his father collects it. It was Arthur Bannerman's plan to build a museum that triggered off the public brawl between them a few years ago—no doubt when you were still at school, my dear girl. The old man won that one by the skin of his teeth, but public sympathy was on Robert's side, and most of the family, too. If Robert thought his father was going to give it another try, I imagine he'd rush home to put a stop to it. Of course, I don't suppose any of these rumors will have spread to Caracas, as yet, unless some unkind soul were to pass them along. . . ."

Sir Leo flicked a half-inch of ash off the end of his cigar and contemplated it carefully. "So foolish of the Americans not to allow Cuban cigars into the country. You don't prevent the Colombians from bringing in cocaine, or the Japanese from swamping you in cheap motor cars. That's one thing to be said for Venezuela—they are deeply anti-Communist, but they don't suppose smoking inferior cigars will topple Castro. Well, it's been a very nice lunch, but I must be on my way. . . ."

Sir Leo stood up with considerable difficulty and waved his cigar over them, as if in blessing. "I'm staying at the Carlyle," he said huskily as he kissed Alexa's hand, after wrenching it toward him. "In case you should have something you need to tell me."

Then he was gone, making the equivalent of a hundred-yard dash toward the Pool Room—no doubt to put in a few minutes of table-hopping there—leaving behind him an aroma of cigar smoke and men's cologne.

Simon glumly called for the check. "I think you'd better have a heart-to-hearter with your friend Arthur Bannerman," he said. "The sooner the better."

"I hope he doesn't laugh at me." She found it difficult to take Sir Leo Goldlust seriously as a threat.

Simon looked at the pile of money in front of him, sighed, and added another twenty. He was not parsimonious when it came to his own pleasures, but he resented having to pay for other people's. "I don't think he'll find it funny at all," he said. "You'll see."

"Damn!" Arthur Bannerman said. "I thought we'd been so careful! Tell me again exactly what that son of a bitch Goldlust said."

Bannerman paced back and forth in front of the fireplace, his hands behind his back, frowning. He paused from time to time to blow his nose. Ever since their walk in the rain, he had been suffering from a cold which he seemed unable to throw off. He looked tired and drawn, and no amount of sleep seemed able to restore him to his usual high level of energy. It was not like him to complain of being tired, and still less to call anyone "a son of a bitch." She couldn't help noticing how pale he was; she wondered if he was angry with her.

"How the hell could he have found out?" he asked.

"Arthur, stop pacing. Come and sit down."

"Don't tell me what to do! Do you think it was Wolff? I always thought it was a bad idea to tell him anything. I can't think why you insisted on it. . . ."

"If there's one thing Simon is good at, it's keeping secrets. Please, Arthur, just sit down and try to relax."

"You always stick up for your friend Wolff."

She was surprised by his anger, but more surprising was the note of petulance behind it, as if, quite suddenly, he had become an old man, suspicious, irrational, quick to lose his temper and blame other people for whatever had gone wrong. "Arthur," she said, her tone as conciliatory as she could make it, for he was clearly spoiling for a fight, "Simon's exactly that—a friend, nothing more."

His jaw shot out. "It's not so long since he was more than that, is it?"

"I don't think my past is any of your business, Arthur. We're not married. Even if we *were*, it still wouldn't be any of your business."

Bannerman sighed. "No, we're not married," he said slowly. "You're quite right." He dropped down beside her on the sofa and closed his eyes for a moment. "I don't know what the hell's the matter with me," he said. "I feel my age today, and then some. Stiff, tired, grouchy . . . I'm sorry."

"Have you seen a doctor?"

"Not yet, but I will, I promise. It's this damned cold, nothing more.

He'll tell me to spend a day or two in bed and drink plenty of fluids. I don't need to spend a hundred dollars to learn that."

"It might be worth doing anyway."

"I haven't the time. And I don't believe in babying oneself. Never have." He put his hand on her thigh. Even through the cloth of her skirt it seemed unnaturally warm. "The truth is that what you tell me about Goldlust shook me a bit. Of course I'm a damn fool. Somebody was bound to see us sooner or later, and put two and two together."

"What will happen if he does tell Robert?"

"A great deal of unpleasantness."

"Why not just tell Robert to mind his own business for once, and see what happens?"

"You underrate him. You must never do that. Robert is shrewd, manipulative, and ruthless. When I was running for the Presidency, I let him handle certain areas of my campaign. He went out and hired a bunch of Cuban ex-CIA types, thugs really. They put together a string of prostitutes to proposition Nixon and Rockefeller delegates, if you please!"

She giggled.

"There's nothing funny about it," Bannerman said rather stiffly.

"It seemed funny to me. Oh, I can see it was *wrong*."

"Wrong? It was an *outrage*. And it was bound to come out sooner or later. Which is exactly what happened. And it's not as if it was done by some overzealous campaign official, a Haldeman or an Ehrlichman. It was my own *son* who was responsible. The more often I said I didn't know a thing about it, the more I sounded like an idiot or a liar. I might have survived it, these things happen in politics, but like all of Robert's schemes, it ended in tragedy."

"Tragedy?"

"One of the delegates committed suicide when he heard they'd taped his—ah—tryst. Flung himself off the balcony of his room and landed by the pool."

She felt a cold chill. "That's awful," she said. "But Robert couldn't have known that would happen."

"He might have guessed. It wasn't that he didn't think about the possibility, he's too smart not to have—he didn't *care*. The man's death meant nothing to him, I believe."

"What did you do?"

"I covered up his part in it as best I could, I'm ashamed to say, just as I've always done. The Cubans turned up again, ironically, working for Nixon—they were caught in the Watergate burglary. I should have washed my hands of Robert, but I couldn't stand the thought of a son of mine disgraced in the eyes of the world."

She put her arms around him. If there was one thing she had learned about him, it was that he had a deep need for physical affection, but was ill at ease when it was given to him. At first she had thought he didn't like being touched, but then she realized that he simply wasn't *used* to it, had grown, as it were, used to the shell of his dignity. He accepted her embrace stiffly, as usual, then relaxed and let her hold him. "Oh, damn!" he muttered. "I should have known this was too good to last."

"Please don't say that."

"It's no reflection on you. I've been pretending to myself that things had changed. But they don't."

"Yes they do. They've changed for me."

"And for me, my dear. What I meant is that Robert doesn't change."

"He may never hear about us," she said. "Leo Goldlust may just be fishing. And really, what can he say? You've been seen around town with a young woman? You're still thinking about the museum? I wouldn't think either of those things is exactly going to shock Robert, is it?"

"You don't *know* the boy," Arthur said darkly. "I have some measure of happiness in my life at last, thanks to you. I will do whatever I have to to protect it."

"You're not going to make a deal with Leo Goldlust, surely?"

"I am."

She was shocked. Arthur Bannerman had seemed to her a symbol of some kind of rectitude, a man who would never make the kind of moral compromises that other people made every day.

He coughed, caught his breath, and coughed again, until he seemed unable to stop. For a moment she thought he was about to choke, and she began to pound his back, while he signaled her weakly with his free hand—though whether he was trying to tell her to stop or continue harder she didn't know. His face was dark red, almost purple, and his eyes had a vacant expression; then his breath came back slowly, in anguished gasps. She wished she knew the Heimlich maneuver. Why did one always think of these things too late? Bannerman dabbed feebly at his face with the handkerchief from his breast pocket. "I'm all right," he groaned. "Stop hitting me."

"I was only trying to help. Are you *sure* you're all right?"

"I said so, didn't I?" He was still breathing hard, wheezing and coughing in short bursts, but his color was returning to normal. He looked furious. He hated the small indignities of life, and had once confided in her that he had never eaten anything but vegetables and bread at banquets during his presidential campaign for fear that he might choke on a chicken bone or a piece of meat in front of hundreds of people and the television cameras. "A glass of water, please," he said, his voice weak.

She rose and got it for him.

"You're going to bed," she said firmly. "*Now!*"

"I shall do no such thing."

"*Now*, Arthur. I mean it."

"Oh, all right," he conceded. "Anything for peace and quiet." He made it sound as if he was giving in to her whim, but she could tell he was relieved—that he *wanted* to go to bed and rest, provided he could pretend he was merely humoring her and not surrendering to his own weakness. He got to his feet, walked unsteadily into the bedroom, and lay down with a grateful sigh.

"Wouldn't it be better to get undressed?" she asked, following him in.

"Not necessary. I'll just lie down for a few minutes, catch my breath. We'll go out to dinner. You must be starving."

"I'm not starving. I'm not even hungry. And you're getting into bed. Undressed, if I have to undress you."

"Don't be ridiculous. I'm not a child. I can undress myself."

"Then do it." She had never spoken like that to him before, but to her surprise he didn't react with anger. Wearily he rose to a sitting position and pulled off one shoe, not even bothering to untie it. It seemed to take him ages. She sat down beside him on the bed, and untied the other, without any protest on his part, then removed his jacket. His breathing was still harsh, and occasionally he held his breath as if he were trying to prevent another coughing fit. He offered no resistance now, and not much help.

She had seldom undressed a man—it was usually men who wanted to undress her—and the intricacies of male clothing were unfamiliar to her. It was one thing to help a man out of his jeans and his sweater, but quite another to struggle with Arthur's tightly knotted tie, his cuff links, his waistcoat and his suspenders. She was amazed at the number of buttons he had. She had always thought of men's clothes as more sensible than women's, but struggling with the stiff buttons of Arthur's shirt and waistcoat changed her mind on the subject. He put his arms up with a groan so she could pull off his shirt and undershirt, then lay back as she tugged off his trousers. She uncovered half the bed, and helped him roll over, then covered him up. "Lot of fuss for a damned cold," he said, but his heart wasn't in the objection. He looked happy enough to be in bed at last, having accepted the inevitable.

"It's not just a cold, Arthur. It may be the flu."

"Damn the flu. A good night's sleep and I'll be right as rain." He tried to give her a jaunty grin, but it didn't come off. There was the faint suggestion of a smile on his face, but he seemed too tired to make it carry any conviction.

"We ought to take your temperature," she suggested.

"I never have a temperature. It's all nonsense. Stop playing the nurse, and come and sit down beside me instead."

"I'll do better than that," she said, and slipping easily out of her dress, in one quick motion she pulled off her panty hose and got into the bed with him. There were advantages to being a woman, after all!

She had expected him to be burning up with fever, but instead he was so cold that she instinctively put her arms around him to warm him up. He seemed happy to be held, and for a few minutes he seemed to doze. Just as she thought he was asleep, he started to cough again, less seriously this time. She helped him to sit up a little, and pushed a couple of pillows behind his back while he took a sip of water. "I feel like a goddamn invalid," he complained.

"Well, you're not, but take advantage of it while you can."

He chuckled. "I wish I felt up to it." He turned to look at her. "You think I exaggerate about Robert, don't you?"

It was exactly what she thought—that and the fact that she wished he would think more about her and less about Robert—but she shook her head.

"No, no, I can tell . . . and it's easy to understand. Parents always exaggerate, one way or the other. Their children are either devils or angels. Your father thought you were an angel, from what you've told me, then, when he discovered you were merely a perfectly normal adolescent girl, he was furious and disappointed."

"Well, that's not quite it." Was this the moment to tell him the truth? she wondered—but it didn't seem right. Then again, lying in bed, when he wasn't feeling well, might be the ideal time to dispose of the subject once and for all, but before she could make up her mind, Bannerman had returned to the subject that seemed to interest him most.

"For all his faults, I've favored Robert over all my other children. There was always more *in* him—not more of *me*, necessarily, I don't mean that, but more potential, more energy, a sharper mind. When he was a child, he idolized me—he expected more of me than I did of myself. When I was with Robert, I could never show the slightest sign of fear or hesitation, because I knew he'd be disappointed. I remember once, when we were out hunting, I jumped this damn huge stone wall, without the faintest idea of what was on the other side, only because Robert was watching me and would have been upset if I'd gone around it, as everybody else was doing—quite sensibly, by the way. I remember thinking, 'My God, I'm going to kill myself just so Robert will be proud of me!' "

He paused for breath. "I felt a terrible guilt for having such a thought, but I could see him on his pony, can see him still today, with those bright blue eyes staring at me, full of pride and excitement, but with something else there as well, something darker. . . ."

"How old was he, Arthur?"

"Oh, I don't know. Ten, perhaps twelve. A beautiful child on a nicely turned out little pony, a dappled gray with a lovely white mane and tail. Mephisto, the pony's name was, because he was a handsome little devil and knew it. I remember it well, bought it from Cornelius Arbogast, down in Clinton Corners, when his daughter got too big for it—paid a thousand dollars, which was good money for a child's pony in those days. . . . Anyway, there was Robert, in jodhpurs and a velvet hunt cap, looking deadly serious, as he always did, with a groom riding beside him, just in case, and I thought, 'The boy wants me dead.' "

"He may not have been thinking anything of the kind."

"Indeed? I always felt, you know, that he could never forgive me for the fact that he wasn't the eldest, that John came before him. . . . And then, too, Robert's a romantic, always was. He loves danger, loves taking risks, and I suppose when he was a child, I let him think I did, too, because it was the easiest way of gaining his affection. But the truth is I don't, not by Robert's standards, anyway."

He lay back and closed his eyes for a moment. She hoped he would sleep, but he was restless, as if he had some need to tell her his feelings about his son.

"When I decided to run for the Presidency, you know," he continued, in a low voice, "Robert wanted me to win far more than I did. I'm not so sure that I didn't go into it more to please Robert than myself. It was the highest jump of all, don't you see, and there was Robert, urging me on, producing political experts and pollsters with printouts that proved mathematically I could win. Well, I wasn't about to show weakness in front of my son, so I threw myself into the race, just the way I'd once thrown myself over fences and stone walls in the hunt field, and of course I came a cropper.

"I remember when the Secret Service came to discuss protection with me. I've no respect for them at all, by the way—FDR got shot at, so did Truman, Ford, and Reagan, and of course JFK was killed, so I wasn't much interested in hearing how they proposed to protect me, since I didn't believe they could, but I noticed Robert *was*. Of course, expertise of any kind fascinates him. He's what you might call an energetic listener—gives whoever's talking such concentrated attention that it makes them nervous, or they come away feeling Robert was hanging on their every word—but I felt a chill down my spine, just the way I had over that goddamn fence, and I thought to myself, 'Well, if anybody's going to be interested in hearing everything there is to know about the assassination of presidential candidates, it will be Robert. . . .' Unjust, you'll say."

"I don't know. I might say that, yes; it's a distinct possibility."

"Exactly what I felt. And yet, I couldn't help noticing that the prospect of my being assassinated by some damn maniac was something Robert could discuss in just the same cold-blooded way as the secret servicemen. They were very much against the idea of my walking into crowds to shake hands, and frankly, I wasn't overjoyed at the prospect myself, not after Robert Kennedy's death and the shooting of George Wallace, but Robert looked at them with absolute contempt and said, 'My father is not going to be elected by showing he's afraid of the voters —besides he's *not* afraid of any goddamn thing!' "

He laughed, started to cough again, and took a deep breath. "Typical, isn't it? Robert was determined to stand up for my courage without even questioning what I might think about it. *His* father wasn't afraid of a goddamn thing—*couldn't* be—and that was that."

"And was it true?"

"Not really. Oh, I'm proud enough to be stubborn, and fatalistic about death—I'm no coward—but you couldn't be a candidate then, or now, without sometimes allowing yourself to imagine what could happen. Robert always had more pride in me than I had myself. He never forgave me for losing the nomination."

"I thought you lost it *because* of him—the prostitutes?"

"I might have lost anyway. It was Nixon's year, not mine or Nelson's. But Robert's activities made it certain I'd lose, yes. He doesn't see it that way. In his view, I should have toughed it out. He saw my decision to withdraw as a failure of nerve. I became his fallen idol."

"It doesn't seem fair. You didn't *make* him idolize you."

"Didn't I? Who can resist being worshipped by his own children? You're right, I didn't make Robert idolize me, but I did nothing to prevent it. I'll tell you something else: when he was a young man in college, he took up polo and became a damned fine player. Dangerous sport, you know. Used to play it myself, and I was pretty good—one of the ranking players in America, as a matter of fact. One day, in Palm Beach, Eduardo Texeira invited Robert to play on his team, so Robert and I found ourselves playing against each other. I told him not to hold back just because I was his old man—jokingly, you know—but I took one look at his eyes and I knew I was going to be in trouble. He *had* to win. It wasn't a game for him, it was a duel. I've never played harder, or taken more chances, but no matter what I did, there was Robert blocking me, riding me off. . . .

"Polo's a vicious sport, you know. Or perhaps you don't. Imagine hockey on horseback, everyone riding full gallop, knee to knee. There's no such thing as a minor injury in polo. I remember, in the very last chukker—we were leading, I forget by how much, but it was very narrow—I thought I had a good, clear shot, then Robert rode into me, damn near had me off my pony, spun around and took a shot, and I suddenly thought, 'My God, he's going to aim straight for my face!'

"I think he had the same thought. I could see it in his eyes, and I *knew*, without a shadow of a doubt, that in the next second or so I'd be dead—then something in Robert snapped, his will, perhaps, and he swung his mallet and duffed. Missed the ball altogether, which no player of his caliber could possibly do, so I rode in, took the ball, scored a goal, and we won.

"I never played polo again, after that. I've often thought that Robert may have wanted nothing more. He may only have wanted to beat me at something I was good at, and perhaps drive me out of the game altogether—and he succeeded. But it's also possible that he may really have wanted to kill me, and didn't have the nerve, when he got the chance."

She moved closer to him, struck by his calm, as if the notion of his own son's trying to kill him were something perfectly understandable and straightforward. "You don't think that's a bit melodramatic?" she asked.

"Not a bit of it. Children quite often wish to kill their parents. Freud merely elaborated on the obvious. Did you never have a homicidal thought about your father? But perhaps girls are different. . . ."

She felt a chill pass through her, so sharply that he noticed it. "I hope you're not coming down with the same thing that I've got," he said.

"No," she said. "I'm all right." But she wasn't. The stories about Robert were frightening, not so much because of what he had done, or had wanted to do, but because Arthur seemed to have no feelings about them. The truth was, he still loved Robert more than his other children, and it was altogether likely that Robert still loved his father.

She felt, quite suddenly, not so much a need for sex, but for reassurance. She slipped out of her bikini pants and began to stroke Bannerman, who seemed a little surprised. "I'm not sure I'm up to it," he said regretfully.

"Oh, I think I can take care of that," she whispered.

He chuckled and moved over onto his side with a groan, while she pressed herself hard against him.

"It's no good, I'm afraid. I'm a sick man."

"Not that sick. Wait and see."

"It may be a long wait."

But it was not. On one level, she was a little ashamed of herself for coaxing a sick man into sex: on another, she wasn't at all sure why she wanted to. To please him? Perhaps. She thought it likely that he wasn't half as sick as he thought he was, and that his cold had simply depressed him—a state surely made worse by dwelling on Robert's shortcomings. Nothing cheered a man up more quickly than sex. To please herself? There was, she had to admit, something sexy about nursing him—a combination of her power over him and his vulnerability—but it was reassurance that she sought more than sexual pleasure, a need for comfort and closeness that could only be satisfied, finally, in one way.

Whatever her motives were, Arthur responded at last, with a certain amount of coaxing on her part, though, to be absolutely honest about it, not more than a lot of men half his age required. She pressed her back against him, fitting herself against his body, like a piece in a jigsaw puzzle. She moved just enough to bring him to a climax, then lay still, hoping he would sleep. She felt at peace, safe, here in bed with him, but of course it was false security, she knew that—the morning would end it. Being in bed with a man was a truce, not a peace treaty, but it was better than nothing, and she was grateful for it.

But he was still not asleep. "Don't let me forget," he whispered hoarsely.

"Forget what?"

"First thing in the morning. I must see to it that Leo Goldlust is offered the job he wants."

"You'd make him the director of your museum?"

She felt him laugh quietly, then catch his breath. "No, but a hint will be sufficient."

"What will you tell him?"

"I?" He seemed surprised. "I shan't say a word, my love. That's not at all the way things are done. You'll have to learn."

He took her hand and held it tightly. "Arthur Bannerman," he said, referring to himself in the third person, as he sometimes did when he was talking about what he could and could not do, "never talks to anyone directly about matters like that. Someone else will call Sir Leo and suggest that I'd like to see him on his return from Caracas. There may be a hint of a most important post at some time in the future. Goldlust will understand. If he shows any signs of impatience, no doubt we can find a nice little place for him at the Foundation, searching for worthy European artists. A handsome honorarium, travel expenses, a little stock tip from time to time, just to whet his appetite. . . . Why buy a man when you can lease him?" He gave a chuckle, then began to cough again.

This was a side of Arthur's character that seldom emerged in her presence. She thought of him as the upright WASP of all time, stately, dignified, moral to the core, which was how he liked to appear anyway. But he could be devious and cunning when he chose to be, all the more so because whatever he did, he would be firmly convinced that he was acting out of principle. She had devoured every book she could on the Bannermans and was surprised to discover that as a "cold warrior," in his middle age, he had been involved in the CIA, though he seldom talked about it. He was a shadowy link between the world of espionage and the larger world of big business, the universities, the foundations and the old moneyed aristocracy of the Northeast, one of the "wise men," whom every President consulted. The Bannerman name had been used to cover plots and coups, to aid "friendly" Latin American dictators and overthrow "unfriendly" ones, to make sure the "right" politicians in Europe (anticommunists) received secret campaign funding. Bannerman research grants had gone to such promising young academics as Henry Kissinger, Herman Kahn, Zbigniew Brzezinski; Bannerman donations had financed conservative think tanks, right-wing newspapers and magazines all over the world, endless citizens' committees to support the cause of worldwide democracy, in the persons of the Shah of Iran, President Marcos of the Philippines and General Jiminez in Venezuela. . . .

Arthur Bannerman dearly loved a dirty trick, provided it was in the patriotic interest—or, she had no doubt, in what he would regard as the interests of the family. Would he have hesitated to order just the kind of thing Robert had done at the Miami convention, with such unfortunate results, if it had been directed against left-wing supporters of Fidel Castro or people who wanted to expropriate Bannerman holdings in Latin America, rather than to discredit Republican delegates? She thought not.

"You make it sound as if you're going to have the poor man eating out of your hand," she said.

He yawned. His voice was sleepy now. "Yes," he said. "Work behind the scenes, like Cyrus. Get what you want before other people even know you want it." He snored briefly, the congestion in his chest making his breathing harsh. His eyes were closed, and for a moment she thought he was talking to himself, his voice so low that she could hardly hear what he was saying. "You'll have to learn," she thought he said, a note of urgency in his voice. "You'll have to learn how to protect yourself . . . better than I have . . . I hope you'll understand . . . I hope you'll forgive. . . ."

His voice trailed off, merged with his breathing; he was fast asleep at last, leaving her to wonder how she was going to get to sleep herself—for it was not much later than eight or nine o'clock, and she could hardly get up, or even move, without waking him. In the dark, she wondered who he had been talking to? Robert? Himself? One of the other children? And what was it for which he wanted to be forgiven?

He stirred, and she stroked him gently. The best thing for him was a good night's sleep. Then, quite clearly, as if he were dreaming, he said, "I'm sorry, Alexandra, but it's the only way."

She was awake half the night herself thinking about it, but in the morning, he seemed to have recovered his strength and couldn't remember at all what he had dreamed about or what he had said.

"HEAT," HE SAID GLUMLY, dabbing at his forehead. "I've always hated the goddamn summer in New York."

"I'm surprised it bothers you. You don't go outdoors much."

"That's exactly my point. Air-conditioning—it's an artificial way to live. When I was a boy, we opened the windows and turned on the fans. In those days a gentleman put on a straw hat and a white suit on Memorial Day and wore them through Labor Day. How many people do you see today wearing a boater—one of those flat straw hats with a black ribbon? You probably can't even *buy* a decent Panama hat anymore. My Uncle John had a beauty, so light you could fly it like a paper airplane. You knew where you stood then. In the summer it was hot, and the body got used to it. Nowadays, you have to wear long johns to go into a restaurant."

He walked to the window, moved the slats of the venetian blind apart with his index finger, stared out at the street, and sighed. "The truth is," he said, "that one only came into the city in the summer when one had to. These last few years, I've holed up here like a badger in his den, winter and summer. And you? You're spending the summer like me. I'm sure this isn't what you're used to."

He waved toward the antique desk covered with files, printouts, and papers, the museum-quality paintings on the walls, the furniture that was designed as art rather than out of any serious concern for comfort. On the far wall, opposite the windows, hung a Chagall tapestry. How many apartments in New York, she wondered, had a living room big enough to contain it? A fire burned in the fireplace, despite the fact that it was nearly one hundred degrees outside. Arthur loved fires—his servants were under strict instructions to keep one going wherever he was and to turn the air-conditioning up accordingly.

"You can't have spent all your summers in the city, can you, these last few years? It's amazing the things I don't know about you, now that I think of it. Do you like swimming? Do you ski? Do you go to the beach in the summer?"

"I'm not sure *what* I like," she said cautiously. "I've never really had the time to find out. When Simon and I were—" she struggled for the right word—"together, he used to rent a house in East Hampton every summer, but I think it was mostly because he thought it was what he was supposed to do. We didn't go there much—only when there was a party he didn't want to miss. I liked the sun. I used to love going off by myself to lie down on the dunes, but I wasn't crazy about the sea. Maybe it's because I come from the Midwest, I don't know—but the sea got on my nerves. I'm not much of a swimmer."

"I used to love the sea. Still do. I have a cottage in Maine, Greyrock it's called. Wonderful place. Wake up in the morning and there are seals on the rocks. Tell me, could you get away for a week? From your job, I mean?"

She nodded. "I could. Sure. Simon wouldn't mind." The idea of going away with him was something she had been looking forward to for some time—besides, he clearly needed to get away himself. Grey-rock she knew about—she had learned about all of Bannerman's properties, from the house in Palm Beach to the hunting lodge in the Adirondacks—an endless list of places nobody seemed either to use or to be willing to sell.

Arthur had gone over these in detail with her. He had never completely recovered from his cold, and there were many evenings when he was simply too tired to go out, and he filled in the time by explaining to her the intricacies of the fortune and his plans for it. Even now, at the beginning of summer, he seemed tired, slept badly, and often had trouble catching his breath. He still refused to see a doctor, all the more stubbornly since she kept urging him. He knew a dozen people, he claimed, who had been stricken by the same virus, it was going round all over town: Elliot Derwenter had been in bed for months; Channing DeWitt, Cordy's black sheep brother, had missed the Kentucky Derby, the Preakness, and the Belmont because of it, for the first time in thirty years; old Mrs. Douglas Fairchild had placed herself in quarantine in her own mansion for fear of infecting her dogs. . . .

Strangely enough, Alexa had met nobody who complained of the virus and had come to the conclusion that it affected only the rich and the elderly. Whatever it was, it did not slow Arthur down when it came to what interested him. He worked his way through the paperwork he had set in motion with furious energy, filling in gaps from his memory, devouring lists, charts, and diagrams, tearing his way through annual reports, scribbling impatient instructions to bankers, brokers, trustees, the staff in the family office, earnestly explaining to her what he was doing and why until his voice was hoarse.

"It beats me what the two of you are doing," Simon remarked in wonder, "the amount of time you spend together . . . I mean, if you were both young newlyweds, okay, for a month or two—but Bannerman's an old man, for Christ's sake. Are you trying to *kill* him?"

She didn't feel like explaining the truth to Simon—not that he would probably have believed it. By Christmas, she had become as familiar with the terms of The Trust, the very heart and soul of the fortune, drawn up at the turn of the century by Cyrus Bannerman himself, as Arthur was, not to speak of the innumerable lesser trusts that depended from it, like fruit from some golden tree. She was no lawyer, but it was impossible not to admire the intelligence of the man who had drawn up this web of interlocking documents, trying to think ahead to every possibility that might one day affect his descendants, or threaten the integrity of his fortune.

She had never thought much about the fortune itself. Why should she? It was a lot of money, and what more did one need to know about it than that? But as Bannerman reviewed it, using her as a kind of sounding board for his own concerns, she became aware of its complexity. The heart of the fortune was not money in the banks, but the shares in the great American corporations that had been fledgling enterprises when Cyrus Bannerman first invested in them—not that his investments were always welcomed by the owners, for, like the camel that stuck its nose in the tent, the rest of him soon to follow, a small investment from Cyrus often led to a quick, ruthless takeover, without any of the niceties imposed in later decades by the SEC. Teddy Roosevelt, and later Presidents, had forced Cyrus to break up his mining monopoly in an age when people joked that Cyrus Bannerman owned everything that was underground except bodies and oil, since he had conceded the former to God and the latter to John D. Rockefeller; but as he divested himself of the mines, he used the proceeds to buy up a huge share of American industry.

He had helped finance Walter Durant to create General Motors in order to spite Henry Ford, whom he hated; he owned significant shares of DuPont, Corning Glass, General Electric, IBM, United States Steel, Baldwin Locomotive, General Foods, 3-M; his foresight had been so acute that no new invention escaped his attention, from the electric light bulb to the radio. But that, of course, was the problem. The industries which had merely been a gleam in an investor's eye, or an entrepreneur's, when Cyrus Bannerman was in his prime, made the family rich beyond all reckoning by the time he was an old man, and continued to do so right through World War II and into the sixties, but by the seventies, they were faltering.

Cyrus had thought of everything, but even he had not imagined an America which would be buying its cars from Japan, Korea, and Germany, in which steel, railroads, shipbuilding were dying industries, and where commodity prices were buffeted by cheaper imports from the Third World.

Worse still, for years, nobody in the family had been willing to face the fact that Cyrus might have been wrong in the long run, or that being right for sixty years was enough for any man. Only with great reluctance had Arthur's father made changes in the family's investments, since he regarded Cyrus's dispositions as sacred, and Arthur himself had been only a little less reluctant. Besides, as he explained to Alexa, poring over the printouts, the Bannerman name made this kind of decision even more difficult. Of course, they should have sold their shares in GM sooner, but was that not like announcing to the world that the Bannerman family no longer had any confidence in America's ability to build or sell cars? They had gotten out of Big Steel when it was far too late, but the sale of the Bannerman family's steel shares was widely viewed as the final blow to the industry, the *coup de grâce*. The Bannermans had *social* responsibilities—and that was exactly what Robert refused to understand!

"He has twenty-twenty hindsight," Arthur snapped, but she couldn't help thinking there was more to it than that—Robert had been right, and his father had been wrong: much of the Bannerman fortune had remained invested in the Rust Belt long after it should have been moved into Silicon Valley, high technology, the service industries.

What surprised her most was the discovery that she did indeed have a head for these things, and that they interested her. Money as something to spend—on the human scale, so to speak—hardly interested her at all, but money on the Bannerman scale was like a gigantic Monopoly game, except that the properties were not only real but in many cases buildings she walked past every day. Soon she knew the assets of the fortune in almost as much detail as he did, and she began to understand his concerns for its future.

SHE WATCHED NOW as Arthur wiped his face again with his handkerchief. The air-conditioning was turned up so high that she was always cold, and she had left several cardigans around the apartment to throw over her shoulders; yet Arthur seemed to be suffocating much of the time, as if the machines weren't running at all. Sometimes he complained that the humidity made it hard for him to breathe, other times that the air was too dry. When he went outside, he complained about the polluted air, the heat, the exhaust fumes, and found it difficult to walk for more than a few blocks. At night he slept fitfully, either too hot or too cold, awakened by occasional fits of coughing that left him gasping for breath. During the day he worked at his desk, tired to the point of exhaustion, but too stubborn to take a nap—to the point where even David Roth took her aside to suggest she should persuade him to slow down. Roth looked menacing even when he was being sincere, but he clearly meant what he had to say. "He's pushing himself too fucking hard," he whispered. "These things take time. I've got hundreds of people to evict. This isn't Russia. I can't do it overnight!"

Despite her initial dislike of Roth, she quickly grew to trust him. A man who lived in secrecy himself, he was perfectly willing to accept other people's secrets without asking questions. There was no charm in him, he seemed to have been born without any sense of humor at all, but he knew quality, and would never settle for anything else. His name made even the toughest contractors shiver—he was, even now, not above getting down on his hands and knees in one of his thousand-dollar suits to find a slab that was a quarter-inch too thin, or a duct that wasn't up to specification. When Roth was around, Arthur seemed to shed ten years—he loved plans, blueprints, and architects' drawings, and she was surprised to find how knowledgeable he was. "I'd have made a good Pharaoh," he told her proudly. "If you had a Moses," Roth added.

Without Roth there would be no museum, and Arthur was determined to have work on "his" museum started before his sixty-fifth birthday, so he accepted Roth into the secret world he and Alexa shared. Roth often came late at night, having telephoned from his car, to bring Bannerman the latest news from his side of the project, much of which seemed to consist of putting pressure on city officials and judges.

True to his word, Arthur had talked to his friends at the banks, and Roth was, as he himself put it, "up to the gazoo in credit again," and building everywhere. The two men seemed to relax in each other's company, perhaps because they shared the same obsessive drive, or perhaps because, for different reasons, both had so few friends. Roth, the loner who trusted nobody, and Arthur Bannerman, who had cut himself off from everybody, were content to sit and stare at the model of the building each of them, for quite different reasons, was committed to construct. They seldom spoke. Arthur would nurse a Scotch; Roth, who didn't drink—indeed seemed to have few of the human weaknesses except greed—smoked a cigar.

Occasionally Roth would get up and run his hand over a detail of the model. "I could use a rose-quartz travertine for this," he would say. "The real thing, quarried blocks, not some inch-thick shit—I'll get you a sample." Or, without rising, he would study the model with narrowed eyes, his head cocked slightly to one side, and say, "All that stone carving's going to be a bitch to do right. You've got to carve deeper as you get higher, or you'll never see it from the street. . . ."

Roth knew stone, Roth knew steel, Roth could see the flaws in an architect's plan or model in a single glance. He was the only person with whom Arthur could share his dream in detail. It sometimes occurred to Alexa that he was doing with Roth what he was doing with her—just as she was learning the intricacies of the fortune, Roth was learning everything there was to know about the plans for the museum, as if Arthur intended to delegate the supervision to him.

Arthur stood there now, in front of the model, looking much the same as he always did, except that there was an urgency about him that she hadn't noticed before. "Can you be ready to go to Maine in two days?" he asked.

She nodded. The sooner he got away from New York and took a rest, the better. Besides, this was a new stage in their relationship, a sign that they might, eventually, be able to live the way normal people did, instead of conducting a secret life, most of which took place in this apartment.

"I hate to leave all of this unfinished," he said, glaring at the piles of paper, the plans, the model.

"It can wait, Arthur," she said.

"Of course," he said. But he didn't seem convinced.

7

Arthur's passion for anonymity made his travel plans seem like the movements of an army in wartime. The idea of flying "commercially" did not even occur to him, but on the other hand he was not about to use the Bannerman Foundation airplane that served the needs of the executives and staff. "I might as well announce my plans to Mother—and probably Robert, too," he grumbled. "I've been trying to get rid of the damned thing for years, but these days you can't hire good people if they have to stand in line at airports. . . . Never trust anybody in the Foundation, by the way. Anything you tell them goes straight to Robert."

Instead, he placed a call to one of his fellow Harvard Overseers and was immediately offered Morgan Guaranty's Gulfstream. "Not as nice as mine," he said, "but one can't look a gift horse in the mouth."

It seemed very nice indeed to Alexa, who noticed that the crew treated Bannerman with the kind of deference that would have been appropriate for the Pope, without ever mentioning his name.

"Amazing," he said, sipping a Scotch and water. "An hour and a half from New York to Camden! When I first came up here, it was all trains." He finished his drink and looked out the window. "I miss trains," he said. "Airplanes don't interest me at all. My father wouldn't travel any way that he couldn't sleep in his own sheets. . . . Damn. Nostalgia is the first symptom of old age."

"Oh, I don't think so. What's the second?"

He leaned over and gave her a kiss on the cheek. "Thanks to you, I'm not suffering from the second. We're coming down."

They stepped out into bright sunshine, though the temperature was cool enough, despite the sun, to make her wish she had a sweater on. The small airfield was deserted except for an elderly man wearing work-pants, a flannel shirt, and a red deerhunter's hat, who waited for them, leaning against an ancient, rusty station wagon. To her surprise, he showed no particular deference to Bannerman, as the pilots transferred the baggage to the car. "Better hurry," he said. "Fog's coming in."

It seemed to her unlikely—the day could hardly have been clearer.

"It's been a long time," Bannerman said. "You don't look a day older."

"Hogwash. I'm already getting my goddamn Social Security checks. You, too, damn near, except you don't need 'em as much as I do."

"Surprised you cash them, Ben."

"If the Government's fool enough to hand 'em out, I might as well collect like everybody else. Now they've got these goddamned food stamps, too. Half the freeloaders in the county are in the IGA Fridays, loading up on beer, off your taxes and mine."

"Ben, let me introduce my, ah, friend, Miss Alexandra Walden. Alexa, Ben Kidder."

Kidder shook her hand with a grip of iron. He gave Bannerman a look that made it clear just what he thought of an old fool traveling with a young woman, then opened the car door for her. He didn't bother to open Bannerman's.

They drove through a countryside that was new to her, but at the same time familiar—the New England village, with its white houses and prim church steeple, the background of countless movies and television shows. They passed a village green, where the war memorial was exactly where she expected it to be. Ben and Arthur Bannerman sat silently side by side on the front seat, apparently having exhausted their capacity for conversation. Arthur, she could not help noticing, was more at ease than she had ever seen him. Despite his dark suit and white shirt, he looked more at home here than in New York.

"How's the fishing?" he asked.

"Stinks."

"You said it was rotten ten years ago. Finished, you said it was, I seem to remember."

"Yup. Well, now it's damn near true, what with all the crap they're pouring in the bay, up past Bangor. How are the kids?"

"Just fine!" Bannerman said enthusiastically. "Couldn't be better."

"Is that a fact?" Ben glanced in the mirror. "Been a long time since we saw Cecilia. She'd be about the same age as Miss Walden now, I guess."

"Thereabouts," Bannerman muttered uncomfortably.

Kidder stopped the car beside a dock marked "Private" and moved their bags onto a small white fishing boat. Bannerman helped her over the gunwale into the cockpit, then went to the stern and cast off as Ben started up the engine. A moment later, as if to prove Ben's knowledge of the local weather, they were in a thick, chilly fog, which had appeared, it seemed to Alexa, from nowhere. She was not particularly frightened by it, if only because neither Ben nor Arthur seemed in the least concerned, but her stomach reminded her that she hated boats. She wasn't sick, merely cold and uncomfortable, but she felt a distinct possibility that she *might* be sick at any moment. She thought about throwing up over the side in front of Ben and Arthur and willed her stomach back into order.

Arthur plunged down into the cabin with a nimbleness that she had never observed in him before and returned a moment later with a couple of yellow slickers. "Too big for you," he said, "but put one on anyway. You look a little peaky."

She slipped into it gratefully. She wondered what he meant by "peaky." She could feel drops of moisture on her face, surely playing havoc with her makeup. Her hair remained straight in any humidity, thank God, but she wished she had had the foresight to tie it up in a braid.

She looked at Arthur to keep her mind off what might at any moment become real misery. In the yellow slicker, his white hair beaded by moisture, he looked twenty years younger. Leaning against the side of the cockpit with a pair of binoculars around his neck, he and Ben might have been brothers, big-boned, hawk-nosed, with the same weathered red complexions and bright blue eyes. Ben was a rougher version, thinner, less polished, but cast from the same mold. The Bannermans, she reminded herself, were of New England stock. Somewhere in their past were whalers, fishermen, men who farmed plots of land that produced more rocks than potatoes.

She had read enough of the Bannerman family's history since she had met Arthur to know that Cyrus's father had run away to sea as a lad—shipped out on a whaler, returned a couple of years later to take up farming in Massachusetts, then, driven by some less disciplined version of the same ambitions that would drive his son, abandoned his family and his home to become an itinerant salesman of patent medicine and part-time lay preacher. He was the black sheep of a family that otherwise had produced a steady succession of sharp, flint-eyed Yankee traders and farmers, with an unlovable talent for buying up their less fortunate neighbors' properties at rock-bottom prices.

A dark shape materialized out of the fog, on the right. "Whiskey Island," Arthur shouted, above the chug and clatter of the diesel. "We used to picnic there—remember, Ben?"

"Eyah." Kidder spat over the side. "Long time ago."

"You're a touch close, I'd say, Ben."

"Nope. I'm in the channel. You was the one who run aground on her, summer of 'sixty-three. Miss Cecilia got knocked overboard, I remember. Never cried a bit. I told the wife, 'You'd think a man with a billion dollars to look after could remember where the goddamned rocks were, after twenty years of sailing those waters. . . .' "

"Ah, those were the days!" Bannerman smiled broadly. "We had some damned good times."

She felt cold, not just from the damp fog, but from the feeling of being excluded. Whatever Arthur's memories were, they had nothing to do with her, and it galled her more than slightly. Still, she knew better than to spoil his mood, even if she couldn't share it.

She looked down and saw beneath the surface the rocks—if not *the* rocks Arthur had run aground on, rocks, anyway. She had no way of guessing how deep the water was, or how close to the surface the rocks were, but they seemed to be only inches below her. Any one of them looked big enough to tear the boat apart. She was about to cry out in alarm when a buoy appeared out of the mist, so close that she could have touched it. A seagull was perched on it, staring at her malevolently, its feathers beaded with moisture. "Dead on course!" Arthur cried, his booming voice strangely magnified by the fog.

The water was deeper now, a bottomless black depth, somehow more frightening than the rocky shallows. She had never been on the water long enough to be scared of it, and the fact that she was—and that there was no way to get off it—made her even more miserable than the fog.

She felt a movement in the air on her cheeks. Arthur's oilskin flapped like a flag, and the water, which had been as flat as a sheet of glass until now, however darkly threatening, sprang to life in long rows of waves. As if a magician had waved his wand, the fog lifted.

Perhaps a mile or so ahead—it was hard to judge the distance—was a rocky island covered with dense woods. At first it seemed uninhabited —or, to be more exact, uninhabitable—then, as Kidder's boat rounded the point, a house appeared. It was painted white, with green shutters, typical New England farmhouse style, but its size was breathtaking. It was impossible to imagine how it could have been built here, in such a Godforsaken spot, on an island miles from the mainland. She could make out porches, a widow's walk, a long dock with a gazebo at the end of it, an ornamental greenhouse, boathouses, but it was the main house itself that held her attention. She could not begin to guess how many rooms it might have. Fifty? A hundred? It was big enough to be a good-sized hotel.

"There's the cottage," Bannerman said. Then, perhaps sensing that she felt alone, a stranger in a world that was part of his past, he came aft, crouched down beside her and put his arm around her.

"It belonged to my wife, you know. Her father, old Jock Merrivale, built it. Jock used to sit there in that gazebo on the dock in his old age, in blue blazer, white pants, and a Panama hat, and watch his grandchildren and their friends bathing in the sea. My God, if he'd lived to see a bikini, the sight would have killed the old boy. You see the harbor? Blasted out of solid rock. Deep enough for a destroyer. And the breakwater? Granite blocks, each one as big as a goddamned house, brought down by barge from Bangor! Of course, all that was built before the crash clipped the Merrivales' goddamn wings," he added with satisfaction. "Are you cold?"

"A little."

"We'll have you warm in a few minutes. A drink, a good fire, early supper. How's your stomach?"

"Holding up. Why?"

"I should have asked how you felt about boats."

"I didn't know how I felt about them. It's a new experience. I'm still not sure."

"Well, luckily for you, I'm past my sailing days. I used to sail a Safe Harbor Thirty single-handed here, and not too many people can do that. My hands are too soft for that now. Damn shame I let it all go."

"You could start again."

"I might," he said, with a jaunty grin. "I just damned well might!" She had never seen him so cheerful.

They entered the harbor, drifted past the breakwater that Merrivale had built, at such expense and trouble, and came to rest at the end of a long dock. She slipped out of the oilskin, grateful to be rid of its clammy embrace, climbed a wooden ladder and stood still for a moment, feeling her legs tremble, happy to be on dry land, or at least within walking distance of it. Bannerman followed, grinning like a boy, then Kidder, who seemed to have no difficulty climbing the steep ladder while carrying the bags.

Bannerman took her arm as they walked the length of the long dock, then led her across a magnificent lawn, in the center of which stood a flagstaff flying the American flag. At its base was a large cannon.

"Jock Merrivale was a patriot," Bannerman explained. "When he was in residence, he fired the cannon every night at sundown as the flag was lowered. You had to stand to attention, too, whatever you were in the middle of doing. It's not a custom I've continued."

"Well, at least there are no neighbors to object."

"No. The nearest inhabited island is about five miles away. Safe Harbor it's called—inappropriately enough, since people have been running aground on it since the sixteen hundreds."

A gray-haired woman appeared on the steps to greet them, Ben Kidder's wife, Alexa guessed. If she was surprised to see Arthur Bannerman accompanied by a young woman, she kept it firmly to herself, though Alexa could hardly help noticing how sharply she was being scrutinized. Here, however, at Greyrock, Arthur Bannerman could do no wrong—these were his people, loyal to him, and it was noticeable that he did not treat them like servants.

All the same, she felt somehow a little dismayed by it all. In New York their life was restricted, but here, for the first time, she was entering Arthur's world, a world of huge houses, servants waiting, sometimes for years, to make him comfortable. She did not see how she would fit into that world, if the time ever came, or what he would expect of her.

She huddled in front of the huge fireplace, sipping a cup of tea, feeling, more than she had ever felt in her life, as if she were swimming far out of her depth. . . .

"MAGNIFICENT, ISN'T IT?"

She nodded, sleepy and admiring. The view *was* magnificent—all the money in the world couldn't buy a view like this one—but of course only money could preserve it or keep it for the exclusive use of just one family.

Leaning back against a rock, Arthur seemed a different man—younger, healthier, far more physically active than he was in New York. His cough had vanished, his color was good, he slept like a baby now. He wore an old Viyella shirt, baggy chinos, a pair of Topsiders that looked as if they had gone to Harvard with him. It was not just that he had the right clothes for the place—it was as if he had never worn anything else.

They sat in the lee of the wind, as he put it, in a rocky cove, with blankets spread on the shingle beach. Kidder had brought them here in his boat, laid the picnic basket and a cooler on the ground, then had gone off, leaving them a battery-operated radiophone to summon him for the return trip. They were as alone as it was possible to be, except for the seals which, as promised, surfaced from time to time to stare at them with friendly curiosity. She tossed a few sandwiches in their direction—Mrs. Kidder had prepared a picnic sufficient for a dozen people, perhaps even a dozen seals—but unlike the seals in the zoo, these had no gift for catching food in midair, or perhaps simply didn't see the point. They waited until the food was in the water and snapped it up as it floated past their noses.

"We'll have a storm tomorrow," Arthur said. "Mark my words. Maybe sooner."

"I don't believe it. It's beautiful." It was not only beautiful, but so warm that she rose and took her sweater off, then sat down beside him in the sun, her shirt unbuttoned to the waist.

He put his arm around her. "You'll see. We should have gone to Jamaica or Puerto Rico. You can count on the sun there. The family owns hotels there, you know—huge damned places with golf courses, beaches, condominiums. . . . I must remember to go over all that. Father believed strongly in investing in Latin America and the Caribbean. He was always suspicious of Europe. I built those places, you know. Hired the architects, went out there with the surveyors, dealt with the locals. He put me in charge when I was twenty-five, right after the war, and I did a damned fine job."

"That explains why you and Roth get on so well together. I like it better here, though."

"So do I. But I'd like to see you in a bikini, by a pool."

"You're not that old, if that's what's on your mind."

"I don't suppose I'll ever be too old to enjoy looking at you, my dear. Still, sixty-five is sixty-five." He looked grim for a moment, and was silent, as if he were trying to make up his mind about something. "It's probably not the moment to tell you," he said at last, "but I think I've made up my mind what to do."

"To do? About what?"

"The Trust," he said sharply. "On my sixty-fifth birthday I'm going to call my children together and tell them that on my death they'll each receive their trusts, plus an additional sum, but the bulk of the fortune itself will become a charitable trust, with each of them having a single vote on the way the income is used. There will be a governing body, with at least two outside directors, and myself as chairman. I'll appoint someone to succeed me before I'm seventy, perhaps in the family, perhaps not. . . . There are a lot of details to be worked out, but that's the general picture. Each of the children will be rich—*far* richer than they are now—but no single Bannerman will ever have power over the whole thing."

"What makes you think Robert will accept that?"

"I'll make him accept it," Arthur said grimly. He stared at the horizon. "I want it done, Alexa. I want it done *now*, while there's still time for us to enjoy ourselves. Once things are in place, we can travel, do what we like. . . . What do you say?"

She was startled by his decision; she knew just how much trouble it would cause. It was the last thing she wanted to talk about now that they were away together for the first time. "I'll go anywhere you want," she said. "I've never been out of the country. I haven't seen London, Paris, Rome. When I was a child, I always dreamed of traveling, but I never got further than New York."

She could not help being happy that he had included her in his future plans, more emphatically than he had ever done. All the same, there was a quality of daydreaming to his conversation, almost as if he didn't want to spoil the pleasure of the moment by making things too precise.

Nor did she. She lay beside him on the blanket, feeling the warmth of the sun and his arm around her shoulder. The picnic hamper was open at their feet—a huge, antique wicker-and-leather contraption, with rows of mysterious, old-fashioned implements in gleaming silver, strapped into the inside of the lid—boxes, something she took to be a spirit lamp, a teapot, sterling silver cutlery, crystal wineglasses and monogrammed china. Bannerman had brought along a perfectly ordinary plastic cooler, with ice, a bottle of Scotch and glasses—the picnic hamper was apparently a kind of stage prop, more important to Mrs. Kidder's sense of things than to his.

"It's damned hot," he said. "I wouldn't mind a dip."

"The water must be freezing."

"Brisk. I hate warm water. It's like swimming in soup."

"You don't have a pair of trunks, anyway."

"Oh, damn that. This is my own island. There's not a soul around."

"Arthur, you can't go swimming with all those seals."

"The seals will vanish the moment I step into the water. They're the least aggressive animals imaginable, my dear. Why do you suppose sealers find it so easy to club the poor brutes to death?"

Alexa shrugged. The heat was quite extraordinary, with the sun beating down on the rocks and not the faintest trace of a breeze. If he wanted to swim, she thought, let him.

She wriggled out of her jeans, pulled off her shirt, and lay back against the blanket, wishing she had brought a bikini along, but content enough to sunbathe in her underwear. She had drunk one glass of white wine with her sandwich, more because Arthur had gone to the trouble of opening the bottle than because she really wanted it, but the result was that she felt as torpid as the seals, now basking motionless on the rocks a hundred yards away, their eyes closed.

He strode manfully into the water, splashing forward until it was knee-high. She closed her eyes and heard a loud splash. "Splendid!" he cried out, though in a voice that suggested agony rather than pleasure. She had put her hand in the water of Penobscot Bay on the way over, on Kidder's boat, and that had been enough for her. It seemed to be just above the freezing point—cold enough to explain why the seals preferred to bask on the rocks in the sun.

She dozed, feeling the heat on her naked back—she had unfastened the straps of her bra—drifting back and forth from thoughts about Bannerman and his family to no thoughts at all, on the edge of consciousness rather than asleep. The heat was like a heavy weight, pinning her to the ground, but not unpleasant, though she knew she would soon have to get up or she'd be burned. She gave herself a minute or two more, then, quite suddenly, she felt a chill. She opened her eyes. The sun had slipped behind a cloud, and she was cold. This was not the tropics, after all—the heat was deceptive. When the sun was directly on you, you were warm enough, even hot, but the moment it was covered, you were reminded that this was Maine.

She reached behind her to refasten her bra, then sat up and looked out over the bay. The water had turned from a cheerful blue to a dark gunmetal gray, the horizon had vanished, and a stiff breeze, springing up from nowhere, it seemed, without any warning, was raising an uncomfortable-looking chop. In the distance, out beyond the rocks, there were streaks on the water. She felt her stomach lurch at the thought of the boat trip back.

Then it occurred to her that Arthur was nowhere in this seascape. The rocks were there, beginning to glisten as small waves broke against them. The seals were there, stirring now, with occasional yelps at the sudden interruption of their sunbath. On the shingle between the blankets and the water, Arthur's clothes lay neatly folded, weighted down with his Topsiders. It seemed to her that the distance between where she was and the water was smaller than she remembered. Was the tide coming in? How long had she been dozing?

She felt panic beginning to suffocate her. She shouted his name, as loud as she could, but if there had been any reply, it was drowned out by the barking of the seals. She shouted again, conscious that the wind was stronger now, carrying her voice back to her, the waves beginning to splash against the rocks as if they meant business.

She stood there on the unfamiliar and now threatening beach, shivering in her underwear, trying to convince herself that Bannerman was playing some kind of stupid, macho practical joke on her, warming herself with anger at him. There was a burst of noise from the rocks, but it was only the seals, finally resigned to the change in the weather, diving and sliding into the water with snorts of disgust. Her anger evaporated.

She forced herself to think logically. If he had been swept away by the tide or the currents, there was nothing she could do. On the other hand, if he was in any kind of trouble, and still conscious, he would try to reach a rock and cling to it. She would have to explore the rocks, going as far as she could without actually swimming—for she didn't swim well enough to survive for long in this water.

She plunged into the water up to her waist, terrified by how cold it was, feeling her legs go numb almost instantly. Her bare feet slipped on the moss and seaweed, but she kept going, moving out toward the rocks where the seals had been sunning themselves a moment ago. Once or twice she slipped into a deeper spot, desperately dog-paddling until she found her footing again. She skinned her knees, scraped her hands, broke her fingernails, but somehow she kept going until she had reached the big rocks at the far point of the cove.

Beyond its shelter, the wind howled at her. The sea was streaking into long strips of foam, the water around her was black now, completely lifeless. She had gone as far as she could—she knew it would take all her remaining strength to get back, wasn't even sure that she *could*. She was crying now, the salt of her tears mixing with the salt from the sea until she was almost blinded. A wave hit her, sent her flying against a rock, so hard that she didn't even feel the impact, though it took her breath away. Had she broken a bone? There was no point in thinking about it. She clung to the rock, moaning, smelling the fishy odor the seals had left behind them, her hands grasping a piece of seaweed while the waves tried to knock her off her feet.

She pulled herself around the rock, trying to get in the lee of the wind—was that the phrase?—to catch her breath. She reached behind to steady herself and felt her hand touch something soft and yielding. She pulled it back with a yelp, astonished to find in herself a reserve capacity for fear. Did seals bite?

Then it dawned on her that whatever she had touched was hairless. She turned around, to find Arthur, clinging to the other side of the rock. His eyes were wide open, but he seemed unable to speak, and his breath came in long shallow gasps. There was a deep gash on his forehead, but what frightened her most were his fingernails, which were a dark blue, almost purple, in livid contrast to his white hands, as he clutched the seaweed to hold his head above water.

It took all her remaining strength to pull him clear of the rock. She knew little of life-saving techniques, and less still of medicine, but it was clear to her that he would die of exposure if she didn't get him back to shore. She could not lift him—he was too heavy for that—and he seemed unable to help himself. He was, she told herself, a dead weight, and the phrase echoed in her mind.

With each step she took, his head slipped under water. She looked at the distance between herself and the shore, and decided that she would have drowned him long before she got him back to safety. She slipped her arms around him and turned him over, so he was floating face up in the waves, then crouched down in the water with her arms around his chest, holding his head as high as she could and walking backward toward the beach.

She slipped, she stumbled, she sank, sometimes she even found herself swimming clumsily, holding him with one arm while she paddled with the other, certain they were both going to drown. She wanted to say something encouraging, but her teeth were chattering uncontrollably, and she gave up the effort. She could hear herself sobbing, so loudly that the sound drowned out the wind and the waves, until finally, with one last heave, she beached him on the shingles, so hard that she was afraid she had broken his back.

She pulled him as far out of the water as she could, then ran back, pulled the blanket out from under the picnic basket, sending it flying down the beach, with all its expensive knickknacks, and wrapped the blanket around Bannerman's body. His ankles were still in the water, but she had done her best.

His breathing was getting deeper. A good sign or a bad one? She didn't know. She lay beside him, sheltering him, trying to give him what little heat her body could provide.

His lips worked, and she put her ear against them, straining to pick up his words. "You're kidding," she thought she heard him say in a hoarse whisper, but that couldn't be right. "Kidder!" he said, more loudly. "Radio!"

She had forgotten about the radiophone they had brought on shore with them. She cursed herself for her stupidity, then told herself that there would have been no point in calling Kidder until she had found Arthur and rescued him.

She ran back to where they had picnicked, panicked briefly when she couldn't find the instrument, then ran to the overturned basket and fished it out from the sodden, jagged mass of broken glass and wet sandwiches. Rain was falling now, in stinging sheets, punctuated by the occasional flash of lightning. She wondered how dangerous it was to be standing here, soaking wet, holding a radiophone with its aerial pointing straight to the sky. She was enough of a farm girl to know what lightning could do. She pulled the telescoping antenna out to its full length and waited for the flash that would singe her or burn her to a crisp. Then she realized that she didn't have the foggiest idea how to use the damned thing. It had buttons on it like a telephone, and a digital readout that glowed a spectral green. There was an illuminated rectangular bar marked "Send." She held it down, put her mouth close to the machine and shouted, "Mr. Kidder! Ben! Help!"

There was a fierce crackle of static that almost deafened her, then Kidder's voice came through, clear as a bell. "Don't shout," he said. "You damned near broke my eardrums."

"You've got to get here right away!"

"I'm on my way. Started out as soon as I saw the weather changing. Getting wet, I guess?"

"Kidder, Arthur was swimming. He nearly drowned. I don't know what to do. Please hurry!"

Kidder's voice came back, serious now. "How bad off is he?"

"Very. He's still alive, but only just."

"Cover him up. Keep him warm. Squeeze his chest to get the water out. Can you hold out for fifteen-twenty minutes?"

"I don't know. Can't you get a helicopter or something?"

"Not in this storm, Miss Walden. You cover him the best you can, and pray."

She ran back to where Arthur lay, covered him with her body and—for the first time since she was a little girl—prayed.

She was still reciting the Lord's Prayer over and over when Kidder waded ashore what seemed like a lifetime later.

HE LAY PROPPED HIGH on the pillows, his face as white as the sheet, his eyes closed. His forehead was bandaged, giving him the appearance of some hero general wounded on the battlefield. It needed only a somber group of officers standing around him to complete the picture.

She sat beside him, shivering, unable to warm up despite the fire, countless cups of tea, and even a glass of brandy, which merely made her choke and splutter.

Bannerman's breathing was normal, he held her hand tightly, like a frightened child, as he dozed fitfully. His fingernails were still blue, but a paler shade. She hoped it was a good sign. Outside, the storm lashed against the windows. The trees groaned and creaked in the gale-force wind, and from time to time the house itself shuddered, as if it were alive. In the last few hours she had developed an antipathy to the Maine seacoast which, she suspected, was very likely to last a lifetime.

She had been sitting beside him for over two hours, while the Kidders came and went to report on the progress of the storm, which had knocked out the electricity and the telephone lines. The Kidders were in their element. For the island people, she realized, the sea provided a year-round soap opera. Mrs. Kidder could and did rattle off drownings, shipwrecks, epic storms, and heroic rescues by the yard.

A sharper gust of wind shook the house and sent sparks flying in the fireplace. Bannerman opened his eyes and looked at her. "You're the one who ought to be in bed," he said. "Your hand is still as cold as ice."

"Hush. I'm all right. You're to lie still until Ben can fetch a doctor from the mainland."

"I don't need any backwoods doctor. A cramp—that's all it was. Swimming in cold water—it could have happened to anyone."

"People don't pass out from a cramp."

"Banged my head. Damn near drowned. Awful feeling. Do you know what I thought, clinging to the rock? I thought: Isn't this typical of Robert's luck? I'm going to drown before I have a chance to rewrite my will."

"It's really *that* important to you?"

"Oh, yes. No doubt about it." He squeezed her hand even harder. "I had the most awful pain. Never felt anything like it."

"Ben Kidder thought you'd had a heart attack, Arthur. I did, too."

"There's not a thing wrong with my heart."

"All the same, it won't do any harm to lie there and rest until the doctor gets here. . . ."

"Damn the doctor! I won't be treated like an invalid."

She was about to lash out at him—she had not saved his life, she told herself, merely to be shouted at for being concerned—then she noticed his expression. It was one of fear. Fear of what? she wondered. Of being told the truth by a doctor? Or of *her* knowing it? And what *was* the truth? Perhaps nothing more than the fact that he was a sixty-four-year-old man with a sixty-four-year-old heart. If he hated weakness in others, how much more must he hate weakness in himself.

His outburst, oddly enough, seemed to have brought the blood back to his cheeks. It also, apparently, brought back his natural good manners. "I'm sorry," he said. "I shouldn't have raised my voice. I behaved like a damn fool and you saved my life." He shook his head. "As a boy, I had a cousin who drowned in these waters. Of all people, I should have known better." He reached up and stroked her cheek gently. "You were damned brave out there, you know. Braver than I had any right to deserve."

"I was scared out of my wits."

"You had your wits about you well enough to find me. *And* get me back to dry land. Not too many people could have done as well." He gave a smile—the first since he had left her on the beach for his swim. "Not everyone would have *wanted* to rescue me, I daresay."

"Shout at me again, and I might not do it myself, the next time."

He smiled, then closed his eyes for a moment, his mood changing, the corners of his mouth turning down.

"I *did* think about Robert out there—and how ironic it would be if I drowned," he said. "But that wasn't the only thought I had. You know, you're supposed to see your whole life pass before you in slow-motion when you're drowning—so they say, anyway—but nothing of the kind happened. I was a little disappointed, matter of fact. I thought to myself, instead, 'Damn, I'm going to lose Alexandra!' And quite suddenly I felt strong enough to swim for that rock. I could *see* it, mind—oh, not more than a few yards away—but I couldn't reach it, not to save my life. Then I thought of you, and the next thing I knew I'd bumped my head against the bloody thing. Remarkable, isn't it? You saved my life, you see, not once, but *twice!*"

"I'm going to do it a third time, by telling you to lie back and get some rest."

"I shall do nothing of the kind." He sat up briskly, then groaned. "Damn!" he said. "Weak as a kitten. Listen to me. I'm going to ask you a question. I want you to give me an honest answer. All right?"

She nodded. It was not the kind of game she liked. Usually when people started to make a song and dance about honesty, they were about to tell you something you didn't want to hear, or ask a question you didn't want to answer. Talk about honesty and serious questions made her want to plead the Fifth Amendment, but something about the urgency in his voice made it clear to her that he meant business.

"What I have to know, Alexa—I want the damned truth, mind—is: Do you love me?"

She stared at him. His expression was as serious as a judge's, the blue eyes fixed unwaveringly on hers. She closed her eyes and sat, silent, for a few moments. She felt panic grip her, as it had in the waves, as well as a slight resentment at being put on the spot this way. Then she realized that there was only one way to answer. "Yes," she said quietly.

"That's all I need to know. You don't like saying it, do you? You *won't* say it, in fact. Never have. Is it me? Or is there another reason?"

"It's got nothing to do with you, Arthur. I've said 'I love you' to people and not meant it. That's an awful feeling. And when I've said it and *meant* it, it's never brought me anything but grief. Or grief to the person I said it to, which is worse."

"Well, I'd agree that 'I/love/you' is perhaps the most overused phrase in the English language. Grandmother used to tell a wonderful story about that, as a matter of fact. It seems that shortly after she'd married Cyrus, she waited until he had sat down at the breakfast table one morning, and said, 'Cyrus, do you really love me?'

"God knows how she found the courage to ask. Anyway, Cyrus spread his napkin on his lap, cracked open his boiled egg, and said, 'Listen to me: I loved you the day we met; I love you now; I will always love you. Those are my final words on the subject and I never want to hear about it again!' "

He laughed, and so did she, happy to see him returning to normal, cheered suddenly at the image of Cyrus Bannerman, in his stiff collar and high-button shoes, laying down the law to his young bride in what must have been the one and only romantic discussion of their marriage. "Perhaps Cyrus and I would have made a good match," she said.

"Well, he had an eye for the ladies—though he always stuck to the straight and narrow. He liked to have a few good-looking young women around the table at Kiawa, and he could be quite the charmer, when he wanted, with them. Yes, you'd have got along well with the old man. He didn't waste words, and he never made a promise he didn't keep."

She looked at him a little warily. "Am I going to be asked to make a promise?"

He nodded. Laughter seemed to have drained him of his newfound energy. "Several," he said, a bit grimly.

"Shoot."

"The first shouldn't give you a problem. This—ah, incident—never happened. Not a word of it to anyone, ever."

"You know I wouldn't talk about it, Arthur. But what about the Kidders? Mrs. Kidder obviously lives for gossip."

"I daresay. In the winter that's all there is to do here—that and making Christmas wreaths. The Kidders will do as I say, however. Up here, believe me, the gentry have no secrets from the locals, but the locals never talk to outsiders."

"What's the next promise, then?"

"The next one is harder. My sixty-fifth birthday is less than a year away. That gives me time to make all my arrangements for The Trust. Oh, I may draw up a temporary document between now and then, just to be on the safe side. I don't intend to go swimming in ice-cold water again, you may be sure, but it *did* occur to me out there that I was a bloody fool not to have put my intentions down on paper. In any case, I want you to put up with our present relationship, unsatisfactory as you may find it, until then."

"I wasn't planning on going anywhere, Arthur. I didn't save you from drowning just to walk out on you."

"No, no, I didn't think that. This hole-in-the-wall life we lead . . . the damned silly secrecy . . . you don't like it. I can't blame you. Neither do I."

"I haven't complained."

"No, and I'm grateful. But silence is sometimes a form of complaint. Anybody who's ever been married knows that."

"I haven't been married."

"Of course you haven't," he said quickly. "I'd forgotten. It's not what it's cracked up to be. . . . Well, never mind that. I want you to promise me something else."

"Anything."

"No, no, this is quite specific, and you're not going to like it. You know what my intentions are, for The Trust, for the family, for the future. . . . It's something we'll share together, but if for any reason we can't . . ." He hesitated. "What I'm trying to say, Alexa, is that I want you to help carry out my wishes if I'm not able to."

She stared at him. "Why wouldn't you be able to?"

He glared at her. "Because I might be dead, damn it. Or disabled."

"I don't want to think about that. It's not going to happen."

"Of course it's not. But it might. It's just a contingency plan, as they say."

"It's morbid."

"Not a bit of it. Give me your word, then let's forget about it. I'll promise anything you like in return. Even go on the wagon."

She laughed, willing to humor him. "You don't have to go that far, Arthur," she said. "I promise, if that's what you want, but all I ask is that you go and see your doctor, when you get back, for a full checkup, like a sensible man."

"You strike a hard bargain, but done."

"And do what he tells you."

"Damn! I'd rather you'd asked for diamonds. I hate doctors."

"I know. Maybe next time I'll ask for diamonds."

He was half asleep already. "Yes," she heard him say softly, as if he was already dreaming, "you'll have to think about the diamonds . . . Vanessa still has them . . . so many things to think about. . . ."

It seemed to her an odd thing for him to say. It was a habit he'd fallen into, when he was tired, as if he were talking to himself. "You'll have to deal with the Foundation," he would mutter, in the middle of a conversation late at night about something else, or "You'll need to take a close look at Mother's trust," he might whisper as he was falling asleep.

She knew how obsessed he was by all his responsibilities—or by the fact that he had ignored them for so long—so it did not surprise her that his mind went on working, finding new things to worry about, or going over the same old ground, even when he was sleeping. . . .

All the same, she couldn't help wondering why the diamonds, whatever they represented, were suddenly so important to him.

SHE DID NOT PUSH HIM. He had appointments with lawyers, bankers, people who advised him on taxes, people whose whole lives seemed to have been devoted to studying every detail of the Bannerman family's financial affairs, the way Orthodox Jews studied the Talmud. Bannerman did not divulge his plans to any of them—he merely gave the impression of a man trying to catch up on things, an absentee landlord, as it were, finally getting around to making a thorough inspection of the stock and outbuildings. No matter how complex the subject, he insisted that it had to be reduced to one typed sheet of paper, a lesson he had learned from his presidential campaigns. His people complained, protested, swore that it was impossible, but in the end, being Arthur Bannerman, he always got his way, and she saw it made sense. "Let *them* do the goddamned work," he told her. "That's what they're paid for. I don't want an essay, or a Supreme Court brief, or a whole bunch of meaningless facts and figures. I want the numbers, the problems, the options. I learned that from Ike. 'A good general is a good manager,' he told me, and he was right. Don't ever forget it."

It seemed to her unlikely that she would ever need to know it, let alone put it to use. Arthur, she thought, was full of good advice lately. Having survived a near-drowning and a storm, he was "on a high," as Simon would have put it, full of energy, briskly wading through piles of one-page memos as if he was enjoying every minute. It was a week before she reminded him of his promise. Predictably, he frowned. "I gave you my word," he said shortly.

"But you haven't made good on it."

"I have an appointment for next week. Blumenthal's a busy man. The best he could do for me was Monday. After all, the feller has patients with serious problems to deal with."

She let it drop. She was quite sure that Arthur had failed to communicate any anxiety or concern and had passed it off as a routine checkup —no doctor, however busy and famous, would fail to make room in his day for Arthur Bannerman. Still, if there was anything wrong, Blumenthal would find it. She wished she could pick up the telephone and tell him what had happened, but she knew perfectly well that Arthur would never forgive her for interfering. Unlike Arthur, she had an absolute faith in doctors, never having been sick herself.

Besides, there was no denying that Arthur appeared to have recovered completely. His color was good, he slept like a baby, he moved at a pace that tired her out.

There was, she decided, no cause for concern.

"FIT AS A FIDDLE," he said, giving her a kiss at the door.

"Did you tell him what happened in Maine?"

"Of course. He put it down to exhaustion, hypothermia, shock. Blumenthal gave me a clean bill of health."

His face radiated a bland satisfaction, his voice was reassuring. She didn't believe a word of it. On the other hand, she told herself, if there was anything seriously wrong, the doctor would surely have put him in the hospital, if only for tests. In any case, he was not a child—she could hardly ask him for a note from the doctor.

He went to the bar, took a bottle of champagne out of a silver cooler, and popped the cork with his thumbs.

"I thought you didn't like champagne," she said.

"I like it well enough. It simply gives me gas. However, it's the appropriate thing for a celebration."

"What are we celebrating?"

He poured two glasses, clicked his against hers, then picked up the cork and rubbed it behind her ear. "Supposed to bring you good luck," he said. "Blumenthal didn't just examine me. He did a blood test, too."

"A blood test? What's there to celebrate about that?"

"You ought to have one, too."

"Why on earth would I want to do that?"

He gave her a smile, at once shy and sly. "Ah. I'll tell you why. Because in New York State, you can't get a marriage license without a blood test." He gave a delicate cough. "What it amounts to is—I'm asking you to—marry me."

She stared at him for a moment, trying to come to grips with the question—and her own feelings. At first she thought he was joking, but practical jokes were not in his nature. She swallowed her glass of champagne in one gulp, which gave her an immediate lightheaded sensation that she regretted. "Are you sure?" she asked, more cautiously than she wanted to.

He refilled her glass. "Sure? Of course I am. We've known each other several months. You've saved my life. Many marriages have been made on much shorter acquaintance than that. Besides, I love you."

"How long have you been thinking about this, Arthur?"

"Oh, it's not a hasty decision, rest assured. I've thought about it for some time. I simply decided there was no point in waiting any longer. Of course, you may not want to—I quite understand that. But for my part, it's something that would make me very happy."

She didn't know what to say. She hardly even knew what she felt. She had been careful, all along, to put the future out of her mind. Marriage was a possibility she had refused even to think about, a commitment so binding—and in this case, with such unimaginable repercussions—that it frightened her. Marriage would make her one of his family—Robert's stepmother, she realized with dismay. She knew he wanted her to embrace him and say "Yes," and she felt guilty for not doing so, but at the same time she felt a faint, nagging resentment at being put so abruptly on the spot.

She said, "Well, I'm flattered—and a little shocked, I guess. What about your family? I can't see them accepting me with open arms."

He laughed. "No, neither can I, more's the pity! But for the moment they won't know, you see. I've given the matter some thought, and what it boils down to is a little game of the carrot and the stick. When I call them all together at Kiawa on my sixty-fifth birthday—they'll *have* to come for that, even Cecilia from her Godforsaken refugee camp—I will then present them with the arrangements I've made for dealing with The Trust. The carrot is that each of them will be treated generously—*very* generously—even Robert. They will also have to accept *you*, my dear, as part of the package. To put it bluntly, that's the stick."

"That doesn't seem a good way of making them like me, Arthur."

"Oh, I wouldn't worry about that. Time may do it. Or not. The object isn't to make them *like* you, Alexa. It's to make them accept the marriage with the minimum of fuss and intrigue. There *will* be storms, I don't doubt it, but once it's clear that they each stand to lose something like twenty-five million dollars if any one of them makes trouble, they'll come around quickly enough. Robert will be furious, but given his financial situation, he's in no position to fight. Cecilia . . . ah, well, Cecilia will have to be talked around to it. That won't be easy. As for Putnam, I don't suppose he'll care one way or another."

"And your mother?"

"She's a realist. I won't say she'll be pleased at first, but I see no reason to think she won't come to like you, provided you don't interfere with the way she runs Kiawa—which you're far too sensible to do. All this is beside the point, however, if you're going to turn me down."

He tasted his champagne, grimaced, and went over to the bar to pour himself a Scotch. "Naturally," he continued, "we'd have to draw up a marital agreement. I would expect to create a considerable trust for you. Money should not enter your decision—I know it would not—but I have to point out that you will eventually be a very wealthy woman in your own right. I can see you're embarrassed by my bringing it up, but you have to understand that the subject of money doesn't embarrass *me*."

"I'm not embarrassed. I just don't know what to say."

"Try saying 'Yes,' why don't you?"

"It's not that easy." She wished there was time to think about it, but she knew there wasn't.

"Is it the difference in age? I'll admit that's a problem. When you're thirty-five, I'll be, my God, *seventy*-five! And the men in my family live a long time—you could be an old lady yourself before you become a rich widow."

"No, it's not that. I don't care how old you are, and I'd love to be married to you. What scares me is your family, Arthur. I don't know if I can deal with them. Or even if I want to try."

"You wouldn't have to face them by yourself. I'd be there to help. And there's no need to see them often, alas. There are worse things to be than a Bannerman, you know."

"It's sure not marrying into the family next door, is it? It's like marrying *royalty*. I'd have to live up to it—to other people's ideas of what's right or wrong for a Bannerman. It would be like living in a glass bowl, on display."

"You have my word that I will make it as easy as I can for you. In any case, once the future of the fortune is settled, there's no earthly reason why we can't live quietly and happily, out of the public eye. I have a lot to do. I shall build my museum—that's something we can do together. We'll travel, enjoy ourselves, do what we damn well please. . . ."

"You make it sound easy, Arthur. But it won't be. The moment the news is out, the press is going to be on my case. They'll talk to everyone I've ever known, rake up every bit of dirt and gossip they can find. . . ."

He shrugged. "Let them. I don't give a damn, and neither should you."

She swallowed hard. If there was ever going to be a moment to tell him the whole truth, this was surely it. But she couldn't bring herself to do it, couldn't find the right way to put it in words. "Arthur," she said, "I've done some things I wish I hadn't," she whispered. "Things I'm ashamed of now. . . ."

Bannerman's complexion darkened, his jaw stuck out in anger. "I don't care, and I don't want to know! Who the hell is perfect? You will be my wife. Nothing else matters to me. Is that understood?"

She was at once astonished and frightened by his outburst—frightened because of its physical effect on him, which went far beyond the flushed cheeks and the raised voice. His hands were trembling, his lips had taken on that blueish tone she had noticed in Maine, and he seemed to be struggling for breath.

Every possible problem in marrying him flashed through her mind, like warning signals blinking furiously in the dark. His children would be bitterly opposed to the marriage; the formidable Mrs. Bannerman (she already guessed there could only be *one* "Mrs. Bannerman" and it would not be her) would hate her on sight; she would be plunged into responsibilities she had no desire to handle, and wasn't in the least equipped to: the fortune, the houses, servants, family problems. . . . And what about her past? Whatever Arthur might say now, he would not be pleased if it were exposed—not to speak of what his family would say.

"Damn it, Alexa, I love you. I want you as my wife. You owe me an answer. Yes or no?"

She heard his voice through the muffled fog of her own fears, heard it and knew there was no way to go backward from here. If she said no, he might forgive her, but the relationship would never be the same. At some level, she was furious with him for changing things between them without warning, but at another level, she understood that he was offering her, in a single leap, wealth, security, social position, the power to do whatever she wanted to—he was handing it all to her on a silver platter. And anyway, she loved him, she told herself. That was what mattered most, the *only* thing that mattered in the end.

She had taken risks in her life before, but nothing like this. There were a hundred reasons, thousands perhaps, to say no, but instead she heard herself say in a small, quiet voice, "Yes."

WHEN ARTHUR BANNERMAN wanted something to happen, it happened quickly.

On Tuesday, the day after he had asked her to marry him, he spent the morning at the Harvard Club, in the writing room, lunched quietly with Baxter Troubridge, whom he found, unsurprisingly, in the bar, paid a rare visit in person to the manager of the Rockefeller Center branch of the Morgan Guaranty Trust Company, used that gentleman's private office to make a few telephone calls, and had himself driven home to change before meeting Alexa at the apartment. All this he told her over dinner at Lutèce, where they ate upstairs at a corner table discreetly hidden behind a screen.

"Was Baxter drunk?" she asked. She was a little drunk herself, Arthur having insisted on a bottle of champagne.

"Baxter is never drunk, in the ordinary sense of the word. His system simply requires a certain level of alcohol at all times, like oil in the motor of a car. To his credit, he knows exactly what that level is. It's been some time since I saw him. I'd forgotten what a bore he is. He sent you his best, however. He's discovered several branches of the Walden family spread through New York State. I hadn't the heart to tell him there wasn't any connection. Pity, though. You'd have two Episcopalian bishops, a mayor of Rochester and an Assistant Secretary of the Navy in your family tree. . . ."

"I can live without them."

"So I should imagine. As a Bannerman, you'll have all the family tree you can handle, and more relatives than any reasonable person could want, bishops and all. . . . I can't think why the French always spoil a perfectly good steak by putting sauce on the damned thing." He saw André Soltner, the proprietor-chef, beaming at him from the doorway and gave him a hearty smile. "Très, très bien!" he shouted, nodding his satisfaction, then set about scraping as much of the sauce as he could off his meat as soon as Soltner's back was turned. "Could you be free at lunchtime tomorrow?" he asked. "For an hour or two?"

"Well, sure. Why?"

"I spoke to the governor. Quite a nice feller, for a Democrat. We are going to be married tomorrow, at one o'clock, in the chambers of Judge Rosengarten. Jack will take you to have a blood test done first thing in the morning—it's all been arranged. There'll be no fuss, no press. We go to the court building on Foley Square, drive through to where the judges park, take a private elevator, and leave the same way. . . . You don't look too happy about it, I must say."

"I hadn't expected it to happen so soon. I don't even know what to wear."

"My dear, it's a civil ceremony. I don't believe it's necessary to fuss."

"A girl ought to dress up for her own wedding."

"Yes, of course." He seemed, she thought, a little abrupt for a man who had gotten what he wanted, as if he had a lot on his mind.

He pushed the plate aside. "The day after the wedding," he said, "we're going to sign some papers. I've had them drawn up by a young lawyer—for obvious reasons, Courtland DeWitt is out of the question. In the meantime, there are a couple of things I want you to have."

He brought two envelopes out of his pocket. He opened the first one and took out a small key. "Morgan Guaranty. Rockefeller Center office. Ask for Gerald Summers, the manager."

"Why, Arthur? What's it for?"

"In case anything should happen to me, you are to take this key to Summers. He will take you down to the vault, where there is a safe-deposit box in your name. Do it immediately. Do you understand?"

"Well, yes, but why? Nothing's going to happen to you."

"I hope not. I'm *sure* not. I have no reason to believe so. But it's a precaution. One does not buy an insurance policy because one intends to die next week, after all—not, of course, that I've ever *had* an insurance policy. . . ."

"What's *in* the box, Arthur?"

"Papers. Instructions. There's not one chance in a million you'll have to open it, so don't worry. However, don't lose the damned key. It's all the identification you'll need."

He put the key back in the envelope, sealed it and handed it to her. "On a more cheerful note," he said, opening the second envelope, "this is for you. A wedding present."

He took out of the envelope a magnificent diamond ring. There was no elaborate setting, merely a thin band of gold surmounted by an enormous round-cut diamond.

Bannerman slipped it on her finger with the delicacy of a jeweler, and nodded. "Seems to fit," he said with satisfaction.

"Is it like the glass slipper? If it didn't fit, I'm the wrong person?"

He laughed. "No, no, it's been in the family for years, but there's no particular magic to it that I know of. The stone was a gift from Cecil Rhodes, after grandfather put up some of the capital to open the South African gold mines. Cyrus had it made into a ring for my grandmother, but she never wore it. She left it to my mother, who gave it to Priscilla. It doesn't exactly have the pedigree of the British crown jewels, but you'll be the fourth Mrs. Bannerman to own it."

She stared at the diamond, trying to imagine how much it was worth. Probably more money than her father had ever made in a lifetime of hard work. For the first time, the idea that she was about to become "Mrs. Bannerman," in fact, seemed real to her.

Strangely enough, the diamond did not cheer her up. The ring was like an object from another world, nothing to do with her. She doubted that she would ever feel it belonged to her.

"You look as if you're about to cry," he said.

"I don't mean to. And I won't. But I don't think I'll ever get used to wearing it."

He smiled. "You'd be surprised." He raised his champagne glass. "To a long and happy marriage."

She clicked her glass against his and drank. She looked down at the ring and wondered what married life would be like. In the immediate future, she guessed, there would be little change in the way they lived. But once Arthur had confronted his family, brought her to Kiawa, revealed her publicly to them and to the world as his wife, what then?

She stared at the diamond, as if it could show her the future, but it flashed back at her, cold, bright, and curiously sinister.

THE DAY ITSELF PASSED like a blur. She was taken for a blood test at dawn by Jack, who seemed to regard the marriage—for naturally he was in on the secret—with calm amusement. He had always treated her with gentle courtesy, but there was some indefinable change now in his attitude, a slight, very slight but still perceptible, increase of respect. Alexandra Walden, girlfriend or mistress of Arthur Bannerman, was one thing, but a new Mrs. Bannerman was quite another. He sat stiffly in the front seat, and instead of his usual calm way of doing things at his own languid pace, leaped briskly from the car to open the door for her.

She passed the morning at work feeling mildly lightheaded, and delighted that Simon, as was so often the case, hadn't bothered to come in. She had dressed, wisely, she thought, in a pale cream skirt and jacket, a Chanel copy, which seemed exactly right for the occasion. She carried the ring in her handbag—she could not bring herself to wear it. What if it were stolen? What if she *lost* it, God forbid? Every half hour she looked in her handbag to make sure it was still safe. Would she get used to wealth? she wondered. Her first brush with it had made her nervous as a cat.

It was not until she found herself standing in the judge's chambers, with Jack behind them as the witness, that the marriage became real to her. She put her signature to the documents, grasped Arthur Bannerman's hand and stood before the judge as if she were about to be sentenced for some crime, hardly even hearing his words. At some point she said, "I do," but she could not remember it. She had a dim picture of the judge, whose face expressed a certain skepticism about the whole procedure—or perhaps, she thought, he was merely envious of Bannerman, a man of his own age, marrying a woman in her twenties. There was an American flag at one side of him, and a New York State flag at the other, and directly behind, a signed photograph of Franklin Delano Roosevelt, which Arthur glared at in frank distaste. Then it was over. Arthur kissed her, the judge shook her hand, and she was in the car, on her way back to the office, the wife of one of the richest men in the country.

The diamond ring was still in her handbag. She had forgotten to put it on.

. . .

THEIR WEDDING NIGHT was uneventful—curiously domestic, in fact. Arthur seemed tired, even irritated, which she attributed to the fact that his lawyer had been obliged to put the signing of the papers off for a day or two. "Damned red-tape pusher," Arthur complained. "He's as slow as Courtland." They ate off trays and watched a movie on television. "I think I'm coming down with a cold again," he said. "I'm damned sorry. Not much of a wedding night."

"Well, it's not as if it's our first night together. Don't worry about it. Anyway, you do look tired."

"Yes. I'll take a couple of vitamin Cs, make an early night of it, kill it in the bud."

He slept soundly, but he seemed no better in the morning, and even stayed in bed while she got dressed for work, which was not like him at all.

"The judge's chambers were too damned warm," he complained. "I can't stand overheated rooms. Never mind. We'll go out tonight. Too early in our marriage to start sitting home every night in front of the television set."

"I don't mind."

"I do. And you soon would."

"I'll have to go back to my apartment for some clothes after work."

"We'll need to talk about that. Do you intend to keep on working?"

"Of course I do."

"For Simon? I could set you up with something much better, you know."

"I like what I'm doing, thank you. When we have a real place to live and don't have to hide out, I'll reconsider."

He conceded the point. He seemed too tired to argue. "Fair enough," he said slowly, each word an effort. "I've never believed in women sitting at home in a gilded cage. I'll pick you up at your apartment at seven." He coughed deeply, his breath returning in gasps, with great effort. She wondered if she should stay with him, but she knew he wouldn't hear of it.

Twice during the day she telephoned him, keeping her voice low so that Simon wouldn't overhear, but both times Bannerman was out and, therefore, she presumed, better.

At seven, when he arrived at her apartment, he did indeed look better, in that his face was flushed now instead of pale. He gave her a kiss, more like his own ebullient self again. "How does it feel to be Mrs. Bannerman?" he asked.

"So far it doesn't feel any different. I was happy before. I'm happy now."

"I'm *dee*-lighted, as my father used to say." He poured himself a Scotch and sat down heavily. "I've had a busy day," he said. "Stopped off at the bank, then I went around to put a fire under that damned lawyer. These people think there's all the time in the goddamned world. . . ."

He sounded irritable. Colds did that to people, she told herself—they did it to *her.* "You still look tired," she said.

"Well, hell, I *am* tired. Took a couple of pills, but they knocked the stuffing out of me. I'm not sure we weren't better off in the days when doctors prescribed hot lemon tea and a spoonful of honey for a cold."

There were dark circles under his eyes, and he did indeed seem to be moving stiffly, as if his bones ached. "Look," she said firmly, "we don't need to go out. Lie down, have a rest. I'll make us something to eat."

"I'm not hungry myself, but I promised you dinner."

"Don't be silly. There's all the time in the world for that."

To her surprise, he nodded. She had expected him to put up a fight, but he seemed happy enough to give in—a sure sign that he certainly wasn't feeling up to par.

"A little nap won't do me any harm," he said. He slipped off his shoes, removed his coat, and lay down on the bed. Almost immediately, he was asleep.

She let him sleep for over an hour—it could only do him good. Then it occurred to her that he might just as well spend the night here comfortably. She went downstairs, found the car, and rapped on the window. Jack lowered it.

"Evening, miss—ah, ma'am, I mean . . ."

"Mr. Bannerman's asleep, Jack. His cold seems worse. I've put him to bed. I don't think he'll be going anywhere, so you may as well go home and come back in the morning."

He looked doubtful. "You sure, ma'am? I don't mind waiting."

"I'm sure. I'm not letting him get up."

Jack laughed. "It's a change, somebody telling *him* what to do. But you're right. You tell Mr. Bannerman to stay in bed. You're the boss now. Good night, ma'am."

She watched the big black car vanish silently down the street, then went back upstairs. Arthur was awake, lying back on the pillows.

"I feel a damned sight better," he said. "Nap did me the world of good."

"You're about to take a longer one. I sent Jack home. Now get out of those clothes."

"Nonsense! I shall do no such thing."

"Arthur, just once, as a wedding present to me, do what I tell you to. What's the point of getting up when you feel rotten?"

"I feel like a million dollars," he said defiantly—an odd phrase for a man who had several hundred million—but when he sat up, he closed his eyes for a few moments, breathing hard as if he had just come off an exercise machine. "Perhaps you've got a point," he conceded grudgingly.

"You're damned right I do." She helped him out of his clothes, covered him up, then went off to undress, remove her makeup, and make a pot of tea. When she came back and slipped into bed beside him, he was dozing lightly, his eyes only half closed. "No damned pajamas on," he muttered. "I feel like a fool. Hardly decent, for a man my age . . ."

"Oh, have your tea and stop being silly."

"I'd prefer a Scotch, but I'll let myself be bullied just this once." He sipped his tea gratefully, it seemed to her. She rather liked him this way, mildly helpless and compliant. Did she have an instinct for nursing? No, that wasn't it. Arthur was rarely malleable, and there was a distinct pleasure in having him briefly under her control. She decided to make the most of it. By tomorrow he would be back in charge again, no doubt, arranging things, giving orders, making decisions, running her life, as well as his own, as usual.

"This is a hell of a honeymoon," he said. "I'll tell you, though, we shall have one, you wait and see, a humdinger. We'll get all the damned papers signed, then go away for a few days, a long weekend, somewhere warm, not like Maine. I know a place in California, in the desert—absolutely charming, very private. We can ride up into the mountains, eat lunch under the palm trees, by crystal springs. I haven't ridden in ages. It would be damned good for me. And *after* my birthday, you'll see! We'll go round the world, that's what we'll do. . . ."

He fell silent for a few minutes. "By God, you've made me a happy man," he whispered gently. "Given me a whole new life, at an age when most men are getting ready to call it quits."

She leaned over to kiss him, but before she could say "I love you"—for the words were, at last, on her lips—he was sound asleep.

She read a little, then turned out the lights. At midnight, or perhaps later, he stirred restlessly. She put her arms around him. "Go back to sleep," she said.

"That's all I seem to do lately. Do you still have the key I gave you?"

"Of course I do."

"I'm just asking." He seemed—she searched in her mind for the right word—*fretful*. He pulled himself up with some effort into a sitting position, rubbed his face with his hands as if he were trying to wake himself up, and took a deep breath. "There's so much to tell you," he said. "Things you have to know."

"Well, there's plenty of time, Arthur. What kind of things do you mean?"

"Things about the fortune. About the family."

"There's no hurry."

"Take Robert . . ."

"No, don't start in on Robert, Arthur, or you'll be awake all night."

He paid no attention. "No," he said. "You'll have to listen. I've put off telling you what you have to know—oh, for so many reasons. Mostly, I suppose, because I was worried what you'd think of me. I meant to talk to you about it in Maine, but I never got around to it. Well, for some reason, I've got the nerve to do it now, so I'm going to tell you what there is between Robert and me."

"I know what there is."

"You know nothing," he said sharply, then took her hand and held it firmly. "I'm sorry. I didn't mean to raise my voice. It's not easy for me to talk about this."

"You don't have to."

"I must." He closed his eyes. "You're my wife now. I had four children," he began, almost in a whisper.

"I know. There was a son who died in a car crash, wasn't there? John."

"John, yes. Poor John. Of the boys, Robert was my favorite. I doted on Cecilia, of course, as fathers will on their daughters, but Robert was my favorite, and by God he worked hard for my approval. He had *guts*, Robert did."

"And John?"

He did not seem to have heard her. He was lost in his own memories. "Putnam was the baby of the family. I never expected much of him, and so he never delivered much. Never mind, he has a good heart, Putnam does, he's *decent*. But John was special. He hated the fortune, you know, even wanted to change his name so people wouldn't know he was a Bannerman. I used to have terrible fights with him. Oh, now, when it's too late, I can see his point of view, I even share it. I should have let him do what he wanted to do—change his name, go out in the world to find himself. He'd have made a good teacher, John would have, he had the passion for it, the way with words, a kind of stubborn honesty. Instead, I fought him. Insisted he go to Harvard. . . ."

"Well, that doesn't seem like the worst thing in the world. I mean, most parents would feel the same."

"The night of his death, we had a *terrible* fight, one of those family dinners at Kiawa that goes from bad to worse. I can't even remember what it was about. Nothing and everything. Foreign policy, politics, the morality of wealth. I thought John was goading me, though in fact he was just speaking his mind honestly. Robert tried to calm things down between us—he was fond of John, though he didn't agree with him on most things. And, of course, he envied him. . . ."

"Arthur, even people who aren't rich have these problems. You should have heard what *my* father had to say to my brothers about the fact that they weren't interested in being farmers. . . ."

"Yes, yes," he said impatiently, unwilling to be diverted. "John had been drinking. Well, so had I. John wasn't a heavy drinker, you understand, but the pressure of the evening was getting to him. Sometime after dinner—we were in the library, I remember—I told him, 'If you're so damned ashamed of the name and the fortune, get out of the house!' "

He shook his head, like a fighter who has just taken a heavy punch. " 'You're goddamn right I will,' John said. I can hear him still. He slammed the door behind him and left, just like that. It was the last time I saw him alive."

"Oh, dear. It *is* a terrible story, but . . ."

"That isn't the worst part, Alexandra. Nothing like. Robert said, 'He's too drunk to drive,' and of course he was right. So he went outside, had an argument with John, who was insisting on driving, and finally managed to push John out of the driver's seat. Robert told me this, afterwards, of course. . . ." He sighed. "I don't know where they intended to go—back to the city, I suppose, but they never arrived."

"An accident?"

"It was a rainy night. The Taconic is a dangerous road when it's wet. John had one of those damned foreign sports cars—he was mad about the bloody thing. The car struck the barrier just a few miles south of Nine Partners Road, skidded broadside into a station wagon. The man driving it was killed. So was his nine-year-old daughter."

She was silent for a moment. There was nothing to say. It was a tragedy but a common one. Where she came from everybody started driving at sixteen; by the time you reached twenty-one, someone you were with at school, a boy or a girl you knew well, was bound to have died in a crash. Like casualties in a war, you tried not to think too much about it. "And John?" she asked softly.

"Dead. Instantly."

His hand was inert, a lifeless object. She wished he would stop torturing himself and go to sleep.

"Robert . . ." He coughed. "Robert had been driving, as I told you. He'd had the good sense to fasten his seat belt, and the good luck to remain conscious. He realized what an accident like that could do to his political career. In short, he moved John's body behind the wheel."

She stared at him. His face betrayed no emotion. He might have been talking about yesterday's lead story in the financial section of *The New York Times.* "So John got the blame?"

He nodded. "Robert told me what he'd done. Told me all about it, quite calmly." He paused. "And I let him get away with it. I didn't tell the police Robert had been driving when they left the house. Well, why destroy the boy's future? I thought. Why ruin his life? I'd lost one son. I didn't want to destroy another."

"I can understand that, Arthur."

"I didn't calculate the cost. Cecilia, Putnam, my mother, everybody knew I had quarreled with John and let him go off driving his car even though he'd been drinking. . . . 'Criminal irresponsibility,' that was the phrase Mother used. But I had given Robert my word, don't you see? I'd promised him I'd keep the secret—and until now I have."

She understood now the strained relationship between Arthur and his children, his exile from his beloved Kiawa, the estrangement between him and his wife, the coldness of his family. . . . He had taken on himself Robert's guilt, lived up to his bargain with Robert, at the cost of much that he loved—even at the cost of love itself. And then, of course, Robert had turned against him, so he had sacrificed all that for nothing.

"From everybody's point of view," he continued, "it was a clear-cut case against me. I had been drinking, I lost my temper with John, I allowed him to drive even though *he* had been drinking. I as good as killed him, not to speak of the poor feller in the other car and his little girl."

"But then why isn't Robert at least grateful?"

"It's too much gratitude for anybody to bear. I know the truth, and he can't forgive me for knowing it. Or perhaps it's as Oscar Wilde said: 'No good deed goes unpunished.' " He laughed again, harshly. "Except that it wasn't a good deed."

"Your *intention* was good, Arthur. That counts for something, surely?"

"Does it? I destroyed my family for the sake of my son. I don't call that good. Even Cecilia, who loves me more than is good for her, left then, for Africa. She couldn't forgive me for John's death." He fell silent.

"Why have you told me all this?"

"Because you ought to know the truth. About me. About Robert. The State Police never believed a word of it, you know. They're not fools, and they see plenty of accidents. In the end, I spoke to the governor, made a few calls, paid a huge settlement to the family of the man who was killed—but the main thing was that they weren't about to contradict Arthur Aldon Bannerman. My *name* saved Robert, ironically enough. The superintendent of the New York State Police actually came to Kiawa and handed me the investigator's file, which made it quite clear what had really happened. 'You'll want to keep this, Mr. Bannerman,' he told me. The investigator had recommended indicting Robert for vehicular homicide and falsifying evidence. I took the file, of course, and thanked him."

He sighed deeply and closed his eyes. He looked exhausted, and his voice was becoming low and raspy, like that of a heavy smoker. "I feel better for having told you," he whispered. "Much better. There should be no secrets between us."

It was the perfect time to tell him hers.

"Arthur," she said quietly, "I have a story of my own, maybe even more shocking than yours. . . ."

Then she realized he was asleep, his breathing low and regular. She pulled the covers up over his chest, turned off the light and curled up beside him.

AN HOUR OR TWO LATER, she felt him stir. At first she thought his cold was making him uncomfortable, but then as she put her arms around him, she realized that wasn't the case. "I love you," he whispered. "Old as I am, I love you."

"You don't seem to be *that* old."

"Never, I hope."

She knew he needed a sign from her that she wasn't shocked or disappointed in him, that she could hear his worst secret and still love him. She wondered if he would do the same for her. It was a risk she would have to take, tomorrow.

For tonight, however, she pressed herself against him. He put his arms around her, and, while she herself was not aroused, she could feel his arousal. Certainly it could do him no harm to make love, she thought, if that was what he wanted. Besides, surely it was a good sign? She adjusted her body to his, guided him into her, let him move at his own speed toward a climax. She was happy enough to give him a moment of pleasure, particularly since it seemed to signal that he was feeling better. "Come," she said, and reached down to touch him.

He groaned, a deep, guttural sound of satisfaction, and shivered. She waited for him to stroke her hair, whisper something—he was usually the most affectionate and grateful of lovers—but to her surprise he did nothing. Charitably, she put it down to his cold and the pills.

A few minutes passed. She was growing uncomfortable with his weight pressing against her. She moved away slowly, trying not to wake him and, as she did so, felt a curious inertia in his body—a dead weight that was unmistakably different from that of a man who was merely sleeping.

Her mind refused to accept it—refused even to consider it. She could not bring herself to try to wake him, but then, she told herself, she *must*. He might be unconscious from the pills. He might have had a heart attack. He might be playing a practical joke. But even as the implausibility of this last thought struck her, the truth was beginning to solidify in her mind, blocking her will to move, blocking out everything except a sense of panic.

She was not afraid, she did not even feel pain or grief—only a chilling certainty and a sense of complete helplessness. She lay there for what might have been half an hour or more—it was hard to tell—then her reason began to return slowly by degrees. She must do *something*, after all. . . .

She got out of bed and turned on the light. Arthur was lying on his side, his eyes open, his lips slightly parted. The ruddy color had returned to his skin. He might have looked perfectly healthy, not at all the pale, ill man he had been only a few hours ago, except that there was not the slightest sign of life in him.

She knew she should have called for an ambulance, rushed him to a hospital emergency room where they could apply electrodes to his chest, give him oxygen, take heroic medical measures. . . .

But she also knew that it would have been hopeless then, and was even more hopeless now. His eyes told the story, and the story was death—final, irreversible, beyond any miracle of modern medicine, beyond any doubt. The eyes were untroubled, clear, totally devoid of life.

She wondered if he had known about it? Was the hasty marriage because of something he had learned at the doctor's? Had he guessed it could end this soon, and possibly like this? She felt betrayed, but she refused to blame him.

She pulled the sheet over his head and sat down to think. She did not cry. She was beyond tears, too deeply in shock to give in to them. "I love you," she heard herself say over and over again, but it was too late now.

PART THREE

A
TIME TO
MOURN

8

DeWitt's Wall Street office gave the impression of having formed itself over the decades. It was a dark, gloomy room, with the shabby look that only time can produce, the perfect place for the rich to bring their secrets. The only splash of bright color was an American flag hanging from a stand behind DeWitt's desk, next to a formal portrait in oils of Cyrus Bannerman, the cold blue eyes staring with what appeared to be contempt at the rows of DeWitt's law books ranged in a breakfront on the opposite side of the room. Alexa felt herself sinking into a pit of depression at the thought of having to listen to DeWitt—or maybe it was the sight of the Bannerman patriarch glaring out of the gilded frame at her as if she were an interloper. The eyes seemed to follow her, like those in Day Keane's paintings of children.

"It's been like a bad dream," she said. "I keep thinking I'm going to wake up and none of it will have happened."

"Quite so," DeWitt said mournfully, his eyebrows at half-mast, his expression that of an undertaker extending his sympathies to somebody pricing a cheap funeral for a loved one. "It's all been most unfortunate."

"*Unfortunate?*" Her nerves were on edge. It did not seem to her the appropriate word.

He tried another. "Distressing?" He jingled the change in his pocket. "Painful," he said at last, nodding as if he were pleased with himself for having hit the right note.

"It's certainly been painful from *my* client's point of view," Lincoln Stern said brusquely, as if Alexa was not present. Stern took every opportunity to prevent her from speaking for herself, and she was beginning to resent it.

DeWitt sniffed. "No doubt. And for the family. Let's sit down, shall we?"

They all sat, Alexa and Stern on the sofa, DeWitt facing them across the coffee table, on an antique chair that looked far too small and spindly for him, his bony knees crossed in what looked like an agonizingly uncomfortable position, exposing black socks with a faint red pattern to them—just the kind of thing Arthur despised.

Whether by design or by accident, she decided, DeWitt had provided his clients with just the right symbols to put them at ease—Cyrus Bannerman and the flag. For those who might still have doubts, there was a scattering of framed photographs: DeWitt towering glumly over a grinning Nelson Rockefeller; DeWitt shaking hands with Eisenhower; DeWitt, a martyr's expression on his face, in earnest conversation with Nixon.

She felt her mouth go dry at the last photograph in the row: Arthur Bannerman, younger and trimmer than she had ever known him, was descending the steps of his campaign plane, his arms raised as if he were giving a papal blessing to the crowd. Behind him stood Robert, barely out of his twenties. Father and son had the same features, but some microscopic alteration made Robert's face seem harsher than his father's.

She wondered if it was just a trick of the camera—after all, Arthur's face had the flesh of middle age, whereas Robert's was thin, the skin drawn tautly over the bones like that of an athlete in training. There were dark circles under his eyes, as if he hadn't slept for days, although the candidate himself looked rested and relaxed. Standing next to Robert was DeWitt, his face reflecting a well-bred disdain for his brother-in-law's efforts to please the common man.

It occurred to Alexa how little she really knew about these people—even about Arthur. She knew about his family only what he had told her, and it wasn't enough for the position she was in. There was no place in her knowledge of them for this photograph, or for the one next to it, a happy family picnic at some horsey event, Arthur and DeWitt in their country tweeds standing on either side of a beautiful woman in riding clothes. Alexa dimly recognized her as Arthur's wife, Priscilla. A couple of Labradors sat at Arthur's feet, staring up at him lovingly.

DeWitt's eyes flickered toward the photograph. He didn't miss a thing. "Oxridge," he said. "Nineteen sixty, I believe. Or thereabouts. Priscilla went home with the Blair Trophy. That was the year she took Dunwoody to the Garden. My God, she was a fine horsewoman!"

"So Arthur said."

"Did he?" He flicked his narrow moustache with his forefinger. "I never thought he paid much attention to it, frankly. I'm surprised he talked to you about her."

"He talked to me about a lot of things, Mr. DeWitt."

"I daresay. Ah, here's coffee."

A secretary came in, bearing a silver tray with an antique coffee service. Not for DeWitt the ordinary office mugs or Styrofoam cups. He had fine English bone china, and, judging from the aroma, the coffee was freshly brewed and not from a machine. She had caught the look in his eye when he talked about Priscilla Bannerman, whom he obviously admired. Had he envied Arthur his wife? Did he feel that Arthur had treated her badly? Was that the reason that the two men disliked each other?

Stern cleared his throat on her behalf. "For the record," he said, "I was opposed to this meeting. I still am. The situation seems to me perfectly clear. There is a will. My client, the widow, is the principal beneficiary. The late Mr. Bannerman placed his affairs largely in her hands under the terms of that will. We naturally expect full and complete disclosure of financial information. . . ."

DeWitt held up his hand. "Hold on," he said. "The purpose of this meeting is only to have a chat. The family is—I think understandably —upset. Eleanor—Mrs. Bannerman—is particularly upset—*outraged* might be a better word—at the continuing speculation in the press about the, ah, circumstances, of Arthur's death."

"My client has—very much against my advice, may I say—kept a low profile. She hasn't told anybody about the marriage. In my opinion, a press conference would clear the air."

"Really?" DeWitt said, drawing the word out. "Well—none of us will ever forget the field day the press had over Robert's divorce, thanks to you. I can't say, Mr. Stern, that the Bannerman family is pleased at your new client's choice of counsel. No offense meant, of course."

The two men glared at each other over their coffee cups. Once again, Alexa thought, she might have spared herself a good deal of difficulty had she known more Bannerman history. She wondered if Stern had been a good choice. Simon had recommended him as a real fighter, and David Roth had seconded the choice, but it had not crossed her mind then that a fight was the last thing she wanted. She had been won over by Stern's courtesy, but his combativeness was as offensive to her as it was provocative to DeWitt, and, she thought, largely unproductive. She should have guessed, too, that the fact that Stern had handled Vanessa Bannerman's divorce from Robert had created bad blood between himself and DeWitt. If only she had paid more attention to Arthur, whose skill at handling people was remarkable, when he was in the mood . . . It was too late now. She decided to put a stop to the two lawyers' squabbling, at any rate. "Look," she said firmly, "could we kindly get on with it? I came here to find out where I stand."

DeWitt formed a steeple with his fingers, his expression grave. "Where *you* stand? Our position is that you stand nowhere."

"Oh, come off it, DeWitt," Stern snapped angrily. "We have a will. We have a marriage certificate. She stands on bedrock."

"Bedrock? There exists a will. It's there on my desk. A carefully prepared document, fine-tuned over the decades by the best lawyers in the country, and brought up to date once a year to take advantage of every change in the law and the tax code. It was submitted for Arthur's review less than six months ago, and he approved it. *That*, sir, is his will, signed, properly witnessed and notarized—not some piece of paper he may or may not have written in haste at the Harvard Club after a drunken lunch with Baxter Troubridge, in circumstances that raise serious doubts about the state of his mind."

"There was nothing wrong with his state of mind," she said, her voice rising despite her determination to keep calm. "And it wasn't a drunken lunch."

"*Any* lunch with Baxter Troubridge is a drunken lunch. We should have no trouble proving that in court, if we have to." He drew a slip of paper from his pocket, put on his reading glasses and smiled at her grimly. "Arthur's bill for the lunch," he said. "Two soup du jour, one chef's salad, one cold-cuts platter, coffee for two, *six* Scotches and two brandies. Two of the Scotches were doubles, by the way. Not exactly a teetotalers' lunch, is it?"

For the first time since meeting him, Alexa looked at DeWitt with a certain respect. He had done his homework, or somebody had done it for him. Even Stern was silent, his eyes half-closed as he turned De-Witt's ace over in his mind.

"I'll bet you Baxter Troubridge drank most of that," she said. "Arthur might have had a double before lunch, sure, and maybe a single with his salad. Not more. He'd cut back on his drinking."

"Actually, Arthur had the cold cuts. Didn't touch them, according to the waiter. Even at *your* estimate, young lady, he would have had three Scotches on an empty stomach. Maybe more. And possibly one of the brandies. Not exactly the proper frame of mind in which to write a will for *any* estate, let alone this one."

Stern had recovered his pugnacity. "The law does not require a sobriety test for a last will and testament, DeWitt. You know that perfectly well. Do *you* keep a breathalizer around here for signings?"

"Two drunken old men in the Harvard Club," DeWitt said calmly. "It won't wash, you know, Stern. Arthur didn't know what he was doing. Troubridge didn't know what he was signing." He again made a steeple with his fingers. "The writing of a will is to be approached with reverence, not on the spur of the moment after a boozy lunch. And of course the one thing Arthur shouldn't have been doing was boozing with his crony Troubridge. He was a very sick man—as I expect you knew, young lady."

She was astonished, and only managed to hide it by sheer luck. "I knew nothing of the kind," she said tightly. "He seemed perfectly healthy to me."

DeWitt raised an eyebrow. The moustache gave a small sympathetic twitch, apparently of its own volition. "He confided in you about Priscilla, but he didn't tell you about his heart? Forgive me, I find that hard to believe."

"He never mentioned it."

Stern held up his hand. "Enough," he said. "We're not here so you can cross-examine my client, DeWitt. I don't give a damn about his health and I don't give a damn what he had for lunch. He wrote out a new will. He had as much right to change his mind as anyone else."

"Booker and I will certainly put that to the test, Mr. Stern."

"Do what you want. We have the will. We have a marriage."

"Ah, yes, the *marriage*," DeWitt said, drawing the word out slowly, an expression of mild distaste on his face. "The marriage is something we'll want to take a close look at."

"What's to look at? If you want a copy of the marriage certificate, we'll provide one."

"Thank you, but that won't be necessary." DeWitt produced another slip of paper and held it up as if it were something dirty that he didn't want to touch. "Witnessed by his chauffeur," he said, shaking his head. "I'm not sure I'd put any more faith in him than I would in Baxter Troubridge, if I were in your shoes."

"Mr. DeWitt, I'm not going to sit here and have you imply Arthur and I weren't married."

"I imply nothing. I am merely asking questions."

"Which my client won't answer, DeWitt. Anyway, what I'm hearing is merely a nasty mix of innuendo and threat."

"If that were the case, Mr. Stern, then you would surely be the first to recognize what is, I believe, widely acknowledged as *your* style."

"Please!" Alexa said firmly, beginning to dislike both lawyers almost equally. "I didn't come here to fight—or answer questions. I don't want to hurt Arthur's family."

"Hurt them? What a strange thing to say! Arthur Bannerman was a sick man, dying, in fact. His own doctor will testify to that. He was on medication and drinking heavily. Against doctor's orders, I might add. In what one can only describe charitably as a *confused* state, he was rushed into a hasty marriage ceremony and persuaded to write out a new will not more than forty-eight hours from the time his doctor gave him bad news about his heart. A day later he died, in circumstances too distasteful to discuss. Based on this sordid sequence of events, you lay claim to one of the greatest fortunes in America. And yet you tell me you don't want to *hurt* the Bannerman family! What more could you possibly do to them, may I ask?"

She stared at DeWitt, hardly even listening to what he was saying. "Did the doctor really tell him that he was dying? When was that? Two days before we were married?"

"Of course he did," DeWitt snapped impatiently. "I spoke to him myself."

She sat silently for a moment, letting it sink in. She stared at DeWitt through a film of tears, which she struggled to hold back. She tried to remember what he had been like the day he had seen his doctor at her urging, for what he described as a routine checkup. He had not seemed particularly anxious about it. When she met him that evening he had seemed perfectly relaxed and at ease, playing solitaire in front of the fireplace, surrounded by catalogs of art auctions, with a half-finished drink on the card table. "A clean bill of health," he had boasted. "Damned waste of time and money."

It had never occurred to her that the reason for his sudden decision to marry her—and for the speed with which he arranged it—might have been the knowledge that he could die at any moment. Before he'd gone to the doctor, had he been thinking of the future in terms of years —with good luck, a decade or more? And when she found him playing solitaire that evening, had he known his future was measured in months, perhaps even days?

Why hadn't he told her? she asked herself sadly. But of course he wouldn't—couldn't. It was part of his code. He would have had a horror of her thinking of him as an invalid. He would marry her now because there might not be time to do it later on; he would draw up a will quickly, in case he died before there was time for a full, formal change in his plans to dispose of the fortune; he would leave it to her to put his wishes into effect because he could no longer be sure there would be time to do it himself. . . .

"I *said*, I spoke to the doctor myself," DeWitt repeated loudly, as if she were deaf.

She hated the sound of his voice, the grating, pompous tones of a man infatuated with his own importance. DeWitt, she suspected, was a bully when he thought he could get away with it—and he clearly thought he could get away with it when dealing with her. "I heard you," she snapped. "You're suggesting that I knew Arthur was dying and pushed him into marrying me and writing out a new will."

He backed off a notch or two, warily. "I suggested no such thing, but the thought had occurred to me that he might have been—" he paused, then took the plunge—"taken advantage of."

"I object to that, DeWitt!" Stern said. "My client isn't here to be insulted."

"And I'm not insulting her, I hope, Counselor. I'm merely expressing an opinion about my late brother-in-law's state of mind. Let me make it clear that the Bannerman family bears no ill will toward your client." Why, she asked herself, could neither of them refer to her by her name? "They are merely concerned with the integrity of The Trust. And with protecting their rights from what would appear to have been the sudden and capricious act of a dying man."

Stern shrugged. "Sudden, maybe. Capricious, we deny, and you can't prove."

"*Capricious*, Mr. Stern." DeWitt made no effort to conceal the contempt in his voice. "This isn't your normal estate, you know. We're not discussing a few hundred thousand dollars here, or some garment-manufacturer's will." The moustache formed a thin, straight line above the narrow lips. Did he have it dyed black? she wondered. "This is The Bannerman Fortune we're talking about!"

Stern sat up straight, his eyes blazing. "Don't throw 'garment manufacturer' at me, DeWitt!" he shouted. "I know what you're trying to say, and I won't put up with that from a Wall Street lawyer who hasn't had an original legal thought in decades!"

DeWitt puffed up like an angry turkey-cock. "I implied nothing, Mr. Stern. I have the greatest respect for your people. Some of the most valued members of my own staff . . ."

"Shut *up!*" Alexa's voice was so loud that it surprised her—and silenced Stern and DeWitt, as well. "Both of you. I'm not interested in the money."

There was a moment of silence. DeWitt half-closed his eyes as if he were thinking wise thoughts, and cultivated his moustache. Stern shot her a fierce warning look. "For God's sake, let *me* do the talking, Alexa," he pleaded.

"No. I didn't marry Arthur for the money. I married him because he asked me to—because he *wanted* it. The Bannerman family and I are going to have to live with each other."

"Is that so?" DeWitt's eyes wandered around his office, as if he were looking for something. They settled on the half-open door to his conference room, then came back to rest glumly on Alexa. "Mr. Stern is quite right to protect your interests, young lady. That's what you pay him for. But, have you considered the expense of fighting this all the way through the courts? Not to speak of the time, the trouble, the publicity?"

"That's none of your business," Stern said.

"True. But I'm a reasonable man. Speaking off the record, and without prejudice to whatever position they may take in the future, the family is prepared to be reasonable, too. Litigation is like war—the last and the most expensive way to resolve a dispute. A negotiated settlement is always better than putting things in the hands of a judge and jury, particularly where a family matter like this is concerned. I might be able to persuade them to be generous, in the right circumstances. Very generous."

"What circumstances would those be, Mr. DeWitt?" she asked, beating Stern to the punch.

"The so-called new will would have to go by the board, of course . . . for a start."

Stern shot her a warning glance. "I don't believe my client should comment on that."

DeWitt cleared his throat noisily. "Oh, quite," he said. "That's what we lawyers are for. To discuss the undiscussable."

Alexa tried hard to master her impatience—and anger. She was tired of being referred to as "young lady" or "my client." She did not see the future clearly—she would have to take it step-by-step—but she was not about to give up without a fight. "I didn't come here to bargain, Mr. DeWitt," she said firmly. "I want to meet Arthur's family. To *talk* to them. Not through lawyers. Face to face. To tell them what Arthur had in mind."

DeWitt looked shocked. "That's out of the question."

It was too much for her to bear. She stood up, gathered her belongings, and stared at DeWitt. "Then there's nothing more to talk about," she said. "I'll take my case to the press."

To her surprise, it worked. DeWitt's Adam's apple bobbed. Apparently she had struck home. The Bannerman family was deathly afraid of publicity. She filed that fact away for future reference. She could not help noticing that DeWitt himself was afraid. Of whom? Robert? Old Mrs. Bannerman? Why?

DeWitt's eyes bulged. "You wouldn't do that, would you?" His voice was strangled. "A *media* circus? What would Arthur have said?"

"I don't have any idea. If they won't reason with me, I'm going to tell my story to the world, that's all I know."

Raising her voice didn't come easily to her, especially to a man of DeWitt's age. The earth did not open up to swallow her, however—if anything, DeWitt seemed impressed by her outburst. "I'll give it some thought," he said reluctantly. "I can't say more than that. It's not up to me."

"I'm not going to wait for long, Mr. DeWitt. I don't like the idea of a press conference any more than you do—and I don't want to fight the family in the courts, either, unless you make me. But I'm not going to sit and let myself be treated like an outcast."

"Twenty-four hours, DeWitt," Stern snapped. "After that, I'm filing papers to demand full and complete financial information for my client. And calling a press conference to announce she and Bannerman were married."

DeWitt stood up abruptly. "I *said* I'd think about it."

Standing up, Alexa thought, DeWitt looked a little more impressive. He towered over her. He walked her to the door and shook her hand. "Thank you for coming by for a chat, young lady," he said.

She looked him straight in the eye—or as straight as she could manage, given his advantage in height—smiled politely, and said, "I'm tired of being called 'young lady,' Mr. DeWitt. I'd prefer to be called 'Mrs. Bannerman,' from now on, if you don't mind."

He blushed—whether from embarrassment or anger, it was hard to tell.

She heard—or thought she heard—a familiar sound. She almost looked around for Arthur. It was recognizably his laugh, a deep, booming bark, like distant thunder.

She decided she was imagining things and turned away, Stern at her side, to leave DeWitt to his problems while she was still ahead on points.

"You shouldn't have laughed. She must have guessed you were here, listening in."

"So what? She'd have guessed it anyway from the way you were looking over your shoulder all the time."

"It's most improper. I wish I'd never agreed."

"This is war, Cordy. Whose side are you on?"

"I don't need to be lectured about my responsibilities, after forty years as a lawyer."

"And just how far would you have gone as a lawyer without the Bannerman family as a client? I'm sorry to offend your legal sensibilities, but I have to know what she's like."

"Well, then, you heard the girl. What did you think?"

"She had *you* on the ropes, old man."

"Nonsense. I'll admit she was more aggressive than I expected her to be. She seemed a timid little thing the first time I met her."

"*Did* she? She married Father, got him to change his will, and turned up uninvited at his funeral. That doesn't sound timid to me, Cordy. She was smart enough to pick that son of a bitch Stern as her lawyer, too."

"I wasn't impressed by the way Stern handled himself."

"He let *her* do the talking. I thought that was a good move on his part. Not many lawyers are smart enough to do that. Don't underestimate him, Cordy. He screwed me to the goddamned wall over Vanessa's financial agreement."

"A legal aid lawyer could have 'screwed you to the wall,' as you put it, under the circumstances, Robert. I'd call her bluff, if you want my advice."

"Would you now? Why?"

"Let's say she goes through with it—and she might not. But say she does. She holds a press conference, gives a few interviews, there's a quick blaze of publicity—not a picnic, but it's probably going to happen anyway. The point is, the more she talks to the press, the more we'll know, and the better we'll look in court when we get there."

Robert Bannerman lit a cigarette, then shook his head sadly. "No way, Uncle Cordy," he said. "In the first place, Grandmother wouldn't like it a bit. No more would I. It's too damned risky. Why let her have the opening shot? When we have something to use against her, we'll give it to the press. Until then, the less said, the better."

"What makes you think we'll find anything? She seems like a perfectly straightforward young woman to me."

"There's no such thing, Cordy. It's just a matter of digging."

"And if there's nothing to dig for?"

"As we sow, so shall we reap—as dear Emmett would say."

"I did *not* hear that, Robert."

"Fine. I'm not going to get into an ethical debate with a lawyer. In the meantime, we'll just have to give her what she wants."

"I'm not sure that's wise."

"I'll tell you what's not wise, Cordy. What's not wise is to let her go public with *her* story before we have one of our own. I owe a lot of money to a lot of people, and most of it was loaned to me because everybody knew I was going to inherit the Bannerman fortune one day, the whole goddamn kit and caboodle. I'm going to run for the governorship—no, don't give me a lecture on politics, I know more about that than you do—and I'm going to *win*. I can't do it without money, lots of it, and I can't raise money if I haven't paid back the debts of my last campaign. Do you read me loud and clear? I'm not going to have little Miss Walden, or whatever her goddamned name is, telling *The New York Times* that *she* controls the estate. It's *mine*, Cordy, and I mean to have it. God knows, I waited for it long enough." There was a flash of anger in his eyes.

"But not patiently, Robert. You know what your father thought as well as I do."

"He's gone. We shall have to learn to do without his advice. And yours, if necessary."

"Don't threaten me, Robert," DeWitt said nervously.

"It's not a threat. If Miss Walden wins, the first thing she'll do is to take the family's law business away from you, Cordy. You know that. And Eleanor isn't going to live forever, you know. I'm your only bet, unless you want to go back to hustling clients in your old age."

"I'm a wealthy man, Robert," DeWitt said without conviction.

"With expensive tastes. Anyway, Uncle Cordy, what you mean is that you have a wealthy *wife*. If dear Aunt Elizabeth knew what *I* know about you . . . that nice little apartment you keep in the Carlyle Hotel, for example, that *she's* paying for, if she ever bothered to look at the accounts of her trust . . . But why should we quarrel, you and I? We have the same interests. You want to keep the family's law business in the family. I want to keep the fortune in the family."

DeWitt blinked. "You can't blackmail me, Robert," he said, but it was bluster.

"Bullshit! Show me a man who wants his wife to think he's faithful, and I've got him by the balls." He rose and stubbed out his cigarette. "Tell the lady we'll meet with her."

"*We?* Eleanor will never agree. You know that."

"Miss Walden knows it, too. She's not a fool. Tell her Cecilia, Putt, and myself will meet her. That will be enough to keep her quiet for a while."

"And if she insists on meeting Eleanor?"

"Oh, for God's sake, she *won't*, Cordy. She's got sense, even you can see that. Tell her Grandmother is ill. Tell her she's still in mourning. Tell her whatever you like; it's not going to be a problem."

"What makes you think Cecilia will agree?"

"That's my problem. Cecilia will just have to bite the bullet. We're buying time, that's all."

DeWitt stroked his moustache as if he wanted to be sure it was still there. "I wonder, is it *wise* to involve Cecilia?" he asked.

"Wise?" Robert gave him a look that would have turned most people to stone. DeWitt, who was used to it, merely turned a reddish shade of purple.

"In her emotional state, I mean."

"If she can put up with several thousand starving Ugandans for a year, she can put up with Miss Walden for one hour."

DeWitt summoned up his courage, puffed out his cheeks, exhaled, and bit the bullet. "Perhaps," he said slowly, then with a rush, "I think you'd do better to stay away from the young woman altogether, frankly. The best strategy is to challenge the will. It's a defective instrument. Very vulnerable, in my opinion."

Robert's voice was cold. "Is that so? What does Booker think?"

"I haven't consulted Booker."

"Well, I did. He seemed to think the will might stand up."

"I have more experience in this kind of thing than Booker does. The courts hate documents that aren't drawn up by lawyers."

"And if we lose?" Robert's tone made it clear what he thought about losing.

"My professional judgment is that we won't."

"Forget your professional judgment! Is there *any* chance we'll lose?"

"There's always a chance, yes," DeWitt muttered unwillingly. "A slim one, in my opinion."

"I don't care how goddamn slim it is, Cordy. I need a sure thing. Not a decision that depends on how some goddamned Democratic clubhouse politician-turned-judge feels about handwritten wills. Particularly when the Republican front-runner for the gubernatorial nomination is involved."

"Front-runner?"

"I aim to *be* the front-runner, Cordy. There isn't time to gamble everything on a long, slow haul through the courts challenging the will. We have to go for the *marriage*, Cordy. If the marriage doesn't stand up, the will doesn't matter a damn—doesn't even exist."

"I'm perfectly well aware of that, Robert. We'll go over the marriage with a fine-toothed comb, starting with Jack."

"Oh, for God's sake!" Robert said. "What's Jack got to do with it?"

"He witnessed the marriage. We'll need to prove that Arthur was unduly influenced. He may have been too drunk, for instance, to even know what he was doing."

"And what if he wasn't? They were married by a judge, remember."

"It's still a possibility. It has to be explored."

"It's slow. It's chancey. I don't think most jurors are going to feel marrying this Walden girl is proof of mental incompetence. Not male jurors, anyway, not with legs like hers. The problem is we don't really know a thing about her." He drummed his fingers on the tabletop for a moment, then got up and started to pace around the room, like a prisoner in a cell. "Send Booker to Illinois."

"Booker? To Illinois? Whatever for? Your father and the Walden girl were married here."

"Because she *comes* from Illinois, Cordy."

"Let me remind you that Eleanor told you to keep out of this, Robert!"

"What she doesn't know won't hurt her. And you're not going to tell her a goddamn thing, or I'll torpedo your sex life so fast you won't know what hit you! My people can get everything from Ms. Walden's bra size to the names and addresses of her boyfriends here, but I don't see them doing so well in some Godforsaken Midwestern hick farm town."

"What makes you think Booker would do any better? And what do you expect to find?"

"I don't know what there is to find. There's always something, though. And Booker is perfect. He is a lawyer, he's smart, he's got good manners, he doesn't come off as aggressive or pushy. Listen, if he could get Cecilia to fall in love with him, he can probably get Miss Walden's friends and family to open up without too much trouble. He looks honest."

"He *is* honest."

"He's also ambitious. If you waved the possibility of a senior partnership in front of his nose, do you think that would encourage him?"

"It's too soon to offer Booker a senior partnership."

"Oh, come off it. If Cecilia had married Booker you'd have made him a senior partner on the spot. Anyway, you don't have to *make* him anything, Cordy. You just have to mention the subject casually. Let Booker put two and two together for himself. I can always drop a hint."

"I won't have you interfering in my business, Robert."

Robert stopped pacing and glanced at DeWitt as if he had lost interest in him. "That's understood," he said in a bored voice. "You handle it your own way, Uncle Cordy. Whatever you think best. But get Booker to Illinois on the double, and let's find out who we're dealing with."

"You sound as if you were sure of finding something."

Robert paused, his hand on the door. "Do I? All I know is what I hear on the news. She left home at seventeen to come to the big city."

"Lots of girls do that."

"I'm aware of that, thank you," Robert snapped. "They come here to become models or actresses, I've fucked dozens of them. But here's the interesting thing, Cordy. *Miss Walden never went back!* I read an interview with her mother, in the *Post*, just a few lines, before she cut the reporter off. Mrs. Walden hasn't seen her daughter in over six years, Cordy. Not for Christmas, not for Thanksgiving, not *once.*"

He opened the door and waved goodbye, a cynical grin on his face. "I have a nose for this kind of thing, Cordy, and it tells me there's something fishy about Ms. Walden. Maybe they don't *want* her at home, old man. Let's find out why."

ALEXA RANG THE BELL of Robert Bannerman's Park Avenue apartment, feeling a little like a female Daniel entering the lion's den. Still, she could hardly complain—she was here by her own choice, and over the vehement objections of Stern. She herself wasn't completely sure that she knew what she expected to achieve—or rather, she couldn't put it in words without sounding naive, even to herself. She did not expect to charm them out of their hostility—she knew there was too much at stake for that—but at least she hoped to prove that she wasn't the scheming adventuress they clearly thought she was.

A maid took her coat and led her down a shallow flight of steps. She had a brief impression of a room that had all the warmth of a first-class passenger lounge at a major airport, then stopped short at the sight of Robert Bannerman, who stood waiting to greet her, looking so much like his father that she almost gasped with the shock.

Standing slightly behind his right shoulder was Putnam, the youngest of the Bannerman children, looking very unlike his father and older brother. Arthur's features had been severe and aristocratic at first sight, and Robert's dashing, but in Putnam the same elements seemed merely to produce a boyish quality, good-natured and trusting, perhaps a little on the mischievous side. He reminded her, for some reason, of a large, friendly dog, a Labrador perhaps, or a Newfoundland. He was at least a couple of months overdue for a haircut by the standards of his family, and had cut himself shaving, leaving a small spot of blood on his shirt collar. He still had the look of a college boy, right down to the well-worn tweed sports jacket and scuffed loafers. One of his socks was a slightly different color from the other—the mark of the bachelor who doesn't have a servant.

"My brother, Putnam," Robert said. "Cici—Cecilia—is a little late."

"As usual," Putnam said.

"You're in no position to talk." Robert smiled, the quick, indulgent smile of an elder brother, but his voice had the sharp crack of authority. Putnam, she noticed, did not smile back. His expression was one of long-suffering resentment, held barely under control, as if he had grown out of the habit of being bossed around by his big brother and wasn't finding it easy to get used to it again.

The maid appeared. Alexa asked for a Perrier. Robert ordered a Scotch on the rocks with a splash of water—exactly the same thing that his father drank. She wondered if there was any significance in that. He had his father's way of talking to servants, too, she noticed—not exactly impolite, but brisk, impersonal, without eye contact, as if they were invisible, a manner that could never be learned, because it came from having grown up surrounded by people whose only job was to look after you.

"I'll have a beer," Putnam said, smiling at the maid with a directness that made it clear he didn't have his father's—or his elder brother's—gift for treating servants as invisible. She wondered if it was a natural democratic impulse, part of his rebellion against the Bannerman family's standards, or just a tactic to annoy Robert. If it was the latter, it was instantly successful. "This isn't a goddamned fraternity house!" Robert snapped. "We don't have any beer."

Putnam smiled, happy to have succeeded in provoking his brother, and asked the maid for a martini with laborious courtesy. He seemed to have perfected a whole repertory of small ways to annoy Robert—warfare by pinpricks, she thought.

"Cecilia isn't too happy about this," Robert said. "I hope you'll make allowances for that. She's still very upset."

"I understand." She looked him in the eye. "So am I."

He nodded. "Of course. Frankly, I had to pull out all the stops to get Cecilia to come. In the end, it was Booker who persuaded her. He'll be coming with her." He smiled. "For *moral* support, you understand."

She frowned. Stern's instructions had been adamant. If a lawyer was to be present, he had to be there. "That's all very well," she said, "but I thought we weren't going to have lawyers here."

Robert smiled. "He's coming as a member of the family."

"He's not a member of the family."

"I agree with you, but Cecilia treats him as one, when she's in the mood. Do me a favor, please. Go along with it. You'll understand better when you've met Cecilia."

Alexa nodded. It was not so much that she was convinced—it was simply that Robert sounded so much like his father that she found it easy to give in.

"You have nothing to fear from his presence, believe me, Miss . . . " He paused and shook his head. "Would you mind if I called you Alexa?" he asked. " 'Miss Walden' seems deliberately provocative. Besides, there are those of us for whom there's only one Mrs. Bannerman. Since Mother's death, anyway."

"Alexa is fine with me."

"Good. Then please call me Robert. Whatever our differences, there's nothing to be gained by a lot of unnecessary formality." He glanced at the door, then quickly at his watch. "You come from Illinois, don't you, Alexa," he said, with a diplomat's gift for filling in the time with small talk. "Farming country?"

"Yes."

"Father wanted to be a farmer, did you know? When he was a boy, he loved the farm better than anything else at Kiawa. Couldn't drag him away. Grandfather finally had to lay down the law to him—as a Bannerman, he couldn't expect to spend the rest of his life bailing hay and looking after cattle. I think he'd have been better off looking after the farm while somebody else looked after the fortune, but that wasn't in the cards."

He made a small gesture of regret, though his ironic smile seemed to hint that he found his father's interest in farming eccentric, or perhaps simply inappropriate.

"He missed Kiawa," she said. "He talked about it a lot."

Robert sipped his drink reflectively. "*Did* he now? Mother always complained she couldn't get him to stay there for two days on end." There was the sound of voices in the hall. Robert gave Putnam a quick, warning glance, like a sergeant signaling the arrival of an inspecting officer, then rushed to the door to greet his sister.

Alexa had the impression that the temperature had dropped instantaneously, as if the very presence of Cecilia Bannerman, even on the other side of the door, was enough to make her brothers nervous, though in different ways. Robert's expression was one of genuine concern—so much so that Alexa would have expected an invalid to appear, if she hadn't already seen Cecilia Bannerman at the funeral. Putnam's was harder to fathom, though she thought she detected a hint of exasperation and even jealousy, combined with the nervousness of a small boy who hasn't done his homework and is waiting for the teacher's arrival.

Alexa rose. Robert went to the door, put his arm around his sister and led her to the center of the room, leaving Booker to trail behind. No, Alexa corrected herself, his arm was not just *around* Cecilia, he was clutching her, as if she might fall down at any moment without his support, his fingers twined so tightly in hers that his knuckles were white.

The object of his concern did not, in fact, look particularly fragile to Alexa, or likely to collapse. She was tall, sinewy, and deeply tanned, with the same bright blue eyes as the rest of the family, and roughly cropped, sun-bleached blond hair. She did not seem particularly pleased to have Robert fussing over her, but it was hard to tell—her expression had a kind of natural sulkiness, as if the world had been disappointing her for a number of years and she saw no reason to expect it to change.

If she had bothered to put on a little makeup, done something about her hair, and worn something more glamorous than what looked like an old black knee-length skirt left over from her college days and a black turtleneck, Cecilia would have been a stunning woman. Alexa wondered at what point in her life she had decided she didn't want to be, and why. She wore no jewelry except for a cheap man's wristwatch, and her fingernails were cut short and squared off, like a man's, the cuticles just ragged enough to suggest that she chewed on them from time to time.

They stood in uncomfortable silence for a moment, while the maid fetched a drink for Booker—who looked as if he needed one—and a glass of orange juice for Cecilia. Booker, at least, had the grace to come over and shake her hand, though warily, as if he might at any moment be accused of disloyalty.

Robert Bannerman, as the eldest of the family, clearly felt obliged to break the ice. "Cici," he said, his voice so soothing that it was almost a whisper, "this is, ah, Alexa."

Cecilia stared at Alexa, bit her lip, and sat down, her knees and ankles firmly pressed together in the best finishing-school style, her hands clutched in her lap, the knuckles white. "How do you do?" she said, through clenched, perfect teeth.

Alexa did not expect sympathy from Cecilia Bannerman, but the outright, bitter hostility Cecilia didn't even bother to conceal set her teeth on edge. "I am as well as can be expected, thank you," she said. "Believe me, this is as difficult for me as it is for you, Miss Bannerman."

"Difficult? What makes you think this is difficult? Embarrassing, certainly, but not difficult. Father was a man. I have no doubt he had mistresses. He did not bring them to Kiawa, or oblige us to meet them."

Alexa reacted as if she had been slapped. "I was *not* his mistress," she snapped. "I was his wife."

"You *were*, in fact, his mistress. Now you *claim* to have become his wife, at the last minute. Let me be honest, since you've forced this meeting on us. Nobody, least of all myself, would have begrudged poor Father whatever comfort he wanted in his old age. He was entitled to his pleasures, after all. In the right circumstances, I would even feel some gratitude toward the woman who had provided them for him, but that is quite another thing from being asked to accept her—*you*—as a member of this family."

Once, when she was in school—she might have been ten or eleven years old—a girl had accused her of having stolen her pen which, as luck would have it, was a dark-blue ballpoint with a feed store logo imprinted on it, identical to hers. Alexa had felt, in successive waves like the tremors of an earthquake, shock, guilt, fear, then anger—anger above all at herself for having felt guilt and fear, since she was innocent. As she stood there, willing back the tears, she had wished she were a boy. Any one of her brothers, in similar circumstances, would have used his fists. It was perhaps the only time in her life when she had wished to be a boy. To her horror, the same feelings ran through her now. She would happily have pummeled Cecilia to the ground and banged her head against the floor until she cried for mercy, but instead, once again, she felt shame and guilt, turning to anger. She counted to ten, and to her surprise, it worked. "He loved me," she said, her voice level, trying not to show her dislike. "And we were married, Miss Bannerman. You're going to have to accept that, because it's true."

"I don't *have* to accept anything of the kind. I came here because Robert asked me to. I will do anything I can, anything I have to, to see that he gets what is his, but what affects *me* is your claim to my father."

"Cici, enough!" Robert said. He was standing behind her with his hands on her shoulders, as if he were pressing her down to prevent her from rising. "You'll upset yourself," he whispered. "It isn't worth it."

"I think we should hear what—ah—Mrs. Bannerman has to say." Booker's voice was carefully neutral. He rushed the words "Mrs. Bannerman," as if he hoped they would pass unnoticed, but instead they produced a long silence, during which everyone stared at him in shock. Cecilia's look seemed to Alexa likely to turn Booker to stone, but he merely blushed.

Robert, standing beside his sister where she could not see him, gave Alexa a wry smile and a shrug. "Booker's right," he said. "We're here to talk. I think you must tell us what's on your mind—Alexa."

"What's on my mind first of all is that I'm not going to sit here and be insulted like this."

"I apologize. You have to make allowance for the fact that this has come as a great shock to Cecilia—to all of us. None of us had any reason to suppose Father contemplated taking such a sudden—drastic —step."

"It wasn't meant to be drastic. And I'm not so sure it was all that sudden. He was going to break the news to you all on his sixty-fifth birthday."

"That would have been almost a year from now. Do you mean that he intended to keep the marriage secret that long?"

"Yes. He was determined to. He'd thought about it very carefully."

Cecilia closed her eyes as if in pain. "I don't believe he thought about it at all. He was drinking too much. He was old, tired, and sick, and you took advantage of his weakness. I knew my father better than you did. He would never have done anything like this if he'd been in his right mind."

"I knew him better than you think, Miss Bannerman. He knew *exactly* what he was doing. It's painful to me to have to say this, but if the three of you had been closer to him in the past few years, I don't think he would have married me. The fact is, he was lonely."

Robert retrieved his drink from the coffee table. He sat down beside Cecilia, slipping his hand over hers, as if she needed the constant reassurance of his touch.

Nobody wanted to be responsible for the consequences of making Cecilia unhappy, not even Robert—or *more* unhappy, for her unhappiness was the glue that bound them all to her in the first place. The one thing Cecilia couldn't afford to do was smile.

She wasn't smiling now. There were dark circles under her eyes, and her lips curved down in anger. "Lonely?" she asked, in a voice that was surprisingly low and husky—a voice which would have been sexy in any woman who wasn't so determined *not* to be sexy as Cecilia was. "*Lonely?*" She drew the word out theatrically, as if Alexa had just invented it, or perhaps misused it in some way. "You know nothing about it. I would have stayed home to look after Father if he'd wanted me to, and he knew it."

It seemed to Alexa doubtful that Arthur would have wanted to be "looked after" by his daughter. "He wasn't an invalid," she said. "He didn't need to be 'looked after.' He was just lonely."

"He was drinking heavily," Cecilia said.

"He was *not* drinking heavily," Alexa insisted, holding her hands together tightly, the knuckles white, as if she were trying to prevent herself from physically attacking Cecilia. "He drank a little bit more than was good for him, but he cut way down after we met."

"He was drunk when he took you to the Metropolitan Museum trustees' dinner," Cecilia said. "Uncle Cordy saw him. He said Father's behavior scandalized people."

"He had a couple of drinks, and we danced. What's scandalous about that? Mr. DeWitt doesn't know what he's talking about."

"Courtland DeWitt knew my father for more than forty years. I imagine he would know if he was drunk or sober."

"Your father didn't like Courtland DeWitt, and the feeling was mutual. Mr. DeWitt isn't exactly an impartial witness."

"I don't think you knew Father well at all," Cecilia said. "Courtland was his closest friend. Either you're inventing his opinions for reasons of your own, or he was so ill and drinking so heavily that he didn't know what he was saying half the time."

"Cici, please. This isn't getting us anywhere." Robert's tone was not so much demanding as pleading, but it seemed to do the trick. Cecilia bit her lip and subsided into sulky silence. "We'll take it as given that you knew Father," he said. "I'm a little surprised to hear you say he felt 'lonely,' as you put it. He did everything he could to drive us away, even Cecilia—and she was the closest to him of us all. Well, Father always had a terrible temper, and as he grew older, and the drinking got worse, he simply couldn't control it any more. It's not a pretty thing to say about one's own father, but he was consumed by anger—on the subject of his children, anyway. Every time we talked, I was afraid he'd have a stroke or a heart attack, and I can't say I'm surprised that it finally happened. He simply wasn't rational. Hadn't been for years. Certainly not since John's death, anyway."

"He held himself responsible for that," she said evenly, looking him right in the eye.

Even though he had brought the subject up himself, the mention of John's death was enough to make Robert wary, she noticed. "Did he?" he asked. His expression was cautious, his eyes flickered nervously, unlike his usual steady gaze. "Let's not get onto that subject. I'm merely saying Father wasn't reasonable when it came to his children."

"He was the *most* reasonable man I've ever met. As for his temper—in all the time I knew him, I never saw him lose it once. I'm not saying he was a saint, but he certainly wasn't the drunken monster you're making him out to be."

Robert's attitude was suddenly more conciliatory. Was he afraid she might bring John's name up again? He seemed determined not to provoke her, at any rate. "I did *not* say Father was 'a drunken monster.' I'm merely saying he had a temper."

"*I* never saw it, Mr. Bannerman. The man you describe doesn't sound like my husband." At the word "husband," Cecilia's mouth pursed like somebody who had just bitten down unexpectedly on a piece of lemon. Robert continued to smile diplomatically.

"Call me Robert, please," he said gently. "We agreed. Was he still angry at me?"

"Yes, but he regretted it. He felt it had been his fault. He wanted to put it right, but he thought it had gone too far, that it was too late."

"He was probably correct on both points, Alexa. And Cecilia? Was he prepared to forgive her for running away to Africa?"

"He didn't seem to feel there was anything to forgive. He missed her. He talked about her often."

"Did he now? He seems to have talked to you about us a lot." There was an edge of suspicion in his voice.

"Well, you were—are—his children. You were always very much on his mind."

"Is that a fact? Tell me, if we were so much on his mind, why do you think he proposed to overturn a family tradition on his deathbed and hand control of the fortune over to you—if the new will is valid?"

"It *is* valid."

"That remains to be seen."

She realized that Robert was cross-examining her, but somehow she didn't mind. She had only to shut her eyes, and it was Arthur she was talking to. Nor was there anything in Robert's voice to suggest that he was hostile. His tone was soothing, apologetic, genuinely curious. His piercing blue eyes—so very familiar to her—registered his sympathy, his respect for the difficulty of her position, even a certain degree of friendliness.

Cecilia, who had withdrawn her hand from Robert's, apparently having had enough of the finger squeezing, sat like someone in a trance, an expression of mild disgust on her face, while Putnam and Booker, still on their feet, hovered behind her protectively.

"I don't think I should discuss that," Alexa said. "I mean, where we go from here, legally, that's something I have to talk to Mr. Stern about. Look, try to understand: What your father did with the will—that was as much of a surprise to me as it was to you."

"A pleasant surprise?"

"No, not at all."

Cecilia made a noise that sounded as if she were about to choke. "Oh, *really!*" she said.

Alexa's anger was so apparent that Cecilia's eyes glinted in triumph, pleased that she had struck home at last.

Robert ignored Cecilia's outburst, continuing his interrogation as if he were a lawyer ignoring an unruly outburst in court. "It must have occurred to you that by marrying Father you would become a very wealthy woman?"

"I didn't think about it." She thought now for a moment. What she had said was not strictly true—she *had* thought about it, of course, but it had never seemed quite real to her. Given time, she might have begun to think about the material consequences of marrying Arthur Bannerman—but she had not been given time. "Look," she said, "I didn't *know* Arthur was going to write out a new will, and I didn't have the slightest reason to think he'd die, either. I know what he wanted to do with the fortune because he talked to me about it a lot, but I think he'd have done it even if he hadn't met me."

"Is that so?" Robert asked. "Pray tell," he added with an ironic smile.

She wasn't sure whether he was making fun of her, but she decided to ignore it. "He felt he hadn't done enough with it. Enough good, I mean," she added, aware that it sounded too earnest. "His father and his grandfather had been great philanthropists, and he felt he hadn't followed in their footsteps, that he'd let things slide . . . I mean, take the Bannerman Foundation. . . ."

Robert laughed. "*You* take it! A pack of whining pinko academics, pushing and shoving each other aside at the trough for grants."

"Arthur didn't feel that way, exactly. He did think, to quote him, that it had 'degenerated into empty intellectualism,' that instead of doing good, the Foundation was producing nothing but Ph. D. theses and left-wing propaganda, which wasn't at all what his father—I'm sorry, your grandfather—had in mind."

"Damned right it wasn't," Robert said. "Grandfather would turn over in his grave if he knew the Foundation had issued a report recommending that inherited wealth be taxed out of existence!"

"Your father had his own doubts on that subject," she said. "Anyway, since he couldn't change the Foundation, he wanted to start all over again—use the fortune to do good, but on a smaller, more human scale. 'Philanthropy for people, as opposed to institutional philanthropy,' he called it."

Robert looked puzzled. " 'Philanthropy for people'? What the hell is that?"

"It means funding projects that help people directly, instead of creating big institutions that get out of control, like the Foundation." She was again conscious of sounding a bit too earnest, but Arthur had believed passionately in his ideas, and she wanted to convince his children, as he had convinced her. "It means finding out what people need," she explained, "instead of telling them. Your father thought about it a lot. He was looking for a way to get away from what he called 'ivory tower philanthropy.' He wanted the money used to improve people's lives. He loved finding small organizations that were doing things that interested him, it was like a hobby for him. He funded a ballet school in Harlem, a traditional crafts school for the Navaho Indians, all sorts of projects nobody else seemed to care about. He felt he had to touch people's lives somehow, not just build a new library at Harvard or keep a lot of academics busy."

"It all sounds like one of Emmett's crackpot ideas."

"There was nothing crackpot about it. He had it worked out in detail. And, as a matter of fact, he thought Emmett's ideas made a lot of sense. Some of them, anyway."

"And Father's goddamned museum? Was *that* in his plans, too?"

Arthur's ideas had seemed so sensible to her that she was puzzled—and annoyed—by his children's skepticism and hostility. Robert she could understand more easily than the others—as the heir, his pride was injured, and he was being deprived of a fortune that he must have thought of as "his," but she saw no reason why Cecilia and Putnam should be opposed to Arthur's plans. "Yes," she said, "he *was* planning to build the museum, though it wasn't the only thing on his mind. He wanted something which was *more* than a museum, you see. He thought the Museum of Modern Art was sterile, and the Guggenheim even more so. Arthur wanted a museum that would be a community center, that would be self-supporting, that would *involve* people with art, rather than just putting it on the walls. . . ."

"I've heard it all before," Robert said wearily. "It's nonsense. A monument to Father's vanity."

"It is nothing of the kind!" Alexa said, raising her voice. "He had it worked out carefully. I can show you his plans. . . ."

"I wouldn't waste my time looking at them," Cecilia said. "I don't believe Father had the slightest intention of doing these things, and if he did he was mad, or drunk, or unduly influenced by you."

"That is absolutely not true! He was a man of vision. . . ."

"And are you asking us to believe he discussed all this with a total stranger?" Cecilia, Alexa noticed, was determined to avoid eye contact. Even when she was speaking to her directly, she managed to focus her eyes on some far distant point above Alexa's head. "You may have persuaded him to sign a piece of paper, because he was old and sick, but he would never have betrayed his own flesh and blood."

"I was not 'a total stranger,' Miss Bannerman." She allowed her voice to show an edge of anger. "As a matter of fact, your father was deeply concerned about his children—about all of you. He didn't like what the fortune had done to *his* life, and he was determined not to let it happen again."

Robert came over and sat down on the arm of the sofa, his legs crossed casually, looking more like a well-dressed undergraduate than a United States ambassador in his mid-forties. He put his arm around Cecilia's shoulders. It was a gesture that was at once intimate and proprietary—indeed, he behaved far more like Cecilia's fiancé, or former fiancé, than Booker did, and seemed to have developed a whole series of small tricks designed to push Booker into the background, where Robert Bannerman clearly thought he belonged. "Hush, Cici," he said. "Let Alexa talk." He gave Alexa an encouraging smile. "What exactly *were* Father's thoughts? Since he talked to you so freely?"

"He didn't want control of The Trust to be in the hands of one person anymore."

"You know, you're a remarkably tactful young woman. But let's be frank. He didn't want it to be in *my* hands, did he? It was *me* he was worried about, wasn't it?"

She had dreaded telling Robert the truth and was relieved that he had brought the subject up himself. "Yes," she said quietly. "But that's only part of it."

He nodded. He seemed a little sad, but not at all surprised or indignant. "It's an old story," he said. "I won't bore you with the details. Not that they matter now. Father never forgave me for the fact that he lost the nomination. He put the blame on me, but I was only doing what he wanted me to. He tried to strike back at me with this so-called new will. I'm only sorry he dragged *you* into this sordid little Oedipal drama. So I was unfit to look after The Trust, in Father's eyes?"

"He felt that you'd tried to snatch it out of his hands."

He sighed. "I know. It's ridiculous. He wouldn't run things himself—*couldn't*, given the shape he was in after John's death—so I tried to take over the burden. He knew perfectly well what I was doing—I never made any secret of it. With all respect to Grandmother, she couldn't have been expected to do it all herself. I mean, there *are* more important questions facing us than the ownership of a rock in the middle of the Hudson River, or whether the servants at Kiawa should be kept on salary even when they're long past the retirement age and getting social security. When Father got his strength back again—no, let's be frank —when he managed to get his drinking more or less under control again, and came out of his depression—he turned on me, as if I had been going to tear down Kiawa and put up a glass high-rise on the site. I suppose he told you that I'd use The Trust for my own purposes, didn't he?"

She nodded, grateful again that he'd said it himself.

"My God! Cecilia knows better than that. Putnam knows better than that, don't you, Putt?"

Putnam, apparently awakened from his own thoughts by the mention of his name, shrugged. His expression was hard to read, but Robert chose to interpret it as agreement. "You see," he said. "*They* don't think so. Grandmother doesn't think so. DeWitt doesn't think so. It was a figment of Father's imagination. No, no, let me finish, you're not to blame, I know that. You believed what Father told you. Why wouldn't you? It just doesn't happen to be true."

"*He* seemed pretty sure of it."

"Look, it's thirty or forty years of family history. You can't expect to arrive on the scene at the last minute and understand it all. Whether you know it or not, Father was finally getting his revenge on me, that's all—and overturning family tradition as well."

"It only looks that way," she said. "His idea was that I would carry out what he didn't live to do. Look, it's not *my* fault all this happened. If Arthur had lived, he would have done it himself. He was going to tell you about me, then explain his plans. When he learned he might not live to do it, he gave control to me so I could do what he wanted. He *trusted* me, don't you see? I can't walk away from that."

"It's a heavy burden." There was no irony in Robert's voice. It occurred to her that he could have made a terrific actor, but then she told herself she was being unfair. She had no reason so far to suppose he was not sincere. "He gave you control with the intention that you should give it up? He must have trusted you to a remarkable degree!"

"Well—he *did*. I don't know why, and it doesn't matter. I didn't *ask* him to, but I gave him a promise and I'm stuck with it. . . ."

"You don't *have* to be stuck with it, Alexa," he continued. "There are a dozen different ways you can repudiate it and save yourself and everybody else a lot of trouble. We can reach an agreement. Drop your claim, acknowledge that Father was of unsound mind when he drew up this last will. You'll be a rich woman—a rich *widow*. We'll make a settlement—whatever you like, five million, ten million, more if you insist—then go back to the original will, without fighting this thing through the courts. You don't want to spend the next ten years in litigation, do you? And if you win—which you may not—do you really want to spend the rest of your life worrying about the fortune? Or the family, for that matter? Why give up your life to a fight over something he forced on you, without even telling you what he was going to do? It's not worth it! Let *me* worry about Kiawa, and the cousins, and the goddamn Bannerman Foundation and all the rest of it. It's what I was brought up to do, after all."

He gave her a smile. With his deep tan, flawless teeth, and good bones, Robert had the kind of star quality that would have made anyone look only at him even if there had been a hundred people in the room. Next to him, poor Booker and Putnam seemed faded, drab, and out of focus, mere bit players.

DeWitt had put the same proposal to her, less frankly, and with less charm, and she had not been tempted. Robert made it sound so tempting that she almost said yes. Indeed, she found herself nodding while he spoke, as if she agreed with every word. He leaned forward, close to her—no mean feat for a man who was precariously perched on the arm of a sofa—and put his hand on hers, a brief, gentle touch, as if his fingertips had brushed against hers accidentally. "Think it over," he said. "In the long run, it's the best way."

She might almost have given in right then if his hand hadn't touched hers. Not that she was offended—on the contrary, she felt an almost electric shock—but she had only to close her eyes and the voice was Arthur's. Even with her eyes open, what she saw still reminded her of Arthur so strongly that there was no way she could persuade herself to go against his wishes. "I can't do that," she said firmly.

He leaned back, still smiling, though something in his eyes told her that he had reached a decision of some kind. "I think you're making a mistake," he said pleasantly.

Cecilia put a hand over her eyes. "Robert, darling," she said, "do let's end this. You're not getting anywhere. And it's giving me a headache."

"I just want to get a clear picture of what Alexa has in store for us."

"We *have* a clear picture, Robert. I do, anyway." Cecilia turned to look straight at Alexa for the first time. "If nobody else in this family will say it, I will. You took advantage of my father shamelessly. He was angry with Robert. He was disappointed with Putt. He couldn't understand why I went to Africa—didn't *want* to understand. You played on those feelings, fanned the fire, for your own selfish, greedy ends. You stole him from us, and now you're trying to steal the fortune. And to justify what you've done, you're handing us a lot of nonsense about Father's museum and his plans for the family. As if you had any right to dictate to *us!*"

Cecilia paused. She sat demurely, hands in her lap, a pleasant expression on her face, the merest trace of what a total stranger might have taken for a polite smile on her lips. Only her eyes, enormous, filmed with tears and as cold as an assassin's, conveyed any emotion—though as she spoke two bright red patches appeared on her tanned cheeks, giving her face the look of someone who has been out too long for a bitter-cold winter walk.

"Robert may sweet-talk you if he chooses," she said. "I won't, not even for his sake." She smiled, as if what she had to say was something Alexa would enjoy hearing, a compliment, perhaps. Or was it just a habit, an automatic social grace so deeply bred into her that she couldn't drop it, not even in rage? It had not occurred to Alexa before that Cecilia's smile, rare as it seemed to be, was a sure sign of dislike, that it had more to do with showing how perfect her manners were, even to an inferior whom she despised, than any pleasure.

"I'm not going to be sweet-talked into anything, Miss Bannerman," Alexa said, fighting to keep her voice unemotional. She would *not* let herself be provoked by Cecilia Bannerman, she told herself—though she could feel anger building up inside her, like a volcano waiting to erupt. "I'm not going to let myself be talked to like a servant, either."

"Like a servant? Our servants have always been decent, respectable people who know their place. It's the kind of thing you can hardly be expected to understand, I suppose."

"Enough, Cici," Robert warned. "This won't get us anywhere."

"I was brought up to believe in being honest, Robert. I'm sure Miss Walden would expect nothing less."

"I am not *Miss Walden*, Miss Bannerman!" Alexa said, standing up. "I don't give a damn about the fortune, and I don't give a damn what you think about me, but I'm your father's wife—his widow—" she corrected herself—"and until you accept that, I'll fight you right down to the last penny. If it takes a lifetime."

She gave herself the satisfaction of walking out of the room.

ROBERT BANNERMAN, Booker thought, seemed more pleased than not by Alexa's outburst.

To his surprise, Robert had asked him to stay, while Putnam, always the good soldier, was sent off to take care of Cecilia. Now that Robert had told him why, he wished he had been smart enough to go with Cecilia himself. A face-to-face conversation with Robert nearly always meant problems.

"Don't give me any more crap about ethics," Robert growled. "I'm in no mood to hear it."

"It's not even *ethics*, Robert. It's plain common sense."

"I'm not interested in plain common sense just now, either, Martin. If I want a paper-pusher, I've got Uncle Cordy. That's all the son of a bitch is good for. I watched her like a goddamn hawk. She's hiding something, Martin, I *know* it. Stop arguing with me and get out there to Illinois."

"I already said no to DeWitt when he brought it up, Robert. I'm a lawyer, not a detective."

"I don't care what you told Uncle Cordy. This is between you and me, Martin. Have I ever asked you for a favor?"

"Many, many times. And I've always done my best to oblige."

"And have you ever asked me for one?"

Booker sighed. They were sitting in the study of Robert's apartment, surrounded by hand-carved bookshelves for which the decorator had provided the books by the yard. Robert, when he read at all, liked spy stories, and it was part of his secretary's job to keep a supply of the latest ones, in paperback, on the ambassador's night table. The books in the shelves represented what the decorator had thought suitable for an ambassador—yards of history, atlases, encyclopedias, heavyweight biographies, leather sets of the classics, removed only for dusting. Facing them was an enormous television set, on which Robert was watching a football game, with the sound off. "I asked a question," Robert said.

"Yes," Martin admitted reluctantly. "I asked you for a favor, okay?"

"And I took care of it, didn't I?"

"That was a long time ago, Robert."

"What does time have to do with it? Did I whine and complain, or try to talk my way out of doing it? I did not. I talked the girl into keeping quiet. Which wasn't easy. I hushed her husband up. Which was a lot harder. And I made sure Cici never heard a word about it, which is what you *really* owe me for."

"Let's not dwell on details."

"That's up to you, sport. But let's not *forget* them, either, shall we? You had a little problem, I straightened it out. Now *I* have a little problem in Illinois, and I need somebody I can trust. Somebody respectable and smart, who won't get into trouble. If I send some of my people out there to the boonies, it could backfire, frankly. You know what they're like."

"I still don't like it."

"I'm not asking you to like it, Martin. Jesus! Look at that tackle!" They both stared at the screen for a few moments, Robert with the rapt attention of a jock who has never outgrown the passion for contact sports, Booker with the slightly glazed expression of somebody who long ago decided there was no succeeding in life without faking an interest in sport he had never felt.

"Son of a *bitch!*" Robert shouted. "Did you see that?"

Booker signified that he had, and that he was impressed. Usually that was enough to satisfy Robert, but not always.

"Let me spell it out for you in words of one syllable, Martin. How many years have you put in with DeWitt?"

"About ten."

"Eleven, to be exact. Cordy's getting on for seventy, sport. When he retires, you could be legal counsel for the family, for the Foundation, for everything."

"What makes you think he'll retire?"

"I can take care of that, Martin. You do this for me, and it's a promise, okay? I mean, why put in eleven years of doing the real work for Cordy while he pockets the fat fees without collecting the payoff at the end? That doesn't make sense. I forget what DeWitt pulled in from the Foundation last year, but it was in the seven figures, as I remember."

"There was a lot of litigation."

"Which you dealt with, mostly, not Uncle Cordy. But Cordy is the one with the chauffeur-driven Mercedes and the house in Pound Ridge with two tennis courts and six in help."

"I'm still not happy with the idea."

"Who's talking about happiness, sport? Am I happy? Is Miss Walden happy? Does anybody care? Do you want to write off eleven years of toil for Cordy DeWitt and go hunting for a new job? Do you think I want to hand Miss Walden, pretty as she is, three-quarters of a billion dollars and the keys to Kiawa? What's your goddamn problem?"

"Well, *one* part of the problem is that I believe her story."

"What story?"

"I don't think she's a fortune hunter. I think she's telling the truth."

"Oh, for Christ's sake, Martin, so do I. What's that got to do with it? I *like* the girl. I even asked her out to dinner tonight to apologize for Cecilia's behavior, and she accepted. That doesn't mean I'm going to give up control of The Trust, or my chance at the governorship, or let her spend a hundred million dollars on Father's crazy ideas. Grow up! Just because she's a girl with good legs doesn't mean I have to roll over and play dead. I put in my time, Martin. So have you. It's time to collect now."

"All right, all right. But what makes you think this is the way to go?"

"Instinct. The suspicion that she's hiding something. The fact that if we go to court it could take forever, and in the meantime, I can't finance my campaign, I'm in limbo, a fucking *claimant* to what's mine, with a good chance of losing. And don't tell *me* DeWitt thinks we'd win, because you and I both know he's full of shit. She ran away from home, and she can't go back, that's what I think, and I want to know why. When I know why, I'll have some leverage."

"And then?"

"And then I'll apply it, Counselor. You leave all that to me."

"And if I don't turn up anything?"

"We scratch Plan A and move on to Plan B."

"What's Plan B, Robert?

Robert Bannerman stared at the television screen, absorbed, it seemed, in the finer points of an instant replay. "Look at that," he said in disgust. "Two hundred pounds of muscle and he's scared, the son of a bitch. You can't play football if you're afraid of getting hurt. Of hurting somebody. That's the game, Martin. Skill and balls, that's all there is to it. Balls first and foremost. You'd better go see if Cici is all right."

Booker knew he was being dismissed, and he didn't like it a bit. He told himself he didn't need to put up with this kind of shit from Robert Bannerman, and it was partly true. Then he told himself he wasn't afraid of Robert Bannerman, but that wasn't true at all, and he knew it —as did Robert, unfortunately.

Booker was never sure *why* he was frightened of Robert, but it was a fact, one he had learned to live with over the years. In a way, he thought, Robert simply fascinated him, the way dangerous sports fascinate some people. The fear was a challenge, but it still made him nervous, which was part of the hold Robert had on him. You never knew what Robert was going to do, or how far he would go.

"About Plan B, Robert," Booker said, getting up.

Robert did not take his eyes off the screen. "Plan B, old man?" he said gently, as if he had never heard the phrase before.

Booker hesitated. "Don't go too far. I mean, don't get carried away."

"Don't worry so much, Martin," Robert said, switching the sound back on with the remote. "It's just information I'm looking for. No dirty tricks. I learned my lesson a long time ago, in Miami, remember?"

Booker was halfway down the hall to get Cici and Putnam moving before he remembered what Robert was talking about, and when he did, he broke out into a sweat that turned his forehead damp.

He had been a much younger man then, just out of law school, but he could still recall the photograph in the New York *Post*. A group of well-tanned men and women in bikinis and sunglasses, mixed expressions of horror and curiosity on their faces, were being pushed back by the police from the side of a pool. Above them the balconies of a Miami hotel were stacked out of the camera's view. Next to a flowered deck chair, the photographer had caught a pair of feet, one in a Gucci loafer, the other shoeless. The headline read, "DELEGATE'S SUICIDE LEAP: BLACKMAIL PLOT CAUSE?"

Whatever Robert's Plan B was, Booker decided, he would have to make sure it wasn't necessary, for everyone's sake.

ARTHUR HAD ALWAYS AVOIDED "21," as he did any place he might be seen and recognized, but Robert Bannerman was obviously at ease here. The men who greeted him were sleek, middle-aged, self-made millionaires, Alexa guessed, fellows who knew how to make a cash register sing. She recognized a famous Wall Street financier and a couple of major takeover artists who had been in the headlines recently. They were Robert's kind of men, bodies hard from exercise and racquetball, eyes cold, predators taking the night off from making money, accompanied by their wives, mostly a decade or two younger, blond and beautiful, many of whom gave Robert the kind of look that passes only between people who have slept together on the sly, a glance and a smile so devoid of meaning, so deliberately casual, that it was as good as a confession.

Well, she thought, it was none of *her* business. It amused her that the husbands didn't notice anything, but then, they were too busy giving Robert firm, manly handshakes, and anyway, they seemed like the kind of men who probably never paid much attention to their wives in the first place—which probably went some of the way to explaining Robert's success, though not all of the way, since he was, she had to admit, an extremely attractive man—and persuasive, or she would never have accepted his invitation in the first place.

She could not help noticing that whereas his father would have asked for a table where he couldn't be seen, Robert was seated where he couldn't be missed. An endless stream of people stopped to greet him, and he had a word for each of them—a natural politician. A number of them stared at her, apparently aware she was a celebrity of some sort, but not sure who, which was just as well. He ordered briskly, with the usual Bannerman indifference to food, and kept her amused with small talk until he was interrupted by a heavyset man whom she dimly recognized as a wealthy golfing friend of the President.

"The Man says you're going to run for governor?"

Robert nodded. "Run, and win, old man."

"You come on down to Washington, we'll talk politics. It's about time we had a Republican again in Albany."

"I'll do that," Robert said, flashing an incandescent smile. He turned to her as the man walked away, his face more serious. "Father didn't think I could win the governorship, did he?"

"He didn't say."

"You're being tactful. Let's not waste each other's time with tact."

"All right. He thought you'd lose, yes."

"What Father knew about politics could be written on the head of a pin. The truth is, he couldn't stand the idea of my winning a major election, when he'd lost. He absolutely refused to use his influence on my behalf. Any normal father would have been *proud* to help. Look what Joe Kennedy did for Jack and Bobby, for God's sake! Father wouldn't even help me pay off my campaign debts after my Senate race."

"He felt you'd used his name to raise the money in the first place."

"I used *our* name. Why not? I was born with it, after all, just the same as he was. When Republicans nominate a Bannerman, they have certain expectations. One of those expectations is that there won't be any problem about financing the campaign."

"He was pretty firm on *that* subject. He said hell would freeze over before he'd bail you out. I thought he was being too harsh, myself."

Robert smiled—a thinner smile this time, more like the ghost of a smile, as if to show her that he wasn't taking any of this personally. "Well, Father certainly spoke frankly to you. Actually, there's a bigger problem than money." He paused. "What I *do* worry about is a long struggle over The Trust. Airing dirty linen in public is bad politics."

"There's nothing dirty about what happened."

"It won't be seen that way. It's going to be damned hard to run for office in the middle of a major lawsuit. Well, as you say, it's not your doing. Tell me—not that it's any of my business—how does *your* family feel about all this?"

She found herself drawn to him. If she closed her eyes, it was like hearing Arthur speak. In a way, she felt sorry for Robert—it was not he who had insulted her, after all, and the news of his father's death and marriage had certainly come at just the wrong moment for his political career.

"There's only my mother." This was not true, but the less said about her brothers, the better.

He smiled encouragingly, nodding a brief salute to motherhood. "I suppose you can do no wrong in her eyes. It's always the way with mothers." He lit another cigarette—an unfiltered Pall Mall, she noticed. Not for Robert the false security of a filtered cigarette or a low-tar brand. He inhaled deeply, like a man taking a breath before diving. Did he always smoke at this rate, she wondered, or was he nervous?

"Not mine," she said.

"Indeed? Still, she must be concerned?"

"She thinks I can take care of myself."

"Does she? And *can* you?"

"I've managed so far."

He nodded. "Nothing like this, though, I imagine?"

"Worse."

"Ah?" He did not seem interested, but the blue eyes flickered slightly. "You're plucky. You'll need to be, you know."

She laughed. "If I lose, you mean?"

"Oh, no. If you win. Managing the Bannerman fortune is a hell of a job." He looked at her closely, his eyes screwed up against the cigarette smoke. "Do you think we can be friends, Alexa?" he asked.

"Friends?" It would have been easy enough to say yes, but while she might have accepted friendship with Robert Bannerman, she very much doubted that it was what he had in mind.

"I'd like for us to be friends," he continued, taking her hand. "I've got all the enemies I can handle already."

His hand was uncomfortably warm. Or was it just that she was over-reacting to his touch? Get your mind back on business, she told herself, wishing he were less attractive, less like his father. . . .

"I'd like to get to know you better," he whispered. "Much better."

Like his father. . . . She pulled her hand away suddenly. However attractive Robert was—and how could she not be attracted to a younger replica of Arthur Bannerman?—he was *not* his father. She was furious at herself for even *thinking* about Robert, and furious with Robert, though less so, for trying to take advantage of her weakness. "I'm sure we can work together very well once everything is settled between us," she said, a little more stiffly than she intended.

Robert nodded. He removed his hand, out of reach, with the air of a man who's tried one tactic, failed, and has decided to withdraw from the field. "Why don't you take the goddamn money and run, Alexa," he said, his voice all business now. "Name your price."

"I told you before, I'm not a runner. I don't care about the money. And I don't *have* a price."

He laughed harshly. "You sound just like an Aldon. *They* don't care about money either—but they make damn sure their daughters marry people who *do*." His laugh was as loud as his father's, but for the first time she noticed a bitter edge to it. "Seriously, the Bannerman family is no place for a fun-loving girl with a good head on her shoulders! I was born into it, so I don't have a goddamn choice, but why join it when you don't have to? Believe me, being a Bannerman isn't any kind of fun at all."

"I didn't think it was, Robert. Arthur—your father—had very strong ideas about what he wanted to do with The Trust. He thought about it a lot. And it *mattered* to him, Robert. His only fear was that he'd left it too late, and that turned out to be true. I think that's why he talked to me so much about it. I'm not doing this for the fun of it."

He sighed. "Let me guess. A sense of duty? Well, you've come to the right family for that, Alexa. It's the family curse—that and guilt for being so much richer than normal people."

"You make it sound worse than it is."

He shuddered briefly. "You're wrong. Father glossed up the family history for you. And by the time you met him, remember, he'd given up trying to *do* anything about the family, or the fortune."

She was amazed at how little Robert knew his father. Was the same true in reverse? Was Arthur's view of Robert equally distorted? It seemed to her possible. "That's not true, you know," she said patiently, trying to make Robert believe her. "He worked at it—hard. And he cared about it, maybe too much. I don't say he didn't make mistakes, but who doesn't? And I think he sometimes wished he'd had more choices when he was young. Do you know he once wanted to be a painter?"

Robert's eyes opened wide with genuine astonishment. "A *painter*? What on earth makes you say that?"

"He told me so. His father wouldn't let him."

"I'm not surprised. Christ! Can you imagine Father living in some goddamned garret in the Village? Father may have been making fun of you. Or raving."

"He was perfectly sane," she said angrily. "And serious. And he didn't have to live in a garret to paint, did he? He could have lived a perfectly respectable life, and still painted. Look at Wyeth."

He smoked thoughtfully. "What you say about Father's wanting to be a painter—*that's* interesting, if it's true. I wonder why he never mentioned it. It would have made him seem far more human—the heir to the Bannerman fortune telling his father he wanted to paint landscapes, or nudes, or whatever the hell it was he had in mind."

"Perhaps he thought you wouldn't understand."

"I wouldn't have. I still don't. But it's a curiously touching story." He laughed. "I wanted to be an explorer, you know. I saw myself leading expeditions all over the world, naming mountains and rivers after myself—but when I told Father, you'd have thought I'd announced I wanted to be a street musician, or join an order of monks. Out of the question!"

"Why an explorer, of all things?"

"Why not? Perhaps it's in the blood. Cyrus was a kind of explorer—an adventurer, anyway. If he hadn't gone to California via Panama to see what was happening in the mines, he might never have made his first pile. His younger brother was a whaler, you know—went all the way to China a couple of times, ended up shipwrecked in the Fijis, supposedly killed and eaten by cannibals. There was another brother, 'Doctor' Alexander Bannerman, who went West to find gold, got into trouble for trading guns and whiskey to the Indians, and was lynched by a mob in Laramie. Quite rightly, I expect."

Robert's expression softened. "When Father bought the land in Venezuela I was about fifteen. I spent one summer there, herding cattle, camping out in the jungle, going down the rivers to visit the Indian villages, had a whale of a time." He seemed almost to be talking to himself. His eyes seemed focused on some imaginary far horizon, instead of on her. "Of course Father was on the board of *National Geographic*, the American Museum of Natural History, the Explorers' Club, so it was easy to imagine myself leading an expedition somewhere. But there wasn't a hope of anything like that happening, I should have known that. Father laid down the law: Harvard, the Business School, then a few years learning the ropes in the family office. It took me years to discover that the more successful I was at doing what he wanted me to do, the more he'd hate me."

"He *didn't* hate you."

"Excuse me, but I know better. You came in at the end of the story. And only heard one side of it."

"I'm not taking sides."

"You are, you know." A flashing smile—it crossed her mind to wonder how his teeth stayed so white, despite the chain-smoking. Did he visit the dentist once a week to have them polished, or was it simply one more example of fortunate genetics? "You've taken Father's side, hook, line, and sinker, right down to your museum."

"*His* museum, Robert."

He hardly even touched his food. He slipped a cigarette out of the pack, tapped it against his wrist, lit it, wreathed himself in smoke without once taking his eyes off her. "His museum? Yes, of course, but he's gone, Alexa, so I'm afraid it's *yours* now."

For a brief moment she thought she caught a glimpse of open hostility in the clear blue eyes, but if it was there at all, Robert quickly covered it up. "There's no reason for us to lock horns," he said pleasantly. "Let's settle, and get on with our lives."

She was on slippery ground, and she knew it. Stern had warned her not to get into any substantive discussion without him. "Words can't be withdrawn," he had told her, his expression severe—not that it was anything she didn't already know. "You can bite your tongue all you like, but you can't call them back. Mention the word 'settlement,' and Robert will be on to you like a shark after blood. You have to convince him we'll *never* settle."

It was not a position she felt comfortable with, even in Stern's office. Robert was a Bannerman, Arthur's son, and she was an interloper. On the whole, she agreed with him. A decade or so of expensive litigation held no appeal for her, however much it excited Stern—besides, she was beginning to like Robert enough to wonder if Arthur had really understood his own son. The story Robert had told her about wanting to be an explorer she found strangely moving—it had exactly the same wistful quality as Arthur's ambition to be a painter, as if both father and son had discovered at almost the same age that not only could money not buy you everything, it could even stop you from doing what you wanted most to do.

"I couldn't agree to anything that went against your father's wishes," she said. "*Directly* against them," she hedged. "That doesn't mean I'm not willing to talk," she added lamely.

She felt as if she were stumbling along a rocky path in the wrong shoes. Robert gave her no help. He sat there breathing smoke, a smile on his face, his eyes so devoid of expression that she might have been talking Swahili. "There may be—" she struggled for a formal phrase that would commit her to nothing more than the possibility of future good will and that wouldn't anger Stern, and she picked on one of Simon's favorites—"areas of compromise."

"Areas of compromise?" He cocked his head slightly to one side, as if he were waiting for the phrase to be translated. It occurred to her that she might be out of her depth. As a politician and a diplomat, Robert was presumably an expert negotiator. "Such as?" he asked.

"Well, the museum, for example, is *not* an area of compromise."

"It isn't? All right, then. What is?"

The conversation was going faster than she wanted it to. "Control of The Trust? After all, your father's idea was that it should be shared. And put to good use."

"Shared? Yes, of course." He appeared to consider the matter for a few moments. "Perhaps. It's not impossible."

"I'd want to talk to Mr. Stern first, of course."

"Of course," he said gravely. "You must. That's what you're paying him for. And he doesn't come cheap, as I know."

"And I'd want to know that the rest of the family was willing to compromise."

"Even Cecilia?"

She nodded. There was no use trying to reach an agreement as long as anyone in the family held out against it. Robert seemed to feel the same way. "If we get that far, I'll take care of Cecilia," he said. "Don't worry about her."

"And Eleanor?"

"Eleanor?"

"If your father was to be believed, there's no point to talking about anything to do with the Bannerman family unless Eleanor is willing to go along."

Robert chuckled. "On that score, Father was to be believed. Damn right! You don't have Eleanor on board, you might as well not bother to raise anchor."

"Mr. DeWitt tells me she's not seeing anyone?"

"Is that right?"

Robert's trick of answering a question with a question was infuriating, but as character flaws went, it seemed minor compared to the kind of thing of which his father had usually accused him. "I assume you'd know," she said.

"Yes? You're not suggesting you want to talk to Grandmother, surely, are you?"

"I don't *want* to, no. But I think I have to."

"Please don't take this as rudeness, but what makes you think she'll see you? The Bishop of Albany has been trying to see her for years—in vain, I might add—and *he* isn't threatening the family fortune. You met her at the funeral, remember? Surely once was enough?"

"She told me to stay away. But I'm not going to stay away."

"She's not somebody you can argue with, Alexa. Believe me."

"I'm not going to argue with her. I have to try to make her understand what Arthur wanted."

"It's important to you?"

She nodded. "I don't know why, but it matters to me, yes. At the funeral, I felt . . . I don't know, perhaps just that I didn't want her to hate me. And somehow I don't think she *did*. I'd expected to be frightened of her, you see, from what everybody said—including your father—but I wasn't, not at all."

"Perhaps you should have been."

"I don't think so."

"Let's say that Grandmother agrees to see you—which I doubt. What will you tell her?"

"That I'm not the enemy. That I loved Arthur. For a start."

"Those may not be messages she wants to hear."

"I want to give them to her anyway."

Robert whistled tunelessly to himself for a moment. "Let's say I do get her to see you—no promises, mind. Will you drop this business of a press conference?"

Her heart had never been in the press conference. It was Stern's idea, and she dreaded it. Still, she was reluctant to give up Stern's trump card without even consulting him. "I'd have to think about that," she said.

"You tell the world you were married to Father, and it's 'Man the battle stations!' for all of us. No, no, I'm not threatening, I'm merely pointing out a fact. Eleanor will pull up the drawbridge, and that will be it, so far as any sensible dialogue is concerned. Wait. That's my advice."

"I'll talk to Mr. Stern," she said. "We can wait. For a while, anyway."

"Splendid!" He raised his glass and touched it to hers, took a sip, put it down. He seemed relieved and pleased at her agreement, however tentative, but she couldn't help noticing that he was in constant motion, playing with the breadsticks and the silverware, summoning the waiter and the captain, then dismissing them, picking at his food, waving at people he knew. She had the sense that Robert's restlessness and impatience were always seething, just at the edge of control, beneath the ironic smile and the cultivated charm that he presented to the world. It was a quality that appealed to her.

She warned herself to be careful.

9

"Cheer up!" Simon said. "It'll do you good to get out, see some people, enjoy life."

"It still frightens me—the whole idea of going out. They'll know who I am. Somebody's sure to recognize me."

"Well, since you've been on the television news and in every paper in town, of course they will. 'Arthur Bannerman's mystery girlfriend'— in Hugo's circle that will hardly raise an eyebrow."

"I've met him before. With you."

"I know. But Hugo treats everybody as if he'd only just met them. Carter Pierrepoint had an affair with Hugo—I can't imagine why, except that it was something young men used to do in the Sixties, after Yale—and Carter told me that even when he was *living* with Hugo, he had to reintroduce himself every morning when they woke up in bed. Hugo isn't rude—he just can't store people in his memory for more than twenty-four hours."

"I've never liked his work much."

"Well, nobody does, not even Hugo. That's not the point. It's *anti-art*—a colossal joke. Cereal boxes five feet high, with real cereal in them! Hugo doesn't even do the painting any more. He sits on a sofa and tells his acolytes what to do. It's the critics who take Hugo's work seriously, not Hugo."

"What's the occasion?"

"Once a week, the people around Hugo put on a luncheon party just to make sure the world knows he's still alive. Speaking of which, it won't be long before people begin to ask the same question about *you*. It's been, what, a week since he died?"

"More or less."

"A week tomorrow, to be exact. You can't hide out forever."

"I'm not hiding out."

"No? You're living in my spare bedroom, using the service entrance to go in and out of the building, and sneaking in and out of the office on the freight elevator. You go around in sunglasses and a hat, like Greta Garbo."

"I don't want to be interviewed."

"Well, I can understand that. 'Did Arthur Bannerman die in your bed?' It's not a question you'd want to answer, I agree. But face it, you've got a much better story to give them than that. *Tell* it, for God's sake! Stern thinks you should. I think you should. Your friend Roth thinks you should. What the hell are you waiting for?"

"I want the family to accept me. I don't think being on the front page of the New York *Post* again is the way to do it."

"You're living in a dream world. They're never going to accept you. The sooner you start fighting back bare-knuckle, the better off you'll be."

"I don't agree. Cecilia was horrible, okay. But Putnam wasn't hostile. And Robert's at least willing to talk."

"I *bet* he is." Simon leaned back in the car, and glanced at the partition to make sure the driver couldn't overhear them. "He's jerking you off—playing for time."

She frowned. It was not the kind of language she liked, and she was no longer used to hearing it. Arthur never talked like that, and it was one of the many things she liked about him. Even without the sunglasses, however, frowning at Simon was a waste of time. "Look," she said, "in a way it's *my* family, now—even if they hate me. I don't want more headlines and an endless lawsuit any more than they do. It's just what Arthur wanted to avoid."

"He went about avoiding it in a pretty funny way. Listen, I believe you, Alexa. And you're not one hundred percent wrong. Look at the Johnson family—nearly ten years of litigation and over one hundred million dollars in legal fees. Not to speak of everybody's private lives splashed all over the tabloids." He paused significantly.

"I haven't done anything to be ashamed of, Simon."

"Who's talking about shame? Christ, here we are."

The car pulled up before a nondescript loft building liberally decorated with graffiti. They got out and paused before a battered steel fire door painted a startling shade of pink—Hugo Pascal's trademark—and a small sign that read "The Group." Simon pressed a button, shouted his name into a small grille, and pushed open the door with his shoulder as the buzzer sounded. A rusty metal spiral staircase wound its way out of sight above them. They climbed it to the first story, at which point it had been transformed to look like the set of a cheap made-for-television jungle movie. The staircase had been painted bright green, draped in plastic vines and leaves, with dusty, faded silk flowers attached haphazardly. Fake birds molted in the greenery, a plastic parrot dangled from one wire foot, a stuffed monkey with one eye missing leered among the fake leaves. From somewhere buried deep in the greenery around them, a loudspeaker blared jungle sounds.

At the top of the stairs, they pushed through a door marked "No Entrance" and found themselves in a cavernous space, the loft to end all lofts, big enough for a blimp. The walls and ceiling were covered with what looked like several thousand square feet of torn and wrinkled kitchen aluminum foil, clumsily applied over everything. Hanging from the ceiling were various artifacts from Pascal's inflatable-sculpture period: a twenty-foot-long Marilyn Monroe balloon, naked, with air valves for nipples and a shiny zipper in her crotch; "The Cheerleader," a bright pink monstrosity that had sparked off a riot at the 1971 Venice Biennale, when angry feminists tried to set fire to it; a pneumatic Raquel Welch in a fluorescent bikini and shiny cowboy boots, her foot-wide, bright red lips set in a colossal, sexy smile. There were several pieces of sculpture that looked like large lumps of melting plastic, one of which seemed to pulsate with a ghastly life of its own, and several paintings consisting of old pieces of clothing stapled to canvas.

Alexa remembered that Arthur owned several of Pascal's earlier pieces from the period when he was still painting, or stenciling, or whatever it was he had done to reproduce the labels of familiar household products on canvas, grossly enlarged. Since then, like Dali in an earlier generation, Pascal had devoted himself full time to creating his own legend instead of painting. The less he produced, the more famous he became, and the more seriously critics took him.

In the center of the room a dozen or so well-dressed men and women huddled together nervously, like captives in a hostile Indian village, surrounded by Pascal's followers—strange-looking girls with dead eyes, punk hair, and huge, vaguely obscene, dangling plastic earrings, androgynous young men, a sprinkling of older members of The Group left over from the Sixties, looking, for the most part, as Simon whispered, "as if they had been freshly dug up from their graves," the men with hair to their waist and earrings, the women dressed in what looked like old Victorian parlor curtains, and wearing heavy, clanking homemade jewelry like the product of some demented hobbyist. A clutch of greasy-looking motorcycle-gang members were working as waiters, dressed in tight black leather, with studs, chains, swastikas, skulls and crossbones stenciled on the back of their jackets.

One thing you had to say for Simon, Alexa reflected—if nothing else, he managed to amuse. His own fear of boredom was so intense that he could always be counted on to find whatever was new, original, or, in this case, exotic, as if guided by some kind of internal radar.

He pushed into the group of guests, several of them people she recognized vaguely: Chloe Kahn, the critic, with her monocle and her man's bowler hat; Gunther von Sandow, a friend of Simon's, who was married to one of the richest women in America and was said by his friends to be a homosexual, a drug addict, a sadist, and by his enemies, a necrophile; Norman Mailer, whose expression suggested that everyone here would sooner or later find themselves in a novel; Sir Leo Goldlust again, the shrewd little eyes glittering in the vast, suety moon of his face; José Diaz y Doro, a schoolmate of Simon's, heir to a Bolivian mining fortune, who made a practice of introducing himself to women in restaurants or on the street by tearing a five-hundred-dollar bill in two and offering them one half and his card; Aaron Diamond, the diminutive superagent, wearing a pair of glasses so big that they made him look like a barn owl stranded in the daylight. There were several additional celebrities hovering in the background, or what Hugo Pascal would regard as celebrities, anyway: a well-known society figure currently on trial for the murder of his wife, a transsexual tennis star, a TV talk-show host in the middle of a multimillion-dollar palimony suit. "Jesus, what a freak show!" Simon whispered.

It occurred to her that she herself was probably part of Pascal's "freak show"—the girl in whose arms, or bed, at any rate, Arthur Bannerman had died. Diaz kissed her hand; the transsexual—decked out in what must surely be the only Mary McFadden pleated silk flower print dress ever made for somebody over six feet tall with the shoulders of a weight lifter—gave her a firm, masculine handshake; the accused wife-murderer expressed his sympathy for the way she was being treated in the press. ("He should know," Simon whispered.)

Aaron Diamond, his gleaming bald head California tanned to the color and texture of a sun-dried fig, recognized her immediately. "Say the word, I'll sell your story," he growled. "I'll phone Joni Evans or Howard Kaminsky this afternoon and get you two-fifty on the spot. No, what am I talking about? Five hundred, at least! Christ, first serial alone is worth a hundred, maybe one-fifty. . . ."

"I don't want to do that, thank you."

"Suit yourself," he said pleasantly enough, losing interest in her immediately and changing gears with the speed of a Formula One driver. "I met Bannerman once. I tried to get him to write *his* memoirs, but he wasn't interested. Well, you can't blame him—he didn't need the money. Nice enough fellow, but a little stuffy, I thought. Who's the tall gal over there who keeps staring at you?"

Alexa searched the room, saw out of the corner of her eyes a familiar face—the pale skin, the aquiline nose, the well-bred, slightly superior smile—and knew, instantly and without a shadow of a doubt, that it had been a mistake to come here. "Simon," she said, "in the corner . . ."

"Oh, shit!" he said, but it was already too late. The tall woman was moving toward them now, smiling at Alexa as if they were long-lost friends. "So nice to see you again," she said, her elocution so perfect that Aaron Diamond stared at her as if she were speaking a foreign language.

IT WAS BOUND TO HAPPEN sooner or later, Alexa told herself. For nearly three years she had managed to avoid meeting Brooke Cabot, which wasn't all that difficult, since their paths didn't normally cross. Brooke's social life was among her own kind, respectable old WASP families in which the blood had begun to thin and the money had long since run out, people who still "kept up appearances"—membership in the Metropolitan Club, squash at the Racquet Club, the summers at Dark Harbor, the winters at Hobe Sound, the apartment on Park Avenue, and always, somewhere in the background, a house in Virginia or the right part of New Jersey, with horses, barns, and a family history—but now had to work to do it.

These were the kind of people for whom work was a guilty secret, something their parents or grandparents had never expected them to do, had never prepared them for. They did not descend from great wealth, like the Bannermans, but from generations of well-to-do Americans who lived on the income from "family money" and neither touched their capital nor did anything very ambitious with it. Since they did not speculate, they had been, for the most part, untouched by the Crash. It was inheritance taxes, inflation, and World War II that did them in—Brooke's parents among them.

Brooke had pony-clubbed, gone to Miss Porter's, come out as a debutante, graduated from Smith, done the usual genteel year in Europe to study art only to discover that there was nothing left, no way to make ends meet—but unlike most of her friends, she had a certain entrepreneurial spirit, a trace of that daring quality that had brought her ancestors across the Atlantic from England to the New World in the first place. Not for her some graceful, "respectable" job in the Publications Division of the Metropolitan Museum of Art or the Ford Foundation; "I'd rather read for the blind!" she had allegedly said. If she was going to have to work for a living—and short of marriage there wasn't much choice—she was determined to make it pay off.

She was also determined to keep it a secret. To the outside world— the part of it that mattered to her—she would continue to lead the busy life of a young woman with family money, serving on the "right" committees, doing volunteer work for the more fashionable charities, appearing at the usual lunches, dinner parties, and charity balls, in clothes that were "good," certainly, but never outrageously expensive or exotic. Her style was "plain," ladylike, demure, her manners beyond reproach. She always wore white gloves in the summer.

Nobody would have guessed that this quiet, unassuming young woman owned and ran New York's most expensive and exclusive escort service, "The Social Register," whose telephone number was a prized secret among the kind of men who could afford its services.

"It's been a long time," Brooke said pleasantly, shaking Alexa's hand. There was something strangely masculine about the way she shook hands, not in the strength of her grip, which was ladylike enough, but in the way she stood up straight like a Marine sergeant, a resemblance emphasized by her height, feet planted at an exact forty-five-degree angle in sensible pumps with low heels.

Alexa straightened her own back involuntarily and squared her shoulders—not that her posture was bad—by any reasonable standards it was excellent—but Brooke Cabot's standards weren't reasonable.

As Alexa knew only too well, perfection was barely good enough for Brooke, who could count the number of stitches in a seam from across a room. Alexa found herself doing an instant self-inspection in her mind. Her charcoal-gray Donna Karan suit? Fine, but a little too trendy to pass muster, the skirt perhaps an inch or so too short. A white silk blouse? Okay, but Brooke would have made her button it all the way up to the neck. Sheer black panty hose? Brooke would have sent her home instantly; she insisted on stockings in natural skin tones, without seams, of course. Brooke had always been able to make her feel like a rabbit trapped in the road by the glare of oncoming headlights, and had not lost the trick. Alexa forced herself to snap out of it. "You're looking well," she said, and it was true: Brooke had one of those bland WASP faces that never seemed to age, the skin as clean, scrubbed, and healthy as in a soap ad.

"Thank you. So are you. And you've done well for yourself, too, Alexa. Simon, so nice to see you."

"How's business, Brooke?" Simon asked politely. He had a good deal of respect for Brooke Cabot, as a businesswoman first, and above all as somebody it didn't pay to cross.

"Thriving." Few people knew what Brooke did for a living. Simon, with his taste for lowlife, was naturally one of them. She was never exactly open about her business with anyone—for good reason—but it was among her own kind that her secrecy was tightest, and she had long since made it clear that Simon wasn't that kind.

"I've read such a lot about you," she said to Aaron Diamond with her most gracious, garden-party smile. "It's such a pleasure to meet you at last."

"Yeah? What business you in?"

"Business?"

"You just said your business was thriving."

Brooke laughed. She had one of those musical little laughs that sounded as if it had been taught to her in childhood, along with dancing, the right way to sit and fluent French. It was a perfectly modulated social grace rather than a sign of humor. In Brooke's mind there was a right way to do everything, however small or ordinary, and the only right way was the way she had been taught. "I'm in personal services," she said lightly. "A small company, you know, with a select clientele."

Diamond bobbed his head sagely. "You're a smart cookie," he said, then paused, apparently to remember which coast he was on, took his bearings and rephrased what he had to say in his East Coast voice, a curious gravelly mixture of tough-guy Brooklyn Jewish filtered through a fake British accent, which he apparently took for the language of Harvard, Yale, and Groton. "You are absolutely right," he sang basso profundo. "I run my business along exactly the same lines, young lady. I keep it small and classy. I mean, *elite*. People call me all the time, begging me to represent them. You know what I tell them? I tell them, 'Go to William Morris, where you belong.'" Diamond's face glowed with passion. Like most people from the West Coast entertainment world, he talked about himself as if this was a profound religious experience. "I'm too old, frankly, to do things that bore me. Now you take Miss—ah, Waldheim—here. . . ."

"Walden."

"That's what I said. She's got an interesting story. A beautiful young woman, an older man . . ."

"Quite a *lot* older," Brooke said, with a sweet smile at Alexa.

"Christ, Bannerman wasn't all that old," Diamond said, reverting suddenly to his normal accent. "He was sixty-five, tops. Of course, he probably didn't take care of himself the way I do. Still, you take Miss Waldman's story—you've got sex, you've got love, you've got money. With that combination, believe me, you can't go wrong."

"Could we talk about something else, please?" Alexa said. Given a chance, she would have made a run for the door, but she was hemmed in now as the room began to fill with people who either knew the right time to arrive at Hugo Pascal's for lunch was after two o'clock or were simply late for everything on the grounds that nothing of importance would happen until they got there.

At the sound of the words "sex" and "money," Sir Leo Goldlust drew closer, his furtive eyes flickering between Alexa and Brooke, as well as half a dozen strangers pursuing their own conversations at the top of their voices. Large as the loft was, everybody wanted to be in the center of it, where the density of people packed in against each other was that of a New York subway car at rush hour. In the vast open areas, Pascal's bikers were busy setting up tables and fighting among themselves like gorillas at play. A pasty-faced rock group, which had appeared from nowhere, launched into violent song, as if a thunderstorm had just broken out immediately overhead. The noise was so loud that for a moment Alexa thought she could actually *see* the sound waves flashing and pulsating in the stale, smoky air, but then she realized it was just one of Pascal's preprogrammed light shows, a leftover from the Sixties, when he had invented the "happening," or at any rate brought it out of the theater and into the living room.

She felt a dizzy rush, like the onslaught of a migraine headache. The lead singer, a neurasthenic-looking blond with the face of a child-abuse victim and the complexion of an albino, dressed in scraps of tattered lace, black leather, and chains, howled away, the words amplified to the point where they became meaningless noise. It had been warm when Alexa entered the room, but now there was a kind of locker-room fug, made worse somehow by the odors of perfume and marijuana. Cigarette smoke, like smog over L.A. as you approached it by air, drifted in solid layers.

"Alexa's always had a gift for dealing with older men," Brooke said, "haven't you, dear?" There was not a trace of hostility in her voice, but the pale eyes were cold. Brooke forgot nothing and forgave nothing. She could fire anybody who worked for her, in any capacity, for the slightest transgression—but if you quit, you became her enemy for life.

Alexa had quit. With any luck, she might have gone on for years without ever running into Brooke again, but luck had run out. "I'm not sure I know what you mean," she said.

"Oh, I think you do, Alexa." She smiled. "You should always keep in touch with old friends. It's not nice to drop them. We must have lunch soon, for a good gossip."

"That would be nice," Alexa said, though the idea of gossiping with Brooke Cabot brought her out in a cold sweat. Brooke had the skills of a KGB interrogator when it came to getting secrets out of people. Alexa hadn't the slightest intention of ever seeing her again, if she could help it.

"Did you know Mr. Bannerman long?" Brooke asked. "I mean, *before* all this happened?"

"Several months."

"Really? I'm impressed. He had a reputation for being hard to know. I'd heard he was drinking heavily, poor man."

"That's absolutely not true."

"I'm so glad. One hears these rumors. . . . Have you met the family? Such nice people. Dear Cecilia, who's practically a modern Florence Nightingale; and Robert, who's by far the best-looking of them. My aunt is married to one of the Bannerman cousins, so I hear all the family gossip."

"Is that so?" Alexa said coldly, wondering if Brooke was trying to provoke her. She was quite capable of inventing relatives—there might be no aunt, or she might not be married to a Bannerman cousin. Brooke's style was to pretend to know more than you did, to put you off your guard, then pump you relentlessly.

"Did you ever meet Arthur?" Alexa asked.

"Of course, now and then." She gave Alexa her best Cheshire cat smile, a look so feline that one almost expected her to purr. She leaned close to whisper, "He was a client, you know."

Alexa felt a sudden surge of anger. "I don't believe you," she said, loudly enough so that Simon, deep in conversation now with Aaron Diamond, shot her a warning glance.

"Well, it's true. I don't mind telling you, when I heard the news about his death—I had the shivers. I thought he might be with one of my girls. It wouldn't have been the first time it's happened, frankly, and a pretty penny it costs to smooth things over. But then I called the office —*you* remember, dear, how the system works—and we didn't have a booking for him, thank goodness. You're looking very pale, dear. Have you been eating properly?"

Alexa's first impulse was to slap Brooke, her second to tell her that she was a malicious, lying bitch, her third to turn and run for the door, but all three were forestalled by a hush that fell over the crowded room, marking the arrival of Hugo Pascal himself, with his immediate entourage.

The Pope's entrance into St. Peter's for a papal mass could not have been greeted with greater silence. Of course, it was true that Hugo was a legend. He was born in Skokie, Illinois; his father had been a butcher, as well as a drunk and wife-beater, his mother a maid and sometime diner waitress, while Hugo himself had been afflicted with almost every possible childhood disease and misfortune. His homosexuality had made him an outcast by the time he was in junior high school. Almost illiterate, he had a small talent for drawing, and perhaps because of the beatings he had received from his father and his schoolmates, a great capacity for absorbing pain.

Sadists were drawn to the thin, frail-looking, pale young man like moths to a flame, and it was by allowing himself to be whipped, kicked, stomped, beaten, that Hugo Paskalowicz had made his way from Skokie to New York at the age of seventeen, and to a job as an assistant window dresser at Bloomingdale's. Within a year he was drawing shoes for *Vogue* with painstaking accuracy, and in two years his giant cereal boxes, which made fun of the whole idea of art, caught the attention of the more avant-garde critics and catapulted him to fame and fortune. Since then, he had been shot once, stabbed twice, beaten and left for dead behind the trucks under the West Side Highway several times, and survived it all—not to speak of looney starvation diets, fasts, and drugs, so that his mere appearance—the proof that he could still breathe and walk—caused a sensation, even among sophisticated people.

Indeed, Pascal looked so ghostly that it was easy to believe he had just been taken from the grave. His skin was the color of an albino's and deeply pockmarked with old acne scars, his hair was long, straight, and snow-white; it was impossible to see his eyes, since he wore a strange pair of joke spectacles made of heavy white plastic, with one red lens and one blue, the entire frame surrounded by tiny blinking lights.

He wore a hearing aid in each ear—one of his childhood illnesses or beatings had left him deaf—and it was thought by many that he never turned them on, which partly explained the vagueness of his conversation, though others argued that prolonged use of LSD had simply short-circuited most of Pascal's synapses long ago. He wore a black leather jacket, a surprisingly neat white shirt, and well-pressed gray flannel trousers, and was supported on either side by a Hell's Angel in full leather, as if Pascal would fall over if he tried to stand on his own. Behind him stood a motley crew of admirers, "protégés," and the kind of moonstruck crazies who worshipped Pascal and occasionally tried to murder him.

Now, in total silence, he made his way around the room, shuffling from person to person to give each a limp handshake, hardly more than a brief touch of his cold, dry fingers, and a few mumbled words of greeting. One of his acolytes filmed the master's progress, while another dangled a microphone on a long pole in front of him to capture his words. The Dalai Lama could not have been treated by his followers with more reverence.

"Don't provoke Brooke," Simon whispered to Alexa.

"She's lying."

"Probably, but so what?"

"I don't believe Arthur was one of her clients. And he certainly wasn't, after we met. He *loved* me, Simon. Nobody seems to understand that."

"Don't get carried away, for Christ's sake. Brooke's needling you, that's all. Ignore her."

"I'm just so tired of it all. His children treat me like dirt, Brooke Cabot says he was a client and a drunk . . . Arthur wasn't any of those things, Simon. He was my *husband*."

"He wath altho a great collector." She barely heard Hugo Pascal's whisper with the lisp that had caused him so much grief as a schoolboy in Skokie.

Alexa turned to find herself face-to-face with her host, his colored spectacles blinking only a few inches from her face. "I'm thorry for your loth," he said mournfully. "Did he leave you a lot of money?"

"Well, no . . . I mean, I don't know. . . ."

"I expect he did and you're jutht not telling." The glasses hid Pascal's eyes, but there was something about him that was at once naive and knowing, like a shrewd child—and indeed he spoke rather like a child, in a mixture of nonsense and uncomfortably sharp questions. "Don't thell off hith collection," he warned. "It would be a crime to break it up."

"Well, I agree. But I'm not sure it's going to depend on me." She was aware now of the microphone and the camera. She was being interviewed, she realized, and consoled herself with the thought that Pascal's home movies of himself must run by now into thousands of hours of film that nobody ever watched, or would watch— a monument to mindless voyeurism. She hoped that was the case, anyway.

"Tho nice of you to come," he said vaguely, and shuffled on to greet Brooke Cabot with, it seemed to Alexa, suspicious enthusiasm.

She sat through lunch in unhappy silence, while Pascal's tame Angels walked from table to table banging plates down and growling at the guests. She ignored her food—a strange meal that by some miscalculation on the part of the caterer, or of the bikers, began with melted ice cream and ended with a salad, the main course being a plate of pasta so unappetizing that nobody touched it.

Wedged between Sir Leo and Simon, who were quite capable of discussing art prices for hours without boredom, like Catholics telling beads, she had ample time to consider how foolish it was to have come here—now that it was too late.

She heard Simon's voice intruding on her thoughts. "I said, they make a strange pair."

"I'm sorry. Who?"

"Over there. You wouldn't have thought Brooke had anything Hugo would want."

Alexa glanced over her shoulder toward the center table. Brooke Cabot was sitting next to Hugo Pascal, deep in conversation. Both of them were looking in her direction as they talked. Pascal had taken off his joke spectacles for a clearer look at her.

She felt a moment of sheer panic. She should have told Arthur the truth, told him everything about herself. She had meant to, then kept putting it off until it was too late. If he had known, would he have forgiven her? She thought so. More important, though, he would have understood that she was in no position to fight his family by herself for what he wanted.

It was too late to worry about that, too, she decided. Arthur had trusted her, rightly or wrongly.

"Take me home, Simon," she said.

He nodded glumly. "It was my fault, coming here. I'm sorry."

"No, it was mine. I hadn't realized I've become a kind of celebrity, for all the wrong reasons. I'm not used to it."

"Okay, we'll go. The car's waiting downstairs. You can have a rest."

She shook her head. "I don't need a rest, Simon. I've got a call to make."

"I HOPE YOU SLEPT WELL, Grandmother?"

"I *always* sleep well. Why should I not? Unlike some people, I have a clear conscience."

"Of course you do."

"I have no patience with people who can't sleep. Your sister is always complaining that she doesn't sleep. I told her it's nonsense. Sleep is perfectly natural. You get into bed, you close your eyes, you go to sleep. Cecilia takes sleeping pills, I'm sorry to say. Well, what can one expect? A girl her age should be married. There's nothing like a husband for putting one to sleep."

Robert hesitated. Did she mean that husbands were boring? he wondered, or was his grandmother making a veiled reference to sex? The latter seemed improbable, but you never knew with Eleanor.

She had received him at eight in the morning, lying regally in bed, an elaborate breakfast tray on her lap. He knew her habits as well as his own—better, since hers had more or less ruled the family for sixty years. Eleanor rose at six, when she was awakened by her maid with a glass of hot water and the juice of half of one freshly squeezed lemon. What she did between six and seven-thirty was known only to her maid and God, but at precisely seven forty-five she was always back in bed, with her makeup on, her hair in place and her "morning diamonds" fastened round her neck and wrists, ready for the breakfast tray. Her nightgowns had never been seen, of course, by anyone but her maids and the late Putnam Bannerman Senior (though Robert would not have taken a bet on the latter), but her breakfast peignoirs were famous —fanciful, elaborate concoctions of lace, satin, and ribbons that took even the most skilled ladies' maid hours to press, and were made in Paris by a *lingère* who might have learned her trade in the days of Marie-Antoinette. His grandmother must have an endless supply of them, since he had never seen her wear the same one twice—but then she had an endless supply of everything.

She lay back against a white satin bed chair, placed so that she was sitting upright. Her pillows were so heavily embroidered that it was a wonder she could sleep on them, the edges threaded with pink grosgrain ribbons; the counterpane over her legs was so light and fluffy that it seemed about to float off the bed, prevented from doing so only by the breakfast tray with its white wicker legs. The contents of the tray never varied: tea with lemon, in Eleanor's favorite Limoges china cup, one piece of dry toast, half a grapefruit, a vase with a single rose, white in the summer, red in the winter, pink in the spring, and yellow in the autumn, when she felt a spot of bright color was needed to cheer her up.

In the wicker pockets on either side of the tray were carefully folded copies of *The New York Times* and *The Dutchess Freeman*, for Eleanor was just as interested in local news—births, deaths, land sales, the price of crops—as in national news, perhaps more so. Next to the starched linen napkin was a freshly laundered pair of white cotton gloves, since she disliked getting newsprint on her fingers, and a Fabergé magnifying glass in case she had a need to read small type. She read the farm and land sales with particular attention. Over the years, she had bought up parcels of land all around Kiawa as if she were forming a DMZ against developers, and it was rumored in the family that if she lived long enough, the property line would eventually reach the Albany Mall, or possibly the Canadian border.

"What brings you up here so early, Robert? You must have left the city at five-thirty."

"I'm an early riser, Grandmother."

"Not that early, I think. And not without a good reason. Don't tell *me* that you rose at dawn just to come here and ask if I had a good night's sleep."

"No. We have to talk."

"I see. I suppose it's about the girl?"

"Yes."

"That old fool DeWitt tells me that Booker is looking into her background."

"Yes?"

"Stop trying to pretend that you know nothing about it. I can tell from listening to DeWitt that you've been interfering—against my wishes. Thanks to your father, we've got enough troubles, without your machinations."

"I merely gave Booker a little advice."

"Which I hope he was intelligent enough to ignore." She gave him a steely look. "Your poor father indulged you too much. It's made you disobedient, just as I warned him."

"Disobedient? I'm a grown man, Grandmother."

"There's no such thing. All men are boys—they never grow up."

"What about Great-grandfather?"

"Cyrus was the exception that makes the rule. Now tell me why you're here. What sort of trouble are you in?"

"I'm not in trouble. I may have a solution to my problem."

"*Your* problem? Surely you mean *our* problem, Robert? Unless you've had a vision, like Saul's on the road to Damascus, while you were driving up the Taconic, I can't believe you're concerned about the family. You're far too selfish for that."

He resisted the urge to argue with her. It was a waste of time arguing with someone who had enjoyed having the last word for five or six decades. Besides, his selfishness was a matter of record. "Surely it's not selfish to want what's mine?"

"That's exactly what I mean. The Trust isn't *yours*. It belongs to the family."

"I know that. But you don't want it in the hands of Miss Walden any more than I do."

"I want it in the hands of the person who can handle it best, Robert. I grant you that except under the most extraordinary circumstances, I would expect that person to be one of Cyrus's descendants, not a stranger."

"Would you agree that there's some benefit to keeping all this in the family, and out of the papers, for the time being?"

"I suppose so. The scandal of your father's death has made us a laughingstock already."

"If you think *that's* bad, Grandmother, wait and see what the news of his marriage and the new will does. Or the trial, if we challenge the will."

"*If?* Of course we shall challenge it. The publicity will be appalling, but it can't be helped."

"It can be postponed. We can buy time."

"Can we? And for what purpose?"

"To let Booker get on with what he's doing quietly, for one thing."

"That doesn't sound very straightforward to me. Anyway, DeWitt already talked to her."

"DeWitt's not the right person. She doesn't like him."

"That speaks volumes for her good sense. What are you suggesting?"

"I spoke to her myself."

She sipped her tea and stared at him coldly over the top of the cup. "I told you to keep out of this, Robert. DeWitt's a lawyer. If he can't do the job, we'll get a better lawyer. Dealing with the girl directly is bound to cause trouble."

"On the contrary. It's the only way to handle it. She doesn't care about the money, Grandmother—at any rate, she doesn't care about it as much as you might think. She wants to talk to *you*."

She gave him a baleful glare. "You're surely not suggesting that I greet her with open arms as a member of the family? She's a fortune hunter with a fraudulent claim to marriage!"

"I'm not sure that's what she is at all, as a matter of fact. I think all this was Father's idea, not hers, and that she genuinely thinks she's

doing what he wanted her to. That doesn't make her any less dangerous, by the way. More, if anything. But unless we want to watch her
stake out a claim to the fortune on the 'Today Show' or 'Sixty Minutes,'
we'd better talk to her soon."

"You've already talked to her, it seems. What was your impression?"

"That she's a nice enough young woman. She's stubborn—I don't
think she'll back off. On the other hand, I don't think she's out to make
trouble just for the sake of trouble, either. She'd be very good on television. And on the witness stand, too, I daresay."

The old lady closed her eyes for a moment. "I shall never forgive
your father for this," she said. "Stop jiggling your foot." She put down
her teacup with a click of diamonds against the china. "I can't very well
receive the young woman while Booker is trying to prove the marriage
was invalid. That would be dishonest as well as distasteful."

"No, it wouldn't. You can be perfectly honest and outspoken with
her."

"I hope I'm honest and outspoken with everybody."

"Nobody would ever deny that."

She looked at him sternly, but he could tell she wasn't angry. Better
than anyone else in his family, Robert understood his grandmother.
Her mother had been from Virginia, a Southern belle married into a
family of Bostonians, a fish out of water on Beacon Hill. From her
beloved father, Eleanor had inherited her rigid Puritan standards, along
with the absolute conviction that the Aldons and God spoke with one
voice. From her mother she had inherited a strong streak of Southern
womanhood, which explained her belief in matriarchy as the natural
order of things, as well as a certain flirtatious femininity which old age
had done nothing to diminish.

Robert flirted with her, as he flirted with all women, and since he was
the only person in the family who did, she had a soft spot in her heart
for him, which she did her best to conceal.

"I'm old enough to speak my mind," she said. "It's perhaps the only
benefit of age."

"You've always spoken your mind. As for being old, that's nonsense.
You're still the most beautiful woman in the family."

She picked up her magnifying glass and reached across the bed to
give him a sharp rap on the knuckles. "Don't try to win me over with
flattery, Robert," she warned him. "I don't want to meet this gal, and
that's that."

"May I ask why?"

"Because having her up here would be like legitimizing her claim to
be your father's wife. And because I can tell, knowing you, that there's
double-dealing involved, and I won't be a party to that."

"Not even if I ask you to, as a favor to me?"

She thought for a moment. "No. It's wrong. It's foolish. You're being selfish again—putting your election and your campaign debts before the larger interests of the family. I have to think about *all* the Bannermans, including the next generation. I hate the idea of all this becoming a public fight more than you do, but if it has to, so be it."

Robert had not expected agreement—not at first, if at all, and not easily. His grandmother was like a battleship—she could only be moved from her course slowly, and by small degrees.

He smiled at her in his most winning way, knowing that the slightest sign of bad humor on his part would be fatal. "I understand," he said. "No, truly, I do. I think Grandfather would have taken the same position."

"I'm sure he would. He was always straightforward in his dealings, whatever the cost. There wasn't an ounce of duplicity in him."

"Yes. Of course, I wonder whether Cyrus would have taken the same view."

Her eyes narrowed. "Cyrus?"

"Yes. Often, when I'm in doubt what to do, I ask myself what *he* would have done."

"Then I'm surprised you get into so much trouble. Cyrus had a nose for trouble like an old foxhound on the scent."

"He must have had."

"Of course he did," she said, warming to her subject. "When that noisy, demagogic oaf Teddy Roosevelt passed the antitrust laws, he found Cyrus had already split his companies up and dispersed them in different states, totally independent of each other, so the law didn't apply to him."

"I don't suppose Cyrus announced his intention of restructuring his companies, did he?"

"Well, of course he didn't! Cyrus always acted in the strictest possible secrecy. He never confided in anybody. He had hundreds of people, you know, who bought and sold shares for him, so the market would never know what he was doing."

"I think that would be illegal today."

"A lot Cyrus would have cared. He'd have found a way to do what he wanted to. He always did."

"Then what would Cyrus have done about this girl and her claim?"

"He'd have met with her, tried to buy her off, dragged the negotiations on for as long as possible, and used the time to find some way to disprove it—" She stared at him angrily. "You *deliberately* set out to trap me!"

"I was only trying to make a point, Grandmother."

"You're not Cyrus."

"No. None of us is. But we can learn from his example, surely?"

She sighed. "Cyrus was one of a kind."

There was a glow to her cheeks that had nothing to do with powder or rouge, as there always was when she talked about Cyrus. There was never any doubt that Cyrus was the man she admired, not Putnam Senior, who had grown up in the shadow of the old robber, so awed by him that he had never really developed a character of his own.

"Don't you think that Cyrus would have talked to the girl? I don't suppose he'd have simply dumped the whole problem in the lap of a lawyer and left the courts to solve it, would he? I expect he'd have said, 'Do something about it.' Don't you?"

"I don't believe even your great-grandfather ever faced a problem like this," she said, after a moment's thought. "Still, he wouldn't have been shocked. Nothing ever shocked *him*. When he went out to California, you know, the miners were so angry that they hired a local thug to gun Cyrus down. It wasn't that unusual in those days. There wasn't much in the way of law west of the Mississippi, and Cyrus had been sent out to stop the people who ran the mines from stealing the shareholders blind, so he wasn't at all popular. Well, when he heard about it, Cyrus found out who the man was, tracked him down to a saloon, walked right in, and sat down at the fellow's table, cold as ice. 'I hear you've been paid two hundred dollars to shoot me,' he said. 'Here I am. Do it now, if you've got the guts. If not, I'll give you five hundred to go shoot the man who gave you the order.' "

"What happened?"

"I have no idea. Your great-grandfather merely said that he had no more trouble after that."

She picked up a little vermeil bell from the tray and rang it. "You'd better go now," she said. "It's well past the time I dress."

"Will you see the girl, Grandmother?"

"Yes. Not for *your* sake, mind you, Robert. For the family's. I don't want any more of this publicity. I don't want her running off to tell her story to the gutter press, like one of Tommy Manville's wives, or that foolish young Pulitzer woman. We've been spared that kind of scandal so far, thank God." She looked at him intently, head slightly cocked to one side, like an angry bird. "Except for your divorce, of course," she added sharply. "It's my responsibility to prevent another disaster, if I can."

The maid appeared to remove the tray. "After all," she said, dismissing Robert with a wave of her hand, "we don't want the world to think we're just another family of rich people, do we?"

ALEXA WAS SURPRISED that seeing Roth again upset her. His bulky presence reminded her of all the evenings they had spent together, Arthur,

Roth, and herself. When she called him to say she had a problem, he agreed to come at once, but now that he was here, there was a curious sense of embarrassment between them, as if Arthur might walk into the room at any moment and wonder what the two of them were doing together. Roth, too, seemed to feel it—at any rate, he kept glancing at the door surreptitiously.

"Listen," he said, "in real estate, deals sometimes go down the tubes. You got to take your lumps, know what I mean?" He changed the subject quickly. "How much did you pay for this apartment?"

"It isn't mine. It's Simon Wolff's. I think he paid about a hundred and fifty thousand, when the building went co-op."

"A fucking steal. He could get a million today easy, maybe one point five. These old buildings, though, they're a pain in the ass. Once they go co-op, nobody wants to spend money on maintenance. What he oughta do is let me sell this for him, I'll get him top dollar, then I'll get him into one of my new buildings. I got one going up on Central Park South, view of the park, marble Jacuzzis in every master bathroom, central air, he'd be a lot better off."

"I think he's happy here."

"Yeah, well . . ." David Roth shrugged. He'd offered a favor, and it had been refused. He was content. He was wearing, Alexa noticed, a suit identical to Arthur's, but he still had the New York real-estate mind-set, always trying to make a deal, however small.

"Well," Roth said, "he's got those high ceilings here, I guess. What exactly did you want to see me about?"

"The museum," she said.

He stared at her. "The museum? Forget about it. Arthur's dead. I go on to other things. I got a casino to build in Atlantic City. I got a hotel site in Palm Beach, right on the water. It was a nice idea, but these things happen, right?"

"You liked the idea a lot."

"I liked it with Bannerman alive. He could have pushed it through."

"*We* can push it through, David. Still. Even without Arthur."

He blew out his cheeks. "Look," he said, "I wanna be frank with you. . . ."

"Go ahead."

"With Bannerman gone, there's nothing doing. Robert won't build the museum, and whatever plans he has for the site, when he gets around to thinking about it, they won't include me. He'll put up some cockamamie office building on his piece of it, some piece of cheap shit that'll rent out before the walls are dry, and that's it. Arthur had vision. Robert's after a quick buck."

"David, Arthur did you a favor with the banks, didn't he?"

A shrug. "Yeah."

"A big favor."

"Maybe."

"*He* seemed to feel it was important to you. What he told me, and I'm using his exact words, was: 'Walter and David want to cut Roth off at the knees, but I put a stop to it!' He used his clout for you, David."

"So?"

"So maybe you owe him one."

"He's dead."

"I'm going to tell you a secret, David. Arthur said you were good at keeping secrets. Is that so?"

"I done a lot of bad things in my time, kiddo, but I never gave away a secret, not even before a grand jury."

"Arthur and I were married."

"He *married* you?" Roth laughed—the first time she had ever heard him laugh, it occurred to her.

"Why is that so funny?"

He took out a handkerchief and wiped his eyes. "Well, I could see he was nuts over you, no disrespect, but I never thought he'd go that far. Jesus! Does Robert know?"

"Yes, but it's still a secret, for a lot of reasons."

"I'd give a million bucks to have seen Robert's face! Wait a minute, I know what you're gonna tell me next. Arthur changed his will?"

She nodded.

"My mother, God bless her, may she live for a hundred years, ever dies, I'm gonna have my father put under twenty-four-hours-a-day watch. I'm not gonna let a woman come *near* the old man!" He laughed again.

She stifled her irritation. She rather liked Roth, and even if she didn't, she needed him. "The point is, David, we can go ahead."

He turned serious, the pale eyes giving nothing away. "You gotta be kidding," he said. "You're going to be in litigation for the next twenty years, is my guess. And to tell you the truth, I got all the litigation I can handle. I don't need the Bannerman family suing me on top of it."

"If I had control of the fortune, David, would you go ahead? With me?"

He paused and looked at her shrewdly. "Maybe. Sure. It's a great site."

"And if I needed your help? Would you give it to me?"

He thought about it for a moment.

"Arthur helped *you*. He believed you wanted to do something special. 'Roth wants to build something people will remember him for.' That's what he said, David. He thought *you* were a man of vision."

Roth held up both hands in surrender. "Stop already! If it's something I *can* do, I'll do it, okay?"

She leaned forward. "It might mean putting a little pressure on someone."

Roth looked alarmed. "I don't break heads, Alexa," he said. "Whatever people say."

"This would be more in the nature of *real-estate* pressure, David. Buying up a lease, say. . . ."

"Ah," he said, in the tone of a man whom nothing could surprise when it came to real estate. "You came to the right person. *That* I can do."

That's one problem taken care of—or almost—she thought.

She wished it were the only one.

CYRUS BANNERMAN had built Kiawa on a hill so that anybody coming up the Hudson on Commodore Vanderbilt's railway would catch a glimpse of it; and if his intention was to provoke awe among his fellow citizens, he certainly succeeded. It loomed over the river as unmistakably as Mount Rushmore, and not very much less imposing.

The butler inclined his head just a fraction as Alexa entered the hall, where a maid stood waiting to relieve her of her coat. Hall, she thought, seemed an inappropriate word for a space more suited to a railway station or an opera house. In front of her, a broad marble staircase swept gracefully up at least forty feet to the next floor, while high overhead an enormous crystal chandelier was suspended from the domed ceiling. The stairs had been designed for entrances on a dramatic scale—an emperor would not have looked out of place descending them toward a crowd of his admiring courtiers. To one side of the hall, in an antique fireplace large enough to roast an ox and very likely designed with just that purpose in mind, a fire blazed, though not, given the size of the hall, cheerfully. She thought it typical of the Bannermans to keep a fire going in an empty room.

She wondered if Mrs. Bannerman planned to make an entrance down the staircase just to impress her, but then she reminded herself that the old lady had no reason to impress her. She was an intruder here, hardly likely to be given head-of-state treatment by Arthur's mother.

"This way, please," the butler whispered, in a tone that suggested they ought to be walking on tiptoe so as not to wake the dead—and indeed there was something ghostly about this immense, silent room without even the smallest trace of human habitation except for the pointless fire.

He ushered her into a small wood-paneled elevator, closed the brass gates and pulled the handle, making a small ceremony of it—and indeed it was rather like being in a confessional booth, she thought, or what she imagined it to be like, since to her as a Lutheran the very idea was exotic.

She stepped out, then followed the butler down the hall. He opened a set of double doors and announced, in hardly more than a whisper, "Miss Walden, madame."

From inside, a firm, precise voice, betraying no hint of age, said, "Show her in."

Alexa walked inside. Seated in front of the fireplace, Eleanor Bannerman might have seemed dwarfed by the size of the formal drawing room, which could easily have contained several New York City apartments, including Alexa's own. Opulent and richly furnished as it was, Mrs. Bannerman outshone every object in the room—Alexa was unable to take her eyes off her. Mrs. Bannerman's hair was silver-blue and artfully swept up so that it formed a kind of glittering halo around her head, something like the elaborate "beehives" that had been so popular in the Sixties. There was nothing natural about it—it was a work of art that must have taken hours to set, dry, and spray. The effect was not only imposing but almost awe-inspiring, like the headdresses of primitive warriors.

There was indeed a certain masklike quality in her face, made more pronounced by the carefully plucked and mascaraed eyebrows, which had been drawn, perhaps unintentionally, in a way that gave her an expression of permanent, well-bred astonishment, as if the vulgarity of the world was a constant source of surprise to her. She wore, in token of mourning, a Chanel suit of dark-blue moiré silk, almost purple where it reflected the light from the fire, with black embroidered trim. Around her neck was a strand of pearls so large that they looked like costume jewelry, except that Mrs. Bannerman had surely never worn anything worth less than several hundred thousand dollars in her life. Her fingernails were long, pointed, and bright red; her feet—so narrow and small that it was hard to imagine how she walked on them—were shod in elegant blue high-heeled pumps and rested on a small embroidered pillow. "Sit down," she said, in a tone that managed to command without the slightest effort or increase in volume.

Alexa sat, gingerly, opposite her, knees together and hands clutching her purse in her lap, feeling as gawky as a teenager. Between them, like the walls of a fortress, was an antique silver tea service of such complexity that Alexa was hard put to identify a good many of the objects.

"Milk or lemon?" Mrs. Bannerman asked.

Alexa's experience with tea was mostly confined to teabags. "Lemon," she said, on the guess that it was more correct.

Mrs. Bannerman lifted an eyebrow and went through an elaborate little ceremony involving several pieces of silver, presented her with a cup, then poured herself a cup of tea with milk. Obscurely—and resentfully—Alexa felt she had lost points with her choice. She was not here, she reminded herself, to be tested for her social graces.

"Would you care for something?" Mrs. Bannerman waved a tiny, well-groomed hand over what seemed to be an endless profusion of cakes, biscuits, toast, and pastries.

"Thank you, no," Alexa said. "It's very good of you to see me." Instinct told her that Mrs. Bannerman was used to the kind of deference that was normally shown to royal personages and the President of the United States.

"Yes," Mrs. Bannerman agreed. "But then I'm old. A new face is always interesting, however unpleasant the circumstances," she said icily. She sipped her tea. "I fear I was rude to you at Arthur's funeral. I should not have been. I hope you will forgive me. If you made Arthur's last months happy, then I am, of course, in your debt." She managed to convey, without much effort, a wealth of distaste, which Alexa forced herself to ignore.

"I think he *was* happy, yes. Happier than when I met him, anyway."

"Not, mind you," Mrs. Bannerman said severely, "that I *approve* of a man his age seeking happiness." She gave Alexa a basilisk stare. "What can have been in Arthur's head, I can't imagine. He was never happy in his marriage to Priscilla, and I see no reason to believe he would have been any happier in another, had he lived—and had it been real."

"It was real enough," Alexa said firmly.

"That remains to be seen," Mrs. Bannerman snapped. "I should warn you: I don't relish having to go to court to prove that my own son was suffering from senile dementia, but if it's my duty, I will."

"He wasn't senile at all."

"His actions indicate otherwise to me."

"That just isn't so."

"You are being impertinent. Tell me: Why haven't you told your story to the press yet?"

Alexa did her best to sound conciliatory, though she found Mrs. Bannerman infuriating. "I don't want publicity, Mrs. Bannerman. If I did, I wouldn't be here."

Mrs. Bannerman inclined her head, like a bird intent on its prey. There was a certain birdlike quality in her gaze—one of those bright, pretty birds in pet shops, Alexa thought, that one was warned not to get close to because it would bite your finger if you put it through the mesh of its cage. "Why *are* you here?"

"Because I want Arthur's wishes carried out. And because I'm his wife. Perhaps you think I don't belong in this house, but if he'd lived, he'd have brought me here."

"Probably not while *I* was alive, my dear. Arthur was always afraid of me. All my children are—I can't think why. I'm not nearly so formidable as they make me out to be."

Alexa was not sure what to make of this—or how to respond. Was it a plea for sympathy? But that seemed out of character. Mrs. Bannerman struck her as very formidable indeed. She nodded diplomatically.

"A family needs a center," Mrs. Bannerman went on. "Otherwise, it's just a lot of people with the same name who get together once a year for Thanksgiving and Christmas. And for funerals, of course. I have provided that center, oh, for many, many years. Not because I wanted to, I must tell you, but because nobody else did. My late husband was a man of many good qualities—truly a *good* man, in the old-fashioned meaning of the word—but he lived for too long in the shadow of his father. Putnam was in his fifties before Cyrus allowed him any control over The Trust, and even then, Cyrus still had the last word. As for my poor son—he was a house divided."

The old lady stared at Alexa for a moment as if to see whether the biblical phrase had been understood. Alexa gave a nod—the Bible was as familiar to her as it was to Mrs. Bannerman, so much so that at home it had been referred to simply as The Book, as if there were no others.

Satisfied that she was not dealing with a pagan, Mrs. Bannerman continued: "One part of him sought the responsibility of family and wealth, the other to fly from them. His sense of duty was stronger than he received credit for, but it gave him no satisfaction, and it was never quite strong enough. So, for all these years, I have represented—I hardly know what—the continuity of the family, the idea that it stands for something beyond the mere fact of being rich. Or perhaps that wealth of this magnitude must have some larger purpose and meaning, must in some way be a part of God's design. . . . Are you religious?"

"No. I was brought up in a very religious family, but then my father died—and it didn't help."

Surprisingly, Mrs. Bannerman did not seem inclined to argue. "Of course it doesn't *help*," she snapped. "Only clergymen are foolish enough to think that. . . . Robert tells me that you've given some thought to settling this matter?"

You had to keep your wits about you when talking to Eleanor Bannerman, Alexa realized. Her conversation wandered, but then, from out of the blue, she fired directly at the target and scored a bull's-eye.

"In very general terms, yes. I don't want a fight with Arthur's family."

"Indeed? It's exactly for that reason that Cyrus wanted The Trust to pass directly from one heir to the next, without any provision for breaking it up. He had in mind just the kind of disgraceful family fight the Binghams have been going through—children fighting their parents, sisters trying to ruin their brothers, family skeletons being dragged out of the closet. Do you know them?"

"The Binghams? No. I read about it in the papers, though."

"I thought you came from that part of the country?"

"Illinois. They live in Kentucky."

"Ah. There are some quite respectable people in Kentucky. In Illinois, too, I suppose, though I've never met any."

"We like to think so." Alexa took hold of herself. There was no point in getting into an argument with Mrs. Bannerman, whose prejudices were vast and inexplicable. She had not, after all, come here to prove that she was worthy of being Arthur's wife or to be tested for good manners. She decided to be direct. "Mrs. Bannerman, whether you like it or not, Arthur married me. And whether I like it or not, I promised to carry out his wishes. That's what I'm here to discuss."

Mrs. Bannerman's expression was steely, a hanging judge about to pronounce sentence. "I will not be threatened in my own home," she said. "Or elsewhere."

"I'm not threatening you. I would like to have your cooperation."

"In disinheriting my own grandson? In breaking up my family?"

"In doing what your own son wanted to do. After a lot of careful thought."

Mrs. Bannerman drew a deep breath and was silent for a moment. She let the breath out with a sigh. "You're a very stubborn young woman," she said. "However, I have promised Robert to listen to you, and I always keep a promise."

"I'm keeping *my* promise—to Arthur. Surely you can understand that?"

Mrs. Bannerman ignored the interruption. "Provided you keep away from the press," she continued, "I will think over what you've said. Possibly there is a compromise to be found, though I can't imagine what it would be. Compromise does not come naturally to me, I must tell you, but I will do anything within reason to prevent further damage to this family. Do I make myself clear?"

Alexa held her temper and nodded.

"All this is conditional on a number of things," Mrs. Bannerman continued. "One is your silence. I despise the whole idea of all this nonsense about marriage and the new will becoming public knowledge. However, given time and a certain amount of common sense, we may be able to put a good face on things, at least. It might help if you were to go away for a bit while your lawyers work things out with DeWitt. Do you enjoy travel?"

"I've never traveled much."

"Now would be a good time to start. There is much in the world that's worth seeing, though a good deal of it is overrated, in my opinion. In any case, I expect you to keep silent. And of course there must be no unpleasant surprises that might eventually embarrass the family."

There was a creak as the door opened. "I said I wasn't to be disturbed," Mrs. Bannerman said firmly, but there was no reply except for a gentle snuffle. An ancient white-muzzled Labrador, considerably overweight, waddled over and collapsed at Mrs. Bannerman's feet. She prodded it with her toe. "This is Cecilia's brute," she said with surprising fondness. "When the children were still living at home, the house was always full of dogs. Priscilla had dozens of them, and there were Arthur's gun dogs as well. And of course each of the children had one, except Robert. He does not like dogs. It was like a menagerie. Do *you* like dogs?"

"Very much. We always had dogs at home. I never had one in New York."

"That's wise. I'm not fond of the city, and I don't suppose a dog would like it any better." She broke off a piece of fruitcake, fed it to the dog, and wiped her fingers fastidiously with a gossamerlike napkin. "He's grossly overweight and useless," she said. "He's outlived his time." She gave a small sigh. "Perhaps I have, too. Do you think so?"

The question was startling—*meant* to be startling, Alexa decided. Mrs. Bannerman surely didn't expect an honest answer from her, or even care what she thought. Her conversation was a form of shock treatment. Was it just the vagaries of age, combined with loneliness and a monumental ego? The old lady had had her way in the family for more than sixty years, after all, and had once been a great beauty as well. There can have been very few occasions, if any, in the past six decades when anyone had contradicted her.

"I don't believe you seriously want my opinion, Mrs. Bannerman," she said calmly, determined to give an honest answer, "but I don't think so, no. The dog, maybe. Not you."

There was, she thought, just the faintest glimmer of respect in Mrs. Bannerman's eyes, hardly more than a flicker, but still there. Was it possible that she and the old lady might learn to get along with each other? The idea seemed farfetched, but hardly more farfetched than it was to find herself discussing the control of one of America's largest fortunes. She had no clear idea of how to accomplish what Arthur wanted her to. Without his family's good will, she didn't see how she could do anything except perhaps plunge into litigation for which she was equally ill-prepared. If it was necessary to learn to live with Mrs. Bannerman, she would simply have to do it. Whether Mrs. Bannerman would live with *her* was another question.

The dog raised its head, looked apprehensively toward the door, and hid under the sofa. The door opened—to Alexa's surprise, for she imagined nobody ever entered a room in which Mrs. Bannerman was sitting without knocking first.

Mrs. Bannerman seemed surprised, too. She turned to glare at the intruder, but then she smiled—a frosty sort of smile, but a smile all the same. "Robert, dear," she said. "You needn't have come quite yet. I would have called for you."

Robert smiled at Alexa, though there was something about his manner which was disturbing to her—a rigid set to his jaw, a suggestion of tension, or perhaps anger. She didn't know him well enough to judge, but the same expression, had she seen it on Arthur's face, would have caused her to worry.

He bent over and gave his grandmother a kiss on the cheek, with the distant solemnity of a Catholic kissing a venerated relic. She accepted it, but there was no sign of affection to be read on her face.

For some reason, this brief domestic scene chilled her far more than the size of the house. There was something about the Bannermans as a family that frightened her, a coldness, or, to be more exact, an inability to make contact. She had felt it with Arthur, whenever he talked about his children as if they had always been—and still were—strangers to him. He *had* feelings about them, certainly, even strong ones, but he seemed to have no way of communicating those feelings to them, nor they to him. They were stuck forever, apparently, in a formal relationship, like statues in a garden.

"I apologize for interrupting," Robert said. He gave Alexa the grim ghost of a smile, nothing like the warmth with which they had parted after their talk at "21."

He did not sit down. He seemed unable to decide on the right place to sit, apparently reluctant to sit next to Alexa, and perhaps unwilling to give up the advantage of height by plunking himself down meekly next to his grandmother. Under his arm was a thick sheaf of newspapers. He glared at the dog. "Cici should have had that damned animal put down years ago," he said.

"You know perfectly well she would allow no such thing. How is she?"

"She has a headache, so she went for a walk."

"I've never had a headache in my life. Why don't you sit down, Robert, now that you've interrupted us, instead of hovering about?"

"I'm *not* hovering."

"If you're going to stay, sit."

"I don't think I'll be staying. I don't think you should either, Alexa."

She looked up at him quickly, just in time to see how angry he was. He had himself tightly under control—the moment her eyes were on him, he was smiling again, a bland and superior smile that made her stomach churn.

She wondered what she had done, what had happened, but she also felt a sudden surge of guilt, and she knew exactly why. She had begun to *like* Robert Bannerman, to feel that there was—or could be—some relationship between them, and the expression on his face made it clear that this was no longer the case, if it ever had been. "What on earth do you mean?" she asked.

He opened the newspaper with a flourish and held it up. There was a photograph of her, and another, smaller, of Arthur. Above them the headline read, "EX-MODEL CLAIMS BANNERMAN AS HER HUBBY."

Even from a distance she could see that the photograph of her had been taken at Hugo Pascal's luncheon party. She felt, quite suddenly, sick to her stomach with the knowledge that it was her own fault for blurting out the truth where there was every possibility she would be overheard. Of course, Hugo, or one of the people around him, would have leaked her chance remark to the press. Hugo Pascal's real art form was gossip. "I didn't do it on purpose," she said, her throat closing as if she were being choked. "It was an accident."

Robert shrugged. "Maybe so. It doesn't matter, anyway. If the *Post* has the story, so will everyone else by tomorrow. The car is waiting. If you hurry, you might get away from here before the TV people start camping out at the gates."

"It would have come out sooner or later," she said. "It's the truth."

"Is it? We'll see. One thing I'm sure of: If I'd had any idea this was going to happen, I wouldn't have persuaded Grandmother to see you."

Alexa turned to Mrs. Bannerman, who was sitting quietly, her expression as unruffled as ever. "I'm truly sorry," she said to her. "It was a slip of the tongue, honestly. I was talking to a friend. I didn't realize anybody had overheard me." She was surprised how much she wanted Mrs. Bannerman to forgive her, or at least say she understood.

Alexa stood, hating herself for feeling like a child who has just been caught in some transgression—but, facing Mrs. Bannerman, it was hard *not* to feel like a child, as no doubt Arthur had felt, even in his sixties.

She said nothing. There was a long silence, broken only by the dog's snores. Even Robert, who seemed to deal more easily with the old lady than most people did, looked like a member of the Bomb Squad waiting for a doubtful package to explode in his hands.

But Mrs. Bannerman merely rose calmly, neatly avoided the snoring dog, and came around to stand in front of Alexa. The clear blue eyes gave away no hint of her feelings—looking at them, Alexa had the momentary impression that she herself had become invisible. Mrs. Bannerman didn't seem angry; she simply seemed to have erased Alexa from her view. The old lady's perfectly made up eyes seemed to stare *through* her, as if she no longer existed.

Then, to Alexa's surprise, Mrs. Bannerman spoke, her voice precise, unforgiving, a final sentence. "There's nothing more to be discussed," she said. "You do not belong here." She paused. "Please go."

There was nothing further to say. Alexa went, following the butler through the great empty hall out to the graveled courtyard, where the car waited.

It was her worst moment since Arthur's death, and the long, lonely ride ahead of her, back to New York, seemed unbearable—as if she had betrayed Arthur.

SIMON, AT LEAST, was at his best, as he usually was when things turned out badly. He drew her a bath, made her a drink, overcoming her objections, rubbed her neck as she sat in front of the fire in a terry-cloth robe, trying to recover from two hours of silent self-recrimination and guilt in the back of Robert Bannerman's limousine.

The drink, as she had expected, made her feel worse. She would have liked somebody to hold her and comfort her, but the only person who could have done that was Arthur. She even felt disloyal about Simon's rubbing her neck—after all, how would it look if anyone could see her, a recent widow, sitting half drunk (well, no, not even a quarter drunk, if she was going to be truthful with herself), sitting in a bathrobe in front of the fire with her former lover's hands on her? She pulled away involuntarily and took refuge at the other end of the big leather sofa, her feet tucked up under her, her arms around her knees, with something else to feel guilty about.

Simon sighed. He sat down at the other end of the sofa, keeping his distance, and stared at her. "It wasn't your fault," he said.

"I know. But I was careless."

"That happens. The Bannermans didn't like you before. They like you even less now. So what? Why do you care?"

"I care."

"Smart answer. Look, it was a mistake to agree to hide the marriage in the first place. *Everybody* told you that. You should never have promised Robert you would. Now it's out in the open, by accident, and so much the better."

"You just don't understand, Simon. I thought Eleanor Bannerman was beginning to *like* me. I really did feel, for one moment, that she was going to accept me."

"Face it, the only thing you can do that will please the Bannerman family is to get yourself run over by a bus."

"I can't believe that."

"Then try this. Try thinking for a change that you're in the right and they're in the wrong. You *were* married to Arthur. You're his widow. They don't want to accept that. You didn't make the problem. They did. Would Arthur have wanted you to go crawling up to Kiawa with your tail between your legs?"

"I don't know."

"Yes, you do. Personally, I think you should make a settlement, take the money and run—and forget about Arthur's plans for the goddamn fortune. But if you're so fucking determined to carry out his wishes, then *do* it, and stop worrying about whether the Bannermans like you or not. Either you *are* Mrs. Arthur Bannerman or you're not. If you are, then stand up and say so, for God's sake. It isn't anything to be ashamed of, is it?"

She shook her head. "No," she said, "it's not."

"So stop feeling guilty. You're a widow. They owe you, I don't know what, respect, sympathy, *something*, and instead they want you to hide the fact that you were married—because it suits them. The hell with them, Alexa! They'll come around when you've won, and maybe not even then. It's not your problem whether they get along with you, it's their problem. I mean, it's news to me that a marriage in New York State isn't valid until Eleanor Bannerman or Robert has approved it. Right?"

"Right." It was odd, but she felt better already. Simon had put things in perspective. She knew better than anyone that guilt didn't change a thing, or pay for anything you'd done. It was false currency—which bought you nothing in the end. She'd had years of it.

"You're going to get a lot more publicity in the next few days," Simon said. "You'd better be prepared. I hate to say it, but this might not be the best place to be found when the press starts looking for you."

She felt a sudden moment of panic. "Simon," she said, "don't say that. Where would I go?"

"I don't know. Out of town would be my advice."

"That's what Eleanor Bannerman told me."

"Well, she's not wrong, though her reasons are probably different from mine. She wants you out of sight so you can't tell your story. I think you should tell your story, then get out of sight, for your own peace of mind."

"I can't think that far ahead."

"You don't mind my saying so, you'd better start, right now. You can bet that Robert is thinking ahead."

"I don't see what he can do."

"Don't be an idiot. He can do plenty. By the way, David Roth called while you were making your pilgrimage to the gentry. He said he'd taken care of your problem, whatever that means. Oddly enough, he tried to sell me a condo on Central Park West, since he had me on the phone. He told me he'd talked to you about it, and you thought it was a good idea."

"I didn't say that at all."

"I thought not. Do you trust Roth?"

"Yes, I think so. Arthur did."

"Ah," Simon said. "Spoken like a real Bannerman." He stood up, gave her a chaste kiss. "Goodnight," he said. "*Courage!*" he added giving it the French pronunciation, always his language of choice for parting words.

She glanced at him, grateful that he had managed, against all odds, to cheer her up.

"*Courage*," he repeated, with a sad smile. "Something tells me you're going to need it in the next few days."

PART FOUR

THE
FORTUNE

10

Booker huddled in his velvet-collared overcoat in the rental car, watching the windshield wipers battle with the snow. He decided they were losing.

He wondered if he should get out and scrape the windows clear. Then he reflected on the fact that he was wearing two-hundred-and-fifty-dollar handmade English shoes. From the little he could see of the inhabitants of LaGrange, they looked like illustrations from the Sears catalog; the few pedestrians on Main Street were clad in bulky down parkas, galoshes, caps with earflaps, looking from a distance like replicas of the Michelin tire man. Booker's homburg and pigskin gloves lay beside him on top of his briefcase, a gift from Cici years ago; the briefcase was the only object he could have used to scrape the windshield clear.

Cici's attitude toward money had surprised him then, and still formed one of the many barriers between them, though by no means the most serious. She was, he had to admit frankly, *cheap*. She bought her underwear on sale—sensible cotton panties and stretch bras, the kind of things you might buy for a teenage daughter on her way to camp. Even on the rare occasions when she saw something she wanted, a handbag or a pair of shoes, she usually talked herself out of buying it, saying, with no sense of irony, "It's too expensive for me."

Cici confronted the problem of her family's wealth by adamantly refusing to admit she had money, so the purchase of a five-hundred-dollar Crouch & Fitzgerald saddle-leather briefcase, with brass-bound corners, gold initials, a solid combination lock, and enough straps and buckles to tack up a horse, had surely signified real feeling on her part

—or so Booker concluded from time to time in the absence of any more recent proof.

Certainly the briefcase was tough enough to scrape the ice off any number of windows, but he couldn't bring himself to abuse any present from Cici that way—besides, she would treat any damage to it as an insult to her. He turned the defroster up to gale force and trod hard on the accelerator. The inside of the car heated up like the steam room at the Downtown Athletic Club, and gradually the windshield cleared. He put the car in Drive and lurched forward, skidding from side to side in the rutted snow, while 4WD pickups with guns on display in their rear windows raced past him, showering him with slush.

On either side of him downtown LaGrange (was there an uptown?) huddled in the storm like a ghost town. He passed two gas stations facing each other across the main street (how did they both make a living?), an Agway feed store, a Ford dealership, the kind of supermarket you only saw outside New York, enormous, its interior illuminated through the plate-glass windows like Lincoln Center at night. Ahead he dimly saw an old-fashioned brick-and-stone building, larger, more solid and more ornate than anything else in town, and he braked on instinct, slithering to a stop inches from a parking meter. However ramshackle the town, there was only one thing that inspired Americans of the late nineteenth century to build for the ages. He did not even bother to take the envelope with the address out of his pocket. He knew he had come to the right place.

He locked his car and made his way up the steps of the County Courthouse.

"IT'S A REAL PLEASURE," Grimm said, his eyes fluttering nervously toward Booker's briefcase as if it contained some dangerous object.

Grimm wore a tweed suit the color of a dried mustard stain, a matching vest with leather buttons, a button-down shirt, and a paisley tie. He looked like a cross between a college professor and a picture from a Brooks Brothers catalog of the late 1950s. He was much younger than Booker had expected.

His expression was furtive. He had a bland, round Midwestern face, honest, ruddy, and quick to smile, the face of a small businessman from a Norman Rockwell poster except for his eyes, which darted back and forth between Booker and the filing cabinet like those of a man with a guilty secret. There was a glass on the desk, Booker noticed.

"What can we do for you?" Grimm asked.

Booker wondered whether Grimm always referred to himself in the plural. The "we" perhaps referred to Grimm's firm, but that seemed to consist only of himself and a secretary old enough to be his mother. "I want to make some inquiries," Booker said.

Grimm's Adam's apple bobbed. He fixed his sad, watery eyes on the knot of Booker's tie. Eye-to-eye contact seemed to be beyond his powers. "Inquiries?"

"Of a confidential nature."

"Confidential?" Grimm looked puzzled, or perhaps frightened.

"Let me come right to the point. Does the name Walden mean anything to you?"

Grimm shook his head, but his eyes were alert. "There are a lot of Waldens around here."

"He was a farmer. You handled the family's legal business."

"Everybody's a farmer hereabouts, Mr. Booker. I think it was probably my father you're talking about."

"You're Eldridge Burton Grimm?"

"Junior. Dad passed away a month ago."

"I see. I'm sorry. Mr. Grimm . . ."

"Burt."

"Ah, Burt—I'm representing the Bannerman family in a matter that involves a great deal of money."

"Oh," Grimm said cautiously, "*that* Walden. The girl Arthur Bannerman was with when he died? I should have guessed. The town's been full of people asking about her the past couple of days."

"Reporters?"

Grimm nodded. "I haven't spoken to any myself, you understand. Not my place to. She's stirred up a lot of interest, though. Fellow came to see Dad just before he died, wanted to know all about her."

"A *month* ago?"

"More like two or three."

Booker wondered who it could have been and why—it would have been well before Alexa's name was public knowledge. "A reporter?" he asked.

"I don't know. Dad was pretty closemouthed about it. Didn't look like a reporter to me. Too well dressed. Could have been a lawyer, or maybe a private investigator."

"And your father didn't say what he told him?"

"Nope. He kept it to himself. The way he kept most things." He shrugged, as if he were reluctant to admit that his father hadn't shared his confidences with his son. "That's the way he was," he said sadly, then turned briskly back to the present. "So, did Bannerman leave her any money? Is that what this visit's about?"

Booker hesitated. "Maybe. It depends on a lot of things."

Grimm shook his head with wonder. "Little Lizzie Walden hit it lucky at last?" he said. It was hard to tell if he was pleased or not. "She always believed she would. Nobody else did, I know of."

"Can you tell me anything about her?"

Grimm's eyes narrowed. "Am I being retained by your firm?"

"I thought that was clear."

Grimm looked longingly at the empty glass. "Let me buy you a sandwich, Marty," he said. "I'll tell you what I can."

If there was anything Booker hated, it was being called "Marty," but years of service to the Bannermans had taught him the value of self-control. "I'd enjoy that," he said, gritting his teeth, "Burt."

Booker wished he had told Robert Bannerman to do his own dirty work. He *liked* the girl, hard as it was to admit to himself, even hoped that Grimm had nothing to tell him, though already he suspected otherwise. Then he thought about his career compared with Grimm's, about his co-op on Beekman Place, about the BMW 635 in its own spot in the garage of his building, and his easy access to everything the Bannermans had to offer a faithful retainer who *might* one day be Cecilia's husband, the seats at the opera, the black tie invitations to the kind of parties most people only read about, the weekends at Kiawa, the look of respect that came into people's eyes when he said he was representing the Bannerman family—and with a sigh of regret, he rose and put on his coat, to hear Grimm out over the promised sandwich.

"OLD MAN WALDEN and my dad were like this," Grimm said, holding up two unmanicured fingers pressed together.

They were seated together in a booth in the restaurant across the street from Grimm's office in the Courthouse building. At the counter a line of broad backs was turned toward them, flannel-shirted, down-vested. On the coatracks, the one-size-fits-all baseball caps advertised John Deere, Cat Diesel Power, Ralston Purina Feed. Booker's homburg stood out in splendid isolation. He was the only man in the restaurant in a dark three-piece suit and a white shirt.

"Of course Walden wasn't that old, I guess. Maybe mid-forties, or fifty, tops. I guess he just *seemed* old because he took things so seriously. Paid his bills on time, counted every penny twice. Talked very slowly, like words cost money. Didn't say much. Dairy farmers, they get to be like their cows after a while. It makes sense. They spend more time with them than they do with people.

"All the same, he swung some weight around here. His folks had farmed the same place for two generations before him, and farmed it well. They weren't rich, but they were solid, bedrock. He was respected, was Lizzie's dad, but not liked, if you know what I mean."

Booker nodded. He knew what Grimm meant. Much the same could have been said of the first three generations of Bannermans. Grimm paused to take a couple of bites of his cheeseburger. He seemed so pleased at the opportunity to talk to someone that Booker wondered how healthy his law practice was.

"He was tough on his kids," Grimm went on. "Or so Dad used to say."

"Too tough?"

"This isn't New York. Farm people expect kids to pull their own weight. 'Spare the rod and spoil the child' is still the local recipe for child-rearing. Walden bore down hard on his boys. I guess too hard, because all four of them left home, first chance they got. Did pretty well for themselves, too."

"Did you handle their legal business?"

Grimm resumed work on his cheeseburger. He nibbled it fastidiously, without appetite. It occurred to Booker uncharitably that what Grimm probably wanted was a drink, not food. "No," Grimm said shortly. He put his cheeseburger down and stared at it glumly. "Tell you the truth, Marty, there isn't too much legal business around here these days. The farmers are going bankrupt, people are cutting down on dairy products. Whoever would have thought our own government would tell people milk was bad for them? These are hard times."

"Hard times are usually good for lawyers."

"Not here. The banks foreclose, they use their own lawyers. Besides, you start handling that kind of business, folks resent it. Pretty soon, you've got no clients at all. Well, you didn't come here to listen to my woes."

Booker signified that this was the case. "The girl," he said.

"She was a real knockout."

"I already know that."

"Sure. We get a lot of good-looking girls around here," he said, as if they were a local crop. "We had a county beauty queen a couple of years back who got as far as the Miss America semifinals, then dropped her amateur standing to become *Penthouse*'s Pet-of-the-Month. Lizzie Walden was different. My dad once said she reminded him of Garbo, or the way Garbo must have looked when she was a kid. *Her* dad was kind of in awe of her, like he'd planted a row of corn and had one orchid come up in the middle of it. She was her father's favorite, all right. He was hard as a rock, except when it came to her."

"He spoiled her?"

"No, I wouldn't say that. He was old-fashioned, the kind of man who always called his wife 'Mother,' never even smiled at her in public, let alone touch her, but he was just plain *sappy* over the girl. Used to put her on his knees when he drove his tractor, take her to the feed store. They were always together, those two. I think he'd have kept her out of school if he could have, but of course he was a Lutheran, not some kind of religious weirdo, of which, believe me, we have a few around here, and anyway he believed in the value of a good education. My dad told me it damn near broke Walden's heart when he put Lizzie on the school bus the first time, they were that close. Well, I guess a lot of fathers feel that way about daughters—we have two boys, so I wouldn't know—but they get over it. The thing is, Walden didn't get over it. You have kids?"

Booker shook his head. Grimm raised an eyebrow as if to suggest that a man in his forties without children was either suspect or to be pitied.

"Uh-huh," he said. "I guess that's New York for you. Anyway, Lizzie didn't do any of the things teenagers do, so she wasn't exactly popular. She didn't date, she didn't have any close friends, she didn't even try to sneak a cigarette in the girl's room. After school, she'd take the bus home, and her dad would be waiting for her near the mailbox every afternoon. He always tried to make it look like it wasn't on purpose, if you see what I mean—as if he just *happened* to be there with his pickup when the school bus stopped. He used to stand about a hundred yards away, looking at her as she got off the bus with her books, pretending to be doing some chore or kicking the tires of his truck, then she'd walk down the dirt road toward him while he waited for her."

"You seem to know a lot about her."

"Not really. I have a sister a couple of years older than Lizzie, went to school at the same time. She didn't like Lizzie one bit. Thought she was a stuck-up little goody-goody."

"You're saying her father was overprotective?"

"Maybe."

"Did people talk about it?"

"This is a small town." Grimm rolled his eyes toward the counter, where a dozen men were pressed thigh to thigh on the stools, all of them, it seemed, looking at Booker's reflection in the mirror behind the cake stand, as if to indicate how small it was. "People thought there'd be trouble one day. Girls are girls. You can't lock 'em up at home when they're sixteen, seventeen—and if you try, they just do something stupid. That was the local opinion, anyhow. Lizzie's father was determined to build a wall around her, and sooner or later folks thought she'd go over it. Which she did," he added with satisfaction.

"Tell me about it." Booker felt the stirrings of an unprofessional curiosity.

"Not much to tell. She fell for Billy Zuber, of all people."

"Why 'of all people'?"

"Billy was the high school football star—that means a lot in a small town. Personally, I've always thought he was simpleminded. He went to Illinois State, on an athletic scholarship, of course, but he was way out of his league there, sportswise *and* otherwise. Married a girl he'd knocked up—you can't get dumber than that in the age of the pill and the abortion clinic—and ended up back home in his dad's business, insurance and real estate. Has five children, or six, I can't remember. I guess he still hasn't heard about birth control."

"You don't handle his business?"

"We used to, when Dad was alive," Grimm said flatly. "He and Billy's dad were close."

A drunk and a failure, Booker thought. Nothing made him more impatient than dealing with losers, but for the moment Grimm was all he had unless he wanted to drive through the snow to see Mrs. Walden and ask if she'd mind helping him disinherit her own daughter. "She and this Billy became lovers?"

Grimm looked puzzled. "Lovers?" he asked, as if it were a foreign word. "We're not talking about a French movie here, Marty. This is farm country. If you're asking did they go to *bed* together, or do it in the backseat of Billy's car, the answer is probably not, much as Billy would have liked to. She was maybe the one girl in school who would have said no to him, and mean it. They eloped, the way I heard it. It was the big, romantic moment of Billy's life, and he screwed it up."

Booker stared at Grimm in astonishment. "Did you say *'eloped'?"*

Grimm blinked furiously. Booker's urgent, angry whisper alarmed him. He seemed afraid he had said the wrong thing. "Well, that's what I was told," he said defensively. "They ran away together, anyway."

"And got *married?"*

"I don't know about *that*, for sure. They were picked up by the cops somewhere over the state line, at a motel, and brought home."

"Why the cops? How old were they?"

"Christ, I don't know exactly. Billy was seventeen plus, maybe eighteen. Liz maybe sixteen. I don't know that it had anything to do with the law. I think Walden, my dad and Billy's dad just got together and raised a posse. They were heavyweight hitters around here, you know. If the three of them leaned on the sheriff, he'd have done anything they wanted—particularly if it was a question of kids, family, and so on."

"*Could* they have been married?"

"Well, I guess so. Why does it matter?"

"It's just general background."

"Is that so? Well, since Billy is a perfectly respectable married man with a whole bunch of kids, I guess he didn't marry Liz."

"Or he and Liz got a divorce? Or an annulment? Was there any talk of that?"

"Nope. Not that I know of. Tell you the truth, ah, Marty, the whole thing was hushed up so quick nobody ever heard the details. Liz didn't have any close friends to talk to, and Billy was probably sworn to silence on pain of death. He was bundled off to college so fast his feet never hit the ground—which would explain how the present Mrs. Zuber caught him on the rebound so easily!" Grimm laughed. There was a bitterness to his laughter that spoke volumes about his views on the subject of marriage.

Booker waved the present Mrs. Zuber out of the discussion with his cheeseburger. He hated eating with his fingers, but when he'd asked for a knife and fork with his cheeseburger the waitress had looked at him as if he were a visitor from another planet, and half the men at the counter had turned around on their stools to stare at him. Irrelevantly, he remembered that Arthur Bannerman had given strict instructions to his campaign staff that he was never to be photographed eating, and once, when a local entrepreneur managed to present the candidate with a hot dog, Bannerman passed it to Booker, who was obliged to hold it for half an hour until he could dispose of it, the sauerkraut and mustard dripping all over his waistcoat and trousers in the meantime. The things I do for the Bannermans, he thought. "There'd be some record in your files of what happened, wouldn't there?" he asked.

Grimm's eyes flickered nervously. "There's a little problem there," he said.

"Problem?"

"Some of Dad's files are, ah, missing. He got careless toward the end of his life. You know how it is with old folks. He took this one out, you see, when the fellow came to talk to him, and he never put it back."

"And it's never been found?"

Grimm nodded.

Booker wondered if that was the whole truth. More important, he wondered who else had been looking into Alexa Walden's past, and why, and what they had found. He knew how the tabloids operated. They might have been following up on a rumor about Bannerman's affair with a young woman, and then decided not to run the story. There were things about the Bannermans that he didn't know, close as he was to them, but he *did* know that Arthur Bannerman had the power to get a story about himself or his family killed if he put his mind to it. Whatever happened, he guessed Grimm hadn't been told, so there wasn't much point in pushing him on the subject. "I suppose there'll be records in the County Courthouse, won't there?" he said.

"Probably not here," Grimm said uneasily. "You'd have to look in Iowa, or Missouri, I guess. I forget which direction they went."

Booker's heart sank at the prospect of driving farther into the heartland. He had hoped to be back in New York tomorrow.

"Today is Friday," Grimm continued. "TGIF, right? You'd have to wait until Monday. Where are you staying, by the way?"

Booker glanced around the café. "I suppose I can check into a motel," he said glumly. He had seen one on the outskirts of town. It looked like Norman Bates's establishment in *Psycho.*

"Welcome to stay with us," Grimm said, with the expression of a man who hopes his invitation is going to be turned down.

"The motel will do fine."

"Sure," Grimm said, with relief.

"Maybe I could put the weekend to good use. I'd like to talk to a few people."

"Right. Who do you have in mind?"

"How about Billy?"

"No sweat. I can introduce you."

"And her mother?"

Grimm shrugged. "There you're on your own. I don't think I could do that. I wouldn't feel right about it."

Booker nodded. There were limits to how far Grimm would go. Mentally he shaved a few hundred dollars off Grimm's retainer. "You wouldn't mind telling me how to find her, at least, would you?" he asked.

"No problem with *that*." Grimm cleared his throat and signaled for the check. He paused for a moment. "Don't expect anybody to greet you with open arms, Marty," he warned.

"Because I'm a lawyer from New York?"

Grimm shook his head. "No," he said. "Because nobody is going to want to talk about Liz. Nobody's forgiven her for what happened to her dad."

Booker felt a chill run through him. So far Grimm had given him a familiar enough story—the shy, small-town beauty who sparks off a scandal, nothing to get too excited about. Admittedly, the fact that Alexa Walden had eloped, maybe had even been married, was new, if not necessarily damning, but something in the way Grimm mentioned her father's death seemed to hint at something darker and more serious than a teenage escapade with sad consequences.

He felt a curious tug-of-war in his emotions. The lawyer in him wanted to get at the truth and produce results for his client, but at the same time he didn't want to hear it, he *wanted* her to be innocent. Still, he could hardly tell Grimm to shut up. "What did happen to her father?" he asked, surprised at how harsh the question sounded.

His voice must have seemed harsh to Grimm as well. "Well, it may not have been her fault," he said apologetically. "The whole thing was so horrible that it kind of got hushed up."

"*What* got hushed up, for God's sake?"

"Walden's death. About a week after she ran away with Billy, he killed himself."

"Killed himself? Because she ran away?"

"That's what the talk was. That's what some people thought, anyway."

"How did he do it?"

"Shotgun. Made a real mess."

"I can imagine," Booker said, though he couldn't, and didn't want to.

He was a city boy; he knew nothing about firearms except that they frightened him.

Grimm was warming to his subject. On guns, at least, he spoke with authority. "Right in the chest. You wouldn't *believe* what a twelve-gauge shotgun will do at close range. You read about people nowadays buying handguns, submachine guns, assault rifles, all sorts of things for self-defense, but I'll tell *you*, when it comes right down to it, nothing beats an old-fashioned twelve-gauge auto. It'll take a man's head clean off at six feet . . . blow a hole in his chest as big as a soup plate."

"I'm sure," Booker said, firmly closing this line of discussion, which was making him queasy. "You'd have thought that's just what he would have done, though," he said, unable to erase the vision.

"Done what?"

"Shot himself in the head. That's the way most people commit suicide when they use a gun, isn't it? It can't be easy to shoot yourself in the chest with a shotgun, surely?"

Grimm thought about it. "No, it's not," he admitted. "I guess what you'd have to do is to hold the muzzle against your chest with your right hand, and stretch the left hand way out like this." Grimm demonstrated. "Of course, when people are going to kill themselves, there's no telling what they'll do. I had a client who stood in the bottom of a silo, opened the chute, and drowned himself in his own corn. We get long winters around here and some people can't take them. Walden may have been thinking about his girl, you know. He may have wanted to spare her the sight."

"Spare her the sight? You mean—she discovered the body?"

Grimm heaved a sigh. "Not exactly. He did it in front of her."

Booker felt his stomach lurch. "She was *with* him when he killed himself? She *saw* him do it?"

"Yup. That's about the size of it. She was as close to him as you are to me."

Booker closed his eyes and tried to imagine the scene. He couldn't do it—or rather, he couldn't bear it. He felt an overwhelming sadness, an instant understanding of why Alexa was so reluctant to talk about her childhood. As for strength—how many young women could live through what she had, and still survive? Most girls would surely go insane, or break down in some way, but she had moved to New York and started a new life. For a moment he was flooded with sympathy and admiration for her; then he reminded himself that wasn't what he was here for. "What a terrible thing to happen to a young kid," he said. "She must have been—what?—sixteen, seventeen?"

"Something like that."

Booker's lawyerly instincts were returning in spite of himself. If nothing else, the law taught you that few people told the truth—not the whole truth, anyway. Even clients whose interests you were defending lied to you, concealed what they didn't want you to know, left out the things that made them look bad. "Since it was such a terrible thing," he asked, "why weren't people around here more sympathetic? Why did they blame *her*? Her father went off the deep end and killed himself in front of his own daughter, for Christ's sake!"

Grimm fidgeted. "Well, coming on top of her running away with Billy . . . and knowing how her dad felt about her . . . people kind of put two and two together, the way people will. They decided it was probably her fault."

"*Her* fault? She was a kid. I don't see how it could have been, do you?" Even to Booker's own ears, he sounded like the attorney for the defense, cross-examining a prosecution witness.

Grimm blinked uneasily, not quite sure what role he was expected to play. "Well, I don't know that I have an opinion on the matter," he said cautiously. "If you're asking whether I think people are too quick to judge, why, sure. Especially when it's a pretty young girl. Now *my* dad, he held firmly to the view she wasn't to blame. He was real close to Sheriff Karl Ehmer, the *old* sheriff, he's dead now—and Karl told him it was the saddest case he'd ever seen—a lot sadder than people thought."

"In what way? It sounds sad enough the way you tell it."

"I don't know. Dad wouldn't talk about it much." Grimm seemed eager to change the subject. "Hell, you want to see Billy Zuber, we could catch him right now," he said, looking at his watch.

Grimm paid the check, left a tip which seemed to Booker shamefully small, and excused himself to go to the men's room. When he came back, his cheeks were glowing and his whole attitude was more jaunty. Booker was willing to bet there was a hip flask or a flat half-pint of vodka in Grimm's overcoat pocket, and the moment he stepped outside, he was almost tempted to ask Grimm for a swig of it. Sleet and snow filled the air, and the wind whipped at Booker's hat, obliging him to hold it on his head with one hand. "Looks as if we might be in for some bad weather," Grimm said with satisfaction, as if the weather were a tourist attraction offered for Booker's benefit.

"How does Zuber feel about Alexa Walden?" Booker asked, squeezing himself damply into the cluttered front seat of Grimm's station wagon. To his surprise, it was a brand-new Mercedes. He wondered how Grimm could afford it.

"Billy's the kind of guy who doesn't have a bad word to say about anyone, but he's got mixed feelings about Liz, ah, Alexa. I mean, he was a star around here, people thought the world of him—then he ran off with her, and after that things fell to pieces for him. It wasn't her fault, but I'd guess he's got to blame her a little. I mean, he's still here, working in his dad's office, and she's gone off to New York and become rich and famous."

"Famous, yes. Rich remains to be seen." There were dog hairs all over the leather seats of Grimm's car. Booker wondered if he had remembered to bring a clothes brush. In the back seat were several boxes of shotgun shells, a tangle of dog leads, a cardboard carton full of muddy field boots. Clearly, when it came to guns, Grimm knew what he was talking about.

"What did her family think?" he asked.

"I wasn't at the funeral—Dad went, naturally—but I paid my respects afterwards. Christ, you could have cut the tension with a knife in that parlor! Liz's brothers looked at her like they'd just as soon have buried *her*, and her grandmother, old Missus Walden, she was still alive then, she wouldn't even look at her."

"It must have been painful for the girl."

"I guess so. But she never shed a tear, you know. People would have felt a whole lot better about her if she'd cried some."

Booker thought about Alexa Walden at Arthur Bannerman's funeral. She hadn't cried then, either, nor had she cried, according to DeWitt, when she stood over Bannerman's body in her apartment. Eleanor Bannerman, he reminded himself, hadn't cried either. It occurred to him that the two women might have something in common. "She may have had her reasons," he said. "I got the impression that she was too proud to cry at the Bannerman funeral."

"Or too stubborn? She takes after her dad. Always did. Whatever, she didn't show enough grief to satisfy people. Anyway, she stuck it out here until she graduated, then she left."

"To become a model?"

"I wouldn't know. I guess most pretty girls from small towns want to be models or actresses. They look at the magazines and TV and think, 'I could do that,' right? Why waste beauty on *this*," he said, waving a gloved hand at the unprepossessing buildings of LaGrange.

"So she went to New York?"

"I think she went to Chicago first. Tried to get a job as a secretary, then went on to New York. That's what I heard, anyway. Here we are."

William Zuber & Son, like almost everything else in LaGrange, was a one-story building on Main Street, with plate-glass windows through which it was possible to see two sullen girls typing away slowly and resentfully.

"Billy in?" Grimm asked cheerfully, banging the door behind him in a cloud of snow.

One of the girls got up and swayed over to a closed door—another hometown candidate for a *Penthouse* centerfold, Booker thought, at any rate from the rear. Against one wall was a breakfront containing

Billy Zuber's athletic trophies. The other walls were hung with plaques and framed certificates honoring Zuber Senior's community spirit, which appeared to be on a heroic scale. Masons, Knights of Columbus, Rotarians, the Benevolent Protective Order of Elks, the Boy Scouts, and the Illinois State Sheriffs' Association, all attested, year after year, in plastic, bronze, or engraved brass, to William Zuber Senior's fellowship, generosity, and idealism. Sprinkled among the plaques were photographs, all showing a plump, bespectacled fellow, dentures fixed in a broad grin, shaking hands with public officials. Several of them were sheriffs and police chiefs. It occurred to Booker that Billy Zuber's father would have had no trouble persuading the Iowa state troopers to bring his son back.

"Hi there, Burt!" Standing in the doorway to greet them, Billy Zuber looked like a giant, his shoulders almost touching the doorframe, his head grazing the top. Big as he was, he gave no great impression of strength. It was partly because his muscle had softened and was running into the fat of premature middle age, but more because there was a boyish quality to his face, as though the features hadn't yet jelled into those of an adult, and never would. His cheeks were freckled, his thinning sandy hair grew in a cowlick, his smile was still that of the most popular boy in school. There were traces of what must once have seemed like dashing good looks, but they were well advanced on the way to dissolving into the meaningless, flabby smile of the professional salesman. It was impossible to imagine Alexa in the arms of Billy Zuber, Booker thought—and was surprised to realize how strongly he felt about it.

Grimm made the introductions. Zuber's office, once he had lumbered over to his desk to make room for them, was small and bleak, a place for a man who did most of his work on the telephone. There was only one chair for visitors. Booker perched on it, his briefcase balanced on his knees. "This is more in the nature of a favor than business, Mr. Zuber," he said.

"Billy."

"Billy. I'm making some inquiries on behalf of a client."

"In New York?"

Booker nodded. Zuber looked thoughtful. "There's only one person I know in New York."

"Alexandra Walden?"

"I still think of her as Liz. Is she in any trouble?" He sounded as if he wouldn't be surprised to hear this was the case.

"Not necessarily."

"What the hell does that mean?" Zuber looked less pleasant now, a hint of the aggression he must once have had as a football player in his eyes.

"You know she was—" Booker searched for the right word—"quite *close* to the late Arthur Bannerman."

"We get the papers here," Zuber said evenly. "Watch the Tee-Vee news too, believe it or not. We saw Liz every night. Sue-Ellen talked about nothing else for a week. Drove me crazy."

"What did you think?"

"I thought Liz looked pretty good," Zuber said cautiously. "Better than ever, tell you the truth."

Booker thought he detected a note of regret in Zuber's voice. Was he sorry things had worked out as they did between them? Did Zuber sometimes dream of Liz Walden when he was in bed with his wife, or sitting at home watching football on television? There was a photograph of a woman on his desk, a plump, corn-fed matron with short blond hair, all too clearly on the way to becoming fat, almost there, in fact. She was smiling broadly, but there was a certain sadness in her eyes, a hint of missed opportunities that matched Billy's. Had she made a mistake, marrying him on the rebound? Or was it simply that she knew *he* had made a mistake, that she had been merely a hasty consolation prize for the girl he really wanted? Why is it, Booker wondered, that the woman you lost, or the one you can't have, is always the one who haunts your dreams?

He had felt that way for years about Cici after she broke off their engagement and then went to Africa. He did not lead a monastic life— why should he, after all?—but it had always been Cici whose face he hoped to see on the pillow when he woke up in the morning instead of whatever girl it happened to be. He was guiltily aware that Alexa was taking Cici's place in his fantasies—that late at night, when he had taken two Antivans to put him to sleep, reviewed his next day's appointments, and placed his pen neatly on the yellow legal pad beside his alarm clock, it was Alexa's face he imagined on the pillow beside him where he had once dreamed Cici's would be, in those drowsy moments before the pills took effect. He could see, as if she were there in fact, her pale-gray eyes looking toward him with the same curious intensity that had struck him so sharply the first time they met at Bannerman's funeral, and which was perhaps only a trick of the light.

Booker snapped his mind back to attention and heard Zuber say, with a snigger, "She's sure made a name for herself all right. Well, hell, she always thought she would."

"Even when she was a kid? When the two of you ran away together?"

Zuber shook his head. "Shoot!" he said, smiling. "She tell you about that? That was a long time ago." He closed his eyes for a moment, still smiling, at some memory. When he opened them again, he focused on his wife's picture with what seemed to Booker like puzzled surprise, as if he had never seen it there on his desk before, or didn't know who she was. He sighed deeply. "It was her idea, you know. She drove me crazy, telling me how we were going to go to California, where all sorts of wonderful things would happen. Christ, I can't even remember what she said. I was going to teach phys ed, get a job at a health spa or something, she was going to get a job as a model. She had it all worked out. You know how it is—I started to believe in it myself, until we were actually on the road. Say, what does this have to do with Lizzie now?"

"There's some confusion about the late Mr. Bannerman's will. It's my job to straighten it out."

"Is that a fact? What did old man Bannerman leave her?" Zuber asked curiously.

Booker sighed. "If she wins," he said, "the fortune."

Zuber blinked. "How much is that?"

"That's hard to say. Nobody really knows. A lot would depend on how you value the assets. A realistic guess would be somewhere between three-quarters of a billion and a billion, but it might be twice that."

There was a long silence. Then Billy started to laugh. "My Lord," he said, catching his breath. "I guess I should have stayed married to her!"

Booker opened his briefcase and took out a notebook. He had hit pay dirt and wished he hadn't. "Tell me about it," he said.

BOOKER STRETCHED OUT on the bed, knowing already that it was too soft to sleep on and that he was going to be awake all night, with every likelihood of an aching back in the morning.

The room was small and cheerless, the kind of place where a truck driver might catch five or six hours of sleep if he had reached the level of exhaustion where he couldn't drive a moment longer—though judging from the sounds from the room next door, the motel also catered to couples who had no other place to go.

He tried not to hear the groans, moans, and thumps from next door, but *The New Yorker* he had providentially put in his briefcase failed to hold his attention. Outside, the wind howled, bringing with it more snow. The steak he had eaten at the diner across the street formed an indigestible lump in his stomach, making him feel like a sufferer in an antacid commercial. Many people in New York believed that you had to go into the heartland to get a good, old-fashioned, real meal, that you didn't know what steak tasted like until you ate it in corn country, where it was bred. Those people, he decided, were wrong.

He held his breath while the couple next door approached a noisy climax and apparently failed to reach it. Had it been in a motel like this one, he wondered, that Billy Zuber and Liz Walden had spent their wedding night, their lovemaking echoing through the thin walls in those few hours before the police arrived to take them home? He hoped the bed had been larger, given Billy Zuber's size.

Booker opened his briefcase and looked at his notes, reviewing what Zuber had told him, and what he'd managed to get out of Grimm when they got back to his office. Next to Zuber's name he had written a big question mark. Billy Zuber had seemed a nice enough guy, not very bright, apparently dedicated to nothing much except raising the national birthrate a few points.

He picked up his pocket dictating machine, tested it, lay back and pushed the "record" button. He had a pretty good idea of what happened—no proof, of course, not yet, but the best proof was his own instinct, the ability to read between the lines. "If my guess is right," he said into the machine, "Grimm's father screwed up. The old man may have had a couple of strokes, hid it from everybody, pretended he was in good shape when in fact his mind was going. He was senile, or getting there, but crafty, and determined to hang on, that's what Burt Grimm seems to think, anyway, though he doesn't say so outright. And of course with the kind of legal practice the old man had, he *could* hang on. Why not? He wasn't making court appearances. A small-town lawyer can screw up for years before anybody notices. You don't know that a will or a deed has been badly drafted, do you, until somebody dies, or you want to sell the property? And the old man must have been impressive—sort of a midwestern version of John Houseman as Professor Kingsfield, right down to the bow tie and the sharp tongue. No patience with fools, that sort of thing. He probably put on a pretty good show for his clients, and they bought it. Everybody put full faith and credit in Eldridge B. Grimm, and why not? Only the truth was, he was a tired, sick old man, coasting downhill on half his brain cells, if that."

He paused, collected his notes, wondered what the hell he'd do with the tape. "He wasn't getting his work done," Booker continued. "It was as simple as that. He could psych himself up to meet with a client, but afterwards he may not have been able to remember what they discussed, or even make sense out of his own notes. Let's be charitable. He may have *believed* he was taking care of things, but it wasn't true.

"Of course, none of this is based on fact. The facts, if they exist, are on file somewhere in Iowa, unless the mysterious visitor from New York got to those as well. Somewhere there is—or was—a marriage certificate, and presumably some record of a divorce or an annulment, if Grimm Senior actually went to the trouble of doing that. Even if he didn't, it's still likely the marriage wasn't valid. Zuber's vague on the subject, but he and Alexa must have faked their ages somehow. Of course it's quite common for students to have faked IDs so they can buy beer and so on. That wouldn't have been the case with Alexa, but it might be something Billy would do. And he might have been able to get one for her. On short notice? Who knows?

"Anyway, it's probable that their marriage was legally defective. Zuber may have been smart enough to figure she'd never go to bed with him unless they went through some form of ceremony, or maybe *she* insisted on it. As for Grimm, he may just have decided there was no point to unraveling a knot that hadn't really been tied in the first place. God alone knows what a court would decide now. After all, here's Zuber, who married again in good faith, if not in good judgment, and has six kids who *might* be illegitimate. I don't see him as the type who'd do that if he'd had even the slightest fear he was committing bigamy. And Alexa? Would she have married Arthur Bannerman if she knew, or suspected, the old marriage might still be valid?"

He paused, picturing her. "Well, she might," he decided. "Bannerman was like a steamroller when he wanted something. If she'd made an objection, he'd have brushed it aside, rolled right over it—and it may not have seemed like the right moment, anyway, to bring up Billy and the elopement." Why am I making excuses for her, he asked himself?

There was a wild cry from the next room as a snowplow thundered past. He lost his train of thought for a moment in admiration for what seemed to be a heroic sexual performance. Did he suffer from premature ejaculation? he wondered glumly. Was middle age setting in? Lately he seemed to be having the kind of problems that caused women to say things like, "It's all right, don't worry about it," or "It happens to everyone, honest, you're probably just tired." He wondered if they said that kind of thing to Robert.

The thought of Robert made him pick up the tape recorder again. Anything was better than lying here listening to what amounted to the sound track of a porno movie. "The father," he said briskly. "Well, Billy didn't shed much light on him, except to say that he didn't like Walden one bit. That's interesting, only because everybody else speaks well of the man, in a cautious way. Billy's view of him is a little darker. An Old Testament prophet in bib overalls, with the fire and brimstone just barely held in check. Apparently, Billy got a good whiff of it on the few occasions he came round to the house. He said he thought her father was going to take a shotgun to *him*, and he hadn't done anything at that point except take her to the movies. So let's say Walden was overprotective, at the very least, and maybe a little jealous.

"Billy doesn't know much about the suicide. Oddly enough, the deputy who was the first person to arrive on the scene is the current sheriff, a fellow called Plass. Apparently when the old sheriff—Ehmer? —arrived, he and Plass had a big argument, didn't see eye-to-eye on what had happened at all. Billy heard—we're talking rumor now—that Ehmer told Plass to shut up and do what he was told or turn in his badge. Sheriff Ehmer, Bill's father, and Walden were pals—that's probably the wrong word—so I can imagine the sheriff wanting to protect

Walden's family as much as possible—but from what? The man killed himself in front of his daughter! What could be worse than that? The whole town seems to have known what happened, so what was there to hide? I'm going to have to talk to Alexa's mother. And probably Plass, as well. Christ, another day here!"

He turned off the tape recorder and got into bed. He glanced at the telephone. He ought to call Robert, he knew, but he resisted. It was too late, he told himself, well past one in the morning in New York, but that was no excuse—Robert wouldn't care if it were four or five. Then he told himself there wasn't any point in calling until he had some hard facts, but that didn't hold water either. Robert would want to hear the rumors if he couldn't have the facts.

"Always get the facts," he had been taught. Well, he had some, and could guess most of the rest, but it was gradually dawning on him that the problem was he didn't really *want* the facts.

He had no desire to see Robert fail, indeed common sense and Booker's own instinct for order and tradition indicated that Robert should receive his inheritance, exactly the way his father and grandfather had —but he didn't want to see Alexa humiliated or defeated either.

He turned off the light and tried to sleep. Then he sighed, picked up the recorder, and erased the tape.

He felt better immediately and slept like a top.

THE MORNING AFTER her trip to Kiawa, Alexa woke to find the press camped outside Simon's apartment, just as he had warned. She could see Simon was doing his best to be nice about it, but that didn't make the situation any easier, and by the end of the day, Simon had had enough of it. "Staying here doesn't even make sense from *your* point of view," he said patiently. "Surely you can see that?"

She could see it, but she didn't like it. "I can't go near my own apartment. You don't want me in yours. And now you don't even want me coming to work. What I *can* see is that I'm being thrown overboard."

"Be reasonable. Just at the moment, you're the hottest news item in the whole country. It's not so much that I care personally about having the media camped outside my building, or standing around my office with microphones and minicams, but it's killing my business. Christ, you know as well as I do the kind of people I do business with don't want the press anywhere near them. For that matter, I don't want them anywhere near *me*—I'm not exactly looking to have some reporter do the Simon Wolff story."

"I know that."

"Sure you do. You've got to figure that you're being followed all the time. And not just by the press."

She was too distraught to argue. Simon saw private detectives around every corner, but she refused to believe the Bannermans would stoop to that sort of thing. Going back to her apartment to pick up some clothes had been like running a gauntlet. She had refused to confirm or deny the story of her marriage to Arthur Bannerman; but within twenty-four hours there were copies of her marriage certificate in every newspaper, neatly juxtaposed with pictures of her from the days when she had posed for lingerie ads. Even the judge who had married them consented to be interviewed in his chambers, taking the opportunity to give a long-winded homily on the dangers of "May–December" marriages, and an unflattering portrait of Arthur Bannerman's state of mind. ("I wouldn't say he was senile exactly, no, or I wouldn't have performed the ceremony, but he was clearly infatuated.") The Bannerman family contented themselves with a dignified statement deploring the publicity and expressing well-bred doubt about the validity of Arthur Bannerman's "alleged" marriage.

"Look," Simon said, with a shrug to indicate that he was helpless, the victim of circumstances, "if you don't want to find someplace, stay, and I'll move out for a week or two. If we're both in the same apartment, people are going to draw the wrong conclusion. Your own lawyer warned you about that."

"I know." Stern was on the phone day and night with advice, much of it, in her opinion, irrelevant or offensive. She was to move out of Simon's apartment, avoid her own, talk to no one, wear subdued mourning, and accept no calls from the Bannerman family.

"I'll keep you on salary," Simon offered helpfully. "Not that it matters, I guess."

"It matters a lot," she said sharply. "The money Arthur left me and my salary won't even *begin* to cover my legal fees, and even if I win, the whole thing will take years. In the meantime, I'm paying for an apartment I can't use. Oh, what's the use! Stern suggested I move into one of the more 'discreet' hotels, as he charmingly put it—the Carlyle, he thought, or maybe the Wyndham—but I can't afford to live in a hotel, and I'd hate it. Anyway, the moment I registered, somebody would give my name to the press."

"For God's sake, you register under a false name. That's easy. People do it all the time. I'll fix it for you."

"Thanks a lot! My God, Simon, a couple of weeks ago nobody had ever *heard* of me, and now I can't even go to the drugstore without being recognized. I'm beginning to understand how Jackie Onassis feels."

"I suspect that somewhere deep down inside she enjoys it."

"Well, I don't."

"You could just give it all up, you know."

She stared out the window glumly. "But then what? I mean, what do I say? 'Okay, we weren't married, it was just a practical joke'? I mean, Simon, I *married* him, whatever anybody says now. I can't just walk away from that as if it hadn't happened."

"Well, maybe you could, but you won't. If you want my advice, just go away somewhere quiet, leave the whole thing to Stern, and wait for the dust to settle."

"Simon, I'm not going to run away. That was *your* advice, remember? That would be like admitting I'm guilty of something, and I'm *not.*"

"Suit yourself." He shrugged, giving the impression of a man who has done his best and no longer has anything to blame himself for. He got up and poured himself a glass of wine. He was still fresh from the shower, wearing a robe, his hair as yet unmoussed.

One of the things that made living in the apartment difficult for her was the fact that they had been lovers. She could hardly object if Simon lounged around his own living room half-naked, or walked in on her while she was taking a shower to tell her she had a phone call. It was *his* apartment, after all, and they had seen each other naked often enough to make any kind of prudery unnecessary between them.

All the same, these occasional moments of accidental intimacy made her uncomfortable. She sensed that Simon enjoyed them, sometimes even provoked them, and while she found this wearisome—another unnecessary, minor irritation in a sea of real problems—she could find no way to put a stop to it without starting a scene, and a scene with Simon was the last thing she needed at the moment.

He dropped back on the sofa and stretched out comfortably, making no effort to pull his robe tight.

Did he really expect that she would go to bed with him? she wondered. But she knew Simon well enough to guess that more than sex was on his mind. Had he decided that there was a good chance she was going to win, that it might be a good idea to pick up their relationship where they had left it off? After all, she was not just a widow, but potentially a *rich* widow—in fact, if she won, probably the richest widow in the world, unless there was some maharani she didn't know about. Even somebody less calculating than Simon would think hard about that possibility and what it might some day mean.

She hated herself at once for her own suspicion. It occurred to her for the first time that the price of great wealth was probably *eternal* suspicion—that her feeling about Simon was, on a smaller scale, no doubt very similar to the feelings of the Bannerman family about *her*— or the kind of suspicion that had clearly done so much to poison Cecilia's life over the years, for instance, even where poor Booker was concerned.

One thing was certain, anyway: She would have to move out of Simon's apartment. Quite apart from the way it must look to other people, the strain would eventually become intolerable. Nor was staying put while Simon moved out an option. Sooner or later, there would be a price to pay for his sacrificing himself, and she was already in his debt more deeply than she was comfortable with.

"I'll move tomorrow," she said.

"You don't have to hurry," he said, without any pretense that he hoped she would stay.

"No, it's better. You're right."

"You could use Bannerman's little hideaway, you know. You must still have the key."

The idea had never crossed her mind. Now that it had, she wasn't sure she was happy with it. There was something macabre about going back there; on the other hand, it was a lot less macabre than to go back to her own apartment to sleep in the bed where Arthur had died, while the press and the television crews camped outside.

"I don't know if I can do that," she said hesitantly.

"I don't see why the hell not."

"It isn't mine. I don't know if I even have the right to . . ."

"Who's going to stop you? It probably *is* yours, for Christ's sake! Besides, there's a pretty good chance that nobody even knows about it. No offense meant, but if Bannerman was keeping an elegant little love nest in midtown, he wouldn't exactly spread the word around, would he? Nelson Rockefeller had half a dozen town houses that nobody knew about except his bodyguard and the guy who looked after his real-estate interests."

"Arthur was not Nelson Rockefeller."

"Well, sure, I wasn't making a comparison—though a lot of people *have*, face it. I'm just saying that his family probably doesn't have any idea about the apartment, and neither does the press. Nobody would know you were there but the servants, and God knows they must be used to keeping their mouths shut."

"There's just a maid who comes in every day. She doesn't speak English."

"There you are."

"I even have some of my clothes there."

"Better still."

"I suppose," she said doubtfully. "I still don't feel right about it, though."

He shrugged. "If you want to *be* Mrs. Bannerman, you'd better start behaving like her. You married money and power—never mind whether you wanted to or not. Take what he left you and use it, Alexa, or walk away from it right now."

"I'm not going to walk away, Simon," she said, more firmly than she felt.

"I DON'T GET TOO MANY CALLERS," Mrs. Walden said warily. "Did you say Liz sent you?"

"No. I said I *knew* her." Booker felt a certain embarrassment. He was here more out of curiosity, because Alexa interested him, than from any loyalty to his client. It was as if he were an intruder.

"Well, it's nice to meet one of her friends."

Mrs. Walden had not in fact been particularly pleased to see Booker at first. She had not exactly greeted him on the porch with a shotgun, but her face was set in an expression of unmistakable hostility until Booker, shivering in the wind, managed to make it clear that he was not a journalist, and gave her his card.

He had hardly known what to expect when he found his way, following Grimm's directions, to the Walden farm. Booker had imagined something picturesque, backwoods, maybe a little on the primitive side, but the Waldens' house, if it had been transplanted to Fairfield County and given a pool, would not have looked out of place there. White, with green shutters and a Victorian gingerbread porch that ran all the way around it, the house was big by any standards but the Bannermans', and lovingly cared for, though dwarfed by the huge barns that looked to Booker more like factory buildings than anything he associated with a farm.

Mrs. Walden did not exactly fit his picture of a farmer's wife, or widow, either. She bore a striking resemblance to her daughter, with the same high cheekbones, pale-gray eyes and full lips. She looked good for her age, which he guessed to be in her mid-fifties, with a figure that would have done credit to a young woman. He had imagined an old lady, sitting alone in an old-fashioned farm kitchen; instead he found a sprightly matron in a fashionable sweater and a pleated skirt, with her makeup on and her gray hair carefully streaked with blond highlights, in a kitchen that contained every modern appliance known to man.

"The journalists have been just terrible," she said. "Luckily, this snow has driven them off."

"Judging from the papers I read, you don't seem to have said much to them."

"I said *nothing* to them, Mr. Booker. What you don't tell them they can't misquote."

He reflected on the fact that Mrs. Walden seemed to know more about handling the press than most of the Bannermans, who suffered from the delusion that if you told your side of the story patiently enough, some of it would get through.

"It must have been an ordeal."

"Well, it was a change, I'll say that for it. It looked like the parking lot at the state fair, the first couple of days. The cows enjoyed the excitement, I guess—their yield went way up."

"You still run the farm?"

"Those cows aren't there for decoration, Mr. Booker," she said tartly, glancing out the kitchen window. "But I don't run it myself, no. I lease the barns and the pasture. My late husband always used to say it was man's work, and I was happy enough to agree with him. Besides, with the price of milk these days, fool's work is more like it. If one of the boys had wanted to go on, that would have been all right with me, but they're all collar-and-tie types. They had enough manure on their boots as kids to last them for life. I can't say I blame them. I never wanted to live on a farm myself, having been born on one—but then Tom came along, and here I am. I was just like Elizabeth, you know—I just *knew* I'd end up in Los Angeles or New York. I wasn't going to spend *my* life getting up at three in the morning, married to a man who worried more about his dairy herd than he did about his wife. But there you are, Mr. Booker. 'The Lord moves in mysterious ways, His wonders to perform,' doesn't he? Elizabeth takes after me, I'm afraid. When she was just a little girl, I used to look at her and tell myself, 'Well, I'll bet this one is going to get up and go, once she's grown.' Somehow, I could just see it in her eyes."

"And you didn't mind?" Booker asked, as she paused for breath.

"Mind? Good gracious, no."

Booker sipped his coffee. He had expected Mrs. Walden to be frail, perhaps bewildered by the sudden glare of publicity that surrounded her daughter, and had reached out to her, but she didn't seem shaken at all, let alone shocked. The car outside, far from being a rusted wreck of a station wagon or an old pickup truck, as he had expected, was a brand-new maroon Chrysler New Yorker. When he had walked past the living room, he had seen handsome old furniture, a breakfront full of china, a brand-new television set in a handsome wooden cabinet, the latest best-sellers from the Literary Guild and the Book-of-the-Month Club placed neatly on the coffee table, along with the *Reader's Digest*, *Time* and the *Ladies Home Journal*, beside glass plates in the shape of leaves neatly filled with candies and nuts, as if guests were expected at any moment.

"Have you talked to her since all this happened, Mrs. Walden?"

"Well, of course I have." She looked at him shrewdly. "Is she all right? Is she in some kind of trouble?"

"Yes and no. I'm going to be honest with you."

Mrs. Walden poured herself another cup of coffee and came over to sit down opposite Booker at the big, scrubbed pine kitchen table. "Does that mean you haven't been honest so far, Mr. Booker?" she asked.

He felt himself blush. Mrs. Walden had the good courtroom lawyer's way of looking you right in the eye when she asked a question. Her eyes were the same color as her daughter's, which made him even more uncomfortable.

"I represent the Bannerman family," he said.

"You don't look any too happy about it, Mr. Booker. Suppose you tell me what's on your mind."

"Mrs. Walden, did Alexa tell you about the will?"

She nodded impatiently, as if the subject wasn't of any real interest to her.

"If it's valid, she's going to be very, very rich, Mrs. Walden."

"I can't get used to people calling her Alexa," Mrs. Walden said with some irritation. "Or Alexandra." She paused. "I guess all this is my fault. I always used to tell her, even when she was little, 'Get out and make something of yourself.' Well, she did, didn't she?"

"I suppose you could say that, yes." He paused. "There's some question, Mrs. Walden, about the validity of Arthur Bannerman's will. As you can imagine, the family isn't too pleased."

He had touched a raw nerve. "Well, that's just too bad, isn't it? We may not be as rich as the Bannermans, you know, but we go back a long way. My father's family, the Brandaus, came from Pennsylvania originally, near Wilkes-Barre. My great-great-great grandfather, on that side of the family, was a Hessian soldier who deserted and joined the Continental Army. My husband's family came here from Switzerland just after the Civil War, and practically *started* the dairy industry in this county. They all made an honest living, too, which is more than can be said of the Bannermans."

Booker waved this tide of genealogy to one side. Eleanor Bannerman and Mrs. Walden would get along just fine if they ever met, despite Mrs. Walden's opinion of the Bannermans. "You misunderstand me," he said. "It's not that the Bannerman family doesn't think Alexa is good enough for them—well, to be more exact, some of them feel *nobody* is good enough for the Bannermans, not just Alexa. The problem is that she claims Arthur Bannerman left her control of The Trust—the fortune, that is—in his will."

Mrs. Walden rode right past this interruption like a freight train at full steam. "I'd like to know how they think *I* feel!" she said. "My daughter has been treated in the press as if she were a kept woman, or worse. I've got nothing against the Bannermans, mind you, except that they're too rich for their own good, from what I hear, but how do you think I feel about having a son-in-law who was older than I am? It's certainly not what I'd hoped for, let *me* tell you! I think it's disgusting, a man of that age marrying a girl like Liz—then having the bad taste to die in her apartment."

"You *knew* they were married?"

"Well, of course I did! She told me. Called me early in the morning, the night he died, so I wouldn't have to learn about it all from the newspapers. She does have feelings, you know, even if we don't speak to each other very often. She made me promise to keep it a secret. I thought that was silly, and I told her so, too, straight out. I still do. Now it's in all the papers and on television, which I knew would happen. Well, they didn't hear it from *me*, anyway. I warned her then, the sooner she told the truth, the better off she'd be, but she's as stubborn as a mule, and never did pay any mind to what I have to say, though when her *father* said something—which wasn't often—it was a different story."

It was beginning to become clear to Booker why, if she was to be believed, Alexa Walden seldom called her mother. Wearily he held up his coffee cup to distract Mrs. Walden. Interrupting her took strategy and a firm tone. "The truth," he said gently, "that's what concerns me. That's why I'm here. I'm not saying Alexa isn't truthful—but she didn't tell you about her relationship with Arthur Bannerman until he dropped dead in her apartment, and then she had to. And she doesn't seem to have told *anyone* about the fact that she was married before."

"Married before? What on earth do you mean?"

"To Billy Zuber."

Mrs. Walden was silent for a moment, to Booker's relief. She filled his coffee cup and handed it back to him. "Oh, that was just a prank," she said. "It didn't mean a thing in the world."

"Everybody else seemed to take it pretty seriously."

"That was my husband's fault. She'd have come home all by herself in a day or two, if he hadn't stirred up the whole county to go chasing after her. Liz thought too much of herself to waste her life on a fathead like Billy Zuber. She was smart enough to have worked that out for herself long before they reached California."

"But were they *married*?"

"They went to some fool justice of the peace outstate, and Billy talked him into some kind of ceremony, yes, but I don't call that a marriage. I don't know how Billy found the courage. Or the energy. He hasn't shown a bit of spunk since. When my husband found out what they'd done, he was furious."

Mrs. Walden paused long enough to gather her thoughts, or at least to turn them in a new direction. "Sex," she said loudly, causing Booker to blink. "You'd think people who lived on a farm would take a calm view of it. The trouble it causes! You'd have thought a man of Mr. Bannerman's age would have put all that behind him long ago, wouldn't you?"

"His mother takes the same view. So do his children, for that matter."

"Oh, children never understand their parents, Mr. Booker." There was a bitter edge to her voice. Booker had the feeling that Mrs. Walden's chatter was a fragile screen, designed to conceal something, or perhaps to deny it to herself. There was something about her that made him nervous—no, he corrected himself, *she* was nervous. Once you got used to her chatter, the way she suddenly changed subjects, the unexpected, slightly flirtatious attempt to charm, there was an undercurrent of fear that the lawyer in him could hardly fail to recognize.

He had not looked closely at Mrs. Walden, but now that he did, he saw the tiny lines of tension in her face, the strained muscles in her neck, a nervous tremor in her fingers as she lifted her coffee cup. Her gray eyes, so similar to Alexa's, betrayed her. He could read fear there.

About what? To hear her talk, Alexa's elopement with Billy had been a childish escapade, nothing to get excited about—but it had ended in her husband's death under grotesque circumstances.

Somewhere in this tidy, cheerful house, perhaps even in this room, Thomas Walden had stood within reach of his own daughter, held a shotgun to his chest and pulled the trigger. "Mrs. Walden," he asked quietly, "why did Liz run away with Billy?"

Mrs. Walden giggled, a sound which seemed to Booker shockingly inappropriate, until he realized that it was just a nervous reaction to his question. "Well, girls will do these things," she said, fluttering her eyelashes. "Girls do silly things at that age."

"Sure. But why Billy? I wouldn't have thought he was your daughter's type, even when she was a teenager. And why California? What I'm wondering, you see, is whether Billy wasn't the only way she could think of to get as far from here as she possibly could. What *I* think is that running away to California was a lot more important to Alexa— Sorry, Elizabeth—than marrying Billy. Maybe she didn't have the nerve to go on her own, but she was determined to go. And you *wanted* her to go, I think, didn't you? You said so yourself. Why was that?"

"I wanted her to make the best of herself. I didn't want her to be stuck in a small town, like me."

"I don't believe that's the reason," Booker said. "Not the only reason."

Mrs. Walden's face seemed to sag with age. He knew it was just his imagination, but it was as if the attractively groomed matron had suddenly been replaced by a frightened old woman. "You've been talking to Sheriff Plass," she said. "Or listening to Burt Grimm's drunken gossip. Is that it? I won't have you poking in our affairs."

"Listen to me, Mrs. Walden. Your daughter is laying claim to one of the biggest fortunes in America. Whatever it is you're hiding, it's going to come out eventually. Admittedly I'm representing the family, but the truth is, I like Alexa, and I truly don't wish her harm. The best thing for her, in my opinion, is to make a deal. The worst thing for her would be an endless battle in the courts—especially if she has anything to hide. You don't like me asking questions? I can understand that. But you'll like it a lot less if we go to trial and you get a superstar trial lawyer out here, with half a dozen investigators handing out subpoenas and taking depositions."

Mrs. Walden seemed to be staring at a point just above his head, not seeing him at all. Was she looking at the spot where her husband had killed himself? Booker wondered. But there was no way he could bring the subject up directly—which explained, he supposed, why he had never become a trial lawyer. Roy Gruttman or Edward Bennett Williams or Barry Slotnick would have asked her point-blank, and the hell with her feelings. He felt ashamed of himself, but he had to know what had happened here, not for Robert's sake, but for his own—and Alexa's, he told himself. "Were they close?" he whispered gently. "Liz and her dad?"

She nodded, eyes shut as if she were afraid of seeing something.

"*Too* close?"

She shrugged. "He couldn't help it."

Slowly does it, Booker told himself, filled with self-disgust. "Of course he couldn't," he agreed soothingly. "You didn't talk to anyone who could help? Seek counseling?"

"He wasn't the kind of man you could talk to about something like that."

"So she decided to solve the problem for you by running away? With Billy? And her father got her back?"

"I prayed she'd get to California. I didn't think much of Billy, but still, that's what I prayed for."

"And then, when she came back, what happened, Mrs. Walden?"

He asked the question gently and realized immediately that it had been a mistake. Roy Cohn would have shouted it, seized the moment to force the truth out of the witness, but Booker couldn't do it. She looked him directly in the eye, her voice firm again, and said, "My poor husband killed himself. As you already know. He was out of his mind."

Her strength seemed to have returned. She had been caught off guard for a moment, but this was as far as she was going to go—he could see that in her eyes. "You'll have to go now, Mr. Booker," she said, pleasantly enough. She rose and walked him to the door. "It was nice meeting you," she said with mechanical politeness, shaking hands with him. Then, as he stepped out onto the porch, buttoning up his coat against the storm, she turned for a moment in the open doorway, snowflakes dotting her blond-rinsed hair, and said, loudly and clearly, "Please don't come back again."

He had never felt so awful in his life.

"I DON'T CARE if you *are* a lawyer. I don't care who you're working for. You bother Mrs. Walden again and I'll lock you up, understand?"

By the time Booker arrived back at his motel, he found a police car waiting for him, its red light revolving in the falling snow. There was a crest featuring several variations on the theme of corn sheaves, a gold italic inscription that read "Stephenson County Sheriff," and a motto announcing, "Your Safety Is Our Business."

Booker's safety did not seem to be on the mind of Sheriff Plass, a tall, thin young man with the cold, narrow eyes of a Western gunfighter glaring at Booker from under a spotless gray Smokey the Bear hat. Plass's tan uniform seemed to have been dipped in starch—his creases would have wrung admiration from a Marine drill sergeant, and his brass gleamed like gold. At his waist was an enormous revolver, on the butt of which he rested the heel of one large hand. He looked as if nothing would give him greater pleasure than to draw it and take a bead on Booker.

"Lock me up for what?"

"Disturbing the peace. Hell, who knows? I'd find something."

Booker guessed Plass probably would at that. He did not look like the kind of law enforcement officer who spent much time worrying about the Miranda rule. "Get in the car," Plass said.

Booker stared him down. "No way," he said.

Plass sighed. Clearly Booker was not a man to intimidate. "Mr. Booker, it's cold outside, that's all. You want to talk to me? Let's go to my office and talk."

It seemed reasonable enough. Booker wanted to talk to the sheriff, and there was certainly no point in doing so in the parking lot of the motel in the middle of a storm. He reviewed habeas corpus in his mind and got into the police cruiser, resting his head against the wire mesh that formed a cage for whoever was put in the back seat. He bumped his knee against two shotguns locked in a rack next to the driver. Another local believer in the efficacy of the shotgun, he thought.

Plass was silent during the five-minute drive back to the courthouse. He ushered Booker politely through the sheriff's department, which was cleaner than any big city police station, with polished linoleum floors, bright overhead lighting, cheerful colors, new filing cabinets. He poured two mugs of coffee and led Booker into his office, which was hardly more than a bare cell. Whatever Plass's awards, hobbies, and family ties were, he did not make a display of them. He put his flat-brimmed hat directly in front of him on the clean desktop, and stared at Booker. "You've got a nerve," he said.

"What the hell do you mean by that?"

"I'll thank you not to swear, Counselor. This isn't New York. I guess you've got a right to snoop around, since that's what you're paid for, but disturbing Mrs. Walden is a different matter. She's a widow. She's been through a lot—as you know by now. You should have let her be."

"She let me in. I didn't break in. I told her what I was there for."

"I'll bet you did! Burt Grimm tells me that you're representing the Bannerman family?"

Booker nodded.

Plass did not seem impressed. The man had an expressionless face, Booker thought, the kind you expected to see at your car window when you were stopped for speeding.

"Did Mrs. Walden complain about my visit?"

"She called me, sure. That's what we're here for, Mr. Booker."

"Is it? It's not a crime in any law book that I know of."

"Maybe. You're the lawyer. I'm just a cop. In my book, it's a crime to root around like a hog in other people's tragedies. No matter how much money is involved."

"I don't disagree. But if this thing goes to court, it will all come out, and in the most sordid way. You know that. That's why I want Alexa— ah, Liz—to settle. For her *own* good."

"Does she?"

"No, not yet."

Plass blinked, his hostility ebbing slightly. "Strikes me you're playing God, Mr. Booker. That's a common failing among lawyers, in my opinion. Burt Grimm's father suffered from it."

"He thought he knew what was best for people?"

Plass nodded. "I just follow the law, myself, wherever it leads. Grimm and the old sheriff, they tried to get the law to come out the way they thought it ought to, played God right and left. . . . "

"Is that what you and Sheriff Ehmer were arguing about the night you discovered Tom Walden's body?"

"Grimm talks too much, even for a lawyer. I didn't 'discover' the body, Mr. Booker. I was called to the scene by radio, and I responded."

"Grimm said you and Ehmer didn't see eye-to-eye."

"Ehmer and I didn't see eye-to-eye on a lot of things."

"Surely a suicide is a suicide?"

Plass broke eye contact. "I guess so."

An awful thought occurred to Booker. "You were first on the scene, weren't you, Sheriff?" he asked.

Plass nodded.

"It must have been a terrible sight."

"You get used to it in my line of work."

"Sure. All the same, there can't be many people who shoot themselves in the chest with a shotgun?"

Plass moved his hat an inch or two as if he were searching for the exact center of his desk. "Not in my experience," he said. "Not many at all."

"Is it possible to do? Physically, I mean?"

Plass looked at his hat, apparently pleased with its position on the desk, at last. He seemed to relax a bit now that Booker was asking professional questions. "Oh, sure, for a guy with long arms and a strong thumb." He thought about it for a moment. "People do the damnedest things to kill themselves."

"Mr. Walden have long arms?"

Plass hesitated. "About average, I'd say. He wasn't a big guy."

"I see. So he'd have had a hard time doing it?"

Plass seemed lost in thought, as if his mind had taken him back to the scene of the crime. Despite his claim of being used to such things, there was obviously something about Walden's death that haunted him still. "Maybe he could have gotten off one shot, but not a second," Plass said, as if he were resuming an old argument with someone else; then his eyes focused on Booker, and he was all business again. "Anyway," he said briskly, "it's a police matter. It's been closed for years."

Booker glared at him. "What was he trying to do, Sheriff?" he asked. "What was he trying to do to his daughter?"

Plass stood up. He towered over Booker, even with his hat off. His face seemed carved in stone. "Let's just say he got what was coming to him, Mr. Booker, however it came. I'm afraid I have to go now."

"You wrote it up as a murder, didn't you? Then Ehmer, the old sheriff, turned up and made you tear up your report. Old Grimm probably came along, too—or knew about it, anyway. They knew they couldn't get away with calling it an accident, so they decided to make it a suicide, to protect the girl, or maybe just to protect Walden's reputation?"

Plass put his hat back on straight as a die. "Speculation, Mr. Booker. That's all you're talking." He opened the door. "If things had been as you suggest, however, that *wouldn't* have been the right thing, no. The right thing is to stick to the facts, Counselor. The *truth*. The law. Whatever it costs. You should know that."

"And the fact was a suicide who shot himself twice at arm's length?"

"I never said there were two shots, Mr. Booker. You must have misheard me." He glanced down the hallway, where the only sign that this was a law enforcement office was a rack of riot guns in a stout, glass-fronted locked cabinet, with a padlocked chain running through the trigger guards. "Of course, guns are funny things," Plass said calmly. "An automatic can double-fire, or so I've been told. That's why I prefer pump guns, like these."

He held out his hand. "You come back and see us again real soon,

Mr. Booker," he said. "But stay away from Mrs. Walden. She's been through enough, poor woman."

Booker sloshed through the snow back to his motel, checked out, got into his car. He had a few stops to make, including saying his farewells to Grimm; but once he was out of town, on his way back to Indianapolis, he couldn't help noting that a sheriff's car followed him all the way to the county line, to be replaced by another car from the next county all the way to the airport, where a deputy watched as he boarded the plane, his eyes fixed at a point just over Booker's head as if he were looking at something else. Was it a warning, he wondered; or did Plass simply want to make sure he was really going home?

It didn't matter. He had guessed the truth.

What he didn't know was what he was going to do with it now.

BOOKER READ THE CLIPPINGS on the plane. Thomas Walden's death had been reported at length in the LaGrange *Husbandman*, though with some restraint. In a newspaper for which headline news was mostly soybean prices and the fate of the high school football team, the suicide of a prominent local citizen must have posed certain difficulties for the editor, who had tried to avoid outright sensationalism.

Walden, Booker was relieved to find, had not died in the kitchen but in his office, by the barn, "after milking," the reporter was careful to add, as if that made the act less awful because the cows didn't have to suffer. If the story was to be believed—and Booker did not believe it— Walden came in from the barn, took off his work boots, changed into loafers, had a few words with his daughter, Elizabeth, who was going over the account books as she always did in the late afternoon after school, then walked over to the corner, where he kept a loaded shotgun in case a dog started chasing his stock in the fields, and calmly shot himself.

It did not seem probable to Booker, nor apparently to the reporter who, reading between the lines, hadn't believed a word of it.

Booker closed his eyes and wondered why they hadn't tried to pass it off as an accident—perhaps that Walden shot himself while he was cleaning the gun. But of course that wouldn't have worked. Nobody in LaGrange would believe for a moment that a dairy farmer would come in from milking in the late evening after a fifteen-hour working day and start cleaning a shotgun, or that a man like Walden would be careless enough to clean it without unloading it first. Besides, they must have been in a hurry to make things look right before the state troopers arrived—they certainly wouldn't have had time to find Walden's cleaning kit and lay it out.

Did Alexa threaten to tell the truth? If Walden had tried to force himself on his own daughter and she shot him in self-defense, his friends might have decided the best service they could do for him was to make it look like a suicide. *Anything* would be better than charging his daughter with homicide, or second-degree manslaughter, and having her tell her story in court. They didn't want a scandal, they probably didn't want Mrs. Walden to suffer, so they performed hasty damage control and forced the reluctant Plass to go along.

Booker opened his eyes and shuffled through the clippings again. When Plass was made sheriff—another front-page story—he was described as "Karl Ehmer's hand-picked successor," which argued, in Booker's mind, for a deal of some kind. Was Plass to keep quiet about what he had found when he arrived on the scene of the killing in exchange for which one day he would be sheriff?

Or had it been Mrs. Walden who persuaded them to save her daughter's reputation? That was also possible, he thought. He could imagine the three men standing there: Plass tall and grim, knowing the truth and determined to follow through on it; Grimm and the sheriff, shocked not only by what had happened to their friend, but by what they had just discovered about him, trying to sort out what was best for everybody—all of them trying not to look at what remained of Tom Walden after he had received two 12-gauge shotgun shells in the chest at close range. "A hole the size of a soup plate," Burt Grimm had said, and Booker, while he had no experience in such matters, could easily imagine that it had not been a tidy death.

There must have been blood everywhere in that small room—and Alexa huddled somewhere in a corner, trying somehow to come to terms with what she had done. Or so he imagined. The thought chilled him, and he rang for the stewardess and asked for a Scotch, even though drinking on airplanes always gave him a headache.

He went back to the account of Walden's death. There were three photographs on the front page of the *Husbandman*. The first and largest was of Thomas Walden taken at a livestock show, standing next to a prizewinning bull. He did not seem pleased by the victory, nor did the bull. Walden was a good-looking man but apparently not given to smiling—indeed, his expression was rather similar to the bull's, a combination of stubbornness and a quick temper held barely in check.

A smaller photograph of Mrs. Walden showed a pretty young woman with a faintly unhappy expression. Alexa's picture seemed to have been taken from a high school yearbook. She looked exactly the same then as she did now, Booker thought, but she, too, seemed unnaturally solemn, even sad, in the formal portrait. These three people had been bound together in a family tragedy which had ended in an explosion, and some hint of that—or what was to come—seemed to Booker to be stamped on their faces. Perhaps he was reading too much into the photos, he thought, sipping his Scotch.

Was he beginning to understand what made her tick? Was it anything as simple as the fact that Arthur Bannerman had been both a benevolent father figure *and* a lover? Or was it also a question of security, not so much money as the feeling that he offered her a special kind of private world in which everything, at least on the surface, appeared to run according to plan? If so, he had surely played a kind of cosmic practical joke on her by dying in her bed—but not before leaving her with the title to the ultimate security, the Bannerman fortune itself.

In the newspaper files he found a page torn from the LaGrange high school yearbook, doubtless the one from which the photograph had been reproduced. There was a brief paragraph under her name. She did not appear to have had many extracurricular activities to list—she was not a cheerleader, or active in sports, or a member of the drama group, or a debater. "Everybody knows Liz is the person to see if you don't understand a math problem," the writer noted, rather cheerlessly.

Well, Booker reflected, a good head for numbers won't hurt her. Eleanor Bannerman, after all, could outperform a computer when it came to the fortune and could do compound interest in her head. At the bottom of each paragraph was a kind of "zinger" of the "Most likely to succeed" category.

Liz's simply read: "Still waters run deep."

ALEXA FELT LIKE A BURGLAR opening the door to the apartment, and felt even worse once she had closed it behind her and turned off the security system.

Less than two weeks ago, Arthur Bannerman would have been waiting for her in front of the fire, trousers pulled up neatly to protect the crease, his gleaming black shoes planted firmly on the antique carpet. His face would have had that rosy, pink-cheeked glow which most people mistook for ruddy good health.

He always rose to greet her and give her a kiss that was surprisingly formal and decorous, considering the nature of their relationship. Now the apartment was empty—not just empty, but with the special kind of emptiness that only death can produce. That was fanciful, she told herself, but still she knew the feeling, from her father's death—the sense, for a brief moment, that the life had gone out of the house as well. Perhaps it was just a trick of the emotions, or simply that nobody had lived here for nearly two weeks.

Then she realized that the particular deadness of the apartment was only partly in her mind. It was not Arthur's absence she felt, but his *presence:* a pair of tortoiseshell half-moon reading glasses neatly folded on the desk beside the leather portfolio in which his mail was delivered to him once a day, the shaving things laid out neatly on the marble shelf of the bathroom, his silk bathrobe still hanging from the clothes-hook. Apparently it was nobody's responsibility to collect his belongings —or perhaps it was hers.

She lay down on the bed, suddenly exhausted. In a way, exhaustion was a blessing, for it overcame her initial reluctance to get anywhere near the bed. Once she had kicked off her shoes and stretched out on it, she half-expected to roll over and find Arthur lying in it, his head raised by the pillows, reading glasses propped far down on his nose so he could look up over the rims to see her, absorbed in the catalog of some art auction or the financial section of *The New York Times*.

She rolled herself up in a ball, feeling at once lazy and helpless, as if she had the flu or a bad cold. She closed her eyes and drifted for a moment, enjoying the sensation of feeling sorry for herself, the way it was sometimes possible, when she was sick, to give in and simply lie in bed luxuriating in the way her muscles ached and knowing that for the next eight to twelve hours she wouldn't have to use them. . . . She opened her eyes—it seemed to take a great effort—and saw only the plumped-up, unused pillows beside her with their freshly laundered pillowcases and Arthur's initials, discreetly embroidered in one corner of each, white on white, "AAB."

She closed her eyes, and fell into an uneasy, restless doze.

SHE WOKE IN A COUPLE OF HOURS. There were a million things she should be doing, she told herself sternly, but when she tried to decide what they were, they seemed to make up an endless list of trivia.

For no particular reason she was suddenly frightened. She had been alone before—often—but in the past few months she had grown used to Arthur's presence, orchestrating her life, even if from a certain distance, and drawing her into his. Now she was alone in his empty apartment, and, except for Simon, nobody even knew she was here.

She found herself listening for the small noises of any apartment, even one as lavishly soundproofed as Bannerman's pied-à-terre—the whir of the ventilation system, the muted click of the thermostat, the hum of the electric clock, an occasional intrusion of noise from outside when a police car or an ambulance screamed past. She almost wished the apartment were smaller; its dark, cavernous rooms stretched away into infinity in her imagination.

The only way to calm herself was to get up and walk through it, turning on all the lights, but she was too tired to move, and besides, she felt safer in bed than she would walking around. She knew her fear was only a product of fatigue and anxiety, just as she knew hiding in bed was merely seeking the imaginary safety of childhood, when she had sometimes lain awake in the dark, hearing the noises of the old farmhouse as the winter wind shook its windows and made its massive timbers groan, imagining monsters and demons creeping through the attic toward her room. Sometimes it had been so bad that she had crept silently down the hall and slipped into her parents' bed, snuggling between them for warmth and safety, much the way a cat does—a habit her mother discouraged firmly, but her father didn't seem to mind.

The thought of her childhood brought her back to consciousness again, as if her mind were on guard, trying to prevent her from remembering too much of it. There were people who *must* know she was here, she told herself. Her mother, certainly—she might be trying to reach her—Stern, Roth, possibly even Robert Bannerman. Perhaps if people knew she was here, she thought, her fear would go away. It seemed worth a try.

She pulled herself up in bed, picked up the telephone and dialed her mother's number. It would be an hour earlier in LaGrange, and her mother would surely be up, watching television and probably none too pleased to be interrupted.

The phone rang several times before her mother's voice came on the line, clearly annoyed.

"It's me," Alexa said.

"Who?" There was the noise of a commercial in the background.

"Alexandra, Ma. Turn down the TV."

"Oh, Elizabeth," her mother said. "Just a moment." Alexa wondered whether her mother would ever accept the fact that she didn't want to be called Elizabeth, or Liz, or worse yet, Betty.

The background noise dropped to a more tolerable level. "I just can't believe that Joan Collins!" her mother said. "Have you been watching 'Dynasty'?"

"No, I haven't, Mother."

"Well, you just don't know what you're missing. Of course, I suppose in New York there's all sorts of things to do. Not like here."

"I wouldn't know, Mother. I'm a recent widow, remember? As a matter of fact, I'm lying in bed in Arthur's apartment because the press are camped outside mine, so I can't even go home, and if I went out anywhere I'd probably have a dozen reporters following me, along with photographers and television crews. And on top of that, I'm feeling rotten and lonely."

"It doesn't do any good to brood."

"I'm not brooding." Alexa sighed. It had been a mistake to call. This, after all, was the woman who had managed to persuade herself that her husband had died accidentally. She knew better, of course, but she had dealt with the horror by simply pretending it hadn't happened the way it did. Alexa wondered whether her mother sometimes had nightmares, or moments when she remembered the entire grisly event as it had actually been, but if so, she kept these dark thoughts to herself.

She tried a new approach. "Mother," she said, "what would you say if I told you I was frightened and lonely and didn't know what to do?"

"I'd say you should think more positively than that. You're young, you're pretty, and you've got the rest of your life ahead of you. And from what I hear, you stand a good chance to be very, very rich."

"Don't believe what you read in the papers."

"I don't. There was a fellow here talking to me about it just the other day . . . Hooker? A nice young man, for a lawyer, anyway. Or at least I thought he was, at first."

"Hooker? You don't mean Booker, do you?"

"That's it."

"*Booker* was in LaGrange? Talking to *you?* What did he want?" Even as she spoke, she knew the answer to that, and it filled her with fear and anger. "What did you tell him?"

"Not a thing, dear."

Alexa squeezed the receiver so hard against her ear that she felt a sharp pain. "How long did he stay?"

"Well, we had a couple of cups of coffee. Perhaps an hour or so."

An hour or so. Alexa knew her mother well enough to guess that given an hour, she would have talked Booker's head off. "Why on earth did you let him in?"

"I couldn't very well let him freeze to death on the porch, could I? Besides, he'd already seen Burt Grimm."

"He saw that old fool Grimm?"

"No, dear. Have you forgotten? He's dead. Mr. Booker saw his son."

"That's worse." She was wide-awake now, her mind racing. Robert had sent Booker to her home! She should have thought of that. But what could she have done? Nothing. Simon had been right. Sooner or later it was bound to occur to Robert Bannerman that he ought to know more about her than he'd read in the newspapers.

She felt a sense of outrage that Booker—a lawyer, a Harvard man, almost but not quite the son-in-law of Arthur Bannerman, had barged in on her mother like the worst kind of sensation-mongering journalist. "What did he want to know?" she asked. "Did you talk to him about—what happened?"

"What happened?"

Alexa detected, with no particular difficulty, a defiant trace of guilt in her mother's voice, disguised as injured innocence. Her mother did not get many visitors, and practically none from the far horizons beyond Illinois. No doubt she had been grateful enough for Booker's company and quite happy to sit there chatting to him. "About Father," she said, finding it as hard as ever to say the word.

"Well, of *course* I didn't, dear," her mother said automatically and unconvincingly, then hesitated. "Well, the fact is, he brought it up.

He'd obviously been talking to people, Grimm, I suppose, and got quite pushy wanting to know what had happened. I had to ask him to leave, finally. I was a little upset by it. So I called the sheriff."

"You called the *sheriff*? About Booker? What for?"

"I shouldn't have, I know. The sheriff was very nice about it. Mr. Booker just upset me, asking so many questions, that's all."

"Questions about Father? Like what?"

"Oh, I don't remember, dear. Anyway, Mr. Booker wasn't all that interested, to tell you the truth. It was Billy Zuber he wanted to know about, mostly."

"Billy? Why on earth was he interested in Billy Zuber, of all people?"

"He'd been to see Billy."

"Booker went to see *Billy*? Are you sure?"

"Oh, yes. Billy called me about it himself."

"How is Billy?" Alexa asked, knowing her mother's answer would give her time to think, and not much caring what had become of her high school sweetheart, if that was what Billy had been. She had chosen Billy, worked hard to get his attention, and had succeeded, with dire results. She was still astonished, thinking about it, at the sheer daring of her plan. They would run away together, get married, and once that was done, she would be beyond her father's reach. Of course, it hadn't worked out that way. She could hardly have picked anyone less courageous or enterprising than Billy Zuber, who had failed her at almost every level. But why would any of that be of interest to Booker? It was nothing to be proud of, true, but kids run away together every day. Putnam, if Arthur was to be believed, had never spent a full term at any school he had been sent to.

Was Booker simply collecting information that would *look* bad, building up a case against her as a person of low morals? Did running away from home with a boy from school matter, in the eyes of the law? She would have to ask Stern—whom she had neglected to call for two days —but she found it hard to believe any judge or jury would care.

In the back of her mind she was aware of her mother's voice, telling her about Billy's children. How could he possibly have that many? Alexa wondered, counting the years.

Poor Billy, Alexa thought, but then, all things considered, Sue-Ellen, or someone very much like her, was exactly what he deserved. "He wanted to know whether you and Billy were married," she dimly heard her mother say, and came back to full attention with a snap.

"What are you talking about, Mother? I was never married to Billy."

"Of course you weren't, dear. That's just what I told Mr. Booker."

"*He* thought I'd been married?"

"Well, you did go to a justice of the peace, you and Billy. You meant to get married. That's what I told your father—that your instincts were right, even if your choice of young men was poor. 'She wouldn't just run off with a boy,' I told him, 'not unless they were going to get married,' and I was right."

"Yes, but it wasn't valid. Anyway, Father told me that Grimm—the old man, not the son—was going to straighten everything out, if anything needed to be."

"And I'm sure he did, dear. I wouldn't give it a moment's thought."

Alexa focused her mind on the subject while her mother plunged off on a tangent about local news. From time to time she murmured, "You're kidding!" or simply made the appropriate noises of surprise and interest, but she knew these to be essentially unnecessary—her mother would continue until she ran out of gossip or breath, neither of which was likely to be soon.

Familiar names loomed like rocks in the fog, births, deaths, and adulteries drifted past in the haze, while Alexa concentrated on her brief and disastrous fling with Billy Zuber. It was true—she had made Billy promise to marry her out of some ludicrous notion that it would be wrong to run away with him unless they were married, or perhaps because she simply hoped her father would be less angry that way. Billy had done his homework for once and had found a minister of some obscure Protestant sect, who doubled as a local justice of the peace across the state line. He had performed a quick ceremony without asking too many questions and with only a cursory glance at their IDs. They were married in the eyes of God, he told them, with an expression that seemed to suggest he felt God might be making a mistake, but he was less clear about the eyes of the people and the state of Iowa.

She remembered the whole scene with strange clarity—strange since she had not given it a thought for years: the minister in his shirt-sleeves, wearing a hastily knotted and very unministerial tie showing pheasants and ducks in full flight, hurrying the ceremony as fast as he could, either because he wanted to get his twenty dollars or because he was on his way to shoot a few ringnecks before the light went. The latter was more likely, since he wore heavy field boots under his baggy dark cloth trousers, while a grizzled retriever with a red collar dozed at his feet, one soulful eye open, like an inattentive extra witness. There was an American flag hanging from the wall and a framed photograph of Richard Nixon, even though there had been two Presidents since his resignation—which said everything there was to say about Republican sentiment in the heartland.

Billy had not thought to provide a ring, so they were obliged to use his class ring. The lack of a proper ring was somehow symbolic of the whole meaningless ceremony, she thought. If she had *really* loved Billy, she would have been willing enough to go to bed with him without going through a marriage ceremony, valid or not. The fact that she had insisted on it had proved to her even then, as he slipped his class ring on her finger and held it there—it was far too big for her—that she knew she was making a mistake.

How on earth had she, of all people, done it? Billy was a dummy, there was no denying that, but not *that* much of a dummy, while she was the kind of girl who had moral doubts about everything, for whom "leading on" a man was unthinkable, even if she had possessed the wit to do it, which in ordinary circumstances she did not. But of course she knew exactly where she had found the courage and the guile—from the simple fear of what would happen if she stayed at home.

Her instincts about men were poorly developed—the choice of Billy Zuber as Knight in Shining Armor, however reluctant, was proof of that—but they were good enough to warn her that her father's jealous attention was rapidly developing into something more threatening. She couldn't tell her mother—besides, there was never any doubt in her mind that her mother *knew*, at some level of her mind, knew and didn't want to know.

You were supposed to get counseling in situations like that, that's what you always read in the magazines, but from whom? There was no way she could have gone to one of her teachers, or to the sheriff's office, and say that she was afraid of her own father.

Thinking about it now, as her mother rambled on, her voice like the noise of traffic outside, something you heard but didn't listen to, Alexa tried to remember when it had begun—whether there was an exact moment when she had ceased simply to be her father's little girl and became an obsession—but there was no big scene to remember. They had always had a lot of fun together, laughing as she sat on his knees while he drove his tractor, or snuggled up beside him in the seat of the pickup, but then the laughter stopped. Everything *seemed* the same, but it wasn't. There were no more jokes. Her father's touch, which had once been natural, easy, comforting, became something she dreaded, as if his hand touching her leg when he changed gears was burning hot, a leaden, oppressive weight when it rested on her shoulder. If she had run away alone, they would have brought her back—that was what she had thought, anyway, and the irony of it was that she might have done better alone, without Billy. "Mother," she said, "did Dad leave any papers?"

"What did you say?"

"I said, do you have Dad's papers?"

"Of course I do, dear. Whatever for?"

"Because if there's anything there about me and Billy, I want you to find it."

"Well, there's an awful lot of them. What are you looking for?"

"I don't know. An annulment? Anything, Mother."

"Oh, dear. There are boxes and boxes of things. I didn't throw anything out. I'm not even sure where I put it all."

"Mother, you must have been through his papers."

"I left all that to Mr. Grimm. I mean, the deeds to the farm, insurance policies, all that sort of thing was in the bank, your father had it all put away neatly, just the way you'd think he would."

"Just *look*, Mother, that's all."

"Well, if I don't know what I'm looking *for* . . . Why don't *you* come out and go through it all?"

Alexa sighed. It was always the same old blackmail. Nothing in the world could get her back to LaGrange, and her mother knew it perfectly well. Nor was she in fact anxious to have her only daughter back, bringing with her memories that she had done her best to forget. Alexa did not doubt—had never doubted—that her mother loved her but found it easier to do so at a distance, in the comfortable illusion that Alexa had left LaGrange merely to make a career for herself in New York, and not because it was impossible for her to stay. Since this illusion could only be maintained by Alexa's staying away, it suited both of them that Alexa never came home, but it was also necessary for Mrs. Walden to complain about it, as if the matter were entirely Alexa's fault.

Occasionally Alexa wondered what would happen if she said, "Fine, I'm on my way, turn down my bed," but both of them knew it wasn't possible, not yet, and since "not yet" had stretched out for years, it might as well be never. Alexa wasn't resentful. Her mother had found a way of dealing with the horror. Alexa only wished she had found an illusion that worked as well for herself, then considered that being accepted by the Bannerman family might well be it.

"Mother," she said, "if anybody else comes to the door to ask questions, don't talk to them, all right? Call me. Please."

There was a pause. Then her mother spoke, in quite a different voice, as if the real person were coming through, not the absentminded gossip who lived in a world where nothing bad had ever happened. "Elizabeth," she whispered, "are you going to be all right?"

"I don't know," Alexa said softly.

"You haven't done anything wrong, have you?"

"No," she said. "I haven't done anything wrong." She said goodbye and hung up, feeling lonelier than ever. It was beginning to dawn on her that if Booker knew what had happened between her and her father, or even guessed it, he held the trump card, though he might not be aware of it. Not for anything—not even for Arthur's last wishes and the Bannerman fortune—would she make her mother relive that night. There was no way she could let the manner of her father's death become public knowledge, no way that her mother could survive hearing it on the television news, reading it in the newspapers, knowing that her neighbors were doing the same.

Despite her anger against Booker, she willed herself to sleep.

SHE WOKE AGAIN SUDDENLY with the sound of the front door clicking open, and lay still in bed, trying to remember what time the maid arrived. The faint buzz of the alarm system sounded, and she saw the red light on the key pad next to the bed flicker briefly, then turn to green as the code was punched in. She rolled over and looked at her watch, and was startled to see that it was three in the morning.

She sighed and curled up again, hoping to get back to sleep—then she felt a rush of adrenaline and sat up suddenly, clutching the bed-clothes around her. She was a New Yorker—tales of break-ins and burglaries were part of her life, though none of these had ever actually happened to her. She had been frightened of being alone in the apart-ment only a few hours ago, and had dismissed her fear as irrational. Now that there really was something to be frightened about, she was surprised by how calm she felt.

She reviewed her situation. Whoever it was, it was somebody with the key and the alarm code—a security guard, perhaps? But no security guard had ever interrupted them when she and Arthur had spent the night here together. Still, it was a possibility. Should she call the secu-rity company? But she had no idea what the number was, or where it might be written down. She could press the "panic button" on the alarm key pad, but she had no idea what that would produce. It glowed faintly red in the dark, but was it silent, or did it trigger a siren, and how long would it be before the police and the guards arrived? She hesitated to call 911, having heard often how slow-moving and bureaucratic the emergency operators were—besides, it was only a week ago that half the police force, it seemed, had tramped through her apartment to look at Arthur's body.

She sat very still, absurdly conscious of the fact that she was only wearing her bra and panties, while the intruder—if it was an intruder —made his way through the rooms below. Finally it occurred to her that in a few moments he might make his way upstairs and rape or murder her. She quietly lifted the receiver of the phone to push the buttons for 911—she was beginning to realize that the police would be welcome, in fact, to wish they were already there—only to hear a soft voice with a Spanish accent on the line. "I'm in," the voice said. "No problems."

Did burglars make telephone calls as soon as they had broken in? she wondered. Trying hard not to breathe, she listened in. A muffled voice at the other end grunted.

There was a series of clicks, the noise of paper being shuffled, heavy breathing that seemed to go on forever, then the sound of a cigarette being lit, and a deep smoker's cough. "It's not in the desk."

"You're sure? A manila envelope?" The voice at the other end was muffled and opaque, but it sounded vaguely familiar despite the distortion. She wondered if it was Robert Bannerman, and the moment that question occurred to her, she knew she was right.

"I know what I'm looking for," the man with the Spanish accent said gruffly. "I'll look around."

He hung up. She lay there for a minute, listening to the man downstairs as he searched, wondering what to do. If she dialed 911, he would surely hear her voice, and it might be anything from fifteen minutes to half an hour before the police arrived—time enough for him to kill her, if that's what he decided to do. Once he was upstairs, there was no place for her to hide, not if he was a professional, which was very likely. He would certainly search the closets and the bathroom, and in any case, the moment he saw the bed he would know somebody was there.

She smelled an acrid, sharp odor—cigarette smoke, but not an ordinary cigarette, something foreign, a strong, dark tobacco. She heard the click of a light switch as he reached the bottom of the stairs, and without a moment's hesitation she pushed the panic button and was rewarded by a high-pitched wail that pierced her eardrums, and apparently the intruder's as well, for he shouted "*Coño!*" and ran for the front door.

Despite the noise, she sighed with relief. The telephone rang, she lifted the receiver and gave the security guard the code number, hoping that was the correct procedure. The siren stopped. "Who are you?" the guard asked.

"Mrs. Arthur Bannerman."

There was a pause. "I don't have a Mrs. Bannerman on my list, ma'am."

"Try Miss Alexandra Walden."

Another pause. "Okay, ma'am. Any problem?"

"No. I just pushed the panic button by mistake."

She said goodnight and hung up.

She thought of calling Stern, but she wasn't sure what she could tell him, or how much he could do, and was a little ashamed of having hid the problems of her past from him in the first place. Roth, she guessed, might be able to tell her how to deal with Booker, but neither of them was likely to be able to stop Robert if he was determined to expose her. If only Arthur were here, she thought. Then, lying in the bed she had shared with him, it occurred to her that he had foreseen just this kind of situation and had prepared for it.

Without bothering to dress, she went downstairs to the desk the intruder had been rummaging through, found Arthur's address book, and dialed Baxter Troubridge's number.

TROUBRIDGE'S APARTMENT WAS ANCIENT and enormous. What it lacked in style, it made up for in content, as if the furnishings of many houses and generations had been squeezed in so tightly that it was hard to find a place to sit. Paintings of people who were presumably his ancestors lined the walls floor to ceiling; there were stacks of books on the chairs; endless sets of antique china gathered dust on the floor; everywhere you looked there were objects from the Troubridge past, most of them thick with dust.

Troubridge himself, though it was only ten in the morning, wore a plum-colored velvet smoking jacket and a pair of sharply creased gray flannels, and sported on his feet velvet dancing pumps with his family crest embroidered in gold. She counted at least a dozen cats before she gave up; from the odor, nobody had bothered for a long time to clean the litter pans, which were scattered everywhere.

"I'm sorry I called you so late last night," she said.

"I don't sleep much, so it's all right. Luckily you didn't wake Father."

"Father?" She wondered for a moment if it was one of the cats, or if Troubridge was already drunk.

"*He* sleeps better than I do," Troubridge said glumly. "Eats like a horse, too. But once he's awake, he wants to talk, and then there's no sleep for anyone."

She thought about this for a moment. "How *old* is he?"

"Ninety-eight. Luckily, he's asleep now. A young woman as pretty as you are brings out the worst in him."

"You look after him?"

"Oh, Father's not a lot of trouble. Looks after himself, pretty much. Besides, his, ah, *fiancée*"—Troubridge gave the word the full French pronunciation—"lives here too. They moved in with me after Father lost his house in the last divorce."

Alexa stared at Troubridge, wondering if he was making fun of her, and decided he was not. "How old is *she?*"

"God knows. I'm no judge of these things. Fifty, perhaps." Troubridge leaned forward, his expression sad, his eyes moist. "They still do it."

"Do it?"

"Make love." He seemed about to cry. "I haven't in years, but the old goat is still at it, every day." He put his hand on her knee. "I can hear them sometimes."

She backed away. Troubridge's problems were no concern of hers—

nor were his needs. "Mr. Troubridge," she said firmly, "Arthur wrote me a letter before he died."

"Arthur?"

"Arthur *Bannerman*. My husband. My *late* husband," she corrected herself.

"Ah, yes. That's an uncommonly pretty dress you're wearing."

"Thank you. He told me to come to you if I ever had any trouble with Robert."

Troubridge sighed. "Robert. I like the boy, you know. Always have."

"I'm sure."

"I warned Arthur, you know—if I may be frank with you. I told him a man his age shouldn't marry a young woman! Truth is, just between us, it's nonsense. I was merely envious. Wish I could do the same. Warned him that Robert would make trouble, too, but any damned fool would know that."

"Mr. Troubridge, what *exactly* was it that Arthur wanted me to know?"

Troubridge stared into space, a forlorn figure surrounded by cats. "There's a lot of good in the boy," he said. "I never had children myself."

"I'm sorry."

"No, no, no need to be. Look at poor Arthur. Can't say having children made *him* happy."

"Well, I'm not so sure about that. What *did* he want me to know?"

Troubridge shrugged. "Damned if I know," he said. "He didn't tell me."

"He didn't *tell* you?"

"No. He gave me something for you, that's all. 'To be used with discretion,' he said. Where the hell did I put it?"

Troubridge shuffled off, moving stacks of paper, cats, books and folders as he went, muttering to himself in the cloud of dust. From somewhere in the apartment, Alexa heard a curious cackle, a kind of harsh, cracked laughter, followed by the sound of a woman moaning hoarsely. Were Troubridge's father and his fiancée "at it," she wondered?

"Aha," Troubridge cried, and shuffled back, holding a manila envelope. "Knew I had it." He handed it to her ceremoniously. "You wouldn't care to stay for lunch, would you?" he asked.

She shook her head. "I can't, I'm afraid."

"Perhaps some other time?"

"Perhaps."

Troubridge nodded sadly, as if he had expected nothing else. Then he took her hand briefly, bowed his head, and said, "He was my best friend."

He paused for a moment, ignoring the strange noises from down the hall. "I don't know what's in there. Perhaps I can guess what one of them is, but I don't want to know . . . if it's what I think it is. Whatever you do, young lady, be *careful*."

He opened the front door and waited beside her for the elevator, a piece of old-world courtesy which she appreciated until, at the last moment, as she was about to step in, he firmly pinched her bottom.

When she turned, he was gone.

SHE OPENED THE ENVELOPE in the taxi, her bottom still smarting from Troubridge's pinch, and skimmed through the contents. It was a New York State Police accident report, and as soon as she had read the first few paragraphs, she knew what it meant. Arthur had told her what he had done to save Robert, but the State Police memorandum, written in dense bureaucratese, made the events of that night even more chilling. Not, she thought, that she could altogether blame Robert. She knew what it was like to have committed a crime and covered it up—though in her case, it had been done for her. Still, she had numbly acquiesced, while the sheriff, Burton Grimm, and her mother cooked up the story, and later on she was grateful enough, if ashamed.

She understood—who better?—Robert's panicked effort to save himself, since his brother was already dead. It must have taken a good deal of courage, though perhaps not the most admirable kind, to pull himself out from behind the wheel of the smashed car, move his brother's body into the driver's seat, and crawl up a frozen embankment to call for help—which is exactly what the investigators had concluded after studying the crash and the autopsy report. Robert had been driving and had worn his seat belt, which no doubt saved his life; John had been in the passenger seat and had not fastened his. Given his injuries, the police decided that he could not possibly have been driving the car.

She tried to imagine the scene—the car skidding directly into the station wagon, the terrified faces of the man and his daughter, the instant when Robert must have realized that there was nothing to be done, and after the crash, as he slumped in the wreckage, knowing that his elder brother was dead or dying, his decision to save himself . . . and of course the realization that he was heir to the fortune, at last.

She remembered what it was like when she had looked at her father's body crumpled against the wall like an animal that has been carelessly slaughtered, his chest opened wide by the two shots she had fired into him—but others had taken care of her, changing the facts, as Robert had changed them for himself.

She could not bring herself to blame him now. "Let the dead bury the dead," Burton Grimm had said, like so many people finding in the Bible a justification for what he wanted to do—and certainly it was a lot easier for the dead to bear guilt than for the living, so perhaps he wasn't wrong.

All the same, she could understand why these documents mattered so much to Robert. It was his Chappaquiddick, the moment of panic in his youth when he had taken the easy way out and placed the responsibility for three deaths on his brother. The press would gleefully try him for something that had happened twenty years ago, retired state troopers would appear on television to tell the story of how they had been forced to bury their report, learned psychiatrists would give their view of the case on "Nightline" and "20/20," his political career would be destroyed. As for his family, what would they think? They had blamed Arthur bitterly for John's death, still did, because of the quarrel that preceded it, but the news that Robert had been driving the car, not John, would surely shock them—even Cecilia. She wondered if Eleanor knew the truth. Would Arthur have told her? Probably not, she decided.

Well, if Robert could bring the battle to LaGrange—she still burned with anger at the thought of Booker rooting around in her past, then using guile to get her to confirm his suspicions—she could bring it to Kiawa.

She was tempted to ask Stern for his advice, but on reflection she realized that was impossible. What she had in her hands was a family secret. She could not trust anyone outside the family with it.

"THIS MEETING IS MOST IMPROPER," Booker said, though he looked happy enough to be here.

"I know."

"And probably not a good idea. For *you*, I mean."

"Maybe I don't care."

Booker's nervousness was apparent to Alexa. She tried to control her own. It had taken a lot of effort to persuade him to come here, but she had been insistent. Behind the glittering glasses Booker's eyes flickered nervously, as if he were afraid to meet hers. It was not the look of a courtroom lawyer about to cross-examine a witness—there was something soft there that reminded her of a shy boy who wanted to ask a girl for a date and didn't dare.

She smiled at him. "I'm sorry we haven't had a chance to get to know each other," she said. It didn't seem the right thing to say to a lawyer from the opposing side, and Booker looked puzzled. "What I wanted to ask you," she said as pleasantly as possible, "was why you went all the way to LaGrange to bother my mother when you could have talked to me. I didn't think lawyers skulked around doing detective work."

Booker blushed fiercely. "I wasn't skulking," he said defensively.

"What would you call it then?"

"Background research."

"I see. And that includes bursting in on my mother to question her?"

"Perhaps I should have called her first," Booker said glumly. "I'm really sorry."

"I wonder what Arthur would have said about it."

"I have no idea."

"He believed in the direct approach—honesty. I don't think he'd have approved of *his* lawyer spying on people, do you?"

"I was doing nothing of the kind."

"Did he ever ask you to do anything like that, Mr. Booker?"

"Martin. No, admittedly."

"He spoke very highly of you, Mr. Booker. He thought of you as his son-in-law."

"Martin, *please*, Mrs. Bannerman, ah, Alexa . . . I'm surprised to hear that, frankly."

"Why? You were practically a member of his family. He saw more of you than he did of his own children."

"I suppose that's true, but I never detected any feelings of the kind you suggest."

"He was a very reserved man—" she smiled at him—"Martin."

"You could say that."

"I think, at the end of his life—not that Arthur thought it was the end—he was sorry he hadn't expressed his feelings. To you. To his children. That's part of what he had in mind, you see."

"I see. I hadn't thought of it that way."

"Well, he did. Look, you're acting for Robert, I understand that. If we're going to fight this out in court, okay, I can live with that, even if I lose. But do you really think it's fair to rake up a lot of rumors about my childhood? What does any of that have to do with the case? And what gives you the right to hurt my mother?"

"Alexa, believe me, I haven't the slightest desire to hurt your mother."

"Is that so? You don't think telling the world about my father's death won't hurt her?"

Booker didn't appear to have an answer for that. He stared at his shoes. He took off his glasses. He rubbed his chin. "Alexa," he said softly, "I think I know what happened," he whispered. "To your father."

She stared at him in horror. "No, you don't."

"I can't prove it but I'm pretty sure."

Was he trying to draw her out? She felt a moment of panic, trying to guess how much he knew, but one look at his face told her it wasn't a trick. His look of concern was genuine, she decided, and possibly went deeper than that.

She had always thought there was something boyish about Booker, perhaps because he had sacrificed so much of himself over the years to the needs of the Bannerman family, but he looked older today; there were lines around his mouth, and dark circles under his eyes. He looked more handsome than she remembered him, and very tired.

"This isn't easy for me," he said. "I wish we weren't on different sides . . . ."

"Do we have to be?"

"I'm a lawyer. I represent Robert—and the Family. A lawyer isn't supposed to play God, Alexa—as Sheriff Plass told me. . . . I wish I'd never gone to LaGrange in the first place, by the way. God knows I didn't *want* to. But I went, and that's that."

"And now you're going to pass on to Robert a lot of rumors and gossip so that he can use all that against me?"

He sighed. "No, I don't think so. I'm not comfortable with rumors and gossip. I like facts. Anyway, I didn't come here to talk about the damned fortune. I came here to talk about *you*."

"That's none of your business."

"Maybe so. Look, I'm not fishing. I don't think you're going to tell me what happened, and I don't even *want* you to, but what I want to say to you is that you're too damned *hard* on yourself. I thought about it all the way home. I don't give a damn what Plass thinks, or Grimm, or that fat oaf Zuber, or even your mother . . . though, if you want my opinion, your mother feels the same."

She could not lie to him or deny what he had guessed. "No, she doesn't. She blames me. She always will."

"The hell she does. If you weren't so goddamn wrapped up in your own guilt, you'd have seen that years ago. She forgave you. Maybe she never even blamed you in the first place."

She struggled to answer. "Maybe. Yes. I don't want to talk about it."

"We're *going* to talk about it," Booker said forcefully. "Did you ever tell Arthur about this?"

She shook her head. "I wanted to. I tried."

"Well, he'd probably have agreed with me. Frankly, I don't think he liked me a bit, whatever you say, and I wasn't crazy about him, but I'll give him this—he had a pretty fair sense of justice, particularly when it came to family. And he wasn't easy to shock. Not that he didn't screw up badly as a father, mind you, but at least he knew it."

"I tried to tell him. I just couldn't work up the courage. And then it was too late."

Booker polished his glasses and put them back on. "Did it ever occur to you that he might already know?"

"Know? How could he?"

"Alexa, I've had two days in LaGrange to think about all this. I don't believe your father committed suicide, but I'm not going to press the point with you. One thing I do know, and it's puzzled me a lot, is that somebody was out there in LaGrange before me, while old Grimm was still alive, *three months* before Arthur married you. At first, I figured it might have been an investigator for one of the tabloids, but the more I thought about that, the less it made sense. As it happens, I took Burt Grimm out for a few drinks the last day I was there, and he told me the man who'd been to see his father looked like a Wall Street lawyer, English suit, expensive shoes, Harvard accent, the works. Reading between the lines, this man passed out a lot of money for the privilege of spending a few hours in private with the old man and taking one file away with him. Which would explain why Burt Grimm has no business to speak of but drives around in a new Mercedes. If you care to know what I think, Arthur guessed there was a problem about your father's death, and maybe with your marriage to Billy as well, so he sent somebody out there to find out the truth and bring home the documents. I think he *knew*, all along. I think he forgave you."

"He can't have."

"Why not? He was shrewd. And he loved you. I think what he did was put Grimm's file in the fireplace, as a present to you, and maybe a lot of other papers as well. That's probably why Burt Grimm was so sure I wouldn't find anything at the County Courthouse—and pretty worried in case I went there to look and might ask why some things were missing. For what it's worth, by the way, I agree with Arthur."

They sat in silence for a few minutes. She did not need Booker's absolution, nor did she put much faith in it, but she was grateful all the same. "Thank you," she said.

"But you don't forgive yourself?"

"No. Maybe I will some day. You're the first person who's said it."

"I think if you'd told Arthur all about it, he'd have said the same."

"I wish he had."

"You'd have believed him?"

She nodded. "I *trusted* him, Martin. He was the first person—since my father—I ever really trusted."

"And that's why you feel you have to win for him?"

"Yes."

He sat glumly. "I've never been here before," he said. "No matter how long you work for the Bannermans, there are still things you don't know. And I *do* work for them, Alexa."

"I know."

"I've put myself in an unconscionable position. A conflict of interest. Perhaps I ought to give up the case, leave DeWitt, I don't know . . . it's a lot to give up."

"You don't have to give it up. Not for me."

"I wasn't thinking of you. I was thinking of the ethics of the situation. I could be disbarred for sitting here talking to you like this." He shook his head as if he couldn't believe the sheer stupidity of what he was doing.

"I won't tell anybody. I promise."

"As for LaGrange, I don't know what the hell to do."

"You do what *you* think is right, Martin. What you have to tell Robert, you have to tell him."

"Well, that's *my* problem. I wish . . . " Booker started to say. Then he paused, looked at his watch, and stood up.

"You wish what?"

"We weren't on different sides, for a start."

She got up. He shook her hand formally and picked up his briefcase. "Can I give you a word of advice? If there are any other, ah, little problems in your past, I would advise settling, *now*. Robert will find out about them, sooner or later, with or without my help. Pick a number, settle, and run."

"There aren't any other problems, Martin."

"I'd heard . . . well, never mind what I'd heard."

He paused at the door, looking serious. "If Arthur did what I think he did, don't throw it away, Alexa. It was a gift of love. Maybe the most important thing he could give you. Who would have thought the old man was capable of a romantic gesture!" He looked back at her.

"When all this is over," he said quietly, "perhaps we can get to know each other a little better, talk about something other than the Bannerman fortune. . . . I'd like that, you know."

She would too, she thought. The more she saw of Booker, the more she liked him, but she could hardly even imagine an end to her immediate problems. It might be years before matters were resolved, if ever, if Stern was to be believed, and Booker, despite his evident affection for her, was on the other side. "Perhaps," she said, allowing him—and herself—a moment's hope. "It could be a long time."

"I'm a very patient man. I'll take that as an expression of guarded optimism, if you don't mind."

She smiled. "I don't mind."

"Good." He paused. "Take *care*, Alexa," he said. "I *mean* it."

He let himself out. The moment the door clicked behind him, she started to cry, as if she were trying to make up for all the years when she hadn't, as if it were the day of her father's funeral, and she'd done then what she really *wanted* to do, as if she were at Arthur's grave, and hadn't stubbornly held her feelings back from showing in front of his family.

She knew now how much Arthur had loved her. She would not fail him, no matter what it took.

.   .   .

BOOKER STARED GLUMLY AT HIS SHOES, avoiding eye contact. He wasn't sure himself which side he was on any more, for the first time in his life, and it produced an effect similar to nausea. "She seems to have led a pretty ordinary life," he said, as firmly as he could.

"I should have sent somebody else."

"They wouldn't find anything that I didn't, Robert. Nothing that matters."

Booker sighed to himself. He had never held out on a client before, let alone a member of the Bannerman family. He felt like a man walking a tightrope across Niagara Falls.

"No boyfriends?"

"The high school football star. I talked to him. A perfectly nice guy, wishes her well. Listen, what difference would it make if she'd slept with the entire team? She's not a candidate for sainthood."

"Well, I must say it doesn't sound like much. You're not holding anything back, by any chance, are you, sport?"

"Why would I do that?" Booker hoped his guilt didn't show.

"I can't imagine."

"Well, I'm not."

"I should hope not," Robert snapped impatiently. "Tell me about—what's its name?—LaGrange?"

"Well, it's a pretty typical midwestern small town, you know."

"Spare me the travelogue, Martin. I'm not planning to visit it."

"What I meant was that it's a typical small town . . . a lot of gossip. Everybody knows each other."

"And what was the gossip about the beautiful Miss Walden?"

"Nothing much. I talked to her high school sweetheart, a fellow called Zuber."

"And?"

"They ran away together, it seems."

"Aha! A sex scandal. That's something, anyway."

"Well, it wasn't exactly a *sex* scandal, Robert. They only got about a hundred miles before their parents brought them back. Everybody was pretty upset, but not for any good reason that I can see. It was all fairly harmless."

"How old was she?"

"Sixteen or so. Just the age when kids do that sort of thing."

"Are you putting out your shingle as a child behaviorist on the side? Get on with it."

"Well, shortly after that episode, her father died. Killed himself, actually."

"You call this an *ordinary* life? How did he kill himself?"

"He shot himself. He appears to have been depressed, angry, something of a Type-A personality."

"You're trying my patience, Martin. When I want a psychological profile, I'll ask for one. Did he kill himself because she ran away?"

"It may have been a contributing factor, yes."

"Is that why she never goes home?"

"I think so, Robert. Bad memories and a strong dose of guilt. I talked to her mother, in fact. Alexa took her father's death very hard, but I don't get the impression that anybody blames her for it but herself. I've started some inquiries, but I'm not sure they'll produce anything you're looking for."

"Damn," Robert said. "I was hoping for something better than that." He sighed. "Have you seen the papers?"

"Most of them."

"Unbelievable trash, isn't it? We're on the front page of every goddamned tabloid in the country with the story of her marriage. Christ, the day before yesterday, the story even made the front page of the fucking *New York Times!* We can't go on forever saying 'No comment.' Ted Koppel called me to appear on 'Nightline.' There are reporters camped outside my apartment. At least two people propose to write a book about it. The President called, by the way."

"The President of the United States?"

"Of *course* the President of the United States, Martin. What other President is there? He wanted to thank me for taking the budget crisis off the front page! We've got a stand-up comedian in the White House. Even that miserable hypocrite Beau Randolph called, as if he was still a member of the family! To think that that son of a bitch actor, without a brain in his goddamn head, is running for the governorship of California. And may win it. *Christ!*"

"How is Eleanor taking it?"

"Don't you worry about Eleanor, Martin. Try worrying about *me* instead. Leaving to one side control of the fortune—just what is all this going to do to my chances of getting nominated? *I'm* the one who has the problem, and all you're worried about is how Eleanor feels."

"And Alexa? What's she doing?"

"Luckily she still hasn't talked to the press. She's vanished, in fact, but that just creates an additional mystery for them. I've come across a couple of interesting things about her life in New York, by the way—*very* interesting. Of course if we start slinging mud at her, who knows if it won't backfire?" He laughed, the familiar Bannerman roar. "There's a mixed metaphor worthy of a politician! I must be slipping."

"What *kind* of thing?"

"Have you ever heard of a gal called Brooke Cabot?"

"No, should I have?"

"Brooke's a madam. Rather a special one."

"Special?"

"Well, I don't mean that she caters to special tastes, though I suppose she does, or used to, within reason. What's really special about her is that she's a Cabot—a genuine Puritan descendant, with a pedigree long enough to satisfy even that old fart Baxter Troubridge. She went to school with Cici, matter of fact. Good breeding and no money is a sad combination, Martin, and that's Brooke's problem, poor girl. I've known her for years. Well, a couple of nights ago she phoned me out of the blue. Brooke isn't the kind of person who phones to chat, not with me at any rate, and she doesn't solicit business by telephone. She said she wanted to meet me, said she knew something that might be—and I quote her—'mutually profitable.' " Robert chuckled. "Reading between the lines, I'd say she knows something about our Miss Walden."

"Oh, surely not. I can't believe that." The shock in Booker's voice was audible.

Robert seemed amused by Booker's reaction. "It wouldn't surprise *me* a bit," he said. "You're shocked? You're an innocent, Martin. A lawyer can't afford to be a prude. Let me tell you, there are plenty of perfectly respectable women in society who once turned tricks. I'm not talking about *whores*, you understand, in the full meaning of the word— though there are a few of those, too. The young women who work for Brooke are well-bred and perfectly respectable in every way that matters, except in what they do for a living—but then you could say the same for most bankers and practically everybody of any importance on Wall Street."

"You sound as if you admire her."

"Well, I do, rather. If it's true, it's the best thing I've heard about Alexa so far. I'm not a moral man, Martin, as you may have had occasion to notice—except when I'm making political speeches, of course, when a certain amount of hypocrisy is required of a man. I'd be relieved to learn that Alexa Walden shares my view of morality. I'd be quite prepared to like her for it if she weren't at my throat."

He looked closely at Booker. "Are you all right?"

"Of course I am."

"You look a little shell-shocked. Has little Miss Walden managed to charm you, Martin?"

"Not at all," Booker said, astonished at how easy it was to lie. "I just wouldn't have thought her the type."

"I would. It explains a lot, when you come right down to it—how she met Father, for instance. Somebody's going to have to talk to Brooke."

"I suppose so."

"I was thinking you might go and see her."

"*Me?*"

"Why not?"

"I don't think I could do that, Robert."

"And why the hell not?"

"It's not a lawyer's job."

"No? Or is it just that you don't want to hear the truth about Miss Walden, Martin? You screwed up in Illinois; now you don't want to talk to somebody who may have important information for us. Whose side are you on, Martin?"

"Yours, as you know perfectly well."

"No. I don't know anything of the kind. Don't try to fuck *me*, Counselor. I have enough clout to make sure no decent law firm in New York would take you on. I can have you ambulance chasing or taking on tenant-landlord cases in the South Bronx, if I put my mind to it, and I will, so don't you ever forget it."

Booker dabbed at his forehead. "I was merely trying to suggest that you might want to hear what she had to say firsthand. And that she might talk more freely to somebody who wasn't a lawyer."

Robert looked thoughtful. "You're right about lawyers. I hadn't thought of that. But I can't see her, Martin. It's just too goddamn dangerous for somebody who's running for office. She could be under investigation, the cops could be following her, she might even be wearing a wire. You know what a pain in the ass the Manhattan DA is, for Christ's sake! I can't risk it."

Booker sighed. There was something to be said for doing it himself, he decided. At least he'd know if he'd been wrong about Alexa all along. Besides, he was developing a strong curiosity about her, ever since the trip to Illinois. Her personality was like a puzzle to which he had found some of the pieces, but not enough to complete the picture. He understood what had happened with her father, but nothing of what had happened to her since then, or what had led her to Arthur Bannerman. "I'll go," he said.

"Of course you will. And soon. Call her right away." Robert lit a cigarette and glared at Booker through the smoke. "There's one other thing," he said. "I've been meaning to ask you to go through Father's files in your office. And also to see if there's a list of his safe-deposit boxes anywhere."

"I don't think he had any that I know of. Why would he? He hated banks. A bank would be the last place he'd trust."

"I'm looking for something. I've gone through his apartment with a fine-toothed comb, I've been all over Kiawa, and I've looked in every goddamn drawer in the apartment. I've even had the archivist go through Father's papers at the family office, and everywhere I've come up dry as a goddamn bone."

"If I don't know what it is, I can't help you."

Robert glowered. "It's a document, Martin." He hesitated. "An accident report from the New York State Police. The date would be, oh, November 1967."

Booker recognized the date as that of John Bannerman's death, but had enough self-control to keep the thought to himself. "A police report?" he asked.

"Correct. Did Father ever mention it to you?"

"No. He never brought it up at all. I once asked him about John, and he changed the subject. What's in the report?"

"Never mind what's in it. It will be in a sealed envelope marked 'Confidential,' I'm pretty sure of that, maybe with my name on it. It's of purely, ah, historical interest. If you find anything resembling that, don't open it, just bring it to me immediately."

"DeWitt might have it."

"No, Courtland is the last person Father would have given it to. This was strictly between the two of us."

"I'll have a look. It may take some time."

"This is *important*, Martin."

"An accident report? Why?"

"Just find it if it's there, okay?"

"Miss Walden may have some of his papers, you know. It's quite possible . . ." Booker paused in mid-sentence, astonished at the look on Robert's face. It was an expression he had never seen on Robert before, would never have expected to see, but there was no doubt about it—even his tan faded suddenly, making his complexion seem sallow. For one brief moment, Robert seemed *afraid*, almost terrified. Then, with what seemed like a major effort, he recovered, drew on his cigarette, inhaled deeply. He gave a laugh—a short, sharp bark without any trace of humor at all. "No," he said, "I can't believe even Father would have done *that*. It's a family matter, Martin. Father would have kept it in the family."

It occurred to Booker that from Arthur Bannerman's point of view, Alexa *was* a member of the family—one he trusted more than Robert, for that matter—but he thought it prudent not to say so.

"IT'S *SO* NICE OF YOU to come and see me," Brooke said sweetly to Alexa.

She was seated like an illustration from Emily Post, knees pressed firmly together, her demure little black leather high-heeled pumps parallel-parked and neatly touching.

Despite her height, Brooke was built rather like a bird, with such fine, thin limbs that it was a wonder she could walk at all. How she had survived a WASP boarding school childhood, with field hockey, riding lessons, and gym, and still managed to grow up with such perfect, tiny ankles was a mystery of genetics. Every bone in her body seemed as translucent as old china, and as beautifully shaped. Her eyes were jade green and piercing, set a little too close together in her face. She was not beautiful: the ruler-straight nose and thin lips gave her face a Puritan severity that she accentuated by wearing her blond hair short, almost like a man's.

"I've been meaning to call you since we met," Alexa began.

Brooke bared tiny, perfect teeth in what passed, for her, as a smile. "I'm glad you did. Finally," she added.

"Well, I've been busy."

"Yes, so it seems. However, one should never be too busy to remember old friends, surely?"

"We weren't friends when we parted."

"We had a misunderstanding, Alexa, dear. I'll admit I lost my temper just a *tiny* bit. So did you. But I don't believe in holding a grudge."

Alexa smiled back to indicate that she too was able to forgive and forget—though in fact she would just as soon make it up with a rattlesnake as with Brooke Cabot. Theirs had not been a minor misunderstanding, after all, or a spat between friends. Brooke's good manners and white gloves did not prevent her from running her business with an iron hand, and she had made all sorts of threats when Alexa walked out on her—threats which Alexa had taken seriously at the time, and still did.

Brooke had been then, as now, cool, businesslike and bossy, so ladylike in every way that Alexa's doubts about the job she offered her had seemed not just unreasonable, but positively shameful. Brooke's office might have been that of a high-class employment agency, right down to the motherly receptionist who presided over the elegant waiting room and the impressive rows of pale-pink filing cabinets, which, as Alexa was subsequently to discover, were empty, since Brooke didn't believe in keeping records where anybody could get at them.

Alexa had worked briefly for her as an "escort" when she discovered that she couldn't make enough money modeling to pay her share of the apartment she lived in with another girl. A roommate had suggested it, and Alexa resisted the idea for weeks until, finally, when it was a choice between working as an escort or going home, she put on her most respectable clothes—a pleated skirt, a blouse with a high collar, and a tweed jacket, the kind of thing she might have worn to a weekend at somebody's country estate, had anyone ever invited her to such a thing, and walked up two flights of stairs to the offices of "The Social Register" for an interview.

Brooke had a way of talking about her business as if it were a kind of social service, a mission to the lonely rich or well-to-do, rescuing them from the solitude of their hotel suites or co-ops, where they might otherwise take to solitary drinking or watching X-rated movies on television to the detriment of their health and moral tone. After all, where was the harm in going out to dinner with a charming gentleman from Tokyo, or Dubai, or Fort Worth? Men did not like going out by themselves, it was a known fact, and The Social Register provided handpicked escorts for a handpicked clientele—for Brooke made it clear that her clients were chosen with as much care as her employees, accepted only on the recommendation of at least two existing clients, and even then only after a careful interview conducted by Brooke herself. "Our clients understand that this is an *escort* service," she had said firmly to Alexa, looking her right in the eye. "Nothing more, nothing less."

There had been a good deal more—working for Brooke, Alexa discovered, was like stepping into one of those animal traps with a one-way entrance and no exit. Brooke not only had charm, but an instinctive ability to discover and exploit your weaknesses, whatever they were and however well you tried to hide them, a strange capacity for appealing to your loyalty, even when you had none, as well as a ladylike way of making you look and feel like a fool for opposing her, or even questioning her.

Alexa had been afraid of her then, and had more to fear from her now. She took a good look at Brooke, with her sweet smile and her cold green eyes, artfully posing against a wall covered with paintings and engravings of earlier Cabots, and reminded herself that *she* was the widow of the late Arthur Aldon Bannerman, who, if nothing else, had taught her how to look the rest of the world straight in the eye without blinking. A Bannerman, he said, always laid it on the line—and was she not by marriage a Bannerman?

"I don't hold a grudge either," she said firmly. "You told me if I left you'd make sure I regretted it. I haven't regretted it so far. I seem to remember that you promised to destroy me if I didn't do what you wanted me to. That was your exact word, I think: 'Destroy.' However long it took, you said."

"I don't remember saying anything of the kind, Alexa. That doesn't sound like me at all."

"Then you have a very selective memory. In any case, it doesn't matter. That was the past. It's the present I'm concerned about."

"I don't know what you're talking about."

"I think you do. I think you're sitting on what you know about me and waiting for the highest bidder. That would be Robert Bannerman, I suppose. Or perhaps the tabloids? But I don't think you'd go to the tabloids, would you? Just a word to Robert, perhaps even a hint. What would he do for you in exchange, I wonder?"

"You have a very unpleasant mind, Alexa. I'm shocked."

"I doubt it. If the press found out I'd worked for you, they'd have to know about you, too. We'd be in the headlines together. You can't want that. So it has to be Robert."

Brooke gave her a level stare. "I have nothing to hide—or gain. I sold The Social Register a long time ago. I have no connection with it at all. I did keep a few records, of course. Just to be on the safe side. People who worked for me, and so forth."

"I see. I'd heard you were still in business, though."

"I have a few business interests, yes, of quite a different kind. None of them is any concern of yours."

"Maybe. Maybe not. You've always had a better head for business than I do. That nice little brownstone you rent on East Fifty-first Street, for example—three floors and a ground floor office—you got it very cheaply."

Brooke smiled, this time without showing her teeth, the kind of smile that could cut ice. "I don't know what you're talking about."

Alexa drew a slip of paper from her handbag. She had asked Roth for a favor, and he had delivered. "It certainly has a lot of telephone lines. You wouldn't be operating one of those telephone services, would you? Dial-a-sex, with an Eight Hundred number? I suppose that would explain the name 'The Answered Prayer Corporation'? All that equipment would be expensive to move, I guess. And you'd never find the kind of space you have, in such a discreet location, for the kind of money you're paying, not the way rents are these days."

"I fail to see where this is leading."

"What I'm trying to tell you is, you have a new landlord," Alexa said.

"I don't understand."

"The previous owners of the building just sold it."

"To whom?"

Alexa studied David Roth's note. "The Dovidel Real Estate Corporation," she said. "If that helps."

"Dovidel?" Brooke lifted a perfectly penciled eyebrow. "What a strange name. I don't see what any of this has to do with me. Buildings change hands all the time. I have a perfectly good lease."

"Do you? There's a clause in it about the purpose for which the space is let. In the small print, on the third page. The lease can be canceled if the premises are used for 'an illegal or immoral purpose.' I don't know what arrangement you had with the previous landlord, but your new one may not want to continue it."

"And the new landlord is?"

"Let's just say he's a friend of mine."

"I see." Brooke's face registered a wide range of emotions, none of them particularly pleasant. She finally settled on a saintly smile. "You were always cleverer than you seemed," she said. "I should have remembered. That's why I was so upset when you left. If I understand you correctly, you're threatening to put me out of business?"

"I'm not threatening you at all. I'm simply offering you a deal."

"That's what everybody says who's making a threat, Alexa. Do you know, I'd like you a good deal better if you threatened me openly? Never mind. What exactly am I to do to prevent your closing me down?"

"Don't talk to Robert Bannerman about me. Or anyone else."

Brooke nodded. She was a realist. She had been accused of many things, but never of failing to look after her own interests first and foremost. "Robert is sending somebody around to see me, you should know," she said. "Some lawyer named Booker. I don't think I should cancel the appointment, frankly. Robert would just send someone else who might be harder to deal with, not a legal type. I'll just tell this Booker he's been misinformed."

"*Booker?*" Alexa could not keep the shock out of her voice. She wasn't in Brooke's league when it came to dissimulating her feelings. She was appalled, not only by Booker's new treachery—for she had believed him to be sincere—but at her own bad judgment for thinking he was telling her the truth. She had allowed herself to be lulled into revealing the one thing she had never told anybody, not even Simon, and here Booker was, the same day, doing Robert Bannerman's dirty work, this time with Brooke Cabot.

She felt such a rage that for one moment she thought she was going to be sick. She had *liked* Booker, too—been touched by what she thought was his sheepish affection for her. Was there nobody she could trust? It didn't seem much to ask. Yes, she still trusted Arthur, she reminded herself. Given that, there was no choice but to plunge on alone and do what he wanted her to do. With some effort, she turned her attention back to Brooke, who, she noticed, looked scared to death.

"Are you all right?" Brooke asked, with what seemed to be genuine fear.

Alexa took a deep breath, and counted to ten. "Of course I am," she said, with as much composure as she could summon up. "Why?"

"The expression on your face . . . you looked so—angry. I won't tell Mr. Booker anything, I promise."

Alexa nodded. A promise from Brooke might not be binding, but if she had accidentally thrown the fear of God into her as well, there was a good chance she would keep silent.

"You'll make sure I don't have any trouble with your Mr. Dovidel, whoever he is?"

"I'll take care of it."

"Thank you. And by the way. I was only joking about what I told you at Hugo's luncheon—Arthur Bannerman was never a client of mine."

"I never thought he was," Alexa said coldly.

.   .   .

IT WAS NOT THE FIRST TIME that Booker had been exposed to Robert's anger, but still he was shocked by his sudden rage, since Robert usually managed to conceal his feelings under an even layer of polite sarcasm. His eyes were narrow blue slits, his hands trembled, his cheeks were flushed. He gave off an aura of violence.

"She said *nothing?*" Robert shouted. "How dare you come back with nothing!"

He stood facing Booker across the living room, his features distorted with anger, and for a moment Booker thought he was about to launch himself across the room and attack him physically. Booker's instinct told him to retreat slowly, as if he were facing a dangerous animal, but he held his ground. Brooke Cabot had been polite and apologetic. She had known Alexa a couple of years ago, they had been friends, she had heard a few rumors about her, friendships with older men, that sort of thing, but on tracking down the rumors they had proved to be untrue or exaggerated. Booker's relief had been so great that he had given almost no thought to what Robert's reaction would be, and, to his surprise, his divided loyalties gave him a curiously clearheaded kind of courage. "Nothing," he repeated flatly, expecting to be pummeled in the next moment.

There was a moment of silence; then Robert flung his glass with such force that it was as if all his tension were absorbed into the movement. Booker ducked, but the glass had not been aimed at him. Robert had sent it, with the unerring accuracy of a natural athlete, straight into an antique wall mirror, which shattered at the impact, crashing to the floor and sending shards of silvered glass flying through the room like shrapnel. It occurred to Booker that if a piece had hit his jugular vein, he would probably bleed to death on the priceless Aubusson rug, and also that, since they were in Arthur Bannerman's Fifth Avenue apartment, the mirror was probably worth several years' salary.

He heard an odd sound and realized it was Robert laughing. "My God!" Robert said. "You should see your face."

Booker put his hand to his cheek, expecting to feel blood, but there was nothing.

"No, no, I meant your *expression*, Martin," Robert said cheerfully. "It was worth every dime of whatever that goddamn thing cost to see it, let me tell you."

Booker thought he had never hated a man so much. Robert smiled, apologized, mixed him a drink, brushed a few pieces of glass off the sofa, and sat down, cocking one leg jauntily over the other as if nothing had ever happened. "Somebody got to her," he said. "I'm sure of it."

Booker sat down gingerly. "What makes you think so?"

"A profound understanding of human nature. Well, it's my own fault. I didn't move fast enough. I should have gone myself. I might have wrung the truth out of her. It would have been risky, from the political point of view, but maybe worth the risk." He lit a cigarette. His hands were steady now. Except for the glass all over the rug, there was no evidence of his outburst. He seemed in good spirits and at peace with the world. It occurred briefly to Booker that Robert was crazy, but he dismissed the thought. Robert was under stress, he told himself, and surely entitled to a tantrum.

"Well, then," Robert said, "what are our options?"

Booker took a deep gulp of Scotch. He was not a drinking man but he felt the need for it. He was about to take a second gulp, then decided better not. "Settle, or challenge the will in the courts. We could do both. Challenge, and pick the right time to settle."

"I'll talk to Eleanor. I'd prefer to fight her in the courts if it doesn't take too long. She might back down in court."

Booker nodded. He didn't think Alexa would back down at all, but it didn't seem worth saying.

"And our chances?"

"It's hard to say. There are precedents." He left it unsaid that they were weak ones.

"And the papers I asked you to find?"

"Not a trace, Robert. I've had people searching everywhere."

Robert put out his cigarette and stood up. "Be careful going out, Martin," he said gently. "Don't slip on the glass. If you'll excuse me, I have a call to make."

Booker stepped gingerly over the pieces of glass. It was only after he was in the elevator that he wondered who it was Robert planned to call.

"I HATE THE SMELL of those damned things," Robert said.

The man standing beside him made no effort to put his cigarette out. He did not look at Robert. His eyes were fixed on the lights of the 59th Street Bridge, as if it were the most beautiful view in the world. "Americans worry too much about smoking. Why?"

"Don't you read? It's bad for you. I wish I could give it up myself."

"Americans worry too much about health, I think. Cancer? It's an old man's disease. Where I come from, nobody expects to become an old man. So everybody smokes." The accent was Spanish, the voice soft, deep, with a conspiratorial undertow eddying beneath the placid surface. He spoke as if every word had great weight, a burden not to be released without careful thought.

"Health apart, it's good politics. I never smoke in public any more. These days a cigarette costs you more votes than adultery."

"Americans worry too much about that, too. A leader should have many mistresses to show his power. I have lived here twenty-five years, and still I don't understand American politics."

"You helped change them, in your day, I seem to remember."

The man gave a harsh laugh. "Change? What change? Castro is still in Havana, I am still in Miami. Your Presidents change, but for Cubans nothing has changed. You fight Communism in Angola, in Nicaragua, in Vietnam, you give arms for the Afghan *muzhaddin* and the Israelis —but for us, *nada*, go fuck yourselves. Maybe we should have been born Jewish, then *we* could have the F-16 fighter planes and the state-of-the-art antitank rockets."

"I'm not unsympathetic, Ramirez."

A sigh. Ramirez put out his cigarette, neatly field-stripped it like the soldier he was, or had been, and lit another. "What does that mean, please, 'not unsympathetic'? That's diplomats' talk. Kenn–ee–dee"—he pronounced the name slowly and with venom—"was 'sympathetic,' Johnson, Nixon, Ford, Reagan, even that gutless *cabrón* Carter, were all 'sympathetic,' but Castro is still sitting in Havana making speeches, and our people get arrested by your Feds every time they try to buy a case of guns."

"Well, you can't blame Nixon for being pissed off with you after Watergate."

"It was his fault, not ours. My men were asked to do a burglary. They did a nice, clean job. Who would have thought the White House didn't have the sense to take care of the Washington police, or the guts to get the men out of the country once it went wrong? Amateurs! Bunglers!"

Ramirez's voice was husky with contempt. "Conspiracy is a serious business, not a game you can call off because it rains, like baseball." He smiled, his teeth, white and regular, like marching soldiers gleaming beneath the dark, full moustache. "So, the girl," he said, getting back to business. "I have observed her. Not a disagreeable task, by the way."

"No. Not disagreeable at all."

"We put a tap on her phone. And also on Señor Wolff's. As you know. You have the intercepts."

"Yes. Nothing earthshaking there."

"Well, that's not our fault, Excellency. You order a phone tap, we give you a phone tap. What the subject says on the phone, that's not up to us. It's like fishing. You put down a hook, maybe you get a minnow, maybe a shark, maybe nothing."

Robert nodded. He knew better than to be sarcastic on the subject of Ramirez's wisdom. In the first place, Ramirez knew what he was talking about, his tradecraft was impeccable; in the second place, he was a dangerous man, and not just because of his volatile Latin temperament. Even among hardcore danger freaks, the CIA arms'-length-contract guys who ran covert missions in Nicaragua, the sanctioned thugs who performed "political" hits in Salvador, the shadowy counterterrorists who were indistinguishable from terrorists (and very often the same people), Ramirez was viewed in much the same light as a hand grenade

with the pin removed. Ramirez was "said" to have hit squads still operating in Cuba, he was rumored to have been the man who "supplied"
Lee Harvey Oswald to kill JFK, although supplied to whom was a subject never even whispered about, and there were people who swore he
had been seen standing over Allende's body, with a gun in his hand,
shortly after the assassination.

His reputation was so fearsome that few people would employ him,
and it had been Robert's decision to use him for his father's first presidential campaign that cost Arthur Bannerman, in the eyes of many
politicians, his chance at the White House. Ramirez and his men had
tapped telephones, cut off the air-conditioning in Hugh Scott's suite,
punctured the tires of Richard Nixon's limousine so that he was late for
a major speech, hired prostitutes to entice key delegates to special
rooms where they could be videotaped for instant blackmail, and were
rumored to have put LSD in the punch at Stassen headquarters.

Ramirez received over a million dollars from the Bannerman campaign fund for his services, thanks to Robert, and his activities brought
him to the attention of the Nixon team, and thus, eventually, to a
leading role in the Ellsberg break-in, the Watergate burglary, and the
abortive attempt to firebomb the Brookings Institute. Although not a
man much given to gratitude, Ramirez had a soft spot in his callused
heart for Robert, who had brought him back into the big time, and,
provided the price was right, there was almost nothing he would not do
for him, or arrange to have done, for now Ramirez was more of a
contractor for violence than a man of violence himself, having risen,
in the American way, to ownership of a Miami real estate agency, a
Mercedes-Benz dealership, several restaurants in Cuban Miami, half a
dozen office buildings, a flourishing motel, and an aviation company
which specialized in leasing aircraft for flights to and from Colombia.
He was contemplating the acquisition of a small bank in Fort Lauder-
dale with major growth possibilities, and correctly assumed that a word
of recommendation from Robert Bannerman would do wonders with
the Florida State Banking Commission.

"I searched her apartment," Ramirez went on.

"And?"

Another smile, as if Ramirez had just found a long-lost friend. "She
has refined taste in lingerie, I would say. What always interests me
about American women is this quality of *hidden* eroticism. You understand, in my culture, the erotic is on the surface, because of the climate. Women bare their shoulders, wear tight dresses, and so on.
Because of the heat very little is concealed. But here, you never know
what goes on beneath the raincoats and sweaters. Behind the Puritan
facade, there are all these fantasies of nylon and lace. It never ceases
to fascinate me, frankly."

Ramirez on the subject of American women was more than Robert wanted to hear in the middle of the night in a playground beside the East River. "And the document?" he asked brusquely.

"Not a trace," Ramirez said cheerfully, his eyes gleaming. "It was a long shot, I told you." He chuckled with self-satisfaction.

"You're sure?" Robert asked suspiciously.

Ramirez was offended, but he smiled gently to show that he was prepared to forgive Robert what he certainly would not have forgiven anyone else. "I'm a professional, Excellency," he said, his voice full of hurt. "I can tell you that the young lady takes the pill, wears a size Thirty-four–B bra, has about six thousand dollars in her checking account, and has an expired Illinois driving license, but so far as documents go, I didn't find any."

"I apologize."

"Between friends no apologies are necessary," Ramirez said, in a tone that suggested Robert might not be the kind of friend he had in mind. "So what do we do now?"

"Keep looking."

Ramirez shrugged. "And if we don't find it?"

"Christ!" Robert said, "I don't know. Booker screwed up completely, the lily-livered-son-of-a-bitch! And time is running out."

"You should marry her, Excellency. Then you'd have no problems."

Robert laughed bitterly. "Don't think it hasn't occurred to me, but I'm not even sure it's legal. . . . I've tried to win her over hard enough, God knows, but she's stubborn as they come. . . . No, you'll have to find the goddamn document, that's all there is to it." He lit a cigarette and tossed the match into the children's sandbox, to Ramirez's evident disapproval. "If you can't, you'll just have to terminate her, Ramirez," he said. He laughed again.

Ramirez did not laugh back.

ALEXA DID NOT EXPECT to reach Eleanor Bannerman on the telephone easily, and she was not disappointed. A succession of servants reported that she was "unavailable," for one reason or another.

Alexa left her telephone number and settled down to wait. An hour later she decided she was wasting her time. Should she rent a car, drive up to Kiawa, and confront Mrs. Bannerman? It was a daunting prospect, but there might be no alternative. But if the old lady wouldn't speak to her on the telephone, there was no reason to suppose she would see her, either.

The telephone startled her, and she picked it up gingerly, half hoping it was someone else, but there was no mistaking the crisp voice or the tone of righteous indignation.

"I understand you wish to speak with me," Eleanor said.

"I *have* to." Alexa tried her best to match Mrs. Bannerman's firmness, but was conscious that she fell short of it. "It's important for both of us," she added.

"Now that Arthur's so-called marriage is public knowledge, thanks to you, I would have thought it more expedient to communicate through our lawyers."

"I don't think this *can* be communicated through our lawyers, Mrs. Bannerman. It's about Robert."

"Anything concerning Robert you should talk to him about, surely? He's a grown man."

"Mrs. Bannerman, I can't talk to him, not about this . . . this is very difficult for me."

"Honesty is never difficult."

Alexa envied Mrs. Bannerman's absolute certainty that she was always in the right and had an answer for everything. It was easy enough to understand why Arthur, even when he was running for President, had always broken into a cold sweat at the news that his mother was on the telephone.

"Before he, ah, passed away, Arthur gave me some of his papers."

"He didn't pass away, pass over, or pass out. He died. At my age I don't require a euphemism for death. Such papers as he may have given you rightly belong to the family, and should be returned. Have your lawyer send them to DeWitt, or Mr. Booker."

"Arthur was anxious about these. Mrs. Bannerman, what Arthur gave me was the State Police report on John Bannerman's accident."

There was a long silence, broken only by what Alexa thought was a sigh, though it might have been static on the line. "That foolish man," Mrs. Bannerman said, with less than her usual snap, then fell silent again.

"You know what's in it, then?"

"I have no idea," Mrs. Bannerman snapped, her vigor restored. "All I know is that you're trying to destroy this family. If you're proposing to blackmail me with this supposed document, I warn you not to try."

"I'm not trying to blackmail you at all. Or destroy the family! Robert's been trying to blackmail *me*, as a matter of fact—he sent Booker out to Illinois to threaten my mother."

"Your mother?" Mrs. Bannerman exclaimed, as if she were surprised to hear Alexa had one. "I warned Robert to keep out of this. Have you discussed this document with anyone at all?"

"No." Alexa paused. "Not yet," she added.

"Perhaps you're more sensible than I gave you credit for." There was a pause. "You'd better come up here at once."

"Well, if that's convenient . . ."

"It is not a question of my convenience. As it happens, it is not convenient at all, since I'm expecting the whole family here, but it appears to be necessary. I will expect you this evening before six. You'll stay, of course. It's much too far to drive back after dinner." Mrs. Bannerman's tone made it clear that this was an order. "Don't think this means I am accepting your claim," she added. "I am merely doing what I think is in the best interests of the family."

"So am I."

"I find that hard to believe," Mrs. Bannerman said darkly, and hung up.

"I HOPE THIS IS SATISFACTORY, MA'AM," the elderly English butler said. "The Duke of Bedford stayed here—the present one, of course, not his father. And Colonel and Mrs. Lindbergh, though that was before my time here." He bowed his head slightly toward a silver-framed photograph in which the young Lone Eagle and his bride stood timidly on the lawn at Kiawa, flanked by Eleanor Bannerman and her husband. Standing beside Putnam Bannerman was a young boy who she guessed was Arthur; to her disappointment, she could see no resemblance between the man she had married and the grinning child in old-fashioned knickers and long socks.

The maid who arrived the instant the butler had beaten a hasty retreat also called her "ma'am," and hoped that everything was satisfactory. Alexa said it was—after all, it had been good enough for Mrs. Lindbergh and the Duke of Bedford—and was given a quick tour: a small sitting room, overlooking the endless lawn, with the Hudson River visible just above the bare early-winter tree line; a bedroom with an immense four-poster bed, the kind in which people were born, gave birth, and died; a bathroom which was comfortable, but by no means opulent, as if to make it clear that the Bannermans and their guests were not the kind of people to spend any more time here than was absolutely necessary. "Dinner will be at eight," the maid said, her eyes firmly fixed on the floor. "Cocktails are in the downstairs drawing room at seven. Will you need me to help you dress?"

"Dress?"

"Oh, it won't be formal, ma'am. Old Mrs. Bannerman—Mrs. Bannerman, I mean—always wears a long dress for dinner, but it's not black tie for the gentlemen."

"I think I can manage by myself."

"Well if you do need help, just ring. There's a bell by the bed. Or if you want your bath drawn or anything . . . My name is Lucille, ma'am, and I'll be looking after you. Would you like tea? It's that time of day."

Alexa glanced out the window where the light was fading fast under a dark sky. Despite the fact that the lawn was big enough for several football fields, there was not a single dead leaf in sight. She tried to imagine the number of gardeners that must be necessary to sweep the neat gravel paths, vacuum the immense lawns, brush the endless flagstone terraces and marble steps, trim the miles of hedges. . . .

In the dying light, the grounds of Kiawa had the glassy perfection of a painted backdrop. In the far distance where the lawn met the woods, she saw a figure move as if somebody was coming home after a walk. The man—she was sure it was a man, from the way he stood, hands in the pockets of his jacket just like Arthur—stopped, turned toward the house, and stood for a moment, staring, it seemed, right at her windows, then moved across the lawn at a steady, unhurried pace, vanishing into a pool of shadow. "Is Robert Bannerman here?" she asked.

"Mr. Robert arrived a few hours ago, ma'am. From the city," she added, as if New York were a remote and mysterious place known only to the Bannermans. She drew the curtains against the night and plumped up a few pillows—not that they needed plumping—one quick look was enough to tell Alexa that Eleanor Bannerman's standards of housekeeping were on some superhuman level beyond normal experience. "Tea would be nice," she said.

After Lucille left, Alexa went into the bathroom and unpacked her makeup. There was something about Kiawa that depressed her—not so much its size, she thought, as the fact that she was a stranger here, an intruder, in fact. Even if Arthur had lived to bring her here, she did not think she would ever have felt at home. Anyway, she had the feeling that Arthur was perhaps the last Bannerman, except for Eleanor, for whom Kiawa represented "home" in any meaningful way—and even he had preferred not to live here. For his children it was already part of the family past—none of them lived here or even showed much interest in visiting. And yet, she thought, if you took it away, the Bannerman family would no longer have a center. They would still be rich, of course, as individuals, but there wouldn't be the same kind of awe that was attached to their name; which came in part from ownership of this magic, privileged kingdom where dead autumn leaves were swept up as they fell and the ordinary customs of twentieth century America did not apply.

She heard a knock at the door and called out, "Come in!" There was a tinkle of silverware against china as the tray was put down. "Thank you—Lucille," she said, feeling, as she always did, a fraud whenever she talked to servants, and particularly *these* servants, who seemed to have been preserved in amber from the days of "Upstairs, Downstairs," or perhaps perfected as part of some experiment, like the Stepford Wives. She did not think she could ever get used to being waited on hand and foot by Lucille, or to find the right tone with her—and at

Kiawa there must be a hundred or more people like Lucille, their lives devoted to taking care of the Bannermans and their guests. Where did they *live?* How much were they paid? What happened when they retired? Who looked after such things? It was like being on a well-run cruise ship with no officers. The Bannermans, she supposed, never questioned these things, or even noticed them.

She walked into the sitting room, and heard a familiar voice say, "Milk or lemon?"

"What are *you* doing here?" she asked. She should have been frightened, perhaps even angry, but she wasn't. Robert looked so much like his father that it seemed, for a moment, perfectly natural for him to be there, sitting on the sofa, in front of the tea tray.

"I didn't know you'd arrived," he said, smiling. "When I heard, I took the tray from Lucille, and brought it in myself. I'm not above the occasional spot of physical labor. A man of the people, you see."

Had Robert only wanted to startle her, she wondered, with what amounted to a practical joke? It didn't seem in character. He poured the tea. He was still smiling, but his eyes were looking at her sharply. "The *real* question is what *you're* doing here," he said.

"Your grandmother wanted to see me."

"*Does* she? I had the impression *you* wanted to see *her*. About what?"

Did he know? Had Eleanor warned him? Alexa thought it improbable. Mrs. Bannerman did not seem the type to take anyone into her confidence, not even Robert, until she knew all the facts. "It's about some of your father's possessions," she said lamely, hoping Robert would pass over it.

He seemed to. "Does this indicate a thaw on your part?" he asked, as if he didn't care one way or the other.

"Maybe. Has *she* thawed any? Have you?"

"I'm always open to negotiation, Alexa. That's what diplomacy is about."

She changed the subject. It was Mrs. Bannerman she wanted to talk to, not Robert. "Was that you in the garden?" she asked.

"That is *not* the garden, my dear Alexa. That is the Great Lawn, to distinguish it from the one behind the house, which *is* called The Garden, for some reason. But yes, that was me."

In his country clothes he looked, if anything, more dashing. Actually, there was nothing particularly informal about them. He wore a tweed suit, a checked shirt with a plain tie, elegant walking shoes that looked as if they had been made by the best of London shoemakers and lovingly polished for decades.

He held up a plate of sliced lemon. She shook her head. "Milk," she said.

"You're following Eleanor's example, I see."

"Why were you looking up at my windows?"

"Why? Because they were lit. It's been a long time since anybody stayed in these rooms. It's sad, really."

For a moment, she felt his sadness, believed in it. She was almost tempted to hand him the document, make peace, accept his terms, whatever they were—then he put his teacup down, stood up, and went to the window. "You don't want any of this," he said. "Why are you fighting for it?"

"I'm not fighting. I'm carrying out your father's wishes."

"His wishes? I've spent my whole life hearing about his wishes. Now he's dead, and I'm still hearing about them. Just for once I'd like to hear about *my* wishes."

She couldn't see his face, but his voice was sharp. His good temper had vanished in an instant, and there was something frightening about the intensity of his voice. Then he turned around, his good humor apparently restored. "I must change for dinner," he said. "We'll talk later."

She watched him go, wondering what his ironic smile meant. He was such an expert at concealing his feelings that he sometimes seemed not to know what they were himself. Had he come here as a peace offering, or just out of curiosity? Perhaps he didn't know himself, but whatever it was, he had apparently decided against it, and left with it unsaid.

She had no reason to fear him, she told herself, but all the same, she took the police report on John Bannerman's death from her handbag, rolled it up, and slipped it into one of her calfskin Jourdan boots, then stuffed the boots with Kleenex, feeling a bit silly for doing so. Still, she thought, if Arthur had chosen to keep the document secret, the least she could do was to follow his example.

She drew her bath—were there people, she wondered, who seriously asked the maid to do it for them?—and began to get ready for dinner. She would wear a dark-gray Donna Karan knit dress, simple, unobtrusive, with a neckline that was neither prim nor revealing, and a hemline that was low enough, she hoped, to seem respectable to Mrs. Bannerman, and still attractive to Robert. She decided not to wear any jewelry. Eleanor Bannerman would certainly outshine her in that respect. She lay back in the bath, feeling cut off from the world and rather enjoying it. The press could never hound her here, she had no immediate responsibilities. Lucille and the rest of the staff would take care of her every need. It occurred to her that there was a great deal to be said for being rich—not, of course, that she *was* rich yet.

She heard a gentle knock on the door, then Lucille's voice, as she hung up the freshly ironed clothes and fussed with the tissue paper. It would be easy, she thought, to get used to living this way. She felt suddenly ashamed of herself, even guilty, for worrying about how she looked. . . .

All the same, when she finished dressing, putting up this time with

Lucille's presence hovering in the background to help out if she was needed, she couldn't help thinking that she had never looked better.

She slipped the diamond ring on her finger—she thought of it as her wedding ring—squared her shoulders, and went down to meet the family—her family!

MRS. BANNERMAN WAS SEATED in the center of the drawing room, wearing an ankle-length evening dress with long sleeves of silver-gray moiré, which Alexa, with a trained eye for such things, recognized as a Balenciaga. Despite her years, Eleanor Bannerman did not dress like an old woman, but she had the sense to cover what couldn't be disguised. Long sleeves hid her arms, the immense bracelets and rings took the eye away from her hands, and a diamond necklace, several strands wide, concealed a good part of her neck and bosom. Her earrings alone would have kept a family of four above the poverty line for a lifetime, and though she did not wear a tiara, she sat so upright that Alexa almost imagined she saw one fixed in the waves of perfectly coiffed silver-gray hair that must have taken the maids all afternoon to achieve. She examined Alexa carefully, head to foot, the sharp little eyes taking in every detail without the benefit of glasses.

"Come and sit down beside me," she said. The politeness of her voice did not conceal the fact that it was an order. "Will you have a drink?"

"A Perrier, thank you."

"You will not shock me by drinking. My mother was a teetotaler. I am not."

"I wasn't worried about shocking you. I just don't drink very often."

"Well, that's all right. I'm not in *favor* of it, you understand. My poor brother was a slave to drink. Of course, men of his generation and class were expected to be drunk a good deal of the time, and he lived up to that expectation. My husband was an exception, I'm happy to say. Today, I believe, it's drugs. You don't take drugs, do you?"

Alexa was startled. Mrs. Bannerman always took the direct approach. "No. I mean, I've tried marijuana, but I didn't like what it does to me. So I don't do it."

"I'm not prying. I'm merely curious. One hears so much about drugs nowadays, but nobody I know takes them. I suppose Putnam smokes marijuana, given the bohemian circles he moves in. He often looks as if he's about to doze off on the rare occasions when I see him here, but that may be sheer boredom, I suppose. If I asked him, he'd almost certainly deny it. You didn't deny it. I find that interesting, though I do not approve, of course."

"I don't see any point in lying. Anyway, in my generation, I guess everyone has tried drugs at least once, if you count marijuana as a drug."

"I don't know if I do or not. My foolish grandson Emmett made quite a stir by leading a campaign to 'decriminalize' marijuana—how I hate these ghastly new words!—but then nowadays, the Episcopalian Church seems to be run by lunatics and radicals. I could tell you stories about the Bishop of Albany that you wouldn't believe. But then you're a Lutheran, I seem to remember, and I have the impression that the Lutheran Church still retains some small vestige of common sense. I'm wandering. . . . Ah, thank you."

Alexa took her Perrier from the butler's tray. Mrs. Bannerman sipped delicately from a fine antique stemmed glass. "Sherry," she said. "I always have a glass of sherry before dinner, and one glass of wine during dinner. Never more, never less." Mrs. Bannerman seemed to treat drinking as if it were a duty, to be performed with exactitude. "We shall be dining quietly," she said, "just the three of us. Cecilia has gone off to New York. Young Mr. Booker, whom you know, is taking her to a play. Or so she tells me. Frankly, it would do Cecilia no harm to kick up her heels a bit, in my opinion."

Mrs. Bannerman's natural chattiness and instinct for hospitality seemed to have temporarily got the better of her dislike—either that, or she was simply starved for company, Alexa decided. It also seemed more likely to her that Cecilia had gone to the city simply to avoid seeing her. Apparently Mrs. Bannerman thought the same, for she added, "Perhaps it's for the best, her not being here. In view of her feelings about you."

"I understand her feelings."

"I don't see how," Mrs. Bannerman snapped, reverting to hostility. She stared suddenly at Alexa's hand. "That was Priscilla's ring," she said accusingly. "It's been in the family for generations."

"Arthur gave it to me. It was my wedding ring."

Mrs. Bannerman's expression was that of a snake about to strike. For a moment Alexa wondered if the old lady was going to demand it back, but Mrs. Bannerman gained control of herself. "You have brought disruption and disgrace into my family," she said, with an icy calm that was worse than if she had lost her temper. "Now you are here to bring me more bad news. In comparison, the fact that you are wearing a ring to which you have no right hardly matters, I suppose. Let us get down to business. What are the contents of this report that Arthur was at such pains to hide? John was driving while intoxicated and killed two people as well as himself. Robert was lucky to survive. How much worse can it be than that, I wonder?"

"A lot worse." Alexa summoned up her courage. "John wasn't driving."

Mrs. Bannerman put down her sherry and stared at her.

"Robert was driving, you see. After the accident, he changed places with John. . . ."

Mrs. Bannerman did not seem to be listening. Her face did not reflect surprise or shock. The only sign that she heard was that her cheeks turned a darker red than mere rouge could produce. It was anger that Mrs. Bannerman was feeling, but at whom? Alexa prepared herself for the onslaught, but nothing happened. Mrs. Bannerman's cheeks went back to the color of her makeup, and she lifted her glass of sherry with a steady hand. "Robert?" she asked quietly.

Alexa nodded.

"You're sure? This can be documented?"

"I can show you the report of the investigation. It's all there, in black and white. There doesn't seem to be any doubt."

"The police can make a mistake. Most of the local troopers are lazy oafs who didn't want to stay home and farm. Or they used to be, anyway."

"Maybe, but there doesn't seem to have been any question at all. Besides, Robert *told* Arthur—he admitted the whole thing. That's why Arthur had the report removed from the files. He covered up what happened for Robert's sake."

Mrs. Bannerman closed her eyes. When she opened them, they did not seem to be focused on Alexa, but on some faraway point in the past.

Mrs. Bannerman stirred restlessly. "It's not an easy task to be the head of this family," she said. "Arthur must have thought he was doing the right thing, but of course he wasn't—he was merely doing the *expedient* thing. And he did not tell me, which was the most foolish thing of all."

"Perhaps he couldn't."

A small sigh. "Perhaps so. Possibly I asked too much of him."

"You never had any idea?"

"Of course not," Mrs. Bannerman snapped. Then she paused. "I had a strong suspicion that *something* was being hidden from me, if I am to be completely honest. But I didn't know what it was." She sighed again. "Perhaps I didn't want to know."

She looked at Alexa sharply. "The tragedy is that poor John's memory has been tarnished. All these years we've had to live with what he did, and now you say he didn't do it at all."

"And you all blamed Arthur for quarreling with him that night."

"Yes. What a great burden Arthur took on himself. And how needlessly. By hiding one tragedy, he created another—many others. He should have confided in me."

"Would you have forgiven him?"

"I would forgive anyone who told me the truth. And who had the best interests of this family at heart."

"And Robert?"

"I am very fond of Robert, but John was twice the man he is. In any case, Robert seldom tells the truth, and he thinks only of himself. Shocking as this news is, I'm sorry to say that I'm not surprised now that I know it."

"What are you going to do about it?"

"Surely the question is, What are *you* going to do?"

"I want Robert to stop digging into my personal life or hounding my family. The last is the most important. I won't have my mother disturbed again. If she is, then I *will* use this against Robert."

"I will talk to him."

"I don't want us to be enemies."

"Enemies? Do you have me in mind or Robert?"

"I don't want to be anybody's enemy."

"I deplore what has happened, but I am glad you came to me with this news rather than going to the press. I cannot say I like you, but you have behaved sensibly, as I should have done. Which is more than I can truly say for Arthur. As for Robert, I do not think he will forgive you, but he will not go against my wishes."

Mrs. Bannerman's reaction was a good deal more reasonable than Alexa had expected. For the first time she found herself drawn to the old woman—a good deal more than the members of her family seemed to be—but then, she hadn't grown up at Kiawa under the supervision of those sharp and unforgiving eyes. "If I could run away from all this, I would," Alexa said. "Tomorrow. Tonight."

"You've considered that?"

"All the time."

"But you haven't. Why not? I wonder."

"I'm doing what Arthur wanted me to do, that's all. I can't run away from that. Well, I could, but I won't."

Mrs. Bannerman gave a ghostly chuckle. A faint smile crossed her face, making her look much less forbidding and years younger. It occurred to Alexa that Mrs. Bannerman only respected you if you fought back, which nobody in her family seemed able to do. "Spoken just like an Aldon," Mrs. Bannerman said, pleasantly enough. "Walden? Aldon? I wonder if there is some remote connection? That's the kind of question that old fool Baxter Troubridge spends his days laboring over."

"My father's family came from Switzerland. I don't suppose there's a connection."

"No." Mrs. Bannerman seemed disappointed. "Ah, here's Robert." She smiled at him, but her eyes were cold.

Robert did not appear to notice. He had changed into his usual darkblue suit. His face was still deeply tanned, despite more than a week of New York in the late autumn. Did he use a tanning lamp? Alexa wondered.

He bent over and kissed his grandmother, shook Alexa's hand and went over to stand in front of the fireplace, just the way his father had whenever he entered a room. The butler brought him a tray with a glass and a small crystal decanter just big enough for two drinks. "I went for a long walk this afternoon," he said. "I'd forgotten how beautiful it is. I don't care if I never smell another tropical plant again. If the President went down on his knees, I wouldn't go back to Caracas."

"I hope you would go wherever he sends you," Eleanor said firmly. "Much as I despise the man."

"I would prefer to serve in Albany, Grandmother," Robert said, giving Alexa a wink. "Grandmother is a royalist at heart."

"Nonsense! I believe in property rights, that's all. As did the Founding Fathers."

Mrs. Bannerman's tone was so sharp that Robert looked alarmed. "So do I," he said. "But things change. Even the rich have to adapt."

"I'm not against *change*. I'm against giving up what's worth preserving merely because it's hard to hold onto. It's not change I mind—it's surrender."

"It's not surrender to think ahead, surely? Where's the sense, for example, in refusing to develop land we can't even see?"

The mere mention of developing land had brought two spots of color back to old Mrs. Bannerman's cheeks. She appeared rejuvenated as well, as if an argument on a subject she cared about gave her new energy. "I won't discuss it, Robert," Mrs. Bannerman said angrily. "I won't *have* it discussed in my house."

The Kiawa Development Plan, Alexa remembered, had been high on the list of Robert's crimes in his father's eyes, and had divided the Bannerman family into warring factions. It had been at Eleanor's insistence that Arthur finally came out of his self-imposed isolation to take back full control of the fortune and send Robert off to Venezuela, where he could do no harm except to American foreign policy in South America, which in his father's view was beyond even Robert's ability to damage.

Strangely enough, Eleanor had forgiven Robert, whose idea it had been to develop a corner of her beloved Kiawa, and blamed Arthur, who had saved the estate. And that was not the end of it, unfortunately. Emmett DeWitt preached an inflammatory sermon against Arthur's indifference to the social needs of the poor, which found its way into the newspapers, and Arthur had been obliged to pay the developers' costs, which ran into the millions, and to defend himself against a blizzard of lawsuits, as well as incurring the undying wrath of Barney Roth, the most powerful real estate tycoon in New York. Saving Kiawa had cost Arthur money, personal embarrassment, and great aggravation—yet Robert still appeared to most people as the victim.

"Just as you say, Grandmother," he murmured soothingly.

Happily, the argument was ended by the butler, who appeared to lead them in to dinner, most of which took place in a silence made all the more acute by their surroundings.

The gleaming mahogany table could easily have seated forty people. With one end set for three, it looked even bigger, stretching away like the deck of an aircraft carrier. On the dark paneled walls were hung vast, gloomy old masters, mostly Dutch still lifes of fruit, vegetables, and game birds. Alexa knew they were valuable—knew their *exact* value, in fact, since Arthur had asked her to go over the inventory of the family's collection and bring it up-to-date—but they did nothing to stimulate her appetite. Under the picture lights, dead pheasants, ducks, grouse, as well as larger animals of the chase, rabbits, deer, wild boar, and innumerable fish, stared at her with sad, accusing eyes. Only one of the six chandeliers was lit, but there was a blaze of candlelight on the table, as well as a fire in the fireplace, as there was, it seemed, in every room in Kiawa. A cluster of maids hovered in the gloom at the far end of the room, like geese gathering on a pond at dusk.

After dinner, Mrs. Bannerman, who had hardly eaten anything, said goodnight and withdrew, leaving Robert and Alexa to themselves in the drawing room. The old lady showed no signs of fatigue—it occurred, uncharitably, to Alexa that her departure was deliberate. Perhaps she hoped that the two of them would work matters out by themselves, given a chance. If so, it was a forlorn hope. Robert's veneer of charm had thinned as the evening went on, possibly because of his drinking, and he did not seem in any mood now to negotiate a compromise.

"You and Grandmother seem to have hit it off better than I thought," he said, taking a deep drink. There was an edge to his voice, as if he felt he was no longer in control of the situation, or perhaps felt simple resentment that his grandmother still hadn't told him why Alexa was here.

"I'm not afraid of her as much as I thought I was, that's all."

"Really? Not many people have ever said that." He took another drink, then refilled his glass from the decanter. She guessed that Robert prided himself on handling his liquor well; but he seemed almost determined to get drunk tonight, as if he *wanted* to lose control of himself. "It takes courage not to be afraid of Grandmother," he said. He gave her a knife-edged smile. "But of course we *know* you've got courage."

"What makes you say that?"

"Coming up here in the first place. And it must have taken courage to leave home after what happened there. I admire that kind of courage."

She wondered how much Booker had told him. "It wasn't courage," she said.

"You lived through a terrible tragedy and walked away from it. *That* takes courage. I know."

"I don't know what you think happened," she said, "but you shouldn't have sent Booker to LaGrange to bother my mother. You had no right to do that, Robert. She isn't part of this."

He continued to smile, but it was nothing more than the reflex action of a man who prided himself on self-control. He wasn't drunk, but he had reached the stage where he couldn't completely hide his feelings. "I don't think you're in a position to criticize when it comes to meddling in other people's affairs," he said sharply; then he laughed, a quick, uneasy laugh, and changed his tone. "Booker exceeded his instructions," he said. "I was as shocked as you are."

She stared at him. "I don't want my mother hurt," she said firmly. "I'm still willing to accept a compromise over the fortune, but *only* if it's one that I think your father would have approved."

"Yes? As far as your mother is concerned, rest easy. But in the long run, you can't hide the past, Alexa, whatever is in it. You're famous now. The press will drag it all out, sooner or later."

"Not unless somebody points the way to them, Robert. And if someone does, I'm not the only one who's going to be worried about the past. Your father made sure of that."

The moment she said it, she realized it was a mistake, but of course it was too late. If Robert had any doubts about who had the document his father had held over him for so long, he knew the truth now. For an instant, she thought he was going to throw his brandy glass at her, so strong was the look of hatred on his face; then he simply erased the look as if it had never been there.

She said goodnight, and they shook hands formally, Robert as charming and relaxed as ever, but as she left the room she saw him reflected in a mirror, lounging against the mantel, his eyes following her.

THERE WAS A FIRE in the fireplace and the sitting room was warm. She opened a window and heard the sound of a car on the gravel, voices, then a silence that was hard to get used to after years of living in New York. She sat for a few minutes by the window, as she had often sat in her room at home. In New York you only heard noises loud enough to rise above the hum of traffic and people on the move. As a child, she had been able to hear all the small, low-pitched sounds of a farm, the movements of the animals in their stalls, the occasional mooing of a restless cow, a sudden screech as one of the cats pounced on its prey, the wind in the cornstalks. Here, too, once you got used to it, the silence was deceptive. She could hear the dry rustle of the autumn leaves stirring in the wind, a dog barking somewhere in the distance, an owl calling to its mate.

For a moment she felt strangely at home. Perhaps, she thought, the truth was that she had never belonged in New York, or any city. She heard a fox bark, a sound she hadn't heard in years, and was delighted that she still knew what it was. At home, the fox would have been making its way toward the chicken run, hoping to avoid the dogs; here it was probably fed by the gamekeepers to keep it alive and healthy for the hunt—still, a fox was a fox, whether it lived on Kiawa or in Stephenson County, Illinois. It was one of the things she had hoped someday to share with Arthur, a country dweller himself, in his own way. He had talked about coming back to Kiawa with her and living here. He would take up riding again, go for long walks, resume life as the country squire he had always wanted to be before the pressures of being a Bannerman drove him out into the world to find a place for himself beyond the family. She wondered if he would have done it. She thought so, and she thought, too, that she would have liked it.

Then, as she hung up her clothes, she had the sudden feeling that something was wrong. She had a sharp sense that her privacy was being violated, and the kind of irrational fear that sometimes comes over the most sensible people late at night, perhaps while getting out of the bath or going into the kitchen for a glass of orange juice, when, even though one knows one has drawn the curtains and put the chain on the door, one still feels lonely and exposed, and hurries back to bed to curl up under the covers. She thought for a moment and realized it wasn't that. She had the sense that her things had been moved, ever so slightly, while she was at dinner—that the room had been thoroughly searched. Everything was where she had left it, but not *exactly*—as if a ghost or a poltergeist had been at work.

She told herself she was imagining things, but still the odd feeling persisted that somebody had been here, carefully, methodically going through her things. She could not prove it—she had not taken any of those precautions you read about in novels, the hair artfully placed where a searcher would disturb it without noticing, the clothes folded a special way so it would be easy to tell if they had been moved—but still she *knew*. She stuck her hand in one of her boots and was relieved to find that the envelope was still there, and immediately felt paranoid.

It occurred to her that Lucille would probably have tidied everything up when she turned down the bed for the night and left Vanessa's clothes. Given the spirit of perfection that reigned at Kiawa, that was likely.

It was only as she was beginning to doze off that she realized there was a smell of tobacco in the room, the sharp, acrid, familiar scent of a foreign cigarette. Then she was asleep, and the thought left her.

. . .

"I'M IN A GAS STATION, at a pay phone," Ramirez said to Robert, his voice muffled. "It's safe to talk."

"What is there to talk about? Have you found the goddamn document?"

"Not yet."

"You've lost your touch," Robert said furiously.

"I can't find what isn't there, Excellency."

"It's *here*, goddamn it, I feel it in my bones."

"*Nada*, Excellency. I assure you."

Robert's temper flashed. He had put too much faith in Ramirez. As usual, he had been betrayed. "Don't '*nada*' me," he snapped. "Our arrangement is *nada*."

"We had a deal. . . . "

"Fuck the deal! I expected *results*, Ramirez. You screwed up. You can kiss your goddamn bank goodbye. No more favors. From now on you're on your own with the Florida Banking Commission, and the IRS and Immigration, too."

"You can't do that," Ramirez said, as a statement of fact, his lack of anger more chilling than anger itself—though Robert did not seem to notice.

"You watch me! Do what I told you to, or a ton of bricks is going to fall on your head, Ramirez." Robert banged down the phone, content.

He had no doubt that Ramirez would redouble his efforts. You could always rely on a man who was greedy—experience had taught him that.

ALEXA HAD DECIDED, at some point in the night, to go home in the morning, wherever "home" now was—there seemed no point in exposing herself to further hostility from Robert or his grandmother—but when Lucille brought in her breakfast tray, an unaccustomed luxury, she found an envelope on it, with a brief note of apology from Robert. In the same loose scrawl as his father, he regretted his behavior. "Grandmother and I," he wrote, "both feel that it might be in the best interests of the family if you could stay, perhaps for a day or two, and see if we can find some common ground that will avoid a protracted fight in the courts. If you think there's even the smallest possibility, I will do my best to try. I hope you will give us this opportunity."

The letter was signed "Cordially, Robert Bannerman," and there was no denying the cordiality of its tone. Alexa wondered briefly if Mrs. Bannerman had dictated it to Robert, but she decided it didn't really matter. The letter was a peace offer, and she had nothing to lose by treating it as such. She sent word through Lucille that she would stay, and spent the morning alone, walking over the property, or as much of it as she could cover, searching out the places that Arthur had described to her, constantly surprised to realize how much of what she was seeing seemed familiar to her from his descriptions, as if she had been here before.

From time to time, a car arrived—Mrs. Bannerman had warned her lunch would be a family gathering, so she was prepared for the worst when she followed the butler into the dining room.

So, apparently, was everybody else, judging from their expressions— particularly Cecilia, whose rage was evident. Only Mrs. Bannerman herself appeared at ease. Alexa's arrival had coincided, by ill luck, with one of those rare occasions on which Mrs. Bannerman gathered her immediate family under one roof, and she had been unwilling, as usual, to alter her plans. Alexa was here as a guest, however unwelcome, and she would be treated as one, whether she liked it or not. Her presence at luncheon was as nonnegotiable, in Mrs. Bannerman's view, as Cecilia's, and since it was her house there was no arguing with her. It occurred to her that this might also be Mrs. Bannerman's way of mak- ing—or enforcing—peace.

Mrs. Bannerman had informed her that lunch was to be "informal," whatever that meant, but if this was so, Alexa found it hard to imagine what a formal luncheon here might be like. The table was elaborately set, there were fresh flowers everywhere, including a massive arrange- ment in the center of the table that effectively prevented any of them except Emmett and Robert from looking at one another without strain- ing their necks, and the usual lineup of neatly starched maids trying to keep out of Mrs. Bannerman's field of vision.

She had chosen to wear a wool jersey dress, assuming that "informal" surely meant something quite different to Mrs. Bannerman than it did to the rest of the world, and was relieved to find she had been right. Mrs. Bannerman wore a jaunty pink Chanel suit with gold embroidery on the jacket, matching pink shoes, and her daytime diamonds; Robert was resplendent in a beautifully tailored blazer and a tie that signified his membership in some exclusive horsey association judging from the many gold-embroidered horses prancing on it; while Booker, looking glum, wore his usual three-piece lawyer's suit, apparently unwilling to risk wearing anything more countrified among people who could tell the right tweed from the wrong kind at a hundred yards. Putnam had caused a stir by turning up in an old tweed jacket and a pair of blue jeans, and had been sent upstairs to find a pair of gray flannel trousers; while Cecilia, as usual, looked as if she had bought her skirt and blouse out of a catalog, which was probably the case. Like everyone else at the table, she tried to give the impression that Alexa's presence was normal by ignoring her. Even Putnam, who smiled at her nervously, did not want to be the first person to actually *speak* to her.

Alexa had not seen Emmett without his robes, but even out of the pulpit his clerical identity was lavishly, if eccentrically, maintained. He wore a plain black suit that would have identified him as a clergyman anywhere, but just in case there might be any doubt, he wore a priest's collar above a bright azure shirtfront—or whatever that particular piece of clerical garb was called—draped over which was a crudely made white dove of peace and a fine antique-gold cross on a chain made from what appeared to be tabs from soda cans. Emmett's eyes, enlarged by his thick glasses, were the same color as his shirtfront. He had made a fuss on his arrival about wanting to have his Puerto Rican cabdriver seated at the luncheon table, but Alexa had the impression that he wasn't entirely serious about the idea, since he gave in without too much protest. "Jesus has as much right to sit at this table as anyone," he said, unfolding his napkin. There was a startled silence. Even Robert could not deny the truth of this.

Cecilia frowned. "If He appeared, I'm sure we'd ask Him to sit down, Emmett, but I think your driver's name is probably pronounced 'Hey–zus,' isn't it? I thought we dropped that subject."

"I was making a point."

"Well, it's a damned silly point," Robert said peevishly. "What we would do if Jesus, the Son of God, appeared here has no bearing on bringing a Puerto Rican cabdriver—a *gypsy* cabdriver at that—in to lunch with the family."

"Would it make a difference if he were a medallion driver?"

"For God's sake, Emmett, of course it wouldn't! He's a taxi driver, not the son of God. Even you can see the difference."

"He's a poor man. So was his namesake."

"What the hell does poverty have to do with it? We respect Jesus because he was God's son, not because he was poor."

"You don't think it's significant that God chose to have His son born into poverty when he could just as well have had Him born a prince?" Emmett's eyes glittered with lunatic intensity. His voice was thin, reedy, but embarrassingly loud, more suited to the pulpit than the dining room.

"That will do," Mrs. Bannerman said sharply, but without any trace of anger—apparently she regarded Emmett as somebody to be indulged up to a point, like an idiot child. "It's not for us to question God's motives, Emmett. In any case, I won't have religion discussed at the table."

Emmett's Adam's apple bobbed violently. Perhaps it was the clerical collar, but he seemed to have more neck than he needed. "As you wish, Grandmother," he said, tamely enough. "Of course I've always thought the servants should eat with us, too. We're all equal, in the eyes of the Lord."

"That's not religion, that's politics," Mrs. Bannerman snapped. "I won't have politics discussed at table either. Particularly radical politics."

The soup, like most things at Kiawa, required full attention. It was a jellied madrilene of some sort, and served with an endless number of accompaniments—a lemon wedge, sour cream, chives, black pepper, red caviar—so that every time you thought you were ready to eat it, a waitress appeared at your elbow with yet another silver platter. Except for Emmett, who spooned his up as if he hadn't eaten for days, the rest of the Bannermans ignored their soup altogether. Out of politeness, and because she didn't want a lecture from Mrs. Bannerman, she tasted hers and found it completely lacking in any identifiable taste.

"A simple country meal," Mrs. Bannerman said, as if they were all enjoying it. "It's such a beautiful day that I thought we'd have an indoor picnic—the sort of meal the French do so well. Your mother used to love that kind of thing, Cecilia. She adored France, poor woman."

"I don't remember anything about it," Cecilia said mulishly, determined not to please.

Why "poor woman," Alexa wondered? Because she had died young —or young*ish*, anyway—or because she hadn't been able to live in France? Arthur, she remembered, hated France, and especially French cooking. If Priscilla adored France, she could hardly have married anyone less likely to share that passion.

"When are you going back to Africa, Cecilia?" Emmett asked. From anyone else the question might have sounded rude, but Emmett's manner, and his clerical garb, made him seem like a kind of innocent whose questions were simply direct and guileless. Since it was impossible to offend him, nobody seemed to take offense at what he said.

"Soon, I hope, Em. It depends."

"Of course you're doing no good there. It's no use just *helping* people without organizing them to confront their oppressors. They should be out marching against imperialism and colonialism, instead of being spoon-fed."

"Most of them are too weak to stand, Em, let alone march. And who are they going to demonstrate *against*? They've already got an anti-colonialist, anti-imperialist, Black government, and it's starving them to death. Frankly, you don't know a thing about it."

"I know about injustice."

"I doubt it. Anyway, you know nothing about Africa."

"Uncle Edward loved Africa," Mrs. Bannerman said, with her usual habit of twisting any subject of conversation back to her family. "He spent half his life there on safari, and shot the Big Five I don't know how many times over. The natives worshipped him. I think they named a lake for him, or a waterfall, I forget which. I expect it's all changed now." She nodded at the butler to have the iced bowls of soup removed.

"Missionaries ruined it all," she said darkly. "That's what Edward believed, at any rate."

Neither Cecilia nor Emmett seemed about to defend the missionaries, Alexa thought, momentarily distracted by the arrival of an immense silver bowl with a starched white napkin on top of it, carried on a silver tray by the butler himself. Since she was a guest, she would be the first to be served, and could not help wondering just what it was. The bowl itself offered no clue: its contents might have been cold or hot, solid or liquid, soft or hard. Since they had just been served soup, it seemed to her unlikely that it was liquid, but then Mrs. Bannerman had eccentric ideas about a great many things, and perhaps believed that a cold soup should be followed by a hot one.

She didn't want to ask, nor did she want to make a fool of herself, but the butler was already beside her, his face slightly red from the effort of carrying the heavy silver. There were no serving utensils on the tray. Had he forgotten them, she wondered, or was she expected to use her fingers? Hoping that she was not about to be the victim of a practical joke, she cautiously lifted a corner of the napkin and reached in with her fingers. Whatever was in there was cold, round and slippery. She grabbed one and hoped for the best. "Hard-boiled eggs, madame," the butler said, as the one she had picked up slipped out of her fingers and rolled across the table toward Robert.

He retrieved it and handed it back to her, smiling. "Grandfather was fond of hard-boiled eggs," he explained, the first person at the table to acknowledge her presence. "It's something of a tradition on the luncheon menu." Indeed, she noticed that everyone took an egg casually, sprinkled it with salt, and ate it, except for Mrs. Bannerman, whom it was hard to imagine eating anything with her fingers.

"Some traditions are worth keeping," Emmett intoned. "Others are not. I think we respect tradition too much—oh, not the eggs, of course. Though what a waste, to boil dozens of eggs for seven people, when there are whole families starving."

"I expect the servants eat them, Em," Putnam said. "Probably they make egg salad."

"The poor get the leftovers of the rich? *That's* your idea of the social compact?"

"Oh, for God's sake, Em, lighten up. The servants aren't poor, anyway." Putnam stared at his cousin as if he had noticed his appearance for the first time. "What's that god-awful chain around your neck?"

Emmett preened like an ungainly bird smoothing its ruffled plumage. "It was made by one of the maximum-security prisoners in Attica. I visit there regularly."

"They let *you* in?"

"They can't keep me out. I'm a clergyman. The poor fellow who made this for me is a political prisoner."

"What's he in for?"

"He's alleged to have held up an armored car. Another victim of the system."

"That's not the fellow who shot the two guards and a state trooper, is it?" Putnam asked. "Mohammed something?"

"He is now Andrew Young Smith. He's become a born-again Christian. A very impressive man, condemned to life imprisonment by a racist society for an act of self-defense."

"I thought he executed the guards? Made them kneel down, handcuff each other, then shot them in the back of the neck? I seem to remember that's what the *Times* said."

"The *Times* is an organ of the establishment. You can't believe a word in it."

"Your grandfather felt much the same way after 1932, when the *Times* came out for Franklin Roosevelt," Mrs. Bannerman said, as usual bringing the conversation firmly back to where she wanted it.

Emmett hesitated, on the brink of pointing out that his criticism of the *Times* was from a very different point of view than his grandfather's, and Alexa could sense that everyone—even Robert, who tried to ignore most of what Emmett had to say, as if it were beneath his dignity to argue about—was waiting expectantly for Emmett to bring Mrs. Bannerman's wrath down on his own head. Emmett apparently thought the better of it and let the moment pass. He turned his attention to Alexa instead, apparently feeling it was his Christian duty to bring her into the conversation.

"You're very quiet, ah, Alexa," he said, hunting like everybody else for the right way to address her. "Surely Uncle Arthur must have shared his opinions with you?"

"Of course he did. I happen to have some of my own, too."

"One gathers they include wasting a fortune on a museum."

"Arthur didn't think it was a waste."

"But since you have your own opinions, what do *you* think?"

"I think he had every right to presume his wishes would be carried out," she said firmly.

Emmett glared down at her, the very picture of Protestant rectitude. "That's an evasive answer. I thought better of you. If the courts decide in your favor, which I pray God they won't, would you build Uncle Arthur's folly, as he wanted you to, or make some more reasonable use of the money? After all, there are children starving in New York, Alexa, not just Kampala."

"He knew that, Emmett. I know it, too. That was Arthur's whole point—he wanted the fortune *used.* He wanted to change people's lives with it. The museum is only a part of it. And it isn't an extravagance at all. If you combine a museum and an office building, and have a plaza and plenty of public space, the cost of the museum is about equal to the tax advantages you get on the office tower. We worked all that out. Then, if you license the reproduction rights to the artwork, and sell the reproductions on a large scale, with a mail-order catalog, for instance, the museum pays for itself. Arthur was very excited about that part of it—'bringing art to the people' was what he wanted to do. I suppose once the whole complex begins to make money, the profits could be turned over to some kind of charitable foundation. I don't see why not."

There was a moment of silence as they all turned this over in their minds, without visible enthusiasm, till Emmett asked: "Was that Uncle Arthur's idea, or yours?"

"Well, mine . . . the last part, anyway."

"It's a very shrewd one," Emmett said with a hint of admiration. "I had much the same idea myself, as a matter of fact. I wanted to sell the air rights to Saint James's Episcopal and use the income to start a charitable foundation, but needless to say, the Landmarks Commission and the archbishop stood in the way of progress, as usual."

"I thought it was your parishioners who put a stop to it," Robert said. His expression was as bland as ever, but his eyes gave away his anger. Emmett, in his clumsy way, had blundered onto the subject of the museum and given Alexa a chance to seem reasonable and intelligent.

"The attitude of the parishioners was most un-Christian, I admit," Emmett said. "Fortunately, they have very little to say about it." Emmett, Alexa noticed, shared the family's attitude toward opposition, a combination of arrogance and high-minded obstinacy. His opinions might be to the left of the rest of the Bannermans, but his view of the world was the same—he knew best, and anyone who disagreed with him was hopelessly wrong.

He helped himself to a piece of salmon from a platter on which there lay a whole fish, cooked, sliced, then artfully reassembled without its bones to look as if it were lying freshly caught on a bed of greens. Alexa had ignored it, both from a Midwestern dislike of fish and a real repugnance to eating anything that still had a head, eyes, and a tail. DeWitt had no such fears, or perhaps he was simply hungry. He ate rapidly, as if he were afraid that at any moment Robert might take his plate away.

" 'Art to the people,' " he said, between mouthfuls. "It has a certain ring to it. Not that I'm in favor of museums as such, but the notion of combining greed and cultural snobbery to provide money for the poor is an interesting one. I mean, when you come right down to it, that's what New York has become, hasn't it? People who've made money in real estate trying to buy the social graces? And what better way to do it than with art?"

He chewed on his salmon for a few moments, evidently taught as a child that everything should be chewed at least a dozen times before swallowing. "You know, Robert," he said, at last, having done justice to the mouthful of salmon, "this young lady has a good head on her shoulders. It's a better idea than I've heard for ages from this family."

There was a longer moment of silence—the calm before the storm—then Robert said, very quietly but clearly, "Shut the hell up, Emmett."

"Don't speak to your cousin that way, Robert," Mrs. Bannerman said in a voice that suggested they were ten years old.

"I will *not* have Emmett sticking his nose into my business," Robert said. "Or preaching to me. I don't need a lecture from a crackpot in my own house."

Emmett's normally ruddy face turned white. "It's not *your* house, or your money, either," he said. "The Trust belongs to the family."

"My father inherited it from *his* father."

"Yes, and though I had a good deal more respect for Uncle Arthur than you did, I don't think he handled the responsibility all that well—not if you look at the figures. Still, give him his due, he did *not* regard it as his personal fortune, Robert. He thought of it, quite rightly, as something that belonged to the whole family, as a trust that should be used to do good, on behalf of us all."

"I will not have you criticizing Father," Cecilia chimed in. "Particularly in front of a stranger."

Emmett tried his best to look apologetic without giving ground, while Robert tried to catch Cici's eye and hush her up. "I was *not* criticizing him, Cecilia," Emmett said. "He did his best. I have always said so, unlike some at this table. Perhaps it was not enough, that's all. As for Alexa, she is hardly a 'stranger,' surely?"

"She is to me. I'm here only because Grandmother asked me to be, or I wouldn't sit down at the same table with her."

"I'm not a stranger," Alexa said firmly. "Mrs. Bannerman invited me here. Your father married me. There's no law that says we have to like each other, but I'm not going to disappear just to please you."

Cecilia's nerves had been sending up small storm signals as she played nervously with her silverware and moved the glasses in front of her back and forth. Her complexion, which was still darkly tanned, took on a curious, blotchy pallor, and her eyelids were puffy, like those of someone who suffers from hay fever in the pollen season. Booker reached across the table from time to time to give her an ineffectual pat on the hand, but failed to calm her. She slapped his hand out of the way. "Stop that!" she told him sharply. He blushed and hid both hands under the tablecloth.

"You know, you have to hand it to Father," Putnam said, as if his mind had remained behind during the last few minutes. "If he'd explained the museum to us as reasonably as Alexa did, I don't suppose there'd have been so much objection to it. I remember, years ago, when he was first thinking about it, I talked to him about having a photojournalism collection, and he seemed pretty interested in the idea. Then, later on, he wouldn't talk about it at all. He knew we were against the project, so he simply hid it away from us. I thought he'd lost interest."

Alexa wasn't sure whether Putnam was an ally or not, but he gave the impression of a certain neutrality. He was not unfriendly—she simply presented yet another family problem which he would prefer to avoid.

"He never lost interest," she said. "He certainly hadn't forgotten about your photographs. He showed them to me. He was very proud of your work. When he started to think about the museum again, the first thing he told me was that he was going to have a permanent wing of photojournalism as art—a 'Hall of Living History,' he wanted to call it."

The butler appeared beside her with yet another tray—this time a large game bird of some kind, roasted, sliced and put back together in its original form, with its head and tail feathers raised as if it were still alive. She waved it away, wondering why the chef seemed to feel that every dish should be an exercise in taxidermy, as well as *haute cuisine*. She wished she had eaten her hard-boiled egg.

Putnam's blue eyes seemed troubled. "He was really going to go ahead with all that?" he asked. "I had no idea."

"He was *determined* to. He wanted you to be a part of it, as a matter of fact."

"Why didn't he ever mention it?"

"He was a very proud man. He thought you were all against it. He wouldn't have wanted you to think he was begging for your support. At least, I suppose that's what he thought. He didn't tell me everything."

"Oh, for God's sake, Putt," Robert said. "You're like Cecilia's dog. Throw you a goddamn bone and you roll over. I'm sick and tired of hearing about Father's goddamn museum."

"Please don't swear at table," Mrs. Bannerman said.

Robert seemed on the verge of explosion—he was a grown man, after all, and must certainly not enjoy being treated like a child, on top of all his other problems, but when it came to his grandmother, he seemed to have herculean powers of self-control. He sighed and took out his feelings by glaring at the butler with such ferocity that the poor man nearly dropped the tray.

"Well, there are worse things than a museum," Putnam said boldly. "At least Father wanted to *do* something. Make his mark."

"Make his *mark?*" Cecilia's voice rose, causing Booker to snap to attention like a guard dog on the alert. "Why is it that everybody in this family has to make his mark? The first thing anybody tells us is, 'Well, it's all very well to have been born a Bannerman, with all that money, but what are you going to *do* with your life?' Look at Father. He didn't *have* to go off and run for the Presidency. Mother begged him not to. . . . And she was already sick. That's the one thing I can never forgive him for, much as I loved him. Not to have come home when she was *dying.* . . ."

"Cici, he may not have realized she was dying. You know that." Booker's eyes flickered toward Robert. A warning? Alexa wondered. Or a plea to calm Cecilia? Everybody seemed to have forgotten her presence, even Cecilia, who was clearly bringing up an old, familiar grievance.

"Cici," Robert said, in the low voice one might use for calming a horse, putting plenty of space between his words, "let's not go into that again."

But Cici was not to be stopped. "I'll never understand it. We let him know, and he didn't come."

"It wouldn't have made any difference if he had."

"It would have, to her, Robert! You know it would. You gave him the message, and he went on to Kansas City anyway, or wherever it was, to make a speech to the Young Republicans, so she died without seeing him. . . ."

"It was a presidential campaign, Cici. We've been through this a thousand times. You have to understand what it's like on a campaign."

"Still, you gave him the message and he ignored it."

"He didn't *ignore* it. He simply underestimated the urgency. He felt he had to make that speech. And if it hadn't snowed that night in Kansas City, he'd have been back in time."

It struck Alexa that Robert, in his measured voice, might be telling less than the truth. She knew Arthur had blamed himself for not flying immediately to his wife's bedside, but he had also implied that it was not his fault—that it was another of those things that stood between him and Robert. Had Robert failed to pass on the message? Had he not conveyed the urgency of it because he wanted his father to make the speech? Either was possible, but what was almost certainly true was that Arthur would have taken the blame on himself and protected Robert, because that was what he had always done. There was no other explanation for the fact that Robert was prepared to defend his father's behavior in this instance, however lukewarmly. It had been *his* responsibility, and his father had shouldered the burden of guilt for him—and more important, the burden of silence.

Her eyes locked with his for a moment, and she caught a flicker of fear, as if he suspected his father had told her the truth; then he turned to Cecilia. "There's no point in raking up old troubles, Cici," he said, almost pleadingly. "We've got plenty of new ones."

But Cici, once launched on her grievances, was not easily deflected. "The point is," she went on, "he felt he *had* to prove himself somehow.

As a Bannerman he couldn't just stay put and be with Mother when she was sick. He shouldn't have gone into politics. Everybody in the family was against it."

"That's not true, Cici," Putnam interrupted. "Robert was his campaign manager, for God's sake! I was too young to have an opinion, but John was all for it. He didn't agree with Father's politics, but he still thought Father would make a damned sight better President than Nixon or Harold Stassen, and he was right."

Robert chuckled, apparently relieved that Cecilia had dropped the subject of their mother's death. "God, yes!" he said. "I can remember John and Father arguing about politics as if it were yesterday. John wanted him to run on a peace ticket, remember? Father was outraged. But, you know, he took John's advice on a lot of things. Ecology, civil rights, environmental issues, he'd sit and listen to John for hours on any subject except the Cold War and Vietnam. John made him read Rachel Carson's book, and damn near made a convert of him! Of course it wasn't hard—Father preferred a clean river to a chemical plant any day, and had no respect at all for big business. 'Greedy bastards,' he used to call them. 'They'd sell the national parks—or their mothers—for a one-point jump in the price of their stock.' No, I would say John wasn't *against* Father's running at all. He had high hopes of winning him over all the way by the time he got to the White House."

"I didn't realize he listened to John. I thought they fought all the time."

"Well, you were too small, Putt. You didn't know. John was the only one who could argue with Father and get away with it.

"I miss John," he added with a smile. He seemed absolutely sincere.

"We *all* miss him." Cecilia's voice was tremulous now. "Father wanted *him* to make his mark, too. And look what happened."

"It was an accident, Cici. Let it be." There was a note of anxiety in Robert's voice now, as if he regretted having allowed the subject of John to come up in the first place. "We were talking about the museum."

"The hell with the museum. It's just another one of Father's grandiose obsessions, a monument to himself when he didn't need one. He couldn't leave well enough alone. If he hadn't insisted that John go back to Harvard . . ."

"Cici, *please!* Not now."

"Not now? Why not now?" Cecilia glared at Alexa. "Because *she's* here? Is that it? That's the final blow, of course. We have to sit down at table, in our own house, with some girl that Father might just as well have picked up on the street, for all we know."

Alexa was too startled to react, but at least four voices shouted, "Cecilia!" in various degrees of horror, while Emmett closed his eyes as if in prayer. Mrs. Bannerman's voice carried the most weight—not enough, however, to stop Cecilia from flinging down her napkin and walking out of the room, banging the door behind her and narrowly missing the butler as he sailed through with yet another silver platter, on which Alexa desperately hoped not to see the head of any animal. A suckling pig or a calf's head, she thought, would be more than she could bear, worse even than Cecilia's insults.

"I'll go talk to her," Booker said, rising to his feet.

Mrs. Bannerman glared at him frostily. "You will do nothing of the sort, Mr. Booker. This is not a cafeteria, or whatever they're called." Out of the corner of her eye, she caught Emmett rising as well. "You, too, Emmett," she snapped.

"Cecilia's nerves . . ." Emmett said.

"Fiddlesticks. Sit down. It's her *manners* that she should pay more attention to, not her nerves. She was always a sulky child, and now she's an adult behaving like a sulky child. I will speak to her later myself. You're not eating much," she said, suddenly switching her attention to Alexa. "I hope you're not one of those young women who's always on a diet?" Her tone was as frosty as ever, as if Alexa had insulted the cook.

"I'm not very hungry, thank you."

"If you're not well you should take a nap after lunch," Mrs. Bannerman said, in a tone that suggested she was giving an order.

"Actually, I think I ought to make a few calls."

"Calls?" Mrs. Bannerman looked puzzled. "Ah, *telephone* calls. Use the study. There's a telephone there, and you'll be perfectly private and comfortable."

"I thought we might have a talk later on, Alexa," Robert said. "If you're up to it."

"Of course she is," Mrs. Bannerman said, glaring at Alexa. "You can clear now," she told the butler, as he opened the door and glanced in.

Alexa studied the silverware in front of her, hoping the meal was coming to an end. Judging from the fact that there was only a spoon and a fork left, with any luck the next course would be dessert. "If we're going to discuss anything in detail, I think I'd want Mr. Stern here," she said firmly.

Mrs. Bannerman nodded. Alexa's remark had been aimed at Robert, but his grandmother had a habit of answering before anyone else could, like a third player on a tennis court who rushes in to take a ball away from the players. "You should feel free to have whom you like, of course."

There was a moment of silence as the dessert arrived—an enormous and elaborate pudding, at the heart of which seemed to be a decorated crème caramel. Alexa, who did not have a sweet tooth, shook her head, and noticed that Mrs. Bannerman, despite her criticism of diets, did the same. Booker, ever anxious to be polite, helped himself to a small serving. Robert waved the butler away impatiently, and Putnam filled his plate like a greedy schoolboy. Mrs. Bannerman beamed at him. "*Gâteau Saint-Honoré*," she said. Her pronunciation of French was awesomely precise. "I remembered that it was one of your favorites when you were a little boy."

"Nursery food," Robert said contemptuously. "I'd have thought you'd have outgrown it by now, Putt."

"Some things you don't outgrow, Robert."

"Alas." Robert's eyes followed the butler as he left the room. It was just dawning on Alexa that the Bannermans governed their conversation by the movements of the servants, with a sense of timing that would have done credit to professional actors. Matters which could not be discussed in front of the servants were delayed until they left the room, by some kind of collective instinct. Mrs. Bannerman seemed to have an exact knowledge of how many minutes it would take until the servants appeared again. There was never an embarrassing break in the conversation—Mrs. Bannerman effortlessly guided it into a harmless channel for as long as was required, using her inexhaustible fund of small talk.

The door shut behind the butler, and Robert turned to Alexa, instantly dropping the subject of Putnam's taste in food. "We ought to talk before we sit down with our lawyers," he said. "No hurry, of course. At your convenience."

It struck Alexa as odd that Robert appeared content to let things drag on slowly, pretending she was a guest on a country weekend. Did he feel delay was to his advantage, and if so, why? Perhaps it was as simple as the fact that this was his home, his "turf," as Simon would say. It occurred to her that she had meant to call Simon as well as her lawyer.

Robert nodded, ending further discussion with a frown as the butler entered—at last!—with coffee. "It's great weather," he said, as if he were playing the perfect host. "A shame not to take advantage of it. You don't ride, do you, Alexa?"

"Not really, no."

"*You* might think of going out with the hunt, Robert," Mrs. Bannerman said. "They'd be delighted to see a Bannerman in the field again. Though I must say it's all changed for the worse since your father was Master. A lot of New York lawyers and stockbrokers with weekend houses up here . . . shocking seats, most of them, and poorer manners. And the women! Hard-faced blondes with too much makeup, looking for husbands."

Robert smiled. "Just what I need, Grandmother."

"Oh, get on with you! Anyway, it would be a good gesture. It *is* supposed to be our hunt, you know."

"I don't know . . . I don't think I have the clothes."

"All your riding things are upstairs, Robert. Maitland can have them ready for you in a moment."

"Perhaps. Actually, I'll tell you what I *would* like to do, since I'm here at the right time of year. I'd rather leave the foxes to the New York lawyers and their hard-faced ladies, and bag a few pheasant. I've missed that. Apart from polo and soccer, the Venezuelans don't have much in the way of sport, as we know it. The President of the Republic took me out shooting with him, but it meant putt-putting down some frightful jungle river in a fancy canoe, killing everything that moved on the banks. Not *my* idea of sport. I'd enjoy a day out in the field."

"Talk to McGiverney, then. He's *dying* to have someone shoot. He's always complaining that the place is overrun with pheasant. On the other hand, he won't stop breeding them."

"How about it, Putnam?" Robert asked cheerfully. "Game for a shoot? Five dollars a bird, for the biggest bag?"

"Christ, I don't think so, Robert. I haven't fired a gun in years. And if you remember, I never liked it all that much."

"You were a damned fine shot, though. Come on. It'll do you good."

"Oh, all right." Putnam gave in reluctantly but inevitably, as he always did with his brother.

"Alexa, you'll join us?" Robert asked.

"I don't know how long I'm going to be here."

"We'll do it tomorrow, if the weather holds. You'll have a good time, I promise you."

"Well, maybe," she said, feeling the pull of Robert's enthusiasm. There was something about the way he looked directly at her while he was talking that made it hard to resist. Besides, she had fond memories of tagging along beside her brothers through the acres of corn stubble during the pheasant season, with the dogs running excitedly in front of them.

It was odd, she thought, that her humanitarian feelings stopped short at pheasant, for some reason. She had never liked eating them all that much, sharing her father's view that a chicken made a better meal and was a lot less trouble to kill; but it had been one of the few things her brothers did that she could share in, and despite her dislike of blood and killing, she always had a good time, running hard to keep up with their longer stride, making a fuss over the dogs, carrying a big Thermos in a bag slung over her shoulder—for it was often cold in the early morning when they set out, a thin silver crust of ice on the ground that crunched under their feet and melted away once the sun was up over the horizon.

"If you like," she said. "Sure."

"Good," he said, with such relief in his voice that she wondered for a moment what he would have said if she'd refused.

IT WASN'T UNTIL she was in the study that Alexa realized this must be the room in which Putnam Senior had laid down the law to Arthur, and Arthur to his own children, the very room, in fact, where he and John had their final, fatal argument.

She sat down at the desk, feeling dwarfed by it. Cyrus Bannerman had been tall, and he had ordered his furniture accordingly. The surface gleamed with polish, six feet by three of antique tooled leather. Here Cyrus, no doubt, had once pored over his ledgers, and Putnam Senior had tried to run his billion-dollar fortune all by himself. This was in fact the same desk that had so impressed Arthur as a child and behind which he had determined never to be trapped when he grew up. There was a telephone on it now, an old-fashioned instrument without buttons or multiple lines, the kind of telephone you saw on television in late-night movies of the Forties.

She dialed Stern's number and was put through to him immediately. "Where in God's name have you been?" he asked.

She explained about leaving Simon's apartment.

"I know all about that. I told you not to go there in the first place. This is like a divorce case—the old-fashioned kind, before this damned new equity law, when what mattered was appearance rather than reality. The husband moved out to the Hampshire House, the wife stayed in the apartment, both sides hired private detectives, and everybody was supposed to be celibate until the papers were signed. Divorces were a damned sight more interesting when they were about sex and money, not just money. Why didn't you go back to your apartment?"

"The press was there. I didn't want to be interviewed."

"Well, that's sensible. Where are you now?"

"Kiawa."

"Kiawa? Are you mad?"

"I had to discuss something with Mrs. Bannerman. A piece of family business." She wondered if she should tell Stern about John's death, but decided that for the moment it was better kept between herself and Eleanor.

"Family business? It isn't your family. Not yet, anyway. If you don't tell me what you're doing, I don't see how I can represent you."

"I know. It was wrong. But I had to do it. Anyway, I think it worked."

"She talked to you? What was her attitude?"

"If the rest of the family were as reasonable . . ."

"The rest? Who's up there?" His voice rose with alarm.

"Putnam. Cecilia. Emmett DeWitt. Robert."

"*Robert?* My God, Alexa, be careful."

"Careful of what?"

"Careful of what you say, to begin with. Careful of everything. How's the atmosphere?"

"Well, a little tense. The only person who's made any real difficulty is Cecilia. I think Mrs. Bannerman wants us to come to an agreement. In fact, I was wondering if you could come up here so we could all sit down and discuss it."

"An agreement? I'd say we have a damned good case without giving up a thing. I think we'd win in court, hands down. And it would give me a good deal of pleasure to see Courtland DeWitt's face when we do."

"That's what worries me. I'm not sure I *want* to win that way. Not if the family will accept what Arthur wanted."

Stern's voice was cautious. "I suppose there's no great harm in talking, provided that it's without prejudice. What does Robert say?"

"He seems to be in favor of an agreement. He's been quite reasonable about it, in fact."

There was a long silence. "*Has* he?" Stern said. There was a note of caution in his voice, as if he wanted to say more than he could. "I'd better get up there right away."

Simon, when she reached him, sounded alarmed, too, and even more cautious. "I tried to call you," he said, "but it's a goddamned unlisted number. I left messages at the Bannerman office, at the Foundation, everywhere I could, but nobody seemed to know how to call Kiawa. Or maybe they just weren't willing to try. I thought maybe you'd gotten up there and been locked in a tower, like the Prisoner of Zenda. You *could* have called."

"I didn't think you'd be worried."

"Of course I'm worried. You're in enemy country. Though I suppose you can't come to much harm from the old lady. At least Robert isn't there, I assume."

"Yes, he is."

"Oh, Jesus! He *is*? Listen, be careful."

"Of what?"

"Not on the telephone. Is that uptight son of a bitch Booker up there, too?"

"He came up with Cecilia. I don't know about uptight, but he's turned out to be a rotten, prying little sneak."

"Well, be careful of him, too. Listen, I'm coming up there. I'll be up by dinnertime, okay? Maybe sooner. Make sure they don't set the dogs on me or anything."

"Okay. I'll have to ask Mrs. Bannerman."

"Don't ask her, Alexa. Do yourself a big favor and start *telling* her. It's your house, not hers, remember?"

"I don't think of it that way. I'm sure *she* doesn't."

"You'd better start."

"Mr. Stern is coming up, by the way."

"Great! It sounds as if you're getting somewhere. I'll call him and bring him up myself. And Alexa—keep your mouth shut until we get there."

He rang off abruptly. She was about to say that she wasn't at all sure Lincoln Stern would enjoy being hurtled from Manhattan to Kiawa at a hundred miles an hour, but it was too late. She was left holding the receiver, which buzzed, then clicked again. Was Simon, for once in his life, right? *Was* somebody listening to her calls?

She decided she was being paranoid.

IT WAS CHILLY OUT in the late autumn afternoon, but Robert wore no overcoat and didn't seem to notice. He loped along, taking great strides, just like his father, his hands deep in the pockets of his jacket, while she struggled uncomfortably to keep up, wishing she weren't wearing shoes with high heels. "Grandmother seems to have taken something of a shine to you," Robert said.

"I hadn't noticed."

"Didn't you? Well, but it makes sense. She was once an outsider in this family herself, you know—a young woman, damned attractive, coming to Kiawa as Putnam Senior's blushing bride—though I don't suppose Eleanor actually blushed, do you?"

"I don't think we're at all alike. For one thing, she didn't come from a farm in the Midwest."

"No. She was an Aldon, and we all know about the Aldons. To hear her talk, you'd think God was an Aldon. And who knows? Maybe He is. It would explain why the world is so fucked up, I suppose. Anyway, the Aldons weren't rich. They 'had money,' as the phrase used to go. And they didn't need to work for a living—they *served* instead. Did you know that at one time there were no less than seven Aldons in the State Department telephone directory? FDR once complained that if State took on any more Aldons the whole department might as well be moved to Boston to save them the trouble of commuting."

He laughed, setting off a raucous echo from the crows in the woods beyond them. "But the Aldons didn't have a fortune," he continued. "They certainly didn't have anything like Kiawa. Probably wouldn't have *wanted* anything like Kiawa, come to that. Who can blame them?"

He waved in the direction of the house, which loomed behind them as they crossed the garden, its vast institutional bulk glowing in the last light, so large that one of the early astronauts, a local Dutchess County boy, had been able to make it out with his telescope while orbiting the earth, and had commented on the fact on television, to nobody's surprise.

"You could have those goddamn things for your museum," he said, pointing to the horizon, where a series of Alexander Calder steel mobiles, each the size of a large house, rose against the darkening sky like grotesque visitors from space in a Hollywood sci-fi epic. Cattle grazed in between them contentedly.

"Father couldn't find anyplace else to put them," Robert went on. "Grandmother wouldn't have them anywhere she could see them from the house, so he stuck them in the pastures. I suppose they're worth a fortune?"

"I'm not a judge. Simon would know. But a lot of money, yes. Millions. How many, I couldn't say." Had Robert just conceded the museum? she wondered. Apparently. "I'd take them," she said. "Arthur had in mind putting one or two of them in the plaza."

"They won't be missed by anyone here except the cows." He paused, squinting at them. "Let's say you build your museum. Then what?"

"I don't know what you mean."

"That's what Father wanted—his damned museum, one more cultural white elephant in New York City. Fine. That's what *he* wanted. What do *you* want?"

"It's a lot more than the museum he wanted, and you know it. I want all that, Robert—and I want to be recognized as Arthur's widow. After that, I suppose I'll go on and make a life for myself somehow. I haven't thought about it, really."

"Well, you *should* think about it," he said sharply. "Are you going to live in Father's apartment, for example, and take a stab at the New York social world? Just having the Bannerman name isn't enough, you know —not for that. You'll have to give the right parties, make your name in the right charities, cultivate all the *grandes dames* and the society journalists, dress the part, wear the family jewels. It shouldn't be hard. You start with good looks, money, and the right name. What the hell more do you need? A lot of people would give their eyeteeth for what you've already got. Or *almost*. Christ! Put some effort into it and you'll make Brooke Astor look like a dowdy old has-been. Young, beautiful, rich— you'll be Queen of New York!"

"I don't think I'd want to do that at all," she said angrily. "I'm twenty-four. I'd like a *life*, maybe a marriage and children, the kind of normal things everybody wants."

"*Normal?* If you wanted a normal life, you picked the wrong goddamned family to marry into. Normal people don't lay claim to a billion dollars or build museums in midtown Manhattan. If you think some nice, normal feller is going to marry you one of these days, when you're over your goddamned grief-stricken widowhood, forget it. Money does strange things to people's lives. Look at Sunny von Bulow and what happened to *her.*"

"Robert, I am *not* an heiress looking for a title. I've earned my own living since I left home."

"Yes? But then you met Father, which rather changed things, didn't it? You're in no position to read me a lecture on inherited wealth." He stopped and stared at her—not exactly a hostile stare, but with a trace of hostility just beneath the veneer of easygoing charm, as if he had just noticed, for the first time, that she might fit in very well here at Kiawa, or that her beauty and intelligence were formidable weapons. His smile was perfect, but automatic—it couldn't be called icy or threatening—it merely conveyed nothing, except perhaps a moment of self-doubt, which he quickly covered up.

"Well," he said, "all that is your business, not mine. Grandmother wants a settlement," he added quietly. "She wants it all over and done with, as quietly and quickly as possible."

"And you?"

"I don't seem to have much of a choice, do I? It's really a question of whether you and I can deal with each other, isn't it?"

"I hope we can."

He did not reply. Ahead of them was a flight of steps. At the top, half hidden by the trees, was a strange-looking little building which reminded her of a gingerbread house.

"The Doll House," Robert said. "I'd almost forgotten it was here."

"What on earth is it?"

"Great-grandfather had it built when Katherine and Elizabeth were born. A playhouse, I suppose you could call it. Everything's half-size, built to the scale of a child."

"I'd love to see it. Is it open?"

He hesitated. "Well, yes," he said. "It might be."

He climbed the steps and fumbled in the decorative fretwork for the key. Despite his hesitation, he knew exactly where to find it. "Still in the same place," he said. "Nothing ever changes at Kiawa."

He unlocked the door, doubled over, stepped in and switched on the lights. Alexa followed him in, astonished to find herself in a child-size Hansel and Gretel house. The effect was mildly hallucinating—the furniture was built for children, but the house was alarmingly complete, with drapes on the tiny windows, a miniature table, even a well-appointed kitchen, with everything in it the right size for a girl of six or seven. At any moment, she felt, the White Rabbit might appear through the doorway, consulting his watch.

She had expected the place to be damp and musty, but like everything the Bannermans owned, it was immaculately kept up by some unseen hand as if it were used every day. Rows of dolls, most of them rather old-fashioned, sat on the spotless shelves, a miniature tea set was on the table, a small glass cupboard contained children's books and games. The ceiling overhead was richly decorated with painted flowers and birds, all in bright colors, and the general effect, she thought, was a little like being inside a cuckoo clock. She bent over and peeked through the window. Built on a hill, the playhouse commanded a remarkable view. She could see the entire main house, even with a little effort, by counting floors and windows, her own suite of rooms.

Behind her she could feel Robert's presence, magnified by the small space. For some reason, the playhouse no longer seemed amusing, but sinister. She could not help feeling, somehow, that it was a hideaway and that it was no accident her own windows were so clearly in sight. She felt, quite suddenly, trapped.

Two flashes of bright light appeared in the wall mirror, then vanished. "A car," he said, to her relief. "Your friends are arriving, I think. We'd better go."

She nodded. She wondered if she was suffering from claustrophobia —though it was not, in fact, all that small a space she was in. Still, she and Robert suddenly seemed to fill it up as if they were giants.

She walked to the door, while Robert drew the curtain. Seen against the tiny furniture, he seemed grotesquely enormous.

"I don't suppose anybody but the staff has been here in thirty years or more," Robert said. "A typical Bannerman folly, like Grandfather's teahouse, which I'll show you tomorrow."

He opened the door for her and turned off the light, but not before her eye caught a collection of incongruous objects right behind him, sitting on a shelf between two dolls—one in what looked like a Victorian nightdress, the other in a lace evening gown, both pairs of wide-open porcelain eyes the same startling bright blue as those of the Bannermans: a pair of modern high-power night binoculars in military khaki, a tape recorder, and two fresh packs of Gauloises next to a brass ashtray full of cigarette butts.

LINCOLN STERN GLARED DOWN at her from his towering height, his thumbs in the armholes of his vest as he paced the room, exactly as if she were a hostile witness. "You're as headstrong as the Bannermans," he said. "You've got a good, strong case. Let them challenge it. Time! That's what wins cases. Time and patience. Look at the Rockefeller girl who married the Marqués de Cuevas, then left her fortune to her husband's lover . . . it's dragged on for years, the children are middle-aged now, and half the witnesses are dead. The side with the most patience will win the lion's share, mark my words."

He had downed a tumbler of Scotch as soon as he arrived, and his facial muscles still seemed frozen, as if he had clenched them all the way from the city to Kiawa. She had forgotten what the experience of being driven by Simon was like to the uninitiated. Stern was recovering now, but at first he had looked as if he might drop to his bony knees at any moment and kiss the ground in gratitude that he was still alive, like a voyager of ancient times reaching the shore at last after months at sea. His eyes still had the glazed, faraway look of a man who has been staring at death for two hours. Simon lay stretched out on a sofa behind him.

"I want to settle this," she said. "Now."

Stern gave her an avuncular smile. "Of course you do," he intoned soothingly. "Perfectly natural. But this is a complex issue. I have only just begun to probe the surface of what's involved. There are hundreds of millions of dollars involved. Even if DeWitt were to cooperate—and he won't until we go to court and make him—it would take years to get a clear picture, and God knows how long to draw up a document that I'd be willing to let you sign."

"I'm not going to wait years."

"We don't even have a clear picture of the assets, Alexa. It would be a most unprofessional thing to do. Why the hurry? You sound as if you're afraid of something."

She thought about it. "I *am* afraid," she said. "I don't know why. Maybe it's this house." She paused and stared out the window, thinking of Arthur. "I thought we'd have a wonderful life together," she said sadly. "Oh, I know all about the age difference, but I thought I could handle that. We'd travel, we'd build the museum, we'd open up the house in Palm Beach, I'd make him happy. I mean, that wasn't so farfetched, was it? I wasn't *wrong?*"

"Not at all, I would say. Speaking as a contemporary of your late husband, he was a very lucky man to find you. And you're right: if he *had* lived, poor man, you would never have needed to know about the trusts or to deal with his family. Whatever Bannerman intended, and I think he was unduly optimistic, I suspect his family would have remained estranged from him, more so, if anything, and that he would have decided, very sensibly, to make a life for himself with you instead of worrying about it. However, it didn't happen. He left you with his problems, and possibly with his fortune. What you do with them is up to you."

"For two weeks I've tried to make sense of it all. I thought I'd do what he wanted me to do. What *he* would have done. But I can't put right all the things Arthur did to his children or didn't do, going back to before I was born."

"That's true, but it has no bearing on your right to the fortune."

"Yes, it does. It isn't *mine*. It's the family's. Robert asked me what I was going to do with the rest of my life, and I realized I didn't have an answer."

"You've been having a heart-to-heart with *Robert?*" Simon asked, from the depths of the sofa. "Was that wise?"

"Yes. I can't just ignore him. Anyway, he was right. The sooner all this is over, the sooner we can all go on and do whatever we're going to do."

"And what *are* you going to do, Alexa?" Simon asked.

"I'm going to stop hiding, for one thing. I've had two weeks of it, and that's enough. Did you know that Robert sent that sneak Booker to see my *mother* and poke around LaGrange?"

Stern looked solemn. "I'm surprised Mr. Booker would have done such a thing himself. One would have expected him to hire investigators. What exactly was he looking for, by the way?"

"Any dirt he could find. But when I realized he'd gone and talked to my mother, I think I knew right then this had all gone too far. I want it over with. I'm tired of trying to hide my family secrets, and I don't want to know any more of the Bannermans'. Who knows? Maybe Robert will make a terrific governor, if that's what he wants to be."

Stern shook his head. "He wants to be President," he said glumly. "God forbid! Albany would never satisfy him. Alexa, I understand what you're feeling, but you haven't thought it through. In my judgment, a court would confirm the validity of your claim. At worst, if the Bannermans fought you to the wall, you could still settle for a fortune. Who knows? Twenty, thirty million dollars, maybe much more."

"I don't *want* the fortune split up," she said firmly. "That's the one thing Arthur would never have allowed. It's exactly what he wanted to avoid."

Stern sighed deeply. "You've been under a good deal of stress," he said. "That is not a good frame of mind in which to make decisions, let alone concessions."

Simon chuckled. "Mr. Stern," he said, "I think you're missing the point. Alexa's beginning to believe this *is* her family, so it's hard for her to fight them. Isn't that so?"

"I don't know, Simon. Please shut up."

"Surely you didn't bring me all the way up here just to have me shut up? I assumed you wanted my advice. And Mr. Stern's, of course."

"I wanted your support. As a friend."

"Ah. Well, I'd support you if I thought you were doing the right thing, but frankly, I think you're off your rocker. If you let Robert know you're willing to make a deal, he'll take it as a sign of weakness, that's all. He'll agree to anything you say, then bit by bit he'll take control until he's pushed you out. If you threaten him—which I hope you're smart enough not to do—he'll fight back, as hard as he can. Mr. Stern is absolutely right. Arthur left the fortune to you, right or wrong. Let Robert dispute it. Wait for *him* to propose a deal. He will, you know, sooner or later. He doesn't have a choice."

"Sound advice," Stern said grudgingly. "You're sitting pretty. Why get up?"

She gritted her teeth. Homely advice appeared to be a specialty of Stern's. "I am *not* sitting pretty. I am sitting, in fact, nowhere. I don't even have a home to go to, unless I want my photo—and my address —on the front page of the New York *Post*. Robert seems to feel we can work together, share control in some way, and as long as Arthur's wishes are respected, I'll agree to that. I don't want a court fight, and I don't want any more publicity. Sit down and talk with Mr. DeWitt, Mr. Stern. See what he has in mind. If it's anything like what we discussed, I'll take it."

"It weakens our case," Stern said. "It weakens our case immeasurably."

"I don't care. Just do it. He's probably in the library right now."

"I thought this *was* the library," Simon said. "It's got enough books."

"This is the study. There's a library, a drawing room, a sitting room, God knows what else. Somewhere there's a ballroom, as a matter of fact, and I haven't even seen it." She rang for the butler to show Stern the way.

"I'll do as you wish," he said. "I'll make it as clear as I can that anything we discuss is without prejudice to our position. We are exploring possibilities, nothing more." He gestured to show how insubstantial the possibilities were, as if he were tossing pancakes. He paused for a moment, towering above her, his expression as melancholy as his namesake Lincoln's. "Tell me, though," he said, "do you *trust* Robert? I have to know."

She stared at the fire. The paneled room was dark, but not at all cheerless. The rows of leather-bound books gleamed in the shelves, the paintings were illuminated by picture lamps.

Strangely enough, it was one of the few rooms she had been in where there was no photograph or artifact of Cyrus Bannerman. Instead, here was a small and not particularly skillful portrait of Putnam Senior's mother, painted while she was still a young woman, presumably before Cyrus had made his fortune or was just beginning to make it. Her hair was pulled back severely, revealing a strong brow, her black dress was buttoned to the neck even more primly than the conventions of the time demanded, and she wore no jewelry of any kind. She had the same mouth as Robert, and something about the way it was set, combined with those dark eyes under full brows, made it clear that she was a woman not to be taken lightly, and that if she had lived to old age she might have been just as formidable as Eleanor.

"I think so," she said, looking at the portrait, in which, it seemed, the subject had managed to veil so much of herself from the artist, but the smile on her face was ambiguous, hinting of something more complex and secretive—exactly the same smile that Robert had most of the time, pleasant, but not entirely convincing or easy to read. All the same, Alexa was determined to take him—and his smile—at face value. "I have to trust him," she said. "He's Arthur's son."

But she couldn't forget what she had seen—or thought she had seen —in the Doll House.

DINNER WAS NOT MADE more festive by the arrival of DeWitt, who was full of bustling self-importance and glaring at Stern and Simon Wolff— though to everyone's relief, Cecilia was absent, pleading a migraine headache. Mrs. Bannerman indicated her disapproval of weakness by telling the butler not to bring Cecilia a tray. "If she's got a headache, she certainly shouldn't eat," she snapped with satisfaction, making it plain that however large Kiawa was, not a tray, probably not even a cup of tea, left the kitchen without her knowing it.

For reasons best known to herself, Mrs. Bannerman fussed over Simon from the moment he appeared with Alexa and Lincoln Stern for drinks before dinner. "You must be exhausted after your long journey," she said to him after he had shaken her hand. She spoke very slowly and loudly, enunciating each syllable as if she were giving an elocution lesson.

"Well, not really," Simon said, confused. "I had a rest, as a matter of fact, but I'm fine."

"You're young. You recover fast. I would find the change in climate disturbing, but I suppose you're used to it."

Puzzled, but pleased to be treated with such unexpected graciousness, Simon glanced around for help, but found none. "There's not such a big difference, actually," he said.

"I hope they've made you comfortable, Mr. Wolff." She pronounced it "Vulf," in the German manner, turning it into something foreign and exotic. "If there's anything you need, let me know, and I'll explain it to the servants."

"Well, I think I can manage, Mrs. Bannerman, thank you. . . ."

"I think it's a shame that here in America nobody speaks a foreign language, while most foreigners speak such *good* English. A great pity, don't you think?"

"Perhaps," Simon said desperately.

"You're too kind. I shall put you next to me at dinner. If there's anything you don't understand, you must ask me. Alexa should have let me know and I'd have had the chef prepare something special for you, to make you feel at home. Ah, well, perhaps tomorrow, if you're staying."

"She thinks I'm a foreigner," Simon whispered to Alexa.

"I don't see why. I only said you were in the art business."

"Maybe she thinks all art dealers are foreigners," Simon said, but before he could pursue the matter, Mrs. Bannerman, playing the perfect hostess, called him back to her side to subject him to a detailed inquisition on the value of the Bannerman paintings, speaking so slowly and loudly, and with so many pauses in case repetition was necessary, that she might have been talking to a child.

Was Mrs. Bannerman eccentric, or merely having a good time at Simon's expense? Alexa wondered. There seemed no way to know. Simon was in such awe of her that he was gradually, obediently, turning himself into a European for her benefit, as if at any moment he might lean over and kiss her hand or ask for cold ham and cheese for breakfast.

"I have to talk to you," Booker said.

She turned to find herself facing him, at close quarters for the first time since her arrival. "I can't imagine what you'd have to say that I'd want to hear. If it's another apology, I don't want it."

"Well, I do owe you an apology, but that's not what I wanted to say."

"The hell with your apology, Booker! You sneaked around LaGrange spying on me, you forced your way into my mother's house, then after you came around to show your *concern* for me, you went off digging for dirt with Brooke Cabot. I trusted you! You ought to be disbarred."

"I can understand how you feel."

"I doubt it. I can see now why Cecilia went to Africa instead of marrying you. I'd go to the North Pole, if I had to."

"Listen to me, please. I *agree* with you. I'm sorry. You have to leave."

She stared at him. "What do you mean, 'have to leave'? What are you talking about?"

"Just take my word for it. Robert's not going to make a deal with you. I can feel it in my bones."

"That's not what Mr. Stern tells me. It's not what *Robert* tells me, for that matter. Anyway, I hate the word 'deal.' We're trying to negotiate an arrangement that will save both sides an expensive lawsuit and a lot of unpleasant publicity. A 'deal' sounds cheap and nasty." She paused. "Or maybe it just sounds cheap and nasty coming from *you*."

"Look, you don't like what I did, I understand. I didn't like doing it. But who wanted it done? Have you asked yourself that?"

"I have. Robert has already apologized. He also mentioned that you went far beyond anything he'd told you to do. He was shocked that you went to see my mother."

"Shocked? He wasn't shocked at all. Listen to me: Go back to New

York. Let Stern stay here. Go after dinner. Simon can drive you back. *I'll* drive you back."

"I don't have any intention of going. I think you're just making trouble, maybe because Cecilia asked you to, or maybe because you're just a born troublemaker. Either that or you've got some ax to grind of your own."

"Alexa, you're making a mistake."

"Am I interrupting? What mistake?" Robert glided into touching distance like a sleek cruiser pulling into a dock past smaller, less powerful vessels.

"We were talking about Mr. Booker's skills as an investigator," Alexa said.

Robert laughed, though he gave Booker a stare that brought a glaze of mist to the poor man's glasses. "Water under the bridge," Robert boomed. "The first lesson of politics is to forget what happened yesterday. Did Booker tell you that Stern and I had a good chat?"

"No, he didn't."

"Well, he should have. DeWitt joined us, and we made some real progress. I can't say DeWitt was much help, but then whenever was he? Booker, there's a good feller, would you let us be, for a moment? Thanks."

Booker withdrew reluctantly. "Don't forget what I told you," he said, with desperate urgency, it seemed to her.

"To tell you the truth, I've just about had it with Booker," Robert said. "He far exceeded his authority in running off to LaGrange like that, and now he's behaving in a very peculiar manner. If it weren't for my sister, I'd have gotten rid of him long ago. Of course, she won't marry the poor man, but she also won't let him go. It did occur to me to ask if there was something personal between the two of you."

"Personal? Of course there isn't. I only *met* him two weeks ago, at your father's funeral. What makes you ask that?"

"Oh, I wasn't thinking of *you*, I was thinking of him. From the very first, right there at the goddamned *funeral*, for Christ's sake, I think he was attracted to you. Easy to understand, but in damned poor taste. You probably didn't notice, given the occasion, but I did. He's an odd feller, Booker. When you didn't respond—and why the hell should you have?—he turned against you, quite sharply, in fact. I'm going to have to cut him loose, I'm afraid. He's simply not trustworthy." He sighed. "Grandmother seems to like your friend Simon," he said.

"She thinks he's a foreigner."

"Yes, well, of course, in a way he *is*, isn't he? So is Booker. That's his problem. He's been part of the family for years—or as good as—yet he still doesn't *belong* here. Look, your fellow Stern and DeWitt are going to spend the day tomorrow putting everything down on paper—I expect

Stern will discuss it all with you tonight after dinner. We'll spend a day in the field tomorrow—the weather's supposed to be marvelous—and who knows? By the time we get back, we may have something we can both sign. And more important, live with."

"Booker isn't included?"

"Frankly, I think better *not*. The sooner he goes back to New York, the better. Besides, Stern won't want to be outnumbered. If DeWitt has Booker with him, then Stern will have to bring somebody of his own up from the city, and we'll have a dozen lawyers doing the work of two. When all this is over, there's no reason why we can't get to know each other a little better. Much of what we both want will depend on a good relationship between us. We can disagree—I'm sure we will, from time to time—but as friends, as equals."

"That's exactly what I want. Nothing more. Or less."

"Well put." He patted her shoulder. "We're going to get along just fine." He glanced around the room. "Emmett," he sighed. "God, it would have amused John to see him here. He used to tease poor Emmett the way a bullfighter teases a bull!" Robert knocked back his Scotch and grimaced. Had he been drinking hard? Like many big men —like his father—he seemed able to consume a lot of alcohol without showing much effect, but it did occur to her that whenever she saw him he was either finishing a drink or starting one. "John liked Emmett," he said, as if that were a miraculous feat, almost saintly. "Of course, John liked everyone," he added, with an edge of contempt, or perhaps envy. "And everyone liked *him*, the poor son of a bitch." He shook his head. "Grandmother doted on him. He could do no wrong."

"Why 'poor son of a bitch'? I thought you liked him, too."

"Correction. I *loved* him. 'Poor son of a bitch' because he's dead. You can't get unluckier than that."

"It still bothers you, after all these years?"

He nodded. "When I'm here, I think about it. It's one of the many reasons I don't come here often. You can understand that. I imagine it's why *you* don't go home, isn't it?"

She stared at him for a moment, wondering how much he had guessed from what Booker told him, and more important, what he was trying to say. "You mean my father's suicide?" she asked, surprised that she was able to say the word. "Yes. That's the reason why I don't go home. But John didn't commit suicide, did he? It was an accident."

"Of *course* it was an accident," Robert said with vehemence. His eyes narrowed, as if he were looking at her hard, trying to memorize her features. He might have been a witness confronted with a police photograph, concentrating on whether this was the right woman. "You were with your father when it happened, Booker told me?" he said, taking her hand, squeezing it hard. "A terrible thing."

"I don't want to talk about it, Robert."

"No, no. That's the point I'm trying to make. I was *with* John. Sitting right beside him. We both know what it's like, you see. We've each been through the same experience."

"Maybe. I really don't want to talk about it."

"I can understand that. Nobody ever wanted to talk about John's death, either—least of all me. Father virtually took an oath of silence, as if it never happened. And yet he talked to *you* about it. Did he tell you the whole story? Paint the scene? Poor John, getting drunker by the minute, in this very room, Father building himself up into a rage, with Grandmother, as usual, pretending that everything was perfectly normal, just your usual Bannerman pre-dinner family chat, only would somebody just slip out and tell Maitland to keep the servants away for a few minutes, and hold dinner until she rang? . . ."

Robert *was* drunk, she decided. Drunk and angry, but still in control of himself. He must have hated the meeting with Stern, hated having to be pleasant while he bargained away what was, in his mind, his own inheritance, made room in the family for a stranger, accepted finally the fact that it was this or a long court fight that he might lose. He had hoped she'd give in under pressure, or that Booker would produce something solid enough to *make* her give up—and now, finally, it was over, or almost, and the most galling thing must be to know, as he surely did, that it was only her willingness to settle that would make it possible for him to keep his position and his place in the family, that he was accepting his partial victory at her hands, as a gift, while she still held the winning card.

"He told me about it, about everything. He trusted me, Robert. More than my own father did. More than anyone ever has."

He smiled, or tried to, for his expression was more of a grimace, perhaps because of the drink. "Ah," he said, a little thickly, "trust! It's a wonderful thing! I envy you." The smile gave way to his usual bland expression. "I'm not good at trusting people, myself. Or so I've been told."

"You could learn."

"Maybe." He gave a loud laugh, which seemed to her more sinister than humorous. "I may need a helping hand, though," he said, winking.

She edged her way, as politely as possible, away from him. Perhaps because she did not drink herself, people who drank too much made her nervous—and besides, Robert's comment about trust reminded her of the document, which she still hadn't decided what to do with, and which was obviously on his mind. Of *course* he couldn't trust her, so long as she had it, but could she trust him enough to hand it over to him? She could have it copied of course, but that would hardly be an act of good faith.

If things worked out between them, *when* (for she was an optimist) she had learned to trust him, she would give it to him.

In the meantime, the safe, sensible thing was to hold onto it, she decided.

SHE SLEPT UNEASILY, kept awake not by the dinner, of which she had eaten very little, nor by the conversation, which had mostly been dominated by old Mrs. Bannerman explaining American customs, history, and folklore to Simon, but by Robert's unexpected remark.

Did he really think they had something in common—two people who had killed someone they loved, both in a sense "accidental deaths," but in fact, though it was a word she never applied to what had happened between herself and her father, "homicides"? Robert had driven carelessly, and cost his brother and two innocent people their lives.

She—but she refused to consider what she had done, refused even to let her mind wander in that direction.

Around her the big house creaked and groaned, full of small, odd noises, like a ship at sea. It was strange, she thought, that something so huge and substantial should produce any noise at all, as if one of the Pyramids might produce the same kind of nighttime noise as an old farmhouse in the wind. She could hear the creak of wood as the temperature dropped a few degrees, the stir of trees against a slate roof, the hum of air in the heater vents, from somewhere far away the sound of a pump or a fan, the padded footsteps of a servant making the nightly rounds—for there was always somebody on call here twenty-four hours a day, as if it were a hotel, and a push of the button on the bedside table would—eventually—summon somebody, in case one wanted a pot of tea or a cup of cocoa, or simply, in Mrs. Bannerman's case, wanted to know what time it was.

Tomorrow, she decided, when her business was completed, she would leave right away, get Stern or Simon to book her into one of the more discreet midtown hotels, the Dorset, perhaps, or the Hampshire House, and stay out of sight for a while. Gradually, step by step, she would return to normal life.

No, to be more exact, she would start a *new* one, for things would certainly not be the same. She would need an office to oversee the building of the museum—Simon could help with that. With time, perhaps, she would be accepted as a Bannerman, as indeed Mrs. Bannerman had all but done. And then what? She refused to think that far ahead.

She closed her eyes and heard, quite suddenly, the noise of people walking on the gravel outside—two people talking.

The voices were hushed, but it sounded like a man and a woman.

Then they died away and she fell asleep, telling herself that there was no reason to think they were talking about *her*.

"IT'S CRAVEN SURRENDER, Robert—nothing less."

"It's common sense, Cici," Robert said wearily. "I don't like it any better than you do."

"She's a scheming little tramp, and you're giving in to her. I never thought I'd live to see the day."

Robert sighed. They reached the end of the graveled courtyard, then turned to walk back again. He could not see her expression in the dark, but her eyes were gleaming, as if she were crying. "If we let it drag on, Cici," he explained patiently, "she might win. Father *did* marry her."

"I refuse to believe that. Or accept it."

"Belief has nothing to do with it. Booker thinks the marriage is valid."

"Oh, I could just *kill* Martin!" Even in the moonlight, Cecilia's eyes flashed with rage. "He's been *useless*. I can't imagine how I could ever have let myself think of marrying him. But *you*, Robert, *you're* the real disappointment! You're allowing her to walk all over you, just because she's a pretty girl." She paused. "In a common sort of way."

"She doesn't look common at all, Cici. I quite like the way she looks. Ramirez—you remember him?—even suggested I marry her!" He laughed. "Not a bad solution to the problem, actually."

"That's disgusting!"

"I'm joking, Cici."

"I don't find it funny. Surely you can *do* something, Robert, instead of trading jokes with your Cuban friends."

"It's not that easy. She's smarter than you give her credit for, Cici. She's got some documents in her possession that I'd very much like to get back."

"Do you mean to say that she's *blackmailing* you, Robert? Is that the reason for your spinelessness?"

"Not exactly blackmailing me, no, Cici. 'Threatening' might be a better word."

"With what?"

He was sorry now that he had brought the subject up. If Cecilia knew the truth about John's death, she would never forgive him—he feared the possibility of her learning about it far more than the effect it would have on his political career.

"Political stuff," he said, as casually as possible. "Father gave it to her. Unwisely."

"Can't Ramirez get it back? You used to say he could do anything." Cecilia had met Ramirez when she was hardly more than a child, in the old days, when he was still a certified hero to tough-minded patriots who believed the Bay of Pigs landing would have succeeded if Jack Kennedy had had the guts to send in air cover. That had been her father's opinion at the time; like many wealthy Americans Arthur Bannerman had been happy to invite the dashing Cuban hero into his home, and to write out a check for *la causa*. Ramirez's subsequent descent into the world of political assassination and contract killing had escaped Cecilia's attention. On the rare occasions when his name came up, she still talked about him as if he were a kind of Hispanic, anti-Communist Sir Galahad, a reputation he had lost almost as quickly as he gained it.

"He's failed so far. We had some pretty harsh words."

"Put a *fire* under him, Robert! Father used to say that if the Kennedys hadn't lost their nerve, Ramirez would have reached Havana and sent Castro packing."

"Cici, Father changed his mind about that while you were still pony-clubbing, for Christ's sake. God knows, I've done my best. I've got Ramirez up here, holed up at the Merry Hours Motor Inn, but he's produced nothing."

"He's *here?*"

"Forget I told you that. The less you know about it, the better. It's all under control."

"Well, tell him to get cracking, then," Cecilia said sharply.

He regretted that he had ever agreed to discuss things with Cecilia, but it was too late now. He should have known better than to suppose that she would ever give her blessing to a compromise with Alexa. "I'll do my best," he said glumly, to end the conversation.

Cecilia took his hand. "Nobody could ask for more," she whispered.

CECILIA'S REPUTATION FOR FRAGILITY was a family tenet of faith, except to Cecilia herself, who knew better. In a different age, she would have been well cast as a Roman mother, or sister, or daughter, she thought —at any rate, one of those stern, vestal figures who pointed out the way of duty to the men in her family.

It was also her opinion—unshared—that Robert was too gentle for his own good; she blamed herself for having fled to Africa to escape from the family and the fortune, leaving him to face the world alone. Had she been home, she would have urged him not to try to take The Trust away from his father—or, if he was going to do it, she would have stiffened his backbone so he succeeded. She could tell that he was weakening now that the girl had taken advantage of his good nature, that Ramirez was probably weaseling out of whatever he had promised to do.

She thought about it as she undressed and slipped into her cotton nightgown, enjoying once again the feeling of being cold, after all those years in Africa. Still, it was her duty—self-appointed, to be sure—to be there, helping the poor, and a Bannerman always did his or her duty without complaint. If nothing else, her grandmother had taught her that, and it was the major satisfaction of her life—perhaps, she thought without bitterness, the *only* one.

If Robert couldn't get Ramirez to do what he'd been told to do, she would do it herself. That was her duty, too. She reached for the phone and dialed.

IT WAS NOT A HAPPY GROUP that gathered for breakfast, but Robert, whose idea the day had been in the first place, did his best to liven it up, like a suburban corporate wife who feels a crucial dinner party has gotten off to a bad start and sees her husband's chances for promotion vanishing as the conversation falters and dies. Not normally an early riser himself, Robert moved around the dining room cracking jokes, shaking hands boisterously, and telling everybody what a wonderful day it was going to be. And indeed, it did show promise of being a wonderful day, at least as far as the weather was concerned. Outside, Nature was doing her best to live up to the Bannermans' standards. A fine, pale autumn mist was rising to reveal a delicate frost that melted at the first rays of the sun, making the fall colors look as if they had been freshly painted overnight especially for the occasion. At the far edge of the Great Lawn, half a dozen deer grazed peacefully, their coats a rich dappled orange in the early morning light.

"The only *point* to these things is the breakfast," Putnam groaned, as he sat down beside Alexa. Indeed, there was an array of silver chafing dishes on the buffet at the far end of the dining room that would have done credit to a cruise ship. A day of sport in the Bannerman family proceeded along lines laid down firmly in the preceding century. A small army of unseen servants had been up since long before dawn, preparing an elaborate breakfast, assembling picnic hampers, loading guns and ammunition into the cars, grooming dogs, even bringing pheasant in cages from the farthest reaches of the estate where they were bred and raised, just in case the quantity of birds on the ground proved disappointing. Nothing was left to chance.

"You're not eating?" Putnam asked.

Alexa looked at his plate and shuddered at the sight of eggs, bacon, sausages, and pancakes. "It reminds me of my childhood," she said. "Except that breakfast then was at three, not six."

"I'd forgotten you're a product of the farm belt," Putnam said, his cheerfulness getting on her nerves. "Now that I think of it, there are more things I *don't* know about you than I *do*, except for what I've read in the newspapers, and as a journalist, I know better than to believe most of that."

She tried hard to pay attention. "You're not working as a journalist any more, though, are you?" she asked.

"How did you know that?"

"Your father said so."

"Ah. I keep forgetting. Well, no."

"Why not?"

"There's nothing I want to shoot. I took pictures of the war. After you've covered a war—a *real* war—everything else seems boring, pointless, faded out. Presidential campaigns? The hell with all that." He shoveled his breakfast in as if a full stomach might cheer him up.

She sipped her coffee while Putnam polished his plate with his final pancake, with the slightly morose expression of a man who has been looking forward to a big breakfast and now that he has eaten it, faces a day of guilt about the calories and cholesterol he has consumed.

"Why are we doing this?" she asked.

"Why? I ask myself the same question. Because Robert wants us to, I guess. As usual."

"Is that enough for you? All the reason you need?"

"It used to be. Maybe it still is. Look, he's my brother, whatever you think of him. If he wants to play the country squire—for *your* benefit, I suspect—now that he's home for the first time in four or five years, fine, let him. Who am I to spoil his party?"

"You think he's doing all this for *my* benefit?"

"Not entirely, but yes. He likes to stir things up, and there's only a limited number of ways you can do that at Kiawa. Robert can't sit still, so the prospect of a whole day talking about the deal you two are going to cut is more than he can stand. He likes to organize people, run things, keep everybody busy. He'd have made a pretty good general if he could have skipped the grades from private to four stars. I mean, *look* at him! He's in his element. The servants have been up all night, half the estate is out there making sure there are enough birds, he's even invited some of the local gentry, people he really despises. It's a demonstration that Kiawa is still his, not yours, that's all."

"I never thought it *was* mine."

"Well, if Father's will is to be believed, it *is* yours. And welcome to it, so far as I'm concerned. God, there's DeWitt, looking like a poster for Ducks Unlimited."

The dining room was filling up now. Cecilia had appeared, clad in a tweed skirt and several layers of sweaters, and looking very cross indeed. DeWitt looked like an illustration in an expensive sporting clothes catalog in camouflage pants, heavy boots, and a jacket of tan khaki and suede festooned with pockets, cartridge loops, straps, leather laces for hanging game, padded leather patches for cushioning recoil. An extra pair of glasses hung around his neck on a chain, and he carried a green Tyrolean hat. This was not a group, she noted, that wore old corduroy trousers and down parkas for bird shooting, nor did they follow the Midwestern rule of wearing red in the field. Robert, deep in conversation with DeWitt, wore a well-cut tweed suit, and so did his neighbors, most of whom were staring at their surroundings with awe when they were not sneaking glances at Alexa. Even Booker was fully tweeded up, though in some mysterious way the texture and cut of his tweeds seemed ill-chosen, or perhaps his clothes were simply too new. She wondered what Simon would be wearing. He had probably overslept.

Putnam winked at her. "There you have it," he said, with a glance at Booker, apparently reading her mind. "The rich have suede patches sewn on their clothes when the cloth has worn through. It's a way of saving money—don't throw out a good suit so long as there's life in it. They'd never buy a *new* suit with suede patches—that's merely *style*. Poor Booker has never learned the difference. You have to be born to wealth to appreciate the fine line between well-used and shabby."

"I thought he and DeWitt would be working today. I know Mr. Stern's expecting DeWitt."

"And he'll get him. DeWitt will be back by ten, at the latest—the country gentleman, red in the face, ready to talk business after a couple of hours of expensive sport. DeWitt doesn't like this any better than I do, but it's part of his image. He goes trout fishing every year, you know, makes a big deal of it, but I don't believe he enjoys it one bit. If he caught a fish, he probably wouldn't know what to do with it. Ah, here comes Robert, loaded for bear."

"We're in luck," Robert said, beaming. "A beautiful day!" He spoke as if he'd arranged it personally for her, along with the breakfast. "Slept well?" She expected him to gloat, now that he'd eliminated her threat, but his face gave away nothing except good will.

"I never have any trouble sleeping, myself," Putnam said. "It's staying awake I have to work at."

"Not you. I was talking to Alexa."

"As a matter of fact, I didn't sleep all that well," she said. "I don't know why."

"Too much going on, I expect."

"No, it wasn't that. It's as if the house were haunted. I don't mean that *really*, I don't believe in that kind of thing—but it's as if somebody was *there*, in the room, you know. . . . "

Robert laughed. "Haunted! No, there's never been any suggestion of that. There are no Bannerman ghosts that I know of, unless Grandmother is summoning them at night without telling anybody. Ready to go?"

She nodded.

"I asked them to give you a twenty-gauge. An English over-and-under of my mother's, matter of fact. Is that okay?"

"I'm not planning to shoot."

"I thought I'd heard somewhere you were good at it." He gave her a knowing smile, as if they shared a secret. "A pity, since the gamekeeper has gone to the trouble of cleaning it for you. And you, Putt?"

"Count me out. I'm carrying a camera. Maybe I'll do a story on blood sports of the rich."

"You will do nothing of the kind, Putt. That's an order."

"I was joking."

"I don't take that kind of thing as a joke. I take it as a threat."

"Jesus, Robert, look on the bright side, you'd win the NRA vote."

Robert's sense of humor did not seem to extend to Putnam, or perhaps to the public-relations aspect of bird shooting. He stared at Putnam for a moment, then shook his head as if he were rejecting serious advice. "I'll get the NRA vote anyway," he said. He took Alexa's arm and walked her out of the room. "I slept like a log, myself," he said proudly. "I always do."

It seemed an odd thing for him to say, she thought. He did not look like a man who had slept well. There were dark circles under his eyes, he had cut himself shaving, and there was a certain high-strung tension in his manner, as if he had not been to bed at all. He looked, she decided, like someone who had spent the night in dissipation, then taken a couple of pills to keep him going through the day. Even his complexion was a shade paler than usual. She wondered why.

Simon materialized from the gloom of the hallway holding a cup of coffee in his hand and looking at the cold, bright sunlight through the door as if it had been put there just to annoy him. He wore a stylish black leather jacket, gray flannels, and dark glasses, and looked as if he were on the way to a rock concert or just coming home from one. "Christ, it's early," he said.

"You missed breakfast," she said.

"I didn't miss it. You've forgotten—I never eat it. I'm not sure I'm up to this."

She had no difficulty in guessing how Simon had spent the night. An early bedtime in the country held no attractions for a man who usually stayed up until three or four and liked to spend his evenings surrounded by as much loud noise and as many bright lights as possible. Only a heavyweight dose of whatever drug he was taking these days, plus a couple of sleeping pills, could have seen him through a night of solitary boredom, and his face was so pale that the Bannermans' neighbors, busy making sure they had their hats, gloves, scarves, shooting sticks and pocket flasks, stared at him as if he were, in fact, Kiawa's ghost. He took two small blue capsules from his pocket, popped them into his mouth and washed them down with black coffee. "For my allergies," he explained, closing his eyes for a moment. He shuddered, turned suddenly a shade paler, if that was possible, and sighed. "I'm not sure I ought to go out there in all that pollen."

Robert took his arm and towed him toward the door. "Nonsense," he said, "you *have* to go. Alexa would be disappointed, and so would I. Anyway, the pollen season was over a month ago. There's nothing out there but good fresh air."

It struck Alexa as odd that Robert should be so insistent. She found it hard to imagine that he really cared whether or not Simon went with them, but he *did* seem to care, strangely enough. Like a cruise director, he was determined to get everyone involved in what he had planned for the day, and was not about to accept holdouts, however reluctant. It was as if he wanted the largest possible number of people present, and had even invited his neighbors whom, she correctly guessed, he had been avoiding for years, and who seemed astonished to be there, and so nervous in Robert's presence that they looked like a small school of fish in the presence of a shark. Clearly, whatever the rest of the world thought of Robert, his neighboring landowners were wary of him, perhaps from previous experience, and gave the impression that they were afraid he was about to play some kind of practical joke on them.

"A few hours in the fresh air will do you a world of good," Robert said, pushing Simon toward one of the cars, and Simon, whose will-power was at its lowest ebb in the early morning, gave in glumly.

Robert placed Alexa beside him in an open Jeep and led the small convoy down the drive. "Do you know the form for these things?" he shouted.

She shook her head. The woods stretched beyond them in their bright colors, and the air was so clear that the low hills of the Catskills, which must be thirty or forty miles away, beyond the Hudson, looked as if she could reach out and touch them. Far overhead, a massed V-formation of geese made their way noisily toward some farmer's corn-field. She wondered how she had ever been able to live in the city, and at the same time she knew this was an illusion, that after a week here she would be as eager to get back to New York as Simon was. "Where I come from," she shouted back, "people walk out in the cornfields and let fly when the dog raises a bird. It isn't a complicated sport."

"It's not so different here." He pointed to an upland ridge of trees, mostly pines, mixed with bright red maples. "On the far side, you see, there'll be beaters, working their way through the brush to drive the birds toward us. On this side, there'll be the dogs and their handlers, to spot the birds. With any luck, a good many of the birds will come out of the tree line, straight overhead, full speed—the best shooting there is, for my money, and I've shot grouse in Scotland, dove in South Carolina, larks in Spain, and duck in Alaska. . . . Here we are."

He stopped in a cleared field that resembled a military encampment. There were a dozen or so pickup trucks and vans, a small tent, even a portable toilet. Fifteen or twenty men waited, most of them with dogs, while two of the servants from the house set up coffee, tea, and a bar in the tent. Robert helped her out of the Jeep and produced a tweed shooting jacket for her.

"At home we wear red," she said.

He laughed. "That's hardly necessary here. Everyone's experienced. You watch out for the other feller, and he watches out for you. There's a scarf in the pocket, which you might want to put over your hair. You'll get cold otherwise, and it helps to muffle the sound!"

She took the scarf out, a beautiful cashmere square from Hermès, patterned with the feathers of various game birds. She put it over her head, tying it at the throat. In the olive-and-brown hunting coat and the russet scarf, it occurred to her, she was remarkably well camouflaged, but clearly hunting clothes in the East were intended to blend with the scenery rather than to stand out in vivid contrast to it. As in so many other ways, the rich sought invisibility, it seemed, even in their sports.

McGiverney, the head gamekeeper, was not the type who might have interested Lady Chatterley, she decided. He would have fit right in at home, a big, beefy man, with the narrow eyes of a state trooper and the kind of ruddy complexion that comes from a lifetime of outdoor work and drinking. His handshake was like a bear's. "Mr. Arthur was a good shot," he said, then fell silent, leaving it to her to wonder if this was a form of condolence, or as much as she was ever likely to get from him in the way of recognition as Arthur's widow.

"Not the last time I saw him shoot," Robert said.

The gamekeeper was apparently not in awe of Robert. "He had an off day, Mr. Robert. In his prime, he was the best shot in *this* family." He reached into his truck, brought out a gun, broke it open, and handed it to Alexa. "You know how to handle a gun?" he asked.

"I'm not going to shoot," Alexa said firmly.

McGiverney shrugged. "Up to you. *Mrs.* Arthur—the *late* Mrs. Bannerman, she was one hell of a shot, when you could get her away from her horses, wasn't she, Ambassador? Mr. Arthur was real proud of her in the field. You stick close to me. I'll take care of you," he said to Alexa.

"I'll be looking after the young lady myself, McGiverney."

"Anything you say, Ambassador," McGiverney said with an edge of dislike, handing Robert his gun. He walked off like a sergeant inspecting his troops, splitting the party up into pairs, and giving each a man with a dog. "Those who ain't shooting," he said, "stay well behind the guns where we can see you."

They formed up in a rough line, in twos. Simon, Alexa noticed, had managed to arm himself, apparently determined, now that he was there, not to be left out of things. To the best of her knowledge he had never hunted before, and though he was in the habit of carrying a pistol, she had always assumed it was more of a psychological prop than anything else, since he had never fired it. She guessed that the only reason he was carrying a gun was to avoid having to stand with the other spectators—or perhaps he simply wanted to annoy DeWitt, whom he had chosen as his partner. But no, she thought, Simon was clever enough to let DeWitt do the shooting, and gain points as a good sportsman.

They moved forward at a leisurely pace while the dog ran in zig zags in front of them, an aged Labrador with a graying muzzle, too experienced at the game to get overexcited, and apparently quite capable of doing his job without the whispered orders and low whistles of his owner, a grizzled old man who looked as if he slept in the kennel with the dog. "Who is he?" she whispered to Robert.

He shook his head. "One of the locals. McGiverney rounds them up when he needs them. We're only ninety miles from New York City, but this is still real country. There are people up here who wouldn't eat meat if they didn't poach deer. There are parts of this county that make *Deliverance* look like Beverly Hills. . . . Get ready!"

The dog was at the tree line now, about fifty yards away across the rough, stubbled field, motionless on point. His owner shifted the plug of chewing tobacco in his mouth and said, "Git closer." Robert took her by the elbow and together they ran forward, stumbling on the ruts and hummocks of the open field; then there was a noise like a rocket going off, and before she had even registered the direction of the sound, Robert had raised his gun and fired twice. She did not even see the bird until it dropped to the ground with a heavy thud. The dog, who obviously did not believe in wasting energy, strolled over to it at a leisurely pace and brought it back to its owner in its mouth.

"How's that, McGiverney?" Robert shouted, over his shoulder.

"Hit 'em in the head, Mr. Robert, and they make better eating. No point breaking a tooth on shot. Your dad used to bring them down so there was never a mark on the meat."

Robert looked grim. "Damn," he said, under his breath. "For two cents, I'd . . . " But whatever he was prepared to give two cents for was drowned out in a burst of noise. From the other side of the wooded ridge Alexa could hear dogs barking, men shouting, the occasional squawk of a pheasant, while from the trees in front of them, pheasant were launching themselves into a barrage of gunfire. It was as if a small, noisy war had broken out, and quite suddenly, she felt sick. She closed her eyes and saw her father lying on the floor, his hands on his chest, as if he were trying to hold the blood back, damming it in his hands, his eyes wide-open, his face already white with the pallor of death. She had missed the moment of his dying, and perhaps he did, too, mercifully. He simply slipped from one state to another with no sign. She could smell the familiar odor of gunsmoke, hear the familiar noise of a shotgun firing close by—though the shots were nothing like as loud as they had been in an enclosed space. She felt herself trembling, growing faint, as if the noise of the guns were pressing straight down on her brain.

"What the hell's the matter with you?" Robert asked, lowering his gun, slipping on the safety.

"I can't stand this. It was a mistake. I have to go."

He grabbed her arm. "Are you going to be sick? They're only birds, you know. They're bred for this."

"I can't explain it. I must get out of here."

Robert paused for a moment as if he were thinking out a problem, then he took her by the arm. "Come with me," he said. He pulled her toward the wooded ridge and set off toward a low stone wall in front of them. "You sit down over here," he said. "I'll go through the woods to the other side, and organize a truck to take you back to the house. It's safer than going back to where people are shooting."

It did not seem safer to her. The moment they were in the woods, they would be invisible to anyone who was shooting in that direction—and, in fact, spent shot was already pattering down from the trees overhead. Robert seemed to know what he was doing, however, and she was too shaken to argue with him. He helped her over the stone wall and pointed down a short, steep slope covered with dead pine needles, at the end of which was a pile of stone. "Down there. Sit and wait," he said. "I'll follow the trail. Take your time."

She had no wish to be left alone. She guessed it was only a hundred yards or so to the far side of the woods—and she felt ashamed of her sudden attack of panic. She felt better now that she could no longer see the dead birds.

Would Arthur have cared whether or not she carried a gun, or took a shot at a pheasant? She thought not. He had never made her feel that he expected her to live up to his first wife's standards in anything. She smiled at herself—it was the second time she had thought of herself as Arthur Bannerman's "second wife"—an indication, if nothing else, that she was at last beginning to accept her role, even if others didn't. . . .

Robert stood a few feet away from her, carrying his gun, breach open, over his arm. There was no great significance to the moment, his expression anxious. For no reason, she shivered. She looked up, thinking perhaps that a cloud had passed over the sun, but the sky was bright blue above the autumn foliage.

Robert hesitated, as if he wanted to say something; then he turned and moved down the trail, disappearing quickly into the woods. She felt exposed and lonely. Then she reminded herself that he was probably right; she would be safer if she walked down to the spot he had chosen than standing on the ridge. She could hear shots behind her close by, and an occasional patter of birdshot in the leaves above her, but she felt no real sense of danger.

She followed the broken stone wall, her feet slipping on the damp, dead leaves. Just beyond the rough trail was a tangle of stones around a big fir tree of some kind, a blue spruce, she guessed. It was not a tree that grew in her part of the country, and it reminded her of something out of a children's book, its branches so thick and dense that it looked like a solid cone, a tree for dwarfs and gnomes and giants. At one time a house must have been here—she could see the outlines of a rectangular foundation and a stone well, close to the tree, overgrown now with thorn bushes. She skirted it, then stopped for a moment.

She felt a chill run through her. She could actually feel, under the borrowed scarf, the hairs on the back of her neck stand up, as she stood, unable to breathe or move, rooted to the spot. She told herself not to be silly—that it was just a delayed reaction to the shock of the gun going off beside her, the dead bird, the sudden memory of her father's death. She took a deep breath, but instead of the odor of pine needles, there was something else, something that made her even more uneasy, a familiar acrid, burnt smell, which she found hard to place.

She took another deep breath; then it came to her that it was the smell of a cigarette, but not an ordinary cigarette. The smell was somehow foreign, much sharper and stronger than that of any domestic brand she knew. Then she recognized the distinctive odor of a Gauloise, and at the same moment she remembered she had smelled the same odor in her room, as if somebody who smoked Gauloises had been there while she was at dinner.

Just as she had known someone had been in her room, she knew now that she was not alone. It occurred to her that she was standing on a wooded ridge, while half a dozen people with shotguns were firing behind her. Of course, there was very little danger of being hit, she knew that—they would be firing high into the air as the birds passed over them, not firing into the woods, but there was always the possibility of an accidental discharge, a hasty, impatient finger on the trigger, or a safety catch that was off when the shooter absolutely believed it was on. . . .

She turned her back to the stone wall and started to move down the slope. Then, as if fear had intensified her senses and frozen the air around her in silence, screening out the shots and the noise of the dogs, she heard with absolute clarity the sharp metal-on-metal click of a gun safety. She knew it could be no other sound. Somebody else might not have heard it, for it was anything but loud, or might have mistaken it—but she had heard that same quiet, sinister, deadly, final click in the moment of silence before she pulled the trigger and fired at her father, heard it as loud as an avalanche or a burst of thunder, without even feeling her thumb press the checkered steel catch forward. She had not felt its sharp edges, or noticed the pressure on the ball of her thumb as it resisted—for a safety catch was designed to require a conscious physical effort. She had simply heard the click, as her father must have, in that fraction of a second before a much greater noise deafened her. . . .

In her mind, the one sound preceded the other. She did not *think* it out—she was hardly thinking at all—but some inner reflex made her anticipate a shot. She spun around, just in time to see a man rise from the stone wall around the old well, and was not at all surprised to see him raising a shotgun to his shoulder.

She saw him with unnatural clarity: a swarthy face, dark glasses, a slash of black moustache, a seaman's knitted watch cap, but in camouflage colors, pulled down over his head, a mouth set in determination, or perhaps irritation that she had reacted so quickly, for he had apparently intended to shoot her in the back. "*Mierda!*" she thought she heard him say, and that too seemed to make sense, for there was a Latin look about his face—the luxuriant, macho fullness of the moustache, the slight jowls, the olive skin—something unmistakably tropic, more suited to palm trees than the firs and maples he had chosen to hide among.

She had this thought firmly in mind as she dived for the ground, and it stayed with her as she heard the shot and felt the air sliced as if by a hot knife, directly over her head. She knew better than to stand up and run, and, anyway, she had no strength in her legs, which was perhaps what saved her, for the instinct to get up and run for dear life was natural, and would certainly have killed her. Instead, since she was on a downhill slope, she rolled, slipping into a low, shallow, leaf-filled trough, which erupted in front of her face in a shower of dead leaves, dirt, and debris as the second shot hit the ground a few inches in front of her face.

"Bitch!" the man cried, this time in English. She rolled over the edge of the trough, then let herself slide down the sharply inclined slope of the clearing, pushing as hard as she could with her feet. The leaves were slippery and the slope was steeper than it looked, and she was quickly sliding downhill, out of control, bruising herself against rocks and tearing her clothes on thorns. She could feel her face stinging from cuts and bruises, but she could only hope that she made as difficult a target as possible—which seemed to be the case, for the next shot hit a few inches from her thigh. She could feel the heat and even a few pinpoints of intense pain—she knew she had taken a few shot in the flesh—but by now she was almost out of killing range. She made a desperate lunge for the bushes at the far end of the clearing, felt one shot go by her so close that a few stray pellets whipped through her down vest, scattering feathers around her as if she were a bird that had just been wounded.

She was moving fast now, and by the time the next shot whistled over her head, she was in the bushes, crouched and crawling as fast as she could, tearing away at the branches in front of her, falling, scraping her knees, getting up again, until she reached a culvert, into which she fell with a loud splash, covering herself with mud and slime.

She realized that she was sobbing, crying, struggling for breath, making far too much noise. She had covered nearly fifty yards like a toboggan bumping down a hill out of control, and now, at least, she had found some cover in which to hide, if she could force herself to be silent. She could lie in the mud, motionless, and hope the man wouldn't follow her down here, or wouldn't find her if he did—or she could start to move. She had an instant picture of him standing over her as she lay there, putting a shot through the back of her neck, and her scalp crawled, as if she could feel the muzzle of his gun touching her right at the base of the skull. She started to move blindly, on her hands and knees, and soon found herself burrowing more deeply in the tangled second growth and brambles, slipping faster and faster down a steep runway. She was crawling on rocks now—this must be a stream bed when the rain was heavy or the snow was melting off—and her progress should have been painful, except that fear seemed to have anesthetized her. She squeezed between two mossy boulders and paused to catch her breath.

Immediately ahead of her, almost close enough to touch, a startled hound stared at her, having apparently wandered into the woods for a drink. She lay still and hoped it wouldn't bark, but the sight of a human being, however bedraggled, apparently reminded the animal that it wasn't doing its job. It gave her a look of abject apology and made off into the bushes on its way back to its master. She couldn't have moved if she had wanted to. She had reached such a state of panic and exhaustion in the past thirty seconds—for it could hardly have been more than that since the stranger fired his first shot—that she was now prepared to lie here and let him kill her if he found her.

"Shit," she heard him mutter, astonishingly close. She forced herself not to scream, holding her breath as if she were trying to swim under water. Then she heard his footsteps crashing through the undergrowth in the opposite direction, faster and faster, until it was clear at last that he had abandoned the chase and was running away.

She lay there for some minutes, as the facts of the matter pressed in on her, as heavy as the boulders on either side. Somebody—the same person who had searched her room—had made a deliberate and savage attack on her life. It was a fact so wildly improbable that she could hardly bring herself to accept it, and now that she was safe, she had a guilty feeling, as if she were a child who had imagined some improbable threat to explain a torn pair of blue jeans, or why she was late for school. But the pain in her thigh, now that she was able to feel it, was undoubtedly real, and when she reached down to touch the place, she winced.

If a few stray pellets could do that to a nonvital part of her body, what would it be like to receive the whole load in her back at closer range? But, of course, she of all people *knew*, all too well, what that was like. She would have been knocked to the ground, face first, her lifeblood running out of a wound in her back the size of a plate. Death might not have come instantaneously, but it would not take long.

And when she was found? When she was found, it would naturally be concluded that a stray shot, fired accidentally low into the woods, had hit her as she was standing on the ridge—a foolish place to be, of course, while people were shooting just the other side of it, just the kind of stupid thing a city girl would do. An astute trooper, or more likely the coroner, might have questioned the severity of the wound and given some thought to the possibility that the shot had been fired at close range, but hunting accidents were not subjected to much scrutiny, particularly when everybody involved was wealthy. There was always the possibility that somebody might have barged into the fringe of the woods to take an unsporting point-blank shot at a bird on the ground—it happened, even among people who were brought up to know better. The State Police would doubtless want to protect the Bannermans and their guests from the embarrassment of a full-scale investigation—and what was there to investigate? She had run off into the woods and put herself in the line of fire while Robert Bannerman was off getting a vehicle to take her back to the house. He had advised her to move down the slope, where she would be safer, and he was nowhere near her when the shot was fired. . . .

She bit her lip. As a scenario for her death, the hunting accident could hardly be improved upon. If she had not reacted instinctively to the click of the safety, she would be lying on the ground, less than a hundred yards from here, at the top of the slope, dead. It came to her quite suddenly that the only reason she was still alive was simply that her would-be killer had to make her death look like an accident—he had no interest in tracking her down in her hiding place and blowing her head off. Once he had failed to stage a fatal accident, he was no longer sure what to do, which explained the hesitant way he had followed her.

She was in pain, her clothes wet, torn, covered with leaves and mud, but none of that was anything compared to the knowledge that only one person could have set this up. She could hardly bring herself to believe that Robert, with whom she had almost reached an agreement, had all along been planning to kill her—but there was no other explanation. She could hardly believe the whole thing had happened, now that it was over, but she could see the empty shotgun shells lying among the dead leaves, the brass ends gleaming in the dappled sunlight, and feel the blood running warm down her thigh. A minute ago a total stranger had tried to murder her in cold blood—it was a *fact*, as real and solid as the trees around her.

Her mind searched for alternative explanations—that it was a mistake, that somebody had perhaps meant to frighten her and gone too far, that it was just a case of mistaken identity, or even that the gunman was a psycho, some lunatic who was simply waiting for the first person to come within range, like the snipers one reads about in the newspapers—but she knew better. The killer had been waiting for *her*, had been watching her—for she remembered the field glasses in the playhouse—had even been in her room.

She had no idea what to do. Go to the police? But this was not New York City. She could not simply dial 911 and wait for the arrival of a couple of patrolmen or a detective. She would have to get back to the house, telephone the local police or the troopers, wait for them to arrive, then bring them back here to explain what had happened, by which time, very likely, the spent cartridges would be gone. They would ask if there were any witnesses, and in the end, it would be her word against Robert's, if she carried it that far. Did she really want to try to tell a couple of country bumpkins that the United States Ambassador to Venezuela, great-grandson of Cyrus Bannerman and gubernatorial candidate, had planned to have her shot by some kind of South American terrorist, and would they believe her for one instant? She doubted it. Stern might believe her story—even, just possibly, Booker—but not the local police, certainly not when confronting Ambassador Bannerman himself, with his cold eyes, his superior smile and his easygoing, natural air of authority, as if he had been born to give orders to lesser men, which was in fact pretty much the case. It would not be easy to persuade *anyone* that he had tried to kill her, let alone the local law.

She could hear the sound of a vehicle moving slowly over rough ground behind the trees—presumably Robert was returning with a truck and a driver. Was he expecting to find her dead, on the ridge, next to the stone wall, the apparent victim of an unfortunate hunting accident? What would he say when he saw she was alive? More important, what would *she* say? Accuse him point-blank of murder? She wasn't sure she knew how to say it, wasn't even sure she *could* say it. She needed help, she decided, before doing anything at all.

She scrambled up the slope and into the bushes, praying, absurdly, that she wasn't touching poison ivy, climbed the stone wall, and emerged at a run onto the plowed field, gasping from the pain in her leg. She heard a shot close by and a lot of shouting. Through her tears and her tangled hair, she could see figures running toward her. "Damn silly bitch!" she heard somebody say indignantly. Then Simon materialized out of the blur, put his arms around her and asked, "Are you trying to get yourself killed, for Christ's sake?"

She started to laugh, a high-pitched laugh bordering on hysteria, which seemed to be coming from somewhere else, beyond her control. Then she grabbed Simon's coat, her fingers digging into the soft leather, shaking as if she had just been hauled from freezing water, and whispered very softly, as if she hardly believed it herself, "Somebody just tried to kill me."

Once the words were out, she felt a rush of relief and at the same time, a sudden fatigue and weakness, so overpowering that she was afraid of fainting or falling.

She closed her eyes. She heard Booker's voice, full of concern, or perhaps alarm, DeWitt's squawk of astonishment, like a bird's, and then she was in a car, bumping over the rutted tracks, on her way back to Kiawa.

"I NEED HER BLUE CROSS NUMBER, major medical and social security," the lady behind the desk said firmly.

"For God's sake, she's been *shot!*" Simon said. He and Booker had brought Alexa straight to the emergency room of the local hospital, despite her protests, breaking the speed limit all the way. Simon was at his best when his taste for drama was satisfied, and a gunshot wound, however minor, was just the kind of adventure he thrived on. He had driven, while explaining to Booker how to make a totally unnecessary tourniquet out of Alexa's borrowed scarf. He and Booker had dragged her, still protesting, but more feebly, into the hospital, but their dramatic entrance had no effect on the emergency-room receptionist at all. "If she can stand, she can fill in a form," the woman snapped.

"She *can't* stand!"

"She looks to me like she's standing."

Booker elbowed Simon to one side. "I don't think you understand," he said. "This is Mrs. Arthur Aldon Bannerman."

The woman's eyes opened wide behind her harlequin glasses. She took them off and let them dangle on her ample bosom by a chain. "Well, mercy's sake, why didn't you say so? We can deal with the paperwork later, of course." She abandoned her post in a hurry, and a moment later a doctor and two nurses appeared with a Gurney, lifted Alexa onto it, and took her flying through the big swing doors at a run. "You can't come in here," the doctor said to Booker and Simon, who were following.

Booker did not even pause. "I am the attorney for the Bannerman family," he said. "This gentleman is a trusted business associate of Mrs. Bannerman's."

"Ah, in that case . . . Well, stay out of the way and try not to touch anything."

Alexa lay still as she was transferred to an operating table, and she closed her eyes as the bright overhead lights were turned on. Her wounds did not seem serious to her, but she was grateful to be here, if only because it postponed making a decision about what to do. Could she accuse Robert face-to-face of trying to murder her? And yet she would have to, she knew that—she could hardly ignore what had happened. And what was to stop him from trying it again? She winced, as the doctor cut away her blue jeans, and washed off the dirt. "Puncture wounds," he said. "Birdshot, it looks like. Mostly superficial, a few of them deep. I'm going to give you a local anesthetic, which will hurt a bit. Then we'll get them out."

"Is she in any danger?" Simon asked.

He laughed. "They're a long way from the heart." Then he remembered who his patient was, and assumed a more serious expression. "No, no danger. The young lady may have a few scars, but nothing a cosmetic surgeon couldn't fix, if they bother her. Here we go."

She felt the needle pricking her skin. "Good girl," the doctor said. "I'm going to leave you for a few minutes to let the area go numb. Have you reported this to the police, by the way?"

"The police?" she asked.

"It's a gunshot wound. GSWs have to be reported. It's the law."

Booker nodded. "I can assure you, Doctor, that we'll take care of the formalities. Of course, we'd like to avoid any publicity, as you can imagine."

"Oh, sure," the doctor said warily. "There's no hurry. I'll be back shortly."

"What makes you think he isn't calling the police or the newspapers right now?" Simon asked.

Booker directed his eyes at a discreet plaque on the wall. It read, "In memory of John Aldon Bannerman—a gift of Arthur Aldon Bannerman." He gave a somber smile. "It's ironic. This is where they brought John after the car accident. He was dead, of course, DOA, but they did their best, even though the facilities were pretty primitive, so Arthur bought them a whole new emergency room, state-of-the-art. It's probably the best-equipped emergency facility between New York City and Albany. Around here, the Bannerman name is still magic." He took off his glasses and wiped them clean. "So what happened?"

Alexa could feel the pain in her leg ebbing. She had been cold before; now she felt warm, almost too warm, and relaxed. "I told you," she said. "A man tried to kill me."

Booker put his glasses back on. His expression was severe, judicial. He seemed to her, quite suddenly, years older, no longer the legal lapdog. "You're sure it wasn't an accident?"

"An accident? He was standing there, shooting at me. He'd have hit me if I hadn't stumbled. And when he missed, he kept right on shooting."

"How many shots?"

"Four or five, I think."

"You don't remember precisely?"

"Of course I don't. I was scared out of my mind. Why on earth does it matter?"

"It matters to me. If you weren't telling the truth, you see, you'd have given me a precise number of shots."

"I'm not lying."

"I know. You say the man seemed to you Hispanic?"

"Hispanic? Yes, I guess so."

"Might he have been Cuban?" Booker's expression suddenly changed, as if he had remembered something.

"Maybe. He said something in Spanish, when he missed. It sounded as if he was swearing."

"Would you recognize him if you saw him again?"

"I hope I don't. But I think I probably would, yes. He smokes some kind of foreign cigarette."

"Gauloises," Booker said. "He's about my height, stocky build, hawk-like nose, a thick black moustache, usually wears wraparound dark glasses?"

"You know the man!" she said. She tried to sit up, felt dizzy, and lay back again.

Booker was cautious. "I might," he said grimly.

"Who is he?"

"His name's Ramirez." He sighed glumly. "I'm in a tricky position, Alexa. As a lawyer, I have a responsibility to protect my client, but I don't think it extends to this sort of thing. Ramirez worked for Robert. They go back a long time. They have close connections still."

"*How* close?" Simon asked.

Booker stared at his muddy shoes. "I think there's a point at which

I'd prefer to stick with the lawyer–client relationship. Let's just say close enough."

"Close enough to have me killed?" Alexa asked.

Booker nodded. "Maybe," he said.

"I just can't believe he'd do it," she said. "Not *kill* me."

"I myself find it hard to accept Robert is that *stupid* or that evil. Frankly, I feel responsible. I didn't tell Robert everything I found out in LaGrange, you see, or what I guessed . . ." He gave a discreet cough. "About your father, and so on. I thought I was saving you from *character* assassination." He frowned. "I hadn't realized how far he might go if I didn't deliver."

"Didn't deliver?"

"Didn't deliver the goods. About your marriage. About your father."

"*What* marriage?" Simon asked. "And what about her father?"

The door opened, and the doctor came in with the nurse. He approached Alexa as if she were some kind of precious artifact, now that he knew who she was. "Close your eyes, Mrs. Bannerman," he suggested. "Think of something nice."

She tried. The probing was not, in fact, painful at all, though the feel of the instrument made her queasy. She heard the metallic clink as the doctor dropped each shot into a tray, but despite his advice, nothing pleasant came to her mind. She had known, of course, that Booker had been sent out to dig up whatever he could find in her past, but it had never occurred to her that he might not have passed what he had discovered on to Robert. She understood at last Robert's strategy: Delay things by seeming to agree on joint control of the fortune, build up a case against her so he could either blackmail her into submission or destroy her in the press—and if all that failed, as it had, simply eliminate her. She had missed in his character what must have been there always, a combination of duplicity and total ruthlessness.

Arthur had warned her about it, but she had assumed he was exaggerating. Should she run away now, go away somewhere, Europe perhaps, and let the lawyers sort things out? But to do that would be to let Robert get away with murder, or attempted murder, anyway. And what was to stop him from trying again?

"This may cause you a little discomfort," she heard the doctor say, and the next thing she felt was a stab of pain so sharp that she had to hold her breath to prevent herself from screaming. She opened her eyes and saw him leaning over, sweat on his brow, his eyes grossly enlarged by the magnifying spectacles on his nose, his surgical gloves covered in blood. The bright lights overhead dazzled her, giving her an instant headache, but she supposed the worst was over. She let out her breath and closed her eyes, then felt an even sharper pain, going deeper and deeper into her leg as he probed.

Quite suddenly, she felt nothing at all. She saw—or thought she saw, through a kind of fog—Arthur, dressed in his usual dark-blue banker's suit, standing beside her, looking down, an expression of concern on his face, but not just concern, something else also, a firmness, even a trace of impatience.

She reached out to touch him, and felt a hand grasp hers. She realized instantly that it was not Arthur's. It was smaller, much smaller, the fingers long and narrow, a beautifully-tended hand, but with the swollen joints of old age palpable just under the skin. "I came here as soon as I heard," Eleanor Bannerman said.

"I'm sorry. I thought it was Arthur."

"Yes?"

"I really thought he was *there*. . . ."

"Of course." Her voice became more gentle, surprisingly so. "I sometimes used to see my late husband—oh, for months after his death. I'd go to sleep, and there he'd be, lying in bed with his reading glasses on." She paused. "Then he faded, you know," she said sadly.

Alexa's head throbbed. She found it difficult to concentrate on what Mrs. Bannerman was saying. "We haven't had a shooting accident in a very long time," Mrs. Bannerman went on. "Not since Willie Auchincleck, silly man, shot one of the beaters. Are you in pain?"

"No, not really. It hurts a little."

"I should think. But your expression is not that of someone who 'hurts a little.' It is that of somebody in great pain. It shows in the eyes, you see. Pain, I mean. It's quite unmistakable. One sees it in horses when they've broken a leg. I saw it in the eyes of Arthur's first wife, poor thing, when she was dying of cancer."

"I'm not in that kind of pain, Mrs. Bannerman."

"No? Well, that's good. But then—what kind *are* you in?"

"I don't know if I can tell you."

Mrs. Bannerman tapped a long, cold fingernail against Alexa's wrist, like the scratch of a bird's talon. "I think you *must*. Mr. Booker is standing downstairs with a face full of gloom. I know what it means when lawyers look gloomy. Like doctors, they don't like giving bad news. Since the doctor here—an obsequious little toad, but quite competent, I am assured—has told me that your wounds are superficial and he foresees no complications, the bad news can hardly concern your health."

Alexa gathered her courage. "It wasn't an accident," she said.

Mrs. Bannerman showed no surprise, nor did she seem shocked. "I see," she said.

"A man tried to kill me. He was hidden in an old well, by a stone wall. . . ."

Mrs. Bannerman nodded. "I know the spot. There's a big spruce next to the old well, I remember. What on earth were you *doing* there? You don't shoot pheasant in the woods."

"Robert took me there."

There was a long silence.

Mrs. Bannerman sought the button for the nurse, who stuck her head in through the door immediately. "We should like some tea, please," she said.

The nurse, a plump young woman, seemed about to say that she wasn't a maid, but one look at Mrs. Bannerman changed her mind. "Tea?" she asked, as if it were an exotic request. "I'm not sure . . . "

"Thank you," Mrs. Bannerman said firmly, as the nurse disappeared. "So that's why Mr. Booker was looking so grim," she said.

Alexa was astonished at old Mrs. Bannerman's calm. Had she taken it all in? Did she understand what Alexa was accusing Robert of? For a moment she wondered if Mrs. Bannerman had aged overnight, as old people sometimes did. One look at her eyes, however, was enough to tell her that senility had not suddenly struck. If anything, she seemed more composed than usual, as if an attempted murder were just another small disturbance in the orderly progress of life at Kiawa, like a housemaid breaking a cup, or an old tree falling in a storm.

"You're quite sure this man was shooting at *you?*"

"Absolutely sure. I saw his face."

Mrs. Bannerman sighed. Her expression was fixed, as if she was steeling herself to hear more bad news, as no doubt she had done all her life.

"Did you know him?" she asked.

"No," Alexa said. "But I know who he is."

There was a rattle at the door, and the nurse appeared, bearing a tray with tea. Mrs. Bannerman thanked her, though she glared at the tray as if she had never seen a teabag before. Once the nurse had gone— and she seemed anxious to get away from Mrs. Bannerman as fast as possible—she poured two cups of tea and handed one to Alexa. She sipped hers with an expression of well-bred disgust. "It's not what one's used to, is it?" she asked, "but never mind. What are you going to do now?"

"I've been thinking about that."

"So I would suppose. You've spoken to the police?"

"Not yet."

The door opened and the doctor stuck his head in, smiling nervously. "I think the patient should get some rest now," he said apologetically.

Mrs. Bannerman gave him a withering glance. "Kindly go about your business," she snapped. "And surely the mere fact that you are a doctor does not free you from the obligation to knock on a lady's door before entering?"

"Well, yes. I mean, no. Of course I can come back later."

"By all means."

The door shut. "What an impertinent little man," Mrs. Bannerman said. "However, he's probably right. You should rest."

"I'm all right, really."

"You look feverish to me," Mrs. Bannerman said with the snap of authority that made all her opinions absolute. "You don't think this could possibly have been the work of anarchists, or a madman?"

"No. I don't think so at all."

Mrs. Bannerman stared into the far distance. "Neither do I. That being the case, your duty is to tell the police."

"I know."

"I'm sure you do."

"But I wouldn't want to go to them with anything I couldn't prove."

Mrs. Bannerman stared at her unblinkingly.

Alexa paused. "Well, the truth is," she said, "I'm not sure I'd even want to go to them with something I *could* prove. Not if it affected the family."

Mrs. Bannerman nodded. "That's not an easy decision to make," she said. "Or one to take lightly."

"I've made it before—or had it made for me, when my father died."

Mrs. Bannerman showed no curiosity. She simply waited, one eyebrow raised.

"I can't help asking what Arthur would have done," Alexa went on. "Or would want me to do."

"I do not believe he would have wanted the family exposed to more publicity. Not if it could be avoided."

"*Can* it be avoided?"

"I think so," Mrs. Bannerman whispered. "In a family like ours, many things are best kept secret. It's a great responsibility. One I have borne for many years myself." She was silent for a moment, as if she was thinking about the past. "Of course, justice must still be served. The wicked must be punished, even if we do it in our own way, without the help of the police and the courts."

"I'm not sure I know how to do that."

"In this case, you have only to fulfill Arthur's intentions, I think," Mrs. Bannerman said briskly.

She settled her gleaming coat over her shoulders. In the drab little hospital room, she looked like some splendid example of medieval costumery in a museum exhibit, a reminder of some long-forgotten age of splendor and luxury. "It is not an easy task. You might do better to walk away from it."

"I know. But I can't."

"Because?"

"Because I promised Arthur."

"He's dead," Mrs. Bannerman said sharply, as if dying was a sign of weakness. "You surely don't believe he's going to be waiting for you on the other side to ask you if you built his foolish museum, or what the state of the Foundation's portfolio is?"

"No, I don't believe that. But a promise is a promise."

Mrs. Bannerman opened the door. "Well, then," she said, "you'd better get some rest. I believe you'll be able to leave the hospital tomorrow. I'll have my car sent for you."

"I'm not sure I want to go back to Kiawa. Not right away."

"Nonsense," Mrs. Bannerman said crisply from the doorway. "Where else would you go now?"

ROBERT WAS SWEATING, as he turned the situation over in his mind. Things went wrong. People screwed up. You bit the bullet and got on with it. It's not over till the fat lady sings, he told himself—though he had a hollow feeling in the pit of his stomach, not so much from fear as from the sheer rage that Ramirez, of all people, should have gone off the reservation. Had the man lost his mind? By what twisted logic had he decided Robert wanted him to carry out an assassination?

There was nothing for it but to put a good face on things, he decided. Brazen it out and live to fight another day—if nothing else, politics taught you that. What, after all, could the bloody woman *do?* Go to the police? There were no witnesses. An unknown assailant had shot at her, a poacher, perhaps, surprised in his work, or an escaped convict—there were always escaped convicts in Dutchess County, which boasted of innumerable state prisons and hospitals for the criminally insane. He had left her to fetch a vehicle, since she felt unwell, and when he came back, she was gone. Had he heard shots? Of course he had! There were a dozen people shooting pheasants on the other side of the trees. There was no reason for anybody to connect Ramirez's crime to him, he told himself firmly.

He parked outside the hospital, leaving the car in a space marked "Handicapped Only," and fixed his face in an expression of concern. He did not pause at the visitor's desk—after all, he as good as owned the hospital. On the second floor, in the corridor, he found Booker and Simon, pacing up and down like a pair of expectant fathers. Neither of them seemed pleased to see him, but that was to be expected. Booker, he decided, would have to go. He was smart, but he simply didn't understand *loyalty,* Robert told himself, but then how could he? You were loyal to your class, and Booker was out of his, had been from the very beginning.

"How is she?" he asked.

Booker looked embarrassed, Simon hostile. For a moment, it seemed they might bar the way to her door, then Booker coughed and said, "She's doing well." He paused. "I'm not sure she wants to see you."

"Why the hell wouldn't she want to see me?" Robert asked, with an expression of astonishment, even hurt.

"There's reason to believe this wasn't an accident."

"Well, of *course* it wasn't. It seems perfectly clear that we're dealing with a lunatic or an escaped convict. He might have fired at any one of us. If I hadn't walked away from where he was hiding to fetch a car for Alexa, he'd probably have shot at me. The whole thing is a goddamn outrage. Who would have believed that an armed trespasser could hide out at Kiawa? It couldn't have happened in Grandfather's day."

"What makes you so sure it was a lunatic?" Simon asked.

"What else could it have been?" Robert did not wait for a reply. He knocked on the door and entered.

Alexa was propped up on the pillows, her eyes closed, and for a moment it occurred to him that she was dead, but that was merely wishful thinking, and besides, looking at her, he had no great wish to see her dead, convenient as it would have been. She was a splendid-looking girl, no doubt about it, despite the scratches on her face and hands. He thought, not for the first time, what a pity it was that they hadn't met under different circumstances.

"I came as quickly as I could," he said.

She opened her eyes. She did not seem particularly startled to see him, or afraid. That was a relief. He had not expected her to scream, or anything like that, but you never knew what women would do, and he had no desire to be embarrassed.

Then it occurred to him that it might have been better if she *had* screamed. The gray eyes were cold, remote and unforgiving.

"What on earth happened?" he asked, sitting down beside her. He was close enough to touch her hand, but decided against it.

"A man tried to shoot me," she said calmly.

"So I heard. But who? Why?"

She said nothing. Not a good sign, he thought. "Have you given the police a description?" he asked. "The sooner it's done, the more chance there is of catching him."

"Not yet."

"Booker should have dealt with that, damn him," he said indignantly, "instead of lounging in the corridor. I'll do it myself. If you're up to it, I can have the State Police over here in a few minutes." It would not make any difference, of course; he knew that. Ramirez might have gone crazy, or slipped when it came to marksmanship, but he was the master of the contingency plan—escape was the first thing he thought of in any job. By now he would have changed cars a couple of times and be well on his way to Canada or New York, by the back roads. He would have a woman with him. It was one of his rules that the police never paid much attention to a man and a woman together in a car. The domestic relationship was their norm, and they were unlikely to suspect or question it.

"I don't think they're going to find him," she said. "Do you?"

"That depends on how clearly you saw him." With any luck, Ramirez would not have given her a look at his face. It still baffled Robert how the man could have taken matters into his own hands. Well, never mind, he *had*. But, so long as there was no proof, it was merely her word against his, and although there would certainly be sympathy for her, it was still the word of a fortune hunter and a nobody against a United States ambassador.

"I saw him quite clearly," she said. "It's not a face I'm ever going to forget."

Damn! he thought. Ramirez should have worn a ski mask—but of course he was too sure of himself for that, the crazy son-of-a-bitch.

"All the more reason to hurry, before this fellow gets too far away," he said. "God knows who he'll shoot next, if he's a psycho."

"He didn't look like a psycho to me, Robert."

"I can't imagine how he got on the estate without being seen. We've never had guards, not since Cyrus's death. Well, the world is changing. We may have to change with it."

"I don't know how he got onto the estate, Robert, but I know where he was hiding. He was in the Doll House. I saw his cigarettes and his binoculars when you took me there."

"Surely not," he said, wishing she were less observant. "How could he have gotten in? There was no sign of a break-in that I recall."

"There wouldn't have to be, if somebody told him where to find the key, would there?"

"It sounds farfetched."

She nodded. Her expression was difficult to fathom. It was, in fact, rather the *lack* of any discernible expression that made Robert nervous. "It *is* farfetched," she said. "Eleanor was here a few minutes ago, you know."

He was surprised, and only barely managed to conceal it. He had counted on seeing Alexa first, then going back to Kiawa to make sure Eleanor heard his version of events before anyone else's. The thought of his grandmother sitting here chatting with Alexa brought him out in a cold sweat. "She would have been upset, naturally," he said as calmly as he could.

She looked at him without anger, he thought, even with a disturbing hint of regret, like a woman saying goodbye to someone she might have loved, given a chance. "Robert," she said gently, "you know what happened, and I know what happened. Eleanor knows, too."

"*Knows?* So far we know nothing," he blustered.

"I know as much as I need to know." She paused. "I know the man's name, first of all. Ramirez. Does that ring a bell to you? The man who worked for you in Miami."

He blinked. "Ramirez?" he asked, as if he was having a hard time placing the name. "That was a long time ago. I can't remember the name of everybody who worked on Father's campaign."

"Robert," she said quietly. "I know all about Ramirez. He's the man who's been searching my room, isn't he? The man who smokes those disgusting cigarettes? You used him in Miami, and it cost Arthur the nomination. Your father told me all about it, you see. When Ramirez couldn't find the document you wanted, you told him to kill me, didn't you?"

Her voice was so quiet and calm that a second or two passed before he understood the full meaning of her accusation. "Good God!" he shouted indignantly. "You're overwrought. Understandably, mind you. I don't even know what document you're talking about. And you can't possibly imagine I would have you killed. I'm not in the Mafia, you know."

"No. I believe *they* don't usually shoot women, do they? I would have *given* you the document, Robert. If we'd made a deal, as I wanted us to, I'd have handed it over to you, to burn, or lock away, whatever you wanted to do with it. I didn't even make a copy, you know. I wouldn't ever have *seen* it, if you hadn't sent Booker out to LaGrange to talk to my mother."

"I did no such thing."

"It's too late to lie any more, Robert. Once I've given Ramirez's name and description to the police, they'll find him and when they do, he'll talk. You know that. He's not going to do twenty years in prison or let himself be deported back to Cuba just to protect you, is he?"

Robert felt as if he were strangling. How did she know so much about Ramirez, he wondered? Booker again! He was sure of it. He took a deep breath, knowing there was only one way out. "You haven't talked to the police yet, then?" he asked, trying to make the question casual.

"Not yet, no." Her eyes were cold.

He knew that only the truth could save him. He was at her mercy. "Very well, Ramirez *was* working for me," he admitted. "I had to have that damned police report. There was never the slightest suggestion of having you hurt in any way, though. You surely *can't* believe I'd do that?" For the first time, his voice was pleading.

"Why not?"

"Because you know me."

"Yes. I *do* know you, Robert," she said, letting her anger show. "And I think you're telling me the truth, as a matter of fact, at last. I think you'd have *liked* to see me dead, probably still would, but I don't think you have the guts to do it, probably not even to order someone else to do it for you."

"It's not a question of guts."

"No? What is it a question of, then? Ethics? Morality? Humanitarian scruples?" She paused. "I'm going to tell *you* something, Robert, which may surprise you—something I never had the courage to tell your father. You sent Booker off to see what he could find out about me at home, but I don't think he gave you what you were looking for. Or if he did, maybe he just didn't tell you the whole story. You see, when I was seventeen, my father tried to attack me."

"Good God!" Robert cursed Booker silently. He should have been told! Trust Booker to come back without the goods. All the same, he wondered what that had to do with the present. "I had no idea," he said uncomfortably.

"Oh, you may have guessed a little of it. Booker must have told you *something*, even if he didn't give you your money's worth. I'll tell you the truth, Robert. Father was obsessed with me—couldn't take his eyes off me, couldn't keep his hands off me, ever since I was a little girl. I knew it was wrong, but I didn't know what to do about it. Children never do, do they? Oh, don't misunderstand me. Father never actually abused me, but he *wanted* to, and I knew it. The worst is that there were times, when I was older, thirteen or fourteen, when I wanted him to, or thought I did. He tried to run my life, more than most parents, I mean. So I ran away."

"I know all about that."

"Do you? Maybe. Maybe not. Anyway, Robert, it doesn't matter. When I was brought home, my father was furious. He let it build up for days, and then one night, in his office, next to the barn, whatever it was that was holding him together must have snapped, and he tried— to rape me."

"Awful," he muttered mechanically, wondering where all this was leading. "What did you do?"

She looked at him and smiled—an ambiguous, Mona Lisa smile that might have meant anything. "Do? I shot him, Robert. Twice. In the chest."

There was more to come, and he knew it. If Booker had brought him back that story a week ago, he realized, he wouldn't have had to bring in that bungling oaf Ramirez. On the other hand, why was she telling him now?

"What I'm trying to tell you, Robert, is that you are going to leave Kiawa, leave the country, and leave me alone. Otherwise, I will kill *you*. I've done it before, you see, to somebody I loved. I *don't* love you, so it should be a lot easier. Do I make myself clear?"

"That's ridiculous," he said, but something about that calm smile told him that she meant just what she had said.

"No. My father thought I wouldn't pull the trigger, you know. I wish I hadn't, but I did."

"I will not be threatened," he blustered.

"It's not a threat. This is a promise, that's all, a little secret between the two of us."

He was silent for a long time. His eyes made it clear he believed her. It was not so much the threat that did it, but the final realization that he had lost. "I see. Well, I'd better be on my way. You're going back to Kiawa, I assume?"

"I don't think it's any of your business where I'm going, but yes, I am. For the present. Then I will move into Arthur's apartment, I think. It's too big for me, but it seems silly to stay in my own."

"I suppose so." There was no interest in his voice.

"I don't think we're going to meet again for a long time, Robert. I think it's better that way, don't you? And please don't forget what I told you. I meant it. I always will."

He stood up. It was strange, she thought, but suddenly he no longer reminded her of Arthur at all. She supposed the physical resemblance was still there, but she couldn't *see* it any more. He even seemed shorter to her, as if defeat had shrunken him. "Are you going to talk to the police?" he asked, in a low voice, almost begging.

"I haven't decided. I will have to think about what's best for the family."

He stood in the doorway for a moment, then nodded. "And the document?" he asked.

"I think I'll keep it, Robert," she said gently. "Just to be on the safe side."

He stared at her, as if she were a total stranger. He seemed almost amused. "It's odd," he said. "You sounded just like Eleanor when you said that." He smiled grimly, cleared his throat, as if he had something more to say, then changed his mind, gave her a nod, and left.

She lay in bed for a few minutes, trying not to think about what she had done. She heard the door open. She did not open her eyes. "Are you all right?" she heard Booker ask.

"Yes," she said tonelessly.

"When you feel up to it, shall I get the police here?"

She did not answer for a long time, but finally she shook her head, surprised at how much effort it cost to move it. "No, Martin," she said. "I don't think we need to do that." She paused. "I think we'll keep it in the family." Then she closed her eyes and let herself fall asleep.

She had done what Arthur would have wanted her to do. What Eleanor would have done.

She was content.

THE CAR SWEPT DOWN the long driveway, slowed as it reached the graveled oval in front of the steps. The chauffeur opened the door and she stepped out. The silence was extraordinary—the huge house loomed as if it were lifeless, deserted, the only noise the sound of her shoes on the gravel. At the top of the steps, the butler waited to take her coat. She could not remember his name. She would have to learn that kind of thing. Arthur had once said that while most people could afford to forget names now and again, no Bannerman could. People expected more of a Bannerman, or felt that something must be owed for the privilege of all that money.

In the hall—that great, empty room, with its fireplace always lit, like some kind of eternal flame—Putnam stood, surrounded by his luggage, which looked more like that of a teenage backpacker than a grown-up Bannerman.

"You're going?" she asked, with a sense of regret. She did not know Putnam well, but what she knew of him she liked.

"There's no reason for me to stay. Robert left in a rush, looking strung out. I gather the two of you are not going to be partners?"

"Partners?"

"Split control of The Trust. Your lawyer, what's-his-name, is still here, by the way. You must be running up a hell of a tab."

"Robert and I *have* reached an agreement, as a matter of fact, Putt."

"Yes?"

"I'm going to do just exactly what your father wanted me to do. Robert is going to live with it."

"I *see*. Well, I never held out much hope for a partnership between you and Robert, personally. It's not like him to give up so easily, though . . . to give up at all, in fact. What the hell happened out there in the woods?"

"A minor accident."

He raised an eyebrow. "Another family secret? No, don't tell me about it, please."

"There's nothing to tell."

He gave her a searching look, then nodded. "Okay. That's the Bannerman way, all right."

"Will I see you again?"

"I suppose. You're going ahead with the museum?"

"Yes."

"Then we'll talk." There was a sound of tires on the gravel outside.

"There's my car." He shook her hand, stiffly and formally. "Take care," he said. He paused, as if there was something else he wanted to say. "Nobody wants all this, you know," he said quietly, glancing around the hall. "Oh, for Cyrus and my grandfather, this was it, of course, this and 'The Fortune' "—he said "the fortune" with irony, putting it in caps. "Always the goddamn fortune! Maybe we need an outsider. Father might have reached the right conclusion the wrong way, do you see what I'm saying? Or by accident, who knows?"

He leaned over—it was easy to forget how tall he was, since he had neither his father's presence, nor Robert's tight arrogance and stiff bearing—and kissed her on the cheek. "Good luck," he whispered. "I hope we get to know each other."

She watched him go—a nice, talented man, who would surely have made more of himself if he hadn't been born to a trust fund that produced several hundred thousand tax-free dollars a year—then she walked upstairs and knocked on Eleanor Bannerman's door.

"Come in." The voice was as sharp as ever, but Eleanor herself seemed to have aged. Sitting beside the small fire in her elegant little upstairs room, she had taken on the fragility of her own beloved porcelain collection. "Sit down beside me," she said. It was not a command this time, but a request. "Putnam has gone?" she asked.

"Yes."

"Cecilia will be going soon, I expect."

"Back to Africa?"

"It seems so. So much for Mr. Booker's hopes. Such as they were. Did you tell Putnam what happened?"

"No. I saw no reason to."

Mrs. Bannerman nodded approvingly. "And Robert's part in John's death?"

"I don't see any reason to change things, do you? For years, Putnam and Cecilia have believed it was Arthur's fault. I think they ended up by almost forgiving him—Putnam, certainly. So long as Robert behaves himself, why confront them with the truth at this late date? What good would it do?"

"Cecilia, at any rate, might like you better if she knew. She might forgive you for taking what she thinks of as Robert's inheritance."

"Yes. Perhaps. Or she might dislike me even more. But why destroy her faith in her brother? Arthur took the blame for Robert when he was alive. Surely he can continue to now that he's dead?"

The old lady gave a nod. For the first time since Alexa had met her, old Mrs. Bannerman seemed tired. "It's a wise decision," she said quietly, almost whispering. "Cecilia may never forgive you. That is a possibility. You should not expect a miraculous reconciliation. There is no great harm to that, by the way. Her dislike of you may even push her to make a real life for herself, who can say?"

She paused, then placed her hand on Alexa's, the bones so fine and brittle that they might have been made of glass. "The real burden is not looking after The Trust. The real burden is in knowing what others aren't strong enough to know, and living with that knowledge—keeping it to yourself so they don't *have* to know. Arthur had that strength—though, my God, what it cost him! He kept Robert's secret, even from me. And I, in my life, I have kept many secrets. Who knows? Perhaps the best thing you can do for Cecilia is to let her keep her illusions about Robert. If she needs to love him and to hate you, then you will just have to accept that."

"It seems sad."

"Much of life *is*. I talked to Robert. I do not think you need to fear him. Not any more. That, too, was sad. I love him, and I will not disguise from you that I had hoped to see him taking his father's place. But he cannot. Oh, not merely because of the will, of course. That is merely paper, fodder for lawyers."

"What will he do?"

"He is going back to Venezuela, for a while, where he belongs. Then, I think, perhaps another ambassadorship. I do not believe he will seek his party's nomination for the governorship. Perhaps next time, once things have settled down. . . . A little travel and work would do him good, I think. As for you, you had better get back to the city. I have asked DeWitt and Mr. Booker to start gathering you the information you'll need. You will have a lot to learn."

"I've learned a lot already."

Mrs. Bannerman withdrew her hand. She sat composedly, ankles touching, hands together in her lap, her expression distant, as if she had reached some peace with herself, or perhaps the past. "Not nearly as much as you think you have," she said sadly. "Not nearly."

11

The heavy rain stopped just as they came out of the church, turning to a fine drizzle that kept the rest of the mourners hidden under their umbrellas. Emmett DeWitt was the only object of color in sight, in his bright clerical robes. He stood for a moment, his glasses still misted by the intensity of his sermon and the heat in the church.

"One would have thought Robert would be here," he said.

Beside him, straightening her veil, Alexa stood, the two of them alone on the steps for a moment. "He's traveling," she said.

"All the same . . . Eleanor's funeral . . . "

"He's not well, Emmett. Just at the moment, he's in hospital, in Marrakesh, I believe. He sent a cable."

"Is it drink? From all accounts, he's been going to pieces steadily ever since he resigned the ambassadorship. Damn shame he gave it up."

"He didn't have a choice, Emmett. Not after he was caught out having an affair with Señor Guzman's wife. It's not often that an American ambassador makes headline news in a sex scandal. The President was furious with Robert."

"Poor Robert," Emmett said, without sympathy. "A pointless life. Polo, drinking, women . . . his problem is that none of the Bannermans is cut out to be a playboy, not even him."

"Perhaps that's only one of Robert's problems," she said. "We'd better get on with it."

Emmett recognized the voice of authority. He took her arm and descended the steps. Behind them, Cecilia and Putnam Bannerman appeared from the church, Putnam uncomfortable as he always was on family occasions, Cecilia glaring straight at the back of Alexa's head, unforgiving and not caring who noticed. They descended the steps together and passed between the lines of mourners, their umbrellas rustling like trees in the wind, as Emmett led them to the Bannerman Pie at a pace which made the older members of the family pant for breath, as if it were a race.

Alexa walked briskly beside him, her veils fluttering behind her. She approved of the pace. Eleanor, she knew, would not like to be kept waiting.

SIMON AND STERN STOOD TOGETHER, sheltering under Simon's golf umbrella, with its red and green Gucci stripes. "I wish it were black," Stern said. "It seems out of place."

"It *is* out of place. So are you. So am I. Let's face it, we're both out of place here."

Stern seemed reluctant to admit he was out of place anywhere. He changed the subject. "How's the museum going? Have you gotten used to being a museum director yet?"

"Up to a point. Respectability doesn't come easily to me, so far. Henry Geldzahler wrote a scathing piece about me in *New York* magazine. I suppose that means I've arrived. To be attacked is a sure sign of being taken seriously in New York. I wanted to sue, but Booker talked me out of it, quite rightly."

"He's come a long way, Booker has."

"Yes. Well, responsibility is what does it, I guess. With DeWitt retired, he's carrying the full load. He's been terrific with the museum. You know he's been named to the board, as chief legal counsel?"

"*And* to the board of the Foundation. There's no telling how far he'll go."

"Only one person knows that," Simon said. An eavesdropper would have heard a tone of awe in his voice.

"A-men," said Stern solemnly. "Amen to that."

EMMETT DEWITT'S VOICE CARRIED FAR, as if the drizzle were amplifying his reedy tone, so that it boomed over the Pie and out to the woods beyond. He had every need to raise his voice to its full operatic strength, for there had never been so many mourners, not since the death of Cyrus himself, which only a handful of people here had been alive to mourn.

"Ashes to ashes, and dust to dust," he shouted hoarsely, concluding his service. He stood in prayer for a moment, standing even taller because he was on a mound of earth. A sea of umbrellas stretched before him, glistening. He bent down, filled the silver trowel with a little dirt, and flung it into the open grave.

He handed the silver implement to Alexa, the same one that she had seen used at Arthur's funeral. She lifted her veil and gently poured a spoonful of dirt into the grave. She had been crying, he noted with approval. He knew how fond Alexa had been of Eleanor. One of the few who were—for Eleanor Bannerman had lived so long that her death was a kind of anticlimax, and few people remembered her, except with fear or curiosity. Many people outside the family thought she had been dead for years.

Things would never be the same with Eleanor gone, he thought, but then he watched Alexandra Bannerman walk away from her mother-in-law's grave, dressed head to foot in black, with a heavy veil covering her face, and wasn't so sure. The sea of umbrellas parted before her, opened a path for her as the Red Sea had once parted for Moses. The umbrellas dipped and bowed on either side of her as the cousins, the relatives, the far reaches of the Bannerman family pushed themselves forward to touch her hand, introduce themselves, say a word of condolence or respect.

David Roth, eyes downcast as if the entire ceremony were alien to him, walked behind her. His involvement with the museum—and with Alexa Bannerman—had brought him not only profit, but the respectability that had eluded his father. His building had earned him praise from critics, architects, even the mayor, and on the strength of it, he had moved out of the shadows and into the limelight, appearing on talk shows, in the gossip columns, at parties, often with Alexandra Bannerman, as she was now always referred to in the press, as his companion. Not only had his ghosted autobiography, *Vision: The Story of a Builder*, made *The New York Times* bestseller list, but there was talk of its being made into a miniseries, even rumors that Roth would play himself in it, which he did nothing to discourage.

Martin Booker, hatless in the Bannerman tradition, now walked beside her, whispering names she didn't know, warning her of any problems or requests she might have to deal with. From time to time, she touched him with her black-gloved hand. Some people supposed that Alexandra Bannerman was in love with Roth, others that she was in love with Booker, but she led her life with such perfect discretion that nobody could really say, except Alexandra herself.

One thing was sure, Emmett knew: both men were in love with her, but his money was on Booker.

ALEXA DID NOT LOOK BACK as she left the Pie. She had greeted everyone who expected to be greeted, shook every hand, remembered everybody's name, even down to the most distant cousin.

The most important members of the family would be staying to dinner. She had chosen the menu, carefully arranged the seating. Everything was in its place, down to the last detail. Even the Bannerman diamonds had been returned and were safely back in the vault, where they belonged, thanks to a settlement that was too generous for Vanessa Bannerman to refuse, as well as a discreetly worded threat, conveyed in person by Alexa, to have her arrested for theft the next time she set foot in the United States.

She put her hand on Martin Booker's and squeezed his gently. He was the one person she trusted, the only one she could imagine one day replacing Arthur—but this was not the time or place to let him know.

She tried to remember if there was anything she had overlooked, anyone who had been ignored.

After all, she was the head of the Bannerman family now.